THE WALLACE

'You give me leave to speak, my lord?' Bruce asked the Steward.

At that man's nod, he turned. 'I have heard what is proposed, my friends,' he said. 'And I too say that a Guardian of the Realm should be appointed. But not myself, who has fought no battles, earned no plaudits, am but untried amongst you. Only one man, at this juncture, can fill Scotland's need today. Only one man will the people follow. That man is William Wallace of Elderslie. I name you Wallace as Guardian!' It was though a dam had burst, and the emotion of the men surged free in clamour. The shout that rose seemed to shake the very hills.

It was some time before Bruce could make himself heard again. 'Hear me – hear me, my friends. Wallace has rid us of the English. But they will be back. And he needs must do it again. Nothing on God's earth is so sure than that they will be back . . .'

The Wallace

Nigel Tranter

CORONET BOOKS
Hodder and Stoughton

First published in Great Britain in 1975
by Hodder and Stoughton Limited
a division of Hodder Headline PLC

10 9 8 7 6

ISBN 0 340 21237 3

Printed and bound in Great Britain by
Cox & Wyman Ltd, Reading, Berkshire

Hodder and Stoughton
A division of Hodder Headline PLC
338 Euston Road
London NW1 3BH

PRINCIPAL CHARACTERS

IN ORDER OF APPEARANCE

WILLIAM WALLACE: Second son of Sir Malcolm Wallace of Elderslie.

MASTER JOHN BLAIR: Benedictine monk.

ROBERT BOYD: Farmer.

EDWARD LITTLE: Nephew of Wallace. Son of small laird.

MARION BRAIDFOOT: Wife of Wallace. Daughter of Sir Hugh Braidfoot of Lamington.

ADAM WALLACE: Cousin. Son of Sir Richard Wallace of Riccarton, head of family.

MASTER THOMAS GRAY: Parish priest of Libberton, Lanarkshire.

LORD JAMES STEWART: Lord of Renfrew. 5th High Steward of Scotland.

MASTER ROBERT WISHART, BISHOP OF GLASGOW: Second of the Lords Spiritual.

MALCOLM, EARL OF LENNOX: Great Celtic noble.

STEPHEN MACGREGOR: Vassal of Lennox.

MACFADZEAN: Servant of Lennox.

FAWDON: Irish servant of Lennox.

SIR JOHN GRAHAM: Son of the Graham chief, Sir David Graham of Dundaff.

MEG DRUMMOND: Perth prostitute.

SIR JOHN BUTLER: English knight. Deputy Governor of Perth.

PATRICK AUCHINLECK OF THAT ILK: Cousin of Wallace.

SIR THOMAS LEARMONTH OF ERCILDOUNE: Eccentric laird, known as Thomas the Rhyme.

SIR HUGO DE MORELAND: English keeper of Lochmaben Castle.

SIR WILLIAM DE HAZELRIG: English Sheriff of Clydesdale.

SIR ANDREW MORAY: Lord of Pettie and Bothwell, heir of Moravia.

SIR ALEXANDER LINDSAY, LORD OF CRAWFORD: Great noble.

ROBERT BRUCE, EARL OF CARRICK: Eldest son of Lord of Annandale, later King.

SIR WILLIAM DOUGLAS: 5th Lord thereof.

ALEXANDER SCRYMGEOUR: Dundee burgess and soldier. Later Standard-Bearer.

DUNCAN MACDOUGALL OF LORN: 2nd son of Alexander, Lord of Argyll.

SIR NEIL CAMPBELL OF LOCHAWE: Chief of Clan Campbell. *MacCailean Mor.*

MALCOLM MACGREGOR OF GLENORCHY: Chief of Clan Alpine.

SIR RICHARD LUNDIN OF THAT ILK: Scots knight.

SIR JOHN RAMSAY OF AUCHERHOUSE: ditto.

MASTER WILLIAM SINCLAIR, DEAN AND COADJUTOR-BISHOP OF DUNKELD:

SIR WILLIAM RUTHVEN OF THAT ILK: Former Provost of Perth.

LORD HUGH MACDUFF: Uncle and Tutor to the young Earl of Fife.

GARTNAIT, EARL OF MAR: Great Celtic noble, brother-in-law of Bruce.

JOHN COMYN, EARL OF BUCHAN: Lord High Constable of Scotland.

SIR JOHN COMYN, LORD OF BADENOCH: Chief of the great House of Comyn.

SIR JOHN STEWART OF MENTEITH: Sheriff of Dunbarton and Perth. Uncle and tutor to young Earl of Menteith.

MASTER WILLIAM COMYN: Provost of the Chapel-Royal, brother of Buchan.

MASTER WILLIAM LAMBERTON: Chancellor of Glasgow Cathedral, later Bishop of St. Andrews and Primate of Scotland.

LORD NIGEL BRUCE: Brother to the Earl of Carrick.

JOHN BALIOL, KING OF SCOTS: Exile.

PHILIP THE FAIR, KING OF FRANCE:

ENGUERRAND DE MARIGNY: Intendant of Finance. French administrator.

SIR SIMON FRASER OF OLIVER: Scots veteran soldier.

RALPH DE HALIBURTON: Border laird.

JOHN STEWART: Nicknamed Jack Short, a young esquire.

SIR JOHN DE SEGRAVE: Grand Marshal of England.

SIR PETER MALLORY: Lord Chief Justice of England.

Part One

CHAPTER ONE

The man stood, weeping. If weeping describes the dry-eyed, deep and tearing sobs which racked his enormous frame, in an extremity of sorrow, pain, hurt. The three men with him eyed him askance, or sought not to eye him, afraid almost to look on his distress. Not that they were ashamed, embarrassed. They were, in fact, terrified — terrified of their friend.

The scene was indeed terrible. But it was not the scene which frightened them. It was the big man weeping, sobbing. Most things this man did, he did with his whole heart and mind and faculties — and that could hold its own alarm for the less committed. When his emotions were strongly aroused, subsequent action could be swift, shattering, shocking, indeed — not in sheer impulsiveness nor mindless violence, but in intense, calculated vehemence. For this was a man of thought and assessment equally as of action — a rare combination, in itself apt to make others uneasy. Just as in reverse as it were, his gentleness, kindliness even patience, could be as unexpected, insupportable in its implied demands on others.

Yet the three others loved him.

William Wallace's lips were moving. 'God in Heaven help me!' he whispered. 'God in Heaven — help me!' He raised two great hands up and forward and open, towards that scene of horror, but higher. 'I need . . . Your help.' His hands and arms, like his entire huge frame, were trembling, so that the ground they stood on seemed to shake in elemental accord.

For long moments he stood so — and his companions scarcely drew breath. Then, suddenly jerking both hands higher still, he reached over in a single swift and sure movement, above and behind his bare head, to whip out with the harsh shriek of steel, the mighty two-handed sword sheathed at his back. In a great sweeping arc he brought its five feet of length over and down, and, as its tip nearly reached the ground, released his grip on its hilt to catch it again expertly, halfway down the broad blade, and so to raise it aloft before him,

9

cross-shaped hilt and guard forming the sacred symbol. There he held it, still, unspeaking — and no sound save the faint residual crackle of fire, and the ululant howling of a hound in its desolation, broke the hush of the warm afternoon.

Unspoken, the fearsome, fatal vow was made, there in the quiet green Ayrshire valley — unspoken because it required no words, no detail, no explanation. For life and death, for ever, for eternity, the vow was made, the decision reached, the compact sealed, the task dedicated. And his witnesses, Master John Blair, Benedictine monk, Robert Boyd, tenant-farmer, and Edward Little nephew and small laird's son, stared destiny in the face and shivered.

After a little, still not trusting himself to speech, Wallace lowered the sword, and moved forward, heavy-footed, towards Carleith Tower.

It was a small place to have undergone so notable a visitation, a simple square keep of but three storeys and a garret, of no more than twenty-five feet measurement, crowning a grass-grown artificial motte or mound, some twenty feet high, the soil for which had been dug out to form a deep surrounding ditch, into which a lade from the nearby Killoch Burn had been led to fill a moat. Within the ditch, but below the mound a high stone wall arose, square also but rounded at the corners, the paling for this pele-tower, pierced only by a single gateway, to the west, at the end of a drawbridge across the ditch. This gateway stood open, the heavy oaken and iron-bound doors wide but undamaged. The bridge was down. A pall of blue smoke rose lazily in the warm early autumn air from all within — even from the square keep on its mound, for it was not a stone tower but built of stout timbers, only coated with whitewashed clay to protect it from blazing arrows. It was not blazing arrows that had done this. The whitewashed walls were still comparatively unscarred. This fire had been lit from within, as had the fires which had destroyed the lean-to domestic buildings and stables built against the curtain-walling around the mound. There had been no arrows, no assault, no fighting, here.

None of all this held the gaze of the four young men, as they paced so slowly forward. It was the bodies which appalled them. Dead bodies were none so rare a sight in the Scotland of 1296, admittedly; but these were perhaps exceptional. When the drawbridge was let down, the portcullis apparatus here projected two long timber beams, from which the chains depended.

10

These beams had been used as gibbets. Hanged men, likewise, were not a scarce sight, under the Lord Paramount Edward's rule; but hanged women and children were less common, especially hanged as were these.

There were fourteen bodies, or parts of bodies, swaying gently on ropes. Old Cunninghame of Carleith himelf, the laird, had pride of place, and hung, not from one of the beams, but from the keystone of the arched gateway itself. The newcomers knew it was he from his girth, he being a large and bulky man, heavy, in his late sixties — for his white-bearded head, sadly reddened now, did not hang below his shoulders, but was kicked into a corner of the entrance. The rest of him hung by an ankle — they all did — in particularly ignominious postures. None, it seemed, had died by hanging.

The laird, however, was the only one who had retained any of his clothing. His son, Dod Cunninghame — whom the four young men had, in fact, come to see — had not lost his head, only his genitals and all his limbs. His younger brother Rob, likewise, but also partly disembowelled. Something horrible had been stuffed into his open mouth.

But it was the women who had them all but vomiting. Lady Carleith, twenty years younger than her husband, her three daughters and two serving women, had all suffered alike — at least, in appearance. All hung upside-down, naked; all had their breasts sliced off; and all had stakes or axe-shafts or other, wooden handles projecting upwards from between their thighs. Five children, the offspring of Dod and a married sister — whose husband was a prisoner captured at the defeat of Dunbar and awaiting ransom — aged from two to eight, had merely been hacked to pieces and the parts strung up anyhow, in bundles.

The flies were a humming dark cloud about all.

Forcing himself to look, not to hurry past eyes averted, William Wallace still dared not speak. John Blair, the monk, was muttering Latinities in an unending, incoherent gabble; Edward Little, whose far-out kinsfolk these were, was mouthing incessant obscenities with tears streaming down his cheeks; Robert Boyd, hard man, kept smashing a clenched fist into an open palm, again and again and again, as eloquence enough

A paper was affixed to one of the half-doors, held in place by a reddened dirk. It was only roughly penned, and in blood — probably no better ink was readily available — and not very legible, for the blood had run and clotted. But the intimation was clear enough, and brief. It said, in Norman French:

'*King Edward's Peace.*

These failed to do homage to the King's Grace, as commanded.

So suffer all traitors.

God Save the King.'

Wallace ripped the paper from the timbering, and crushed it in convulsive grippings of his huge hand. Then he paused, smoothed it out again, and folded it, to tuck it away inside the calfskin leather sleeveless jerkin which he was wearing in lieu of the steel jack and chain-mail which was his more usual travelling garb in these unsettled days of English Edward's Peace — for this had been more in the nature of a social call than any expedition. He led the way through the gateway into the courtyard.

Here all was the expected ruin and chaos, with smouldering thatch and straw, scattered clothing, smashed furnishings and implements, dead and charred poultry and dogs littered on the cobblestones, in the doorways of the burned-out stables and outhouses, on the steps up to the keep. The horses and cattle had gone, as worth driving off. Life remained only in the shape of a single grey wolfhound, a red gash on its shaggy flank, whose baying to the uncaring sun-filled sky had warned them from afar, even before they saw the smoke, as to what to expect at Carleith Tower. Now it stood over the body of a mutilated child, which somehow had escaped the hanging-up process, and snarled in white-fanged fear and hatred at the intruders.

But it was not so much to the surviving dog or its small forlorn charge that the young men's eyes were drawn, but rather to the round well-parapet in the centre of the cobbled yard. Out of this, as though from a stuffed and bursting sack, sprouted legs and arms and torsoes, some clad, some naked. The fact that they so protruded, from a deep well-shaft, told its own story.

Here was the answer to the question of why the scatter of cothouses, thatch burned and ravaged, which the visitors had had to pass along the Killoch burnside approaching the Tower, had held neither occupants nor bodies. All the cottar-folk, farmhands, shepherds, cattlemen, wrights, smith, miller and the rest, of a little self-contained community amongst these Ayrshire-Lanarkshire border hills, with their families, had been driven in here, to their laird's courtyard, and slaughtered *en masse,* rather than outside in penny-numbers, their bodies crammed down the well, where the lairdly family had been elevated on ropes. There might be thirty or forty or more, in that well. No small group of marauders could have done this; it must have been a sizeable company of soldiery.

They were not so very far from the main highway from Ayr to Lanark, here at Carleith, four miles up the dead-end valley of the Killoch Water from Mauchline. The young men had themselves ridden eastwards from the Ayr district that morning — and they had passed no body of troops. Therefore the perpetrators of this outrage, in all probability, had gone on eastwards towards Lanark, a score of miles further through the empty hills by Muirkirk and Douglasdale. There was almost nowhere else they could have gone, to shelter for a night secure, for a fairly large party of English in a country hostile if largely subdued, sullenly repressed. Only the large towns, garrisoned, offered safe lodging for the invaders. Ayr was the headquarters of the Percy, Warden of Galloway and Ayrshire; and Lanark the base of his principal deputy, Sir William de Hazelrigg, new-styled Earl of Clydesdale and Sheriff of Lanark. The company who had done this thing were almost certainly, then, on their way from Ayr to Lanark.

After a minute or so of stunned reaction, Wallace pulled himself together and took charge. Digging any sort of graves for all these dead was out of the question for four men. They took the top bodies, shamefully reluctantly at first, out of the well-shaft, until there was a sufficiency of space below the parapet, and this they filled in meantime with charred thatch and straw from the stables. The half-dozen dead thus removed, they carried out to the drawbridge, where they cut down the ghastly things which hung there. They found blankets and plaids from the sacked keep, and in these they wrapped all the remains, as reverently as they might, and took them to a sort of small re-entrant of the moat, a grassy hollow to the south, slightly higher than the water level. In this they placed the bodies. All kneeling, Father John said a disjointed, broken-voiced prayer of committal and Christian burial. Then they filled up the hollow with more thatch and straw, and dug out a layer of soil to cover all, hacking and shovelling at the earth with the muscular fury of strong men who desperately needed physical action of some sort, any sort, to relieve something of their pent-up emotion.

Then they went back and said another prayer over the wellful of victims. Robert Boyd put a crossbow-bolt between the eyes of the snarling, half-mad, wounded wolfhound, since they could by no means either approach or aid it.

There was nothing else that they could do here — whatever fell to be done elsewhere. Apart from the praying, they had scarcely exchanged a score of consecutive words with one another throughout. Words, muttered half-formed curses apart, were as inadequate and valueless as they were emotive, liable to release an embarrassing flood. But as they strode away from Carleith Tower, towards their horses left by one of the cot-houses, William Wallace paused at the bridge-end, and looked back.

'God aiding me, the men who did this evil thing will go to answer for it. To a higher court than Edward Plantagenet's!' he said, deep-voiced, 'And, thereafter, we will seek to cleanse this good land of, of ...' The deep voice cracked and broke. He could not go on. Nor required to. He swung away abruptly.

'So be it,' John Blair took him up, quietly. 'In the name of the Father, of the Son and of the Holy Spirit. Amen.'

Mounting, they rode back down the empty valley, to head eastwards, for Lanark.

*   *   *

It was the dove-grey of a quiet September evening before they reached the hill-terraced town of Lanark, above the deep gut of the upper Clyde valley, its climbing narrow streets already beginning to be dominated by the towering stark stonework of the New English castle being built, on the site of the older strength on Castle Hill, by the equally new and self-styled Earl of Clydesdale, the Cumbrian Sir William de Hazelrigg, Sheriff of Lanark under Edward Longshanks' improved administration for the occupied Kingdom of Scotland. Away in the foothills, Lanark was less conveniently sited than Ayr on the coast, so Percy, Governor and Warden of all the South-West, did not base himself there. But it was strategically important too, lying at the north-west extremity of that vast upland area of wilderness known as The Forest, more properly Ettrick Forest, which covered so much of the southern part of Scotland, providing a buffer between the Borderlands and the populous and fertile central belt — and a notorious refuge for the numerous outlaws, broken men and fugitives from settled authority.

Lanark, although fifty miles from the Borderline, was a frontier town, and the English treated it accordingly. This summer of 1296, it swarmed with soldiery.

It was not a place that William Wallace and his friends would have chosen to frequent in the circumstances, especially not to leave his recently wed wife in. But she was undoubtedly safer here, in her family's townhouse, amongst her own folk, than she would have been anywhere else that her footloose and presently homeless husband could have installed her. It was their misfortune to have wed just before the time that Edward Plantagenet had decided to end the sham semi-independence of King John Baliol's puppet government, to strip John of his powers and freedom, and send him a humiliated prisoner to England, taking over with an iron hand the rule of the northern kingdom for himself. Included in his edicts was the peremptory requirement that all land-holders, officers, magistrates and men of substance take the oath of allegiance to himself, Edward of England, no longer merely as self-appointed Lord Paramount, but as King — not of Scots, since he no longer accepted Scotland to be a kingdom — but of England, under pain of death. Most, at least in the southern part of the country, had done so, however reluctantly and with inward reservations. Sir Malcolm Wallace of Elderslie had refused — and had died for his pains. It was wise, therefore, for his sons Malcolm, William and John, not to make themselves prominent, not to claim any lands, even those most rightly their own, not to identify themselves meantime with houses, offices, positions. They were not exactly outlaws — yet; but they were marked men. Will most especially, for sufficient reason. In the circumstances, the new bride, daughter of Sir Hugh Braidfoot of Lamington, was best remaining in her father's house, since he was one of the majority who *had* taken the oath.

The four young men avoided the main streets of the town, crowded with strolling and drunken soldiery — and such of the local women as would associate with them. Wallace was apt to avoid busy places anyway, these days. He had a distinct physical handicap, when it came to associating with other folk; he was six feet seven inches in height, broad in proportion, and in consequence stood out head and shoulders in any company he kept. It went without saying that this was a great trial to a young man who very frequently had need to be inconspicuous, anonymous, before the present ruling authorities in Scotland.

He was, in fact, a highly unsuitable husband for Marion Braid-foot, or any woman — at least in some respects.

So the newcomers slipped into Lanark by back ways, left their horses at the rear of an obscure alehouse in the South Vennel, in the care of Robert Boyd — and Wallace's huge sword with him, hidden, for such a thing to be found on any Scot would be as good as a death-warrant — and found their way across to the North Vennel and so by a lane to the garden-door of the Braidfoots' house in the Castlegait, near the High Street. Normally the family would be at their country home of Lamington Tower at this harvest season; but it was remotely set in The Forest foothills, ten miles to the south-east, and in these unsettled times the laird preferred his womenfolk to be in the security of the walled town.

Even the back-door of the house had to be unbarred and un-chained cautiously to let the trio in — a sign of the said times. And it was a man with hand on dirk-hilt who gingerly opened to them. But there was no mistaking the towering figure outside in the dusk, and the serving-man admitted them at once, and cheerfully, raising his voice to shout for Mistress Mirren, that here was Master Will, by God! It was himself, the Wallace. Master Will had come.

There was a cry from somewhere in the depths of the quite large house, and the sound of light running feet. Into the stone-flagged kitchen raced a laughing, wide-eyed young woman — wide-mouthed also for, as well as seeking to gasp aloud her gladness, she was gasping for breath, being in fact in no state for running, six months pregnant, and heavy with it. Otherwise she was a slender, almost fragile-seeming girl, the more so of course when seen beside her large husband, with great, gentle brown eyes, oval features and luxuriant dark hair, her small head poised proudly on a long and shapely neck. She flung herself bodily into Wallace's arms, and he raised her high, high, until her head was all but touching the curve of the smoke-blackened, stone-vaulted ceiling, holding her there — but gently almost reverently, before lowering her pan-ting, laughing person so that their lips could meet and cling, her feet still some fifteen inches from the floor. But on this oc-casion, vehement and fervid as was the love and warmth of his greeting, the laughter was all on her side — although that man could laugh as loud as any. It was almost three weeks since they had seen each other.

16

As women will, she sensed something different, and her gurgling, kiss-interrupted laughter faded. She drew back her comely, flushed face a little way, to peer at him.

'Oh, Will! Will dear — how good!' she got out, the first coherent words she, or he either, had managed to enunciate as yet. 'My love, my love! But . . . there is something wrong? Amiss? What is it, Will . . .?'

He set her down carefully. 'I am sorry,' he said, and nodded slowly. 'Aye, Mirren — there is something amiss.' He glanced over at the others. They were glad to take the hint, and followed the serving-man out into the passage and along to the front part of the house.

'You are well, at least,' she declared, eyeing him. 'It is not that. Are — are you in trouble, Will? Again?' And, when he shook his auburn head, 'Of a mercy, then — let me look at you! Before — before you tell me. Just let me look at my husband I see so little of. When there is so much of him!'

He mustered a smile at that, as she looked him over. And he was good to look at, not handsome in the accepted sense but with features pleasing as they were strong, an open, candid face, warm blue eyes under a broad but not high brow, and a fine head of slightly curling auburn hair kept sufficiently short so as not to get in the way of the great sword which was so frequently sheathed at his back, its hilt rising behind the pillar of his neck. For the rest, his nose was on the short side, and both his upper lip and chin on the long side, with a beard kept short and neatly trimmed. That he was massively built goes without saying; but there was no surplus of flesh to him, no heaviness in proportion to his gigantic frame. And, strangely, for so active and vigorous a young man of twenty-six years, little appearance of muscular tension or bracing; on the contrary, rather an air of physical calm, relaxation, the more unusual in one of this man's reputation.

Presently he told her something of what they had found at Carleith. He did not dwell upon the details; but nor did he gloss over the scale and vileness of what had been done. That it was not so much the horror itself, but some significant and vital effect on the man himself, however, she was quick to realise. Great-eyed, urgently, she gazed at him, seeking to control the words, the pleas, even the denials which all but sprang to her lips.

'And you?' she said, at length. 'This evil means — what? To you, Will?'

17

He was as slow to answer her, to put into actual words his committment, his vowed total committment. But she had to know.

'I cannot stand by, Mirren,' he said quietly. 'I must do something. Carleith cries to Heaven for vengeance. But — it is more than vengeance that is required. Punishment, yes. But it is *cleansing* that this land and people need. Cleansing, not only of these savage invaders, but of this realm's own inner spirit. Its soul — if a nation may have a soul. The soul which cowers under this tyrant Edward's iron lash, the spirit which accepts tyranny, savagery, insult, shame. Aye, accepts — for Carleith is not the first such shame. I could name a dozen others. And what of Berwick? 17,000 died at Edward's sack of Berwick, men, women and bairns. For what? To cow us, for an example. That we should bow to tyranny. We did not bow at once — the folly of Dunbar showed that. But we have bowed and cowered, since. It must not go on.'

'Yes, Will. God knows it is true. But — what can *you* do? One man. One unimportant man — unimportant, save to me! Not a great lord, not a noble, landless. What could you do?'

'I could do *something,* God aiding me. And I will,' he said. 'Someone must — or we *deserve* to be trodden down under the Plantagenet's heel. Deserve it, I say! I have much — a powerful body, a strong right arm, wits enough for some few to follow me. I can wield a sword . . .'

'Aye, these you have. That you have done already. And are a marked man, in consequence. But that was different. Oh, Will . . .!'

'That was different, to be sure. I have slain Englishmen, yes. In wrath. In revenge. Because they attacked me, taunted me, insulted me. Or harmed someone of mine, or in my sight. But that was . . . me, just. Myself. *For* myself. A man defending himself, striking back, refusing to bend the knee. No more than a man angry, Mirren. But — now it is different, yes. I have sworn an oath. If I am to respect myself ever again, I must now *act.* Not merely against this arrogant Englishman, or that. But against what they stand for. Against the invader — not just this cruel assassin or that petty ruffian. Do you not see?'

'I see, yes. Oh, I see, Will! I see you going away from me again. Going into grievous danger, fighting. Being hunted by the English. Being caught, it may be. And then, and then . . .'
She gulped and could not go on.

18

Unhappily he considered her. He could not deny anything of what she had said. He could only grip her arm, and shake his head, wordless.

She knew her man too well to seek to argue with him, to try to convince him against his own considered judgement, his conception of his duty. He might have been called an obstinate man. She sighed — and then closed with him again and, folded within his huge embrace, sought to tell herself — although not him — that she was still the most happy and fortunate young woman in all broad Scotland.

In time, they moved through to the others, eating in a pantry. Sir Hugh was at Lamington with his sons, helping to get in the precious harvest — for famine was never far away when war was about. The second Lady Braidfoot was bedridden upstairs, and only Marion's two younger stepsisters were at home with her cheerful girls in their mid and later teens, now bombarding Ed Little with questions and sallies — though restrained a little by the priestly character of their other guest. Not that John Blair appeared any solemn monkish figure; indeed bore no evidence, meantime, of a monk, whatsoever, in dress or bearing. Clearly the girls had been restrained from rushing through to the kitchen, no doubt highly unwillingly, and now hurled themselves upon their brother-in-law in typically uninhibited welcome.

Wallace gathered that his friends had not told the younger girls about the Carleith massacre. He commended their judgement.

Nevertheless, the thought of it and its consequences was still very much in the forefront of his mind; and when the girls were away preparing more food, he told his companions what he wanted. They were to slip out, presently into the town. They were not kenspeckle, recognisable, as was he. Try to find out in the wynds and closes, the alehouses — aye, and the whore houses — what party of military had come in from the South-West that day, who the leaders were, and anything about them. Some folk would know. There might well be evil, shameful boasting. Men would have loot, mementoes. Somewhere in Lanark, almost certainly these butchers were to be found. Their officers would be installed up in the old castle, and safe; but their men would be celebrating in the town. The night was young yet.

So presently, their bellies filled, Blair and Little excused

19

themselves, the first to go relieve Rob Boyd at his vigil in the South Vennel alehouse yard; all to gather what information they might. Then the two younger girls were packed, protesting, off to bed. And William Wallace could be alone with his wife.

Just before midnight Rob Boyd was first to come back. His news, gleaned at the alehouse and elsewhere, was interesting but general rather than particular. Hazelrigg had gone to Ayr to confer with Sir Henry Percy, the Warden. There was word of a revolt in the far North-East, in Buchan and Moray on the fringes of the Comyn country, led, it seemed, by young Sir Andrew Moray the Pantler's nephew. It was apparently serious for troops were being summoned from far and near to send north. As well as from Northern England itself, large numbers were said to be coming from Galloway. Some had already arrived this afternoon, a company of light cavalry — whether on their way further north or no was not known. It could have been these that had been at Carleith. Lanark looked like being important in this business not merely as a staging-post on the way North, but because the great de Moray family, Hereditary Pantlers and amongst the most important in the land, as well as owning the vast northern lands from which they took their name, were also Lords of Bothwell, here in Lanarkshire. The powerful Bothwell Castle lay only some eighteen miles to the North-West; and though it was held by an English garrison, its large demesnes supported a great many men who might rise in arms at the behest of their young lord — the old lord, his father, being safely in an English prison, like his brother, the Pantler. Bothwell, therefore, fell to be given a major demonstration of English might and authority; and Lanark was a convenient base for operations.

This news had a notable effect on Wallace. The fact that there was revolt arising, even so far away as Moray land, was enheartening indeed — especially in that the English evidently anticipated that it might spread here to the South-West. If the tinder was so dry as they seemed to fear, then now was clearly the time to strike the spark. Was he the man to strike it? And if so, how?

John Blair arrived back an hour later, his dark and rather hooded eyes gleaming with a sternly damped down excitement. He was the eldest of the four men, a younger son of a wild house, the Blairs of Balthayock in the Carse of Gowrie, with whom Wallace had become friendly while at college in

20

Dundee — for Will too had been intended for the Church, like so many younger sons of the lairdly class. The latter's activities in Gowrie, however, particularly in the matter of one of King John Baliol's English minions' son, one Selby, had effectively put an end to his studies, theological and other, and he had had to flee the area and come back to his own South-West. But he and John Blair had remained in touch, a dark, lean, quiet man, of a well-hidden but smouldering intensity. That he had news now, was evident.

'Fenwick!' he said, briefly. 'Sir John Fenwick.'

The effect on Wallace was extraordinary. He rose from his seat on the settle beside his wife, abruptly, and so stood. He did not speak. He had a gift for silence, that young man. But his gaze was eloquent, demanding.

The other nodded. 'There is no doubt, Will. The only company to have ridden into Lanark from the South-West this day, the only company of any size from anywhere, was two hundred men commanded by Sir John Fenwick. They came by the Douglasdale road. As did we. In early afternoon. Fenwick it was who savaged Carleith.'

Wallace let his breath out in a long and quivering sigh. 'Fenwick!' he said. And again, 'Fenwick.' Slowly he looked round at them all. 'This, then is fate.'

'The hand of Almighty God!' the monk amended.

Boyd smashed his fist down on the table-top, as sufficient comment.

Marion Braidfoot bit her lip. If she had had any least hope of deferring trouble, danger, harsh involvement, for her Will, this put an end to it. She knew, as well as the others, that it was Sir John Fenwick, one of the Percy's Northumbrian vassals, who had captured Sir Malcom Wallace of Elderslie, Will's father, at Loudoun Hill, six years before, and thereafter slain him with his own hand, as a traitor who had refused to take the oath to the Lord Paramount Edward — this in John Baliol's Kingdom of Scotland. This had been the reason for the Lady Wallace's flight with her sons, from Renfrewshire to Dundee, where her brother was a priest. This had been the beginning of the Wallaces' troubles. And now, Sir John Fenwick was here in Lanark.

'I believed the man in England. These three years,' Wallace got out.

'The Percy has brought him back. He is Percy's man. He has come from Carlisle, they say — not from Ayr, as we thought.

21

By Dumfries and Sanquhar and Mauchline. With this squadron of light horse. His men are roistering in the town — North Country Englishmen. They make no secret of what they did. At Carleith. They were making for Ayr — but were met by a messenger from Percy at Mauchline. To come on to Lanark. To escort an especial convoy from Lanark back to Ayr. Tomorrow.'

'But ... why Carleith?'

'Young Dand Cunninghame the eldest son, has escaped from his English prison, they say. Unransomed. This would be ... a lesson! Possibly Fenwick had some old score to settle, from the days he was garrisoned here. Carleith was not on his route of march.'

They considered that for a little, silent.

'The convoy?' the big man said, presently. 'What is it? So, important?'

'I have heard a dozen tales of it, in the town,' Blair answered. 'It has been assembling here, for days. Men say it contains the spoil ravaged from a score of towers and houses. Hundreds of sumpter-horses are being gathered and requisitioned, to carry it all. Whatever it is, it is precious to Sir Henry Price. No ordinary troop horse is sufficient escort. This two hundred light cavalry, under his vassal Fenwick, are to bring it to him at Ayr. Before they continue northwards for Moray. So his men declare openly.'

Wallace's blue eyes narrowed. 'Tavern talk may be less than accurate. But in the main, it could be true enough. The convoy leaves when? Tomorrow? Or today, is it?'

'So it is said. But two different men mentioned also Strathaven to me. They said another such convoy was assembling there. They said some of the troopers talked of collecting this also. So Fenwick and the escort could be going north-about. For Ayr, by the Avon valley. Over Loudoun pass and down the Irvine Water. Not the way they came, by Douglasdale. If it is true ...'

'Loudoun ...!' Wallace breathed. It was at the pass of Loudoun Hill that his father had died.

'Will ...!' Marion faltered. 'Oh, Will — think! Think well! Two hundred trained soldiers. A great company. Not for such as you ...'

He moved over, to squeeze her shoulder, reassuringly. 'I will think well, yes, lass. Never fear, I will consider no folly. This is too great a matter, too important for foolishness. Perhaps, as Father John says, with God's hand in it.' He turned. 'It is four-teen, fifteen miles to Strathaven. More perhaps. By Clyde and Nethan Water, over Stonehouse Muir and down Kype Water. Rough marching. With a long convoy of laden beasts, that is half-a-day's march. Fenwick's squadron have come far. From Cumberland. They will not move at daybreak tomorrow, for a wager! They might even rest for a day. But if they ride tomorrow, they will not ride early, I think. So, with all that long stretch of empty hills before them, they will halt for the night at Strathaven.'

As his friends nodded, he went on. 'From Strathaven to Ayr is not far off forty miles. Say thirty eight, up Avon, and down Irvine Water, then south at my uncle's house of Riccarton. Laden packhorses will not do that in a day, across the hills. They will halt the second night at Galston. or Hurlford. If they ever get so far!'

Breaths were caught at that last sentence, and the manner of its enunciation — even if the young woman's was a gulp.

'They must cross the pass below Loudoun Hill. As my father did! As all travelling that road must do. A dozen uphill miles west of Strathaven. They will not be there, even with an early start, before noon, the day after tomorrow. That is, if they indeed go by Strathaven. Saturday. We have a whole day and a whole night, a half-day and a half-night, thirty six hours. Perhaps more — but we cannot count on it. Between here and Ayr and Irvine, aye and Douglasdale, we have friends, many friends. The houses of my father's brother and my mother's brother. Rob — your home of Kilmarnock breeds stout lads. Ed Little's folk are at Irvine. You, John, do not belong to these parts — but Holy Church has resisted the English better than most. I have heard them call the Red Friars' Monastery of Fail a nest of vipers! You might go stir them up. Thirty six hours, my friends, to be in what strength we can muster, at Loudoun Hill! How say you?'

The two men did not require to say anything; their ex-pressions were sufficient. Marion Braidfoot's little wail was sad, but she did not make other protest than the single plea. 'Sleep?' she said. 'You must sleep. For what is left of this night.'

'We shall have other nights for sleeping, lass,' the man told her, but as kindly as he might. 'Tonight is for hard riding. We have a great opportunity, I think. If what John has learned is

23

truth. It may not be. Street gossip is scarce the most sure information to fight upon! But it is all that we are given. And we would be worse than fools not to put it to the test. This of Strathaven has the ring of truth to it. For none would choose to ride to Ayr by Strathaven, unless for some especial purpose. Lacking that word, I would have much doubted. But Strathaven, Loudoun Hill . . . and Sir John Fenwick, all three! If it is not a sign from Heaven . . .!'

'I see naught of Heaven in this,' Marion said simply. But she left it at that. 'When do you leave?'

'Now, Mirren — now. While Lanark sleeps. While no men are on the roads, to ask us our business. We go tell Ed — and then ride.'

She rose, and came to cling to him, wordless.

The others moved, for the back door.

'Forgive me, my love,' her husband murmured into her dark hair.

'God take care of you, Will,' she whispered back, into his broad chest. 'For *you* will not . . .!'

CHAPTER TWO

It was cold up there on Loudoun Hill, waiting, although it was only late September. A thin smirr of rain on a chill wind blew off the Firth of Clyde, and the heavy clouds were low, blanketing any warmth from the forenoon sun. They were at quite a height, of course — just over the thousand-foot level, with cold wisps of the cloud-skirts frequently drifting across them. William Wallace did not complain, since this weather gave them fair cover from observation. Not that they were likely to be observed up here in the hill-top fort; but others coming up to join them, reinforcements, might have been seen — and he very much hoped for such others. So far, there were only thirty two of them, all told, and it lacked but ninety minutes till noon.

He himself, and his party of eighteen had been here since just before dawn — and had found Rob Boyd and a dozen Kilmarnock men awaiting them within the brokendown, grass-

24

grown ramparts of the Pictish fort. All had climbed here on foot, horses left hidden and tethered down in a hollow below the north face of the hill, the far side from the pass and the road — for this was no place for horses. Their Pictish ancestors had had excellent eyes for strategic sites; — the Damnonii Caledonians, according to the Romans who had failed to conquer them. Loudoun Hill was one of the finest defensive positions in all Southern Scotland. Only, of course, defence was not its present holders' objective. The hill was an isolated, slender, conical peak, rising out of the wide boggy and lifting moorlands; and out of its South-West flank the infant River Irvine was born on a waterlogged shelf of mosses and reeds, quite quickly to form a deep V-shaped winding ravine. And up this ravine the road from Ayr to Strathaven climbed, on to Hamilton and eventually, to Glasgow. Out of the ravine, it crossed the boggy wide terrace by a crooked and narrow causeway, and then entered a sharp defile directly below the hilltop itself — although almost four hundred feet below. There was perhaps half-a-mile of this, the steep and rocky sides a place for goats, the road having to share the constricted floor with a small burn, this now running in the other direction, eastwards, one of the headstreams of the Lanarkshire Avon — indeed the border between the shires of Ayr and Lanark was at the east end of this pass. The old Pictish fort crowned the pointed summit of the hill, and was approachable, without actual scaling, only from the north, the hidden side, and that only after much peat-hag and bog ploutering.

Wallace's waiting party, as well as being grievously small, was distinctly divided — as so much of Scotland was divided these days. In this case, it was because of the composition of the group which Wallace himself had brought. It contained two of his own cousins. Adam was the eldest son of Sir Richard Wallace of Riccarton, his father's elder brother, and head of the name — aged eighteen; Ranald was the eldest son of his mother's brother, Sir Ranald or Reginald Crawford of Crosbie — aged nineteen. They were fine, vigorous young men both; but Boyd's Kilmarnock burgesses' sons and apprentices eyed them askance. For Sir Reginald Crawford was Sheriff of Ayr — had been from before English Edward's time, and still was; which meant that he had elected to co-operate with the hated invader. He declared that he could better serve the people of Ayrshire that way than by letting another English appointee, like Hazelrigg, tyrannise over them. Not all thought as he did. And Sir Richard Wallace of Riccarton, although less co-operative, had indeed signed the infamous Ragman Roll at Berwick only a month before. The two lairds' sons did not agree with their sires' attitudes — but theirs was not the responsibility, of course. The fact that they were here, with a few of their fathers' servants, was not enough to reassure some of the Kilmarnock burghers, whose views and attitudes were more clear-cut.

Wallace himself occupied this prolonged waiting period in seeking to keep the peace between his suspicious adherents, planning tactics for varying eventualities, scanning the eastward approaches for an enemy presence, and watching and praying for vitally necessary reinforcements to arrive in time.

Just before noon, nine men did make an appearance, just as the clouds began to thin and clear, and a watery sun broke through. It was John Blair, with a party from Fail Monastery, including two stalwart monks and five serving brothers. Also Master Thomas Gray, priest of the Lanarkshire parish of Libberton, who had happened to be visiting at Fail and offered to help, as it were, on his way home. None of this group looked today any more ecclesiastical than did Blair himself, all having equipped themselves with steel jacks or leather jerkins, two even having rusty helmets of a sort. They were variously armed, like the others with spears, swords, dirks and two crossbows.

The new arrivals were welcome for more than the mere increase in strength, for most of them were somewhat older than the company already assembled, and being men of religion, drew a certain amount of respect from Boyd's young townsmen. And since they accepted the lairdly party without question, they served as a sort of catalyst between the other groups. Wallace was especially glad to see his friend, whose counsel and aid he much valued.

The weather cleared rapidly thereafter, and the prospects became extensive on all hands, from this lofty viewpoint. Wallace grew concerned about the sun glinting on steel, and giving away their presence, ordering his people to smear peat-mud on all metal equipment. Not that there appeared to be anyone to give them away to, in all that wide panorama of hill and moorland. Sheep and a few shaggy cattle seemed to have those far-flung uplands to themselves, along with the peewits, the shouting larks and the wheepling curlews. A sense of anti-climax began to become evident on Loudoun Hill.

Then, almost an hour after noon, the arrival of Edward Little and a party of ten, from Irvine, revealed how erroneous judgements about the emptiness of the landscape could be. Wallace had put out single watchers at vantage points some way out from the hill-top fort itself; but even so, none of these gave warning of the approach of their reinforcements until they were within some four hundred yards of them — indication of the tricks of dead ground, and of the ability of men to blend into a broken and wild terrain. Little, of course, had endeavoured to make his approach as unobtrusive as possible; whereas the enemy they waited for would be unlikely to do anything of the sort, in the circumstances. But it was a lesson not lost on Wallace, at least, on the need for increased vigilance, and for making sure that every quarter of the terrain was kept under scrutiny, as far as was possible.

The enemy, to be sure, were expected to come along the open road, far below — and that road could be seen intermittently for miles now, to the east, snaking across the purple heathery moors. But there were many gaps in that vision, inevitably, where it disappeared into hollows or little valleys, where the lie of the land produced dead ground and ridges intervened. The fact that they were looking for two hundred horsemen and over one hundred pack-animals should surely make observation along a narrow road no mere matter of chance?

Although Wallace was disappointed that his nephew — who was only one year younger than himself — had only managed to bring ten men with him from the town of Irvine, he was glad indeed to have his company fully assembled. They numbered now only a total of fifty two. He had hoped for twice that, at least. Still, it was a force of sorts, and all were volunteers, their presence here showing that they were willing to take a major risk. All knew what their fate would be, should they fail and thereafter fall alive into English hands. They believed, of course, that they had kept their venture a secret — this was the major reason why there were no more than fifty two of them. But a secret known by fifty two could conceivably have been learned by one or two others. And if only one man, or woman, was to talk, treacherously or merely foolishly, then they had reason to watch their flanks urgently, as well as the road from Strathaven.

But as the afternoon wore on, any urgency was hard to sustain. The Loudoun moors remained as apparently devoid of the

27

presence of man as ever. On all hands, doubts began to be expressed. Was it all a false alarm? Were the stories in Lanark's streets merely wine-inspired folly? Had the convoy gone by Strathaven, at all? Were Wallace's calculations as to timing hopelessly agley?

There was no sure answer to any of these queries, of course. They could only wait — and hope. They could even wait until the next day, the big man declared, if necessary.

It was Wallace himself who eventually first caught sight of the gleam of sunlight on steel, in late afternoon, away to the east. His cry drew all eyes. Soon there were many flickers and flashes for all to see — three miles away, perhaps, amongst the purple and brown moors. Many men were there, armoured men.

'Fenwick made a late start from Strathaven!' the big man cried, unable to keep the quiver out of his voice. 'Now to see that he makes a swift entry to Hell!'

They had, perhaps, half-an-hour. They had had plenty of time to make their plans. The narrow pass steeply below them was half-a-mile long. Wallace divided his company into three. The smallest party, six only, under young Ranald Crawford, he sent off eastwards, behind the hill, to put themselves in a position to rush down and seek to block that eastern end of the pass, at a given signal. The second group, of a dozen, the strongest men muscularly, under Robert Boyd, he sent to creep directly down the rock hill-face, which he himself had thoroughly prospected that morning. They were to disperse themselves, spread out along the face, about half-way down, and be ready to roll down loosened rocks and boulders — again at a given signal. The remaining thirty four he took with him down the North-Western flank of Loudoun Hill.

At the hummocky base, they worked their way round to the level, boggy flat at the western end of the pass. Wallace divided his strength again. He sent ten men under the priest, Thomas Gray, stumbling, leaping, floundering out over the rushes, deer-hair-grass and bog-cotton of the marshy shelf to a scrub-grown knoll of firmer ground a couple of hundred yards from the mouth of the defile. Here, amongst the birch and hazel scrub, they were to raise the old banner which Wallace had brought along for the occasion, the white saltire on blue of Scotland's St. Andrew's Cross; and to show themselves openly — indeed, by constant movement and scurrying amongst the trees, to make themselves seem many times their number. With his final two dozen he hurried on round to the jaws of the pass itself, where he disposed his men on either side of the track, hidden in the burn-channel, hollows, behind boulders and bushes. He himself took up a position on the north side — the burn was on the south — with John Blair, where they could see much of the way along the gut of the defile — and also could be seen from Gray's knoll. There was no cover here, so they pulled up some whins and bracken from nearby, and piled it so that it looked natural enough from the road. Behind it they would crouch. Wallace prayed that in this dispersing of his little force he had acted wisely. He reckoned they might have ten minutes more, in hand.

They had nearer half-an-hour, in fact, before the first horsemen appeared in sight, steel breastplates and spear tips catching the now slanting sunlight, two men side by side. Wallace held his breath as the next pair came into view, immediately behind — and then the next and the next. He was not satisfied to let out his breath until he saw the fifth pair, in full knights' armour these, though with their helmets this warm afternoon, slung over their saddle-bows. Another pair of men-at-arms rode immediately at their heels. It was as he had hoped for. Unsuspecting — and why *should* they suspect in this cowed land? — Fenwick and his friends had not put forward an advance party. This Wallace had feared — and it could have complicated matters considerably. The narrow track through the constricted floor of the defile inevitably forced the enemy into no more than two abreast. With two hundred men-at-arms and some hundred pack-horses, this would make a very long column. How would Fenwick have divided his men?

It soon became apparent that he had a full troop at least, up front with him — a hundred men perhaps, before the first of the sumpter-animals appeared, each pair led behind a single trooper. That would dispose of another fifty or so men-at-arms. Leaving the remaining fifty to form a rearguard. Just about the normal arrangement any military commander on the march would make. As far as today's ambush was concerned, however, it effectively halved Fenwick's fighting strength. Wallace had only, therefore, about a hundred effective cavalry to vanquish, at this stage.

And it was the effectiveness of even these that was the vital matter. At the moment they were strung out, in pairs, for something like three hundred and fifty to four hundred yards at a guess. Which meant that, so long at the fighting was confined within the pass itself, or its mouth, only the front few files could be in action — for the rear files could not turn off the track, because of the burn and the steep rocky slopes. This situation did, of course, affect the ambushers also, to a lesser extent since they were afoot, restricting their concentration of attack. In choosing this battleground, Wallace had taken all this into account. Now, he had to see whether his accounting, together with his timing — which was desperately important — was approximately correct.

That timing was now the big man's urgent preoccupation, as he crouched behind his cover, with Blair. He must not let the excitement, the fury that welled up in him at the near presence of the man who had slain his father in cold blood, who had made a shambles of Carleith, affect his judgement. Thirty seconds too soon, equally with thirty seconds too late, could mean the difference between possible success and bloody ruin. And so much more was at stake than even the lives of some two hundred and fifty men in the pass under Loudoun Hill, he knew in his bones.

Pray God none of his untried ambushers lost their heads, any more than he did, and moved or showed themselves before his signal.

He had chosen his present stance with the greatest of care. The first riders should not be able to see the banner or Gray's group, out on the flats, until they were at least level with his hiding place, even allowing for the fact that they were mounted, and so higher placed. But, equally, nothing ought to prevent them from seeing it within a few yards thereafter. If they did not see it, they must *hear* it . . .

Bent most painfully for so big a man, who must yet be able to see clearly and to get to his feet swiftly, Wallace saw the first pair of riders come level with him, at a jog-trot, only three or four yards away. They looked tired, bored, non alert. Certainly they were not scanning the cover at the sides of the track, nor indeed the more distant prospect. The couple behind were chatting, voices raised above the clip-clop of hooves, the jingle of harness and the creak of leather. Wallace's gaze switched back over three more pairs, to the two knights. He had never seen Sir John Fenwick, but he was said to be a handsome, black-avised man — and the younger knight was distinctly fair

30

of head. The other was he then — dark, long faced, clean-shaven, hooknosed, with a supercilious expression and a glitter of the eyes, discernible even at thirty yards. The watching man all but choked.

He jerked his glance back to the first file, now well past him and giving no alarm. The late afternoon sun was, to be sure, now slanting in from the west and almost directly into the riders' eyes, something Wallace had not planned for, in a noontide ambush. He dared not let this go on, even another ten seconds — or his plan would not work. If it would work, anyway? He required a bunched grouping of the enemy, not a column of pairs, only a few of which could be attacked, and leaving those behind to come on and ride down the attackers. The whole thing was a most delicate operation in time and motion.

Stretching his hand behind him, awkwardly, he waved back and forward, not up and down, a white rag, twice, briefly, and swiftly withdrew it again, beseeching the Almighty that His reverend servant Gray would see it and the horsemen so close at hand would not, behind the whins and bracken.

He had barely got his hand back to his side — and to the hilt of his drawn sword — when high and clear and ululant the horn's call rang out its challenge and signal, to echo hauntingly from all the enclosing hillsides. And now, at last, the convoy was alerted. Everywhere within sight horsemen sat up, staring ahead into the dazzlement of the sun. The first files, now fully thirty yards beyond Wallace's stance, raised hands to shield their eyes, peering. Then they shouted, and pointed, pulling up their mounts.

Sir John Fenwick did not pull up. He spurred forward, past Wallace, jostling aside the two pairs of troopers in the way, to get to where his front men had halted, his knightly colleague close behind. There they drew up, likewise, to stare out over the marshy flat to the scrub-covered hummock. There was not much breeze to blow out the Saltre flag, so Gray had stretched it out over a couple of bushes. It was plain enough — as were the men running and waving and shaking their swords in and around the scrub beside it.

Fenwick barked orders, turning in his saddle to wave up urgently his following files of men-at-arms, before swinging back to consider that terrain. He was a veteran captain, and could not doubt that the ground ahead was marshy and soft, once off

31

the track. But it was unlikely to be deep bog, in such stony land, nothing that horses could not get through, however slowly. He had to make the decision, crucial both for himself and for Wallace. The big man could almost hear the other's mind working.

Then crashes and shouting from far behind jerked all heads round again. Boyd and his strong men, in answer to that horn's summons, were hurling and prising loose their boulders and rocks, to send them bounding down up on the long thin line of packhorses and men far below. What the effect would be was anybody's guess; but it all sounded sufficiently alarming and terrible, men screaming and horses neighing in fright.

Fenwick was faced with another decision — which could affect his first. He could see more or less from whence the rocks were coming — and could likewise see that nothing very effective could be done meantime against the hurlers, away up there. He turned to face the front again, biting his thin lips. Then he whipped out his sword, and started to bellow new orders.

Some three dozen or so men-at-arms had now accumulated round the knights in the mouth of the pass, jammed tight, necessarily, as herrings in a barrel. The younger fair haired knight was sent forward with most of them, not in any charge but in a rather gingerly advance, to pick their way across the swampy flat to Gray's position. An under-officer with two or three others, was sent back hot-foot, to turn round following files of troopers, rescue the precious baggage, warn the rearguard, and send forward information. Sir John himself, like a good commander, remained where he was, in an approximately central position, where he might exert a measure of control over all, about ten men still at his side. Wallace would have done exactly the same.

The big man gave the under officer sufficient time to get well away from the scene, and then jumped up at last from his crouching, cramped position great sword raised high 'A Wallace! A Wallace!' he shouted, and leap forward. And everywhere, on either side of the track, his men followed suit, springing out of the burn-channel, from behind bushes and boulders.

'A Wallace! A Wallace!' they cried, irrespective of their own names and allegiancies.

Wallace himself was by no means the nearest to the mounted group. In fact, he was one of the furthest away. But seeing him, and recognising him for what he was, the leader, Fenwick spurred his splendid horse towards him, sword weaving.

32

Edward Little happened to be quite close to the knight. With no foolish inhibitions about leaving Fenwick to his uncle, he leapt in, sword in right hand, dirk in left. The other saw him come, but had no intention of being diverted. Without drawing rein, he made a vicious sideways slash at the younger man. Little, anticipating this, ducked low, lower than any mounted man's sword could reach unless he actually leant down from the saddle — and leaning so is one of the many things an armour-clad knight just could not do, sheathed in steel as he was. The sword whistled harmlessly almost a foot above the other's head.

Little did not straighten up — although he maintained his forward motion. This was war, not any chivalric tourney. Risking no return slash of Fenwick's blade, he flung himself almost under the horse — and his dirk flashed up, to plunge and rip. The bay stallion screamed and reared high, knocking the man below over in its pawing, lashing agony, amidst a cascade of blood and entrails, and so tottered on its hind legs a few terrible yards before heeling over and crashing.

Fenwick was a trained cavalryman. There was a drill for this, even for a man largely encased in steel. Maintaining an upright position he kicked his feet free of the heavy stirrups and, while his mount was still rearing, slid down backwards, half over its rump. He made an awkward landing, but on his feet, and managed not to overbalance. He was able to jerk aside, clear, before the brute crashed.

So he stood, swaying, face to face with William Wallace. John Blair was only a yard or two behind his friend.

The big man, seeing Little's move and the beginning of its results, had paused, to survey at a glance the engagement as a whole. As instructed, should a detachment of the cavalry be enticed out towards Gray's trap, about half his men here had gone leaping off into the marsh after the already floundering and scattered horsemen. It was bad ground for men on foot — but not nearly so bad as for men on horses, a quagmire of mud, peat broth and green slime amongst tussocks of reeds and deer-hair-grass. Men could jump from one to another of the tussocks, horses could not. The foot would catch up with the cavalry. And the priestly party was already issuing from the hummock to meet them.

Nearer at hand, Wallace's men were, in the main, following Little's tactics, and attacking in the first instance the unprotected horses rather than the part-armoured horsemen, seeking

33

to disembowel the poor brutes with their dirks, and so bring the riders down. The men-at-arms had long lances as main weapons — which could be deadly in a charge, or with ample room for operation; but in this cramped situation on the narrow track, and against men whose aim was to get under the horses' bellies, they were fairly useless, indeed something of an impediment. Most of them quickly discovered this, and threw the lances from them, to draw instead their short cavalry swords. But by that time, not a few were on collapsing, dying mounts.

Wallace, satisfied, addressed himself to his personal enemy. Fenwick and he were now more evenly matched, for though the knight was encased in steel, his sword was much the shorter, and he had less than the big man's reach. Moreover, in the flurry he had not had time to don his helm.

Sword fighting, with the then heavy weapons, was no delicate art; but Fenwick's blade, being vastly the lighter as well as the shorter, did allow him greater scope for manoeuvre, variety of stroke and speed of play. On the other hand, one shrewd stroke of Wallace's great brand, and there would be no recovery.

Both perceived this — and also the fact that the knight, being older, and clad and constricted in heavy steel, would tire the sooner. Fenwick, therefore, drove in right away without any preliminary skirmishing and circling. He lunged straight for the younger man's throat, above his jack or breastplate and, as Wallace stepped back and swung his blade round and down in a protective sweep, leapt to the left swiftly, changed the direction and style of his thrust, and stabbed low for the other's unprotected right thigh beneath the leathern jerkin.

It was a near thing, and had the knight's blade been three inches longer, it would have succeeded.

Fenwick stumbled forward a little, with the force of his thrust, and if Wallace could have used his weapon to good advantage, then he could have finished the fight. But a five foot long, double-handed brand weighing a dozen pounds cannot be tossed about like a dirk, even with wrist muscles such as the younger man possessed; it could not be jabbed or poked either, save by a carefully controlled movement, but only slung and slashed. Requiring room for this, Wallace leapt well aside, sweeping the weapon high in an arc again.

They circled round each other more cautiously now. John Blair and Ed Little could have come to their friends aid, but judged that he would not have wished that. They went to join the larger mêlée instead — though continuing to keep an eye on this personal duel.

Wallace made the next attack with a swinging leftwards, down-slanting swipe to the knee, designed to make the other skip — a difficult movement for a man in full armour. Fenwick achieved it, after a fashion, all but tripping in the process. But this blow was not just a swipe — it was a controlled figure-of-eight swing, which came back and up, right-handed all in the same motion. It struck the other on his left arm, with a loud clang, all but knocking him over. If it had not knocked him aside, it would have finished the fight there and then, for it swept on and up over the steel shoulder and missed slicing the bare head only by an inch or two. Its residual force carried Wallace himself round, staggering a little, and Fenwick had the opportunity to recover his stance. But now his left arm hung limp within its chain-mail sleeve.

The older man was panting now, sweat streaming down his dark features. But he well perceived the handicap of the other's weighty brand. He shortened his own blade in his steel-gauntleted fist, and rushed — as fast as his armour would allow — straight in at his large opponent, to get inside his guard before the mighty weapon could be upraised sufficiently to crash down on him effectively. Wallace leapt backwards again, with all his speed and energy — and he was surprisingly light on his feet for a man of his size; even so he was not quick enough altogether to avoid the rush, and the point of the other's sword bored into the toughened hide of the younger man's jerkin just under the uprising left arm, at the side of the jack. The leather, the slight sideways angle of the knight's thrust — probably caused by his damaged left arm — and Wallace's own jerk away, took the main force out of the jab, so that the sword point slid away without actually penetrating the man's flesh, although it ripped hide and clothing and scored the skin, spinning him round.

Wallace scarcely felt the pain, then. But the spin around to the left had its own result. It put him in a better posture *vis-a-vis* Fenwick who, still on the impetus of his rush, came lurching past. The knight tried to stop himself — but would have been wiser to allow himself to go on, out of range. For the big man had maintained, through it all, the upswing of his brand, and now suddenly was in a position to bring it driving down, half-turned, on the back of his opponent's bare head. Down the mighty blade smashed, cutting through hair and bone and brains, cleaving the dark, sardonic head in two, right to the neck bone. Sir John Fenwick collapsed slowly, part held up by his armour, into a horrible jerking twitching mass of blood and flesh and steel.

One debt was paid.

Wallace turned away from what he had done slowly, emotionally rather than physically exhausted. But this was no state of mind for a commander of men. Drawing great breaths, he looked to the larger struggle.

His friends and colleagues nearby did not appear to require his assistance. Most of the ten men left with Fenwick were already prostrate. Only one remained on his horse — and he was galloping off westwards along the track, flogging his beast's rump with the flat of his sword. One or two of his fellows were still fighting, beside their fallen mounts, but even as Wallace watched, one of these went down and the other surrendered, throwing away his weapon.

Out in the bog all was a slaistering confusion. All semblance of a cavalry attack on the hummock area had disappeared. Individual troopers and Wallace's men were milling about over a wide area in an indescribable, floundering chaos of mud and peat, all leg and foot movement reduced to a ridiculous slow motion by the quagmire, men up to their knees, horses worse. None would actually sink deeply for there would be rock and stone not far down; but a worse place to fight in would be hard to imagine. There was no sign of the younger knight.

Some of the enemy had turned back. Some had dismounted, and were fighting on foot. Some were frankly fleeing. There was not much doubt as to the outcome, especially as some members of Wallace's nearest group, finishing their bloody business on the track, were hurrying out to the aid of their friends in the bog.

The big man turned, to gaze eastwards along the pass. Nothing could be made out, with any clarity, of what went on there; only that the floor of the defile was packed with a confused mass of men and horses. Wallace forced himself to clear, constructive thinking. The main numbers of the enemy were still along there, not only undefeated but not having been in action. Only thirty odd were accounted for hereabouts; therefore sixty odd, apart from those involved with the pack-train, were still to be dealt with. And that not counting the rearguard. But they had lost their leaders, lost the initiative, lost coherence and control. And some, surely would have become casualties to the crashing rocks?

He made up his mind. There were one or two riderless horses, which had not been disembowelled. sidling around. He ran to one, reddened sword still in hand, and hoisted himself onto it.

'John!' he yelled. 'Get a horse, and follow me. Ed — take charge here. When you have disarmed these, send to me all the men you can. Along the pass. Quickly. Ready to take to the braesides. You have it?' And slapping the grey's haunch with his open left hand, he rode off, kicking the beast to a canter.

The nearest of the enemy were about three hundred yards away, men-at-arms sitting their horses, more or less inactive, mainly facing the other way, uncertain with no clear orders, no sure objective. Obviously there was complete confusion ahead. Boulders were continuing to come bounding down in terrifying fashion along there, and the noise of them, with the screaming, whinnying and shouting, was daunting in the extreme. No doubt Fenwick's under-officer was there, trying to bring some order into the situation, but without much evident success.

Wallace thought swiftly — he had to, with only hundreds of yards to cover. The track ahead was packed tight with mounted men. They had no room to manoeuvre, no space in which to wield spears or even swords. If he descended upon them, only three or four at the most would take his impact, protecting the others behind — but at the same time, immobilising them. Most would not be able even to see what was going on at this end. Sixty horsemen cramming a hundred yards or so of road, stationary, watching those bounding boulders. What would be the effect of even a one-man charge at their backs?

The man knew his decision before ever he reached any actual conclusion. He dug in his heels, spurring his mount on to as near a gallop as it could manage under his weight, and waved his huge sword round and round above his head.

'A Wallace! A Wallace!' he bellowed, and thundered directly at the enemy rear.

Men turned to stare. And a strange sight he must have made, a single but enormous young man bearing down on them, auburn hair streaming, mighty brand whirling, shouting challenge — a strange sight, but alarming for those who must take the impact and who were wedged tightly, unable to engage the attacker on equal terms, or to either dodge or bolt. The first four would have been better actually to ride out to meet the charging giant — but perhaps that was asking too much of ordinary men-at-arms fighting somebody else's battle. Moreover, Wallace was not quite so alone as he thought — for John Blair was now pounding along only fifty or so yards behind — and who knew how many more might be appearing after?

In fact, what those first four did was reasonable enough. The two nearest the burn-channel leapt from their saddles, straight into the shallow water; while the pair at the other side jumped down likewise, and began to scramble up the steep bank, out of the way. It was less than heroic — but sound common sense. Only, it put the next four or so into almost the same position as they had been in — save that these had four uncontrolled horses between them and this raving madman.

Horses, like other God-made creatures, have their own instincts towards self-preservation — and perfectly good eyes and ears into the bargain. These four would see one of their own kind being driven headlong down upon them, and would have no doubts that immediate avoiding action was necessary. Without riders to force them to any other course, and misliking both the burn and the steep braeside, they turned to bore in eastwards amongst the others away from the menace. It was not a bolt, since the press precluded that; but it was pushing, jostling, hood-lashing and positive action nevertheless — and markedly infectious.

As a result, when Wallace smashed into that wall of horseflesh and men, it was not nearly so solid or unyielding a barrier as it might have been, since most of the first dozen or so animals were seeking to go in the other direction — and not all their riders were seeking vehemently to change their minds. The great sword, whirling in the traditional bent figure-of-eight swing, left side, right side, slash and slice, was no incentive for harassed horsemen. Many more elected to jump clear, like the first four. Others were so tightly wedged that they could not do so. The sword got some, others went down under trampling, rearing, flailing hooves. Some even found themselves safely behind the storming maniac — and there was another yelling, charging Scot to cope with, John Blair, looking wholly secular.

The effect of all this on the troopers ahead was progressively more traumatic. They did not know what was going on, *could* not. All they knew was that they were being attacked in the rear — where their leaders should have been — and by how many they could not tell; and that this attack was pushing them on towards the area of those hurtling rocks and the shattered pack-train. It would have been a super human under-officer who could have turned those fifty or so remaining men-at-arms into a disciplined fighting machine, there and then. They could see men, their own mates obviously, scrambling up the hillside to the south, to get out of harm's way. Not a few thought it an excellent idea.

Wallace, hoarse with yelling his slogan, recognised that this could not continue. He was making practically no progress at all, now, brought up by sheer pressure of flesh and blood, animal and human. His brand was still flailing, but he was finding it increasingly difficult, even with its five-foot length, to reach any more victims. None of their swords could reach him either, of course — but that was scarcely relevant. He could now hear Blair whacking and slashing behind him; but the same conditions would apply to him. So far, the charge had been an extraordinary success. But stalemate was almost upon them — for none of Little's people would be able to reach them for long minutes yet, at least. And stalemate must be wholly to the advantage of the enemy, inevitably, as they learned the number of their assailants.

Wallace drew on all his lung power to yell for Rob Boyd to join in, to leave off stone-rolling and come down to the attack.

It is improbable that, in all the shouting and screaming and neighing, Boyd could have heard. But, though two hundred feet higher, he himself was no more than some three hundred yards from the bottleneck mêlée, and could see approximately what went on. Moreover, his men were running out of suitable stones to dislodge and roll. He drew his sword, roared the order to break off the advance and led the way, scrambling and slithering down the steep slope.

There was only a dozen of them — although that might not have been entirely apparent to the English in the gut of the valley. But they added a new dimension to the struggle, and to the feeling of being trapped, front and rear. The boulders and rocks stopped crashing down. The way along the pass was, therefore, for the moment free — apart from the litter of dead, maimed and milling men and beasts therein. It would take minutes for the former stone-rollers to reach the track, for it was a difficult descent. There was time for men on horses to escape from this hellish place. Like a plug suddenly pulled from an all but bursting tank, the pressure was removed. Flight was possible. A sort of panic relief took over. Men-at-arms started to disengage themselves and stream away eastwards, lashing their mounts. The tight wedging began to ease at that side. Men could move again — but only in one direction. In but a comparatively few seconds, all who could were spurring away down the pass, the way they had come, riding down dismounted and wounded men, leaping fallen pack-horses, cursing any who got in their way. By the time Boyd and his stalwarts got down, there was nobody left to fight — save those who had abandoned horses for the opposite braesides. Cheated, after these they went climbing.

Wallace, somewhat bemused by this abrupt and complete victory, did not pursue. There was little to be gained by so doing. But he sent Blair after the fleeing enemy, to discover how Ranald Crawford and his little party were faring at the east mouth of the defile. If there was a fifty-strong rearguard, they would have been able to do but little. Their instructions had been to cause a delay and diversion, if possible, not to indulge in heroics.

Meantime, with Boyd's people chasing dismounted escapers up the hill, the big man was left alone on the scene — or alone as one upright — suddenly inactive, an extraordinary situation which he could scarcely credit. Almost at a loss for what to do now, he decided that he had better ride back, westwards, to see that all was still going their way at that end. Only now did he begin to feel the pain of the skin-deep score on his left side.

He met Edward Little and Thomas Gray, with most of their men, coming down the track at the trot, to his aid — and found them quite incredulous at his report of the flight of the enemy main body. They had to see to believe — like an earlier Thomas — and Wallace turned back once more, with them, after learning that all was well at the west mouth, and a small group left under Adam Wallace, with about a dozen disarmed prisoners and the wounded.

Boyd's men were mainly returning to the valley floor, now, with such few prisoners as they had been in time to catch. Most of the dismounted men-at-arms had escaped, un-doubtedly — but this was not important.

In a state of suspicion and euphoria mixed, they all went to inspect the central pass area, with its shattered pack-train.

It represented a scene of prolonged and extensive chaos and

horror, hard to look upon in cold, or cooling, blood. The rocks and boulders had inflicted terrible damage on the close-ordered ranks below. Everywhere mangled horses and men, dead and wounded, lay littered, their panners and packs scattered, crushed, burst open. Many pack-horses still stood or roamed about, more probably than were down, though many also undoubtedly had followed the fleeing cavalry. Dismounted men lurched and staggered around, likewise, seemingly aimlessly, though some were seeking to catch and ride off on frightened sumpter-horses. Ed Little was for urgent pursuit of these — but Wallace saw no point in it. There had been a sufficiency of killing; prisoners were only a problem and embarrassment to them — and anyway, the more of them who escaped to tell the tale of their defeat, the greater, more alarming, that defeat would become, since none would seek to minimise the odds against them, the terrors they had had to face. This day's work had been not merely for vengeance, but for a light, a beacon, to rouse cowering Scotland. The more enemy who escaped, therefore, the greater the blow to English morale, and lift to Scottish.

If only doubtfully, in the main, the others accepted that. They went on to put the wounded horses out of their misery, do what they could for the human wounded, and inspect the captured booty.

It did not take them long to discover the nature of the contents of the pack-train which Sir Herry Percy, the Warden, had been so anxious to bring safe to him at Ayr. The burst sacks revealed that it was mostly the loot of churches, abbeys and religious houses — lamps, censers, crucifixes, candlesticks, chalices, lavers and the like, in gold and silver with gems. There were bags of rings, holy ornaments, begemmed miniatures of saints. Chests of jewel-encrusted copes, chasubles, dalmatics, stoles, even mitres. There were chestfuls of coin, also gold and silver. Here were the raped and ravaged treasures of Holy Church from much of Southern Scotland, spilled and scattered over an Ayrshire hillside, in the mire of peat, in the blood-stained waters of the burn. Appalled — for sacrilege was a greater horror to these men than was the death or injury of their fellow Christians — they stared at the evidence of wicked avarice and shameful impiety, Master Gray openly weeping.

Wallace was less affected than some, though shocked. In the present circumstances, he preferred the Church Militant to the

41

Church Magnificent, and believed Thomas Gray and John Blair worthier representatives than those from whom all this had been filched; though he was the first to admit that the Church in Scotland had been in the forefront of resistance to the Plantagenet — much better than the nobility and gentry — hence this pillage, no doubt; but it had been a passive sort of resistance, in the main, so far, a refusal to co-operate, a rejecting of edicts, a preaching against, rather than any active or concrete campaign. Leadership in the field, as it were, had been as absent amongst the Lords Spiritual, since Dunbar, as it had been amongst the Lords Temporal — unlike the fierce and warlike Bishop Beck of Durham, who was one of Edward's senior commanders.

All this sacred treasure was, in fact, an embarrassment and problem to the day's victors. They could use the coin, undoubtedly; but what to do with all the rest? The last thing Wallace wanted was to saddle himself with loads of heavy valuables demanding transport and guarding. On the other hand, it was unthinkable that it should be allowed to fall back into English hands. He would have to think about it . . .

He had more to think about than that — the wounded in particular. According to Little, none of their own men had been slain, at the west end, but four were quite sorely hurt, all in the bog fighting. And one of Boyd's townsmen had broken a leg in a fall while rushing down the steep braeside. But these were as nothing to the battered and mangled English wounded, casualties of the rock bombardment in the main, whose moans and groans disfigured the early evening calm. They could not just put them out of their sufferings, as they did the horses; nor could they, in humanity, merely leave them lying there.

He ordered about half of his available men to give immediate temporary succour and care; the others to gather together the uninjured horses, both pack and riding, and to bring the baggage and loot — also captured arms and good usuable armour — to a central point. This was going to take a long time, he feared.

John Blair rode in from the east to report that all was well at that end. Ranald Crawford and his party were marching up, with a fair number of prisoners, mainly fleeing troopers whom they had intercepted. By making a demonstration, and actually lighting a grass and heather fire in the mouth of the pass they had been able to hold up Fenwick's rearguard for a con-

siderable time without any true fighting — until the refugees
had come streaming down from the west presumably with tales
of terrible things behind. Very quickly the rearguard, thereafter, had evidently decided that if a hundred and fifty and
more in front could not cope with the menace forward, then
their mere fifty or so could do nothing about it. After a little
they had turned and trotted off eastwards, as though washing
their hands of the entire affair. It looked as though there would
be no rally in that quarter.

Wallace, faced for the first time with the many problems of a
victorious commander, paced the trampled and bloody track
back and forth, thinking them out. When his cousin Ranald
Crawford arrived, with his half-dozen, he called a council-of-
war of his principal lieutenants, to explain what he proposed
and to seek their views.

He saw it this way. By tomorrow, the occupying forces in
Lanark and Ayr would be out searching for them, by the next
day, half Southern Scotland. Those of them who were prepared,
and able, to campaign further, to try to widen and strengthen
the fire they had lit today, must make a quick escape into
Ettrick Forest, there to establish themselves. Others, like the
men from Fail Monastery, who had heavy responsibilities and
could not just drop everything meantime, must go back to their
own places, as secretly as possible under cover of night. The prisoners, disarmed, would be given charge of their own wounded,
with a few of the sumpter-horses to carry them, and let go free.
The Fail party would take their own Scots wounded with them
to the monastery, and tend them there. Also take the bulk of the
treasure, and store it until happier times. He and the Ettrick
group would take some of the money, and the best of the arms
and armour — all of which might prove very useful. They
would move just as soon as possible, for they had to get their
own horses hidden on the North-West side of this Loudoun Hill.
They could do nothing about burying the dead; the English
could do that tomorrow. Was this a reasonable course of
action?

None could better it, save in minor details. It was decided
that just over a score would follow Wallace into the Forest at
once, and others would join them there later. All would do their
utmost to stir up vigorous reaction, in their own communities,
to this blossoming of revolt. The impetus must be maintained
and increased.

It was almost dusk, with cloud building up again, before they left the pass under Loudoun Hill — the English party of freed prisoners and wounded sent off eastwards, and very surprised to be so. There were some score of them comparatively unharmed and about thirty wounded. Nearly fifty dead were counted. Which meant that approximately half of Fenwick's force had fled. They would undoubtedly have to contend that a very large force had attacked them — whatever the released prisoners said.

On his way out, as Wallace reached the body of Sir John Fenwick, he took the knight's richly chased sword from the already stiffening fingers within the steel gauntlet, and with a single fiercely controlled movement, snapped the blade across his bent knee. It was quite likely to be the same weapon which had slain his father.

CHAPTER THREE

The forest of Ettrick, in golden autumn, was a splendid place for fugitives and hiders — but less convenient for campaigners and for stirring up revolt, Wallace discovered. He and his friends had achieved the safety of the upland glen of Cow Gill, under the mighty mass of Culter Fell, near the Lanarkshire-Peebles-shire border, where the chances of their being surprised, or even found at all, were as remote as the glen itself. Wallace had chosen this position for various reasons. Although hidden deep in the hills, it was approachable — or leaveable — in three directions — by the Culter, Lamington and Wandel Waters, from respectively the North-West, the West and the South-West; but also it had a back door, for the agile at least, over to the upper Tweed valley in the Drumelzier area. It had three additional advantages, in that it was within reasonable range of the Braidfoot lairdship of Lamington — it was in Lamington parish, in fact — Thomas Gray's parish of Libberton, to the North, and the Crawford district to the South-West, where Ranald Crawford had kinsfolk. Supplies could be obtained by night from sympathisers in these places; news and reports also.

All of which was good. But security and comfort were not Wallace's prime objectives. He had not come to Ettrick Forest to hide away, or even to use it as a base for limited forays — as did so many outlaws of one sort or another. The Loudoun Hill attack had been intended to be the start of a campaign, and the present hiding merely a necessary interlude for regrouping and gathering strength in approximate safety. But security and opportunity proved, as so often, counter-productive. The Cow Gill glen was inevitably a backwater as far as news, influence and effective exploits were concerned — and frustrating accordingly.

One of two small raids were, in fact, mounted from here, on isolated English-held positions, mainly small motte-and-bailey castles and towers along the main North-South route between Lanark and Carlisle, by upper Clydesdale and Annandale, some successful, some less so — one indeed a complete fiasco. Their most rewarding venture was the attacking and routing of another convoy, in the Dalveen Pass near upper Nithsdale — only military stores, but a telling blow, which would no doubt worry Percy. But all this was scarcely setting Scotland alight.

Wallace fretted. All accounts made it clear that the effects of Loudoun Hill had been spectacular — but mainly towards the state of mind of the English overlords. They were impressed, obviously — but angry rather than alarmed, it seemed. And they visited their wrath on many innocent folk — which was no doubt part of the reason why the Scots reaction was distinctly muted. Generally, from what could be gleaned from informants, the common people were delighted at the successful affront put upon the usurpers; many of the gentry, likewise. But no uprising followed, no large scale demonstrations, no flood of volunteers for revolt. Worst of all, in the circumstances, the great lords and nobility, who in the feudal polity controlled the main means of revolt, armed men, horses, money, not only showed no elation, or even sympathy, but some actually condemned the affair as an outrage and banditry. They had the most to lose, of course — unless a poorer man's life was considered of major value.

So the English grip tightened rather than eased, reprisals were the order of the day, and the Scots as a whole awaited developments doubtfully.

Marion Braidfoot had come to Lamington Tower, to be near

her husband — she would have joined him in the Cow Gill glen, pregnant as she was, if he would have allowed it, pleased so to do — and so they could see each other more frequently than before, when Wallace had divided his lodging between his uncles' houses of Crosbie and Riccarton; this was one personal advantage to accrue. Marion, through her brothers, was in fact one of the most valuable channels of information. From her, amongst other things, they learned that none of the parties returning from Loudoun Hill had been intercepted; and that the monastic group had reached Fail in safety, with the wounded and treasure — and remained apparently unsuspected. In some agitation, Marion had also broken the news that Wallace himself had been declared outlaw, and a price set on his head; presumably no others had been identified, since his was the only name outlawed, as yet.

If that large young man was fretting, impatient, and somewhat disappointed, in the month that followed Loudoun Hill, it was because reactions were so comparatively modest on the Scots side, not that they were non-existent. In fact, quite a number of enthusiasts did come to join him in the Forest, mainly young men — some indeed, like his cousins, little more than boys. One, John Cleland, was another far-out cousin, son of Cleland of that Ilk, in North Lanarkshire. It was notable how many of the sons of chiefly and lairdly families were prepared to venture all, where their fathers and superiors were not; for though none of the great lords and nobility sent representatives, by mid-October Wallace had been joined by, amongst others Adam Currie, son of Currie of that Ilk, from Annandale; young Alexander Auchinleck of that Ilk, from near Ayr; Hugh Dundas, son of Dundas of that Ilk, in Lothian; and Roger Kirkpatrick, Younger of Closeburn, in Nithsdale. He was indeed building up a junior officer corps, of a sort, for his venture. But where were the seniors? And the men they had to lead, the large numbers of men necessary for any effective campaign? Only the lords could supply these in any quantity. The odd serving man and forester was all very well, like the few apprentices and burghers' sons from towns such as Kilmarnock, Ayr and Irvine; these were useful for guerilla tactics, and Wallace had nearly a hundred of them assembled in Cow Gill glen by this time — and finding them difficult to keep fed, occupied and keen. But such would never serve to cleanse Scotland of the invader, never be able to challenge proud Edward Longshanks' might. For that, they must have the retinues of the great lords, the nobility's trains of men-at-arms.

One great lord, in the South-West, might have been expected to be prepared to help — Sir William Douglas, Lord of Douglasdale and Avondale, a man of spirit and fire, nicknamed the Hardy. But he, unfortunately, was a prisoner in England. He had commanded the key castle of Berwick, and at Edward's siege and sack of Berwick town had managed to hold out in the fortress high above the blood-soaked streets. But after the fatal Battle of Dunbar, with all the rest capitulated, he had surrendered to the Plantagenet personally, on honourable terms — and whenever he had marched out into the hands of the First Knight of Christendom, had been seized, humiliated, shackled with iron and set to walk, on foot, with scullions leading him, all the way to his English prison, as example of what happened to those who chose to oppose the King of England. This for lordly 'traitors'; the rest of his garrison, of less than noble rank, had merely been slaughtered there and then. Sir William had left only a wife and children at Douglas Castle, so there was no help to be looked for there.

With the days shortening, and winter approaching, when the outdoor life in the Forest would scarcely be practical politics for any large numbers, Wallace decided that he must attempt a different role. Instead of addressing himself to the English, he would address himself to his own lord. His father had been a vassal of Sir James Stewart, Lord of Renfrew, Bute and Kyle Stewart, fifth Lord High Steward of Scotland. He would go to Renfrew, and seek to persuade James Stewart to what was surely no more than his duty. As a vassal, or at least a vassal's son — or brother, rather, since his elder brother Malcolm was now the vassal — he had a right to approach his lord.

Renfrew Castle was nearly forty miles away to the North-West, in the settled low country of the upper Clyde estuary. It would be a perilous journey for an outlaw and wanted man as kenspeckle as William Wallace. Therefore he would travel alone by night as far as possible, and in a begging friar's gown and hood.

Marion, indeed almost all his friends, sought to dissuade him — or at least to let them go with him as a large and strong escort. But he was adamant — he must go, and alone. He took emotional leave of his wife, and set out one chill October evening, with staff and begging bowl, to follow, not the Clyde itself but hidden and unfrequented routes parallel with the river's valley, to the North-West.

*   *   *

In the village of Paisley, only three miles from Renfrew — and from Wallace's old home of Elderslie likewise — he called at the great Abbey, where he had a kinsman as Prior, and made discreet enquiries anent the occupants of the fine castle above the short River Cart, three miles to the north. Yes, the Lord James was at home; but he was currently entertaining the Prince Bishop of the Palatinate, Anthony Beck of Durham — and all knew Beck as one of the most dangerous and savage men presently in Scotland. The Steward was married to the Lady Gelis de Burgh, sister of the Earl of Ulster, one of King Edward's greatest friends, a situation which had both advantages and the reverse, through having to associate closely with certain of the English overlords. Few imagined that the High Steward of Scotland would enjoy the company of Bishop Beck, whether or not his wife did.

The Prior advised his young kinsman that, if see the Lord James he must, he should go to Renfrew Castle discreetly, at the evening angelus. The Lady Gelis was a notably pious woman and took religious observances very seriously — her husband less so. Beck, being a bishop — although a blood-thirsty one — might be expected to attend the lady's services while her guest, whereas the Lord James was something of a backslider and tended to absent himself, save on Sundays and saints' days. As ever, Wallace's size would draw attention to him, and it was highly inadvisable for him to be seen by Beck or any of his minions.

Accordingly, the young man, still in his tattered friar's habit, walked on to the burgh of barony of Renfrew, through its narrow streets and down towards the shore of the Clyde estuary, where, on a mound overlooking the Cart's confluence with the greater river and the little huddled port there, rose the towers and curtain-walls of the Steward's castle. He presented himself at the Watergate, not the main entrance, just as the angelus bell was sounding, and declared that he came from the Abbot Dungal of Holywood, in Nithsdale, with a message for the Lord James in person, and sought interview. The gate porter was a stranger, and presumably did not know him either. Though he eyed the tall monk curiously, he went off to make enquiries. Presently he returned and Wallace was admitted, and led to one of the flanking towers of the large quadrangular establishment, passing on the way the chapel from which singing was echoing.

Here a major-domo recognised him at once — for Elderslie was only a mile away — and greeted him warmly — although he subconsciously lowered his voice to do so. After a brief exchange, he went off to inform his master, on the floor above.

When the visitor was escorted up the winding stair, he was shown into a small, comfortable chamber, with rich hangings and many books, somewhat over-warm from a well-doing log fire, where a long, dark, lean-faced man with cadaverous features, of late middle years, pored over parchments on a table, quill in hand. He looked up thoughtfully, and though his face was set in gloomy lines, his eyes were large, brown and luminous, almost soulful, and matching but strangely with the rest of him. This peculiar looking man pursed his lips, sighed, and then shook his head — less warm a welcome than that of his major-domo.

'Will Wallace,' he said. 'Man — you should not have come here.' He had a somwhat wet and indistinct delivery, his tongue rather too large for his mouth. 'This was ill done.'

'I had to see you, my lord,' Wallace said simply bowing briefly. 'How else could I do so?'

'As to that, I know not,' the other said, laying down his pen. 'But you are a proscribed outlaw — and I am Sheriff of Renfrew and Bute, amongst other things!'

'You are also my feudal lord, sir, I your vassal. I have a right, have I not, to come into your presence? Moreover, my outlawry is by English proscription and law, not Scots. And you are High Steward of Scotland. In the absence of the King of Scots, principal officer of this realm.'

'Do I not know it!' the older man answered testily. 'I need not such as young Will Wallace to tell me of it. But I am sore hedged about, walled in, watched as by hawks. Beck is here, roosting in my house — and why, think you? Not for love of James Stewart! And you, after what you have done, come seeking my presence!'

'I have come discreetly, at least, my lord. None knows of my presence here, save Pate Denniston there. That is why I came at this hour.'

'No doubt, no doubt, man. But you have not won *out*, yet!

49

And you have come wanting something from me, I swear! My aid?'

'*I* do not require your aid, my lord. But Scotland does!' the younger man declared forcefully.

'Tcha! Scotland! What is Scotland, today? Tell me that, Will — what is this Scotland which requires my aid, at the risk of my head! It is — or was — a realm, yes. An ancient realm, which has grown weary. Done. A name on old parchments. A throne that has tottered. A pack of squabbling nobles. A Church which is but an empty shell. That is the Scotland of which, God pity me, I am High Steward! And you would have me put my head in a noose for it?'

The big man looked troubled. '*Is* that Scotland, my lord?' he demanded. 'What you say may be the kingdom, the realm. But it is not the *nation*, surely? It is Scotland the nation I say needs you, and such as you. What of the people? The folk. And the land? The burghs and villages, the farms and the folk in them? Are these not Scotland, also? And worth fighting for?

Curiously the Steward scanned the younger man's face. 'Folk ... are but folk!' he said. 'Whoever rules them. Be it Edward Plantagenet or John Baliol. And the land is the lords' — who will cut each others' throats for more of it! And support the king who serves them best. Edward Longshanks is a strong king. In Edward's peace a man's lands may lie secure. And his folk on them.'

'So long as they pay tribute to the tyrant usurper!'

The Steward glanced about him fearfully. 'Hush, man — watch your foolish words! Men have been torn limb from limb for less than that! And I have watched them.'

'Yet it is the truth, lord. Free men will never bow the knee to Edward and his cruel lackeys. Therefore, those who do are no free men. And it is the free men who will, who *must*, save Scotland.'

'And you believe, Will that what *you* have done — waylaying and slaying Fenwick, and stealing his baggage train — is like to save this Scotland of yours? Many have already suffered for that act.'

Wallace nodded, unhappily. 'Fenwick slew my father,' he said. 'I am sorry if the innocent have suffered for what I did. But I say, nevertheless, that it required to be done. That if more would do likewise, fewer would suffer. And in the end we could drive the invader from our land. 'After all, we do not outnumber the English by twenty-to-one! More. They say that there are not more than 30,000 English troops in all Scotland. And yet we suffer them to grind us into the ground — *our* ground!'

'There are 30,000 trained soldiers, man, well-armed and disciplined. And well led. They hold all the great castles and walled towns. Against such, what can we do . . .?'

'Fifty of us routed two hundred of such trained soldiers at Loudoun Hill, my lord — and saw little of discipline or good leadership.'

'Fifty? I heard that there were six hundred of you!'

'Fifty-two, my lord — including myself. And half of us did not strike a blow! None trained to arms — apprentices, townsmen, even monks. The folk of Scotland, sir. Simple folk — not great nobles.'

The Steward's great eyes considered him thoughtfully.

Wallace came a pace forward, eagerly. 'My Lord James — you talk of trained and disciplined troops, Men-at-arms. Every lord in Scotland has such at his command — horsed, armed, trained. His retainers and fighting tail. If they would but agree to fight the English, instead of each other, the invader could be driven out in a matter of months.'

'If, man — if! They will never unite. If they could not do it before Dunbar, they will not do it now.'

'Because Edward knows it and plays one off against another, giving one lands, offices the other wants, offering them English estates, pensions, to hold them. Are all blind, not to see? My lord, Edward can take away, as easily as he gives. Yet our noble Scots lords sell their freedom, and their country, for such largesse, stolen from better men!'

The older man held up his ink-stained hand. 'I think you forget yourself, sirrah!' he said, voice quivering a little. 'And to whom you speak. As well that *I* am not such as you describe! Or you would be in my pit forthwith!'

'I am sorry, my lord. I crave your pardon. I was carried away. All are not so. But . . . many are. And since Dunbar, none has raised a hand against the enemy.'

'All are not, perhaps, so sure as you, Will, who is the enemy! Who does young Bruce of Carrick now see as his enemy? Edward, who has befriended him? Or John Baliol, who sat on the throne he believes should be his own father's? Or John Comyn, whom he hates, who also sought that throne? Who does

Malcolm of Lennox call enemy? The English — or Lame John MacDougall of Lorn and his Highlandmen, who raid his Lennox lands? Who is Cospatrick of March and Dunbar's foe — the Plantagenet, or the Border thieves and mosstroopers, Kerrs, Turnbulls, Scotts, Elliots, with whom he is at constant war?'

'But — is that not what I am saying, my lord! These are all Scots. Yet they fight each other, rather than the invader.'

'They have always done so — and always will. Under a strong king, like our late Alexander of blessed memory, they could be held in check. But not under that empty tarbard, Baliol! They need a firm hand — and Edward supplied it. If any thought to kick against it, he would lay himself open to be savaged by the others. And they have the example of my good-brother, the Douglas, who did hold out against Edward. Where is he now?' The Lord of Douglas's first wife had been the Steward's sister. 'No — they will never unite, Will.'

'Some might, sir. Under a leader. One they must respect. And who better than the High Steward?'

'Havers, man — havers! Not to be considered. I am a peace-able man, no soldier. A man of the pen, not the sword. I am the *Steward,* not the Constable.'

'The Great Constable of Scotland is a Comyn. The Earl of Buchan. Kin to King John Baliol. He will not raise sword against Edward.'

'Nor will I, boy — nor will I. Not to put John Baliol back on the throne Edward gave him, and then took away.'

'Yet he is our lawful and anointed leige lord, crowned at Scone on the sacred Stone. No English prison can change that.'

'God's Death — you are as bad as my lord of Glasgow, Will! Harping on the same broken string! Though Wishart is old enough to know better.'

'You will do nothing then, my lord? I came to you, as vassal, believing you noble, a true man, my father's friend as well as lord . . .'

'What can I do — tell me that? What happened to your father could happen to me. And worse, more swiftly, since I am watched as he was not. I will not draw futile sword to cut my own throat! And for what? For a notion, outworn as an old boot — that you call Scotland!'

They looked at each other in silence for a long moment.

Wallace sighed. 'If you will not lead, my lord — at least will you not sound out others more, more warlike than yourself? As Steward, the greatest of the great officers-of-state, as a former Guardian of the Realm, you surely have some right, some claim, some duty. I need men-at-arms desperately . . .'

'*You* need? You, Will Wallace, a small knight's son, barely out of boyhood — you need lords' men-at-arms! And would have the High Steward of Scotland gain them for you?'

'Yes,' the other agreed, simply. 'Since no other will take the lead, I will. Have done. Will continue to do. Until a better man stands forth . . .'

'Or until you dangle on the end of a rope — and be fortunate if only that!'

'Perhaps, yes. But . . . I have taken a vow. And will not rest while it remains unfulfilled.'

'God help you, then!'

'Amen. But — you will not?'

James Stewart wagged an exasperated greying head. 'Save us — you are an obstinate devil, Will. Like your sire! See you — this I will do. I will sound out some of the hotter spirits amongst the young lords. Secretly — aye, fell secretly! Lindsay of Crawford, Boyd of Cunninghame, young Lundin, my own brother perhaps. It will take time — for I must not draw attention to myself, or the others. But the winter is near on us — no time for war. Come you back to me in the spring. Mind, I promise nothing. But I will do what I can.'

'I thank you, my lord — from my heart.'

'Do not — since I cannot think that I serve you well! But this *I can* give you, Will, meantime — good advice. Get you away from the South-West. Your hiding place in Ettrick is known. Beck talks openly, boasts, that they will have you, and other outlaws, before the first snows. Clearly a move is planned against you. Get out, while you have yet time.'

'Get out where, my lord? The Forest is large, inhospitable to cavalry. Are we not as well there as anywhere?'

'They can put a ring of steel round you. Nor will you sustain hundreds of men in those bare hills in winter. They will tighten the ring, till they crush you. And you will have achieved nothing, cooped up in Ettrick.'

Wallace had already discovered the truth of that, at least. 'What, then?' asked.

'See you — it may be that I am an old fool, to advise you

53

thus. But it seems to me that if any revolt against the English power is to come to anything, it must be on two fronts, at the least. They must be forced to split their strength, to look back as well as forward. Young Andrew Moray, another hot-head, has risen, in the North. I have heard that he is heading south-wards — south and west. For Perth. At a guess he is making for Lennox. Earl Malcolm is his kinsman. And Malcolm now needs help against Lame John MacDougall of Lorn — whose mother is a Comyn, and kin to Baliol. If you could join with Andrew Moray . . .'

'Aye. But any strength I may have, where I am known, is here in the South-West. In Ayr and Lanark and Renfrew. In the Lennox and Perth and the North, I am but a single, unknown man.'

'Then come back to the South-West, in the spring. You cannot campaign in the winter months, forby. See Moray, if you can. Plan joint action. And then return. If Lennox would aid you, all might be changed. And he might, for he did join the drive against Carlisle, at the time we lost Dunbar. He has paid fealty to Edward since — but, then, so have I! Perforce. See you Lennox first. John of Lorn calls himself Edward's friend — which may cause Lennox heed you the more!'

Wallace nodded. 'I thank you again, my lord. For your advice, your good-will. I shall do as you say. But — back there, you named another name. My lord Bishop Wishart of Glasgow. You said that I was as bad as he? Does that mean that he also chafes under the yoke?'

'Do not we all, boy! But, yes — Wishart is hot against the English. At his age, and a man of God, he should have more sense. Beck knows it, baits him, humiliates him. Wishart, I fear, but digs his own grave . . .'

'Pray God for more Wisharts!' the younger man said.

'Aye,' the Steward acceded grimly. 'But, if you have a notion to have a word with the Bishop, boy — as I jalouse you have — mind your step. For he is watched even closer than am I — since he has not the advantage of a wife in Edward's favour!'

'I will watch, my lord. And now, if you will permit that I take my leave?'

'Aye, Will — go. And God go with you — despite your head-strong foolishness! Do not think that I disesteem what you have done, or what you would do. It is folly, but gallant folly. Had I been thirty years younger, perhaps ... ! But, off with you, then — and of a mercy's sake go as discreetly as you came! You stand out like a lone tree on a ridge!'

'One thing more, my Lord. We captured much gold, at Loudoun Hill. We have it hidden away. Gold is but metal — and I prefer steel! But that hidden gold might help speak more loud to some of your young lords ...!'

Next afternoon Wallace presented himself at another great house, the Bishop's Palace near the Stable Green Port and the mighty cathedral church of St. Mungo, in Glasgow. He had not taken quite such elaborate precautions here, for he was not known personally in Glasgow, and the crowded narrow wynds and lanes of the Bishop's burgh were full of monks and friars, as well as seafarers, watermen and Erse-speaking Highlandmen, besides the citizens, providing good cover for even very tall strangers. There were many English soldiers too, to be sure, most wearing the gold cross on blue of the Prince-Bishop of Durham, who had elected to make his headquarters here.

The young man had some difficulty in gaining access to Bishop Wishart, for the two prelates much disliked each other, and Wishart's palace had presently something of the aspect of an armed camp. But with Beck temporarily absent, conditions were a little relaxed, and Wallace gained entry to the kitchen wing, facing High Kirk Street. But getting from there to the Bishop's own quarters was a slow and protracted business. Eventually he had to reveal his name and true identity — whereupon he was eyed with some alarm and apprehension, while a chaplain hurried off to acquaint higher authority.

Thus it was that Robert Wishart himself presently came to find his visitor, rather than the normal procedure, in the lesser refectory of the palace, which was as far as the young man had attained. The Bishop was a small but stocky man in his early sixties, ruddy of complexion, with keen twinkling eyes and a markedly misleading air of diffidence. Son of a Mearns laird, he looked a countryman rather than the second most important of the Lords Spiritual in Scotland.

'Wallace?' he asked. 'Will Wallace — Sir Malcolm's son? God rest his soul!' He searched his guest's features. And, as the big man had to stoop low indeed to kiss the episcopal ring, he patted the bent auburn head a little. 'Aye, a worthy son of a worthy sire, I hear, I declare that you honour my poor house, my young friend — I do so. How can I serve you?'

55

Much heartened, Wallace straightened up. 'I come to you, my lord Bishop, for guidance,' he said. 'Knowing of you as a leal man, and true — and no lover of the invader. Such are none so common in Scotland today, I find!'

'More than you think, my son, I do believe. But — come you away, where we may be more private, lad. I trust all within my house. But it is not seemly that we should converse here, before all this gawping, open-mouthed clan! One would think that you were the Devil, and I his Satanic Archangel Lucifer, by their faces!' The little prelate's smile, and diffident manner, robbed that of all offence, as he led the way, by vaulted passages and corridors, to a panelled sanctum and a flagon of wine.

'Tell me how you wrought it at yon Loudoun Hill, my son,' Wishart demanded, almost as soon as the door was closed. 'I ken the place fine, and its potentialities. But I'd hear the blessed tidings of it from your own lips, young man.'

His heart warming to this little man, Wallace launched out upon a suitably modest and edited description of the action against Fenwick — saying something of what led up to it, also, as well as its frustrating aftermath. The Bishop listened enthralled, frequently questioning and seeking elaboration of detail. Oddly enough, he did not seem particularly interested in the mention of the Church treasure recovered.

'So now, my lord — you will perceive why I have come to you,' his visitor concluded. 'I have been to my lord and High Steward, and achieved no great deal. From you, perhaps, I may learn what hope there is of rousing some of the lords of this realm? If Scotland is to be saved, men-at-arms are necessary, horsed and trained, who can fight a campaign, not just a skirmish here and there. In great numbers. And only the lords can supply these.'

'I know it, my son — all too well,' Wishart said. 'But — they are all afraid. Edward's hand is heavy, and grievous. And they stand to lose all. Moreover, they require a leader. A leader of stature.'

'Who does not stand to lose all? Some must be made of sterner stuff, surely?'

'No doubt. But even these require to be *shown* that they might succeed. It is my prayer that your own fine ensample at Loudoun Hill may spur on some. If only a true leader would arise! These great lords will only rally to one of their own kind. I know them well, who am no great lord's son.'

'And is there none who could be roused, my lord Bishop? To lead?'

'I cannot see one, my friend — as yet. The Bruce would be the best — the Lord of Annandale, son of the old Competitor for the crown. Since he is of royal descent. But Robert Bruce is but a feeble chuckleheaded man, all words and pride but no deeds. His son, young Robert, Earl of Carrick, has more spirit — no doubt inherited, with his earldom, from his lady-mother, who was a bold woman. But he has been all but brought up in Edward's Court. They say that the Plantagenet loves him better than he does his own son, the Prince of Wales. I fear there is no hope, there. The Comyns are of the royal line, also, and John Comyn of Badenoch bold enough. But they are kin to King John Baliol, and will not rise against the English in this situation. Buchan the Constable, the same. Cospatrick of March and Dunbar has great lands in England, and will not risk them. Malise, Earl of Strathearn is Buchan's good-brother, and a weathercock. MacDuff, Earl of Fife is only a youth — although I heard but two days back that his uncle Hugh MacDuff has led some sort of insurrection in Fife . . .'

'MacDuff? I had not heard of this. The Steward did not speak of it. If this is true it would be good news indeed. One of the most ancient, proudest houses in Scotland.'

'Aye. But the Lord Hugh is scarce of the stuff of heroes, I think. Head-strong, yes — but hare-brained. Ill tempered. I know him. I see not many of Scotland's lords following him as leader, my son. Malcolm, Earl of Lennox is, it may be, the best hope. His is of the old Celtic polity, like MacDuff, but a man of more stature and worth.'

'The Lord James spoke of him, also. But has he not taken oath of fealty to Edward?'

'Aye, twice. But — who has not? Few indeed. Even I, after a fashion! Your father, and Douglas, did not — and paid the price. Such oath, sworn at the sword's point, need not carry a deal of weight! Me, I would gladly absolve any from that oath, in the name of Holy Church!'

The younger man looked doubtful, but did not challenge that statement. 'And what of Holy Church itself, my lord?' he asked. 'How much aid can we look for in our struggle, from Scotland's Kirk?'

'More than from her Lords Temporal, at least, young man. The Church has already lost much. But it has not bowed — or only in a measure, that worship may continue. We have no great hosts of men-at-arms. But we seek to keep alight the flame of resistance all over the land.'

'Yes — and I rejoice at it. But the Church *could* find men, if it would. It found me some, from Fail and Libberton, at Loudoun.' Wallace hesitated. 'My lord Bishop — I have recovered much of the Church's treasure, stolen from all over the South-West. It lies hidden at Fail Monastery. Would . . . would that help the Church to rise? In arms?'

'It will rise, without that. Never fear, lad. When there is any general rising, Holy Church will be in the forefront, I promise you, treasure or none. Myself, I will ride, with fifty men at my back — and will urge others to do as much. But you cannot ask that the Church *leads* the rising. Provides the leader required. That is no work for a churchman. And a leader there must be. A leader whom the nobles will follow, my son — not a small laird's son, I fear, however bold! Any more than a churchman.'

Wallace nodded. 'I know it, my lord. I have never sought to lead, save my own small band. But if none other will draw sword . . .'

'They will, in time. Do not despair, my friend.'

'And meantime? I am a hunted man, an outlaw. I wait? For this leader to appear?'

'Go you and see my lord of Lennox, my son. He is not of the Norman blood, and less concerned with rank and privilege. He may heed you. See — I will give you a letter, commending you to him. I am his Father-in-God.'

'You are good, my lord Bishop . . .' Wallace said — but he said it with a sigh.

CHAPTER FOUR

The purple of the heather was fading to brown on all the Highland hills, but the blue waters of the great loch reflecting them gave back their colour, along with the blazing autumn tints of the birchwoods and bracken that decked their lower slopes. William Wallace's heart lifted to all the loveliness and colour and sparkle of it, for he was a man who rejoiced in beauty, basically a gentle man, however terribly he could be roused to fierce action. And Loch Lomondside in autumn was beautiful indeed.

He stood on the pebbly shore near the mouth of the Fruin Water, towards the south end of the twenty mile loch, at the west side, waiting, and gazing across to the scatter of wooded islands and the mighty mass of Ben Lomond towering behind, a thin coating of snow, the first of the season, already whitening its proud head. He had been waiting for over an hour, but he was not impatient, with that fine prospect to consider. Moreover, in the Highlands, time was well known to be immaterial. Anyway, all the impatience in the world would not get him out to Inchmurrin Island and its castle before its keeper was ready to receive him. Boats were there in plenty, drawn up on the pebble strand beside him, but all guarded by Highland gillies, who waited as he did. One of them actually played a fiddle, sitting on a thwart of his boat, and the others raised strangely melodious voices to join in the recurrent refrain, in some lilting Gaelic air which Wallace found soothing and to his taste. There was a time for haste and action; equally a time for stillness, acceptance, musing. The boatmen had greeted the tall man in the begging friar's robe civilly enough; but none would row him the half-mile out to Inchmurrin before the required signal came from the castle walls. This was not the sort of place on which a man could descend unannounced or in a hurry. When Wallace had arrived, and said that he wished to proceed to the island for interview with Earl Malcolm, polite nods and agreement had been accorded him; and a kilted youth in a light skiff, little more than a coracle, had paddled off, presumably to convey the message. Since then, nothing. But then, although only some fifteen miles north of the Clyde, at Dumbarton, this was the Highlands.

Inchmurrin was the largest of the islands in the loch, over a mile long and rising to a wooded ridge of some height above the wimpling waters. On the extreme South-West corner of it, directly across from the green headland where Wallace stood, the Earl of Lennox's principal castle crowned a bare rock knoll, a fantastic site for a great house. It was not so very large, as castles went, nor as seat for so great a potentate; but it seemed to dominate all the southern end of the long loch — if anything under Ben Lomond could be said to do so. It had no central keep, like most castles Wallace knew; but its curtain-wall was high, not much lower than the squared flanking towers oddly and irregularly placed to fit the contours of the rocky bluff. From one of these a red-and-white banner flew, with lesser pennons on the other squat towers, a gay sight in the golden late-October sunshine.

Wallace had crossed Clyde at Glasgow, and walked here in two days, sleeping at churches in Kilpatrick and Strathleven. He felt a long way from Ettrick Forest — although he could have seen it from Ben Lomond's top.

Presently a disturbance behind drew all eyes, and arrested the fiddler's bow. A mounted cavalcade was emerging from the birch-scrub and juniper thickets of the lower slopes, no doubt come out of Glen Fruin, which opened hereabouts. One of the boatmen raised a curling long horn to his lips and blew a prolonged ululant note, which echoed and re-echoed from the encircling mountains. Before the last echo died away, it was answered from the castle walls. Somebody had come who gained quicker service than William Wallace.

The newcomers were huntsmen, riding shaggy Highland garrons and dressed in stained and faded tartans. Gralloched deer hung over the backs of ponies, heads dangling. There were half-a-dozen of these, and thereafter rode a better dressed group, in tartans also, doublets and trews, but cleaner, with calfskin, sleeveless jerkins. They also were mounted on the broad hooved garrons necessary for the mountain sides. Grey shaggy deerhounds loped at heel. Attendants came behind, three with hooded hawks at wrist, others carrying bows and spears and nets.

This cheerful party clattered down to the beach. Wallace felt eyes upon him, for disguise or none, he was inevitably an outstanding figure. One of the gentles, a dark flashing-eyed young man, said something which drew a laugh from the others. And a slender, fine faced man of early middle years, called out in the Gaelic, to the boatmen, asking who was the mountainous monk, and what did he want — money, for a wager?

Wallace knew the Gaelic; indeed frequently spoke it. He raised his voice. 'I have a letter from my lord Bishop of Glasgow for the Lord Malcolm, Earl of Lennox,' he said, in the same language. 'I seek passage out to yonder castle. And will pay money for it, if I must!'

'I can save you the trouble, and cost, Sir Friar,' the slender man answered, dismounting. He held out his hand. 'I am Malcolm mac Maldwyn mac Aluin. How fares the good Bishop? In his nest of vipers!' He laughed. 'You will not object to me calling the English so, I think — since you too speak God's own good tongue?'

'Indeed no, my lord,' Wallace assured. 'I could call them worse — since vipers at least stay in their own place!' He drew Wishart's letter from his ragged robe, and handed it over.

The other eyed him keenly, glanced at the superscription and seal, and asked if a reply was required?

'I do not know, my lord.'

The Earl broke the seal and spread the paper, to read. In moments he looked up quickly, intent, staring indeed. 'Wallace?' he jerked. 'William Wallace! You . . . you are Will Wallace? Of Loudoun Hill?' It was noticeable that he now spoke in English, the language of the letter.

'Aye, my lord Earl. Brother to Sir Malcolm, of Elderslie.'

'*Dia*! Then here's my hand, friend Wallace!' the other exclaimed. 'And myself proud if you will shake it! Here is a day to be remembered, when Will Wallace comes to Lennox!'

'You are kind, my lord . . .'

The gentry, all making much of Wallace now, embarked in a number of the small boats, while large flat-bottomed scows were rowed across from Inchmurrin to take the horses and the slain deer. Wallace went in the Earl's own boat, for nothing, it seemed, was too good for the man who had rubbed English noses in the mire of Loudoun Hill. There did not appear to be any doubts about Malcolm of Lennox's sentiments and allegiances, at all events.

The island greatly interested the young man. It was larger than it had seemed from the shore, and obviously full of folk. Houses and cabins were dotted everywhere amongst the tall old pine trees, with every available patch of soil, however small, tilled. Other islands to north and west were in use also, one supporting a church and burial ground, another the kennels for hounds and dogs, a flattish grassy one for the horses, and so on. All had their quota of cot-houses and cabins. Some had been artificially extended, built out with platforms of logs and piles; some were wholly artificial, indeed, true crannogs. There were about a dozen in all, a small secure kingdom in the great loch, populous, busy, domestic, in strange contrast with the vast spaces of the empty mountain wilderness all around.

The castle itself, high on its rocky knoll and separated from the rest of its islet by a deep artificial ditch spanned by a drawbridge, was unlike any Wallace had ever visited. It was a sort of walled town in miniature, within the twenty-five feet high parapeted curtain-walls with the flanking towers. There was a gatehouse at the drawbridge end but no central keep or stone donjon; instead a whole series of single-storey buildings, mainly of timber thatched with reeds, large and small, lean-to against the curtains and dotted all over the quite large expanse of enclosure, at varying levels dictated by the outcropping rock surface of the knoll. Under different roofs were a great hall, lesser hall, dormitories, kitchens, bakehouse, brewery, armoury, laundry and so on. It was a self-contained community, with enclosed well, even a small garden with fruit trees within the enceinte, all with infinitely more space and comfort than was apt to be provided by the stern stone towers of the usual castles. Wallace had heard of these Highland chieftains' strongholds but never visited one. Lennox, one of the great earls of Scotland, would not call himself a Highland chief; but he was of the ancient Celtic stock, and evidently preferred the old ways.

The Earl was a widower, but there was no lack of hospitality and welcome at Inchmurrin. The guest was given a sort of cottage to himself, where he could at last doff his friar's robe, with a serving wench to wait on him, offering to wash his feet and otherwise comfort him. He fed at the Earl's own table, at the dais end of the long, low lesser hall, with its peat fires at each gable and only holes in the roof for the smoke, its open rafters and reed straw in consequence rather hazy-blue where not soot-blackened. Pipers paraded up and down the courtyard outside, blowing lustily. The feeding was tremendous, such as the visitor had not experienced for many a long day, and the fiery native spirits flowed like water. The effect of all this, after the exertions of the day's hunting, was to send Lennox and most of his company into a dazed and semi-comatose state. Clearly this was not time to approach the Earl on the subject of revolt.

What with the heat, the smoky atmosphere, and a full stomach, together with his days of major walking, Wallace himself was not loth to retire that evening rather earlier than usual. In his cabin, he found the serving girl naked in his bed — warming it for him, as she pointed out. She offered pleasantly to remain in it with him, if so he preferred, on her lord's command; but he

excused her, or himself, with the plea of weariness and preoccupation of mind. He had heard about this comprehensive
Highland hospitality. Helping the warmly rounded but notably
buxom person of his would-be benefactress, rosy in the glow of
the peat fire, into her enveloping plaid, he patted her still prominent bottom and sent her off. She had certainly left the bed delightfully comfortable; and any consequent instinctive masculine regrets that he might have milled over, as to rejected opportunities, were quickly overcome by slumber.

His interview with the Earl Malcolm next day was indeterminate. There was no questioning Lennox's hostility to the
invaders, and his joy over Louden Hill; but he did not commit
himself to anything like leadership or even active participation
in a campaign against the English. Men he might provide,
yes — though how many remained unspecified. But the fact
was, he was preoccupied with a more urgent problem — Lame
John MacDougall of Lorn. The man was harrying all the northern borders of the great Lennox lands, in pillage and
rapine — had been doing so all summer and before. Being kin to
Baliol and the Comyns, he seemed to consider that he could
attack his neighbours with impunity. He even called himself
Edward of England's Admiral of the Western Seas. His father,
Alexander of Argyll, was old and had no control over him. The
Earl went into the wickednesses of the MacDougalls, at length.

Listening, Wallace perceived that Malcolm of Lennox, despite all his fine looks, gallantry of person, influence and undoubted power, was not a strong man. He was, it became clear,
impractical, lacking in decision, probably lazy mentally, something of a dreamer in fact. And it soon became equally evident
that his interest in his guest was not as a means of assailing the
usurpers, but as a stick with which to beat MacDougall of
Lorn. Indeed he actually offered to make Wallace leader of all
his Lennox manpower, if he would carry war and reprisal into
Lorn and Argyll, the reward to be that, after he had dealt with
the MacDougalls he could have the force for use against the
English.

His visitor declined this honour and offer, but tactfully — for
at the least he hoped for some accession of manpower here,
even though Lennox was obviously not going to be the so necessary leader of revolt who was to bring the lords to the point of
fighting. After working on him for some time, he got the Earl to
agree that he could recruit some men for his purposes. But quite

63

quickly thereafter Lennox reverted to his suggestions that Wallace should lead a force against Lorn. Clearly there was going to be a tug-of-war here, with two interests pulling against each other, both hoping to wear down the other's resistance.

The younger man was in a quandary. Both the Steward and Wishart had picked on Lennox as likely to be the most sympathetic to his cause of the great lords — and in fact his sympathy seemed to be established. Like his potential, in power. But more than sympathy was required. To go back to Ettrick empty handed, at the beginning of winter, would be humiliating, and bad for the morale of his band. On the other hand, he would gain little by waiting here for long, however flatteringly hospitable his host. Then, a chance remark of the Earl's changed the prospects. Lennox mentioned the MacDuff defiance in East Fife — not exactly a rising, since the English had not actually occupied that area, save for a small garrison at the ecclesiastical borders of the great Lennox lands, in pillage and rapine — had been doing so all summer and before. Being kin to Baliol and the Sir Andrew Moray, coming from the North, in the Perth vicinity. Although he, Lennox, did not seem to think a lot of MacDuff, he at least was a great noble, also of the ancient Celtic blood, uncle to the Earl of Fife, whose right it was to crown the Kings of Scots. If he could be guided and persuaded to take on the general leadership role, something might be achieved — even if he was only a figure-head. Lennox agreed that the man might be useful, though he did not see him as of the stature of leadership. He conceded that it might be worth while for Wallace to go speak with him — but thought that his suggestions might carry more weight if he had a small armed force with him, and was seen to be continuing his campaign. If he would not move against Lorn, at least there were targets for the Wallace arms in Southern Perthshire, in Strathearn and Menteith. He would lend him a few men for this admirable purpose.

If the other was a little suspicious of this unexpected proposal and offer, he might be excused, perhaps. It was known that Malise, Earl of Strathearn, another of the great earls of Scotland, if admittedly very much in Edward's pocket, was also a hereditary enemy of Lennox's; and Sir John Stewart of Menteith, uncle and tutor of the boy Earl of Menteith, was presently occupying Dumbarton Castle a few miles away, as Edward's Sheriff of Dunbartonshire, of which Lennox was the rightful hereditary custodian. In the circumstances, it might be suggested that Lennox was merely wanting to use Wallace to harry his enemies, of whom he seemed to have no lack. On the other hand, the younger man saw possibilities in the project, a means of giving the impression that all over Scotland there were spontaneous risings against the invader; this, as well as effecting a link with MacDuff. He was prepared to consider it. But he would require men — not only new men from Lennox, but men on whom he could rely as lieutenants. He decided, in his still virtuous bed that night, to send to Ettrick for two or three volunteer aides. It would mean waiting here at Inchmurrin for a few days — but he could use the time to recruit and train some Highlandmen.

His mind made up, he slept with a degree of contentment.

It took a full eight days for an answer to come from Ettrick Forest — in the persons of two of his lieutenants, Thomas Gray, the parson and young William MacKerlie of Cruggleton. Gray had found his Libberton parish too hot for him, with rumours circulating that he had been involved in the recent disturbances, and the English beginning to ask questions. A vigorous priest in his mid-thirties, he had decided to throw in his lot with Wallace, for better or for worse. MacKerlie known to all merely as Kerlie, a young Galloway laird who had been dispossessed by the Lord Soulis, with King Edward's agreement, had been at Loudoun Hill — a cheerful, good-looking and uncomplicated young man. Only these two had come; for Blair Boyd and Adam Wallace were having difficulty in keeping any sizeable nucleus of the band together in this difficult interim period, when nothing vital was happening. They felt that if the group was to be maintained at all, as ever the core of a striking force, no others could be spared to leave it. Wallace had, in his message, only asked for volunteers, and left the decision open for the men on the spot. So he could not complain. But Lennox clearly was not impressed.

Wallace himself had not been idle during those eight days. He had gathered round him a company of almost sixty Lennoxmen, volunteers again, for his proposed winter campaign, mainly young men who, now that the harvest was in and the cattle back from the high summer grazings in the sheilings, were comparatively footloose. None of these, really, were of the stuff of leadership, however, and he had been able to select only three as possible officers. One was a MacGregor called Stephen, from South Argyll, son of a small laird, a quick-silver gallant sworder, whom Wallace judged would do excellently well in a tight situation but who might be less reliable under prolonged and unexciting hardship. Another was a man who had actually served with the English in Ireland as a mercenary, called Mac-Fadzean, but who had sickened of the barbarism which the English troops pursued, as a deliberate policy of terror on the part of their king, and had returned to his home in the Lennox — a slightly older man, but with experience of warfare. The third was an Irishman who had come with him, Fawdon by name, a big, surly harsh man, but also trained to arms and with a hatred of the English, and something of the leader in him however unpopular he might be with the others. With these, and the pair from Ettrick, Wallace had to make do.

On a misty morning of early November, then, he took leave of the Earl Malcolm, who gave him a letter of introduction to the Lord Hugh MacDuff, much advice, good or otherwise, and his blessing. He set off with his company of about sixty, for the North-East.

They crossed in boats to the east side of Loch Lomond, and struck up the valley of the Endrick Water. Lennox had offered garrons, horses; but Wallace decided that, in the skirts of the Highlands, they would be better on foot, with steeps and precipices and peat-bogs to negotiate and torrents to cross. The most direct route to the Perth vicinity would be to cross diagonally over Menteith, on the north side of the infant Forth, and into Strathearn; but since these two earldoms were in hostile hands, hostile to Lennoxmen and presumably to Wallace also, he decided that the Fintry and Gargunnock Hills area, south of Forth, would be the wiser choice, since these were in the hands of Graham of Dundaff and Fraser of Touch, who could be expected to be reasonably sympathetic. This could be very important for a fairly large company which had to live on the countryside yet did not wish to ravage or endanger it.

They covered a good thirteen miles the first day, and camped for the night in an unobtrusive site below Buchlyvie, almost an island indeed, on the southern fringe of the great Flanders Moss, which the Forth's meanderings made out of its flood plain, a waterlogged wilderness fifteen miles long by four across, the daunting and effective barrier between Highland and Lowland Scotland, which had even defeated the Romans. This was MacGregor country, and Stephen knew it almost as well as any man living. They could sleep secure in the Flanders Moss, amongst the fighting wildfowl and the shadowy roe-deer.

Next day, soon after noon, they began to near the far-eastern end of the extensive marshlands, Wallace going warily now. Stirling lay ahead, its proud castle already to be distinguished, skied on its rock — though proud in fact no longer, in English hands, and guarding the vital crossings of Forth. He had no intention, of course, of trying to cross the river at Stirling Brig. But a few miles up-river, there was a place where crossing was just possible for men who did not mind a wetting, called the Fords of Frew — passable when the Forth was not running high. Stephen MacGregor knew it; and the autumn had been a reasonably dry one.

At the farmery of Kerse, below the village of Kippen, about nine miles west of Stirling, where they called to obtain milk and eggs and honey — paid for in good money, for Wallace was well supplied with the gold which had fallen into his hands at Loudoun Hill, and which had greatly aided his recruiting — they received sobering news. They learned that the English knew about the Fords of Frew, and the crossing was watched. Not only that, the invaders had recently built a strongpoint nearby, as quarters for a garrison. The Peel, it was called — the Peel of Gargunnock. And from this the English ravaged the country round about, as well as guarding the fords, savagely, terrorising the entire neighbourhood.

Wallace, of course, was interested as well as sympathetic. If the enemy had gone to sufficient trouble not only to guard the fords but to build this fort, then they must have believed that they had good reason. It would have been easier and cheaper, surely, to make the fords unusable? But that would have denied the use to themselves. Perhaps they perceived a tactical use, as by-pass for the famous bridge at Stirling, for them as well as for others. But against whom were they guarding it, meantime? Could it be that the enemy were seriously concerned about a possible threat from Moray's or MacDuff's forces? Were expecting one, or both, of them to head southwards; and guessed that they would not attempt the heavily guarded Stirling Bridge. If so, then the English were indeed beginning to take the fear of revolt seriously. Wallace's heart lightened at the thought.

At first, his reaction, tactically, was to turn back discreetly, and make for the Aberfoyle area, twelve miles up, and beyond the Flanders Moss, where amongst the heather hills they could get across the stripling river and into Menteith. Then another thought occurred to him. He asked the farmer about the garrison.

The man did not know a great deal, for his farm of Kerse was fully four miles from Gargunnock and he seldom ventured outside the marshes. He had little idea as to how many soldiers there were. All he knew was that they were a particularly ferocious crew, who ravaged, raped, burned and slew at will. And that their captain was called Thirlwall — God's everlasting curse on him! But the folk at Leckie would be able to inform them. They had suffered enough at Leckie and should know! The marshes had saved himself and his . . .

Wallace was not prepared to risk marching on to Leckie, almost three miles, in daylight. They would camp here, amongst the birchscrub and alders; and Thomas Gray would go forward alone, in his shabby priest's habit, and discover what information he could glean from the good folk of that Graham manor.

Gray was nothing loth.

The priest was back with the dusk, with a sufficiency of news. There was a garrison of half-a-company, fifty cavalrymen. But some were always on guard down at the fords — and since it was a day-and-night guard, some were usually asleep during the day. The effective strength at any given hour, therefore, was likely to be considerably reduced. The Peel itself was not a stone castle but a timber construction coated with clay, set on a low artificial mound, or motte, with a high stockade of timber palings around, all provided with a water-ditch or moat, in the usual way. But the drawbridge was normally kept down apparently even at night — since, with Stirling Castle and headquarters only six miles away, who was likely to attack the dominant invaders? Workmen were extending the premises. Discipline was notably lax, however harsh the impact on the local folk.

Wallace decided that it was worth the attempt, to strike a blow here, in an area where so far there had been no trouble for the English, yet where they were evidently anxious about the Forth crossings. He questioned Gray closely as to the situation of the Peel, and its surroundings. It lay apparently at the edge of the marshland, a mile-and-a-half east of Leckie, and half of that distance below the village of Gargunnock, where the track which led to the Fords of Frew entered the Moss. It was almost two miles from the fords themselves; but there was no suitably firm ground for a fort closer, it appeared. This seemed always to have been a defensive area, and not unnaturally, for between the Peel and Gargunnock village was a low conical hillock with the embankments of an ancient Pictish fort on top. It was from there that Gray had scrutinised the Peel.

The party left Kerse just before midnight, and made their quiet way eastwards, skirting the manor and hamlet of Leckie discreetly. They kept away from the marsh-edge now, as far as possible — for nothing is more readily disturbed and gives noisier alarm than wildfowl roused at night. Even in the dark it was not difficult to find Gray's conical hill. There should have been half a moon, but it was a chill, cloudy night — although there was a certain luminosity to which, after an hour or so, their eyes grew accustomed enough to see, after a fashion, for some considerable distance, however indistinct were details, even close at hand.

Within the Pictish embankments on the little hill, they could look down on the darker loom of the Peel some way below, outlined rather eerily against the wan night mists which were rising from the wide Moss behind. No lights showed. Wallace debated tactics with Gray. Not that there was much scope for elaboration. There was, after all, only the one entrance to the place; and though they might negotiate the water-filled ditch, they had no gear with which to try to scale the high paling.

In the end, they merely crept downhill silently — and prayed that the English cavalry kept no dogs. Gray had seen no sign of any — and it seemed unlikely. Bloodhounds were much used by the invaders — but it seemed more probable that, with army headquarters so relatively near, at Stirling. any such would be kept there.

No disturbance, at any rate, developed out of their descent and approach. The Highlanders were adept at this sort of thing, born hunters and clearly used to moving noiselessly at night. Close inspection revealed the Peel's curtain-walls to be approximately one hundred and fifty feet long, and in form of a square, the ditch outside being about twenty feet wide. How deep was the water they could not judge.

Withdrawing a little, Wallace sent a single scout cautiously round the perimeter, to the north side, where was the entrance. The man came back with the news that the bridge was indeed down, but that the heavy wooden doors beyond, to the gate-house pend, where shut and barred. He had crept closer, and peered through the crack between the two halves of the gate, and had been able to see a single guard, apparently asleep, hunched on a bench beside a brazier of glowing coals. There had been no other sign of life.

Thankful that at least the bridge was down, the entire party moved quietly round to the north, and padded with great care across the timbers of the drawbridge — which, though sanded, might conceivably creak.

They all waited while Wallace went forward to examine the fairly massive double-doors, and peered through the slit between them. It was difficult to see details, but he came to the conclusion that there was no actual lock. More important however, there was no doubt that the doors were secured by a very substantial drawbar, a quite normal device, a greased beam which slid into a deep socket-hole in masonry at each side of the gateway, a simple but very effective expedient to keep doors from opening.

Could this be moved in any way? He could see the guard, still most evidently undisturbed, slouched forward on his bench beside the red glow of the brazier.

Wallace inserted his finger through the slit between the doors, to feel. Yes, the draw-bar was greased and smooth, for ease of pulling out and pushing back into its socket in the masonry. If it could be eased, inched, sideways . . .?

He drew his kirk and inserted the point through the slit and into the wood of the bar. Which way to try to push, left or right? He tried to remember on which side was the deep socket for housing the bar, when not in use, in his own old home, the small castle of Elderslie. It had been on the right. If that was normal, he facing *inwards* should try to push this bar leftwards.

With all the power of tremendously strong arms and wrists, he sought to edge the heavy timber sideways, with his dirk tip. It moved perhaps half-an-inch. He tried again. It moved, but less than before. Strive as he would, in that awkward position, with no room for leverage, he could make no further impression. Perhaps it was the wrong direction? Reversing his pressure, he attempted to move it to the right. It went back an inch, and then stopped, however hard he tried. And there was no other slit in the doors, no aperture at the hinges end, to insert a blade.

Then his straining, panting efforts produced a momentary

carelessness, and he dropped his dirk. It did not make the ringing clatter which it might have done, for the drawbridge timbers
were sanded for the sake of horses' hooves; but it produced a
distinct thud. Eye to crack, he saw the guard straighten up, to
stare.

Cursing below his breath, perceiving that all could be lost in
moments, Wallace in a fit of what was little less than fury at an
inanimate object, grabbed at the crosswise timber strapping of
one of the doors itself, and lifted, in an explosion of all his
enormous strength. And with a rending crack the entire half-
door rose. Not only it but the bar behind, bringing with it three
courses of the mortared masonry, at the left, into which it was
socketed. In staggering, homeric violence, the big man burst
forward into the pend, the upraised half-door now bringing the
other half with it, because of the linking draw-bar, and crashed
full length over the ruin of it all, at the feet of the appalled
guard. Over and past him his sixty streamed, all need for quiet
now over. The sentry died with a dagger in his throat, and
collapsed across William Wallace.

There was shouting from above now, where was the little
garret chamber, over the pend, which acted as guard-room and
gatehouse. All duties had been allocated, and it was Kerlie's
men's task to deal with the guard-room and the projecting
wooden gallery which ran round the inside of the stockade as a
parapet-walk.

The others now faced the Peel's interior, Wallace on his feet
again, dirk recovered. It could be discerned that there were four
central buildings, clay-covered, two large, two smaller, in the
inner square, as well as the lean-to stabling and storerooms
which lined the stockade. For a wager, the two larger would be
the mess-hall and the men's bunkhouse — with a murmur of disturbed voices already sounding from the latter. The two smaller
would be officers' quarters and the kitchen, probably.

The kitchen would be the one alongside the mess-hall.

With half of his own group, Wallace ran straight for the
lesser building, while the others made for the dormitory.

He was just too late. He was still a few yards from the door
when it opened, and a man peered out. And for one presumably
just wakened from sleep by the noise of the gate crashing, this
individual acted swiftly. He saw, perceived, leapt back, and
slammed the door shut in Wallace's face.

There might be a back door. He sent three men running

round. Then, wasting no time either, and with the recent example of what his own brute strength was capable, he lowered one thrusting shoulder, took a deep breath, and launched himself forward with all his force and momentum.

With a splintering of wood, this comparatively light door was burst completely off its hinges and fell inward, Wallace staggering headlong after it. This time he managed to keep his feet. Nevertheless he was at a momentary disadvantage, unbalanced and plunging into deeper gloom. His rush carried him onwards, and he all but fell his length over a bed. There was a yell of fright — a female yell.

It was perhaps as well that he did so fall, for the man who had slammed the door had had the further wits quickly to grab for and unsheath his sword, and this he brought slashing down on the violent intruder. Wallace's head or shoulder would have taken the blow had he not collapsed on the bed and its screaming occupant. As it was, the slash glanced off his leather-padded left arm, numbing it but doing no worse damage. Flinging himself off sideways and to the right, the big man managed to get clear before another swipe could be aimed, cannoning into the walling in the process — for it proved to be quite a small room, with the bed taking up much of the accommodation.

Chaos ensued. His men came pouring in after Wallace, and promptly got in each other's way in the confined space. The woman from the bed continued to yell, and another door opened from an inner room and children's shouts were added to the uproar. It was all so dark in here that nothing was clear. Wallace was much put out at the unsuspected presence of women and children, and his every instinct was against seeking to dispatch a man to eternity in the presence of wife and offspring. But since the man was urgently seeking to dispatch himself — and with eyes probably more accustomed to the gloom than were those of the intruder — debate was scarcely relevant. Wallace had only his dirk in his hand against the other's sword, but in that confined space and with the big man's extended reach, that was little handicap. He flung himself across both bed and woman in a sort of vault, recovered his balance at the other side, and so gained a slight advantage. As the other man swung round, sword upraised again, he feinted as though to drive in low, under the captain's guard. The sword slashed down — but as it did so Wallace jerked to the left and backward, then, using the bed itself as springboard, flung himself

72

upon his half-dressed opponent. The dirk rose and fell, and the man collapsed with a choking groan. The woman was screaming and screaming.

It was all over in only seconds, Wallace's men still in the doorway, peering. He thrust out through them. 'Women and bairns to be spared,' he panted. 'Donald — guard them. You others — come!'

They hurried over to the bunkhouse — but most obviously they were not required there. The dreadful work within was all but finished, already — the strong smell of spiritous liquors perhaps helping to explain the ease of it all. In a room at the back of the eating hall, they found Fawdon and five men, with three dead English officers and three young women — one of whom the big Irishman had naked, and was bending over a bed to his will, while his men held the other two, less than gently. Angrily, Wallace dragged Fawdon off, and flung him aside, exclaiming that they did not make war on women and bairns, whatever did the English or the Irish either. He ordered the women to be covered up, taken over to the captain's building and put in with the wife and children. Then he led his group to the kitchen quarters.

All here was under control, with Stephen MacGregor having five more women held fast, and two male cooks — none slain and no opposition encountered. Kerlie came to him, to announce breathlessly that the parapet-walk was clear. Some shadowy men had been seen escaping, racing out and over the drawbridge; but all elsewhere seemed to be dead, dying or prisoners.

Back at the bunkhouse they found a ghastly scene, with bodies strewn everywhere amongst blankets, sheepskins and clothing. Thomas Gray, his sword-ing abandoned, had reverted to his true calling and was now administering a last absolution to the dying, to the incomprehension of his Highland colleagues. It appeared that there were indeed no prisoners.

Sickened a little, but steeling himself, Wallace congratulated his men, and summoned all out from that charnel-house, leaving Gray to his ministrations. If men had escaped, as Kerlie said, they could not assume that they were secure here, even though the Peel seemed to be satisfactorily in their hands. The part of the garrison which was on duty at the Fords of Frew had to be reckoned with.

A muster, out in the courtyard, with reports from the leaders, established the situation clearly enough. First of all, they themselves had not lost a single man, although one or two were slightly hurt. There were twenty-two enemy dead or dying — it was significant perhaps that none were *less* seriously wounded. Apart from the two cooks, there were no male prisoners. As well as Captain Thirlwall's wife there were eleven female camp-followers, willing or otherwise. Clearly the kitchen annexe had been used as something of a brothel. And there were Thirlwall's three children, whom Wallace had orphaned before their eyes.

How many had escaped, then? If the garrison was in truth about fifty, they had only accounted for half. The other half presumably were down guarding the fords — a larger proportion than might have been expected. Although the total might have been exaggerated.

Wallace was faced with a major decision. Either they could decamp forthwith, perhaps setting the place alight behind them as a warning and foretaste for the invaders — which undoubtedly would be the safer course; or they could put the Peel into a condition of defence again, and try to rouse the neighbourhood from it, lighting a larger conflagration on the very doorstep of Stirling Castle — a greatly more ambitious project.

It did not take the man long to make up his mind. Just to slink away and leave Gargunnock, after this easy victory, would be a feeble outcome. The flames of the Peel might lighten the darkness of Central Scotland for a little, but nothing lasting would be achieved for the cause he had embarked upon, by this night's work. His objective, however headstrong and vaulting, was nothing less than to set the entire country alight, not just a part of the Carse of Stirling. He must encourage others by a show of strength and confidence, therefore. They would stay at Gargunnock, meantime.

Decision taken, he wasted no time. First he went to the sobbing, wailing women, all assembled in Thirlwall's house, under guard. When he could gain approximate quiet from them, hating the task, he told them that they would be safe, free to go unharmed, in the morning. He expressed stilted and awkward regret that he had been forced to use such violence and savagery in their presence — especially that of Mistress Thirlwall and her children. This was much contrary to his wishes and indeed his principles. But surprise was vital. And he had not known that there were women and bairns in the fort. Besides, Thirlwall and his garrison were notorious ravagers, rapers and killers of the helpless and innocent, deserving of death by any standards. He made no apology for slaying such — only of his affront to those he addressed and with whom he had no quarrel. This difficult speech over — and received in tearful silence — he went out, and ordered some forty of his sixty men to follow him. The rest he left, under Gray, to deal with the dead and dying, tidy up the fort, and raise the drawbridge behind them, to make all secure.

With MacGregor as guide, Wallace led his party down through the marshland towards the fords. Almost certainly the fleeing men would have come this way. Quietly as they sought to go, however, their progress was marked flagrantly all the way by alarmed quacking wildfowl exploding off in all directions. The MacGregor was right, the English garrison would have been much safer camping on an island of firm ground in these watery wastes than in their walled fort. They went wary for any return of the presumably warned detachment.

Their approach to the fords area, therefore, could scarcely have gone unnoticed. Nevertheless, Wallace sent forward Mac-Gregor and another, as scouts over the last quarter mile, to spy out the situation. These returned, presently, with a negative report. There was nobody this side of the Forth. There had been, until recently, for fires in braziers still burned at the thatched-roofed shelter which the guard had used, and fresh horse droppings were in evidence. They could not see across the river, in the darkness and the mist which was coiling above the water; but fairly clearly the guard had decamped over to the north side, at short notice, and recently. Whether they were still across there, or had fled further, was not ascertainable.

'It is scarcely to be believed — yet the same folly as we saw at Loudoun Hill,' Wallace declared, to Kerlie. 'The escapers from the Peel, to excuse their flight, must needs announce that a great force had overwhelmed them. And if the fort could not withstand such, what chance had the score or so here at the fords? So, as sensible men, they flee also, lacking leadership.'

'Cravens! And *where* would they flee, Will?'

'Who knows? Perhaps all the way to Stirling. That is likely, indeed — a mere ten miles.'

'Then we can expect trouble in the morning.'

'Perhaps. Perhaps not. For some thirty to flee, we must be a greater force than ever! They will *know* nothing of us, where we are from, how we are composed. We might be but the advance

75

guard of an army. Moray's army, it might be, or part of it, chosen to drive south by upper Strathearn and Menteith. They cannot know. I think that they will be careful — they must be. They will send out scouts, spies — but will not venture their strength, until they know what they face. Does that not make sense?'

'And then?'

'By then, we must be elswhere. Or greatly reinforced!'

'Reinforced . . .?'

Wallace did not answer that query.

To make sure about the missing guards, the big man and MacGregor themselves waded, as quietly as they might, across the ford, up to their middles in the icy-cold waters, feeling their way with long sticks. But over there they found nothing, nobody. The Fords of Frew were left unguarded.

They retired to the Peel, Wallace thoughtful — and had to wait while they were duly challenged and the drawbridge clankingly lowered.

Before Wallace slept in that blood-drenched place that night — or early morning — he had decided on his probable course of action, so far as he might.

*   *   *

With daybreak, there was no lying in. The dead were interred in a dryish spur of the moat's ditch, with Thomas Gray's brief intonations, and a modicum of earth put over them. The women and children were turned loose, and even given money to aid them on their way. Wallace withdrew all but a dozen men, under Gray, from the Peel, and took these down into the marshland, where they might remain hidden, in safety. The drawbridge clanked up behind them, and men showed themselves parading on the parapet-walk — most evidently to be seen holding a fortified position. Leaving Kerlie in command of the main force, with instructions to watch the Peel and vicinity from hiding, and taking only the MacGregor as guide, the big man set off southwards, on excellent horses which they had captured in the fort stables.

The rode due southwards, up into the Gargunnock Hills, by deliberately lonely ways, avoiding hamlets and farmsteads and all haunts of men. It was a grey morning of low clouds and no wind. On the high ground, the skirts of the cloud enfolded them, and they no longer needed to fear observation. They

found the old drove-road past the dramatic Spout of Ball-
ochleum, which MacGregor had been looking for, and followed it South-Eastwards across the heathery watershed, below
the quite lofty but unseen summits of Fintry Hill and Cringate
Law, and so down the farther slopes beside the stripling Endrick
Water into the great upland valley of Carron. Here they began
to come into crofting country, quite populous, with herds of
shaggy black cattle on every hillside, herd-laddies watching over
them. This was fairly safe Graham country, remote, a world
unto itself, and the two men dispensed largely with their wary
precautions, greeting all genially but lingering nowhere.

The floor of the wide valley, where the Carron Water and
Endrick Water all but joined, before flowing east into the Forth
and west to Loch Lomond, was fully five hundred feet higher
than that of the Forth and Flanders Moss to the north, but
likewise covered by part-loch, part-swamp. It was a famous
place for bog-hay after a dry summer, and reed thatch in
season. At the western end of it, where thrusting hill-shoulders
on each side challenged each other and narrowed the mile-wide
vale almost to a pass, down which the Endrick poured in
peat-brown flood, on a terrace above the foaming river rose a
strong stone castle, a tall, square, battlemented tower of five
storeys, within a flanking-towered courtyard, a cluster of
cabins and huts surrounding it where they could retain
a foothold — Dundaff, seat of An Greusach Mor, The
Graham.

Wallace had no difficulty in gaining admittance to this
hold — indeed Sir John the Graham, Younger of Dundaff, himself came to greet him warmly when his identity was announced, a fine-featured, sensitive looking young man, slightly
younger than Wallace himself, whose lofty brow and almost
beautiful eyes were redeemed by the hint of strength in mouth
and chin. He was young to have gained knighthood; but his
grandfather, Sir Patrick, had been a prominent supporter of
King John Baliol, indeed had died at Dunbar bearing the Royal
Standard of Scotland — and the unfortunate monarch had been
grateful. The more so as Sir Patrick's elder son, this John's
father, now Sir David Graham of Dundaff, had been captured
at the same battle, and now languished in an English prison, like
so many another from that fatal field.

The young Graham was proud to welcome the victor of
Loudoun Hill to Dundaff — although his lady-mother seemed

77

less enthusiastic, and Wallace sensed a restraining hand. He was agog to hear details of the now famous engagement — and even more excited over the news of the taking of Gargunnock Peel. But when it came to the point of this visit, namely the raising of the great Graham clan to help turn a local success into a national one, the young man bit his lip and hesitated. Nothing would more greatly rejoice him, he declared. But the fact was that, since his father's capture, his uncle Sir Patrick Graham, was really controlling the Graham strength, considering himself too young. His mother, too, was against any action which might bear hardly on her husband imprisoned in England. They were suffering the English arrogance as best they could . . .

Wallace was disappointed — for, apart from the need for the Graham strength, he liked this young man and felt that he could work with him. And the Graham name would have been useful, undoubtedly, in persuading others to make a move. But clearly there was no immediate reinforcement to be gained here — although Sir John promised to approach his uncle, at Cardross to the west, straight away, on the subject. With that, and fervent good wishes, the visitors had to be content. They returned to Gargunnock somewhat discouraged. This was Graham country, and if the Grahams did not rise, who else would do so?

At the Peel they found no change in the situation. No challenge had been offered to the fort, no unwelcome visitors noticed. Reaction from Stirling was not as yet discernible — though it was hardly to be credited that there had been none. No doubt investigations proceeded, however discreetly.

Although roving patrols kept watch on the entire area, that night, there were no disturbances.

In the morning, Wallace made another expedition, with the MacGregor, again through the Gargunnock Hills, but this time in a more easterly direction, for the Touch and Cambusbarron area. The Touch Hills were but the eastwards extension of the Gargunnock ones, and Touch Castle was the seat of Sir Alexander Fraser, a man of some renown. He also had fought at Dunbar, and had been wounded, but only slightly, and had since made his required peace with King Edward — his lands of Touch and Cornton being altogether too close to the great fortress of Stirling for any other course to be practicable. But he was said to chafe restlessly under the invader's heel, and perhaps might be willing to take a chance.

Unfortunately however, Sir Alexander was not at home. Indeed, it seemed that he found Stirling district intolerable these days, and had removed himself to some secondary lands of his in the North. There was nothing to be gained from his steward at Touch, and Wallace returned to Gargunnock, no more enheartened. His efforts at setting Scotland alight seemed to be singularly unproductive.

There was nothing further to wait for at the Peel of Gargunnock, no advantage in lingering, but only danger. As the grey November dusk settled over the marshlands, they withdrew from the fort, turning the horses loose, for they had no use for them, and setting torches to its timbers. They left it a blazing beacon behind them, and moved down into the mosses, to cross the Fords of Frew and head into the Menteith hills to the north.

William Wallace was grievously aware of lost opportunity.

CHAPTER FIVE

His men, at least, were rested, refreshed and in good heart. Marching all night, with the red, winking glow of the burning Peel gradually dwindling behind them, they climbed the rolling, rising ground to the North-East, amongst pasture and moorland and shadowy, stampeding cattle, and by daylight were at the loch of Watston, nearing the Teith. Avoiding the Doune area, which was a seat of the Earl of Menteith, with its bridge, they forded the river near the church of Kilmadock, and made haste to lose themselves thereafter in the green foothill country of the Braes of Doune beyond. They were swinging ever eastwards now, making for the Allan Water, the neighbourhood of St. John's Town of Perth their objective. In mid-forenoon they settled to rest amongst the empty heather slopes above the Cromlix area, the Allan valley below and wide prospects before them, the Highland mountains, snow-tipped to their left, the green Ochils across the high brown shelf of Sheriffmuir, on the right.

The Allan was a lesser stream than Teith or Forth, but it

proved the harder to cross, running narrow but deep. The Mac-Gregor said that, so far as he knew, the only crossing in many miles was at Blackford, where there was a village, an inn and the small Graham castle of Ogilvie. This was on the main road from Stirling to Perth. Wallace decided that they dared not risk crossing this in daylight.

They waited above Cromlix therefore, huddled in their plaids and distinctly chilled, until the November dusk, and then made their discreet way up the strath, Drummond country this side, to opposite Blackford, where one or two lights indicated the presence of houses on the other side. A widening and shallowing of the Allan here, permitted a crossing, on slab rock, with the water no deeper than three feet.

Wallace led the way across. It was a slow process, for the underlying slab was slippery, and there were holes to avoid. He was stamping about, on the far side, to get the blood circulating — for the water was desperately cold, and his wet clothing uncomfortable — when he was alarmed to hear the clip-clop of horses' hooves and the jingle of harness, clearly approaching. With no desire for any confrontation here, so near the village and main highway, he thought of calling for such as were across, with him, to hide wherever they could. But there were men still wading the river, and others not yet started. It was a most unfortunate moment. But, of course the newcomers might be entirely harmless. He had little choice but to wait, warily.

Half-a-dozen riders came trotting up. In the dark it was difficult to perceive details — but obviously these were no High-land garrons; and steel, armour, could be heard clinking. It was the ears, rather than the eyes, which dispelled all doubt however, when an authoritative but very English-sounding voice suddenly demanded who in Satan's name were all these men cluttering up the ford? Answer, in the King's name!

Wallace hesitated no longer. With a great leap he jumped forward and upwards, his arms encircled the haughty speaker's middle, and as the horse sidled and reared, its rider and his attacker crashed to the ground together. The big man was slightly winded, as a consequence, for the other was clad in half-armour, and heavy, falling on top of him.

Kerlie came to the rescue, hauled off the Englishman and dirked the unfortunate under the arm-hole of his jack, all in the same movement. Others in Wallace's band flung themselves on

the five remaining horsemen, troopers evidently, who were so
taken by surprise that they had not even reined round or
drawn their cavalry swords before their shadowy assailants
were dragging them out of their saddles, dirks flickering. It was
all over in a few seconds, with the river-fording still going on
and men at the other side calling to ask what was to do? An
officer, seemingly of esquire's rank, and five men-at-arms, all
dead, was the speedy result of the unexpected encounter.

Wallace, his breath recovered, was now concerned to get
away from the vicinity as quickly as possible. This party of
English might not be missed for some time; on the other hand,
it was an odd time for them to be setting out to cross the Allan
Water westwards, from the Perth road, and it could be that they
were just the advance party of a larger force. Anyway, this was
not a spot to linger at. They hurried off North-Eastwards at
their speediest.

All night they traversed Lower Strathearn, avoiding the areas
of the various castles of the Earl thereof, at Auchterarder, Dun-
ning and Forteviot. There was then the Earn itself to cross,
before daylight, and fords few. MacGregor knew of one near
Mill of Gask. After it, they would not take long to reach the
great Methven Wood, a few miles west of Perth, where they
could lie safe.

That they did. But it was well past dawn before they reached
the outskirts of Methven Wood, after a night of mighty walking, almost twenty difficult miles in unknown country. This
forest was famous as a haunt and refuge of broken men, widespread, thick, teeming with game, deer, wildfowl. They would
eat fresh meat, and feel secure.

They slept the day away — guards posted, nevertheless.

Wallace had come to the Perth neighbourhood for a specific
reason — and he would not learn news of Sir Andrew Moray or
of the Lord Hugh MacDuff, whilst lurking in Methven Wood,
he feared. So that very evening, he left his company under
Gray's and Kerlie's command, and set off alone for St. John's
Town, in his begging-friar's robe once more. Perth was a walled
city, and the gates would be shut at night. But he had gained one
item of importance from one of the outcasts they had come
across in the forest. The porter of the Mill Port was venal, and no
great lover of his English masters. Rob Drummond by name. He
not infrequently let broken men in at his unimportant gate of a
night, for a consideration. He had an interest in a renowned

brothel in the Skinnergait — and apparently had a fellow feeling for a man's needs, as well as for his own pocket.

In the circumstances, Wallace took the friar's habit off when, almost on midnight, he approached the city walls in a drizzle of rain, and bundled it up under his arm. He almost went to the wrong gate, but realised just in time that he was at a major portal, guarded by strong towers, and presumably the West Port. So he worked his way round in a southerly direction, with some difficulty, having to cross two rubbish filled burns or stanks, to this minor access — which was here because the King's Mills, a royal property, were just within, and it was not considered proper that the King's millers should have to seek entry or exit at the ordinary gates, or be bound by other folk's times of opening and closing. This gate-porter, Drummond, was a servant of the millers.

Wallace had to rap on heavy doors. He had to rap a few times, before there was any response, then a barred spy-hole was opened in a wicket door, and a gruff voice demanded what was wanted at this ill hour. The big man replied that he wanted Rob Drummond, gate-porter. The other grunted something inaudible, and went away.

Presently a different voice spoke at the grille, asking who wanted Rob Drummond, why, and where from?'

'I am Will Malcolmson, from near the Ettrick Forest,' Wallace replied. 'Come seeking a kinder country, here in the North. I am told that you can on occasion, aid a man to kindness, here in St. John's Town?'

'Ooh, aye — maybe,' the other returned. 'But — you said Ettrick Forest? Yon's an unchancy place I'm told, man?'

'So I have left it.'

'They say the man Wallace is great there. Slaughtering folk from its ill bounds. Mind, some folk might be the better o' a bit slaughter — I'm no' saying otherwise! But — ken you the man?'

'I have heard tell of him. But I can give you no tidings of him, friend. I have been gone from there some time. Do I gain entry to this town, or no?'

'Can you pay?'

'A sufficiency for what I may get.'

'Aye, well.' The sound of a bar being drawn and a key turned in a lock, and the wicket-door opened. 'Sakes — you fill a big frame, man!' the porter observed, as Wallace slipped within. 'Do they grow many like you in yon Forest?'

'A few. You should see my brothers. But what advantage is over-much body? It takes the more filling and clothing.'

'No doubt. Mysel', I'm content the way I am. Kindness, I think you said you were seeking, in St. John's Town, eh? Kindness, I jalouse, will best be found, at this hour, in a house I ken no' that far away. But ... it will cost a little more, mind.'

Wallace produced a silver penny — which the other took with alacrity. 'That for entry and your good counsel, man. Another of the same if I am well satisfied when you let me out, an hour before dawn.'

'Ooh, aye.' Drummond pocketed the coin. 'It will be mine, for sure. Go you to the third house in the Skinnergait. Ask for *Meg — Meg*, mind. Down this Mill Wynd to the Friary wall, round it and yon's Skinnergait. The third house. It's an ale-house. Meg, mind.'

Nodding, Wallace moved off down the narrow cobbled street of the sleeping town. The place stank to heaven, with pigs snoring in the gutters and having to be stepped over.

He found the Skinnergait without difficulty, and knocked on the door of the third house down, a low-browed place of but one storey and an attic, which smelled of stale ale even from the outside. A shout answered from within, a female shout, which he took to be an invitation to enter. The door opened to his push, and stooping, he stumbled down a dark passage, a chink of light from a slightly open door guiding him.

In this lighted room, where a peat fire smouldered and candles guttered, three men and two women sat at a table. At least, one man sprawled, head on arms in a pool of spilled beer; another lay back, open-mouthed and snoring with a woman, her clothing disarranged to say the least, lying against him, head on his thick shoulder; the third man had a mug of ale in one hand and with the other fondled the very large and white naked breast of the second woman, who sat on his knees, a bulky, blowsy woman, not young, hair as disarranged as her attire — but with a sharp enough eye

'Hey, dearie,' she greeted the newcomer, not moving nor interrupting her companion's caresses. 'Save us — here's a braw lad! See the size o' him — if you can see aught, my billy! What can I do for you, my fine callant? What can Peg Blair do for you, this hour o' the night?'

'Peg? Not Meg? I was to ask for a Mistress Meg.'

'Heck — is that the way of it? No, I'm no' Meg. No' me. But I might gie you a thing or two Meg couldna! Meg Drummond's upby, my swack lad. Awa' up wi' you. Here's a candle. But, mind — I get my siller, forby. The room's mine.'

'You shall be paid, Mistress, never fear. This Meg is up-stairs?'

'Och, you'll find her, easy enough. Eh, Dickon, you fat English gowk!' And she slapped her breast-fondler's hand, but not very purposefully.

'To be sure 'e will. And I do swear she'll find 'im, and no mistake — if the rest o' 'im's the size we do be seeing afore us, eh!' Thickly, slurringly, as the man spoke, it was obviously a north country English voice — presumably one of the soldiers of the garrison.

To the woman's skirl of laughter, Wallace took one of the candles, and left the room to mount the steep stairway which rose from the passage.

At the top of the steps were two apartments, under the rafters. One, the flickering light of the candle showed to be empty, save for the many plaids blankets and old sheepskins strewn over the floor — that, and the smell of unwashed humanity. The other door was not quite shut, and when the man knocked, and pushed it open, it creaked loudly. A voice from within mumbled something sleepily.

Stepping inside, Wallace held his light high. The room was smaller, but it was better furnished, to the extent of having a large bed, a chest and a slop-pail. On the bed a young woman was raising herself on an elbow, to peer drowsily, her fair hair largely covering her face and one shoulder. That was all that covered her, however, for she seemed to be naked. Even at the briefest glance, she clearly was exceedingly well-formed, her breasts, unlike those evidenced below, firm, young and thrusting. She was the only occupant.

The man coughed. 'You ... you are Meg?' he asked, a trace of apology in his voice. 'I was told to ask for Meg'

The girl evinced no signs of welcome. 'It is late,' she complained. 'I was sleeping.' There was weariness in that, something of regret, disappointment, but neither reproof nor outright rejection.

He nodded. 'I am sorry. It is late, yes. But ... I was unable to come earlier.'

She yawned 'It would not do ... another time?'

84

'Not easy, no. To get into this town again. We . . . I am on the move. Journeying. But . . .'

'My father sent you? From the gate?' She pushed the hair aside from her face, but made no attempt to hide herself beneath the bed-clothing.

'Rob Drummond? He is your father?' The girl might be fifteen, sixteen. It was hard to tell.

'Aye. It is well enough for him! I am tired. I have had five men tonight. I am sore, too. At least you sound one of our ain folk — a Scot. The others were all English — and drunken English. But I have had enough for one night.'

He shook his head. 'See you, Mistress Meg,' he said carefully. 'We may yet suit each other. I have come . . . mainly for shelter And to speak with, with a woman. To learn something of this town. I, I am not desperate. For bedding, whoring. You could perhaps give me what I want, without cost to yourself. If I stay with you for an hour or two . . .'

She sat up straighter now, staring at him — and there was no doubting her suspicion. 'What is this you're at?' she demanded. 'What are you saying? You come to my naked bed. At this hour. But you do not want to lie with me? Think you I'm like to believe that?'

'Mistress — tell me. You said that at least I was one of your ain folk, a Scot. That is true. Do you not love the English, then?'

'I hate them!' she said, not fiercely but quietly, simply.

'So-o-o. But . . . your father does not?'

'He does. But he can forget it, if he can get money from them. Through me!'

'Aye. Well, see you — I hate the English too. Or, not the English as folk, but these arrogant and savage invaders whom their proud Edward has sent to grind us down. That is why I am here, creeping into St. John's Town at night. I must seem to have a reason for it — and pleasuring myself with a woman is reason enough for most. For the same reason, I cannot just go away, leave you. Now. Or questions would be asked. You understand me?'

'Is it true? How am I to believe you? It could be but cozening . . .'

'Why should I do that? To what gain? Tell me, Meg — have you heard of the man Wallace? William Wallace, of Elderslie? Your father has.'

85

'Who has not? All Scotland has heard of William Wallace, and what he has done to the English. Are you of his company?'

'I am he — Wallace.'

Her breath caught, and her hand rose to those shapely breasts. 'No! I'll no' believe that! No' here, in St. John's Town.'

'Yes, here. In this room. And endangering my life in telling you, lass.'

'I canna believe it. Why should you come to me, Meg Drummond? You are big enough, to be sure — they say he is a big man. But, but . . .'

'Believe it, or believe it not — I care not. But let me stay awhile, Meg. And tell me what you know, of the English in Perth. Which is what I am here to learn. Living in Perth, and entertaining English soldiery, you will know something of the matter.'

She peered up at him and his flickering candle for long moments, then appeared to make up her mind. 'I will tell you what I can,' she said. 'Not that I ken that much.' She moved aside on the bed, and patted the position she had vacated. 'Come, you,' she invited.

It was the man's turn to hesitate. 'You are tired. And . . . and sore,' he said. 'I can sit on the bed, Meg, well enough'

'You would do better in beside me. None will say that Meg Drummond kept William Wallace out of her bed, when she had let so many Englishry in!'

'Ummm,' he said, a little doubtful at that assertion. But he was not the man to slight any lady deliberately. Blowing out the candle, he sat down, as invited. But obviously he could not lie either on or in her bed in the wet hide brogans he had worn with his friar's robe. So he removed these. Then it seemed, somehow, churlish to share a bed with a wholly naked woman while fully clad himself. So he removed some of his clothing, the girl watching in the darkness without comment. Then he laid himself rather markedly *on* the bed, rather than in it. The other, as markedly, drew the top blanket from under him, and spread it over him, over them both, and lay back with a sigh — but no longer, evidently, of weariness.

She felt most delightfully warm.

So they lay for a while, unspeaking. When the very positively inviting presence, so close beside him, became too much of a preoccupation, the man fell back on conversation. What could she tell him about the English, in Perth, he demanded?

Meg Drummond did not seem to consider this as important a matter as did he, nor her knowledge of any great moment. But at Wallace's assurance and insistence, she dredged up various items of information, recent and not so recent, part of which would be common knowledge in the town, part which she had gleaned in her special relationship with numerous soldiers of the garrison. These items were haphazard and in no coherent order or importance, and most had to be probed for and elaborated upon. But out of them, as the night wore on, the man was able to build up a fair picture of the situation — even though an altogether different but still fairer picture was apt to intrude on his mind's eye intermittently throughout, when he had to call upon a degree of self-discipline in order to maintain first things first. He had difficulty in keeping his hands to himself, too — until his companion's hands also became somewhat restive, when preoccupation tended to get the upper hand.

By then, however, he had gathered that Sir Andrew Moray's army was not thought to be any nearer than Atholl, where it was believed to be awaiting reinforcements from the Earl of Mar, from Aberdeenshire. As to Hugh MacDuff, the girl knew nothing, had never heard of the man. The English commander in Perth was Sir Gerard Heron, a Northumbrian, and his deputy young Sir John Butler, whom Meg described as a stark stirk and bold, an ill man to cross, son to old Sir James Butler who held Kinclaven Castle to the north, where Isla and Tay joined, the last English garrison before the great Comyn lands of the North. She believed that there would be around five hundred English soldiers quartered in the town usually, but more at the moment, for a company was being made up to send as strengthening for Kinclaven, under young Butler, in view of the threat of Moray's advance. This was unpopular with the troops, for that castle was considered to be a dangerous place, exposed and lacking the amenities of the town.

Digesting all this as well as he might under the circumstances, Wallace percieved regretfully that he could do nothing about Perth itself. It was much too tough a nut for him to attempt to crack. But this Kinclaven sounded more interesting, hopeful. He pressed for details.

She was not really very interested in providing them, but he gathered that it was situated some dozen miles or so to the north, guarding the mouth of Strathmore, where the routes from Atholl and Angus met, at the rivers' junction and crossing.

She knew nothing about how many men might be there, but it was said to be a strong hold — and to be strengthened. It was this fact which particularly interested Wallace; but she had no information for him as to when the reinforcing was to take place. Though she imagined that it must be within the next day or so.

Tactical and strategic problems of this sort can be a substantial barrier against temptations of the flesh. The man, even so, found it inadequate.

Meg Drummond could not tell him much more. But she appeared to have a strong sense of duty, and an urge to demonstrate goodwill in other ways.

In the end, Wallace had real difficulty in dragging himself away, with a couple of hours gone — for he had to be out of Perth and indeed back at Methven Wood, before daylight. He assured the young woman of his gratitude — but did not insult her with offers of money. She promised not to mention Wallace's name; also to garner from Englishmen all such further information as she could, and he was welcome indeed to it, as to her bed, whenever he might find his way back into St. John's Town. They parted on the best of terms, with Meg actually coming downstairs to see him off, a blanket wrapped around her nakedness — and spitting like a wildcat at the woman Peg below, when she sought her rooming fee, obviously distressed when the man insisted on handing over a half-merk.

There was no such unrealistic attitude on the part of her father, presently, back at the Mill Gate. He required his promised silver penny for letting the visitor out, but was meticulous in his enquiries as to whether Master Malcolmson had been adequately pleasured and entertained. Wallace could have felled the man for so prostituting his own daughter, but had to forebear. He averred his entire satisfaction, and was told to haste him back.

The six miles to Methven over, he found his camp still comfortably asleep — although the sentries were satisfactorily alert. Wallace altered the situation promptly. Although he himself had had no sleep that night, he had the horn sounded right away. They would move within the hour, he declared.

They did, northwards through the forest and up into the brae country of Redgorton and Luncarty, fording the Almond at Dalcrue.

*   *   *

By mid-afternoon, they were coming down to the great river of Tay, a mile or two short where the Isla joined it from the North-East, out of Strathmore, where they halted in a large wood of birch and oak scrub called Shortwood Shaw, in the Ballathie area. Where the rivers joined was also a great junction of roads, for the Isla came out of the heartland of Angus, and the Tay from Dunkeld and Lower Atholl. Moreover there was a road from the Stormonth, due north, and the high mountain-route by Blair-in-Gowrie over the Pass of Glenshee to upper Deeside. Moreover the Isla, a mountain river much given to spates, brought down a vast weight of stones, which it deposited across the wider and quieter-flowing Tay, thus shallowing it here and creating a well-known fording place, the only one in many a long mile. And at the west side, on a steep mound above this ford, rose the castle of Kinclaven, which the strategically minded King Edward had not taken long to decide was a vital place to have under his control.

Leaving his men hidden in Shortwood Shaw, Wallace, with Gray, Kerlie and MacGregor, crept forward, using all natural cover, to spy out the position, keeping well back from the road, which had followed the riverside from Perth. They got to within half-a-mile of the castle without difficulty; but there seemed to be a mill and cottages scattered around it, and they ventured no nearer. The place appeared to be more of a fort than a castle proper, consisting of high stone curtain-walls with low squat flanking towers at all four angles, with a gatehouse to the west, all set on top of a steep bank. A ramp led up to the entrance, with its gatehouse, but there was a wide ditch here, no doubt water-filled. At present the drawbridge for spanning this was half-up, at an angle. There appeared to be no other access to the place; and certainly no assault up the steep banks was a practical proposition, with twenty-five foot high sheer walling rising above. The parapet-walk of this walling, on the east side, dominated the ford.

Less than elated by what they saw, Wallace and his companions retired into the deeper woodland. It seemed that force would not take Kinclaven; and an effective and possible stratagem would not be easy to devise or contrive.

They mulled it over for long, that evening, considering and rejecting various suggestions. One matter was discovered to be slightly advantageous — a darkness patrol found that the mill and hamlet was in fact deserted, no doubt cleared out by the

English as a security risk. A daylight approach was obviously out of the question; yet the likelihood of persuading anyone to lower the drawbridge, by night, was remote. They came to the conclusion that the early morning might be the best time. It was not infrequently a period of vulnerability for such strongholds, when the night watch were apt to be at their least wary and the day personnel less than fully awake and alert. Moreover, it was then that fresh fuel, food, fodder for the horses and so on, tended to be brought in, and dung and refuse carted out. At such time confusion might be created. But it would be necessary to observe the procedure next morning, so that any attack would have to be delayed till the day following. Which worried Wallace, who was concerned about the alleged re-inforcements from Perth.

They had reached this stage in their deliberations when one of the scouts whom Wallace was always meticulous to post, came running, breathlessly, to announce that a large party of horsemen was approaching from the south, along the riverside road. They were not more than half-a-mile away. A company strong, perhaps.

The big man groaned. On that road, they could only be coming from Perth. And in that strength would almost certainly be the reinforcements Meg Drummond had mentioned, under young Butler, arriving earlier than anticipated. Once they were in Kinclaven, any idea of an assault could be forgotten. On the other hand, to tackle a company of cavalry, say a hundred men, in the open, with sixty men on foot, could be folly. He had done better than that at Loudoun Hill, two hundred attacked by fifty — but these had been convoying a pack-train, the terrain made for an ambush, and the circumstances exceptional. Nevertheless, it was that, or ignominious retiral.

As always, he made a swift decision. Shouting to his men, he went bounding down through the birch and juniper scrub, to the road.

This wound along the bank of Tay for three or four miles hereabouts, very close to the river, with the woodland coming right down to it — not an ideal place for an ambuscade, but possible. Reaching the muddy track, Wallace made a hurried survey, up and down the roadway. No sign of the military yet, for the track wound and twisted, and could not be inspected beyond a couple of hundred yards. This might not be the best spot, but he had no time to look for better. Hastily he divided

his force into two. Twenty men, under Kerlie, he ordered to
cover both sides of the road just to the north, castle-wards. The
bank dropped fairly sharply to the waterside, on the one hand,
the men could crouch under it with every chance of escaping
notice. The bushes on the other side must hide the rest. He took
the remaining forty himself, and ran along southwards for
about one hundred yards, to near one of the many bends of the
road. He dared not risk going further. Placing a dozen men,
under Gray, on the upper, wooded side, he ordered the rest to
string themselves out below the track, on the bank where, after
a moment or two of brief inspection, he joined them.

They had only a minute or so to wait and ponder — indeed,
Wallace could hear the clink of accoutrements and the thud of
hooves before ever he went to crouch below the bank. He
moved along, to lie behind a small thorn-bush there.

What chances had they? The road was so narrow — which
meant that the horsemen necessarily would be, like themselves,
strung out. Within a mile of their fortified destination, they
were not likely to be particularly wary. The river on one side
and the fairly steep wooded slope on the other would prevent
either concentration or dispersal. For a wager, the leader would
be in front. All that might not be much — but it could even the
odds considerably.

The big man called out a low but very urgent warning to his
men.

With a jingle of harness and the clatter of iron-shod hooves,
the first three riders came round the bend from the south. There
was a gap behind. These were only outriders, then. They let
them pass.

A few moments later Wallace cursed, if beneath his breath.
The man in the lead was indeed dressed in knight's armour, a
plumed helm hanging at his saddle-bow — but he was elderly,
with grey hair and heavy purple jowls, not the young Sir John
Butler whom Meg Drummond had mentioned. But this man
displayed, as coat-armour, the three gold cups on red of the
great house of Butler, differenced with a scallop — so it must be
the father, Sir James, Constable of Kinclaven. Meg had said
that the older man was stark and cruel, while the young was
bold and hot-tempered. The latter, then, must be at the tail of
the column — which was unexpected, and could be awkward.

Tensely he counted the files as they came into view, all to his
right hand men crouching, eager, impatient. With Butler past,

ten files were in sight, to the bend. Assessing, he let them ride on. The ten were past, and another ten files in view. They were beginning to string out, towards the rear, lengthening the column. Sixty men only, so far — another twelve files, say, to come. Butler was already almost too far along, forward, beyond the last of Wallace's hidden men. The timing, now, was vital. It was already touch-and-go.

There were not a dozen more files, only nine. And no knight at the rear, as the last trio came trotting round the bend. Unless young Butler was far behind, with a rearguard — surely hardly necessary, in the circumstances? That was good fortune, at least.

Wallace could wait no longer. With a loud yell, he scrambled to his feet, and leapt from behind his bush at the nearest horseman, reaching for his middle, to drag him out of the saddle before he could draw his sword. All along the roadside his men did likewise, from both flanks.

So far as it went, success was with them. They had achieved complete surprise, and major confusion amongst the enemy. With no room to manoeuvre, the horsemen were at a disadvantage. Most of them carried lances, and since these were more quickly brought into action than were swords which had to be unsheathed, they tended to use them but, being seven feet long, they were almost useless in the crush. Wallace's men, darting amongst the horses relied only on their dirks; and with these, when they could not drag off the riders, they slashed the animals' bellies. For some hundred yards and more that roadway became a hellish, screaming, bloody chaos.

But the hundred yards was not long enough. Only some sixty or so of the men-at-arms were engaged, with some five files at the front and four at the rear not covered by the attack. These had time to size up the situation, draw swords, and come to the rescue of their fellows.

It was fortunate for Wallace and his party that there was still no sign of young Butler. For the counter-assault from the rear was hesitant, piecemeal, with no coherent leadership. There was plenty of leadership from the front, with Sir James yelling orders and driving back, sword thrashing. But the driving back to some extent defeated its own object. For such men in the centre, as could get out of the reach of the dirk-wielding Scots, were tending to bolt, and bolt forwards towards the nearby security of Kinclaven Castle. And these found their way blocked by Sir James Butler and his forward files, returning. The result was still greater confusion.

Wallace, his first man down and dirked, sized up the situation in a glance. The rear, where he himself was involved, could be left to itself — as long as no one appeared there to take command. Butler must be his objective. Grabbing a lance from the nerveless grasp of a dying man in process of falling from his horse, he shouldered it, and went pushing forward amongst the press of rearing, plunging, whinnying horses.

He was in more danger from trampling hooves than from men's weapons. Time and again as he fought his way along, dirk slashing, he was buffeted, all but knocked over. His new lance was no help — but he reckoned that he would require it, to counter the longer reach of Butler's sword, from horseback. He could have grabbed a riderless beast and mounted himself — but then he would have been unable to push and sidle on through the crush as he was doing.

He had the best part of one hundred yards to go, and could see only a yard or two ahead at any one time. There were bodies, too, to trip over. It was an utterly blind and incoherent business, and he was able to offer nothing of the leadership required of a commander. But that must wait until he could deal with Butler, or at least negative *his* leadership.

Almost he did not reach Butler. A horseman to the left of him suddenly turned in his saddle and swung down his short but heavy cavalry sword in a sideways slash to Wallace's bare head. He had just time to thrust the lanceshaft between them sufficiently for it to take the force of the blow. The steel sheared right through the wood and left the big man with only half a spear. But before the man-at-arms could recover balance for another stroke, Wallace used the dirk in his left hand to stab in at the other's waist, below the steel jack. With a yittering scream the man sagged, and slid from his saddle. Tossing away the broken lance, Wallace caught the fellow's short sword as he fell. It would be of more use in this press than his own lengthy two-handed brand.

He pushed on, panting.

And now he saw the colourful hues of the knight's heraldic surcoat ahead of him, at last. But not on a horse's back. Butler, like himself, had realised that he was better on foot in that tight packed mêlée, as if he was to win his way to any position where he might take command of the fighting.

93

Furiously Wallace hacked and slashed his way towards the other, the more urgently as he saw more than one of his men go down under the knight's shrewd and effective swordery. Here was a trained and experienced swordsman, protected by excellent armour, and most of Wallace's Highlandmen were no match for him.

Yelling his breathless cry of 'A Wallace! A Wallace!' to seek distract Butler's attention, he came close — and the other perceiving him in the press, as leader, was nothing loth. Men sought to get out of their way, if horses did not.

They reached each other at length — and despite the armour and helmet, Wallace did not fail to estimate that he had the advantage. His borrowed sword might be a trifle shorter than Butler's, but he being much the taller had the reach now the other was dismounted. Moreover, the knight was old enough to be his father, and somewhat stout of build. Also, his armour though it protected him, hampered him likewise, restricting his movement and weighing him down. The older man had been smiting and killing for some time already, and was as breathless as was the other. But Wallace was not wearied with it, only lacking breath from pushing through the horses.

Deliberately seeking to play on the other's weaknesses, the big man leapt in, feinting and jinking around the other, causing him to lash out wildly, to twist and turn in his heavy armour — more important still, to keep turning his head this way and that so that he could keep his opponent in view from the very limited aperture of his helmet, which he had donned at the first hint of trouble. Round and round Wallace danced, his blade flickering — and clearly the knight grew ever more distressed, dizzy, staggering a little, reacting even less effectively. Yet still his sword jabbed and thrust and parried expertly, keeping his opponent just out of range most of the time.

His own breathing now very laboured, the younger man percieved that this would not do. Some of Butler's men were pressing close, to aid their master and tending to distract his own attention. He decided to change tactics. Leaping far back from the knight, he suddenly turned on the nearest of the soldiers and took him wholly by surprise by hurling the cavalry sword directly into the man's face, sending him staggering. Almost in the same movement, he thrust up both hands behind his head, and grabbed the great two-handed blade which was sheathed there, its long pommel at the back of his neck, a circurnstance which had hitherto been no help to him in his leaping and in-fighting. In a single great and much practised sweep he whipped the huge sword out in a flashing arc, and launched himself and it upon the surprised knight — who no doubt thought that he had a brief, but much needed breathing space. Far outreaching the other man, the five-foot-long blade came slashing down in a semi-sideways blow, striking the older man's helmet just at the hinge of the visor, the weakest spot. No light steel could withstand that fearful swipe. The helm caved in and the blade cut deep into flesh and skull. Sir James Butler, swept over by the force of it, keeled sideways like a felled tree.

The fall of their leader had its usual effect on hired men — especially in their reluctance to seek further conclusions with his slayer. Everywhere at this northern end of the prolonged confusion, men began to try to break off and get away. The middle section was already demoralised. The southern end had never been keen — and no better leader appeared there. In fact, the battle was over from that moment, although it took a little time for this to become evident. Disengagement was the order of the day — though many had left it too late.

Gulping great breaths into bursting lungs, Wallace gazed around him. Already men who had stayed on their horses were lashing the beasts round and heading away up the track, for Kinclaven. He forced himself into swift, constructive thought. The castle! This was his chance. Ignoring all else, he stooped over his fallen adversary, and tore off the already torn heraldically-coloured linen surcoat which had been worn over the armour, all red-and-white Butler tinctures. Flinging the tattered and kenspeckle garment round his own great shoulders, he ran to the nearest riderless horse — of which there were now plenty — tossing away his huge brand, only an incumbrance now. Yelling to the MacGregor, who was near him, to follow, and all others within hearing to do likewise, he dug heels into his new mount's side, and sent it after the fleeing men-at-arms at a heavy canter. As he rode, he sought to drape the surcoat over him more effectively. It might just serve.

He burst out of the last of the woodland no more than seventy yards behind the last of the fleeing soldiers. The castle on its mound was only three hundred yards ahead — and the drawbridge was lowered. Glancing over his shoulder, he saw that Stephen MacGregor and perhaps half-a-dozen others were pounding after him on captured horses, not far behind. More, he hoped, would be coming.

He could hear the hollow drumming of hooves on the drawbridge timbers, as the first of the fleeing men raced to safety. Others were strung out behind, over some two hundred yards. Then himself. Could he make it? He lashed his mount's sides with heels and fist. With his size, could he possibly be mistaken for old Butler, in that tattered surcoat? Or young Butler maybe?

He was listening now — listening for the tell-tale clanking of drawbridge and protcullis chains. Would he hear it above the thunder of hooves? Only another hundred or so yards to go.

The last man in front of him clattered over, never glancing back. The Bridge had not begun to lift, nor the portcullis to drop. Sixty yards. Fifty. Seconds only, now. He looked back. Stephen, horse more lightly burdened than his own, had made up some way, a bare fifty yards behind.

Scarcely believing his good fortune, he realised that he was going to make it, that even though the bridge began to lift now, he would get in; for the bridge process was a slow one, and his horse would be able to jump a six or eight foot gap.

In fact, the beast did not have to do so. Whether the Butler surcoat did indeed confuse the gate-porter, or whether the man just lost his head there was no knowing. But the drawbridge remained down and the portcullis up. In a full gallop now, Wallace lashed his beast across, and beat in under the gatehouse arch.

It was a fantastic situation, he recognised. Here he was, alone, in the courtyard of an English-held castle. Men were dismounting in front of him, flinging themselves down from steaming animals. The high curtain-walls were lined with lean-to buildings, with no central tower or keep, only barrackrooms, bunkhouses, a hallhouse, and stables. Some of the formerly fleeing men turned to stare at him, others ran indoors. Some women were in evidence. Dogs barked, people shouted. Wallace, lacking even a dirk now, moved forward at a walk, listening for the clatter of his supporters behind.

'I, William Wallace, call on all here to surrender!' he cried loudly. 'In the name of John, King of Scots!' It was the first time that he had used that phrase.

As still men gaped, open-mouthed — after all, they had seen what this giant had done to the master — the MacGregor came pounding across the bridge and into the courtyard. He at least had a drawn sword. Behind him came the others, not many but fierce-looking, determined, victorious.

'Up to the gatehouse!' Wallace called, to the MacGregor, but as calmly as he could. And to the others. 'All men to be rounded up. Disarmed. Brought to me here. Quickly.' He sat his horse, waiting, a picture of quiet assurance

Nor was his assurance unjustified. More of his men arrived, in twos and threes. No sort of resistance developed within the castle. A couple of priests appeared from the hall-house, to demand, in distinctly shaky tones what was to do? Where was Sir James? Wallace told them, stiffly correct, that they were his prisoners. As were all within this hold. If there was no trouble, full obedience to his orders, there was nothing to fear. All lives would be spared. Everyone, man, woman and child, must assemble before him, at once. All arms be surrendered, in the name of the King of Scots. If nobody else was doing anything in the name of John Baliol, Will Wallace was.

Strangely enough, that was the way it was. By the time Thomas Gray arrived, and Wallace could hand over the priests to him, some nineteen men, nine women and five children — one of the women a proud and hard-faced Lady Butler — were standing in the courtyard before the big man, who still sat his horse like some Roman centurion. Kinclaven seemed to have been left in the care of only about half-a-dozen men, and these, seeing all defeat outside, made no attempt at fighting. Those who had fled here were beaten already, and in no mood to resume hostilities. The promise of their lives was sufficient for all. Kinclaven fell without a blow being struck.

Barely crediting the ease of it all, the victors took stock of the situation. They had lost five men dead, and a number wounded, in the fight at the road. They counted of the enemy sixty-one dead. Wallace set the prisoners to burying all these, there and then, in the water-meadows at the river bank, with the three priests to say the last offices. He collected all the horses and found that they had over seventy of these. Only some few men had escaped, apparently.

He did not want the horses — but nor did he want the prisoners to have them. Forage for all these would be a major problem. As the November dusk settled down, he marshalled all the captives, the women and children and priests with them, and marched them out and over the drawbridge. They were free to go where they would, he told them — but not to stay near Kinclaven. They were all well fed, and would come to no harm in spending a night out-of-doors. They could be in Perth by the morrow's noon, if so they desired. Let them tell Sir Gerald Heron that Scotland had had enough of its English invaders — tell him that William Wallace said so. It would be Perth's turn next.

Some protesting bitterly about being driven out to die, Lady Butler stiff-lipped to the end, the vanquished straggled off along the woodland road.

The horses were then driven out and into the woods, and left to fend for themselves. Then the drawbridge clanked up and the portcullis clanked down, behind them.

Kinclaven's cellars were full of meats and wines, as well as valuables looted from a wide area, again evidently largely from churches. Although the concensus was that they had bought it all cheaply, Wallace grieved for his dead.

CHAPTER SIX

It was decided to make a wary stay at Kinclaven. For one thing, the wounded were in poor state for travel. For another, Wallace was sending out scouts to try to make contact with Moray or MacDuff, or both. That would take time. But he well realised that Heron and young Butler — who was presumably still at Perth — would not be long in seeking reprisals, once the word of the Kinclaven attack reached them. They had perhaps one full day — after which they must look for major trouble.

As at Gargunnock, Wallace was determined not to be trapped within a castle. He moved out next morning, therefore, back into the cover of Shortwood Shaw. The Irishman Fawdon, supported by some others, took this in bad part, protesting that Kinclaven was an excellent stronghold, both secure and comfortable. Wallace was adamant, declaring that it could be a deathtrap. His people being loth indeed to part with the spoils won here, he permitted them to take out the most portable of the booty, and to bury it, for safety, in a woodland glade.

He had more important matters than loot on his mind. The forces such as would be sent against him this time would not be of the sort that he could ambush. He had only fifty effectives now, and they could expect Heron's full strength from Perth and the surrounding area, anything from five hundred to a thousand men. He did not want to have to fight such a force — at least, not without reinforcements. Much depended on how long the English took to descend on them, and how long his messengers took to find Sir Andrew Moray or Lord Hugh MacDuff, and possibly to bring back aid. No aid might materialise, he well recognised, and yet some confrontation become inevitable. Therefore, at one-to-ten at best, he had to try to make the country fight for him, at least while he made a strategic withdrawal if nothing else.

This Shortwood Shaw had great possibilities, Wallace had recognised from the first. It was a fairly thickly wooded hillside, covered in birch, oak, ash and a scattering of older dark Caledonian pines. Here and there were sudden steeps and rocky bluffs. The floor of the woodlands was deep in old bracken, high and entangling. It was impossible territory for cavalry — and almost certainly it would be cavalry which would be sent out against them, at least in the first instance — armoured chivalry, light horse, and mounted archers. In holding down Scotland, the English used little ordinary infantry.

With this in mind Wallace set his reluctant men to the heavy task of constructing a series of barriers — for it was the archers, the English speciality, which worried him most. The barriers they made by cutting birch saplings and weaving them in fence-like structures, backed by turf and soil. They placed these, as far as possible, to link up with the rocky tors and bluffs, these forming strong-points and hinges. When they had finished the first line, some three hundred yards long, with ends based on crags which would be hard for the enemy to turn and outflank, they immediately were started on another about two hundred yards behind — to loud complaint. But the big man was insistent, and almost came to blows with the surly Fawdon — who, although an excellent fighter, seemed to have taken upon himself the role of chief grumbler and spokesman. Wallace assured them that they would go on building such defences for just so long as the English allowed — and would in all probability be very grateful for them, in due course.

By nightfall, the second line was almost finished, and they

99

took their rest around modest camp-fires in a hollow of the woods. Their sentries and scouts had reported no approach by friend or foe.

In chill rain, at daybreak, they were back at work, and had finished a third line when, in mid-forenoon, Wallace took the most consistent grumblers with him back to Kinclaven, where they methodically set fire to the castle, a task which seemed much more to the general taste. The massive stone curtain-walls were impervious to fire, but the lean-to buildings, timber with thatch, blazed satisfactorily. The great column of smoke which rose in the damp air would convey its message to all concerned.

They had a fourth line of barrier erected by evening, and still no sign of the enemy. Heron was taking his time — which could mean that he was gathering fullest strength, reckoning his five hundred at Perth insufficient. It was a daunting thought. Still there was no word from Wallace's messengers to Moray and MacDuff.

When still another wet day passed without incident, Wallace began to doubt his own judgement. Perhaps they were fools to remain here? Was a whole army being gathered, to fling against them — since it was inconceivable that the English at Perth would not institute major reprisals. He would now have been inclined to desert the position at Shortwood Shaw and steal quietly away — but could scarcely leave before his messengers returned, possibly with the requested reinforcements.

That night, the two messengers whom he had sent eastwards, into Strathmore, did return, and alone. They had been quite unable to find MacDuff. They had heard rumours of a band of alleged outlaws, who might be the Lord Hugh's party, operating around Dundee and the Carse of Gowrie, from the fastnesses of the Sidlaw Hills — but though they had searched, they had found no trace of such. They had not dared stay away longer.

Wallace was disappointed in more ways than one. If the MacDuff's company was so elusive, and so little known, it could not be large. It was not a small band of outlaws he had hoped for, but a sizeable force of trained soldiers, lords' men-at-arms.

Still there was nothing from Sir Andrew Moray. Atholl, of course, was a vast area; and Meg Drummond might have been misinformed as to Moray having reached there.

He had kept his men busy during the long wait. Now they had no fewer than five full lines of defence, linked by covered passageways, for retrial, from one to the other. Even fifty men might put up a strong defence on such embattled heights.

The following day, with almost a week passed since they had first come to Kinclaven area, his southern sentries brought Wallace the word both expected and dreaded. A great force was approaching from down Tayside, horsed, many companies strong, seen from the Court Hill. Numbers could not be guessed at, meantime, but it could be termed an army.

The news had, in fact an enheartening effect on the big man. It was the idle waiting and uncertainty which had worried him; the thought of imminent action, even danger, on the contrary renewed his spirit. He sent more sentries and look-outs forward, to various viewpoints, and prepared his little force for eventualities.

His next tidings were that the main body of the enemy had drawn up on the southern outskirts of Shortwood Shaw, nearly a mile away, perhaps eight hundred strong, with much of chivalry and knights' banners. A mounted company of some two troops' strength, say two hundred men, half of them mounted bowmen, was however advancing slowly along the riverside road, probing towards the castle — and the leader bore the red-and-white coat-armour of Butler.

Young Butler, with a debt to pay, had clearly gained permission from Heron to act as advance guard and perhaps bait for a trap. He certainly would not allow himself to be ambushed as his father had been. He would press heedfully for the castle, and seeing it in ruin would turn back, and come searching the woodland, — and his hundred bowmen would be a major menace therein even if his cavalry would not. It was out of the question that the Scots could long escape detection. But it was vital that their flanks should not be turned, their hard-built defences invalidated. It might be wise to do a little decoying.

The Scots had little or no tradition of using bows and arrows for war, unlike the English and the Welsh — only for sport and the chase, partly because yew trees did not grow to the right size in the North. Wallace's party were equipped with nothing of the sort. But they had found about two score of good yew bows amongst the captured armoury at Kinclaven. Unfortunately there had been no great supply of arrows — only about eight or ten per bow. Some of his Highlandmen were used to hunting-bows — but these were much shorter. Taking one himself, and issuing the others to twenty of the most experienced, he left the

101

remaining twenty five or so under Kerlie and Gray to man the first come to Kinclaven area, his southern sentries brought hide just above the road.

It was some little time before the English came in sight, making a very different approach from the previous Butler company. Warily, testing almost each step of the way, they advanced closepacked, four deep, shields up, lances lowered, hands on sword-hilts, bows at the ready. The fully armoured knight at the front bore the Butler arms, and another brought up the rear, with blue-and-gold heraldry.

Wallace let them pass, and then flitted through the trees, above and behind them, keeping carefully in cover.

Before the castle, it did not take Butler long to size up the situation. The smoke-blackened walls and charred timbers of the broken drawbridge, the general ruin and emptiness, may have infuriated him. But it did not delay him. The two knights took counsel, and quite quickly turned back. Watching from well within the cover of the trees, Wallace saw developing more or less what he had anticipated, what he himself would have done. Butler dismounted most of his men, and spread them out in a long line, to move forward on a four hundred yard front, archers interspersed with spearmen. He and his lieutenant remained mounted at the bottom end. They were going to beat out the wood.

So far so good — but it must be only so far. Wallace designed to take the initiative, and retain it, if possible — when he was ready.

He moved his people discreetly back, as yet unseen. It was a blessing that the English did not seem to have brought any of the sleuth-hounds of which they were so fond — not this advance-party, at any rate.

It was a slow retiral, for the enemy were in no evident hurry, and moreover made heavy going of the rough terrain, stumbling amongst the high and dead but still clutching bracken, tripping over roots and fallen timber. These were not expert beaters by any means, nor even expert infantry, and were notably wary, the bowmen especially. They shouted to each other up and down the line as they came — for they had no particular need of silence.

By contrast, going entirely silently, secretly, Wallace moved his party back and back, until they were level with the lines of defence barriers, though considerably below them. This must be where the enemy were halted.

Wallace of course had well chosen his positions beforehand, he had had plenty of time for forethought. He chose a natural hollow on the wooded slope, rather wet, with two small burns flowing into it in channels — but these provided escape routes to higher ground. He had had the hollow strengthened, but not obviously, with scrub and bushes and a boulder or two. In this he installed his archers to wait.

When the line of beaters approached it was distinctly ragged, bunched, strung-out, inevitably.

'Remember — the archers,' Wallace whispered. 'Bring down the archers. Wait until I give the signal.'

This had to be carefully judged — near enough to make sure his amateur bowmen were unlikely to miss; but not so near that the interspersed spearmen would be able to rush their position before fresh arrows could be fitted and loosed. The fact that the enemy line was approaching them sideways on, and was so uneven, complicated matters. Some were fully a hundred yards higher than their own position — and these particularly must be halted. When Wallace uttered the single word 'Shoot!', he was the only man not to aim at an archer. He chose an individual with drawn sword who was very much to the fore in the shouting and directing, presumably an under officer. His arrow transfixed this man just above his jack, clean through the throat—and his shouting ended in a bubbling scream. The score of other arrows winged their lethal way.

Almost a dozen men fell— which was quite good considering the crouching and part-hidden posture of the marksmen, and their lack of practice. The yells and shrieks were appalled and appalling, hell abruptly let loose. There was complete surprise and utter confusion. No attempt was made by the spearmen to make any concerted charge, any charge at all. A few arrows were loosed off, very much at random, by uninjured archers, but these produced no casualties. Most of the enemy either flung themselves flat, or bolted. By the time that the inexpert Scots could fit new arrows, there were few targets to aim at — although Wallace himself — who as a knight's son was well trained in all arms and manly skills — managed to bring down another bowman. The rest leapt, ran, crawled or otherwise got urgently out of range, mainly downhill towards the road. Fortunately those highest in the line were determined not to be separated from their comrades, and hurried downwards also.

It was a good start. But surprise was now expended. They could expect disciplined and intelligent counter-attack — and still from nine times their own number. Wallace praised his archers — but pointed out that they were insufficiently swift at replacing arrows in their bows. The next attack would be serious.

It took a while to materialise. No doubt Sir John Butler was being more careful than ever, whatever his fiery reputation. When it did come, it was fairly stealthy, on a wide front, men creeping uphill bent double, presenting very poor marks even though they made a lot of noise. As they came within long arrow-range, the enemy archers held back, and the spearmen came crawling on, flat as they could. The tactic was obvious, but effective. To gain sufficient elevation to shoot at these crawlers, the Scots would have to rise and show themselves — when the English archers would seek to bring them down.

Wallace had not failed to anticipate this, and had tried to leave a few arrow-slits in the rough barrier. These were not fully effective — but they did allow a few bolts to be shot, and one or two hits made. As well as this, they had had a great pile of stones brought up from the river, large rounded pebbles half as big as a man's head; and these his men now hurled over upon the creeping spearmen. This fusillade could only be haphazard and indiscriminate, but it would be a highly unpleasant hail to be under nevertheless, and had an unsettling effect on belly-crawlers, causing some to dodge and hide, some even to retire — for these were cavalrymen, and ill took this sort of fighting.

It was at this stage that the armoured knights, dismounted now also, showed themselves, in an effort to rally the advance. They could not creep and crawl, even if they would — but on the other hand, their armour protected them from all but the most accurately aimed arrows. Visors down meantime, these two came on, upright, and after wasting precious bolts on their steel-casing, the Scots perceived that their position could no longer be held effectively by a score of men. Wallace gave the order to retire.

Thanks to the two burn-channels, they were able to achieve this without exposing themselves to the enemy, for the channels were fairly deep and hidden amongst high bracken. One man was careless, and fell, pierced by a yard-long shaft; but all the rest got clear away, and were able to make their way uphill to the first line of the main defensive barriers, where they were welcomed by their anxious colleagues.

Clearly it would not be long before Butler's assault caught up with them. Wallace briefly explained the enemy's method of attack, and gave his orders. It was improbable that they could keep the English spearmen from coming close, under the cover of their bowmen; but once they were close, it should be possible to keep them from crossing the barrier, for their archers would then be unable to shoot effectively for fear of hitting their own men. With the five sets of barriers to use, one after the other, the English attack might well falter and fail. Their own bowmen were to station themselves at the ends of the barrier, so as to prevent the enemy archers from working round and enfilading them.

It was well thought out and worked to some extent. But a complication developed, with the arrival of a reinforcing body of English troops under another knight, this one displaying silver-and-black arms. These were horsed, but quickly dismounted under Butler's urgent orders. Their strength appeared to be that of some three companies, perhaps a quarter of them archers. So now the Scots were faced with possibly five hundred men.

The first attack followed Butler's previous strategy, creeping spearmen, with the archers, keeping the defenders' heads down under a vicious hail of arrows. Narrow slits had been left for shooting through, here also, better than below; but these allowed only a narrow field of aim — moreover, the enemy concentrated their shooting upon them, so that more than one of the Scots fell transfixed. The three knights advanced, safely encased, encouraging their crawling men.

Although there was a temptation to rush out and engage them, as they drew close, Wallace restrained his men. The barriers would do half the work for them.

That was perhaps an exaggeration. But fighting off the attackers from behind their defences was a very real advantage — as they were soon proving. Wallace's people had gained plenty of spears at Kinclaven, and the enemy — on their feet now, and blanketing the aim of their own bowmen — had no advantage in reach. Many fell. Some managed to get inside, but were promptly despatched. Most were kept at bay.

The Scots bowmen now had their opportunity, and at a range

at which they could scarcely miss. They did great execution. Wallace himself, bow discarded, made for Sir John Butler, with his lieutenants assailing the other knights. He used his great two-handed sword in this case, flailing it with a tremendous figure-of-eight motion which there was no withstanding. Butler was no mean swordsman, and courageous as a bull with it, but he stood little chance against the enormous reach and terrible five-foot blade, and knew it. He backed away, wisely.

Wallace was not going to be lured out to a position where the English bowmen could mark him. But he risked one sally, leaping forward in a single mighty bound unexpectedly, to bring down his brand on the other's helmet. Unfortunately a tree-branch got in the way, and caught the tip of his sword, deflecting his aim and breaking its force. The sword crashed down on the other's shoulder, insufficiently strongly to penetrate or do more than dent the armour. Even so, Butler was felled to the ground.

An arrow striking Wallace's leather habergeon slantwise warned him that he was taking foolish risks. He flung himself back and over the barricade forthwith. At least he had gained one more arrow — for he had only three left.

It was then that he perceived that his own bowmen had not been entirely successful in pinning down their opposite numbers on the flanks. Some of the enemy archers were already level with the barrier, to the north, and were seeking to climb up the rocky knoll there. From it, they would be in a position to shoot down sidelong upon the defenders. This barrier therefore was no longer tenable.

Reluctantly Wallace blew a gasping blast on his horn, the signal to commence a retiral on the second line of defence. It would be difficult, possibly costly, but they could not remain where they were.

It was costly indeed, for those English archers, Lancashire men by their voices, were experts, and they took a heavy toll of the men struggling up the braeside, who ought to have been taking every inch of cover, zig-sagging and doing everything but run straight uphill as all too many did in their haste. Wallace shouted at them, hotly, and may have saved some. But by the time he was seeking to man the second line, he had only twenty-eight men all told — and four of these wounded.

This could not go on, for though they had brought down far more of the enemy, the odds were constantly increasing. And the main body of the English might not yet be in action. There was nothing for it but to try to withdraw — difficult as this must be. It would have to be a leap-frogging process. They had only twelve bowmen now. As they waited for the next attack to develop, Wallace sent eight of these creeping back to the next, third, line of barrier, to cover a further stage of withdrawal.

Unfortunately whoever had succeeded Butler in the command now, had recognised the Scots great weaknesses in numbers and archers, and was playing the outflanking tactics with his bowmen. He clearly was not going to risk another frontal attack until he had them enfilladed again.

Wallace saw the writing on the wall. Groaning, he gave the signal for the archers above to cover them once more. Then they started another dispersed and semi-secret retiral, without having made any stand.

At the third line he had to follow the same procedure, however disheartening. There could be no stand here, either. His objective now was the fifth and final line — which in fact had never been completed. But it sat along the top of a secondary ridge, on fairly open ground, and there was no higher prominences to overlook and enfilade it. Any last stand must be fought there.

They lost five more men reaching that line, all by arrows, two dead and three more or less seriously wounded. It was strange — or not so strange, perhaps — that it was the leaders who survived, Thomas Gray, Kerlie, MacGregor, MacFadzean and Fawdon. Superior skill, initiative and wits, told.

Now, depressed as he was by their losses, Wallace breathed more freely. For, not only could they not be shot down upon here, but there was a fairly deep and narrow cleft, channel for a sizeable, tumbling burn, to their right a little way, heavily overgrown with thorn and brush. It took a very erratic course, but eventually reached the Tay, and ought to provide a usefully covered escape route — if they could avoid being seen entering it. The fact that it probed back and down, as it were through the enemy's lines, was an actual advantage — for surely none would expect them to flee in that direction. If they could hold this position until the early November dusk . . .?"

That they did not do. Soon the enemy, now under the new blue-and-silver knight, had come up, and started an assault on this last barrier, with the old tactics, archers remaining behind, at long range, to keep the Scots heads down, the temporary infantrymen crawling forward along the ground. With few bowmen, or arrows either, Wallace could do little about this. They could only wait until the attackers were almost upon them, and were at the critical point of rising to their feet, blocking their archers' field of fire, when Wallace leapt up, vaulted over the barrier, and followed by about a dozen of his men, fell upon the English, smiting.

Kerlie and Gray at his shoulder, the big man made straight for the knight in command, ignoring, so far as he could, all others. The rest of his men, forming a sort of mobile hedgehog formation, drew the main attack while the bowmen left behind struck down selected targets. The knight's immediate supporters were yelling 'A Loraine!' now, so presumably that was his name. With all his reach, force and fury, Wallace hurled himself upon this armoured figure, brand upraised, convinced of the wisdom of always seeking the elimination of the commanding officer.

The knight, in fact, had little chance. Hampered and restricted by his heavy armour, tired already by the climbing on foot, unable to dodge or even to run, he could do little against his gigantic, agile and unencumbered assailant. The first two swinging blows he managed to avoid or parry but the third took him clean on the helm, and he crashed to the ground in a sprawling, ungainly heap, and lay still. It was improbable that he was still alive.

Staggering a little with the force of that last blow, Wallace stood for a moment over his foe — an unwise moment. For some of the enemy archers had run forward whenever the Scots had leapt the barrier, and were now comparatively close at hand. One of these seized the opportunity, and sent a shaft at Wallace at no more than a dozen yards range. The big man was moving when it hit him. The arrow missed his throat by a mere inch or so, tore through his beard on the left side, and scored a skin cut on his neck before driving on into the palisade behind.

The pain of it stung Wallace into rage. Swinging round, he hurled himself at the bowman, who was hastily reaching for another arrow. In four mighty bounds he was upon the unfortunate marksman, and parted his head from his body with a single swipe.

This time he did not pause in his running — for there were other archers. Veering round, he plunged back into the main struggle, yelling his Wallace cry — and seeing him coming, confirmed in most of those dismounted cavalrymen the impression that, with their leader fallen, not to mention many of their colleagues, assaulting that barrier in the face of these maniacs was not for them. They began to disengage — and quickly it turned into a wholesale flight.

The defenders did not pursue, but got back over the palisade before long-range arrows could pick them off.

But the Scots were in a bad way. Three more were wounded, as well as Wallace himself. All were very weary. Arrows were practically finished. It was to be doubted whether they could stage another such effort.

Wallace, panting, was allowing Thomas Gray to bind up his profusely bleeding neck with linen torn from his shirt, when someone called out, and pointed. A communal groan arose — as well it might. Men, under banners, many men, were beginning to appear through the trees behind the enemy line; and over to the right, due southwards, another large body could be glimpsed approaching, though further away. Clearly Sir Gerard Heron had decided that he had waited long enough, with the main body.

It was time to be gone, no doubt of that. Sighing, Wallace gave the necessary word. They already knew what to do. Bending low, dodging, to present poor marks, but by no means unseen, they began to retire directly back, over the crest of the ridge. But once over the summit, and for the moment hidden, they swung southwards and raced for the commencement of the gully or ravine which was to be their escape channel, praying that they would not be spotted by any in the farthest-away enemy on the higher ground. They certainly would not be seen by the others.

Whether or not they went unobserved they could not tell. But, gasping for breath and many in pain, they all managed to reach the burn-channel in its cleft.

It was now only a question of crawling down this leafy alley, making as little noise as possible, a wet, slow and uncomfortable process, for they waded and staggered in the burn itself most of the way, and the ravine twisted and zig-zagged. But that was no matter, so long as they were not discovered. And the light was definitely fading now.

It was strange how, although there were hundreds of men not far away, only scores of yards indeed, there was no hint of it down here, no sounds or shouting penetrated above the splash and chuckle of the stream. After the noise and danger and stress of the warfare, it was all distinctly unreal — but very welcome.

Fearing discovery every moment, they worked their way down. But they saw nothing of the enemy, and presumably were seen by none. In places the burn plunged in cascades, small waterfalls, arched over by trees and bushes, and cold and wet as was the negotiation of these, none grumbled.

Wallace could scarcely credit their good fortune when he perceived the road ahead of them, with its bridge of timber crossing the burn. It might well be patrolled, so they dared not cross it while still the light lasted. But they would not have to wait long. Hidden in the bushes they were glad enough to remain still. Wallace had time now to realise how great was the pain of his wound.

There was a fair amount of coming and going on the road, as the light faded — although only a very small proportion of the enemy numbers appeared. The main force must be combing the woodlands and high ground far above, as was to be expected.

Long after it was dark, and after the last clatter of horses, tramping of men, and shouting, had died away from their vicinity, they waited, for safety's sake. Then in file, slowly now, wounds stiffened up and more than ever painful, they slipped across the track and down the bank to the river side. Picking their way cautiously, they moved upstream, towards the ford.

There were camp-fires burning now before the burned-out castle; but when MacGregor, sent forward to scout, came back, it was to report no actual guard on the ford. No doubt this was considered unnecessary, with what amounted to an army camped nearby.

With infinite care the little company waded the ford, up to their middles in the chill water, arms linked with those of the wounded, for support, MacGregor again going in front to ensure that there was no guard at the far side.

Unchallenged, the wet and weary remnant of Wallace's sixty, barely half that number now, found themselves at last in comparative safety, east of Tay, and with all the widespread fastnesses of Cargill Wood before them. They crept into that extensive forest for some considerable distance, Wallace insisting, despite the protests of Fawdon and some others, stumbling painfully in the darkness amongst roots, scrub and fallen trees. At last the big man, himself in much pain, found what he was looking for, a deep hollow, fully a mile in, where they might risk lighting the fire they so greatly needed, moderately secure from discovery. Warmth and rest and food they must have. They could produce but little of the last, there and then; but the first two were now available.

It was long before Wallace slept, nevertheless, weary as he was. Apart from the pain of his wound, endlessly the debate went on in his throbbing head. Had he grievously failed? Had he thrown away good men's lives — as this Fawdon implied? Was he but beating the air, at other folks' mortal cost? This lost day — how was it to be accounted? They were defeated, had fled the field; but it had been fifty against up to a thousand. Steep odds. They had undoubtedly killed and disabled many times their own number of the enemy. They had taken and burned a key enemy stronghold. Sir James Butler was dead, and his son at least injured; the other knight, Loraine, possibly dead also. Adding it all up, it could not be called a debacle. And he, and some of them, at least lived to fight on. But at a cost, a grim cost, tot it up as he would. And how far could he say Scotland's cause to be advanced thereby . . .?

*   *   *

They remained two days hidden in Cargill Wood, undisturbed, whilst the wounded recovered slightly and the exhausted regained strength. Although Wallace's own hurt was fairly superficial, the arrow having missed vital parts by a mere hair's-breadth, it affected him more than he would admit, causing him lightheadedness and a sort of fever. His neck was inflamed around the cut.

They were not all idle during the interval. Food had to be obtained, as well as information. The former, men were sent to secure at some considerable distance, in the Dunsinane and Kinrossie areas of the Sidlaw Hills, well away from Cargill. Wallace, from his college days at Dundee, knew this area well, and was able to direct his messengers. They had plenty of money, still. Information was not so easily come by. They dared not show themselves in the Kinclaven vicinity; and the version of the news their emissaries managed to obtain, at a distance, was uncertain and contradictory. But all tales seemed at one in agreeing that the English main force had returned to Perth, with large numbers of dead and wounded; and that the man Wallace, though defeated and fled none knew where, still had a large force of men with him. The general impression was that he had gone north to join Sir Andrew Moray.

111

The third evening, Wallace deemed it safe to venture out from their refuge. On a night of blustering wind and rain squalls, with moonlight intervals, they crossed the Kinclaven ford once more, and found their way back into Shortwood Shaw. There they located and dug up some of the arms and booty they had won from the castle and buried here, along with some of their own gear. Then they turned their faces southwards, to head back to Methven Wood, west of Perth.

Wallace had been debating this course with himself — although his head was in poor state for the exercise, and he was suffering almost continual dizziness. The simpler and safer move would have been to do what was expected of him, and to go up to Atholl to join Moray. But he was dissuaded from doing so by the thought that such a step would be likely to limit him grievously in his struggle. If Moray came south, to join *him*, that could be excellent; they could meet more or less as equals, and he could retain some authority and independence of action and command. But after the defeat at Shortwood Shaw, if he was to go to join the Lord of Pettie, it would seem like flight, as though he was placing himself under that powerful nobleman's command. He had no least objection to taking a subordinate position; but Moray had not so far shown himself in any hurry to invade the English-held South of Scotland, more concerned perhaps with campaigning against his own hereditary foes, the Comyns of the North. He might well have totally differing views from himself, Wallace, on what was required or advisable. Without any idea as to Moray's plans, he reckoned that it would be unwise to commit himself to the other's commands. Surely he could better affect the situation as an independent commander, however small his party? He had no desire to lose himself in the Highlands of Atholl, however safe. If this was not good reasoning, no doubt he had his fevered head to blame.

So they went southwards, by the same route as they had come. Because of the wounded, they travelled more slowly. It was daylight before they reached the security of Methven's glades.

Here, strangely enough, they obtained no lack of information — although how reliable remained to be seen. The forest seemed to be fuller than ever with broken men, mainly Highlanders from shattered clans, who cared nothing for the struggle between Lowland Scotland and the English, both equally foreigners as far as they were concerned. But there were some amongst them who had a different outlook. These said that Perth was in a state of great excitement, that Heron was to be replaced as Governor of the city, that Sir William de Loraine had died from his wounds but that Sir John Butler was not seriously injured. They said also that English reinforcements were on their way from Stirling and Edinburgh. And that there were rumours of a quite large Scots force operating in Gowrie, which was waiting to cross Tay, by ferry, at its narrowing near Elcho, some four miles east of Perth.

This last greatly intrigued Wallace. It could be MacDuff, at last, seeking to avoid Perth, heading south — even though his own scouts, when in Gowrie seeking food, had heard nothing of it.

He sent Stephen MacGregor, that night, to Perth, via the Mill Port, to discover what he could. But that good man was less successful at this sort of enquiry than at his more normal scouting. He brought back no information of importance, and certainly nothing about MacDuff or the Elcho ferry.

Wallace decided that they might as well go to Elcho, all of them. He must not risk missing MacDuff. It was only some ten miles from their present position, although they would have to make something of a detour. They set out at moonrise, frost glinting coldly — and again there were grumbles.

Passing well to the south of the sleeping city, and over the heights of Tippermuir and Lamberkine, Pittheavlis and Kirkton Hill, to the north side of long Moncrieff Hill, they came to Elcho, on the south bank of Tay just before it began to widen to its long estuary. There was a small Cistercian nunnery here, which maintained a useful service of ferrymen for the crossing, combined with a house-of-refuge for travellers. But there was no sign of a camp, or of any large party having been in the area; and they could scarcely knock up the nuns in the middle of the night, for information. At daylight they were, in fact, warmly welcomed by the holy women, who, like most of the Church, had no love for the invaders, and were more prepared than most to do something about it. They made much of Wallace, loudly singing his praises, having heard that he had recovered much Church treasure at Loudoun Hill; and Thomas Gray they took to their hearts, as a parish priest who was prepared to forfeit all in the cause of freedom. But they could provide no news of any large-scale or significant crossing of Tay, and knew nothing of Hugh MacDuff, or of any force in Gowrie.

113

Wallace had to swallow his disappointment once more.

At least the nuns of Elcho gave them hospitality and shelter, and were able to treat the wounded in better fashion than had been possible hitherto. They were much concerned about Wallace's own condition, declaring that he was fevered and his neck in a bad state. But he would not hear of himself lying up. He had to maintain the momentum of his campaign, he felt, or forfeit anything which had been gained. He sent out more scouts across Tay, into Gowrie — but decided that he himself would go into Perth, that night, to see what he might glean from Meg Drummond. If she had fulfilled her promise, and sought to question her English clients, she might be in a position to give him some of the information he so urgently required. He did not elaborate on the details of his quest to the good sisters.

So, around midnight, in the pale moonlight, he presented himself at the Mill Port, to ask for Rob Drummond. This time the porter displayed an amiable, even ingratiating manner, with much use of the name of Malcolmson, and sly digs of the elbow. Clearly he now guessed at the true identity of his large visitor. He had not reduced his price for services rendered however. He declared that Master Malcolmson would be entirely welcome at the house in the Skinnergait, even offered to conduct him thither personally. Wallace declared, with uncharacteristic coldness, that he would do very well on his own.

At the ale-house, however, the woman Peg, although she greeted him cheerfully, informed him that he would have to wait, for Meg was meantime engaged. Distinctly put out, strange to say, at the thought, the big man was even more so when the large lady coyly offered her own services in place of the girl's. Wallace hurriedly assured that he was in no great haste, and would come back in, say, one hour. In no way offended, the hostess suggested that a beaker of ale would be a better way of passing the time of waiting than in tramping the streets at this hour. Wallace excused himself from that, also, but civilly.

He had a notion that he might pick up some information elsewhere in the city — but as he wandered the lanes and vennels, in fact he saw nobody to speak to but a few soldiers so drunken as to be unintelligible, was barked at by prowling dogs, tripped over pigs asleep in the stinking causeways, and was all but overcome by the effect of the stench on his own splitting head. He could see why MacGregor had been so unsuccessful.

Well under the hour, he was back at the Skinnergait house. Whether the woman Peg had warned the girl, who had got rid of her client expeditiously, or whether there was normally a rapid turn-over, he found Meg Drummond awaiting him. She was obviously delighted to see him, but much distressed at his unhealthy appearance. Any initial disinclination actually to enter her bed, not to say next to disgust with himself in so promptly succeeding some other therein, was quickly dispersed in the face of her simple friendliness, evident admiration and indeed motherliness over his physical state.

She was eager to display her value as an ally, and vehement in her praise for what he had achieved against the English. Listening to Meg, one might have thought that he had achieved a great victory instead of a sore defeat; according to her, his name was now whispered with fear by all the Perth garrison, from highest to lowest, and none knew where his next blow would fall. The folly of this he did not fail to point out, since he did not see how he could strike another blow unless reinforced; but she would have none of it. He, William Wallace, was going to drive the English right out of Scotland. The man's heart warmed to her — as indeed did his body, whatever his mind told him.

Meg informed him that there was talk now, by the soldiers, of a sizeable force of outlaws — as they called them — operating in the Dundee area of South Angus, doing nothing very exciting but giving concern to the English command. The name of MacDuff had not been mentioned, so far as she knew. Nor had she heard anything of a large-scale crossing at Elcho or elsewhere. She said that Sir John Butler was in a raging fury, having lost not only his father but his cousin — for this, it seemed, Sir William de Loraine had been — as well as the wealth stored at Kinclaven. He had sworn direct vengeance against Wallace, and was demanding action from Heron. She had heard no word of the latter being superseded; he was very much in command in Perth, still. As to Moray, the rumour was that he had now turned westwards from Atholl, and was heading up Strathtay — why, was not known.

Digesting all this, Wallace expressed his gratitude, while asking her many questions, most of which she could not answer. She promised, however, to try to gain him the information he wanted. If he would come back in a night or two . . .

The man was doubtful about this, but in the end agreed that he would return, if he could. So much depended on factors

115

outwith his control. She said that she would require at least three nights to gather the sort of details he required — since she could by no means select only customers who were likely to be knowledgeable and garrulous. And it would be better if he came to her own home, in the Potterrow instead of this house. She would make excuse that she was unwell, three nights hence. Then he would not have to risk waiting his turn again.

So it was agreed. He would come if he could. He had decided that he would require a couple of days to comb Gowrie and the Dundee vicinity, anyway, to try to find the elusive MacDuff. And he did not try to refute her strongly declared view that he required much more than any two days rest, that he was in very poor shape, and must take greater care of himself. As indicative of her concern for his physical state, she made it clear that he must conserve his strength in every way, including between the blankets as now — a contention which he was glad enough not to have to disprove. They were both well content just to lie companionably quiet. Indeed for an hour or two, Wallace slept more deeply and peaceably than he had done for the last few nights — and was reluctant when Meg declared that, for safety's sake, he should bestir himself and be gone.

*   *   *

Three nights later, the man was back under the walls of Perth, with more questions for answer — having failed to trace any hint of MacDuff, and almost been captured in Dundee during his quest. He wanted to know if indeed there was any more valid information about this will o' the wisp from Fife; whether his own presence in the area was suspected; whether English reinforcements had indeed arrived; whether the people of Perth could be roused against the invaders, or at least supply him with a company of young men, to aid his task. A considerable and highly unusual uncertainty, lack of direction and faith in himself, weighed upon William Wallace. The fact that he was a very sick man, but would by no means admit it.

He got no adequate answers to his questions, only another large question — and was fortunate that was all that he got. The man Drummond let him in, in the usual fashion, very concerned for Master Malcolmson's state and comfort. Nothing was said about the change of venue from the Skinnergait; presumably Meg had not informed her father — so Wallace did not do so either. Which was as well, perhaps. For when he arrived

116

at the low-browed, thatch-roofed cottage which Meg had described, midway down the cobbled Potterrow, although he was let in promptly at his discreet tapping, it was to find the young woman in a great state of agitation and distress, indeed she dissolved into weeping immediately. In a flood of tears, indignation, regret and sheer fright, she unburdened herself.

He, Wallace, it seemed, was in dire danger. The woman Peg had betrayed them. She had either gone to the English herself, or had told one of her customers, that she, Meg Drummond, was entertaining William Wallace of a night. Soldiers had come for her the morning after Wallace's last visit, and haled her before Sir Gerard Heron. It had been terrible. Sir John Butler had been there, and he was the worst. They had threatened to burn her in a blazing tar-barrel. They had hit and maltreated her. In the end she had admitted that Wallace had been with her, twice. They asked if he was coming back. She said she did not know. They had then offered her favours if she would co-operate in trapping him. They had said that they would give her money, clothes, find a man of property to marry her even — and if not, she would burn. In the end, she had pretended to go along with them. She had admitted that he, Wallace, would probably come back to the Skinnergait house, one night. She had said nothing about this rendezvous here. So the ale-house was being watched, night and day. Fortunately Peg had apparently said nothing about the Mill Port and her father's custom of letting men in of a night, at a price — for she was a partner in this practice, visitors being directed to her establishment. The English assumed that Wallace was somehow entering the city by day, and were watching all the gates — but not by night, when they were closed. She was sorry, sorry — but he had better get back to the Mill Port, and out, while he could.

Grimly the man agreed with her. He declared how grieved he was for all the trouble he had brought upon her — and neither was under any delusion that the trouble was likely to be over for her, whether he escaped or not. He pressed on her what money he had with him, reserving only enough for her father's exit charge — though she was reluctant to take it. He promised that one day, God willing, he would see her again. He specifically absolved her from any need to withhold information about him. Once he was clear of the town, she could tell all she knew, if it would protect her. Take what bribes the enemy offered.

So they parted, in haste. He left his friar's robe behind, in case it drew attention to him — for the woman Peg would know if it. Apparently Meg and her father lived alone in this cottage.

Thereafter, avoiding the Skinnergait vicinity, he approached the Mill Port warily, afraid that the military might have arrived there. But there was only Rob Drummond — who was surprised to see him back so soon. He did not confide in the man, unsure how much he could trust him, but merely declared that his business took him elsewhere without delay. The other nodded knowingly, winked, leered, and let him out. Thankful indeed to hear the gates close behind him, he set off on his four mile walk back to Elcho, mind in more of a turmoil than ever.

He had not gone more than half that distance when he heard a sound which raised the hairs at the back of his neck — the distant baying of a bloodhound, eerie on the night air. That unchancy howling might have nothing to do with him; but it was an odd hour of the night for such to be abroad, and certainly no time for hunting four-legged game. Involuntarily he quickened his stride.

The hound continued to give tongue — and obviously between him and the city. He knew about sleuth-hounds, having hunted with them — though never after men. And whether or no it was on *his* trail, he grew fairly certain that it was getting nearer. Which, since he was now striding at a fast pace himself, must presumably mean that it was with mounted men. A bloodhound would require something bearing his scent, to follow him — but had he not left his friar's robe at the Potterrow house?

He had to cross a sizeable burn, on the north flank of Moncrieff Hill, at Tarsappie; and though it wasted valuable time, he waded down this for some distance, slithering and stumbling, to wash away his scent. Down in the marshy ground near the Tay, he climbed out, and went hurrying away heavily amongst the shadowy cattle of the riverside meadows, sending alarmed brutes careering off right and left.

Suddenly, loud and clear, he heard the hound again, as it came over the Craigend ridge behind him. There could be little doubt now that it was his own trail that was being followed. He was running, now — and each footfall was like a hammer blow in his ringing head.

The noise of the baying died away presently, and the man

118

knew a little relief, hoping that it meant that the animal had reached the Tarsappie Burn and lost the scent. Nevertheless, he kept on running.

He reached the nunnery, with the baying still not restarted behind him — not that he could hear, at any rate. He had his men roused immediately. His trackers might now follow him here; but the chances were that they would eventually come enquiring — and pick up the scent again. He was determined that the nuns should not be made to suffer for having sheltered him, if he could help it. Deliberately he made his men hastily wreck some of the outbuildings, pull up some gates, and scatter furnishing, as though the place had been attacked. The nuns were to say that they had been terrorised into compliance. Thanking them, he hurried his men off in a South-Easterly direction, to round Moncrieff Hill by the hamlet of Rhind, and to reach the Earn. He had trouble with the man Fawdon, in the process. The Irishman contended that this flight was stupid. The nunnery was in quite a strong position, and could have held, at least against any minor attack. If they had been forced to abandon it, they could have crossed the Tay ferry into Gowrie, destroying the ferry-boats behind them. For thirty men to flee before a hound dog, he asserted, was craven folly. Wallace endeavoured to keep his temper. The nuns had befriended them, and should not be made to suffer for it. The ferry-boats were their living. Moreover, if they were hunted, there was no adequate hiding-place in the open fields of the Carse. He knew it well, from college days in Dundee. Methven Wood was the safer refuge — but they would have to make a great detour, south-abouts, to reach it, if patrols were out looking for them. They would follow the Earn westwards.

At the ford of Earn, beyond Moncrieff and Rhind, MacGregor, scouting ahead, returned to report that the crossing was guarded. Whether this was a normal measure, or a sign that tonight a net was being cast wide for them they did not know. Retiring a little, they moved on westwards, along the foot of Moncrieff Hill, parallel with and north of the river.

Presently the westwards jut of the hill forced them ever closer to the Earn. They had reached the Horsemill when they heard the baying of the sleuth-hound behind them, how far it was hard to tell. Kerlie said a mile, Gray half that. There was something baleful, remorseless, about the sound, to agitate even brave and bold men. Of mutual accord, they pressed on at an increased pace — however unsteady Wallace was, now, on his feet.

All too soon, with the baying sound gaining on them, it was evident that the brute was on their trail, and that its mounted masters would be upon them before long. The immediate surroundings were no good for fugitives, the broad, deep and here slow-running Earn on the left, and the fairly steep slopes of Kirkton Hill on the right, with little of cover. Anyway, cover was of only limited value against a bloodhound. Wallace would have been prepared to swim the river; but most of his men could not swim, and the wounded in no state to make the attempt.

As they hurried on, by the light of a fitful three-quarters moon, Wallace was peering about him, seeking somewhere to make a possible stand. He found it near the village of Aberdalgie, where a sizeable burn came in to join Earn. They turned in at this, and went plunging and stumbling up its slippery bed for about three hundred yards, until, in shadowy water-meadows amongst willows, the burn made a major loop, enclosing what was almost an island. It was not much of a strongpoint; but the surrounding meadows were waterlogged at this season, and no use for cavalry. The prevailing water would fault the hound, and the banks of the burn provide a certain obstacle to attack, especially in semi-darkness.

They did not have long to prepare themselves. All too soon the shouting of men and the clank of armour sounded close. Wallace put his best fighters to guard the neck of the little peninsula formed by the burn's loop, and spaced others out left and right, to line the banks at intervals. But with only some thirty men, it could be but a token line of defence. All depended on how many enemy were with the hound. He kept half-a-dozen men with himself to act as a flying-squad, and hurl themselves wherever they were most needed.

The English found them quickly, for it was an obvious refuge. Wallace's heart sank, as it became evident that they were in approximately company strength. The first attack followed immediately, dismounted, an incoherent unco-ordinated affair, which was beaten off fairly easily, at some cost to the enemy. After that they were more wary. Who was in command they could not tell.

The survivors of the first assault must have gained some fair impression of the tactical position, for when the next developed it was more carefully thought out. Two flank attacks were thrown across the meadows, right and left, to splash across the burn in its windings; and while these were being beaten off, the main tight-knit thrust was made at the narrow neck of land between. For thirty defenders it was an almost hopeless situation, and Wallace knew it. He could not fight all three at once. The centre was the more important — so he perforce left the flanks to look after themselves, however hard on the spaced-out defenders. He flung his half-dozen in to help Kerlie, Gray and MacGregor hold the narrow neck.

It was fierce confused, hand-to-hand fighting in a cramped space, in the half-dark with leadership inevitably almost non-existent. Such circumstances tend to favour the defence, but not in a major fashion. It had to be a mere slogging match, with all its dangers to the outnumbered side.

At some stage in the hectic engagement Wallace realised that the enemy commander was in fact Sir John Butler, somebody shouting the name in the press. He sought to beat his way through the struggle, to get at the knight — but could not identify the man in the mêlée.

Presently shouting from the flanks, and even from the rear, made it clear that the enemy had managed to penetrate the defence on either side and were now all around them. Wallace had no option but to shout the command to form an arrowhead formation, tightpacked, with himself at the apex, to try to drive onwards, right through the enemy line. It was an unexpected move on the part of men in process of defeat. But it meant abandoning their position — and those who had got detached, plus the men on the flanks — if any such survived.

The tight group behind Wallace did manage to make their breakthrough, and leaving the burn, with the impetus still upon them, went on running downhill, towards the Earn, stumbling amongst the trees and bracken, a straggling pursuit behind. There was nothing for it but to try to swim the large river, now, as best they could.

But Wallace had underestimated the enemy. There were more of them than he had thought. The riverside was manned. Even so, he would have sought to fight his way through; but when most of his group perceived what he intended, they protested loudly, and refused to commit themselves to the water, dark and deep here. Clearly they were more afraid of the Earn than the English. And here was neither occasion nor time to argue

121

the matter. Nothing for it but to turn around and further surprise their foes by driving back in their tracks. It was only during this turning back manoeuvre that Wallace, still striving to keep approximately a spearhead formation, realised that he had only about fifteen men. Amongst the missing was the Irishman, Fawdon.

They certainly confused the enemy by beating back amongst them again. The running fight which developed as they drove their desperate way uphill to the hollow, with the meadows and the loop in the burn, was a crazy, head long scramble. Wallace was now hoping to pick up some of his own stragglers; but in this he was disappointed. They battled their way through many separate groups of the English, who seemed to be much disorganised and at a loss, unsure whether they had won or lost. Probably, in this process, the Scots inflicted as many casualties as in the earlier struggle in the general bewilderment.

Through only sporadic resistance, then, they beat their way up the little peninsula and splashed over the burn's loop beyond. The main hillside rose above them, and wearily they breasted it, breathless now. This was not the direction they wanted to go — but they had no option. Dismounted cavalrymen were not likely to catch up with them here.

Wallace, head reeling, dared not contemplate the rest of the night ahead.

CHAPTER SEVEN

The fugitives were well up on the south side of Kirkton Hill when Fawdon hailed them from behind — apparently the only survivor of the fifteen missing Scots. How he had escaped, and known where to follow, he did not explain — but then he never was a communicative character. Wallace asked him if he thought they were being pursued still, and he said no they were not. He sounded entirely decided. Pressed for information as to what the enemy was doing, in general, he announced that Sir John Butler had decided to return to Perth.

Despite the state of his wits, this announcement made Wall-

ace think. It seemed entirely improbable. He was well aware
that it was himself that the English wanted. How many of them
had been slain he could not guess; but certainly not sufficient to
make a man like Butler feel defeated. And this of Butler? How
had Fawdon come to name him? Nobody had mentioned him,
thus far. Wallace had only heard the name pronounced during
the fighting. Yet Fawdon was declaring that Sir John Butler had
returned to Perth.

Wallace was not a suspicious man by nature. But he had
never liked, nor greatly trusted, Fawdon. And this curious and
unexplained return, unhurt, making such statements, seemed
questionable, to say the least. It would be as well to keep an eye
on Master Fawdon.

More than that was necessary, shortly. It was the sound of the
bloodhound's baying, once more, after half-an-hour's difficult
contouring of the hillsides, which seemed to spark off the
trouble. It caused Wallace to change course somewhat. He had
been making for Methven Wood. Now he realised that, weary
as they were, they would never reach that far, in time — for
they would have to cross the great plain of Tippermuir first,
where the cavalrymen, with their damnable hound, would be on
ground where they could operate to advantage, could hunt
them and ride them down. They would have to get across Earn
somehow, bend more to the south. And the only fords he or
MacGregor knew were those at Gask and Dalreoch. They had
crossed at Gask two weeks before.

When Wallace announced this change of plan, there were
protests from Fawdon. Unwontedly eloquent, he declared that
it was foolishness. They should press on for Methven Wood,
where they had friends, where they could get rest and food. To
make for the Earn at Gask was further, much further.

With what patience he could muster, Wallace explained, for
the benefit of the others rather than for Fawdon, about the
terrain, the open levels of Tippermuir which they would have to
cross, a death-trap with cavalry closing in on them. He had his
way; but the effort further upset him. He was not at his best, by
a long way.

Presently, in the Dupplin area, Kerlie came to him to report
that Fawdon, lagging ever more behind, was trying to convince
the others not to go on, saying that Wallace was ill, out of his
mind, leading them all to their deaths. They were only sixteen
out of sixty. How many would be alive by morning? Better to

throw themselves on the mercy of the English than continue with this hopeless struggle. Sir John Butler would spare them if they yielded honourably.

They could hear the sleuth-hound's untiring voice, distant but distinct, as Kerlie finished speaking.

Clenching his fists. Wallace turned back, almost falling in his dizziness as he did so. He found Fawdon and four others at the rear, halted.

'What mean you by this?' he demanded. 'With mounted men and a bloodhound on our trail, this is no time for lingering.'

'We go no further,' Fawdon asserted, roughly. 'We are weary, and have had enough.'

'Would you liefer be weary, or dead, man!'

'We will not die. Unless you lead us to our deaths! As you have done the half our number, by God's Mother!' The other, who had been sitting, had risen to his feet, hand dropping to the hilt of his sword.

'You think *you* will lead better?'

'I say yes! I could scarce lead worse. Eh, lads?'

There was an indeterminate murmur from the others.

'You follow me no longer, then?' Heavily Wallace asked it. 'But ... if I made for Methven Wood, you would follow still?'

Fawdon hesitated 'No,' he decided 'We have had enough of you. We'll bide here.'

'Here? Are you mad, man? If you bide here, the English will take you. And that will be the end of you.'

'Not so. The English will spare us, if we yield to them. *You* they will not spare — but us, yes.'

Keenly now, for all his splitting head, Wallace stared at the man. 'So-o-o! That is it,' he breathed. 'How do you know this, friend?'

The other began to speak, and then changed his mind. The hand on the sword hilt switched to his dirk.

Wallace saw it, and tensed. 'I will tell these others how you know, Fawdon. If you will not,' he said. 'You know, because you are already yielded. Back at yon fight, you surrendered to the English. And they promised you your wretched life, and freedom, to betray us! You were to come back to us, to delay us, on the way to Methven Wood, to make sure that they caught up with us. That is why, unhurt, you joined us again. And now ...'

124

Wallace leapt back, less than nimbly, as the other's hand flashed out, with the chill gleam of moonlight on steel — just in time, although he had anticipated an attack. Three paces back he jerked, his two hands reaching up behind his head in fashion which had become almost automatic with him. Then the great sword was out, and he was flinging himself forward again. In a mighty, slantwise blow the blade struck the other man below the left ear, and sheared right through the neck. In a fountain of blood, black-seeming as ink, the head toppled on the wide shoulders, and like a felled tree, the trunk swayed, leaned, and collapsed with a crash.

Wallace stared, suddenly stricken, at what he had done.

There was complete silence from the watchers, until Kerlie spoke.

'You should have done the same, Will, long ago. The man was a rogue and a dastard, as well as a traitor. We are well quit of him.'

Still the big man did not speak. In the quiet, the sleuth-hound's eerie howling sounded, and from no great distance off.

Thomas Gray knelt, and murmured a brief Latinity over the dead man. He rose, and laid a hand on his friend's arm. 'You could do naught else, Will,' he said. 'Sooner or later it had to come — him or you. God be thanked it is Fawdon who lies there, not Wallace! For all our sakes.'

The big man was looking down at his hands and sword, as though neither really belonged to him. 'I ... I am a man of blood!' he muttered. 'I slew ... one of my own. I killed ... a comrade.'

'A Judas!' the priest declared strongly. 'With his dirk drawn against you.'

'I need not have *slain* him. I have become a slayer. With scarce a thought, I now slay! Dead ...?' Wallace stopped, then, and drew a great breath. When he spoke again, his voice was quite different, stronger, harsher. 'No matter now. Time we were far from here. We cannot bury him.'

'Leave him there,' MacGregor said. 'He will serve to distract the hound, at least!'

'Yes. Come then ...'

'See you,' Kerlie said. 'I see use in this. We might make good service of this traitor. I will linger here, hidden, Will. These bushes. The English will halt, for this. The hound will be drawn to the blood — not to me, behind my bush. They will dis-

125

mount. I will learn their numbers, who commands. Better, I might gain opportunity to slay that hound. So all would be saved.'

'It is too dangerous, man.'

'It need not be. See you, they will mill round this body, the hound leading them to it. In the half-dark I could mingle with them, in the crowd of them. They would never look for the like. Perhaps slay more than the hound! A dirk in their leader, Butler or Heron . . .'

'I say it is a sound ploy!' Stephen MacGregor exclaimed. '*I* will bide with you. Two better than one. If we can slay the hound, we all may yet escape.'

Wallace, though doubtful, was still bemused by what he had done. He did not take any strong line and forbid the dire project. The other two said that they would seek to rejoin the rest at or before the Earn crossing, at Gask. Now — they had wasted enough time. Waste no more.

So they parted, and almost at a run the thirteen hurried on — for, by the sound, they reckoned that hound was less than half-a-mile behind. There must be four miles at least to cover before the Gask ford. And running, Wallace tripped and fell, and lay still.

Desperately they clustered round him. He did not seem to be actually unconscious; dazed rather, eyes open but unfocussed, lips moving but no words. The bracken and heather they were running through was full of outcropping rock. It seemed that he had fallen over one and knocked his head on another. Desperately, Thomas Gray brought out the little phial of communion-wine which he always carried, and forced some of it between his friend's parted lips, shaking him even, pleading, urging him to be up and on, or the English would have him.

Somehow they got the great bulk of him to his feet, and moving again, Gray and MacFadzean supporting him at each side. Now he did not seem to know what he was doing, or where he was going. Fortunately, their route at present lay along a high bank above the waterlogged haughs of the Earn, where it was difficult to go wrong, however uneven the going, and with the gaps of incoming burns to cross. One hundred feet above the winding, moon-glinting river they went, a sorry, staggering crew. Once, they passed a tall and ancient stone cross on the very edge of the drop, carved with Pictish symbols and representations — and all crossed themselves, in duty. Was it a good omen, or ill? Gray, who was now having to act leader, said good. They pressed on.

After a while, they realised that they had not heard the hound for some time. Whether Kerlie and MacGregor had succeeded in their endeavour, or whether it was just delay at Fawdon's body which was responsible, they knew not — but were enheartened.

The valley made a sudden narrowing near Dalreoch, and here they were pressed closer to road and river by rocky bluffs. MacFadzean was acting scout now, in MacGregor's place. He came back to inform that he had heard horses' hooves, and was going to investigate. No baying of hounds. Concerned — for no riders were likely to be abroad at this hour of night save enemy soldiers — but glad enough to rest, Gray gave the order to wait.

Wallace stared before him, muttering.

It was some time before MacFadzean came back again, and all were asleep save Gray and Wallace. The Highlander said that there was a company of English cavalry guarding the ford at Dalreoch ahead. They had heard about this ford, which was deeper than that at Gask, only passable for horses usually, save in the driest seasons. He advised that it seemed possible to circle round this party at the riverside, the bluffs allowing a couple of hundred yards — if they went quietly.

Gray woke the others, and they moved on cautiously, picking their way awkwardly amongst large fallen boulders at the foot of the bluffs. After a while MacFadzean announced that he thought they were past the enemy — of whom they had seen and heard nothing. Wallace stared at him, but did not question him. He seemed to be coming out of his daze — but was in a strange state, apparently of shock. He kept looking back, now, at his men, as though their eyes were accusing him, in the darkness.

MacFadzean scouted ahead once more, to prospect the Gask ford, a mile or so further west. There was still no sign of Kerlie or MacGregor.

The Highlander returned — and with the same sad story. This ford was held also, by a smaller party — but still held. And none required to be convinced that they were in no state to seek to fight their way across.

Gray had no alternative but to decide that they would stay on this side meantime. If they lay quiet, with no hounds smelling them out, they might survive. And there was no doubt that the rest was necessary. The old disused castle of Gascon Hall, semi-ruinous, which they had paused at when in the vicinity before, would give them some slight security and shelter. They would go there.

They found Gascon Hall a little further on, on higher ground above the river, deserted as ever save for the owls and bats. There they collapsed in exhaustion — although Gray saw that sentries were posted, with MacFadzean or himself always awake. Wallace remained awake also — but scarcely seemed to be with them. Head in his hands he stared ahead of him, blindly.

All were asleep save Wallace and Gray when, after an hour perhaps, a great blowing of horns disturbed the night. It seemed to come from the north, not from the direction of the river, and went on and on. Those horns, whatever they meant, seemed to have a great effect on William Wallace. They at least made him speak coherently, for the first time since his fall — however odd his reactions. He declared that they most certainly had something to do with his two friends, Kerlie and MacGregor. They represented trouble for them. They were being hunted, the enemy signalling to each other with the horns. They must aid them. *He* had sent these two men to possible death. He ordered two men to go find them, to bring them in, forthwith.

Gray bit his lip. It was a slightly hopeful sign that his friend was at least taking command again; but this was a crazy order. There was no real reason to believe that the horn-blowing had anything to do with the pair who had stayed behind. He said so — but Wallace was adamant. Kerlie and MacGregor needed to be succoured. Otherwise they would blunder into the ford-guards below — if the horn-blowers did not get them first. Two men must go.

Reluctantly, two men were sent off.

They waited — and the horns did not cease to wail. They seemed to come from various points to the north, along the line of the Roman road, in the Findo Gask area. Gray, partly to humour Wallace who was now fretting, tramping back and forth in their vaulted refuge, suggested that possibly it was the enemy, having lost them, were trying to make them bolt from wherever they were hiding. Presumably the hound had indeed been killed, so they could not smell them out. So, many small parties, roaming about, and keeping in touch by horn, would be designed to flush them from cover. Therefore they should sit tight.

Wallace would not accept that — at least, not that they should stay lying secure there, while Kerlie and MacGregor were being hunted. They would *all* go and try to find them.

Gray sought to dissuade the big man — but to no effect. At length, with Wallace insisting that a move be made, he declared that they *could* not all go. What of those he had already sent out? They would return here. What if Kerlie and Stephen did come, and find them gone? Wallace was in no state to travel further this night. *He* must stay here — for a base they must have, or they would never all come together again. He himself would take a group and see what he could discover.

The other acceded — but insisted that Gray took all the men with him, in case they ran into the enemy.

With Gray and the others gone, the big man paced the gloomy stone-flagged vault. Every now and again he raised his hands before his eyes, peering for bloodstains, the blood of a comrade who had risked and fought and suffered with him. Dead by these two hands. He could see no blood — but wherever he looked he could see Fawdon's eyes, accusing, accusing.

Some time thereafter he thought that he sensed movement beyond the broken, ivy-hung doorway. Grabbing up his two-handed sword from where it lay, he rushed out. A man stood in the shadows. It was Fawdon. Wallace cried out. Even as he did so, the apparition detached its own head, and held it out to him. Yelling aloud, the big man went lurching away at a shambling run, every now and again pausing, to turn and flail behind him with the sword. Then on, he knew not where.

Presently he found himself on a high bank at the riverside, in trembling breathless horror, leaning on his sword, as on a staff, seeking breath. If he might cross the black flood, he might shake Fawdon off — like the sleuth-hound. Water — he must cross water. But it was too high, here. He must find a lower place, where he could reach the water. He turned, left-handed — and there, standing beside a bush, was the man, holding out the head to him again, silent, both accusing and appealing.

Wallace broke and ran again — ran eastwards along the riverside road, caring nothing where he went, so long as it was away from that severed bloody head.

He scarcely saw the three horsemen who suddenly loomed up in his path — indeed he would have blundered past them if they had allowed it. But the one in front ordered him peremptorily

129

to halt; and when he paid no attention, reined round his horse to bar the way, at the same time whipping out a sword.

'Halt, I say!' the man shouted. 'In the name of King Edward. Who are you fellow, who runs in the night? Answer me.'

Wallace glanced behind him, rather than at this challenger. He had worse than English horse-soldiers on his mind. He sought to brush past.

The mounted man jabbed with his blade to within inches of Wallace's face. 'Fool! Knave!' he cried. 'Are you crazed? Run mad? Speak, man. Are you of the traitor Wallace's vile crew? Answer me. I am Butler — Sir John Butler. And I command here, in the King's name.'

Wallace did not speak. Instead he swung that long sword of his, which could so easily be mistaken for a staff, in the shadows and half-light, swung it in a curious, lateral swipe, a sort of scything motion, but strong, swift. At their respective levels he could not reach the knight's body; but the leg was different. Butler was not in full armour — or he could not have ridden thus all night — but only in steel corslet, leathern breeches and riding-boots. The sword-blade took him right at the bend of the knee, cut through leather and flesh and bone all three, and came up hard against the wooden framing of the saddle. With an agonised scream the knight cringed, toppled and fell, his own sword hitting the ground just before his body.

Wallace, scarcely noticing the heavy jarring to his arms, turned on the two men-at-arms behind. One of these lunged at him with his lance — and had it sliced in two for his pains. The other was a man of discretion. He reined round his mount and left the scene forthwith. Seeing him go, his companion looked at this broken lance, hurled the half at Wallace, and sensibly followed on.

The big man hardly glanced at the twitching, jerking body of his fallen enemy; instead he peered behind, searching the shadows. Then, still clutching his terrible brand, he clambered on to the back of Butler's fine bay, which still stood in shivering fright, and dug in his heels. Undoubtedly he would flee better, faster, on this good horse.

He drove on, after the retiring men-at-arms, still eastwards.

That he rode into, and through, Butler's guard, at the Dalreoch ford, concerned him not at all. Anyway, they were certainly not prepared for him, none knew who he was or what to do about him; most, actually, were dismounted and sitting

130

round a small fire. At any rate, none got in his way. It was still the water he was heading for. Down to the ford-mouth he rode, and drove the bay splashing in.

Half-way across, his horse part-swimming, snorting in protest, he looked back. Men were congregated in a dark group on the bank, watching; but no Fawdon he thought — no Fawdon.

He beat his mount's flank with his clenched fist as it clambered, streaming, up on to the south bank. Water behind him now, deep, black water. But could he rely on it? A fast horse, too. Were these sufficient . . .?

*　　*　　*

There was no certainty, no clarity, in the man's mind as to the hours which followed. He was not aware of where he went, nor for how long, nor of anything but the need for haste, flight, covering territory. He drove that bay charger until it was foundered, ready to drop, mile after mile after mile — and rode half-turned in the saddle, the better to peer behind him.

When night had faded, reluctantly, into the grey winter's daylight, he was still riding, pounding on, in green rounded hills now, empty, lonely, rearing to infinity, only the sheep and the curlews ahead of him; though it was not what was ahead that concerned him. The hills meant nothing to him, save hostile, inimical ground to cover. He had one aim only, other than to keep going — and that was to cross water, as many rivers, burns, bogs, as possible. Only so could he keep ahead of what he knew pursued him so determinedly. Each water he splashed through was a small relief — no triumph, no sure safety, but a breathing-space. If he lost faith in that, he was finished . . .

But there was no breathing-space for the bay charger. Butler had favoured fine horseflesh; but there were limits for even the purest bred Barbary stallion. High on a south face of one of the green Ochils, near Sheriffmuir, the poor brute's heart eventually gave out. It missed its footing on a wet and mossy apron, staggered, went down on one knee, and pitched its rider over its drooping neck, headlong, before it collapsed and lay still.

William Wallace landed heavily, and lay still also.

*　　*　　*

When next the man had any awareness of himself or his circumstances, he was staring longingly, desperately, across more water, wide this, and fast-flowing. He was on the bank of a

131

broader, greater river than Earn or Allan or any other he had crossed, seeking a way over. He thought that he had been seeking this for long. It could only be the Forth itself. Fawdon no longer pursued him. He was not concerned with Fawdon, any more. But the compulsion to get across the river was as urgent as ever. It was not what lay behind which was compelling the man now, but what lay ahead. Somewhere beyond there was the Tor Wood. Sanctuary, rest, peace, oblivion — the Tor Wood, famed refuge for the hunted — lay there. Of that he was certain. He knew it of old, the Wood. He had an uncle, priest, nearby. At Dunipace. The Tor Wood, across Forth, beyond Stirling — he must reach it. They would never let him across Stirling Brig — not William Wallace. The Fords of Frew? They were far, far, surely. Beyond all gaining.

He asked an old man mending a salmon-net by the riverside where, and how far, to the Fords of Frew — but the creature only stared at him, open-mouthed, lacking all understanding. All he could do was point — point across the wide river, to where a great abbey rose amongst the grassy levels, a square tower soaring amongst many gables. It was in fact a ferry-boat to which he pointed, maintained by the monk of Cambuskenneth; but Wallace did not perceive this. Instead, shaking his throbbing head, he lurched there and then down to the water's edge. The old man shouted, but he paid no heed. Into the cold, grasping river he staggered, wading, and on, until the waters picked him up and swept him away, struggling feebly. His last thought was that he was indeed, going in the wrong direction. The river was taking him seaward, away from the Tor Wood.

*   *   *

It was a wonder indeed, a marvel, that when coherent thought and consciousness of his state returned to him again, it was to find himself indeed in the Tor Wood. The old woman assured him, time and again, that it was so. Her sons, foresters, had found him. Lying half in a burn, deep in this wood; and somehow carried him to her cottage. That was two days ago, apparently. He was William Wallace, was he not? The great Wallace? He had pronounced his name, not once but many times. And Wallace was a big man, all said. Greatly she rejoiced to cherish him, to have Scotland's darling son under her humble roof. She was just a poor widow-woman — but for Wallace she would give her life's blood. Her sons', also. Grahams, they were, ser-

vants of Sir John le Forester, Keeper of the King's Forest of
the Tor Wood. He was safe here, never fear. Although ill — a
sick man. Rest him, then, rest him.

Ask her, and her sons, as he would; beat his muddled brains,
the man could not discover how he came to be in this
Tor Wood. The Forth he could vaguely remember — Cambuskenneth Abbey. For the rest, nothing. They said it was
seven miles from Cambuskenneth, and the deep Bannock
Burn between. But he was here, and safe, and not to fret himself. He must eat, and sleep. His wound was bad, but she had
cleaned it well, and it would heal. She was clever with herbs and
remedies, her man had always said.

For how many days and nights Wallace lay in that cot-house
deep in the forest he did not know. Gradually his mind
cleared — although, as to the immediate past, his memory
served him but ill. But as his wits returned to him, so his distress
and anxiety grew. He had, somehow, deserted his men. He had
run away. Gray, Kerlie, MacGregor, MacFadzean — he had left
them, shamefully, he, their leader. It was scarcely to be believed — and he did not understand it all. But he had abandoned
them, without warning. And now he was lying, weak as a kitten,
in a hovel in the Tor Wood.

He sought to convince his kind hosts of the enormity of what
he had done — but they would not hear of it, shook their heads
over him, soothed, reassured. He was desperately feeble of
body, his neck and all one side of his head greatly swollen; but
as his spirit grew again within him, so grew the pressure he put
upon these good foresters to do more than aid him bodily. At
length he had them persuaded. There were three sons. One
would set off north, for Strathearn, secretly, to see if he could
find Master Thomas Gray and his handful of men, and bring
them back here. Another would go to Dunipace, a village
only some four miles to the South-West, to fetch from there
Master Robert Crawford, the priest, his uncle. The third would
go build a bower of sorts, out in the wood somewhere near,
where he could lie sheltered and secure — but not in their house;
for if his refuge here became known, the English would show
no mercy to his succourers. On this he insisted.

His Uncle Robert was brought, that very evening, in a great
state of excitement. He had not seen his nephew for two
years — but like most others in Lowland Scotland had heard a
deal of him these past months. Now he did not know whether to

praise him as a hero, name him a rash young fool, sorrow over his physical state, or lecture him on the dangers of presumption. Also, on the more practical level, whether to urge that he be got out of the district just as swiftly as possible — or to suggest that the young scapegrace be moved forthwith to the comfort of his own parsonage. Robert Crawford was not really a man for making desperate decisions and taking drastic action, being in fact a scholar rather than a parish priest, of independent means and a contemplative mind, brother of Sir Reginald, Sheriff of Ayr, and installed in Dunipace, a chapelry of Cambuskenneth Abbey more as a sinecure than a pastoral charge. Here he pursued his writings and translations, for he was as noted a Hebrew student as he was a Latinist, and something of a philosopher besides. His philosophy, however, seemed rather to desert him, in the face of this formidable and awkward nephew whom he had very largely educated.

As so often is apt to happen, what started as a loving and sympathetic greeting, a reunion, with even pride implicit — for the good cleric was, in theory at least, an eloquent upholder of the ideas of freedom — proceeded to develop into something of a harangue on youthful follies, dangerous excesses and headstrong behaviour generally, with an undercurrent of reproach for thus stirring up a potential hornet's nest in an area meantime moderately peaceable and decently quiet. And so on.

'Uncle,' Wallace interrupted at last, weak of voice but with something of his old spirit, and laying a hand on the other's arm. 'Mind you when you taught me this, one time?

> *Dico tibi verum, libertas optima rerum;*
> *Nunquam servili, sub nexu viviti fili.'*

If *my* memory does not fail me, that could be translated something thus — 'I tell you of a truth that liberty is the best of all things; My son, never submit to live under any slave's bond.' How say you, Uncle?'

The other had the grace to blink, clear his throat, and amend his stance considerably. He was becoming a self-centred and denunciatory old man, he averred — or old woman, which was worse. He craved forgiveness. But — Will had taken his precepts and teachings to rather more extreme application than he had anticipated! And now what was to be done?

Wallace told him what he planned, here on his couch, and

what he needed — the bower outside in the wood somewhere, a supply of food and drink sent up to recompense and assist these good foresters, clothing, blankets, presently a horse for when he should be fit to move on. And news — desperately he yearned for news, especially of his friends. When his uncle protested at the very idea of the invalid moving out of the cottage into an open-air refuge, in December, and declared that Will would just have to be moved down to the parsonage at Dunipace, his nephew thanked him, but utterly refused. He would be in much more danger there. Besides, he would do very well in the wild-wood, with a sufficiency of cover, plaids and the like, and being fed from the house. Indeed he was much more used to living out-of-doors than in, these days. If his uncle would just send him up the things he needed as soon as possible . . .

His uncle Robert sent more than asked. For the very next day who should arrive at the cottage, bearing the provender and plaiding, than Kerlie and Stephen MacGregor — to a reunion which was all but tearful in its joy and relief.

His two friends, when they could compose themselves to coherent communication, explained that, having heard it reported that Wallace had slain Sir John Butler and fled southwards, to the tune of allegedly swimming the River Forth at Cambuskenneth, they had come after him. They had eventually sought news of him at the great abbey itself, but gaining none had recollected that Will had a Crawford uncle as a parish priest somewhere in this Falkirk-Stirling area. The monks had directed them to Dunipace — and here they were.

Almost too full of emotion to speak, Wallace asked as to the rest. How had they fared? The bloodhound? Had they seen Thomas Gray and his party? He himself, God forgive him, had basely deserted them . . .

Ignoring this last, the others admitted that they had not been in touch with Gray and the rest. They had disposed of that sleuth-hound, just as they had planned, and with ridiculous ease, in fact, none suspecting them as they mingled with the crowd that clustered round Fawdon's corpse. And not only the hound. Kerlie had actually dirked Sir Gerard Heron himself, in the back, while he bent over the body of the traitor. They had escaped into the scrub in the subsequent confusion. Thereafter, they had made their way directly for the Gask ford, as arranged. They had found it guarded — but even as they lay low, watching, soldiers from Dalreoch had ridden up in great excitement, to shout to their companions that Butler had been slain by the madman Wallace, who had then fled across the lower ford, on the stolen horse, and was heading southwards. All the men-at-arms had then hurried away — and left the Gask ford clear for them to cross unchallenged. They had never looked for Gray or the others, assuming them dead or captured.

Wallace did not elaborate to his friends on the strange interlude which had overtaken him after their parting; indeed he was hardly in a position to do so, all being a vague and evil confusion in his mind, a nightmare of unrelated and unbelievable horrors. His uncle had told them that he suffered from a concussion and a fever of body and mind, brought on by his untreated wound, falls, lack of sleep and general exhaustion. He did not seek to counter that, openly — but he had his own reservations. He no longer tortured himself over Fawdon's death; but he did greatly blame himself in that he had fled leaving Gray and his men unwarned.

Kerlie and MacGregor set themselves to aiding the Graham sons in contriving Wallace's bower — and to make it larger now, since it was required to shelter three, not one. They were building it in a hollow, about three hundred yards from the cottage, under a great oak, the roots of which were partially scraped out to form a sort of cave. For the rest, dead bracken and reeds were used, on a framework of branches, to form a thatched enclosure, roofed against rain and wind. In this a fire could be maintained, its smoke led away and dispersed by a series of cunningly devised chimneys and ducts through thick evergreen scrub.

Here Wallace and his friends settled down in fair comfort, and distinct easement of mind. Not only were they unlikely now to bring down reprisals on the heads of the good Graham family; but they had greatly reduced the risk of being trapped, there being back ways out of their refuge for a little more than smoke.

Three days later, the third Graham son arrived back from Strathearn. He had found no trace of Gray and the others. He had been to Gascon Hall and the fords, and had covered a wide area round about, making discreet enquiries. But though the district rang with talk about Wallace and his exploits, nothing was known of the missing party. There was certainly no word of such a group having been captured or slain — and Wallace had to take what comfort he could out of that. The others sought to

reassure him. Tom Gray was the most level-headed and reliable
of them all. Those men were safer with him, they swore, than
they would have been with Wallace himself — who was not
renowned for his caution!

They waited a few more days, in frosty but mainly dry
weather; and then Wallace sent to his uncle for the promised
horse, declaring that he was fit to travel. Master Robert brought
up the beast himself, with notable promptitude — and with
sundry other parting gifts and much good advice. It would be
unfair to suggest that he was glad to see his nephew go; but his
relief was not to be hidden. He did not ask where they were
going — but gave them his blessing.

They took leave of the Grahams in a touching scene. The
sheer goodness of these simple people, their unquestioning loyalty and devotion, was something to warm the heart, their complete ignoring of the risks to themselves an object-lesson, their
love of their country and nation — out of which their ap-
probation of Wallace stemmed — a joy. If Scotland could produce such as these amongst her *ruling* families, the English
would not long remain masters.

They did not say farewell to all the family, for the eldest son
was to act guide for them. They were, in fact, heading now for
his chief's castle of Dundaff, in the Carron valley, some fifteen
miles away — quite far enough for a first move, even with the
horse. Sir John the Graham would welcome them, and put them
on their way to the Lennox — where Wallace had to render a
sorry account of his stewardship.

Young Sir John did indeed welcome them, joyfully, and
promised all aid — but not to head for Lennox. Earl Malcolm
was from home, summoned, like the other Scottish earls and
sheriffs, to attend on Warenne, Earl of Surrey, Edward's Viceroy — in Northumberland no less. To such a pass had Scotland
come that her pround earls must go, cap in hand, out of their
own country, at the call of a jumped-up English captain. No
point in making for Loch Lomondside.

This news was as nothing, however, compared with the
Graham's other tidings. These were that Thomas Gray and the
man MacFadzean were in fact at Dundaff. Not at the moment,
for each day they went scouring the country looking for Wallace. But they were camping in the castle for the time being.
They had arrived a few days before, thinking that perhaps
Wallace might have taken refuge there. There were only the

two of them, yes. The Lennoxmen had gone back home — save
for this MacFadzean.

More relieved than he could say, Wallace, though weary, felt
better than he had done for long. He seemed to be emerging
from the valley of the shadow.

Sir John Graham, it transpired, had no least notion of any
defeat for Wallace. On the contrary, he waxed enthusiastic over
all their doings, even those which seemed like failures. All was
wonderful, according to him, a saga of knightly prowess, a shin-
ing chivalric campaign against overwhelming odds. The
younger man appeared to have contracted a bad case of hero-
worship. Or perhaps his too-early knighting had gone to his
head. His mother was more gracious than heretofore. She had
heard that her husband had been transferred to St. Briavel's
Castle in distant Cornwall. It may be she felt that, so far away,
he could hardly be held responsible for any misdemeanours
committed by his dependents back in Scotland. At any rate, she
treated Wallace kindly — indeed, commenced to nurse him, although he protested that he was no longer in need of such codd-
ling.

Grays reunion with his friend that evening was a joyous
occasion. MacFadzean seemed equally happy. They had, oddly
enough blamed *themselves* for Wallace's going amissing, saying
that they should never have left him alone, at Gascon Hall, in
his then state of mind and body. They laughed to scorn his self-
accusation of deserting them, declaring the boot to be on the
other leg. When they had returned to the ruined Hall and found
him gone, they searched all the area for him. Three days and
nights they had waited there, seeking him, untroubled by the
English, who seemed suddenly to have given up the chase and
returned to Perth. They never discovered the reason for all the
horn-blowing that night. They had heard nothing of Kerlie and
MacGregor. At length a countryman had told them of a
rumour that the man Wallace had slain Sir John Butler with his
bare hands at the Earn, and fled southwards. So they had come,
over Earn and Allan and Forth, seeking him — coming eventually to Dundaff, where they knew he had found Sir John sympathetic. The Lennoxmen, so near home, had tired of this quest,
and gone, save for leal MacFadzean.

The Grahams had no word of either Moray or MacDuff.
They were full of the wickedness, savageries and exactions of
Cressingham, Edward's Treasurer for Scotland, and Ormsby,

the Justiciar; who were responsible for most of the administration of Scotland in the absence of Surrey the Viceroy — who declared that for his health's sake he preferred to live in his own Northumberland. Bishop Beck was another monster — but at least he came and went, based on his see of Durham. Sir Henry Percy, the Viceroy's nephew, at Ayr, was allegedly less harsh and brutal than these others, though a cold fish by all accounts — not one of Edward's own appointments, of course. Edward Plantagenet, who well knew the efficacy of terror mixed with bonhomie, always appointed brutal men as governors, by policy — so that, when it suited him, he might by contrast appear generous, good-humoured. He might be the First Knight of Christendom; but equally well he could be called the Crowned Devil of Christendom. Of set purpose he made the name of Englishman feared and hated.

Agreeable as it was at Dundaff, Wallace did not wish to linger there for long. There was so much to be done — and he did not feel that it could be done from there. Moreover, he longed to see his wife Marion. It was now two months since he had left her, and she would be far gone with her child, *his* child — although he had no least feelings of parenthood. Presumably that would come. It was high time that he returned to her; it had never been his intention to be away for two months. Time he went back to his friends in Clydesdale and the Forest, too. His accumulating responsibilities were beginning to weigh on him. They would head for Lanark, by easy stages. And be home for Yule.

Sir John Graham, agog now for glory and honour and knightly gallantry, wanted to come with them. But Wallace said no — not yet. Let him gather together such company of his Grahams as he could — or that his mother and uncle would allow — and be ready to bring them on when word was sent. This would be of much greater advantage than his personally coming with them now — for there could be no real campaigning until this mid-winter period was over. Somewhat crestfallen, the young knight had to accept that.

So, not hurrying, they travelled southwards and westwards, across the Kilsyth Hills and the Kelvin valley and the high moorlands of Shotts, into North Lanarkshire, keeping ever to unfrequented paths and empty lands. Five days before Christmas they came to Bothwellmuir, where Wallace had a kinsman — and here, within fifteen miles of Lanark, they halted.

They were now in country where he was known, and great care obviously had to be taken. MacGregor and MacFadzean, however, were complete strangers to the neighbourhood; so the two Highlandmen were sent forward to prospect and make enquiries at Lanark. Marion would be unlikely to be at Lamington at this time of the year.

The pair came back next evening, with news which put a damper on any burgeoning Yuletide spirits. Marion Braidfoot was not in Lanark. She was said to be nearer at hand, indeed, somewhere in the Crossford area. And in mourning — double, triple mourning. Her father had died. And she had had a miscarriage, and her infant son had died. Moreover, she believed her husband dead. All Lanark declared William Wallace to be dead, drowned indeed. Details were not lacking. He had been drowned swimming the Forth at Cambuskenneth, after slaying Sir John Butler. The Highlanders had been able to gain no information as to where his wife had gone and why, in her sorrow and loss, save this mention of Crossford.

Dusk as it was, within the hour Wallace was on his way, anxious now almost to the point of distraction. He knew Crossford, of course, a village in the deep inner vale of Clyde, some ten miles upstream and South-East of Bothwell. One of his innumerable cousins, young Auchinleck of that Ilk, newly married, had gone to live at Gillbank, on the Nethan not far from Crossford, he recollected. They would go there. Pate might know.

Auchinleck was only nineteen, and an excitable youth; but even so, Wallace felt that he did not have to stage quite so dramatic a display of shock and dismay at the sight of his relative. His new wife, on the contrary, took the reincarnation calmly — declaring indeed that it was the *English* who had cause to demonstrate such upset over Wallace being alive. She announced that her husband's guests were welcome at Gillbank, to stay as long as they would. They were just in time for Yule.

Patrick Auchinleck at least knew where Marion Braidfoot was. Unable to bear life in Lanark, and her eldest brother and his wife now master and mistress at Lamington, she had gone to her aunt, the Lady Jean Douglas, at Draffane Castle ...

He hardly had the name enunciated before Wallace was off, much after dark as it was. Draffane was only some three miles away, a sizeable house crowning a crag high above a tight bend in the Nethan, a mile above its junction with the Clyde. The

Lady Jean was not actually, an aunt of Marion's but an old friend of her mother's, who, when the first Lady Braidfoot had died at Marion's birth, had largely reared the girl. A widow now, and something of a character, kin to Sir William Douglas, chief of his name, she occupied this eagle's nest of a hold — and would undoubtedly defend it as stoutly as any man.

Wallace chose to go alone on this visit, however loth his friends were to let him out of their sight. He approached the castle on its lofty peninsula warily — for visitors to such places after dark were apt to be looked on with suspicion, to say the least. Moreover, the circumstances of his arrival were unusual and difficult. He did not want to announce his survival to his mourning wife via a gate porter. So he called for the Lady Jean herself, saying that he was a kinsman come to visit. When after some delay, the old lady did come to the gatehouse, and sounding distinctly haughty and suspicious, he called to her, as low-voiced as his words would carry.

'Lady Jean — greetings. You have Marion Braidfoot biding with you, I think?'

'If I have, sirrah — what business is that of yours?'

'The best, lady. Let me in, and I will prove it. She . . . she is not there! With you? Now?'

'No, sir. Why?'

'I would prefer to explain without the shouting, Lady Jean.'

'I cannot see you, man. Your name? I do not know who you are. How do I know that you have not a band of cut-throats with you, seeking our hurt?'

'Only my word, lady. That of a Scot who would by no means sign English Edward's roll!'

'Ha!' The Lady Jean was one of the few land-holders hereabouts who had refused to sign the Ragman Roll of the year before, Her next words were presumably addressed to the gate porter, for a clanking of chains thereafter indicated that the drawbridge was being lowered.

When Wallace came through the gatehouse archway, it was to find the old woman standing under the vaulting, barring the way. At sight of him, presumably struck by his obvious bulk and height, she grabbed the smoking torch from her porter and held it up closer to the visitor.

'Christ-God and all His Saints!' she said, in ladylike fashion.

He nodded. 'You will understand, ma'am, that I'd liefer not shout my name aloud, in this pass. Even at Draffane.'

'Will Wallace!' she gasped. 'We thought you dead.'

'Aye — so I understand. Mirren — how is she?'

'In her body the lassie is well enough. In her mind, a poor thing. But, man ... you were wounded and drowned dead, all men said.'

'All men can be wrong, lady — as when they say that the English cannot be defeated and driven out of Scotland!'

'Aye. You are very much not dead, then, I see!'

'Not yet, no. I was wounded, yes, and sick. But now am almost myself again. I came, so soon as I could. Mirren — where is she?'

'In her room. Abed, I think. She lies much abed. She conceives that she has little to live for. You have been but an ill husband to her, Will Wallace! When I came to your wedding, I little thought this would be the way of it.'

'Nor did I,' he admitted. 'But at least I have not widowed her! Will ... will you break it to her, Lady Jean? That is why I called for you, not Mirren. It will be ... no little surprise.'

'That it will. I give you credit for that much good sense, at least! Yes. I will give her the good tidings — and pray that she keeps her wits! Come you inside. And up with that bridge, Davie ...'

And so, in the first-floor hall of Draffane, Wallace waited, in a turmoil of emotion — and thick stone walls and narrow winding stairs or none, presently he heard the yell from above, whether of joy, hysteria or shock he knew not. Then he heard a strange, choking, gurgling, twittering sound that rose and fell, but came nearer — and the hall-door burst open, and there was Marion, mouth wide, lips trembling, tears streaming down her face. She paused at sight of him, all but stumbled, uttered a sort of wail, and then, as he moved to her, arms out, flung herself at him — and the blanket which she had grabbed up to wrap inadequately round her bed-nakedness, fell off entirely. Into his rain-wet embrace she collapsed, sobbing convulsively.

Clutching her shaking body, stroking her, kissing her hair and brow and the tears from her cheeks, murmuring incoherent assurances, endearments, nonsenses, he found the tears in his own eyes and the choking of his voice scarcely helpful.

The Lady Jean gave them a few minutes; but little to the point had been said when she came in, to talk sense and sanity.

'Dear God — here's a sight, in a respectable widow's house!' she expostulated, but fairly mildly. 'Mother-naked, and no

142

shame in it!' She picked up the fallen blanket. 'Your bed-chamber's the place for suchlike, lassie!' she scolded. 'Forby, you don't want to catch your death of cold just when you've got your man back, do you?' And she wrapped the plaid round the still trembling girl.

Seeing that the pair were still at a loss for adequate words, she went on talking, in businesslike fashion now. 'Here's a to-do, if you like, i' faith! All your mourning and tears wasted, Mirren! He's no' so easy drowned is Will Wallace, it seems. Man — don't stand there like a gowk! Tell us how you contrived it, of a mercy's sake?'

'Yes. To be sure. Indeed, yes It . . . it's a long story. I cannot tell it all now.' He kept his hold on Marion. 'Anyhow, I am too happy, have too much joy . . . To have Mirren again.'

'Yes,' the girl said. 'Yes.' She could find no other words.

The Lady Jean Douglas, looking from one to the other, recognised that this was not the time to get anything worth knowing out of William Wallace. She nodded, philosophically. 'Away up to your room with him, girl,' she ordered. 'You'll maybe win some sense out of him there, who knows! He'll be hungry, too — men are aye hungry. I mean for victuals, mind! Meat and drink — forby they have other hungers, too! I will have Janet put you up a wheen victuals, sustenance. She'll leave it at the door, never fear. Och, I was young once, my own self, mind — little as you think it, I swear! Off with the pair of you, then.'

Up in Marion's room, gradually it all came out. They were not desperate for each other's bodies at this stage; though they had a great need to touch and hold one another, both for the contact and the feel of it, but also from a sort of unspoken dread that if they did not, one might well be spirited away. They had both been under enormous strain, and their health impaired. Passion could wait.

Wallace recounted a very abbreviated version of his adventures, battles, disappointments and illness. He spared Marion word of Meg Drummond; but he did tell her about his killing of Fawdon — and found himself having to insist on how terrible a thing it was for a commander to slay one of his own men, however treacherous. How the story had got abroad that he had drowned in swimming Forth, he did not know. He vaguely remembered swimming in the river at Cambuskenneth; but his mind was almost a blank concerning that period. He could only

143

presume that someone had seen and recognised him, entering the water, and had not seen him emerge on the other side.

In return, he learned how, in Lanark High Street, in November, Marion had suffered a fall when being chased by drunken soldiery, and their child had been born, dead, two days later — the girl's eyes filled with tears again, at this, and he sought to comfort her with typically masculine philosophy that they could make another baby without too much trouble. He was rebuked at some length for his pains. Of her father's death she had little to say, for he had been a stiff, reserved man to whom it was difficult to get close, even for his own daughter. She had come here to Draffane, to her Aunt Jean, when she could stand Lanark and its memories no longer.

Marion was able to tell him, too, something of his friends whom he had left in Ettrick Forest. Under John Blair, Robert Boyd and his cousin Adam Wallace, they had conducted a few small raids, and waylaid a convoy or two. But lacking Will's leadership and enthusiasm, the group had dwindled in numbers; and with the onset of winter weather had gradually dispersed. Blair, Boyd, Edward Little and one or two others were now at the monastery of Fail, where the church booty from the Loudoun Hill ambush had been deposited.

A faint noise outside the door heralded the woman Janet with her tray of cold meat, oatcakes, honey and wine — which Marion, who, after a long spell of eating little or nothing, was prepared to help the man demolish. Thereafter they made love in a gentle but warm and entirely satisfying way.

There were still tears on the young woman's cheeks when Wallace finally kissed her goodnight.

CHAPTER EIGHT

Since William Wallace's physical presence was not one which would readily pass unnoticed, he felt constrained to spend much of that Yuletide of 1296–97 indoors, at either Gillbank or Draffane, in the Nethan valley — a state of affairs in which his wife concurred and co-operated very gladly. It could be that in the process he completed his convalescence both physically and mentally — and certainly spent one of the happiest periods of his life. But this relaxation and comparative idleness did not apply to most of his lieutenants and friends, who were kept busy, summoned from Fail and Ayr and Irvine and Carrick, to confer with him and make plans for a campaign, on a more major scale than anything yet attempted, when the weather conditions would make such possible. Needless to say, all these colleagues, supporters and associates were overjoyed to see their leader again. Most had not, in fact, really considered him as dead, having a typical young men's belief in his, and their own, ability to survive. As well as conferring and planning, they were sent on errands, probes, spying expeditions, up and down that South-West section of Scotland, in order to equip Wallace with an overall picture of the situation, as regards the English occupation and the restiveness or otherwise of the Scots population under it — more especially the reactions of the Scots nobility. Had his activities, in fact, had any rousing effect on his fellow countrymen? And what was likely to be the most useful course to take henceforward?

Little or no news came out of the North, regarding Sir Andrew Moray or the Lord Hugh MacDuff — the latter seeming to have evaporated into thin air, and the former to be uninterested in any intrusion into the southern part of the country. There were encouraging stories of the activities of the Bishop of Moray, who seemed to be a man of vigour — a close kinsman of Sir Andrew. But clearly there was little to be hoped for from north of the Forth and Clyde meantime — anyway, with the Highland passes choked with snow, the low ground waterlogged and the rivers running in high spate, with no forage for horseflesh — or man, for that matter — warfare was almost impossible. For the same reasons, with bridges few and far between and roads all but impassable, the English too confined their activities mainly to their garrison-towns. This was the normal pattern — and Wallace had been very much an innovator in pursuing his hostilities so far into the winter season, discarding horses and using darkness and the land as his allies.

His friends brought word that, though there was nothing like widespread incipient revolt, his activities appeared not to have been wholly fruitless. There were increasing murmurings against the invaders — and consequent increasing savagery on their part. At the monastery of St. Mary's at Fail, into Ayrshire, where Wallace more than once was a nocturnal visitor, the Trinitarian friars were in constant touch with other religious establishments, especially in the sees of Glasgow and Galloway, and he heard much to interest him. Stirred by his exploits — which evidently lost nothing in the telling — more important men were beginning to talk of revolt. Bishop Wishart was undoubtedly foremost in this — Sir Bryce Blair of that Ilk, Sir Richard Lundin, Lindsay, Lord of Crawford, even the Steward it was said, although with the wife he had it was necessary that he be more careful than most. Moreover, the Lord of Douglas was known to have effected his escape from his English prison, and was back in Scotland, vowing vengeance. If only Moray would venture south of the Highland Line. Wallace's alleged death would undoubtedly have a serious dampening effect on these stirrings. Clearly the sooner it was made abundantly evident that he was still very much to the fore, the better.

After some debate it was decided that a really bold stroke was necessary, a major blow at the English occupation; if the blow was such that it might convince certain Scots nobles that their true interests lay in supporting their own country rather than the invader, so much the better.

Curiously enough it was something of an oddity living at Fail who suggested Lochmaben Castle as the best location for such a gesture. This was an elderly knight called Sir Thomas Learmonth of Ercildoune, an eccentric, formerly of considerable renown as a seer and poet, who had prophesied, to the hour, the death of the late and good King Alexander the Third, at Kinghorn's cliff. He had been a vassal of the old Cospatrick, Earl of Dunbar and March; and when the present Earl threw in his lot with Edward of England, Learmonth, or True Thomas the Rhymer, as he was popularly nicknamed, did not require any especial percipience to foresee that the said Earl's Border domain in general, and Ercildoune on the South-East edge of the Ettrick Forest in particular, were likely to be good places to be out of for some considerable time — he being very much a man of peace, despite the consistently doomful nature of his prophecies. So, letting it be believed that he was ill, and retiring to die, he had handed over his lands to his son, and left the East March, to instal himself as a sort of honorary lay-brother at the Trinitarian Monastery of Fail — which, as it happened, had a reputation for good living and capacious wine-cellars. He was indeed exceedingly popular with the monks, for he was excel-

lent company and highly entertaining. He much approved of
William Wallace and his activities — though, naturally, not to
the extent of seeking any part in them. But it was his proposal
that Lochmaben should be the target for this major blow desired. And though he wrapped the suggestion up in dire verse, it
greatly interested the younger man.

> True Thomas does this token make,
> Bruce a step to his throne shall take,
> When the Welshman shall find haven
> In the castle of Lochmaben.

Lochmaben Castle was a very important and strategically-
placed stronghold in mid-Annandale, largely controlling one of
the vital routes in the West March of the Borders. It belonged
to Robert Bruce, Lord of Annandale, 6th of the name, son of
the renowned Competitor for the Throne of a few years before.
The Bruce was a proud man but weak, unsure of his allegiance,
who hated John Baliol to whom Edward Plantagenet, in his
capacity of volunteer adjudicator, had awarded the Scots
throne in the notorious Competition for the Crown — in prefer-
ence to the Bruce claim. Bruce hated Edward also — but not
sufficiently to rise against him, as his old father might have
done. Nothing much was to be expected of the 6th Lord of
Annandale — who would have made as poor a king for Scotland
as Baliol had done; but his eldest son, Robert Bruce, Earl of
Carrick, was a different story, a spirited young man if something
of a playboy, who, although a favourite of Edward's own and
largely brought up at his Court, was known greatly to resent
having had to take the oath of allegiance to the Englishman for
his Scottish lands when his own father should have been King.
As old Learmonth put it, young Bruce was in a swither. If his
father's great castle of Lochmaben was taken from its English
garrison, he would be forced to do something to make up his
mind where his interests and duty lay. It would be apt to put
him in bad odour with Edward, too, who would also have to do
something about so vital a fortress. Let Wallace turn his eyes on
Lochmaben.

That young man accepted the good sense of all this, despite
the flowery language and dramatics of Sir Thomas — but with
much doubt that it was too tough a nut for him to crack. Which
doubts the other pooh-poohed airily, repeating his rhyme as

147

though it were Holy Writ. Wallace understood that the phrase 'the Welshman' therein could refer to himself — Wallace was a corruption of the name Walays, meaning a Welsh-speaking or Cymric Celt of Strathclyde. But the line anent it being a step nearer Bruce's throne intrigued him. Was the old man fore-telling Bruce's eventual gaining of the Crown? Or was it merely one more dramatic flourish? But True Thomas, like many another prophet before and since, refused to be drawn into detail and elucidation. He smugly repeated his jingle, chuckled heartily, and called for more wine — of which Fail seemed to have an unfailing supply — and advised Wallace to be content with what the good God gave him.

Out of much debate with his friends thereafter, Wallace did decide that at least they ought to go and prospect mid-Annandale. If he was going to resurrect his name resoundingly, Lochmaben was as good a location as any. If they could take the castle, in the name of King John Baliol, they would see what the Bruces, father and son, would have to say to that.

It was probably time to send for Sir John the Graham.

*   *   *

And so, on an evening of late January, Wallace and a small party came to Lochmaben in Annandale, from Corhead on the South-Western edge of the Ettrick Forest. Corhead, a small tower-house, was the home of Tom Halliday, his eldest sister's son; and Edward Little, her son by a second marriage, often stayed here with his step-brother. It was only some eight miles, as the crow flies, from Lochmaben. The great castle, and its little redstone town, lay to south and north respectively of the half-mile long Castle Loch — Lochmaben boasted no few than six lochs — in the wide and shallow vale of the Annan. The castle made such strengths as Kinclaven and Gargunnock, even Draffane, seem like children's toys. As well as the natural defences of the loch shore with its steep banks, there were concentric moats with ramparts between, and inner and outer baileys before ever the castle proper commenced. There were six great flanking towers, linked by thirty feet high curtain-walls, as well as the gatehouse-block; and within all, surmounting a rocky mound, was a massive square battlemented keep, with parapet, machicolations and caphouse. From the last, two flag-staffs rose, the tallest flying the Leopards of Plantagenet, the other white scallops on red of Moreland. There was no Bruce banner.

Scarcely encouraged, Wallace and his friends made a discreet survey of the stronghold, as far as they might, perceived no weaknesses or opportunities for surprise, and retired to Corhead.

Here the discussion went on well into the night, with argument, suggestion and objection as to the feasibility of anything being done about Lochmaben, Wallace's friends more or less equally divided for and against trying. Halliday had brought in his farm steward, a man named John Watson, born and bred not only in Lochmaben but in the castle itself, where his father had been chief gate porter to the Bruces. If anyone could get them into the fortress, this man could; but even he could think of no way past the many ditches and ramparts, with the ultimate gatehouse and drawbridge defended against them. Once inside his knowledge would be invaluable — but what use was that, with a garrison of a hundred and fifty men?

Wallace listened carefully, thoughtfully, to the debate, and only intervened in any major way when those hundred and fifty men were mentioned for perhaps the fourth time.

'A hundred and fifty men inside a stout hold may be impregnable,' he observed. 'But *outside* they may be less potent — as we have proved before this.'

Men eyed him, waiting.

'If we could entice this Moreland out, in force, he might leave but few to guard his castle,' he went on, slowly. 'Decoy him away, and we might gain entrance.'

'Ha! A feint?' Kerlie said, 'Could we do it?'

'It would have to be carefully conceived. *All* the garrison, or most of it, would have to be coaxed out. Anything less would be worthless. What would bring Moreland out, with his strength, leaving the castle all but empty? Only something which he believed he could deal with in a short time and *should* deal with, no threat to his base itself. Something far enough away to keep him out of the way for some time — but not so far that he would doubt his ability to get back to Lochmaben the same day. What is he doing here, at this castle? Guarding the central route to and from England in the main, and keeping Edward's so-called peace in Annandale. If we could threaten these functions, we might stir him.'

'An attack on a convoy?' John Blair suggested.

'Say rather the *threat* of attack on a convoy. But not by us. By others. Local, Annandale folk. For whom Moreland is responsible.' Wallace was feeling his way as he spoke. 'Know you any sufficiently committed to our cause to lend his name to such a ploy? Even if he does not have to strike a blow.'

'Harry Kirkpatrick of Torthorwald,' Tom Halliday, their host, put in promptly. 'Brother to Closeburn. He is already at odds with the English — he slew two of them in an ale-house brawl at Lockerbie. He has had to leave Torthorwald Tower — lives in caves up in Eskdale. With a crew of young hot-heads. He is hot-headed enough himself, with a notable temper — but he would aid you in this, I think.'

'Excellent! I know the brother, Sir Roger Kirkpatrick of Closeburn — less than cold-blooded himself! Now, as to convoys? Northward-coming rather than south-going.

The man Watson pointed out that covoys tended to be few and far between in winter time. They could not expect one to come conveniently. Wallace agreed, but contended that there must be considerable traffic between Carlisle, the main English base on the West March, and Lanark, Linlithgow, Stirling, Perth and other mid-country garrisons. An army of occupation must have its lines of communication and supply. Moreover, there was no hurry, for they would require to assemble a sizeable force, and this Harry Kirkpatrick would have to be reached, persuaded, instructed. A week, perhaps — ten days. He had sent for John the Graham — but how many men his mother and uncle would allow him to bring was another story. Surely there would be a worthwhile convoy within two weeks?

Meantime, they all must become messengers, spies, envoys — work for all. With secrecy of the essence.

*　　　*　　　*

It was twelve days later, and into February, that Wallace waited, outwardly calm, confident, inwardly a fret of impatience and doubts, to see the working out of his plans. With a company of about fifty he was hidden in a cleft of the open hillside of Knockspen Hill, above the valley of the Water of Ae. They were some three miles, as the crow flies, from Corhead Tower, and seven miles North-West of Lochmaben. It was not precisely the ideal area for what he envisaged, but to some extent he was at the mercy of circumstances, and he hoped that it would serve. Far below them, in the gut of the valley, they could see movement on the north edge of Knock Wood. This was Harry Kirkpatrick of Torthorwald and his scratch crew

of some sixty Annandale mosstroopers, youths and scal-
lywags — the decoy and bait of the trap. Their numbers, as
whispered to reach Sir Hugo de Moreland's ear in Lochmaben,
were three times that. The convoy they were waiting for was
rather a special one — no less than the womenfolk, children,
plenishings and personal belongings of Sir Henry Percy himself,
Lord of Northumberland, Governor of all this South-West
Scotland and nephew of Warenne, Earl of Surrey, Edward's
Viceroy. Percy had established himself at Ayr, and now intended to make himself more comfortable. It was not an important cavalcade, militarily — but nor was it one which one of
his lieutenants in charge of a long stretch of vital road through
Annandale, would allow to be ambushed. So far as Wallace was
concerned, it was worth the waiting for. He did not make war
on women — but in fact these would be in no danger. The
convoy was necessarily a slow-moving one, and had spent the
night at Dumfries. This had dictated the approximate position
of the present sham ambush — for there had to be time for the
carefully planted whispers to reach Moreland this same morning, and for him to take steps incumbent — not to stop the
convoy, but to reach the ambush-place in time to save it. This
had required considerable calculation, and Wallace had been up
the entire night making dispositions. It was now just after noon
of a crisp, cold February day, with snow brilliantly topping the
high hills but none below 1,500 feet. Knockspen Hill was less
than that.

From their stance they could see a long way to south and
south-eastwards down Annandale — of which this valley of the
Water of Ae was a tributary, and which the road followed.
There was much wood and down there, so that the picking out
of bodies of men at any distance was difficult.

John Blair saw the convoy first — presumably so, at any rate,
since it was coming along the road from Dumfries, not from
Lochmaben, and it was evidently moving at a sober pace. John
Watson, who knew this area like the palm of his hand, declared
that it was in the Shieldhall vicinity meantime, some four miles
away.

Wallace frowned. Four miles only! Even at a snail's pace it
could not take an hour to reach the ambush position — and still
there was no sign of any party from Lochmaben. Had he mis-
calculated? Moreland was cutting it fine, if he was going to act.
Watson pointed out that there was still the Ae ford at Carse of

Ae to be crossed, which would delay somewhat a cavalcade of heavily laden pack-animals.

Anxiously Wallace peered South-Eastwards. If no one from Lochmaben turned up, Harry Kirkpatrick could hardly fail to capture the convoy. But that was not what was required and would achieve little — and possibly damage Wallace's reputation. He would not wish his re-emergence linked with such an incident. And all the planning wasted . . .

Twenty more worrying minutes had to be passed before the keen-eyed Blair spotted the flash of wintery sunlight on steel, well to the east, in the region of Nethermill of Garrel. If this was the Lochmaben contingent — and further glints soon revealed that there was a lot of steel there, a large company — then Moreland, or whoever was in command, must have forded Ae much further down, at Elsieshields, where the river made a major bend eastwards before joining Annan. The reason for coming this way, with Garrel Water also to ford, was not obvious; though Watson thought it might be a little faster, for determined men.

After that first sighting, the lie of intervening land allowed no further glimpses for a good ten minutes. Then they were two miles nearer, and not much more than a mile away — although on much lower ground. They would still not be able to see the convoy from that level.

Now it was clear that it was a large party, possibly two hundred mounted men, with two knights' banners in the lead. This was more than Wallace had anticipated, more than the total garrison of Lochmaben. Watson explained it by pointing out that Moreland's second-in-command was Sir John de Greystoke, another Westmorlander, indeed a kinsman, who was not normally installed in Lochmaben at all, but held the small market town of Lockerbie, a few miles to the South-East, where there was a minor citadel. Greystoke would have about fifty men there; so no doubt Moreland had sent for him, at short notice — which would account for the delay and increased numbers.

This probably was so — but it did not aid Wallace in his immediate problem; the extra numbers were bound to complicate the issue — which was going to be sufficiently complicated as it was.

Then an unexpected development. After splashing across another and lesser burn, which Watson named Clatteringstones, the oncoming cavalry split into two parties, each under a banner, Moreland to head on directly for the Knock Wood in the narrows of the Ae valley, the other to swing due westwards — which would bring them to the Ae also, but much more quickly.

'These go to warn and halt the convoy,' Wallace exclaimed. 'The others to deal with Kirkpatrick's ambush. At least this halves their strength, meantime.'

Now, at length, the watchers had to be ready for action. Wallace waved a white cloth towards a pair of sentinels on a subsidiary spur of Knockspens, much nearer to and directly above the Knock Wood ambush site; they in turn would warn Kirkpatrick — who would, thereafter, wait only long enough for the English to see them, and then make off. That was when Wallace and his group would also make their presence known, in the hope of distracting, possibly dividing, the enemy. After that things would depend on developments.

These were not long in coming, at the rate the Englishmen were riding, under the red-and-white Moreland banner. Soon Kirkpatrick's people were scattering, on foot and in sight of all, up the hill on the far side of the valley, before the cavalry could get amongst them. Moreland's company of about a hundred swept in at one end of the Knock Wood, in excellent formation — and came out at the other in bunches and straggles, but still under control, a disciplined force. From up on Knockspens Hill Wallace could see Moreland reforming his ranks and obviously issuing orders. It looked as though he was not going to allow his troopers to disperse into the hills chasing fleeing individuals, as they had hoped.

The last thing Wallace wanted now was for the Englishman to feel that he had done his duty, retire to meet the convoy, and then, leaving it an escort, retire to Lochmaben. He had got the enemy out of the castle and a fair distance from it; now he must keep them out, and still farther away. He put the second part of his contingent plan into operation, then, by lining his men along a ridge of the hill, where they could not fail to be seen, and raising his horn to his lips, blew a long resounding call, which echoed and re-echoed amongst the hills.

Moreland reacted quickly. After what was presumably a swift assessment of the numbers involved in this new challenge, he divided his company for the second time, sent two men dashing back down the track, no doubt to inform Greystoke, detached perhaps thirty more off westwards, to pursue Kirkpatrick's runners, and turning the rest eastwards, led them directly uphill towards Wallace's stance, half-a-mile above. He was a man of logic and method, obviously, was Sir Hugo de Moreland.

The Scots on Knockspens Hill waited for a little, brandishing swords and shaking fists, defiance personified. But not for too long. Their own horses, like Kirkpatrick's, were hidden on the far side of the hill. With the enemy still about five hundred yards from them, they turned and started to run downhill from their ridge.

The thing was carefully arranged, as always with Wallace. They reached their beasts with ample time to mount and be away before the English could catch up — but not so far ahead as to make the chase seem hopeless. They were, of course, riding the sturdy and shaggy garrons, short-legged hill-ponies, whereas their pursuers were mounted on much taller low-country cavalry horses, in theory much faster animals, but on rough hillsides in fact much less effective because less sure-footed and unused to broken terrain.

It was, then, a decoy chase, a trailing wing enticement, to coax the enemy ever farther away. But it was more than that — it was to coax them into a certain area where, just conceivably, the chasers might even become the chased.

Meantime, all had to be judged to a nicety. They must not let themselves get too far ahead, so that the English were discouraged — but neither must they risk getting caught. They must seem to flee in panic, scattered — but in fact they must act coherently, or the whole project could end in disaster.

Wallace personally was probably faced with as much difficulty as anyone involved, for his weight was a grievous load for any hill-pony, and his long legs practically trailed in the heather and deer-grass; so that maintaining any fairly precise distance from the enemy was no simple matter. And he had to keep an eye on his flock at the same time, to ensure that all headed in the right direction, not easy when they were apt to pass him.

He was aiming for a specific place, some three miles North-Eastwards, where the Clachanbirnie Burn and the Glenkill Water came down out of separate narrow valleys to join in a marshy hub of the hills. Thereabouts, with fortune favouring them, he hoped to play a less ignoble role.

The big man heaved a sigh of relief, with such breath as he could spare, when he saw the double cleft in the green-brown hillside ahead. He kicked hard at the broad flanks of his frothing, panting mount. This was where it was essential that they increased their lead.

There was, he knew, a track of sorts up the right-hand valley, that of the larger Glenkill Water, which led over the small pass of The Donkens to a major drove-road running between Eskdale and Upper Nithsdale. This Glenkill track had a solid causeway of stones laid through the marsh where the two burns joined — and which, at this season of the year, was otherwise impassable for horses. It was all too obvious for any sort of trap, there and then; but later, perhaps . . .

Over the rough turf-grown causeway the Scots thundered, having to bunch now, with the nearest enemy about three hundred yards behind. In the jaws of the narrow, right-hand valley they plunged, now having to string out. The valley was not only narrow, it twisted violently and climbed fairly steeply. That twisting was vital, and their purpose all depended on their next manoeuvres not being seen from behind.

About quarter-of-a-mile up the valley, a small tributary burn came tumbling down the steep slope on the left, carving for itself a quite deep gully in the brae; and as was so often the case, this was thickly grown with scrub rowan and birch. Coming level with this, Wallace raised a hand and threw himself off his horse and into the burn-channel, and without pause, commenced to scramble away up it. Behind him, as they came up, some fifty of his men did likewise, leaving only the last ten or so to remain mounted. These beat on up the winding track, at speed, driving the string of riderless garrons before them. Quickly they were all out of sight beyond the next bend.

The fifty had only moments to get themselves hidden in the scrub of the cleft before Moreland and the first of his cavalry came pounding into view. The knight was only half-armoured, naturally, with his light helm slung over his saddle-bow. He seemed to be a man in his early forties, square-faced, bull-necked, tough-looking. He drove on up the valley-track without faltering, as did his seventy or so men-at-arms, now much strung-out and looking somewhat exhausted.

Whenever the last straggler was past, Wallace and his people were up and climbing. They had to move fast now, however difficult the ground. Using the burn-channel as a ladder, they clambered up the steep hillside. Gasping, they reached the inter-vening ridge, crossed it diagonally at a lumbering, breathless run, and went slantwise down the equally steep slope on the farther, west, side, into the companion valley of the Clachan-birnie Burn.

Wallace, who was still not quite so fit as his usual, was all but dropping when they reached this valley floor, twisting like the other; but he drove himself on, down-stream, and the others with him. There was no track down this one.

Soon they were at the mouth of the glen, and the marshland, again — with here no causeway through it. Hastily Wallace placed his fifty men, grouping them amongst bushes, reeds and scrub. There could be little time left.

Only two or three minutes after they were approximately settled, the drumming of many hooves shook the unsteady ground beneath them. Then into sight down the Clachanbirnie glen came their riderless garrons in headlong stampede, nostrils snorting, shaggy manes and tails streaming. Behind lashing and whooping them on, rode the bare dozen Scots who had remained mounted.

The manoeuvre had been a simple one, although exceedingly tight as to its timing. Almost a mile up the Glenkill valley, there was a gap in the intervening ridge between the glens, a sort of low col or pass. Through this the decoy party had driven the horses, over to the Clachanbirnie Burn beyond, and so back down its twisting valley, doing in fact what the dismounted men had done but by a more level if longer route. It was to be hoped that the English were just behind.

Straight into the marsh the horsemen drove their beasts — and did not throw themselves off their desperately floundering mounts until they were well into its miry middle. By that time the first of the enemy were in sight. Whether Sir Hugo de Moreland, at their head, had any idea that there was no causeway here, or that the bog would sink his cavalry — or whether he just could not pull up in time, with all the pressure of seventy galloping men-at-arms behind — was not evident. But into the green treachery, after his ploutering quarry, he plunged, and his troopers after him. And all around them, Wall-ace's hiding men leapt up, swords and dirks in hand.

What followed was no sort of battle; no more than a mass-acre, a ruthless and bloody slaughter amidst the mud and mosses and slime. If the broad-hooved garrons, used to the hills, floundered and sank, much more so the narrower-hooved, longer-legged cavalry mounts. The men-at-arms were thrown, or jumped, from their saddles, their lances useless, and weighted down with steel jacks and heavy thigh-boots, were stabbed or cut down more or less where they stood. Wallace dealt with Sir Hugo himself and felt not compunction, but almost shame as he drove the great sword down. This was murder rather than warfare — but he reminded himself that Moreland, like the rest of King Edward's veteran captains, was himself a pitiless killer, chosen especially for the task of repressing a whole proud nation, by sheer savagery, rapine and terror. This no time for doubts, he pressed on, blade whirling.

It was all over in a few hectic minutes. Covered in mud and blood, but almost wholly unhurt, the Scots finished off the last of their pursuers, offering no quarter and being asked for none. Then they set about saving the horses, their own and the enemy's, having considerable difficulty in extricating them from the mire. A proud youth of no more than sixteen, reddened dirk still in hand, brought Wallace Moreland's handsome dapple-gray charger, as trophy. To please the lad, and as a gesture for the others, he led the animal to the causeway and mounted — although he would have been better on his own humble garron.

They were still rescuing horseflesh, ever dear to Borderers, when a warning was shouted. Over a ridge to the south a large party of horsemen was appearing, a blue-and-white banner at the head.

Wallace cursed. This could not be Moreland's detachment sent after Kirkpatrick — it had had no knight's banner. It could only be Sir John de Greystoke again, with the second hundred, having left the convoy and come seeking his superior, no doubt at the behest of Moreland's two messengers.

There was no time for any thought-out plan, in this emergency — the newcomers were only half-a-mile away and could see all before them, see any move to decoy them into the marsh.

'Up the Glenkill again!' he shouted, to his people. 'Leave all. Follow me.' And still on Moreland's grey, he spurred back across the causeway.

It was galling to have to flee, thus in face of a new challenge, after such complete victory — but to set sixty untrained men, however courageous, against a hundred professional cavalrymen, in open country, was recipe for disaster. If they took refuge in the marsh and hoped for the best, the English, who always included mounted bowmen in their companies, would be able to pick them off like sitting birds.

So the second chase began — and was a deal less exhilarating than the first, with men and horses tired now. Moreover, the objective of the day was the capture of Lochmaben Castle, not incessant preliminary battling.

Wallace cudgelled his wits. On this track the English horses would be apt to make better speed; it was on the open hillsides that their own garrons would be supreme. So the sooner they were off the track, the better. But they could not leave it in this steep valley — save for the col used previously. They dared not risk that round-about route again; now there would be no time to hide in the marsh. And Greystoke, surely, must have perceived some signs of the fight there, and be wary, even though he would not know precisely what had happened to Moreland's party.

They would have to go on, then, up this Glenkill Water, hoping for a diversion, for a place where he might make the land fight for them. He wished that he was back on his garron, however noble a beast this charger.

At length they were out of the constriction of the valley and into the vast table-land of the Minnygap, with its far circle of enclosing hills, their track snaking to meet the main drove-road which crossed it from South-East to North-West. They certainly did not want to reach that, which would further advantage the enemy.

Wallace perceived the two sets of horsemen in front almost simultaneously, far apart and miles distant as they were, visible on these open uplands. One was coming in from the west, the other from the north. And even at this range, they gave a totally different impression. The first was loosely scattered, ragged-looking, and clearly riding fast. The group to the north was smaller, compact-seeming, with a disciplined look to it. The first could be fleeing, the second merely travelling.

Almost certainly that on the west was Kirkpatrick and his crew from the Knock Wood ambush, presumably being chased by Moreland's thirty-strong detachment. They would be useful reinforcements, even though of doubtful quality. Though of course, their pursuers would also reinforce the enemy. But who were the others? It was too far to be sure, but he thought he could discern a banner at the front. A knightly band, then? If so, a deal more likely to be English than Scots.

158

The obvious course seemed to be to veer towards the western party, to join up. If Kirkpatrick had his promised sixty or seventy, the combined force might give Greystoke pause. But that knight might reckon the thirty additional cavalrymen better value. Weighing this up was difficult. But their garrons would do better, by comparison, off the track. He reined round to the left, waving his people to follow.

An imprecation burst from his lips, presently, as he perceived that Kirkpatrick's party had suddenly veered, in turn, but *away* from them, turning North-Eastwards. The crackpates had probably mistaken them for English — they would not be looking for them up in this area of course: and his own present mount, this handsome grey, would tend to confuse further. Evidently they had not spotted the group coming from the north. If they kept up this new direction, they would run into them.

Wallace altered course to try to close with them again. His grey was not doing so well now, his garron-mounted colleagues catching up all around. Their pursuers, after gaining up the valley, were now dropping a little behind — but still too close for comfort. This was developing into a too complicated race, with the outcome ever more uncertain.

The situation unfolded further. Moreland's detachment, now well over the skyline, might well switch their target. And Kirkpatrick seemed to have become aware of the party approaching over the shoulder of Little Queensberry Hill to the north, and was now veering almost directly northwards himself — the only direction clear of oncoming cavalry. Surely never had this upland tract seen so much hurrying horseflesh.

Wallace still had seen no corner of the land of which he might take advantage. But this ridiculous chase could not go on for ever. They must come to conclusions sooner or later — even if it meant deliberately riding into a bog and fighting it out therein, on foot, where the cavalrymen would suffer disadvantage. Fortunately there were peat-bogs in plenty up here.

He was, in fact, beginning to look for a suitable stretch of marshland, large enough for his purpose, when something about the banner being carried at the head of the south-coming group, now clear enough to be discerned, caught his attention. It was black and gold — and, yes, the charges on it were not round but shell-shaped, scallops. Three golden scallops — Graham. The arms of Graham. It could be none other than young Sir John — and come at an auspicious moment.

This joyful recognition changed the entire position. Now three of the five groups were Scots, and with even a slight advantage in numbers. Say about a hundred and fifty against a hundred and thirty. Hastily Wallace sought to change his tactical thinking. Graham was inexperienced — and Kirkpatrick seemed to have lost his head. Somehow they both must be brought to grasp the situation, and to co-operate.

He could think, there and then, of no other solution than the obvious one — it had to be obvious. He must, in fact, turn and fight — so that the others would perceive the clash and realise what was happening, who was what, and what was required of them. But it might take some time for the thing to become evident, and for these unfledged warriors to react effectively; and he did not want to suffer defeat in the waiting. Somehow he had to counter Greystoke's superiority meantime.

With surprise impossible and only peat-bog to help him, the essential matter was to narrow the front. None of the burns up here were large enough, wide enough, to hold up cavalry. Two bogs, with a narrow way between, would be best; or one bog, with a narrow re-entrant of firmer ground. Not too much to look for, surely? The entire great amphitheatre of the hills was a drainage sump, with consequent prevalence of soft ground after the snows, a womb of waters. They were all already plastered with black peat mire, men and beasts.

He had no time to seek the ideal. A wide expanse of brilliant veridian green, spagnum and similar mosses, lay over on their left. It would have to serve. He pulled round in that direction, shouting to those about him, and pointing. Closer at hand, he saw that there was precious little of even moderately firm ground — but they must make do. Plunging into the green treachery, very quickly his charger was up to its hocks, and deeper, reduced to a floundering uselessness. The others' garrons were better, but not greatly so.

Wallace flung himself out of the saddle, and all around him men did likewise. They sank in above their ankles, but not so far as the horses. Urgently he shouted his commands. Hedgehog formation, as near a schiltrom as was possible, back to back protecting each other, in whatever shape their footing allowed them. It was an odd commander who put all his lieutenants at the front, but he ordered Kerlie, Gray, Boyd, Blair, MacGregor, Halliday and Little, to flank him in the forefront — for he required veterans, shrewd swordsmen, who knew his methods

and did not require continual instructions. The rest were to
pack in behind, close, outward-facing. Cut the lance-shafts first,
hold your ground, keep your backs protected — these were the
only general orders he had time to give, before the enemy were
upon them.

Greystoke and his leading files tried to reach them on horseback, to ride them down. But quickly they were brought to a
realisation that this was impossible. Dismounting, they moved
in for the fight.

Wallace heaved a sigh of relief. As they came up, he had been
looking for mounted archers. He saw a few, not many. Evidently Greystoke was not relying on these — although, if they
all stood back, the bowmen could shoot down the Scots one by
one, without risk to themselves. But there was an advantage in
having a young knight in command. Knights of blood and
family, other than Edward's knighted veteran captains, were at
one in looking down their proud noses at archers, as a kind of
tradesmen, artificers in the game of war, people only to be
employed when more chivalric fighting was impossible. The
sword, the lance, the mace, even the battle-axe — these were the
weapons of gentlemen. Sir John Butler had been otherwise
minded; but he had not been typical.

So the inevitably protracted, ding-dong battle commenced.
The English were faced with a tight, irregularly-shaped formation of some fifty men, with some eight tough and experienced
swordsmen forming a front around Wallace, soft bog all
around. As expected, the enemy came in first with their lances
awkward as the seven-foot-long shafts were to handle, dismounted and staggering in mire. The ash wood was tough, but
it was not proof against flailing steel, and, after a parried thrust,
was difficult to bring to bear again quickly. It was not long
before such lances as remained in one piece tended to be cast
aside in favour of more wieldable swords.

The Scots role had to be almost purely defensive meantime;
but as such it was highly effective. Attack after attack was
beaten off, with the enemy more tired and frustrated after each.

Wallace was too busy to do much glancing around and
behind. He did not know what the Graham was doing, nor
Kirkpatrick either. He hoped that they had both sized up the
situation and were moving in to his aid. If they could see the
elementary advantage of riding around and coming in at the
rear of the enemy, the position would be transformed. There

were the thirty or so English behind Kirkpatrick, of course, who still had to be thought of.

Alas for his hopes. The first Wallace knew of Sir John Graham was when that young man, in handsome if mud-spattered half-armour, spoke to him from behind his own shoulder. He had joined Wallace's group from the rear, dismounted his men, and pushed his way up the formation, to report his presence, sheer satisfaction glowing in his voice.

Wallace was less pleased. Fending off a sword-thrust and following up with one of his own, he jerked back. 'Graham, man — not here! Attack the rear. Get your men mounted. Work round. Threaten their rear. Quickly!'

Sir John looked shattered, opened his mouth to protest, shut it again, gulping, and turned away.

'Is Kirkpatrick as lacking in wits?' the big man cried, to those around him.

None were in a position to answer him.

In a few minutes, however, the frustrated Wallace had reason to feel better, for he witnessed the detachment of Moreland's company, who had apparently abandoned chasing Kirkpatrick, come in to do exactly the same thing as Graham had done, on the other side, circling round from the west to come up behind Greystoke, there to dismount and hurry forward to his aid. It seemed to him incredible that men should be so lacking in the elements of tactics, even by instinct.

Now he had all the enemy before him, and no more effective than they had been before the reinforcement.

In the event, the Graham's delayed encircling move was perhaps all for the best. For Kirkpatrick, with his sixty, however tardy in his return to the scene of action, at least perceived his opportunity, and drove round to the southern side of the expanse of bog from the west, to the rear of the English. He had drawn up there, somewhat at a loss as to what to do next, when Sir John and his well-mounted contingent of about thirty came cantering round, east-abouts — and the young knight, with his reputation to redeem, took charge. Still mounted, and without pause, he led the combined force in a spirited if ragged assault on the enemy rear, shouting 'A Graham! A Graham!'

At last Wallace had the situation he had envisaged and worked for. With a great cry, he raised his mighty brand on high. 'A Wallace! A Wallace!' he yelled in turn, and started to move forward.

A strange advance that formation made, slow, squelching, deliberate — and possibly the more menacing for that. Smiting as he went, Wallace sought to change the formation to that of an arrowhead. And back before its plodding onslaught, the weary cavalrymen fell — to become rudely aware of the mounted assault at their backs, however bogged-down it was becoming.

Suddenly panic overtook the Englishmen. One moment they were fighting as effectively as they could in such circumstances, the next, as though to a signal, all were seeking to flee. Every man sought to grab the nearest horse available, even to fight his fellows for it. Greystoke saw the situation was hopeless here, and fled with the rest.

Chaos followed, with the enemy, mounted and otherwise, hurrying off in all directions — and being pursued by Graham's and Kirkpatrick's men, also in all directions. The horses of Wallace's party were, of course, well to the rear now, and so they could do nothing about any chase meantime. Greystoke, and a group of those closest to him, were going to escape, mainly on the horses of the Moreland detachment.

Furiously Wallace raised hands to cup his lips. 'Graham!' he shouted. 'Graham, Sir John! Gather your men. Lead them, man — lead them! After yon knight — Greystoke. They will win free. After them, a God's name! I want Greystoke dead!'

How much of all that young Sir John heard was not to be known. But the anger, the authority and the pointing hand were not to be mistaken. Hastily the Graham abandoned his personal chase, and called to his men to close in on him. Belatedly and in no very good order, most of his party streamed away after the tight group of the English leadership. Their youthful chief had had an abrupt and less than glorious introduction to the realities of warfare.

Wallace let out a great sigh. 'Save us — have you ever seen the like!' he demanded. 'A slaister in the mud! A fools' cantrip! Bairns' work. Nothing done aright. By myself, or most others!'

'A victory, nevertheless,' his nephew Tom Halliday asserted. 'The day is ours. What more do you want?'

'That was no victory, Tom. That was a nonsense and broil. If we look like the winners, I swear it is by chance and error!'

'You were hard on that young man Graham,' Thomas Gray said, wiping the sweat from his tonsured brow. 'Trained in tourneys and knightly games, how should he know better? All have not your genius for war, Will.'

'You say so? Well, then — I stand rebuked. Aye — I was hasty. He had no orders to work to. He could know naught of what was required. Yet ... it seemed so evident. A babe might have perceived the need!'

'He came to our aid when we needed aid.'

'You are right, friend. I was at fault. I shall seek Sir John's pardon. But, now — we have more to do than stand here in the mud like old men gossiping. Our day's work is still to do!'

Something like a groan arose from those who heard him.

'Have you forgot?' he demanded. 'We did not set out to fight or win battles — even by error! We set off to capture Lochmaben Castle. All that we have achieved, so far, is to decoy its garrison out, and seek ensure that it does not return. That is why I was so wrath when Greystoke was allowed to ride off — lest he won his way back, and shut himself up in Lochmaben again. As still he might do.'

'No, no — Graham will get them, Will. Broken and weary as they are ...'

'That we cannot swear to. God aiding me, I want to be at Lochmaben before Greystoke is, anyway. Kerlie — see that Kirkpatrick and his people look to all those here. And the wounded. Bury the dead. The rest — to horse, my friends. Lochmaben is fourteen rough miles. Let us see how swiftly we may reach it.'

* * *

The short winter's day was all but over when they clattered into and through the town of Lochmaben, in the dusk. The Bruce's castle rose beyond, at the far end of the loch, mighty, menacing. A little way from it, at a hollow of the shore, Wallace halted his hardriding, weary party.

'Even without a garrison, a score of us cannot take Lochmaben by force. Guile is required. Watson, man — slip you forward, on foot. Discreetly. See what is to do. See whether the bridge is up, or the portcullis down, or the gates barred.'

Watson was back in a few minutes, to announce that the portcullis was up, but that the drawbridge was half-up, half-down. The gates seemed to be open. There was no sign of activity.

'That means that they still await the return of the garrison, I think,' Wallace said. 'The bridge only half-up.' He looked behind him, thoughtfully. 'We will wait for a little longer see

164

you. This gloaming light — I could wish it a little darker. But before they light torches. We must not allow Greystoke, or any others, to reach the castle. Ed — gc you back to the outskirts of the town, and keep watch. Warn us if any of the English come. Now — here is my plan. We have Moreland's banner. And this his grey charger. It is a kenspeckle beast. Tom Halliday — you will ride it. I am too large. Here is his plumed helm — put it on. Watson — you know the gate porter, do you not? And by name?'

'Aye — Gideon Jardine. He is head-porter. I've kenned him all my days.'

'Good. Then mount you another of the captured horses. And you, Kerlie, on another — and carry Moreland's banner, be his standard-bearer. John, go with them. The four of you — Moreland and three men-at-arms. Ride to the bridgehead. Watson to shout for the bridge to be lowered, for Sir Hugo de Moreland. Then over at the trot. Overpower the guard if you can. If not, at least keep the bridge from being raised again. We shall not be far behind. You have it?'

Grinning, all assured that they did indeed have it.

After some twenty minutes of impatient waiting, with no word from Ed Little, they decided that it was sufficiently dark for details to be indistinct. But the banner, the plumed helmet and the grey charger would be reasonably clear. The four men were sent forward.

In only two or three minutes they all clearly heard the clanking of the drawbridge chains. Presently they heard the hollow beat of hooves on its timbers. That was enough for Wallace.

'Come!' he cried, and spurred his new mount into a canter.

It was all ridiculously easy, a complete anti-climax. Beating their horses, the fifteen or so men thundered over the bridge and under the portcullis arch, swords out — to find everything quiet and under control. One dead man lay at the door of the gatehouse. Two others, unarmed, stood by, looking bewildered. Tom Halliday said that apart from these, there were only women and children left in the castle. Kerlie and John Blair had gone up to see that the keep door was not barred against them.

They all stared at each other, in the half-light. Lochmaben, one of the greatest castles in the South-West was theirs — with one blow struck. It almost seemed an incidental, at the end of a busy day.

When Sir John Graham and Harry Kirkpatrick arrived

together, an hour or two later, it was to find, with considerable astonishment, the Scottish saltire banner, lit up by blazing beacons, flying above the keep of Lochmaben, and — a nice touch — the Bruce flag flapping beside it, one such having been found in the castle. Half Lochmaben town was there to stare at the sight — and bonfires were beginning to gleam on eminences round about. For this was the first victory where Wallace could have dared anything of the sort. Here the garrison for a whole district was wiped out, a strong fortress won, and no enemy forces in a position to do anything about it for a matter of days, at least. There was a small garrison at Dumfries, and another at Caerlaverock — but not more than fifty in each. Percy at Ayr and Hazelrigg at Lanark, were the nearest English commanders strong enough to tackle Lochmaben — and in the circumstances, they would be apt to move with some circumspection.

The victors made sure that Wallace's name was on every lip. Wallace was not dead. Wallace was back in the South-West. Let the English take note — and the Scots nobility likewise.

One Scots noble, at anyrate, was a happy man that night. Wallace made a virtue out of a necessity. When the gatehouse informed him that Sir John and Kirkpatrick were outside, with their men, he ordered the score or so with him in the castle to assemble in the fire-lit torch-lit inner bailey, and for the drawbridge to be lowered with some ceremony, the portcullis raised, trumpets to be blown. When the two young men came riding in — for Kirkpatrick was scarcely into his majority, two years older than the Graham — it was to find Wallace waiting to greet them, at the head of two ordered lines of his companions.

'Sir John the Graham,' he cried, deep-voiced, 'And Kirkpatrick of Torthorwald — I, William Wallace, salute you! In victory and in honour. This day you have played a part which shall be remembered in Scotland — aye, and furth of Scotland! We have today taught the proud usurpers a lesson — and, pray God, our own countrymen also. For the noble part you and your men have taken in it, I thank you from the bottom of my heart.'

To the ringing cheers of his supporters, Wallace stepped forward to shake the hastily dismounting pair by the hand. The Graham, who had been expecting a rather different welcome, was quite speechless; but Kirkpatrick, a brash young man, hooted, part-embarrassed, part-mocking laughter.

But Wallace was not finished. 'Sir John,' he went on, 'when

last I spoke to you, it was in a fashion unsuitable in a commander, and disrespectful to a knight, and heir to a great and
chiefly house. It did me no credit. In the heat of the battle I
forgot myself, and your situation. I crave your pardon, sir,
before these all — since it was before all that I did offend.'

The younger man clutched the other's great arm, his features
working with emotion. He shook his head — which was as far as
he seemed to be able to go. Wallace was satisfied. 'Up with the
bridge, Sanders,' he shouted. 'Down with the portcullis.
Kerlie — post the guard. For the rest, come you and join me at
dinner in Bruce's hall. The English have left us a notable store
of victuals. Let us do justice to their provision . . .'

CHAPTER NINE

St. Mary's Red Friars Monastery at Fail made an excellent
headquarters for Wallace — much better than could Lochmaben, which might have been turned into a death-trap, and which
he had no intention of trying to hold, appointing Tom Halliday's son-in-law, Johnstone of Eskdale as captain, with instructions to abandon it without hesitation if the pressure grew
too strong. It had served its main purpose. But Fail Monastery
was entirely different. Situated on the edge of the low country
between Lanark and Ayr, it was an ideal spot from which to
keep watch on the English garrisons and their doings. There was
a constant coming and going of monks and friars from other
religious establishments, far and near, which meant not only that
strangers were not very evident, but that news was always circulating. Enmity to the invader could be taken for granted
amongst churchmen; and gratitude towards Wallace for the
rescue of the church plate and treasure at Loudoun Hill was a
strong bond. Add to all that the establishment's reputation for
good living, celebrated by Sir Thomas the Rhymer in one of his
jingles:

> The friars of Fail drank berrybrown ale
> The best that e'er was tasted;

> They never wanted gear enough,
> So long as their neighbours' lasted!

None of the monks, from the Prior downwards — who, oddly enough, was known as the minister — seemed to find this label offensive.

But Fail had this disadvantage — except in an emergency, women were not admitted. Wallace could not have Marion with him, therefore — which meant a deal of night-time travel between North-East Ayrshire and South-West Lanarkshire, over the 25-mile gap.

From Fail he carried out two or three minor raids, as the days lengthened, but all well away from the immediate neighbourhood, on the principle that it is a dirty bird which fouls its own nest. They were minor affairs, designed only to keep up the pressure, to keep men talking about Wallace and revolt, the English in anxiety and wrath, the Scots in hope. For himself, he was planning now a major rising for the late spring or early summer.

The Graham's adherence was now generally known, and it brought in another well-born recruit, Sir Bryce Blair of that Ilk, an Ayrshire laird of broad acres — no kin to John Blair, who hailed from Perthshire. Sir Bryce did not bring many men with him, but promised a large number when the need arose. Meanwhile he was welcome, as demonstration that Wallace was not just the low-born brigand that the English made out, if proud knights such as these were prepared to serve under him.

In March, in the company of the two knights, he made a swift tour round certain of the nobility and landed men from whom he had hopes of support, seeking firm promises of men-at-arms for the rising. Starting with Sir Neil Montgomerie, and his brother, Sir Hugh, of Eaglesham, Sir Alexander Lindsay of Crawford and Sir Hugh de Eglinton, he secretly worked his way northwards. He interviewed the Steward again, and found him less sympathetic than formerly — possibly because he had with him his brother, Sir John Stewart of Bonkyl, who was less cautious in admitting his hatred of the English, but outright in his refusal to look on William Wallace, a vassal, as any sort of leader for noblemen. They would act in their own good time, Sir John averred; indeed their plans were well advanced. But he did not divulge what these plans were, and the Steward was little more forthcoming. He had been south to Surrey's con-

168

ference in Northumberland, of course, along with the earls and sheriffs and had perhaps come home with a somewhat changed attitude.

Disappointed, Wallace pressed on with his visits, in Renfrewshire, West Lanarkshire and Glasgow. He saw Bishop Wishart again, who was admiring of what the young man had achieved, friendly and more hopeful. Glasgow would provide its due quota of armed men, he assured. Indeed there were plans afoot for a major uprising. He could not say more, meantime — all were sworn to secrecy. But matters were moving, at last.

Intrigued, but just a little perturbed, the trio moved on. It looked as though the nobles, or some of them, were at length preparing to assert themselves — but they were not going to cooperate with Wallace and his guerillas.

He had intended to go on to Loch Lomondside to see the Earl of Lennox — but learned at Glasgow that Lennox was nearer at hand than that. He was in fact installed in the royal castle of Dumbarton, the great guardian fortress of the Clyde estuary — of which indeed, he was the hereditary keeper. But previously he had been expelled from there by King Edward, and Sir John Stewart, Tutor of Menteith, a co-operator with the English, installed in his place as Sheriff of Dumbarton — much to the Earls's offence. Now, it seemed, Stewart had been appointed Sheriff and Governor of Perth, in lieu of the late Heron; and Lennox had come back from the Northumberland conference to be keeper of Dumbarton again. It certainly made a more convenient winter residence than Inchmurrin isle in Loch Lomond.

Nevertheless, Wallace changed his mind about his visit to the Earl — perhaps unfairly. It might be that he was growing too suspicious; but it seemed unlikely that Edward's Viceroy would have given Lennox back the fortress which held the keys of the Clyde without some *quid pro quo*, or at least assurances that he could rely on the Earl not to injure his cause. If that was so, then Dumbarton was no place for William Wallace. He came to that conclusion very regretfully, for Lennox he had come to think of as his friend. And while he, of Celtic stock himself, had been prepared to have his doubts about the allegiances of the proud Scot-Norman lords, related as so many of them were to still more proud Anglo-Norman lords — Lennox was not of these, but one of the ancient Celtic earls of Scotland. Instead of going to Lennox, then, Wallace and his companions made a few more calls in the Campsie area and the Kelvin valley, before moving on to Dundaff, where the Graham believed that he could pick up a few more men. Sir John was already twice the man he had been when he left his remote castle in the Carron valley, to go soldiering. His mother, presently, considered the the transformation doubtfully.

It was at Dundaff that Stephen MacGregor found them, after much travel. He brought grim news. Sir William de Hazelrigg, self-styled Earl of Clydesdale — he was no earl, but Edward's sheriff thereof — had hanged young Hugh Braidfoot, Marion's brother. Hanged him on a charge of rebellion — although the young man had done nothing. Undoubtedly it was only because he was Wallace's brother-in-law. Marion had gone to Lanark to help console her stepmother, sisters and sister-in-law.

Wallace and MacGregor left Dundaff at once. The two knights would follow on, with the additional men.

*   *   *

Lanark being only partly a walled town, there was little difficulty in entering it by back ways under cover of darkness. Wallace came to the Braidfoot house in the Castlegait, via its orchard at the rear — and had to wait at the door for a considerable time while his identity was established, bars drawn and chain unhooked, the place secured as though against siege. Marion welcomed him with a mixture of relief and anxiety; for glad as she was to see him, she feared that it all might be a trap, that Hazelrigg might calculate that he, Wallace, would come, and might have the house watched. Her husband admitted the validity of this, but declared that he had had to take the chance. He would leave before dawn, and not be caught in Lanark in daylight.

He learned little more about Hugh Braidfoot's death than he had already heard. Totally unexpectedly, without any warning, Hazelrigg's soldiers had arrived at Lamington and taken Hugh away — for questioning by the Sheriff, they said. Whether Hazelrigg had indeed questioned him, there was no knowing; but he had hanged him that self-same day, without trial. Afterwards, it had been declared that he was involved in rebellion and brigandry — Wallace's rebellion. This was wholly false, for young Braidfoot had taken no part. But Hazelrigg knew that his sister was married to Wallace — and that was enough.

170

Wallace in his sorrow, sympathy and sense of guilt, nevertheless wondered at that. After all, Hazelrigg had known of his relationship with the Braidfoots for long. Why had he waited until now to take young Hugh? He must have had a reason. And it was only common sense to infer that most probably that reason was linked to Wallace's own situation. Had it been merely to bring him here, coax him into the town? And Mirren? Both of them — to Lanark. If so, they had not far to look for further trouble.

Marion grew so anxious for him that she would have had him leave there and then. But he said that, since he was safely in, he might as well stay awhile. The danger, if any, would be when he came to leave.

It was decided that all the Braidfoots were better out of Lanark for a while — though moving the invalid stepmother would be a problem. It had to be done secretly, too, if possible. Wallace would try to arrange it, and quickly.

Mirren and he went to bed.

Perhaps, not unnaturally, they were later than intended in awakening. Indeed, it was the church bells pealing for early morning mass, which aroused them, just after dawn. Cursing, Wallace threw on his clothes. Marion now urged him to stay, not to go, to wait until evening again, and darkness; but he would not hear of it. He would slip out, while the faithful were going to church, perhaps mingle with them.

Taking hasty farewell, he was let out at the back door, the girl clinging to him fiercely before she would let him go.

Through the orchard he ran, and opened the door in the garden wall beyond, to peer out. All seemed to be clear, in the lane there. Slipping out, he turned right-handed. And as he did so, on the left, half-a-dozen men leapt from the cover of a wood-shed, swords drawn.

Wallace had not brought his sword on this clandestine visit to his wife, and was armed only with a dirk. One dirk against six swords was too great odds even for that man. He took to his heels.

He had intended, a few yards along the lane to cut through a couple of cottage gardens and so out on to the open common land of the burgh, where whins and broom bushes would have given him cover. But that would entail climbing two high stone walls, and with these men so close behind he had no time for that. Instead, he darted down an alleyway between the houses, on the right. This led into the main street — and he knew very well that if the back of the Braidfoots' house was being watched, the street front was unlikely to be left unguarded. But such watchers would not be warned, he hoped. If he turned up-street . . .

He gained on his pursuers, down that alley, for his stride was longer than theirs. As he raced out into the street, he glanced right. Sure enough, lined up across the causeway from the Braidwood gable-end was another dozen or so of soldiers.

They saw him at once, of course, and the hue and cry arose. Even so, this group were further behind than were the first half-dozen.

Up the quite steeply-rising street Wallace ran, some forty yards ahead of the foremost — until, in front of him, a hundred yards or so up, he saw more men fanning out from each side, to block the street entirely.

He had only brief moments for decision. The church of St. Nicholas stood there, on the right, its bell now silent but its door still open. With a pause in his running, the man slewed round and dashed for the church's portal.

Inside, he slammed the door shut behind him and dropped the bar with a clang — and the priest, intoning his office, stopped abruptly. Wallace raced down from the back of the nave to the choir, through the worshippers kneeling on the stone-flagged floor — and everywhere shocked and scandalised faces were raised. He lifted a hand as he ran.

'Wallace!' he cried, 'Wallace!' not any war-cry, but a plea for understanding, pardon. A banging and thudding began at the barred door behind him.

In front of the sanctuary he ran, and though he did not pause, he nodded his head towards the Presence Light as he passed — for he was a man of faith, however inadequate. The officiating priest stared, but did not move nor cry out, and the acolyte with the censer gaped open-mouthed.

To the priest's side door he ran, vaulting the altar rail at that end. Opening the door, he paused in the entrance, turned, and raised his hand again, in salutation. Then he closed the door behind him, this time without a slam.

Unfortunately the priest's door led only into a dead-end lane, hemmed in with houses. He darted round the first of the gable-ends but could find no exit, and realised that he would have to

172

go back into the main street. At least, the soldiery all ought to be further up.

He steeled himself to emerge on to the street at a walk, not running, as less eye-catching. But he had only gone a few steps down when a halloo from further up warned him that he was spotted. He began to run again.

It was then that another cry reached him, from just across the street. It was, in fact, Marion, at her own open front door.

'Will! In here!' she called urgently. 'In — and out at the back again.'

He hesitated, if only for a moment. He did not want the English bursting into this house. On the other hand, it would give him an extra precious few seconds. And Marion was already stepping out into the street in her eagerness. He ran to her, and in — and she banged the door shut, and slid the greased bar into its socket.

They wasted no time on talk. He pounded through the house, gripped and squeezed the young woman's arm at the back door, and was out again, leaping up the orchard. At the gate he saw the lane was deserted. Slanting across it he plunged through the cottage gardens, and clambered over the two walls and into the rough common land beyond. Up the slope, amongst the whin bushes and broom he bounded — and began to breathe freely again, however deeply. On this terrain he would outrun any English soldier. Horse he would have to look out for — but such would take time to send after him.

He began a lengthy circling flight, right about, making for the rocky wilderness of Cartland Crags, where he had left MacGregor and where neither horse nor foot would be able to reach him, short of any army and full-scale siege.

That night he was back in Gillbank, and summoning his friends for a council the next day.

It was the next morning that a Braidfoot serving-wench, from Lanark, brought the dreadful tidings. Marion Braidfoot was dead — slain by Hazelrigg, for aiding the escape from justice of her husband, the outlaw William Wallace.

*   *   *

For two whole days and nights Wallace shut himself in his room and would not speak with any, would not eat nor drink. And for two days his friends and colleagues tip-toed about and hardly spoke, themselves, in a state of profound sorrow, disquiet,

173

apprehension. Gillbank was like a mort-house — but with the threat of terrible eruption, explosion in its hush.

Nevertheless, on the third morning, Wallace emerged quiet, sane, not so much subdued as mightily damped down. The first expression of sympathy, by his cousin Auchinleck, was cut short as though by a knife-slash — and after that no one referred to Marion's death.

The big man had never been more practical and businesslike, indeed, Hazelrigg was to die, and quickly. There was to be no delay, no distraction, no possibility of failure. It would be a careful, methodical operation. None were asked whether or no they would take part in its hazards; all were merely, and clearly, informed as to their duties. It was a new William Wallace who had come from that locked room.

A dozen of them would be sufficient, he declared; larger numbers no advantage. They would slip into Lanark that same night, by different approaches, each little group with a target. Hazelrigg occupied the Governor's Lodging, in the requisitioned hospice of the Knights Templar, the best building in the town. His deputy, Sir Robert Thorn, whose position was Governor of Lanark, had a fine house nearby, also in Friars Lane. The captain of the guard would be in the new castle, not yet finished; and most of the soldiery bedded in the old castle, now used as a barracks. A fire at the barracks would distract the guard. Wallace reserved Hazelrigg for himself. He allocated their duties to the others.

They waited until dusk before setting out from Gillbank, for the later in the night the attack, the better. Sir John Graham, arriving from Stirlingshire in the meantime with a score more men, was quickly warned about any display of sympathy, and incorporated in the exercise.

They parted company on the outskirts of the town at around three o'clock on a windy morning. Wallace who had chosen Kerlie to be his own companion, found that his cousin Auchinleck had attached himself, saying that he also had a score to settle with Hazelrigg. They of course knew every alley and corner of Lanark, and had no difficulty in finding their way to Friars Lane and the former Hospice of St. John. This was screened from the street by a courtyard wall, with an arched doorway therein, guarded by two sentries. Further up from them a little way, the trio waited in a dark entry.

It was some time before a ruddy glow to the south, and then

the smell of burning on the night air, proclaimed their message. The sentries, in desultory conversation, did not notice it for what seemed an unconscionable time. Then they both ran out into the street, exclaiming, to stare southwards towards the area of the two castles on their hill — and into the archway they had left three shadows slipped soundlessly. When, in some excitement the pair came back, one telling the other to go warn his lordship that the Old Castle seemed to be afire, his instructions were choked off by an arm crooked round his neck from behind, and a dirk thrust upwards below his jack stilled his voice for ever. His companion was similarly dealt with, without a cry uttered.

The three intruders ran across the flagged courtyard to the main door of the hospice. It appeared to be locked, or barred. Wallace drew back a pace or two, and flung his weight against it, with his entire force. In a splintering of wood it burst open.

Inside, all was dark. With the noise they had made, haste was now vital. They raced for the stairs; the bedchambers would be on the floors above.

They heard a door open up there, and a man's voice demanding authoritatively what was the noise, in God's name? Emerging from the head of the turnpike stair, Wallace all but collided with a heavily-built man, seemingly clad only in a bed-robe. It was too dark to distinguish features — but the Sheriff was heavily-made.

'Hazelrigg?' Wallace jerked.

'I am the Earl of Clydesdale,' the other rasped. Sheriff and . . .' He got no further.

'Then die, murderer,' he was interrupted. 'I am Wallace.' And the dirk rose and fell, with savage precision.

With a groan, the self-styled earl sank to his knees, swaying. Without pause, Wallace ran on. Auchinleck, next behind, stabbed the dying man twice more, as though his cousin might have failed to deliver a mortal thrust.

A young man came lurching out of another doorway, sword in hand, calling out and using the word Father — presumably Hazelrigg's son, whom Wallace had heard much of as an insolent womaniser. He raised the sword as he saw the big man, but, bemused with sleep as he was, he was not quick enough. A leather-bound left arm swept aside the blade, and the already bloodstained dirk rose and fell once more. Young Hazelrigg crashed backwards to the floor.

There were women's cries now, but Wallace was not concerned with them. Leaving Kerlie and Auchinleck to deal with any other men in the house, he ran downstairs and out. He felt nothing, no triumph, no vengeance fulfilled, no emotion of any sort. He was an instrument, that was all, an instrument with work to do, and which had to be effective. The effectiveness, now, was all.

Out in the street he found Sir John Graham hurrying to report. He had not waited for the fire at the Old Castle, but had burned Sir Robert Thorn's house around its occupier. They had cut the Governor down as he ran out. Was Hazelrigg dead? Then — might they not now take all Lanark town, with the leaders gone?

'Take a garrison town with a dozen men, and the garrison roused!' Wallace exclaimed. 'There speaks folly. We have done what we came to do. Now we must be out, while we may.' He raised his horn, to sound the Recall. 'Back to Gillbank ...'

Part Two

CHAPTER TEN

The Seagate Castle of Irvine was guarded like a fortress rather than what it was, the town mansion of the de Eglinton family, in a seaport street. Wallace and his two travel-worn companions had some difficulty in gaining access past the multiplicity of guards, that June evening. It was the Steward's name which eventually gained them entrance, not Wallace's own.

The great hall on the first floor was crowded with a colourful throng, more fitted in aspect for a tournament than a serious council-of-war. Coming in, Wallace and John Blair and Rob Boyd, in their rusty chain-mail, battered breastplates and scuffed leather, looked as out-of-place as mourners at a wedding, amongst all the polished and engraved armour, the coloured heraldic surcoats and furred cloaks. Just within the doorway, they stared at all that galaxy of pride and gallantry and high-born power, at something of a loss.

None appeared to notice their unheralded entrance at first. Most of the company sat around a great central table, laden with wines, fish, meats and sweets, eating and drinking as they argued and debated. And the debate was vigorous, noisy, even acrimonious, with many authoritative voices refusing to be out-talked. The discussion was all in Norman French, of course.

'Ha — Wallace!' It was the Bishop of Glasgow who first perceived them — or at least, first acknowledged their presence. 'Will Wallace!' he called. He actually rose to his feet, small and stocky, but resplendent in armour painted with the episcopal devices of the See of Glasgow. 'Come, man — come, that I may shake you by the hand!'

A silence gradually descended on that large apartment, as everywhere men turned to stare. The Steward looked up from his place near the head of the table, dressed all in sable-black armour; but he did not raise hand or voice to his vassal.

Wallace came into the centre of the chamber, his friends close at each shoulder. He bowed.

'My lord Bishop,' he said. 'My lord High Steward. My good

179

lords all — greetings. This is, I think, a good and great day for Scotland.' he looked around him, with just the hint of a smile. 'And a fine night to be up and doing, sirs!'

No one actually answered that, although there was a certain amount of murmuring and comment, not all of it complimentary it seemed. Who, after all was this second son of a small knight, to make such remarks to his betters?

'As you say, my son,' the Bishop nodded — and since Wallace did not come closer, he moved out from his seat to shake the other's hand. It was a very notable gesture of solidarity and esteem, in that company; but, as notable, Wallace did not fail to perceive, in that the Bishop considered it to be necessary or advisable.

Sir Andrew Moray, Lord of Pettie and Bothwell, now also came forward to greet the trio — which was likewise not strictly necessary, for they had met only a few days before; indeed, it was at Moray's suggestion that Wallace had come from Ettrick Forest to attend at this council in Seagate Castle. It was late June, and at long last Moray had ventured across the Highland Line — but not with his army; prudently, he had left that behind in Breadalbane somewhere, whilst he investigated conditions in the South, both the state of his family's Lowland property around Bothwell, and the effectiveness or otherwise of this movement towards revolt. He was a handsome, well built young man, not yet thirty, with a very slight stoop to his shoulders which gave him a distinctly hawk-like appearance.

Whether or no Sir Andrew Moray considered this a great day for Scotland he did not reveal. But he had intimated to Wallace, four days before, that he had grave doubts as to the ability of the Scottish lords to work together. The Steward, and Bishop Wishart, with Sir John Stewart of Bonkyl, Thomas Dalton, Bishop of Galloway and sundry others, had indeed raised the standard of revolt in Galloway six weeks earlier — to Wallace's great rejoicing. But they had not been particularly successful or aggressive, and had fought no real actions — for, in fact, none of them were soldiers. It was not until Sir William, Lord of Douglas, joined them from where he had been hiding in Dumfries-shire, that they began to achieve results, for he was at least a veteran campaigner, however awkward a man to work with. They had taken a few castles and small towns, and destroyed some English garrisons; but there had been no major fighting, for the enemy did not consider Galloway to be greatly import-

ant and had no large forces there — which was why the rising had
been started there. The Scots army had now worked its way up
the Ayrshire coast to Irvine, again without any serious battle,
and the great debate here was as to what to do now. The trouble
was, all the Scots lords who had at length allowed themselves to
become involved, advocated different courses. Most wanted any
thrust that was made to be in the direction of their own lands,
so that their districts could be cleared of the English first.
Douglas demanded a descent on the Borders; the Steward and
Wishart advocated aiming first at Renfrewshire and Glasgow;
Moray wanted them to move across Forth and Clyde into the
North, to join with his own force and form a real army which
could seriously threaten the English occupation, not just parts
of it.

The pause caused by Wallace's entry was soon over, and
voices were upraised again in dispute. The big man, looking
around him, frowned. This was not a council or a conference,
but a comprehensive bicker. It appeared as though there was
nobody in command. All were too high-born, too assertive of
their own rank and status and quality to accept any other as
leader. The High Steward had the authority, no doubt, but he
was not a man of forceful personality, a scholar rather than a
warrior; and Bishop Wishart, although the second most important of the Lords Spiritual, *was* only a churchman, and son of a
Mearns laird. Wallace recognised a few of the loud-voiced
lords, but only a small proportion — the Lords of Douglas,
Crawford, Cunninghame, Sir Hugh Montgomerie, Sir Hugh de
Eglinton, their host here, and one or two others. They seemed to
be all from the South-West, save Moray; and none looked with
any great warmth at himself. Then his heart lifted a little as Sir
John Graham came into the room. At least he had a friend or
two present.

Near where Graham sat down, and talking to Sir Alexander
Lindsay of Crawford, was a young man, richly dressed, in his
early twenties probably, of medium height but well made, with
broad shoulders and narrow hips. Not handsome but of ar-
resting looks nevertheless, strong, rugged for one so young,
almost bony of feature, with grey keen eyes under wavy auburn
hair the colour of Wallace's own. The big man noticed him in
the throng, partly because of his looks and something of vivid
character therein, partly because he was so obviously looking at
and speaking about himself, Wallace.

He waited a little longer, but not too long, standing there — for no one had suggested that he sit down to the table. He caught the Steward's eye more than once, but that mournful magnate seemed preoccupied with some sorrow of his own. At length Wallace had had enough — for he had work to do that night, if these had not. He raised his hand high.

'Hear me, my lords!' he cried — and when William Wallace wished his words to be heard, his voice could all but raise the rafters of even a castle hall. 'A moment of your time, I pray. Hear me.'

The chatter and argument died away momentarily, more in astonishment and offence than anything else, and he had all eyes turned on him — mainly Norman-French eyes in origin, for little of the old Celtic aristocracy was left in Southern Scotland.

'My friends,' he said into the hush, in a lesser voice, but deep, rumbling, still. 'I have news. I am new come from the Forest. From Ettrick. With news from the East March. Surrey, I am told, has despatched an army north from Newcastle. A great army. Forty-thousand foot no less. Though bare a thousand horse. Under command of Henry Percy. To deal with your rising, my lords.'

There was another and very different hush, as men stared at each other, appalled.

'Forty-thousand . . .!' Bishop Wishart could not disguise the quaver in his voice.

'Aye. So it is time to be up and doing, is it not, my friends? Not sitting here at table.' Deliberately, to give point to the need for action, not comfortable talk, he stepped forward and reached out a hand to grasp and tear off a foreleg of mutton from a roasted carcase on the board. He bit into it, there and then, standing there.

Another voice spoke up, strong, harsh, almost scornful. 'Forty-thousand foot will move but slowly,' the Lord of Douglas declared. 'Ten miles a day, no more. No need to spoil our dinner, man.'

'Sir Robert de Clifford at Berwick has thirty-thousand. Half cavalry. They will be on their way now. In advance of the greater host.'

'You are well informed, fellow!'

'I make it my business to be, my lord. Since my life could depend on it. Captured, lords are ransomed. *I* would hang!'

'That is true, at least!'

A great buzz of talk arose, argument given a new slant.

The Steward, his cadaverous features looking agitated, managed to gain quiet again. 'Certainly these tidings, if true, force us to a swift decision,' he said. 'And since this great host comes from the south, it would be folly, with our small numbers, to go to meet it. We must move north, then. Seek to raise more men.'

'I shall rest happier behind the walls of Glasgow town . . .'

'Rest, my lord Bishop?' Wallace took Wishart up. 'Rest, I swear, is no word for use this night. With much to do.'

'Tonight, man? You would have us move tonight? It is not possible. Such haste would be foolish as it is unseemly. Besides most men will be asleep.'

'So, I think, may be the English!'

'English? What English? What mean you?'

'The English in Ayr, my lord. But a few miles away. We must smite them. Before it is too late.'

'Attack Ayr? Tonight?'

'What folly is this?'

'Is the man mad?'

Everywhere voices were raised in protest.

'That is why I came to Irvine, my friends,' the big man asserted, when he could make himself heard. 'To take Ayr. While Percy is away.'

'The more fool you, then,' Douglas cried. 'Aye — away with you, and take it, man! If you can. Me, I shall finish my dinner. Douglas, for one, does not skulk by night, like some thief or cutpurse.'

'Aye — enough of this. Have done with such talk,' Stewart of Bonkyl said.

'You will not take a town and strong castle by night, Wallace.' That was Lindsay speaking now. 'Think you its walls will be unmanned, its bridge down, its gates open? These English are not as they were at Lanark, unawares. These know we are here, and will be on their guard. You will not take another castle by surprise.'

'No? That is my lord of Crawford speaking, is it not? Then hear this, Sir Alexander. Last night, from Ettrick, I came by Tweedsmuir and over into Upper Clydesdale. By Crawford, indeed. And took your Tower Lindsay in the by-going. Around midnight. Thirty Englishmen now hang from its parapets. That is all its garrison today. It is your house again, my lord

— cleansed of the enemy who held it. You may possess yourself of it, at will. As *I* did, last night!'

Not only Lindsay stared at the giant now, speechless.

'So, my lords — let us to Ayr,' Wallace said, mustering a smile.

Men eyed each other, ill at ease.

'This, this was a notable feat, Wallace,' the Steward got out, sucking in his spittle that went with his over-large tongue. 'And Tower Lindsay is a fine house. But Ayr is quite other. A town. With a great garrison, five hundred men, they say.'

'Nor do *we* go skulking and creeping in darkness. Like broken men and outlaws!' somebody said.

Bishop Wishart coughed. 'Besides, my son, it is against our policy. To waste our precious strength in reducing fortresses and castles. These can wait. When the land itself is ours, they will drop off like over-ripe fruit.'

'You believe so? Then ... you will give me no men, my lords? For this night's attempt? I have but fifty of my own band, here.' Wallace spoke quietly now.

'Fifty or five hundred — it would make no difference,' Douglas snorted.

'My lords — I think that we should consider this more fully,' another voice spoke up, one that had not intervened before. It came from the young man sitting beside Lindsay, the one with the bony, rugged features and the grey eyes. 'I believe that when we move Ayr should not be left behind us untouched. It could endanger us. Moreover, its fall, after Lanark, would be of great cheer, encouragement for all Scotland. I do not know about attacking it by night. Here I have no experience. But assault there should be.'

Wallace was eyeing the speaker keenly. 'Who speaks so, my friends?' he asked. 'I do not know this lord, I think.'

'It is the Earl of Carrick, man,' the Steward said shortly.

'Carrick! Bruce? The young Lord Robert? Edward's lordling — here!'

There were gasps, murmurs, a snigger or two. Bruce set his jaw, but did not respond.

'My lord Earl of Carrick has joined us, Will,' Bishop Wishart explained. 'With, with three hundred men.'

Wallace had not taken his eyes off the younger man, this pampered favourite of Edward Plantagenet. They said that the

184

King even paid his gaming debts for him. But his mind recollected Thomas the Rhymer's prophesy.

'Bruce a step to his throne shall take.'

Had the taking of Lochmaben really achieved this?

'Scotland's case must be better than I had known, then!' he commented carefully. 'But ...' He shrugged great shoulders. 'King Edward, it seems, is a good teacher. In war. *He* would not leave Ayr unassailed. The lord of Carrick is right in this.'

'No!' Douglas roared. 'Failure at Ayr would not only tie us down. It would spell the end of this rising. Until we have mustered a great force, we must keep moving ...'

'Is not that what I urge, my lords? To move. Now!' Wallace demanded. '*I* shall move at least. Here and now. For that I came. Alone, if I must. I go to Ayr. Who comes with me?'

There was a silence. Only Graham, who was already on his feet, raised his voice in the affirmative. For the rest, there was some shuffling of feet under the table, otherwise nothing.

'Very well. A good night to you, my lords. God be with you — and God help this poor Scotland!' Wallace threw down the gnawed leg of lamb, and strode for the door, John Blair and Kerlie almost having to run to keep up with him. Sir John Graham looked round the company of his peers, shrugged, and went after the trio.

*   *   *

Outside, on the beach below the narrow Seagate of Irvine, Wallace was ordering the fifty or so men, who had been waiting for him, to mount, when two others came following from the castle. By the light of a pale crescent moon in the half-dark of a June night, the big man, in process of mounting his own garron, peered at them.

'Who is this?' he asked. 'Ah — my Lord of Bothwell. Or should I say Pette? And, yes — it is the Bruce! What would you, sirs?' That was rather rapped out. William Wallace was a changed man since his wife's death, his mildness of manner burned out leaving only the basic steel.

'I would come with you. To see what fifty men may do. Against five hundred,' the Earl of Carrick said stiffly. 'If you will so much trust Edward's lordling!'

'Trust? I trust my eye, my arm and sword, and God's good mercy, my lord. Little else. But come if you will.'

185

Sir Andrew Moray opened his mouth to speak — and thought better of it.

The two noblemen turned to go for their horses, tethered in the horselines nearer the river-mouth.

'Wait for them, and bring them on, Sir John,' the big man said to the Graham. 'But of a mercy keep them out of my way. Men will die tonight. I would not make their deaths a peep-show for such gentry as these.'

'The Bruce is not all trifler, Will,' Sir John said. 'I have been watching him. He has something to him that the others lack. He was, I swear, the only man in yonder hall who had something of the same quality as yourself!'

'His quality, and mine, are as far apart as north is from south, Sir John. He is one of the great earls of Scotland — and well aware of it. And I am but William Wallace — outlaw! It was the English who outlawed me — but these Scots lords say the same. They *think* the same — Normans all! But, enough. Why waste time on such?' He raised his hand to his men, chopped it down to point forward, southwards, and kicked his garron into motion.

He led his band east-abouts, round Irvine town, to ford the river at Mossmill, and then, skirting the marshlands to the South-East, rode on to the far-flung sandy links of Fullarton and Gailes, along the edge of Irvine Bay, where the moonlight glimmered whitely on the long Atlantic rollers and made silver lacework in the shallows. It was now easy and unobstructed riding, even in the shadows, better indeed than these men were used to. Ayr lay a dozen miles ahead.

As they rode, Wallace's friends discussed the surprise adherence of the Bruce. Could the taking of Lochmaben Castle indeed have been responsible? It did not seem likely — for the English had not been long in retaking it, sending a major force against it, before which their own Johnstone had retired discreetly, as ordered. A quite well-known English commander, Sir Nicholas Segrave, was keeper there now. Bruce would scarcely have found this sufficient cause to turn his coat.

'Sooner or later young Bruce must needs assert himself against Edward,' Thomas Gray declared. 'He must consider himself heir to the throne which his father should have, now that Baliol is demoted and banished.'

'King John may be banished — by Edward,' Wallace interrupted them, almost curtly. 'But he is not, cannot be, demoted.

He has been duly crowned King of Scots, on the Stone of Destiny, our anointed monarch. He cannot be stripped of that position by any, especially an Englishman — even though that Englishman nominated him in the first place, out of malice and scheming. John, although consigned to France, is still King of Scots.'

'A name, nothing more." Edward Little said scornfully.

'Perhaps. But an important name. To us. Anything we do, not to be in brigandage indeed, must be done in that name. Let none forget it. Bruce may have a right to succeed — or, at least, his father may. But Scotland is an ancient kingdom and nation, and John is still its king — or coronations, anointings and vows before God mean nothing.'

Gray, a churchman, could not refute that. But he was not satisfied. 'Facts remain facts, Will,' he contended. 'The throne is to all intents empty. Edward has declared it abolished, and named Scotland one of his own provinces. The Bruces must either challenge that swiftly, or forfeit any claim they may have. And this young one is both proud and spirited, however irresponsibly reared. And he is only partly Norman, partly of the ancient blood, his mother of the ages-old line of Fergus, Lord of Galloway, Countess of Carrick in her own right. He has long centuries of our true Scots blood behind him. Unlike Baliol . . .'

Wallace shrugged. His opinion of all the lordly ones was at a low ebb. 'It may be so. But deeds will speak louder than blood!' he jerked, and spurred ahead.

With the narrow and low-lying headland of Troon curving out into the great bay on their right, the three young noblemen, faster-mounted, caught up with them. Even Moray, the eldest, was only twenty-five, and Bruce twenty-three. They were not received with any display — although Wallace had been working for the revolt of the nobility from the beginning.

They crossed the further links of Monkton and Prestwick, to turn inland and skirt the town of Ayr from the east. It was now well after midnight, and the town itself lay dark and sleeping. But a little way to seaward, the new castle evinced no aspect of slumber, for now fewer than eight blazing beacons gleamed on its high parapets and wallheads, lighting the grey June night ruddily. From this distance it was too far to distinguish men, but no doubt watchers patrolled those battlements. Sir William Douglas had been right in this, at least; the invaders did not intend to lose any more castles by surprise.

187

'English Arnulf does not sleep without watch-dogs!' Graham commented. Arnulf of Southampton was the new acting-Sheriff of Ayr. Sir Henry Percy had taken over the position of Sheriff himself, and after Hazelrigg's killing, deposing Sir Ranald Crawford, Wallace's maternal uncle, and appointing this Arnulf as deputy. With Percy summoned back to North-umberland to confer with Surrey the Viceroy, Arnulf lorded it here in the South-West, with his headquarters in Ayr.

'Even watch-dogs may blink. Or be chained,' Wallace returned.

They forded the River Ayr at Holm, where a sandy islet shallowed it, and circled round westwards again, through a terrain of knolls and broken pastureland, the common-lands of Ayr burgh, back towards the sea. They climbed a low ridge of whins and outcrops, startling sleeping cattle, and dismounted.

Ignoring the three nobles, Wallace gathered his lieutenants around him. Their plans had been made previously — only, they had hoped for more men, many more, from the lords. Now they must make do with what they had — but the plans remained substantially the same, like the leaders. The only change was that one, Scrymgeour, a trained soldier and college friend of Wallace from Dundee, who had joined them after Lanark, was sent with Gray to deal with the castle, he being know-ledgeable about fortifications. The company was therefore divided into three parties, about two dozen each under Gray and Kerlie, Wallace retaining only half-a-dozen with himself. Kerlie and Edward Little were sent off westwards, seawards. Master John Blair, the Dominican and young Robert Boyd, remained with Wallace. That man turned to the high-born trio.

'Come with us, my lords,' he called quietly. 'If creeping and skulking is not too much for your stomachs!'

If the others resented his tone, they did not declare it, aware that they were, in a sense, being tested. Aware also that this man had achieved more than all others put together, in the cause of freedom.

A bare half-mile further, nearer the sea, they were directed to leave their horses, tied up in a leafy hollow. They went on a little, moving quietly, past a pair of cot-houses and across some tilled land, the glow of the castle beacons, now not much more than a quarter-mile off, giving them long flickering shadows. There was some slightly rising ground ahead, dotted with black shapes — some of which proved to be bullocks, but most whin and broom bushes. Here Wallace crouched low himself, waving the others to their knees. The sound of the tide breaking on the shore was close now.

'As far as you may come,' he said to them, low-voiced. 'Wait you here. Do not move from this small ridge, see you, if you value your lives. For any man. not of my band, who moves out there tonight, dies!'

'What do you do?' the Earl of Carrick whispered. 'Why bring us here?'

'You will see, my lord, never fear. Just wait.'

'Is there nothing that *we* can do, Will?' Graham asked.

'No work for knights!' the other returned grimly. 'But if I have not come for you before two hours are past, do as you will. my lords. For William Wallace will be no more!'

'At least you can tell us something of what you plan,' Moray protested.

'I have not time, sirs. All is timed to a nicety. Say that I have a score to settle at Ayr this night. With the man Arnulf and his crew of forsworn murderers. We will endeavour to make the Barns of Ayr mean something other than they do at this present — God helping us!'

'The Barns of Ayr!' That phrase was not lost on any of them even Bruce, who was less well-informed about the fight for freedom than were the other two. Just after the news of the rising in Galloway broke, Arnulf, as Sheriff, had called a justice-ayres, as he named it, and summoned to meet and advise him most of the Ayrshire gentry, including Crawford the former Sheriff. They had come, not to the new and unfinished castle, but to the former storage barns of the common-land of Ayr, a large wooden building requisitioned and used as a barracks for the hundreds of soldiers brought from Lanark. And there, out of hand, Arnulf had hanged them all, the venerable Sir Ranald first, Sir Bryce Blair, Sir Hugh Montgomerie and innumerable others, strung them up from the Barn's rafters, as a warning to all would-be rebels against King Edward's peace.

'The Barns of Ayr lie just yonder,' Wallace said, pointing. And without another word, slipped away quietly, his men with him, leaving the knights to their own speculations. It was unfortunate for the Graham that tonight he was being classed as one of the nobility.

Silently Wallace and his companions ran down through the whins. The loom of a large building materialised before them, vaguely, against the wan sea, with the moon now lost behind clouds. They heard a man's involuntary curse, hastily smothered, amongst the bushes, as he jagged his hand on a whin thorn. All around them, now, Kerlie's men were cutting at the gorse bushes with their dirks, and carrying armfuls of the prickly stuff, to lay it against the walls and doors of the great barn, all in silence. Timber built and thatched, it was both long and lofty, two-storeyed and gabled, perhaps two hundred feet by forty wide, with many doors and windows, for it had had to serve the town's commoners for storing their hay, fleeces and hides.

Wallace found Kerlie at his side. 'Enough, Will, I think,' he whispered. 'Three sentries dirked. One made a squawk — but no alarm. Shall we light?'

'Aye — but mind, all to be lit at once. How many with flint and tinder?'

'Fifteen. A whaup's whistle to be the signal. Then the doors manned.'

'It should be sufficient.' Wallace moved over to near the largest door of the barn — and even his steeled heart quailed within him. But he drew his great sword.

After a little wait, the yittering call of a curlew wheepled out on the night air. And in seconds the flames began to appear, small points of red light at regular intervals around the walls. With fearsome speed they enlarged and spread, leaping, crackling, the whins blazing like torches. In only a matter of seconds, all had run together into a solid barrier of fire, entirely enclosing the building.

The timber boarding walls of the barn were as dry as any tinder, moreover coated with pitch to preserve the wood. They caught alight almost immediately, and the flames went licking up towards the thatch. The crackling became a roar.

It seemed extraordinary to the watchers how long an interval elapsed before there was any reaction from inside. The soldiers must have been heavy sleepers indeed, or drunken — although it probably was not so long as it appeared to the expectant, all but appalled, perpetrators of the fire; moreover the savage and growing snarl of the flames would tend to drown noises within. But at length the screams began, piercing, terrible, muffled as they were by the roaring, but heart-rending and ever increasing in number and volume until it was a continuous dreadful cacophony. The doors began to be flung open, and men appeared at the windows — which were, of course, without glass in a mere barn, hangings removed on a warm summer night, and into which 'the flames licked hungrily.

Outside, however their hearts might be wrenched at the sight and sound, the Scots waited grimly, swords and dirks ready.

Although the barriers of fire, and the menacing figures standing behind it, flickers glinting redly on their waiting steel, held back the first comers to the apertures furious pressure from behind soon forced them out, into the flames and beyond. And there they at least died quickly. Soon men were leaping from every window, many of them already alight as to hair and scanty clothing. None that the flames did not get, survived the steel.

But now the heavy thatch was alight and the terror grew, if that was possible, as blazing fragments fell amongst the packed and struggling humanity. Desperately the struggle to get out intensified — although the contrary effect was achieved, with every exit choked with clawing, fighting men. The smell that was beginning to come from that charnel-house was hard to stomach.

With a noise like thunder the heavy roof fell in, amidst great spouting columns of sparks — and with a horrible suddenness the major volume of screaming and shouting died away, so that individual shrieks could be heard again, thin and high. These, however, did not last long, and in only a few minutes from the first curlew's call, only the rumbling roar of the fire remained. Then another sound split the night, turning the head of Wallace and his men — the shrill braying of a trumpet from the walls of Ayr's unfinished castle, belated but urgent.

'At last!' Wallace jerked. 'I have been waiting for that. They have not been hasty! Now, they will sally out — and pray God, Gray and the Scrymgeour will have them. Arnulf cannot sit within and watch this!'

'Has Gray sufficient men, think you, Will . . .?'

'No. Have we ever sufficient men? Kerlie, and you John — see to all here. I take most of our people to go to their aid. John, when all is over here, go you to those fine lords on yonder ridge, and bring them to Ayr Castle. If we have not taken it, you will know!'

Great voice raised against the noise of the fire, he summoned his men.

They hastened northwards, in the direction of the castle, less than five hundred yards away near where river joined sea — not worth going back for their horses. They could hear the clash of arms as they approached, but it sounded somehow muted, as though the worst was already over, the fighting receding — and since no fleeing Scots had come in their direction, the inference was good.

There were bodies lying near the outer dry ditch, all wearing the jacks and small pointed helmets, with nose-guards, of typical English men-at-arms. Then two Scots they saw, amongst about a dozen others. Nearer the drawbridge bodies lay still thicker. Experienced at reading the signs of war, Wallace calculated that these had been allowed to emerge, when the drawbridge had been lowered, then hemmed in and assailed from the rear by hidden Scots. They had fought their way forward a little, heading for the burning barn, and then been forced to turn back. They had made a stand at the bridge-end. But the bridge was still down, and no living men were in sight — so that stand had been unsuccessful, and Gray and Scrymgeour and their people were within. It was from inside the castle that the muffled sounds of fighting came.

Four men stood on guard under the gatehouse arch, one of them MacFadzean. He assured Wallace that it was almost all over; only the cleaning up left. The actual garrison of the castle itself did not appear to have been more than forty — and these mainly drunk.

There were a few more bodies lying in the inner bailey. At the main building, not so much keep as citadel, two more of Gray's men stood guard, by the light of smoking torches. Grinning, they pointed upstairs. There was a smell of new wood and mortar about, somewhat overlaid by that of burning and of fresh blood.

Up in the great hall above was a dramatic scene. A group of frightened women cowered in a corner. Up at the dias-end, three men stood amidst a circle of drawn swords and dirks, Gray and Scrymgeour standing by. The trio were in some disarray of dress, one large, fleshy, gross, obviously naked save for a bed-robe, one part-clothed, one in most of his armour — and rich armour at that. They looked unhappy.

'Here, Will,' Gray called. 'Here is Arnulf, the Sheriff. Also one Saxby, the captain of this castle. And his lieutenant. We had little difficulty, God be praised. Those of this garrison who were not asleep were in liquor I think.'

'It was well done. And swiftly. But ... what wait you for, with these, my friends?'

'Wait? We kept them for you to speak with.'

'I want no speech with dastards, murderers, betrayers. Hang them.'

Breaths were sharply indrawn.

'Hang them?' Gray swallowed. 'Now? Here?'

'Where better? Save in the Barns of Ayr, where Arnulf and Saxby and their friends hanged my uncle, Sheriff of Ayr, and scores of better men than themselves. But the Barns have served another purpose. This hall will do very well.' He pointed upwards. 'It has stout rafters. But, see you — hanging is no work for a priest, I grant you. Scrymgeour, man — see you to it. Get ropes. And take those women away.'

As Scrymgeour hurried off the heavy man in the bed-robe spoke, thickly. 'Wallace — this is folly, man. You cannot do it. You do not deal so with such as me. I am Arnulf of Southampton, a clerk in orders, one of His Grace the King's trusted servants. You cannot hang the King's officers. Ransom, man. Ransom it is. Since you have me, thus, at a disadvantage, I am worth much to you, in ransom. Master Cressingham, the Treasurer, will pay ...'

Wallace had turned his back. 'Thomas my friend,' he interrupted, 'I repeat — I do not speak with forsworn hangmen. Ask them if they offered ransom to Sheriff Crawford, my uncle. Or to my good friend Sir Bryce Blair. Or to Sir Hugh Montgomerie. Or the others he invited to his conference. Ask him.'

There was a heavy silence in that hall.

They waited for Scrymgeour to fetch the ropes.

'I want the Provost of the burgh brought here,' Wallace said. 'With his magistrates and guild-brothers. Or some of them. Quickly. The town should be aroused now, surely. Adam — go you and bring them.'

More of Wallace's men were now arriving, not a few singed about hair and beard, many blackened by soot and stained with blood, a shabby crew. All watched grimly as Scrymgeour came back with ropes, and nooses were tied round the prisoners' necks. The three Englishmen, recognising that nothing they could say would save them now, faced their end courageously and with dignity. Arnulf was hoisted to the rafters first, without ceremony, his bed robe falling off him to reveal a paunchy

193

white lardlike and quite hairless body, sagging and obscene, which choked and jerked and swung and twirled, to dangle twitching. Saxby went next, and possibly because he was a lighter man, took longer to die. Wallace did not wait for the third execution, but went striding out with most of his men, to see to the state of the fortress and its security.

Presently Adam Wallace found him, to announce that he had the Provost of Ayr and some of the bailies and deacons of trades waiting in the hall, a worried company. Most had already been assembled in the town tolbooth. Back in the citadel, Wallace had barely begun to address the party of half-dressed, middle-aged to elderly burghers, white-faced and anxious, before John Blair came in, leading the three Scots nobles — who halted, taken aback at what they saw hanging from the roof. The man raised his voice. 'My lords — come you,' he cried. 'Here are the magistrates of this good burgh of Ayr. Some of them. And these,' he pointed upwards, 'there is one Arnulf, who called himself Deputy Sheriff. Also the captain of this castle's garrison and his lieutenant.' To the townsmen, he added. 'You, my friends, see before you the Lord Earl of Carrick, the Lord of Bothwell and Pettie, and Sir John the Graham of Dundaff.' He paused, and shrugged wide shoulders. 'I ask these lords to receive this town and castle, in the name of John, King of Scots.'

All stared at him, at a loss. Moray cleared his throat but did not speak. Graham looked doubtfully at the Bruce. That young man, after a pause, found his voice.

'*I* will not, sir,' he said, loudly, clearly. 'There is no King of Scots today. John Baliol was a usurper, and failed the realm. He has vacated the throne. I, for one, can accept nothing in his name.'

Wallace looked thoughtfully at him, tugging his auburn beard — which was notably singed at one side. 'So that is the way of it,' he said. 'All men may not hold as you do, my lord.'

'It may be so. But *I* so hold. And state.'

Men actually held their breaths. Here was a will, apparently sufficiently powerful, forceful, to seek counter Wallace's — and where Wallace was so obviously in complete control. Under those hanging men, who still twitched and swung a little, that would take courage — or an overweening arrogance.

The big man himself might have been debating which. When he answered, his voice, though deep, was comparatively mild.

'Who, then, may speak in the realm's name? The burgh and castle is taken. In whose name, Earl of Carrick?'

'You ever seek an authority in whose name to act?' the other demanded. 'I had not heard that you were so nice!'

'There are some who delight to name me outlaw and brigand, my lord. But all that I have done, I have done for this ravaged kingdom of Scotland, and in the name of its crowned king.'

Bruce seemed to accept that. 'Very well,' he said. 'Then, who better to represent that kingdom, meantime, than the High Steward of Scotland? I shall receive Ayr in his name, if so required.'

The calm assumption that it was he, the Bruce, who accepted and decided, or otherwise, what should be done, was not lost on Wallace.

'Aye. Very well, My lord Earl of Carrick, heir of the House of Bruce, receives Ayr burgh and castle, cleansed of the English invader, in the name of James, Lord High Steward of Scotland,' he intoned impressively, for the benefit of the townsmen. 'Is it agreed?' At least it committed Bruce most assuredly to the cause of revolt.

No one being in a position to say otherwise, the thing was accepted, with nods and shuffles.

Wallace smiled thinly — his former warm smile had suffered a declension since Lanark. 'So be it. My lords, no doubt you will now ride to acquaint the Steward of this matter. Sir John — you could aid me here, if you will. My friends of Ayr — get you back to your town. I want every house searched. For Englishmen. Some there may be yet, in hiding. A great grave is to be dug. The streets and wynds cleared of folk. All to return to their homes. You have it?' Briskly he issued these orders, and stepped down from the dais. 'Now I have work to do.' After all talk of acceptances and the like, it was necessary to show who in fact commanded here.

Bruce and Moray, indeed, took their dismissal as unquestioningly as did the Provost and townsmen.

CHAPTER ELEVEN

The Scots army looked as though it might be celebrating a saint's day, a holiday, rather than waiting for battle. Spread out all along the west bank of the River Irvine, amongst the yellow gorse of the grassy links, the men lazed and strolled and slept in the warm late-June sunshine. They presumably, originally, had been drawn up there in troops and squadrons and companies; but now all semblance of order and readiness was lost, all urgency dissipated. Horses grazed at will, hot and heavy armour was laid aside, some men actually paddled in the cool river. The position was a strong one, admittedly, with the river in front, and beyond that the extensive marshland where the Annick Water came in to join the Irvine just before it reached the sea; but that position could not hold itself.

'Here is utter folly!' Wallace exclaimed, to John Blair and Thomas Gray, who rode at his side, in front of their company. 'With Clifford not five miles off, what do they think? Do they think, at all? All that are needed here, now, are the tumblers and dancing bears!'

'Where are their leaders?' Gray asked. 'I see no signs of the lords.'

'Gone eat their dinner, perhaps! Or seeking better entertainment!'

Their joint company, of about a hundred and fifty mounted men, Wallace's plus Graham's, splashed across the ford, none seeking to challenge them. At the west side Wallace demanded of the first group they came up with, where were the leaders of this, this gathering? Where the Scots lords?

Men-at-arms in various liveries, grinned and shrugged. One, an under-officer, pointed. 'Back at Mill o' Fullarton, sir. They confer, I am told.'

Muttering, Wallace rode on. The Mill was half-a-mile north.

Half-way there, a recognisable figure, finely mounted and armoured, approached, riding fast, the only sign of urgency on all the landscape, his slung shield displaying the golden scallops on black of Graham.

'Ha, Will!' The young Sir John cried. 'Thank God you are come! I can do nothing with them. They will not heed me, or your message. They talk and talk. Mainly of a truce, a parley . . .'

'I know it. I met Sir Richard de Lundin. Riding to speak with Clifford, at Kilmarnock. As their messenger. It is scarcely to be credited.'

'It is the truth, nevertheless. Lundin has gone to suggest a conference. In answer to a messenger, one Livingstone, from the English. Clifford is offering them terms — and they seek elucidation, details. They conceive their case hopeless, anyway. Now that Percy is as near as Lochmaben, and with fifty thousand. He will join Clifford tomorrow. They say we cannot fight these numbers, and must either come to terms or withdraw. I told them your plan. To keep Percy from joining up with Clifford, by taking Kilmarnock. But they would not hear of it. Moray would fight. Douglas and Lindsay also. But most say that it would be fatal. They say that they are in a strong position here, and should make terms from it.'

'God save us from fools! This position could be turned in a couple of hours!'

'I told them that. I said that you had sent me to urge an attack. Drive a wedge between the English forces. But when this Livingstone came from Clifford, offering to talk, they seized on it. Even the Bruce. And sent Lundin to say that they would parley.'

'Clifford is only offering to talk, to use up time, to delay any action until Percy arrives. Surely Moray, or Douglas any man with any experience of war, could tell them that.'

'There is more to it than that, Will. I do not understand fully. But even Bruce paid heed to what Livingstone said. And Bruce, at least, is no fool . . .'

Reserving judgement on that, the big man spurred ahead.

In the cobbled courtyard of the Mill of Fullarton, amongst carts and sacks of grain, they found the cream of South-West Scotland assembled — and in debate even hotter and more vociferous than it had been at the Seagate Castle nearby two weeks before. Never was it more evident how desperately the Scots needed an over-all leader and commander. Nobody was in charge here — or all were. No one, it seemed could decide yea or nay.

Wallace did not so much as dismount from his garron. He

raised the horn at his side to his lips, and blew a blast. It was scarcely respectful to the company, but his purpose now was to galvanise, to shock if need be, rather than to court respect. He obtained momentary quiet, at least.

'My lords,' he cried. 'I sent Sir John the Graham to seek your aid in an assault on Clifford at Kilmarnock. More than an hour past. The townsfolk were ready to rally against the enemy. You have chosen to ignore me, to wait here talking.' His scorn was little disguised. 'Now I hear that you have sent Sir Richard de Lundin to seek terms from Clifford. To seek *terms*! Not only will you not attack, he says — you talk of submission!' He all but spat that word 'Would you parley with the Devil? I cannot believe this is true. Tell me that he has taken leave of his wits, my good lords!'

There was silence. Then a murmur, almost a growl, largely resentful — though some few cheered him.

Leaning forward in his saddle, Wallace changed his tone. 'My lords — there is still time. Order your men to readiness, and I will have Kilmarnock in your hands in two hours. And Clifford cut off from Percy.'

Silence again. This time no growls, but no cheers either.

'You raised armed revolt, my lords. Why? To seek terms at the first approach of the enemy?'

It was Robert Bruce, Earl of Carrick, who answered him, unexpectedly. 'Sir — a new situation has arisen. Did not Lundin tell you? Of this matter of a muster for France? And the English offer? This may change all.'

Wallace looked from the speaker, to Graham, and back. 'What is this? France, you say? I know not of what you speak, my lord.'

'Then hear this. Sir Robert Clifford, Lord of Brougham, has sent this message — that he understands well what caused the Scots lords to revolt. It was, he says, the command from King Edward that all Scots nobles as well as all English ones, should forthwith muster their men and bring them to join and assist him in his war against the French — which seems to be going but ill. None of us here has heard of this command. But it could be so.'

'Edward Plantagenet has temerity enough, I swear!'

'Perhaps so. But here he may have over-reached himself. It seems that the English lords are scarce more eager to obey than would we be. They mislike this war with France. They are tired

198

of war — that I know. This new summons is unwise and unpopular. And Clifford says that the Earl of Surrey esteems it a mistake in policy to apply it to Scotland. Clifford, therefore, and Sir Henry Percy, Sheriff of Ayr, have the Viceroy's authority to declare to those Scots lords and knights now assembled in protest here at Irvine that, if they yield now, disperse their forces and give certain assurances for the future, they will be received back into the King's peace, without penalty. Moreover, Surrey undertakes to seek persuade King Edward that demands for Scots levies for the French war be withdrawn.'

'I say it is a trick!' Sir William Douglas's harsh voice grated. 'A ruse, I tell you, to have us yield without fighting.'

'Why should they so seek to cozen us?' somebody demanded. 'With fifty thousand and more armed men here, why?'

'The English, it may be, want no revolt and fighting in Scotland, while Edward and his main might is in France,' Sir Alexander Lindsay put in. 'Percy and Clifford have men enough to destroy us here, no doubt — but they would rather have peace. Not to fight.'

'If they would treat with us, fifty three thousand men to our four thousand — then we are fools to reject it,' Eglinton said.

'Fools, aye!' Douglas managed to shout all down. 'If we yield. We have a strong position. They are not over-eager to attack. The people of the land are for us. Would you surrender without a blow? Could you raise your heads after, if you did?'

'One lord who speaks the same tongue as I do!' Wallace said grimly.

'And as do I!' Moray added.

By means of beating a staff on the cobbles, the High Steward made himself heard. It was the Douglas he specifically addressed, in his thick, slurring speech. 'Not only raise our heads but our *arms*, my lord! Do you not see it? At this present, we cannot prevail — whatever Wallace says. We may hold off Clifford and Percy, with their horse. But when the fifty thousand foot come up, we are lost. I have been of the opinion that we should hasten northwards, with our force intact. But now, I believe that we might be better to accept these terms. And fight another day, when the odds are less great.'

Bishop Wishart supported him. 'There may be trickery in it,' he admitted. 'But what are we disadvantaged? They make this excuse for us — this of rebelling because we do not wish to take our men to France. Which none of us has so much as heard of! This must mean that they do not want a clash. I say that we should take advantage of this. Rise again, as my lord Steward says, when they and their great host are gone South again.'

'No!' That was Moray, hotly. 'This is betrayal. Did you raise the banner of freedom for this? *I* did not! I will not yield without a blow struck. My lord of Carrick — will you? *You* would not surrender, man?'

Young Bruce took his time to answer that — but when he did so, his voice was firm. 'Submit? Surrender? These are but words, Andrew. There are times to fight and times to talk. If the English wish to talk, I say let us talk. And fight another day, in better case. My lord Bishop and the Steward are right, I think. Today, I fear, we cannot win. So talk.'

'My lord of Carrick says that we cannot win today,' Wallace took him up, from his horse. 'On what authority does he so state? Has he ever drawn his sword in aught more warlike than a tourney?'

There was a quivering hush at such plain speaking. But the young earl did not rise in proud wrath. He spoke, indeed, carefully, restrainedly. 'I am here using, not my sword but by head, my friend,' he said. 'In swordery I yield to you, sir, and gladly. But ... have you *thought* on all this? This of France? It behoves us to think. For it could mean so much. Something which could transform all Scotland's state. Clifford, Percy, Surrey, would not dare to send such message, about the French war being unpopular to the English, unless it was indeed so. Unless they knew that Edward had indeed made a great mistake. Unless, I think, there was near revolt in England itself. All Edward's reign, he has been making war. Against Ireland, Wales, Scotland — now France. It may be that at last his own people have had enough of their blood being shed, their treasure spent. If they are turning, at last — then all could be changing for Scotland. Do you not see it? If this is so, then we should not fight against the English — but rather aid them against Edward!'

Men eyed him, doubtfully.

'How will it change our struggle for freedom, my lord? Wallace demanded.

'It may foreshadow revolt in England. Or, if revolt is too great a word, discontent, resistance. They would not make such

200

offer to us, otherwise, I think. It may be that Surrey would have his fifty thousand back in England!'

'Is that not the more reason to fight them? If they are in two minds. Looking back over their shoulders.'

'I think no. I say that if the English would indeed bring their arrogant king to heel, we should aid them in it.'

'What the English do with their monarch is *their* concern, not ours. Or, not mine. To be sure, it may be yours, my lord! I have feared as much.'

'What, what do you mean, sir?'

'I mean that your conversion to Scotland's cause is something sudden, my lord of Carrick! You have large lands in England. All knew you one of Edward's men. It may be that you are still more concerned with England's cause, than Scotland's!'

There was a shocked murmur, as Bruce raised a pointing hand. 'You doubt my honesty, sirrah!'

'I doubt your interests. Your judgement. Where your heart lies. I doubt the judgement of any man who even for a moment considers submission to the English, my lords!' Wallace stared deliberately round at them all, head high, reproach and accusation both in his eye.

'Curse you . . .!'

'This is not to be borne!'

'How dare the man speak so! To us . . .!'

'My lords — friends,' Bishop Wishart cried. 'This talk will serve us nothing. Wallace is a man of fierce action. He has wrought mighty deeds. But we must take the longer view, here. Consider well our course. For the best . . .' The old man's words quavered away.

Wallace took a major grip on himself. 'I regret, my lord Bishop, if I spoke ill. But — it my be that I speak for other than do you. You all. You, my lord, speak for Holy Church. And these noble lords — who do they speak for? Themselves, their lands, the power of the realm. But who speaks for the folk of Scotland, my lords? Does any here? The folk. The nation. This Scotland is more than a realm, my friends — it is a nation. A people, an ancient people. A people that has been betrayed and sold and spurned. All but forgotten by those who seek the power. But it is the people who will pay for what is decided this day, the people who will be ground under the heel of the tyrant. You lords, I swear, will survive, whoever rules! Even if Scotland is no more, you will still be lords. But not the common folk. Not the *Scots*. Do you ever think of them, my lords? *I*, for want of a better, must be their spokesman this day. And I say, fight!'

Everywhere men eyed their neighbours at a loss. Most were honestly bewildered, knew not of what the man spoke. Was the fellow out of his mind? Had his sorrows turned his wits? Who was it he talked of? The people, the common folk. Who and what, in God's name, were they? Peasants, servants, cottagers, herds, scullions, men-at-arms? What had these to do with the realm? They did what they were told. They were fed, protected, allotted their duties. These needed no jumped-up spokesman, but their own lords. This was a realm, a kingdom — even without a king. What was this talk of a nation? What *was* a nation?

Something of all this was flung at the man on the garron, who listened head ashake.

At last Wallace shouted them down. 'You do not know, my lords, of what I speak? Of who are the Scots, and what is the Scots nation? Here is no time to inform you. But I say that you should ask one of your number — my lord of Carrick! His father claims to be the rightful King of Scots. King of *Scots*, mark you — not King of Scotland. As there is a King of England. My lord Robert Bruce, perchance, will tell you who are the Scots whose king he one day would be! He ought to know, I think! But this I do tell you — few of the Scots are nobles or bishops! For these many others, I make bold to speak today.'

It was Bruce himself who answered, where others merely wagged their heads, shrugged helplessly, or snorted their incomprehension. 'There may be something in what you say, sir — but we will discuss it another time. For it is a large matter. Now, we have decision to make — and no great time left to make it. I say, let us talk with the English. Talk, at length. Learn what we can. Gain time. And while we talk, send messengers privily, to raise the country further. It may be that we will find the English glad to wait. If trouble is brewing in England. Time — let us make time.'

'We shall make better time by remaining free men,' Wallace said, almost wearily. 'The realm, the nation, will be freed by the sword, not by talk.'

'In *your* sort of war, may be. The surprising of a garrison, here and there. The burning of this castle or that. Castles which can be taken again — as was Lochmaben. The raid by night.

This is all we may do with our present support and numbers. It is good — but not good enough, my lords.' Bruce was speaking earnestly, to them all. 'We shall not free Scotland of the English so. They are notable fighters, with many times our numbers. They have their bowmen, their chivalry, their hundreds of thousands, trained in war. Think you we can counter these by night raids, fires and hangings?'

'Is this why you left Edward's camp to join us, my lord of Carrick?' demanded Sir John Graham bitterly. 'To tell us that we could not win? To sap our wills and courage?'

'I did not. I came because I must. Because I saw that I must needs choose between Scotland and England. Not John Baliol's Scotland — *my* Scotland! Wallace has said it, and I say it again. I'd mind you all, my father should be King of Scots today — Wallace's Scots, your Scots, and mine! Let none forget it.'

There was silence in the mill-yard again. Not even Wallace spoke.

'I chose Scotland, I say. But not to beat with my bare fists against castle walls. More than that is required Wits, my friends. We need our wits, by the saints! Wallace here, can do the beating at walls. He does it well. Moreover, I'd mind you, *he* cannot talk with the English. They would hang him out of hand. He knows it.' Bruce jabbed a finger towards the big man. 'It is not so with us, my lords. They offer to treat with us. I say, treat, then. I know Surrey. I know Percy, his nephew. I know Clifford of Brougham. They are not of Edward's wits or Edward's ruthlessness. For I know Edward also! I would not say to treat with Edward Plantagenet, God knows! But these are different. Treat. Talk. Discover what is in their minds. Something worries them, I swear. And let Wallace go fight his own war. With our blessing — for it will aid our talking.'

An extraordinary change had come over the arguing company. Without warning as it were, young Robert Bruce had established himself as a leader not merely the highest in rank there, but a man who had come to know his own mind. He had abruptly grown in stature before their very eyes. It was as though a new voice had spoken in unhappy Scotland. And more important even than the voice, in that leaderless throng of nobles, was the manner.

'There is much in what the Earl of Carrick declares,' Bishop Wishart said, into the hush. 'I believe he has the rights of it.'

'I, too,' the Steward nodded. 'There is wisdom in this, I agree.'

'And I doubt!' Wallace exclaimed. 'I agree with my lord only in this — that the English will hang me if they can! For the rest, I say that you deceive yourselves. Myself, I waste no more time. There is much to be done. If you will not do it, my lords, *I* will! I give you goodday — and naught else!'

'I am sorry for that . . .' Bruce began, and paused. The big man, turning his garron, had halted as John Blair came hurrying, to speak a word or two in his ear.

Wallace looked back. 'You have company it seems! Company *I* would not care to meet! They approach under a flag of truce. I do not congratulate you, my lords. I have no sto-mach for supping with the Devil! I am off.'

The Graham went with him. Moray took a single step to follow, then thought better of it. Douglas likewise. They waited, uncertain.

CHAPTER TWELVE

Wallace's company were in the neighbourhood of Crawford, in Upper Clydesdale, next day, and making for the fastnesses of the Forest, when his rearguard warned him of the approach of a fast-riding squadron behind. Hurriedly he was putting his force into a posture of defence, when a scout brought word that the newcomers rode under the banners of Douglas and Moray. They waited, interestedly.

Wallace noted, as the other company rode up, that the Douglas had something over one hundred men with him. Moray, of course, had only his personal bodyguard, having brought only these from Perthshire. Wallace himself had just skirted Douglasdale, a rich and large lordship where, although its castle was occupied by the English, Douglas could have gath-ered five hundred men had he wished. This, then, was but a token force which approached.

The two nobles greeted the big man very differently — indeed they were very different sorts of men. Moray was civil, affable indeed, almost respectful; Douglas was gruff, aggressive, at pains to make it clear that he was not conceding anything to such as Wallace, and that Douglas was Douglas.

'We have come after you, Wallace, because we are more in accord with your notions than with Bruce's,' he stated baldly. 'Talking is not Douglas's way! And it seemed there is to be talk by the bellyful! I had enough yesterday, by God! I am for some action.'

'I also,' Moray nodded. 'Much that Bruce said is fair, I think. But let these others do the talking. It is not for me. I have a host awaiting me, in the North.'

Wallace inclined his head 'So I thought, my lord. So why ride you southwards into Ettrick Forest after William Wallace?'

'It was my hope that I might persuade you to join forces with me. To turn northwards. We could do great things together.'

'I see . . .'

Douglas interrupted. 'I say that is folly! The English will not be defeated in the North, any more than they will be *talked* into defeat. They must be driven over the Border into their own land. Only so shall we be quit of them. Which means a Border campaign.'

Wallace looked from one to the other. It seemed that they had brought the great debate after him, from Irvine.

'Where are the men for your Border campaign, my lord?' he asked. 'We will not get them from the lords at Irvine.'

'There are many who have not yet risen. Maxwell, Fergusson, Roos, Kennedy, Carruthers. The Johnstones, Elliots, Jardines, Armstrongs and the rest — thieves, but fair fighters! The Galloway clans, Maclellans, MacDowalls, MacCullochs, MacKies.'

'As you say, my lord — they have not risen yet! Nor have we reason to believe that they will. With fifty thousand English on their doorsteps!'

'You will agree that there is more hope from the North,' Moray said. 'I have near three thousand men in arms, many waiting in Atholl.'

'Will they cross into the Lowlands? Highland armies are very well — in the Highlands. But to cross Forth and Clyde they are ever less than eager.'

'Then I — we — must persuade them, sir.'

Wallace eyed the other thoughtfully.

Graham spoke up. 'I say that we should go North, also, Will.

I can gain you many more men in Stirlingshire — but none here.'

Douglas snorted his opinion of the sort of numbers and calibre of men young Graham could enlist — to which the other made meaningful queries about the strength of Douglasdale and Morton.

To keep the peace, Wallace said that they must ride on meantime. Into Ettrick. He had sundry small groups of adherents to assemble from all over the Forest, to complete his own force. They could discuss the matter of their further steps, when camped that night. If their lordships intended to accompany him . . .?

Apparently they did, without actually stating it.

He learned the outcome of the previous day's talking, at Mill of Fullarton. And talking was the word, according to Douglas, empty and endless talk. Though Moray was less critical. They said that Sir Henry Percy had ridden on ahead of his troops, and had arrived at the Mill in person, with Clifford, under the flag of truce. Thereafter a prolonged discussion had dragged on, with Bruce quickly taking the lead on the Scots side — if lead it could be called, since the talking went round and round in circles. It seemed that both sides were playing for time, the Scots as a matter of policy, the English presumably to delay any actual fighting until they had sure word from England as to the situation developing there. For it transpired, from Percy rather than Clifford, that a large and important section of the English nobility were in all but open revolt against Edward and his French plans and demands, certain kinsmen of Percy, and of Surrey, amongst the leaders, pressure to bring the King back from France, and to wind up that adventure, appeared to be the English objective; and no passion-rousing campaign in Scotland was desired at this juncture. Indeed, a united front of the English and Scottish Norman nobility would be the best tactic — since they were both involved in this royal summons to France. So some suitable arrangement at Irvine was advisable.

Douglas hooted his reaction to all such nonsense and trickery. and Moray himself admitted that he was by no means convinced that there was anything to be gained by such debate. But Bruce had told him, afterwards, that there was undoubtedly something in this English disharmony, of which they ought to take advantage; and that if he could, he would spin out these talks for days, while the position clarified, and while more acts of revolt took place in Scotland — which would strengthen their hands at the negotiating table. Hence his presence here, with Douglas.

It all made Wallace more thoughtful than he admitted. It seemed as though they were, in fact, being made to dance to Bruce's tune. Was that, or was it not, to Scotland's benefit?

That evening, in a camp in the hills near where Clyde, Tweed and Annan all rose, they thrashed out a programme. It was mainly of Wallace's proposing, although he gave in to the others on details, and tried his best to adjust to their so varying preferences. Any blow they struck must have maximum impact, he insisted — more than just taking another castle or two was required. They should seek to threaten, frighten or injure the most important Englishmen in Scotland. These were Bishop Anthony Beck of Durham, who acted as a sort of military supreme commander, with direct links with Edward, bypassing the Viceroy, and who, when in Scotland, made his headquarters at Glasgow; and the two clerics who controlled the civil power, in Edward's name — Master Hugo de Cressingham, the Treasurer, and Master William Ormsby, the Justiciar, the former based on Glasgow also, the latter on Stirling. Let them strike at Glasgow, therefore, and seek to unseat two of the trio — which might have a major effect on the Irvine talking, and could well bring pressure to bear on Bishop Wishart and the Steward likewise, since Glasgow was their bailiewick. Then they might turn their attention to Stirling, and though they could never take its mighty fortress, the strongest in Scotland, they perhaps could threaten the Forth crossings which it protected, and which might clear the way for Moray's force to move southwards, and at the same time involve the Grahams.

Douglas, grumbling, agreed at length, with seeming reluctance. But Wallace did not fail to note that he did not volunteer to go and raise another four hundred or five hundred men in the Douglas lands, as he could have done. Nor did the younger man urge him to. Wallace was, of course, faced with the same problem of command, on account of his lower rank, as had concerned him heretofore. If the Lord of Douglas was leading more men than his own contingent, undoubtedly he would assume the supreme command — if he did not seek to do so anyway. The same would apply with Moray, once reunited with his army, inevitably. And Wallace, at this stage, was determined to keep his hands untied, to remain his own master, if possible — for what he considered the best of reasons.

Two mornings later, then, the combined force of about four hundred, all mounted, turned their faces North-Westwards, to make for Glasgow, by Tweedsmuir and the Upper Ward of Lanarkshire.

*　　*　　*

Once out of the security of the hills, they moved only by night, as was Wallace's custom — however little the noblemen approved; and two night rides brought them to the outskirts of the bishop's-burgh of Glasgow, in the Carntyne area, they believed unheralded. It was not a large town, smaller than Lanark or Ayr, being largely composed of the clergy manses of the great Cathedral of St. Mungo and the houses of their innumerable servants, plus the adjoining seafaring and fishing haven on the Clyde. But it was an important place strategically, where the Clyde estuary first narrowed sufficiently to be bridged, and from which the Kelvin, Molindinar, and North and South Calder valleys, as well as that of Clyde itself, fanned out like the fingers of a hand.

Being an ecclesiastical burgh, it was not fully walled, although strongly enough guarded. It certainly could not be surprised, however, by night or by day, by any large force. But it could be infiltrated, especially by night, by individuals or little groups, at scores of points. This was Wallace's plan. He knew the town as well as he did Lanark — Elderslie, his childhood home, was only nine miles off — and personally had worked out every detail. The entire company left their horses in a wood at Carntyne about a mile east of the town, and dispersed in small parties under the strictest orders. Nothing at all was to interfere with silence and secrecy, no distractions or adventures, no easy gains or confrontations to be considered. They would meet in the burial-ground of the Cathedral, amongst the tombs, and all must be there before two o'clock struck on the Cathedral clock, by whatever route they entered the town. There was sufficient time — but none for dawdling.

They had all re-assembled, in fact, considerably before the hour appointed, amidst the shadowy gravestones and monuments below the towering mass of the enormous Cathedral, with the town still unalarmed, although Auchinleck's group had had a scuffle with some drunken soldiery in the Drygate, none of whom survived to tell the tale. One or two others reported challenges from watchmen, to which they had not responded — but no doubt they too would be presumed to be night-prowling English troops. It was probably only a question of time until some idea of the presence of four hundred intruders became evident to the guard-commanders; but so far all was well.

There were two buildings to be taken, in the first place — the Bishop's Palace itself, which Beck was known to have taken over for himself, since Wishart's involvement in revolt; and the Blackfriars Monastery where Cressingham. the Treasurer, was said to be installed — the second-best building in the town. They were both, naturally, near the Cathedral. Graham was given the task of capturing the Blackfriars friary, and its occupants — and with as little general disturbance as possible. Wallace, knowing the interior arrangements of the Bishop's Palace, would deal with that himself. They had far more men than they needed for these tasks; the remainder would surround the buildings and await development.

In the event, the attempt was not entirely successful, in either case. An alert watchman sounded the alarm just before the Palace gatehouse was rushed, and though this could not prevent Wallace's men from gaining entry it gave the inmates warning and time to assess the position — and in Bishop Beck's case, get out. A veteran campaigner and realist, he recognised a state of affairs where he was likely to be at a disadvantage, and abandoned it while opportunity remained, leaving others to deal with an almost certainly deteriorating situation. He fled from an unnoticed postern-door, as the intruders rushed the main doors. He, and one or two of his closest associates, grabbed horses from the stableyard and were off, beating their way through the surrounding cordon. Wallace's people, being all dismounted, failed to stop the horsemen, and were delayed in finding mounts to pursue. Nor was it at first clear that it was Beck himself who had escaped.

On the other hand, Graham captured the Blackfriars Monastery and all within it, with a minimum of trouble — only to discover that Cressingham was not therein, being summoned to see the Viceroy in Northumberland.

Disappointed in all this, and perceiving that he should have recognised the possibility beforehand, Wallace and his colleagues were far from downcast nevertheless. For it did not take them long to realise that, as it were by default, they were masters of Glasgow. There was some small resistance from isolated groups of English clerks, officers and soldiery, one a kinsman of Percy, it seemed — but very little in total, and none of it effective, more of a token than anything else. Glasgow was not a garrison town so much as an administrative centre, relying on the surrounding castles and fortresses of Bothwell, Renfrew, Crookston, Drumsargard, Kirkintilloch and Dumbarton for protection.

So although they had failed to catch Beck or Cressingham, they had given the former a major fright, captured many of the latter's servants and personal belongings; and by taking Glasgow town had no doubt upset the English administration considerably. Which was the object of the enterprise.

Not that there was any point in trying to hold the town. There was a large garrison at Bothwell, nine miles away — to which, no doubt, Beck had fled — and the last thing Wallace desired was to become immobilised in the defence of a town, especially one not readily defensible. They had made their point; now to be on their way.

It was about thirty miles to Stirling from Glasgow, up the Kelvin valley. They cut northwards, however, at Kilsyth and over the hills to Dundaff, in daylight and in one day. There they learned that Ormsby the Justiciar had gone to Scone Abbey, near Perth, home of the Stone of Destiny, to hold justice-ayres — indeed, Sir Patrick Graham, Sir John's uncle, along with other magnates, had been summoned there to attend. So there was no point in making any gesture towards Stirling.

They held another council as to their further moves. Douglas predictably, advocated a return to the south forthwith. Moray, on hearing that his uncle, Bishop David of Moray, was doing great things in the North, with the troops he had left behind, urged that they continue on northwards — after all, Scone was on the way to Atholl, where at least some of his force was presumably waiting for him. Sir John said he required a few days to recruit a further band of Grahams from his wide lands here. Thomas Gray pointed out the notable moral impact of a successful attack on Ormsby while many Scots magnates were in attendance. Wallace agreed with this. They would make a swift thrust at Scone, put the Justiciar in his own dock, for trial, if they could, and then go south with the Douglas, picking up the Graham and his recruits on the way. Wallace was finding that, if he spoke and acted firmly, assuredly, enough, Sir William Douglas would not contest his leadership — meantime.

It was not far off fifty miles from Dundee to Scone, direct; but they could by no means risk going directly — indeed much of the journey would have to be covered by night. The first part, at least, they would traverse in daylight, through Graham's own hills and then across the Forth valley by the Flanders Moss. The Fords of Frew would almost certainly be guarded again; and though their force of four hundred could probably overcome any such obstacle, secrecy would be lost, and warning that there was a large body of men on the move northwards be transmitted to Ormsby. So they put themselves in Stephen MacGregor's hands and he took them north-westwards through the meres and morasses of the great Moss, by round-about and miry ways — to the disgust of Douglas, who called it mud-walloping. There was nothing here to see them save roe-deer and wildfowl — but the crossing took them five slaistering hours.

For the first full day thereafter, they lay hidden in the Menteith hills, near Loch Rusky, south of Callander, waiting for nightfall before crossing the more populous Buchanan lands of the Teith valley.

If these high-summer nights were very short, at least they were never very dark, and progress was not unduly delayed. Morning light found them on the edge of Upper Strathearn, where again they went to ground. This was Drummond country, which might be expected to be friendly; but word of their presence might still be carried to Scone. The following night brought them to Wallace's old haunts in Methven Wood, with Scone a mere seven miles to the east — though with Tay to Cross. This they planned to do the succeeding night, at Derders Ford, two miles north of Perth.

Scone again was not a fortified place, an ancient abbey of the Celtic Church, Romanised, with a community of houses around it, but no town. It served the same purpose for Scotland as did Westminster for England, here was the shrine where its kings were crowned and great ceremonies held. Edward Longshanks had gone out of his way to ravish it the previous year, claiming that he had taken away its famous Stone to London; but its monks remained. It could be crowded indeed, on ceremonial occasions — but even so, most who attended lodged in Perth itself, only three miles downstream. So the township was not large, and the Abbey itself only of moderate size. Its importance lay in its especially sacred and historic character — hence, no doubt, Ormsby's choice of it to demonstrate his authority.

The Justiciar would not be ferrying to and from Perth, nothing could be surer than that. He would have taken over the Abbot's quarters for himself, for certain. In which case there would be comparatively few people about the Abbey at night. A strong guard would be provided, of course, by Sir John Stewart of Menteith, Sheriff and Governor at Perth; but there would be nothing like a garrison.

A discussion with his colleagues confirmed Wallace in his opinion that no special strategy was called for at Scone — other than the sheer surprise which was essential. Douglas, who had been at John Baliol's coronation, knew the lay-out of the Abbey and where the Abbot's quarters lay. The thing should not be difficult.

Nor was it, with four hundred men descending at two o'clock in the morning, without warning upon an unfortified sprawling establishment. All went without hitch, the guard was overwhelmed in only minutes, and the Abbey captured. But Ormsby was not there. Whether, somehow, he had received warning, or whether it was just a matter of chance, he had not returned that night, as expected, from Kinclaven of all places — where he had gone, allegedly to inspect damage, but actually, according to Abbot Henry, to search for the treasure Wallace had reputedly hidden in the Shortwood Shaw; and not the first such expedition, by any means. The Abbot, a cheerful, gnomelike little man, elderly and grizzled but lively, welcomed the night-time invaders of his peace with open arms, expressed his admiration for what Wallace had achieved, his hatred and contempt for Ormsby, fed and wined them all with the best will in the world, from Ormsby's store, in part — but urged a speedy departure from Scone nevertheless. Since the Kinclaven affair, he revealed, there had been a great tightening up of security. Since John Stewart was an able man, though on the wrong side. A system of hilltop beacons had been arranged, for the entire Tay valley and neighbourhood, whereby, at the first hint of trouble, the bale-fires could be lit on prominent points, and within a matter of hours over two thousand men assembled from all over the area, from Dundee to Crieff, from Abernethy to Dunkeld. The first move of such guards as had escaped from the Abbey that night would be to have the beacon-chain lit. By noon tomorrow, the entire Tay valley would be alive with troops. Wallace was made very much aware that he had again failed in forethought.

Sure enough, while still they were eating, pin-points of red light began to appear on the tops of Kinnoul, Kinfauns and Balthayock Hills to the south, flanking the Carse of Gowrie. In a short time, the entire great amphitheatre of the hills was ringed round with fires. The Abbot's advice seemed good to Wallace. They decided on retiral here and then. But first they helped themselves, with the monks' co-operation, to the large store of valuables the Justiciar and his associates had collected and stowed in the Abbot's private rooms — which seemed an apt arrangement, in view of Ormsby's alleged treasure-hunting in Shortwood Shaw. Then they bid goodbye to Sir Andrew Moray, who was travelling on northwards to his own people, excited by the word of his uncle's successes, which had filtered south to Scone. Clearly not many of his force had been sitting idly in Atholl; most were far further north and east, campaigning, with both Elgin and Banff said to have fallen to the Bishop of Moray. Sir Andrew promised, however, to come south again with his entire strength, when the occasion warranted it. Douglas, at least, was glad to see the back of him.

So they left Scone Abbey after only three hours, and were back in Methven Wood an hour after sunrise, richer in pocket and well-fed, and only a little depressed at having failed to apprehend Ormsby, like Beck. All would know that only an accident had saved the Justiciar, as only ignominious flight had saved the Prince-Bishop of Durham. Edward's officers in Scotland would surely be beginning to consider their situation thoughtfully. And the magnates summoned to the justice-ayres would draw their own conclusions.

The following night they returned southwards by roughly the same route by which they had travelled northwards. They crossed the Flanders Moss at the same place, and reached Dundaff in forty-eight hours or so. And there, as well as another hundred Grahams assembled for them, they found tidings awaiting them which had the effect of altering all Wallace's ideas as to the immediate future. These were conveyed by an important messenger, Duncan MacDougall of Lorn second son of the old Highland chief Alexander, Lord of Argyll. He did not come on his father's behalf, however, but on his own, and that of Sir Neil Campbell of Lochawe, chief of that clan; and he had been seeking Wallace across the country for all but weeks. He, and the Campbell, wanted Wallace to come through to the West Highlands to aid them against the English — and against Duncan's own brother. It appeared the Lord of Argyll's eldest son, Lame John MacDougall of Lorn, Lennox's bugbear, had indeed thrown in his lot with the English. Edward had given him English estates, and created for him the high-sounding title of Admiral of the Western Sea; but in fact had imposed on him a fierce Irish mercenary leader named M'Phadan, who was now actually calling himself the Lord of Lorn, and dominating all Argyll and beyond, Lame John MacDougall allegedly a mere puppet in his hands. Sir Neil Campbell, who had been a fellow-student with Wallace at Dundee, and much of whose lands on lower Loch Awe had already been over-run, pleaded that Wallace should come to aid them destroy this arrogant usurper, and all his works. If he would, Sir Neil in turn promised the entire Campbell support in his campaigns against the English in the East and South. Duncan of Lorn also promised MacDougall support.

In this entirely new situation, Wallace perceived an opportunity. Here were lords not only seeking his help but offering a new theatre of war — and an important one, despite its seeming remoteness, since these West Highland chiefs owned great fleets of galleys and birlinns, and so could largely control the narrow seas between Scotland and Ireland; which no doubt was why King Edward had troubled himself in seducing Lame John. The chiefs also had vast reserves of manpower, fierce clansmen un-equalled in the very sort of warfare he, Wallace, was engaged in. If he could gain a swift victory against this M'Phadan and Lame John of Lorn, and then, holding the Campbell to his promise, sail down the Hebridean Sea with a host of High-landers in galleys to the Ayrshire coast, he could utterly trans-form the military situation there. Moreover, he had not forgotten that it was this same Lame John MacDougall against whom the Earl of Lennox had besought his services eight months before. Lennox might have proved something of a broken reed since then — but perhaps he could be brought back to a more suitable attitude by a gesture such as this. A major Celtic army might well be within his grasp.

This was not the only news awaiting them at Dundaff. Bruce himself had sent a messenger to Wallace. They were still nego-tiating at Irvine, extraordinary as it seemed, news from England

and France conflicting and leaving the Englishmen in some doubts. A major blow by Wallace and Moray, in this pass, would be of the greatest help. Especially as Percy and Clifford had put forward a new demand, in their talking — namely that Bishop Wishart, the Steward, Bruce himself and the Douglas, submit themselves in person into English hands, to show their good faith allegedly, but really as hostages; and since Douglas was not available, they would accept his young son James in his place.

The effect of this information upon the hot-tempered Sir William was explosive. He was for the South right away, before these spineless traitors yielded up his son. He would have nothing to do with going to the aid of Highland barbarians anyway; if Wallace proposed to be such a fool, he could do it himself. Douglas was going back to Douglasdale forthwith, to set the Borders alight, if nobody else would. Wallace, now in fact not altogether displeased to be quit of him, agreed that they should part company.

And so, next morning — for Douglas scorned all travel by night; and heading westwards into Lennox, Wallace did not require to use secrecy — the two companies left Dundaff, Douglas and his hundred and twenty riding southwards by the shortest and most direct route under flying banners, the others, less demonstrative but still, with the Graham reinforcements, some four hundred strong, heading up the carron valley for Fintry, the Endrick Water and Loch Lomond, to the Highland West.

*   *   *

It took the four hundred three days of hard riding to reach the foot of Loch Awe, under the frowning mass of Cruachan, by Lomondside, Glen Falloch, Strath Fillan, Tyndrum and Glen Lochy, through a wild and savage but beautiful country of lofty mountains, rushing rivers, forests of pine and birch, vast upheaved heather moorlands and lochs longer than Wallace had ever conceived of — Lomond itself over twenty miles in length. Duncan MacDougall had sent on fast-moving messengers ahead, and at the MacGregor castle of Kilchurn, where the Orchy reached Awe, they found Sir Neil Campbell awaiting them, with three hundred men, and Malcolm MacGregor of Glenorchy chief of Clan Alpine, with another three hundred, a host as wild and untamed as the land they were in, and as colourful.

Wallace and his friends were hardly prepared for the style and dramatic splendour and display of these Highlanders geared for war. Although they themselves were of basically Celtic stock also, they were much more modest, less flamboyant in appearance and behaviour than were the Gaelic warriors from the North-West and the Hebrides. The Lowlanders had long had an instinctive suspicion of and hostility to all such, scarcely looking upon them as of the same nation and race. The appearance of these new allies, now, was such as to confirm their innate Scots prejudice against the highly-coloured and ostentatious. Even Wallace had consciously to adjust his mind. Compared with these, the Earl Malcolm and his Lennoxmen were unexceptional.

The Campbell, who rejoiced in the patronymic of MacCailean Mor, Son of the Great Colin, and whom Wallace had not seen since his college days, was a swarthy young man of sombre good looks and something of a gift for silence, dressed with much less of flourish than were many of his following. He wore a shirt of fine chain-mail over his knee-length saffron tunic, belted in solid gold, but little other symbol of his rank — and only the dark, piercing eyes assured that this was the same rather quiet fellow-student with whom Wallace had sported ten years before.

'My friend,' he exclaimed, dismounting and striding forward, hand outstretched, a deal more effusive than his usual, in reaction. 'Here is a notable meeting. A foregathering which could mean much. For Scotland. I greet you, salute you, Sir Neil. It is long since we last met.'

The Campbell inclined his head. 'I rejoice that you have come to Lorn,' he said. 'My sorrow that it is in so dark an hour.' His softly sibilant, almost gentle Highland voice seemed at odds with the rest of him. He turned. 'Here is Glenorchy,' he said. 'Chief of Clan Alpine.'

The man at his side made a very different figure, older, tall, massively built and just slightly portly, clad in full Highland panoply of tartan plaiding, barbaric jewellery and ornament, bristling with weapons, the whole crowned by an astonishing pointed helmet flanked on each side by the pinions of some sort of hawk, in ancient Norse fashion.

'I am Malcolm mac Gregor mac Hugh mac Iain of Glenorchy, Representer of the Race of Alpin the Royal!' this personage proclaimed, almost trumpeted — and looked dis-

216

tinctly down his great beak of a nose at the Lowlanders as he announced the fact. Then, as though taking pity on their self evident ignorance, he added, 'I am commonly called MacGregor.' He did not extend his hand.

'Ah. I . . . I am honoured, sir. Renown such as yours is to be understood. At the sight of you '

Even that did not dispel the frown from the other's haughty brow. Almost certainly he was unused to having to look upwards to anyone else, physically or otherwise.

Wallace sought to maintain Lowland credit by introducing Sir John Graham of Dundaff and the other leaders of his party, in such pretentious style as he could muster, not troubling with his own identity — but it did not look as though the MacGregor was much impressed. He slightly raised one bushy eyebrow, however, at Stephen MacGregor's dutiful and fervent greeting to his chief.

The Campbell, although entirely civil and even respectful towards Wallace, seemed just a little reserved about the rest. It became apparent that he, and the MacGregor likewise, had looked for many more men than this mere four hundred — by Highland standards a mere raiding party. He indicated as much, though politely.

'All we could detach from other tasks, Sir Neil, I fear,' the other assured. 'We seek to fight on many fronts. But — numbers are not all, my friends. That I have learned well. Most of what we have done, indeed, has been achieved with less than four hundred men. Ten men of spirit, of daring, and using the land to fight for them, are worth a hundred and more who merely do what they are told.' Hastily he added, 'As you will know well.' Raising his glance, however, he scanned the ranks behind the chiefs. 'Not that you yourselves have as many men assembled, my friends, as I had looked for. But fierce and doughty fighters all, I am sure!'

'These are but a small portion of the Campbell strength,' Sir Neil explained. 'I have many places to guard. And it is my large lands at the head of Loch Awe, and over on Loch Fyne-side, where most of my people are and which are over-run by this man M'Phadan. So many are denied to me. I have two hundred and fifty holding the gateway to this country, from Mid Lorn — the Pass of Brander.' He turned and pointed to the great yawning jaws of a mighty gap in the blue mountain barrier some six or seven miles to the west. 'M'Phadan has four thousand facing that pass. Three thousand Irish gallowglasses, with mainly English officers, and one thousand of Lame John's MacDougalls.'

'My MacGregors are not to be measured by their numbers, whatever!' Glenorchy added, stiffly. Although descended from the brother of King Kenneth MacAlpine, who united Picts and Scots into one kingdom with an iron hand, they were not a large clan. But none north of the Highland Line questioned their fighting abilities.

Wallace, although distinctly concerned over the figures quoted of the enemy strength, the largest numbers he had yet had to contend with, did not admit as much, commenting instead on the fame of the MacGregors as warriors. He went on to say that he had hopes of further reinforcements from the East, as he had sent to the Earl of Lennox at Dumbarton, when rounding the foot of Loch Lomond, for aid in this campaign which Lennox was known to favour; but what, if any, might eventuate, and when, he could not tell.

With his accustomed vigour and directness of approach, however, he requested that he might be put into the tactical picture there and then — to which Sir Neil, nothing loth, declared that just a little further journeying, if his friends were not too weary, would be worth a deal of talk. Eight miles, and they would discern the size and complexity of the problem — but eight difficult miles.

Loch Awe was a curiously shaped loch, rather like a very long-handled hammer, the shaft twenty miles in length. The head of the hammer was, however, the foot of the loch. This head was comparatively small. The eastern, or hammer end was blunt, facing into Glen Orchy, and here Kilchurn Castle rose on a mound amongst the marshes of the Orchy river-mouth, under the east end of mighty Ben Cruachan. But the western end of the head the spike or claw, tailed off into a narrow and notably deep valley, which became all but sheer-sided, a great defile, floored by the loch, now only a deep channel of black water. Gradually this shallowed to the out-flowing River Awe, which drained this twenty-five mile sheet of water, and ran for some three miles North-Westwards into the sea-loch of Etive. The mountains rose in fierce, beetling almost precipitous slopes on each side, so close together as to deny all sunlight into the awesome four mile chasm save at noonday, on the northern side a spur of Cruachan itself, on the south Creag an Aonaidh, the

218

Crag of Meeting. Their tremendous cliff-like slopes plunged
straight into the water on the north side, leaving no room for
even the sketchiest road, whilst on the south a tiny, climbing,
twisting track managed to cling, now at the waterside, now high
above it — the only road from the Western seaboard, the Mac-
Dougall lands of Lorn, into the sequestered Campbell and Mac-
Gregor lands at the north end of Awe. This was the celebrated
Pass of Brander, one of the foremost strategic entities in all the
Highland West.

Despite the lack of any road on the north side, it was along
that flank of the loch that the Campbell led the newcomers;
anything else would have required them to have gone over forty
miles round the loch, or taken to boats to cross the water. After
a couple of miles or so, they had to leave the loch-shore and
start to climb. Quickly their track gained height, until they were
some hundreds of feet above the water. Presently this reached a
steep and wooded ravine down which a major waterfall plunged
whitely — the Eas of Cruachan, Campbell called it; and here
even the sure-footed garrons were beaten and had to be left
behind. After clambering down into the ravine and up the other
side, they could only contour the bare steep mountainside
beyond, mile after mile. They could not even see the narrowing
arm of the loch directly below them now, so steep was the drop.

Almost an hour of this, perhaps three miles, and the gloomy
pass began to open in front of them. The effect was extraordinary. From the harsh constriction of the defile all beyond
seemed wide, sunny, open, colourful, with the blue of the
sea-loch giving way to the wider blue of the Firth of
Lorn, isle-dotted, mountain-framed, lovely, an arm of the
Sea of the Hebrides, another world of light and space, to lift
the heart.

But not *their* hearts, this day. For this was Mid Lorn, young
Duncan MacDougall's homeland, but enemy-held. Down
where Etive's sea-loch joined the Firth was the splendid castle
of Dunstaffnage, once a seat of kings, where the Stone of Destiny had rested when first brought from Ireland. This was the
house of Duncan's father, the old Alexander, Lord of Argyll,
now an unhappy, ailing, done man, brow beaten by the insolent
M'Phadan and slighted by his own crooked eldest son, Lame
John — who it appeared, was not present meantime, having
been summoned to London, for France, to be told *his* contribution to Edward's military needs. M'Phadan himself had

taken over for his own use the Valliscaulium Priory of Ardchattan, on the north side of Loch Etive, dispossessing the monks.
As the crow flew, Ardchattan was no more than six miles from
the west end of the Pass of Brander. But the mile-wide loch and
the River Awe's estuary thereto lay between.

Campbell led them on still further along that lofty footpath
amongst the steep-growing heather which was beginning to turn
purple, here over one thousand feet above the pass floor. When,
presently, they could go no further, and the hillside dropped
sickeningly in front of them, with all lower Etive spread before
them like a map, Sir Neil pointed downwards, and there, half-
way down the dizzy descent, crowning a thrusting rock buttress,
was a little castle, a hawk's eyrie of a place which it seemed
unbelievable that men could ever have managed to build there.
And clinging around and about and below it, on ledges and
shelves and less steep aprons, were men, many men.

'My tower of Creag an Eun,' Sir Neil said briefly. 'And my
Campbell guard. All that saves what is left of my inheritance.'

Further down the heady step-ladder of a path to Creag-an-
Eun, the Crag of the Birds, at last they could see directly to the
gut of the defile, where the extreme western arm of the loch, the
claw of the hammer, became the River Awe, a tranformation
marked only by the sudden shallowing and change in colour of
the water, from black to speckled white. Marked too by two
notable rocks, one on either side of the torrent just where it
changed colour and character.

Campbell pointed again. 'Those rocks. It was ever my
family's task and duty to keep a bridge of timber across those
narrows. Great trees were required. None such grew nearer
than Ederline, twenty-five miles away, which might stretch
across. They had to be floated up, a heavy task. As you can see,
we have destroyed that bridge. None now may cross from Etive
to this side. And my archers here can pick off any who would
seek to use the track on that far side — though such would have
all Awe to cross, if they won past.'

'Then you are entirely safe, Campbell!' the Graham declared.
'You have this M'Phadan held fast. This is such a place as I
have never dreamed of. What do you fear?'

'This is my *back* door only,' the other answered. 'More's the
pity, I have others. Others that M'Phadan knows well. The head
of Awe reaches almost to the sea again, at Kilmartin and
Craignish, thirty miles away to the South-West, easy of access.

And northwards, up Etive, a pass leads over the Lairig Gartain to Rannoch Moor — from which they could come down Orchy to me. We have heard that M'Phadan so plans. An assault from both north and south. Hence my call for aid.'

In that crows'-nest of a castle, from its parapet-walk, Wallace long surveyed all the territory stretched out below him, perceiving all its defensive strength — but also its utter impossibility as any sort of battlefield or ground for offensive action. He had not come to Argyll to help defend the impregnable Pass of Brander.

'If the M'Phadan will not attempt to assail you here — as he would be a fool to do,' he said, at length, 'Then he must be coaxed to do so elsewhere, see you. Where he believes his greater numbers must prevail. This is too evident a trap. If we could seem to reverse this trap . . .?'

'What mean you?'

'The enemy will never enter this defile — unless he conceives that it is to trap *you* therein. If you, with your present company and the MacGregors, were on that far side of the pass, down there at the riverside.' Wallace turned 'Where *is* the main enemy host? I see none.'

Campbell pointed. 'In woodland there, at Bonawe. At the head of Airds Bay, on Etive. They have been camped there for near a month. You cannot see them for the trees. But you can see their smoke.'

'I see smoke, yes. I thought it more of yon village. Bonawe, you name it? And M'Phadan is based there?'

'Not M'Phadan himself. He sits comfortable in Ardchattan Priory, across Etive a couple of miles. But he maintains his largest force there, to bottle us up.'

'Good.' It was the big man's turn to point. 'The valley I can just see — beyond the shoulder of this hill across the pass. There is a valley, there. It seems to run on much the same lines as does this Brander, but a mile or so further south. Is that true? And comes down to Etive not far from *this* river. I can see another river gleaming, just beyond Bonawe.'

'That is the Neaunnt River — from Glen Neaunnt. The two rivers enter Loch Etive only half-a-mile apart, yes. The glen strikes up South-Westwards through low hills, to Loch Neaunnt, some six miles.'

'Could men reach that glen unseen? From your Kilchurn? Use it to come down to Etive, unseen? From *your* country?'

'They would have to be ferried across Loch Awe. In boats.'

'Yes. But so would you, would you not? If you were to march down that far side of Brander?'

'To be sure. What mean you? Another force going down Glen Neaunnt?'

'A larger force. Mine. To get behind the enemy at Bonawe, unsuspected. You, in front, the bait. We, behind, to spring the trap. They will not know of our arrival? Not yet?'

'They will learn, in time, no doubt. But not yet, I think . . .'

'Then the attempt must be soon. Before they learn. Tomorrow.'

The Campbell looked doubtful. 'It would require many boats. To carry so many men across.'

'You *have* boats? I saw some at Kilchurn.'

'Aye. To prevent the enemy from being able to cross Loch Awe, if they won so far, I have gathered all the boats from that side and brought them over to our own. But they are not mostly near Kilchurn. Most are scattered, at townships and strands, down the east side of the loch.'

'Then they must be assembled. To opposite the shortest crossing-place. Tonight. We shall work all night, if need be. And tomorrow surprise this M'Phadan. Let us get back, Sir Neil . . .'

The Graham clapped MacCailean Mor on the shoulder. 'My friend,' he said grinning, 'You have summoned up the Devil! Now dance to his tune! I warrant you will require all your breath! As I mine!'

* * *

They indeed made a busy night of it, as up and down the eastern lochshore the Campbell boats were assembled — fishing-craft, scows, rafts, even coracles, anything that would float. They were brought to two assembly points, about a mile apart but some five miles up-loch from Kilchurn, at an area called Sonachan — this because here was the narrowest crossing, so that the ferrying process could be expedited. So soon as a number of the boats were collected, the men began to be carried over — they could sleep on the far side as well as on this. The crossing here was less than half-a-mile. Nevertheless, it was a grievously slow process.

The enormous task of getting the many hundreds of men across was still going on long after sunrise, with the white morning mists beginning to lift off the mountains; at least no horses were required for this project. The Campbell force of about six hundred — Sir Neil had brought back all but fifty of his men from Craig an Eun, leaving only archers, but this extra two hundred were allotted to Wallace — were mainly across, using the greater number of boats, from Upper Sonachan, since they had to move first, to act as bait; but Wallace's company, of approximately similar numbers, using fewer craft, had still fully one-third on the east shore, when there was an interruption. To the surprise of all, quite a large force of mounted men, Lowlanders in the main, arrived on the scene from the east, with only a brief forewarning by Campbell scouts. The Earl of Lennox had, it seemed, decided that this cause, at least, was worth supporting, and had sent a contribution, thus swiftly.

Wallace, fretting to be off and active, did not know whether to rejoice or otherwise at this timely arrival of reinforcements — for they amounted to nearly another six hundred, and ferrying them also would take many hours, however acceptable the extra fighting-men. Another surprise — they came under the command of Sir Richard de Lundin, the same whom Wallace had last seen on his way to Clifford, at Kilmarnock, as the lords' courier asking for terms, at Irvine. An impatient man, it seemed, he had quickly tired of the subsequent negotiations there, and had betaken himself off, northwards, to Glasgow and then to Dumbarton — apparently he was a relation of Earl Malcolm. There he had found Lennox in a mood of renewed doubts, much impressed with Wallace's Glasgow incident and the discomfiture of Beck, whom he hated; moreover somewhat enheartened by the general situation, and so prepared to reconsider his own attitude towards the invaders. When Wallace's request for aid against Lame John and M'Phadan had reached him, he had hesitated no longer — for this, after all, was his own quarrel. He had hastily collected some five hundred men, and Sir Richard had volunteered to lead them. Their assembly had coincided with the arrival of Sir John Ramsay of Auchterhouse, near Dundee, who was actually in search of Wallace, with sixty men of his own. He had been supporting Lord Hugh MacDuff in his rather fitful uprising in Fife and Angus, and had now come from Dundee to plead with Wallace that he would come and liberate that city, which was ready to rise against the invader. So Ramsay had come on, with Lundin, to the Highland West.

The two knights were considerably surprised, but by no

means reluctant, to be drafted into almost immediate action, and told to get their men across Loch Awe just as quickly as humanly possible, dismounted, and come on after Wallace to Glen Neaunnt.

From the west loch-shore, Wallace led his party climbing North-Westwards past the temporarily deserted village of Kil-chrenan, and on up the long slopes, to the small watershed where dark little Loch Tromlie lay amongst the peat-hags. Here he sent Stephen MacGregor, and MacFadzean, with one or two local Campbells, off to the right, to climb to and follow the edge of the ridge directly above the Pass of Brander on this side, and to keep him informed of what went on far below. The main body proceeded to dip into the shallow but deepening valley of one of the feeders of the River Neaunnt.

They struck that river in about two miles, now in a sizeable glen, lined by green birchwoods, a pleasant sequestered place down which the Neaunnt cascaded in a long series of rapids, with one forty-foot waterfall, so that the valley was filled with the sound of hurrying waters. Two more miles of this, and the first of the panting runners from MacGregor reached them, to announce that Sir Neil and the Campbell-MacGregor host had passed the site of the demolished bridge below Creag an Eun, and were emerging into the open western mouth of the pass. So far, no visible reaction from the enemy.

Duncan MacDougall, who was accompanying Wallace, warned him that in only another mile they would issue from the glen on to the flat woodlands behind Bonawe. Satisfied, and sending forward scouts to ensure that they were not surprised by any enemy patrol, he ordered a halt, to await developments.

They rested, in the sunshine of a warm late July day, and men sought to make up on arrears of sleep. But not Wallace. He had Duncan MacDougall describe for him every yard of the land beyond the glen-mouth, drawing plans of it on the coarse sand of the riverside.

It was over an hour before the next courier arrived, to say that the enemy forces were now on the move, eastwards, out of the Bonawe woodland, towards the Campbell position. Also, two many-oared galleys were crossing Loch Etive at speed, from Ardchattan towards Airds Bay. M'Phadan, it seemed, was on his way.

While these expected tidings were being delivered, the residue of Wallace's force, with some two hundred of the Lennox newcomers under Lundin and Ramsay, caught up with them. He had now some six hundred men in that narrow glen, all but choking it. He moved his front another half-mile forward.

Stephen MacGregor himself came to them there, breathless. M'Phadan had joined his force, between three thousand and four thousand strong probably, and was now hastening to fall upon the Campbells before they could escape him back along the narrow twisting path through the pass. There was no sign, that could be observed from above, of any company being left behind to guard the enemy rear.

Wallace nodded grimly. He gave the order to advance, and at the run. Their friends were going to need them, with a minimum of delay. Out of Glen Neaunnt and into the hillfoot woodlands they swept. These were open woods of birch and pine, with much space between the trees. They could cut off something of a corner here. There were no distant views, except intermittently northwards, across Etive. Soon they were running through the litter and squalor of one of the enemy's camp areas. There were some of the inevitable women camp-followers, about, some horses and barking dogs. They pressed on.

There was a good mile of this woodland behind Bonawe, before they burst out into the open; and above the noise of their going and the thudding of their hearts, they could hear the sound of battle in front. Then, at last, they could see ahead, with the jaws of the pass yawning hugely. And in the low mouth of it, the confusion of furious hand-to-hand fighting, the flash of steel and the babel of shouting men.

It all seemed to be chaos, from this angle, of course, a mêlée of struggling figures. But by no means all were struggling — that was the important point. For M'Phadan's vast preponderance in numbers could not be brought to bear on the comparatively narrow Campbell front. The majority of the host, indeed, could only stand by in frustration — as Wallace had foreseen. That man now took time to halt and reform his breathless hundreds, an array twice as large as any he had yet had to marshall. Not that there was much marshalling to be done, for inevitably he would have to attack on almost as narrow a front as had the enemy. But at least they would go in in good order, breath recovered, and with his best sword-fighters flanking himself in the front rank, Kerlie, Boyd, Blair, MacGregor and MacFadzean, Adam Wallace, Little and Halliday. The knightly gentry might take but a doubtful view of

225

this, but Wallace knew what he wanted. He blew his horn to sound the Advance.

Despite the horn, it took the enemy some time to become aware of their approach, since all were facing the other way; and even when fhe rear rank did perceive them, awareness did not communicate itself to the leadership in front for a further interval. Before any adequate reform of battle to meet this new threat was possible, Wallace and his men were upon them.

It was all more or less as the big man had visualised, up there on Creag an Eun the afternoon before. There was only a narrow space as battlefield, between the rushing river and the steep rocky hillside, perhaps a quarter-mile long but no more than one hundred yards wide. Thousands of the enemy, Irish, English and MacDougalls, were crammed into this corridor, with Campbell and MacGregor, now changing from defence to attack, at one end, and Wallace storming at the other. Still the vast majority could not strike a blow. These enforcedly idle ones were now harassed by arrows shot from the Creag an Eun crags above — and although this was necessarily only a minor aggravation, it had a major impact on thwarted men, packed tight, waiting helplessly and unable to hit back.

Wallace's name, shouted almost continuously by his supporters, his vast size outstandingly evident, and the fame of his terrible sword, made their own impressions, morally as well as physically.

Nevertheless, the fight was hot and by no means certain of outcome, for the enemy fought well, such as could bring their weapons to bear, and there were endless supplies of replacements to take over from the fallen, a distinctly disheartening situation for the much-outnumbered attackers as they began to grow weary. The piles of slain became a problem, too as they heaped up at each end of the elongated arena, so that soon the front ranks of both sides were fighting it out unsteadily on top of mounds of dead and dying, which heaved and shifted below them, in a blood-drenched horror. Men were squeezed, or slithered, off, to fall into the river.

For how long this nightmarish struggle would have continued, and with what outcome, with the attackers still outnumbered, is not to be known. But a new development radically altered the situation. This was the arrival, at last, delayed because of the ferrying bottleneck, of the remainder of the Lennoxmen, some four hundred of them. They might have had

226

little or no effect on the position — since they could no more bring their strength to bear on the actual fighting than could much of M'Phadan's force — had not Thomas Gray, left in charge of the rear, taken a swift decision. With what had been done at Loudoun Hill in his mind, he led the newcomers into a precarious climbing and clambering up the desperately steep slopes to the right, the South-West. There were rocks and stones up there, to roll down — although it could only be at the enemy's very centre, lest their own folk might be hit.

It was a slow and difficult procedure, with the four hundred clinging and scrambling like flies all over the cliff-face, and not all making much of it, hopelessly dispersed, but it began to have effect on the enemy almost at once nevertheless, long before any rocks came hurtling down. The waiting men in the centre could see it all, and knew what it portended — arrows to face from one side, rocks from the other, and no escape save out through their own fighting ranks. Or into the river. Suddenly the urge to get out of this ghastly trap became overwhelming for the great huddled mass of forcedly-inactive men. Outwards they began to press and surge, away from the steep slope above, and this newest threat, some pushing against the backs of their engaged comrades and hampering them. But by the very nature of things, most pushed, or were pushed, out on the longest and open side, where there was no containing pressure — to the river. And into the rushing Awe men began to stagger. Soon it became a stampede. Some managed to win out of the raging white waters, compressed by the pass — but most did not.

A comparatively short while after the Lennoxmen's arrival, it was all over — although small groups held out to the last, to be cut down where they stood. M'Phadan himself, a colourful figure with flaming red hair and rich clothing, with a small number of his officers, perceived that what Gray and the Lennoxmen could do, they could do also, and ran off, to start clambering up the hillside on a southerly line, clearly to get down on to the pass path further up, behind the Campbells and Mac-Gregors. In the confusion of dealing with the stand-and-die groups, they were scarcely noticed at first, and it seemed that they would get clear away, when Duncan MacDougall, avid that his enemy should not escape him, gathered a party of Highlanders and went racing after.

All but exhausted, the victors came together, Sir Neil with wounds on brow and shoulder, the older Glenorchy scarcely

227

able to stand upright, Graham limping, Lundin with an arm hanging useless, all splattered with other blood than their own. Wallace himself was unhurt.

'I thank you, my friend,' the Campbell said, shakily, coming forward, hand outstretched. 'With all my heart. Only William Wallace could have achieved this. It is a triumph, a great victory. For this was Edward's main grip on the Highland West. Now that grip is shattered — thanks to you.'

'Sennachies will sing of this day!' the MacGregor chief announced impressively, sitting down suddenly on a boulder. 'Dierdre and the Fionn, yonder, will need look to their fame!' And he nodded his great head in the direction of Loch Etive. But his glance swept round further, on more immediate intent. 'My whisky!' he cried. 'God's death – who has my whisky?'

But Wallace was concerned with more urgent matters than congratulations and restoratives. There was much to be done, as always after battle. He was busily engaged, in the despatching of scouting parties to ensure that no counter-attacks were mounted from the west, supervising the care of the wounded, identification of prisoners and slain, the collection of weapons and valuables, and the commendation of notable acts performed, when young Duncan MacDougall returned, carrying by the long red hair the dripping head of M'Phadan. They had cornered him in a sort of cave some way up the pass — but a shrewdly thrown dirk had taken the creature in the throat and spared further swordery. So died, in a hole in the ground, the man who had terrorised Lorn, Argyll and half the Hebrides.

Presently a move was made down to Bonawe and Airds Bay, where the leadership embarked on M'Phadan's galleys — actually MacDougall's purloined galleys, with Mac-Dougall oarsmen — to row across to Ardchattan, to take over the enemy's base and headquarters. No effective resistance was offered at the Priory, such officers and administrators as were based there, and not involved in the fighting, having discreetly made themselves scarce. But of cooks and scullions there was no lack, also notably splendid provision in abundance, for M'Phadan had been a man who enjoyed his comforts. A celebratory meal was ordered forthwith.

Around the table in the refectory, an impromptu council was held that evening, largely instigated by no less an arrival than that of William Sinclair, Acting-Bishop of Dunkeld. This high-spirited prelate had come on Wallace's trail, from Dundaff, and was much disappointed that he had been just too late to see, even to take part in, the battle. The errand, on which he had crossed Scotland, was to urge Wallace to come back to his See of Dunkeld — which included St. John's Town of Perth — where he promised a strong force of supporters. He believed indeed that they could take Perth itself, God aiding; and with Dundee also ripe for insurrection, they could link up with both Moray and MacDuff, and stretch a line right across the northern half of Scotland, from Lennox to Angus, above which the English would drop away like flies in frost.

Wallace was in a quandary. It was a tempting proposition. And it was highly satisfactory to have even Lords Spiritual coming seeking his good offices, accepting his leadership. On the other hand, he was much preoccupied with the idea of sailing down to the Ayrshire coast with a fleet of West Highland war galleys and clansmen, and striking at the invaders from a totally unexpected quarter.

However, as the discussion developed it became apparent that such seaborne programme would take some considerable time to mount. The Campbell had been denied his coastal lands and havens for long, and did not know how many of his galleys he would be able to recover, or how long it might take him to do so. Duncan MacDougall promised all the galleys and bir-linns still in his father's keeping, or recovered from M'Phadan's minions; but his brother, Lame John, just because he was lame and handicapped on foot and a-horse, was the more addicted to ships, and as so-called Admiral of the western Sea, had the main mass of MacDougall galleys centred on the Isle of Mull, where he could command the seas between Scot-land and Ireland. The regaining of these, or part of the fleet, would not be achieved without something of a campaign. And there was the Clan Donald Lord of the Isles to watch, always ready to pounce if he discerned any weakness on the part of Clan Dougall.

Perceiving that he might well become embroiled in the endless clan warfare of the Hebridean seaboard, Wallace recog-nised realities. Naval activities were not for him, yet awhile. He would do as the Bishop and Ramsay and Lundin urged, go back to the East, and in some strength, and seek to unite the northern half of Scotland against the English.

Sir Neil, in gratitude, said that he could take three hundred Campbells with him, and promised that when he had settled his affairs and was somewhat recovered of his wounds, he would follow in person with as many again. MacGregor of Glenorchy could do no less — though he did not say that he would come east himself. Duncan of Lorn declared that he would need all his MacDougalls meantime, to ensure that there was no English resurgence in Argyll, and to guard against his brother's return; but once conditions were stabilised here, he too would provide men and galleys in large numbers. He asked that, if Lame John would give up his adherence to Edward's cause, no further proceedings would be taken against him, and the two brothers, descendants of the ancient Kings of the Hebrides and Man, could rule Argyll between them for their aged father.

Wallace was calculating the numbers he would be able to take back across Breadalbane with him, as they thus conferred. His own and Graham's four hundred; Lundin's five hundred Lennoxmen and Ramsay's sixty from Angus; three hundred Campbells and three hundred MacGregors — one thousand five hundred and sixty in all. It was a goodly host. And more waiting for him in the East. Also three knights and a bishop in his train. He might do much for Scotland with these.

CHAPTER THIRTEEN

On July 26th, Wallace and Bishop Sinclair arrived at the little town of Dunkeld, clustering round its fine Cathedral on the peat-stained Tay, amongst close shouldering wooded heights on the southern bounds of Atholl. William Sinclair was not a typical churchman, impetuous, active, young for his position — for he was highly-born. Although of episcopal rank, he was only the Acting-Bishop. Old Matthew Crambeth, true Bishop of Dunkeld, had not been able to stomach Edward's hegemony in Scotland, and with the Primate, Bishop Fraser of St. Andrews, had long been in voluntary exile in France, Sinclair, his Dean, appointed to act in his stead. He was the younger son of Sir William de St. Clair of Roslin, one of the proudest of the Norman nobles of Scotland. But his mother was of the Celtic stock, related to Strathearn, and the Bishop was strong for the

Scottish cause, his private lands having been requisitioned by the English.

Much news awaited the Bishop — and in consequence, Wallace — at Dunkeld, for Sinclair had links with innumerable noble families, and was kept well informed of much that went on in Scotland. There was a letter from his superior, Crambeth, in France, to the effect that old Bishop Fraser of St. Andrews had died there. This was important, as it meant a new appointment to the Primacy, and there undoubtedly would be pressure on the Pope, from Edward, to prefer a pro-English nominee. Then there were tidings that Hugh MacDuff and his two sons had been defeated, in an encounter in the Carse of Gowrie, by the pro-English Earl of Strathearn, and were now prisoners in that earl's castle of Auchterarder. Thirdly there were accounts of further victories for Sir Andrew Moray and his uncle, in the North, with Inverness itself taken and Edward's Governor there, Sir Reginald Cheyne, captured. Finally, and perhaps not unconnected with the last, there were fairly circumstantial accounts that Sir Henry de Latham, the English Sheriff and Captain at Aberdeen, was considering changing sides — this word sent to Sinclair by one of the canons there, the Bishop of Aberdeen being a Cheyne, brother of the captured Governor, and, unusual amongst churchman, working with the English.

All of which, good and bad, was of interest to Wallace. If MacDuff was defeated, there would be depression and caution in Dundee and Angus, and the time might not be ripe for any assault there. On the other hand, Aberdeen might be a better proposition, if its Captain was indeed prepared to change his allegiance — though why this Englishman, Latham, should so elect, was a mystery. They would send a messenger forthwith to Latham, to test him out. If Aberdeen and Perth both could be reduced, then Dundee, lying approximately between them, would be much more vulnerable.

Meantime, then, there was Perth — and if support from Perth's garrison could be ruled out, Auchterarder Castle, no mighty strength, would not long withstand attack, and the MacDuffs might be rescued. Bishop Sinclair summoned Sir William Ruthven of that Ilk, who had formerly been Provost of Perth, as had his father before him — Ruthven lying only a mile or so west of the town — for consultation.

Ruthven, a hearty, boisterous man, was enthusiastic over the

231

idea of an attack, especially when he learned of the numbers available for the attempt — for he had debts to pay in Perth. He said that Sir John Stewart of Menteith was highly unpopular — oddly enough, both with the citizens, because of his strictness, and with the English troops, who did not like a Scot set over them, especially a stern disciplinarian. Morale was low in the town, Wallace's fame and reputation high and the auspicies for a successful assault excellent. Wallace declared that it *was* an assault that he had in mind — not any protracted siege. This was only a part of a wide-ranging campaign, in which he sought the collapse of the English control over the entire northern half of Scotland; he could not afford to be pinned down in siege-warfare anywhere. On the other hand, the successful taking of a major walled town would be an important step — so long as it could be achieved quickly. Ruthven swore that it could.

Fortunately, Ruthven himself having helped to plan and strengthen Perth's walls and defences, he was invaluable in planning their reduction. Moreover, Sir John Ramsay was a veteran campaigner and something of an expert on siegery. He promptly set about the construction of what he humorously called 'bestial', sows, rams and other siege engines. Fortunately there was ample timber for the construction round about Dunkeld, also saplings for the making of large quantities of faggots and fascines, needed for filling in ditches and moats. All these could be floated down the Tay the fifteen miles to Perth; the See of Dunkeld gained much of its income from timber thus floated down to the boatyards of the town.

Wallace would not involve himself in lengthy preparations. Four days was all he permitted, at Dunkeld, and then they marched, as usual, by night. By first light, his men had already ringed the unsuspecting town, and were busy filling in the deep outer defensive ditches with the bundles of faggots.

With Sinclair's promised bishopric men, and others from Dunkeld area, plus a small contingent of Ruthven's people, Wallace had now over two thousand. Even so, it was a small number to assail a town the size of Perth, with military experts recommending that any besieging force should be three to four times as large as the defending garrison. But Wallace was determined that it was to be no siege, but an assault; if they had not won Perth by nightfall, he would go elsewhere. There was to be no mining, trench digging and other time-consuming works. All would be concentrated on three points — the main gates, facing south; the Water Port, at the riverside; and, more secretly, the Mill Port, so well-known to Wallace personally.

As the early morning mists cleared from Tayside on that second day of August, and suddenly the presence of the attacking force became evident to the less than alert watchmen, there was panic reaction within the town. Bugles began to blow, shouting could be heard, and then, one after another church bells commenced to ring out in jangling alarm. At this stage, archery was the main hazard for the attackers, and Wallace used such bowmen as he had, mainly Campbells from Loch Aweside, to try to keep the parapets and towers of the two main assault places under fire, to counter any massing of archery defence. Meanwhile most of his men were urgently racing back and forth, with faggots and fascines, to fill in the deep inner ditch, fortunately mainly dry at this high summer period, at these two points, so that their long timber gangways could be run out over the infilling. These were to carry the weight of the sows and rams — the former, protective shields of timber, roofed with hides, to give cover from hurled rocks, arrows and boiling water, under which the battering-rams could operate against the gates themselves, close under the walls. No such preparations were made opposite the Mill Port.

Wallace saw the principal assaults launched at the main and Water Ports with the 'bestial' worked into position without great difficulty or delay. Then, taking a party of his own close fellowship, about one hundred strong, with Ruthven in addition, he moved round to the west seeking to be as unobtrusive about it as possible.

Near the Mill Port, the Town's Lade, an artificially enlarged burn, flowed into Perth by a sort of wall-bridge, its waters used to turn the King's Mills, as well as supplying the townsfolk. This did create a weakness in the walling, but it was fairly well protected by additional defences and hanging gate-like barriers. More important, for present purposes, was the channel of the stream itself, in its shallow depression, nothing which could be termed a valley, but lined with willows and scrub sufficient to offer a fairly covered approach. Down this, Wallace and his party proceeded, and so came to the Mill Port more or less unheralded.

Risking archery, but partly protected by a shield, the big man went forward to shout for Rob Drummond.

233

At the second shout, he was answered — but not by Drum-mond. It was his assistant porter, whom Wallace had seen twice. He announced that Rob had been arrested by the English and locked up in a cell, for aiding him, Wallace. He was to die, they said — like his daughter. Yes, Meg was dead. They had killed her, after Butler was slain.

Wallace took a great breath. Meg, too! Dear God — Meg, too! But this was no time for indulgence of grief.

'Aye,' he said thickly. 'We will avenge Meg, never fear. And save Rob. Open the gate for us, Pate.'

'I daurna, sir — I daurna!' the man quavered. 'There's sodgers near. They'd kill me.'

'I will have this town in a couple of hours, man. My rams are even now battering the main gates. This way will save blood-shed, much bloodshed.'

'I canna. They'd crucify me. I tell you . . .'

'Would you rather be crucified by *my* people, Pate?' the other returned harshly. 'For the good Scots blood you have spilled by holding us up?'

'Na, na. But . . .'

'Open, man — before they are on to us, here. And on to *you*! I promise you, you shall hang, otherwise! And quickly.'

There was no further answer. But in only a few moments they could hear the wicket-door in the larger gates being unbarred.

It was as easy as that. Wallace was the first inside, Kerlie, Adam and Little at his back. They pushed the two greased draw-bars into their sockets and unhooked the chains. The larger gates swung open, and the rest of the hundred rushed in. Wallace sent a messenger back to inform the Bishop and Lundin, before the main gates, and Graham and Ramsay at the Water Port.

Now Sir William Ruthven acted guide, racing ahead down the narrow streets. People were clustered in doorways and at windows and alley-mouths, anxious, questioning. An English patrol emerged from one lane, saw them, came forwards a little — and then, perceiving their numbers and style, turned and fled whence they had come. None followed them, however.

Soon they were in the criss-cross of streets around the great cathedral-like St. John's Kirk, which gave the town its full name. Turning down Shoe Street, they were not far behind the main gates — and could hear the regular thud-thudding of the battering rams and the shouts and screams of men.

And now, instead of runnng, they began, with flint and tinder, to set alight everything which would burn — thatch, woodwork, furniture, mattresses, anything one hundred men could swiftly lay hands on, ignoring the protests of the townsfolk. Swiftly the smoke-clouds arose, and the shouted complaints of the folk with them. Blazing brands tossed on to the summer-dry reed-thatched roofing was not long in turning the centre of the town into a blazing chaos.

The effect was predictable. Everywhere the defenders of the gates and the towers and walls looked back over their shoulders, and saw the town afire. It could only mean that the enemy had gained entrance behind them — no pleasant thought. The defence suffered in consecuence.

Leaving Ruthven and Thomas Gray, with almost half their men, to organise townsmen to both the lighting of more fires, and the general control thereof, Wallace led the rest further eastwards, towards the Water Port. But here they found they were not needed. Graham's and Ramsay's people had managed to batter down that gate, and were now streaming into the town and tackling the wall-defenders from the rear. Joining forces with Graham, Wallace turned back, to seek out and slay Sir John Stewart of Menteith, the Governor and Sheriff.

But this satisfaction was denied him. The royal castle at Perth, which stood to the north, at the end of Sinnergait, was not really a defensive strength so much as a palace. No attempt at a stand was made here, when they reached it; and the few people found still there, servants and non-combatants, declared that the Sheriff and a number of his officers and associates had slipped away, only a short time before, believing all lost, and making for the castle's postern-gate, which opened on to the Tay. It seemed that there he always kept an oared barge in readiness for emergencies. It was understood that he was on his way to Dundee, down the estuary. And so, once again, Wallace gained a swift victory, but failed to lay hands on the man he wanted. Perth did not so much capitulate as collapse piecemeal, as men realised that they were surrounded, outflanked or abandoned. In less than the couple of hours predicted, all was over and the town completely in Wallace's hands.

One of his first tasks, after ensuring that the fire-fighters got the conflagrations under control, was to release Rob Drummond from his cell, along with many other prisoners. He learned how Meg had died, arms and legs tied, and thrown

235

naked into a pool of the Tay — for aiding William Wallace. Her father seemed not bitter, philosophical rather. But Wallace's anger was terrible to see; it was perhaps as well that Sir John Stewart and his cronies had made their escape. Wallace endowed Drummond generously out of the loot captured from the English — all that he could do.

The big man had to swallow his wrath and hurt, to turn his whole mind to less personal matters. It was important, at this stage, to demonstrate that William Wallace could *hold* towns and castles as well as capture them; and Perth was a suitable place on which to make a start. It was highly strategically situated. It was not too large — and being full of religious establishments, monasteries, friaries, nunneries, hospices, owing to its nearness to Scone, was essentially rich and could afford the costs of wall-strengthening, repairs and garrison-support. Wallace would have left Bishop Sinclair in command, but that energetic prelate announced that he intended to take part in the further campaigning, now he had started. Sir William Ruthven, therefore, was made captain of the town of which he had been provost, and urged to recruit as many men as possible in the area, not only for its defence but for additions to Wallace's growing force.

Two days later, as Wallace was about to move off, with some one thousand eight hundred men, a messenger arrived from, of all people, Sir William Douglas. He brought word that Douglas had captured Sanquhar and Durrisdeer Castles and slain large, if unspecified, numbers of Englishman. Also that the craven capitulation of Irvine was over at last, with rumours that Surrey was dismissed as Viceroy, and Percy and Clifford sent stern instructions from the King himself to end all such foolish talking and weakness forthwith, and to prosecute the King's policies with all vigour, or lose their appointments. The Steward, Wishart and Bruce were all now taken into custody, without any sort of resistance apparently, and the Scots lords' army disbanded. It was high time that Wallace and Graham came south, where they were needed, instead of wasting their time amongst heathenish Highlandmen.

Wallace's reaction to these tidings was the reverse of what Douglas advised. If the South was so feeble, then the North must redress the balance. Up here, his lack of lordly rank appeared to be less important. Moray and he now each had substantial and active forces under arms, and bases to work from in

236

Inverness, Elgin, Argyll and Perth. To abandon these, meantime, for the treacheries and uncertainties of the South, would be folly.

They crossed Tay, and headed North-Eastwards into long Strathmore.

At Coupar Abbey, that night, they found its English-appointed Abbot fled and the monks rejoicing to welcome them, like the little town itself. Elsewhere the pattern was the same. At Glamis they were made much of and the bishop's-town of Brechin treated them as conquering heroes. The enemy hold on Angus was obviously very shaky. Montrose fell without a blow, its small garrison putting to sea northwards, discreetly, in a requisitioned ship.

In Montrose citadel they found an old Lion Rampant standard of King Alexander's time; and next day Wallace rode on through the Mearns with this flying proudly at their head, gathering small parcels of recruits from lairds and towns and even monasteries, and accepting allegiances in King John's name — the presence of the bishop and the knights greatly assisting in this. Sinclair made excellent company, and it was hard to remember that he was, in fact, a prelate.

Only the rock fort of Dunnottar, south of Stonehaven, refused to open its gates to them — and for the sake of their reputation, had to be reduced It belonged to a Lindsay lord, but had been taken over by the invaders as a central headquarters for a wide area, an astonishing place, crowning an upthrusting rock plateau jutting into the sea from lofty cliffs, and almost wholly severed from the land by a deep chasm. Fortunately, as so often the case, the English used Scots servants for the menial tasks, ignoring the dangers of subversion in a sort of arrogant assumption of mastery; and during the very first night outside Dunnottar, a scullion was brought to Wallace's couch, to inform him that if he and his men would come follow, in absolute silence, by the same route that he himself had just come, he would have them inside the fortress within the hour. But it had to be done at once, for such was only possible at extreme low tide. The man thereafter led them round the base of the great rearing rock, over the slippery seaweed — where, fortunately, the sigh of the waves drowned the muttered curses and armour-clinking of stumbling men — and presently up a barely perceptible access by a series of weed-hung ledges, and so to a hollowed-out platform on the sheer cliff-face where, at full tide, a boat might tie up. Opposite this, steps cut in the rock led up dizzily to a narrow postern, a door in the face of part-masonry, part living rock. This opened at the scullion's quiet knock, to a youth and a further long flight of steps. Then they were up on the summit plateau, within the walls, one hundred and sixty feet above the waves. Wallace waited quietly there until sufficient of his people had climbed up and assembled, to make the necessary multiple assaults on the different buildings which dotted the uneven site. Then, in simultaneous attacks, they surprised the garrison with minimum difficulty. There were some pockets of hard fighting, but in the main surprise was complete enough to ensure swift success. They found the largest number of troops actually asleep in the parish church, which oddly enough shared this rock with the citadel, men evacuated here from sundry other places, including the Montrose garrison. Packed tight in the church, with fires lit at the only two doors, these yielded with no undue delay. The Bishop was unhappy about fighting and burning in a church — as Wallace himself would have been a year before; but other fires had hardened that large young man to a steely determination.

From Dunnottar's prestigious address, Wallace and the Bishop sent a courier to Sir Henry de Latham, at Aberdeen sixteen miles to the north. They suggested a secret meeting, at Muchalls partway between, the following night — for the advantage of all.

Latham did not appear next night at the rendezvous; but he sent an emissary, a hand-rubbing cleric, who indicated doubts on the Governor's part. Before anything of value could be achieved, he said, his master would have to have sundry firm assurances, arrangements. He was, after all, an important man, a highly-placed officer of King Edward, a man of many responsibilities.

Wallace heard the fellow out. 'Correct me, Sir Priest, if I am wrong,' he said, at length. 'Henry de Latham is prepared to betray Edward Plantagenet. But he is concerned that his payment therefore is adequate, and certain!'

The other spluttered protests, but when forced to it, did not deny the basic reality of that.

'Tell your master, then, sir, that William Wallace does not chaffer over such merchandise, nor buys a man's loyalty. I will have Aberdeen, whether Latham gives it to me, or no. Mind that! I offer him his freedom and one shipload of his belongings,

238

treasure, chattels and friends. If he yields to me without blood-shed. If not, he hangs — as I hanged Arnulf of Southhampton, at Ayr. Tell him that, sir. That is all the chaffering William Wallace will consider. Now — begone, Englishman!'

Hardly was the unhappy cleric away than Wallace was calling for volunteers from his own group — fifty would serve. They had work to do. That day he had not waited idly, but had had scouts probing northwards to Aberdeen, disguised as pedlars. They had reported much activity in the harbour area, with ships being hurriedly loaded with large quantities of goods, valuables, furnishings, hangings and the like, no doubt looted from a wide area of the North-East. Clearly Latham was ensuring a profitable get-away; but if he left the garrison, under better men than himself, to hold the city, then there would be little advantage for the Scots — for all declared Aberdeen a strong place, with natural defences, which might hold out for long. Latham must be made to see things in a different light.

With a hard-riding party of veterans, therefore, the big man pounded up the coast road by a long succession of cliff-tops and fishing-havens, through the August night. In due course they came to the estuary of the Dee, wide, with no crossing save by ferry — one of the principal defences of the city, as the scouts had emphasised. So Wallace turned his people half-right, to the fishing-village of Torry, at the southern tip of the estuary. Here they appropriated about a dozen of the many fishing-boats drawn up on the boat-strand. They took a chance on the loyalty and sympathies of the fishermen, knocking them up and requesting their help. Soon they had many more volunteers than they could use, and many of the villagers, hearing the name of Wallace, insisted in coming along in their own craft, unbidden.

They rowed out across the estuary, on a jabbly sea, with still a couple of hours or so to dawn. All was dark in the harbour and vicinity, and only one or two lights gleamed in the town itself. The tide, naturally, was again almost full out at this time, and the harbour, being partly tidal, some of the vessels were lying high and dry, others moored at quays or in the shallows. Each of the chosen fishing-boats was under the command of one of Wallace's own trusted lieutenants — Adam, Kerlie, Gray, Blair, Boyd, MacGregor MacFadzean, Little and Scrymgeour. Now all these chose their targets, and went boarding.

There were, in fact, not very many men aboard any of the

ships. These were in the main English transports, for the provisioning of the scattered East Coast garrisons, which were most
readily supplied by sea. Most of the crews much preferred to
spend their nights ashore in the brothels, ale-houses and requisitioned quarters. As a consequence, the capture of the shipping
was comparatively simple. Wallace would have liked to extract
the valuables and spoil from the vessels, to restore if possible to
the rightful owners; but there was no time for that. All the ships
had to be fired and destroyed — that was vital. Goods, property,
material things, were of lesser matter — at least to William
Wallace.

By dawn, with most of the shipping in the harbour ablaze,
and alarms beginning to sound in the city, the flotilla of boats
was speeding back across the estuary to Torry. To prevent any
reprisals on the fisherfolk there, Wallace and his party remained
at the village, only sending couriers, to Graham and the Bishop,
to bring on their now-advancing host to join them at Torry.

Latham's clerical messenger found them again, before noon,
in distinct agitation. His master accepted the terms Wallace
suggested, he announced. Sir Henry would sail out of Aberdeen harbour, in one ship, as Wallace rode in at the main gates.
There would be no resistance, if it was agreed that the garrison
would not suffer hurt. He swore that there would be no trouble,
so long as Wallace held to his bargain.

There was no trouble. In mid afternoon the Scots array had
moved to the river-mouth, to start the lengthy process of ferrying across Dee. Even a small defensive force could have held
them up here at Garthdee, almost indefinitely. But nothing of
the sort developed. They rode on into Aberdeen unim-
peded — and wherever the garrison was, it did not make its
presence felt. No crowds lined the narrow streets, though many
citizens peered from windows and doors uncertainly — less
forthcoming than the Torry fisherfolk. Wallace waved and
smiled to them, but with only moderate response. The military
hand had been too heavy here.

At the citadel above the harbour, an elderly hard-bitten
Yorkshire captain of foot waited to hand over command of all,
without ceremony — apparently the highest-ranking officer left,
all his superiors having elected to sail off with Latham. It was
noteworthy that the Governor's ship could be seen turning
northwards, outside the harbour, not southwards. Wallace
would have been interested to know where he was heading and

what were his plans, now that he had broken faith with his liege lord. Presumably he had some understanding or arrangement with some magnate in the North — the Earl of Ross, perhaps, who acted the independent prince in his remote domains, or even Sir Andrew Moray. Such a man was unlikely to burn his bridges without being sure of security on the far side. It was to be observed, also, that Latham had interpreted Wallace's terms in a fairly broad fashion, so that although he took only one large vessel, quite a fleet of small boats escorted it.

Aberdeen was considerably larger than Perth or Glasgow, a city which was the administrative centre for a huge area, of Mar, the Garioch, Formartine, Strathbogie and Buchan. Bishop Sinclair, Ramsay and some others were for making a prolonged stay here, to consolidate, to ensure the firm adherence of all this great North-East, the complete elimination of the English presence therein. But Wallace was otherwise minded. The area, although important, was not really vital in the battle for Scotland, he claimed. The cause would be won, or lost, in the South. Besides, this was really Moray's terrain and responsibility. They had made a gesture, shown that nowhere was safe for the English. But Aberdeen was no place on which to lavish their best energies. North of Forth and Clyde, Dundee, the second-largest city in the land, was a better target, more strategically important in that it could dominate both Angus and Fife and protect the flank of the most vital point of all, Stirling. They could not take Stirling, with its quite impregnable fortress, the strongest citadel in three kingdoms; but Dundee and Fife, in their hands, would lessen Stirling's usefulness to the enemy.

As a token move towards the other point of view, however, Wallace led a swift-moving expedition up the Aberdeenshire coast to Buchan, where the Comyns were based, and where it was said that Latham's ship was heading, at least in the first instance. It was not a major effort, and they were back in Aberdeen in four days; but it showed the flag to a populous area, drove Sir Henry de Beaumont, King Edward's own cousin, out of Slains Castle, and served notice on the Comyn Earl of Buchan, kinsman of King John Baliol, as to where his true duties lay.

Thereafter, leaving Sir Richard de Lundin in command at Aberdeen, the host moved southwards for Dundee.

*　　*　　*

On the way to Dundee, through the Mearns and Angus, Wallace picked up quite large numbers of recruits, from local lairds and churchmen and the burghs, stirred by the accounts of his doings. They also were caught up by two messengers — one from Moray, announcing further successes, in the Black Isle and Easter Ross, teaching the treacherous Earl of Ross a lesson and announcing that Moray was now on his way southwards through Badenoch with an enlarged army. He had heard of the fall of Perth, and proposed that the two forces should meet there, in due course. The second courier was from Lanarkshire, from Cousin Auchinleck, with less cheerful tidings. He informed that Sir William Douglas had been captured, and was now on his way, under heavy guard, for the second time, to London. Bruce also was a prisoner of sorts, at Carlisle, where his father, the Lord of Annandale, had been Governor and was now dismissed, by King Edward's command. Surrey was likewise dismissed, as Viceroy for Scotland — but, was still commander-in-chief of the forces north of York, this for the very simple reason that most of the troops under his command were Northumbrian and Cumbrian levies of his own and his vassal lords. The new Viceroy, FitzAlan, was a very different man, active, aggressive. Wishart was now imprisoned in Roxburgh Castle, and the Steward was thought to be in England. There was nothing for Wallace in the South-West meantime.

Dundee was a different problem from any which Wallace had yet had to face — a large city, walled, with its castle very strong in the centre. He knew it well, of course, from his early years, but was not particularly well-informed as to its defences. Ramsay, whose estate of Auchterhouse lay only a few miles to the north, and Alexander Scrymgeour who was a native, were able to guide him. The walls should cause them little difficulty, they said, for it was really too large a city to defend effectively, and the masonry was very weak in many places. Moreover, the citizens were probably more independently-minded than in any other town in Scotland, and there had been risings without number against the occupying forces. But the castle was very strong, on one of the many hills above the town, and with a large garrison. By its very situation it could not be surprised, and, even though the town fell, might well defy assault for long. There was a new Governor, identity unknown; but since he had been but recently appointed he was likely to be the toughest sort. Sir John Stewart of Menteith was thought to be still at Dundee, also.

Ramsay's and Scrymgeour's prognostications were proved fairly accurate. The host reached the city's outskirts towards the end of August, nearly three thousand strong. There could be no surprise, with numbers such as these; anyway, their progress had been open and indeed spectacular, under the Lion Rampant, all the way. They found the city gates closed against them, as expected, but there was no offensive action. Wallace sent a deputation, under a white flag, to demand the surrender of town and castle, in the name of King John — but this was met only by a shower of arrows. Whereupon he made a personal circuit of the entire perimeter walling, examining all as closely as he dared, out of arrow-shot. There were, as Ramsay and Scrymgeour said, many weaknesses. It ought not to be difficult to effect an entry.

There was no need. That evening a group of citizens appeared in the Scots camp, asking for Wallace. They announced that there were three separate points, unknown or ignored by the English, where entry could be achieved; one, a gate opening into a tannery yard at the cattle-market, and two broken sections of walling, only superficially patched and held up by hoardings on the inside. They would demonstrate where these were, after dark, and the entire town could be in Wallace's hands by morning.

'But the castle?' Wallace observed.

No, they admitted, not the castle. There they could not help. The accursed castle was beyond their grasp — and Wallace's, they feared. It had no known weaknesses.

A few hours later, then, Wallace's troops were inside the walls of Dundee, and fanning out through the town as silently as might be. They managed to take the guards, at three of the gates, in the rear — and these fought bravely if hopelessly; but warning reached the Cowgait Port and Market Port just in time for the defenders there to make their escape. The first managed to disappear into the warren of alleys and wynds behind the harbour; but the second, being nearer to the castle, bolted straight therefore, a party of about twenty men, with Wallace's people hot on their heels. And something of the style and quality of the castle's defenders was then demonstrated. For when these twenty reached the castle-hill, still just ahead of the pursuit, although the drawbridge was half-up and the portcullis raised, when the fugitives yelled for the bridge to be lowered quickly, to let them in, instead it was raised fully to its upright position and the portcullis dropped with a crash into its slots, to shut them out. The hapless men, abandoned, were cut down by the Scots, there before the castle's outer defences, without a hand raised to help them. Clearly whoever was in command was ruthless as he was determined, prepared to sacrifice a score of his own men rather than risk enemy feet on his drawbridge.

The day following, although Dundee, from its provost and magistrates downwards, was waiting and eager to do honour to William Wallace and his men, to present them with the keys of the city, to demonstrate their entire loyalty and enthusiasm, to feast and fete them, Wallace delayed. He spent the entire day examining in detail every aspect of the castle on its hill, every yard of its perimeter and defences, considering every possible approach, any conceivable source of weakness. And could find none. With no possibility of surprise, no likelihood of any ruse being successful, Dundee Castle was safe from assault, its hill-top site precluding the use of any siege-engines which the attackers might fabricate. It appeared that its garrison might only be starved out — and it was no doubt well provisioned, and was known to possess two wells. Wallace was faced with the situation he had always avoided, the need for prolonged siege.

Normally he would have promptly abandoned the situation, and gone elsewhere. But having captured — or, more properly, been delivered — the second city of Scotland, to ride off and leave it would have looked feeble in the extreme. Moreover, that would be to deliver its citizens over to a retaliatory reign of terror — nothing more certain. But there was another aspect of the matter, in that perhaps they were as well besieging Dundee Castle as being anywhere else, that late August of 1297. Wallace had a larger force than ever before; but it was still nothing like sufficient to commence any major campaign of seeking to turn the English out of the strongly-held South of Scotland. And to go back merely to guerilla tactics would be a backward step, mere picking at the problem. He would have to wait for Moray, for any move into the South. So he might as well wait at Dundee. He was, moreover, finding the problems of feeding, and especially foraging the horses of thousands an ever greater preoccupation, something which he had never had to trouble with hitherto. Dundee at least could supply them adequately.

244

So Wallace settled down to encompass Dundee Castle, something he had never thought to do.

It was on the fifth day of the siege that the news reached them. Edward Plantagenet was not wholly preoccupied with his Flanders campaign, it appeared. Wallace and the Scots were to be taught a lesson, once and for all. A huge army had been assembled in the North of England, and was already moved to Berwick, with most explicit orders not to return until it had stamped out the very last flicker of revolt in Scotland, by any and every means. Surrey, since the troops were largely his, had to be in nominal command; but Hugo de Cressingham, the Treasurer, completely Edward's creature, was put in joint-control. And Cressingham, although a cleric, had the most savage reputation in the land, more ruthless even than Bishop Beck. The size of the array was put at eighty thousand, and Percy and Clifford were said to be ordered to join it, from Carlisle and the West, with ten thousand more. The rumour was that Edward had ordered the Steward and Bruce, with Lennox and other Scots lords, to be carried along with this host and forced to take part in the campaign against their own countrymen. Reports gave Stirling as the first objective — as it would be, if Wallace and Moray were the principal targets.

These tidings, of course, changed everything. Dundee Castle became of secondary importance. A decision had to be made, and quickly, as to whether to risk any sort of confrontation with the great army; whether to retire before the invaders in strength, either into the Highland North or West in an effort to lure them into some sort of trap; or whether to disperse altogether, and await better days.

Wallace barely considered the third possibility. The first could only be contemplated if Moray and he could join forces. Moray had said that they should meet at Perth, date unspecified. Within an hour or so of the receipt of the news, Wallace had sent off couriers to find Moray to urge him to get to Perth with all speed and as many men as he could raise. Leaving Alexander Scrymgeour, with about one thousand four hundred men, mainly from Aberdeen, Angus and Dundee itself, to continue the siege of the castle, he was off that same night, westwards for Perth.

There was only some twenty-two miles between the two towns, by the Carse of Gowrie. They reached Perth to find no sign of Moray; but Sir William Ruthven had released the Lord

Hugh MacDuff from Auchterarder Castle, as instructed, and
that elusive individual had forthwith gone to raise another force
in his native Fife. Ruthven said that he had claimed that he
could raise a thousand and more, now that Perth, Aberdeen and
Dundee were fallen. Wallace preferred to believe in MacDuff's
phantom force when he saw it, but he welcomed the possibility
of further support, from any source. They were going to need
every man they could raise. Ruthven said that he had heard
only that morning that Surrey and Cressingham were at Edinburgh, with a mighty army.

While they waited for Moray, and emissaries went out in
every direction to urge and plead for men to rally at Perth, not
to Wallace's but to King John's standard, Wallace himself was
not idle. With Graham and a party of close associates he rode
away southwards to the high shelf-like westwards extension of
the Ochil Hills called Sheriffmuir. From the southern lip of this
area he gazed still further southwards over the green levels of
the Forth, where the great river, almost at its widening to the
estuary, meandered through the wide marshy flats in fantastic
coils and loops. Out of that watery plain, in which Cambuskenneth Abbey lay in one of the loops, soared three lofty
eminences, one on the north side of the river, Abbey Craig, the
other two well to the south and west, the dramatic fortress-
crowned rock of Stirling with a grey town climbing its steep
skirts, the other the wooded Hill of Drip, not so far from Gargunnock and its peel. And in the midst, spanning the river at a
sudden narrowing, the most famous viaduct in Scotland, the
lengthy wooden trestle-structure of Stirling Bridge, with its
mile-long stone-and-log causeway stretching northwards across
the marshes, to the foot of Abbey Craig.

For long Wallace stared at it all, and as the evening light of
early autumn threw long shadows, moved on and down to the
wooded Abbey Craig itself, heedfully avoiding the vicinity of
the quite large enemy post at Causewayhead, northern guard of
the bridge. Under the trees at the craggy top of the whale-back
ridge, he assessed and memorised and examined in depth and
detail. In all the doubts, questions and uncertainties of the immediate future, one matter was assured, certain — the English
army must come here, to cross that bridge. The Fords of Frew
were well enough for a small force of light cavalry; but a major
host required the bridge — and this was the only one before the
impassable Highland mountains.

'If the bridge was cut,' Graham said, 'they could not cross with their heavy chivalry and their thousands of foot.'

'True. But their thousands of foot could build another bridge.'

'We could prevent them, from this side.'

'With their likewise thousands of archers? The river is not a bow-shot wide.'

'What, then?' Kerlie asked. 'If we cannot hold them up here, where can we?'

Wallace did not answer. But he continued to gaze, while the light lasted.

Back at Perth, Wallace fretted, temper short. Where was Moray? Where was MacDuff? Where were all the men his emissaries had been sent to fetch? With what Sir William Ruthven, the Abbot of Scone and some other local magnates had managed to raise, plus the Perth citizen bands, he had almost four thousand people. But even allowing for gross exaggeration in the enemy figures, these were as nothing for the task ahead.

His first lift of the heart was, in fact, the sound of Highland bagpipes and the totally unexpected arrival of Sir Neil Campbell of Lochawe and MacGregor of Glenstrae, from the far West, with almost one thousand of their clansmen, a colourful array on which the good folk of Perth looked askance but which Wallace welcomed almost with tears in his eyes. They had been getting in their harvest, Sir Neil explained, but now were ready for anything. They had not heard of the new great threat, so imminent, and their arrival on the scene was purely fortuitous; but they seemed actually to be the more joyful at the prospect revealed to them.

Surrey was now said to be at Linlithgow, some nineteen miles south of Stirling. That night, Wallace could by no means sleep, but paced the grass outside his tent on the South Inch of Perth. He well knew that what was facing him was the supreme test, making all that had gone before a mere small-scale preparation. And not only in the matter of numbers. The fact was that he would be facing what he had never had to face before, something of which he had no experience, something against which his native wit and all the courage in the world could be of little avail — the mighty mass of the armoured chivalry, the heavy knightly cavalry of a great army, allied to the thousands of archers which the English would be certain to employ, forces they had no hope of even beginning to rival. This would be major war — and Wallace had no training in such a thing. Not a man for doubts, he knew doubts now, and paced the grass.

In the morning, as always, things looked better — especially when his scouts came to tell him that a great host was sighted, approaching from the North, which could only be Moray's. It seemed to be many thousands strong.

'Thank the good God and all His saints!' Wallace cried. 'Thank God!'

CHAPTER FOURTEEN

To do Sir Andrew Moray justice, he was very patient, understanding, even accommodating, when he might well not have been. He and his people were tired, having come in haste all the way from Badenoch, where they had been teaching the Red Comyn, Lord thereof, a lesson — which was, incidentally, only remotely connected with the present struggle, and more in the nature of a family feud. Nevertheless, weary or not, at Wallace's urgent representations, Moray had agreed to come on, almost at once, with most of his horsed strength, the thirty miles or so to the Forth plain, almost another full day's riding. Now, in the evening light, they were grouped on the North-Western shoulder of the Abbey Craig, openly, sitting their horses and looking out over the levels to Stirling. They had, indeed, been there for almost two hours, showing themselves. They ate as they waited; but the saddle-sore weariness ached in their backs.

Not for the first time. Moray voiced his doubts. 'You believe that this is necessary, Wallace? Still? That we wait here. My people are done. The enemy, at Stirling, must know that we are here. What is to be gained by this standing, horsed, idle?'

Many of Moray's knights and lieutenants growled agreement.

'They must believe us to be waiting, yes — poised, a continuing threat to the bridge, my lord,' Wallace insisted. 'Or, at least, the causeway. As I see it, all that we can do depends on them not attempting any crossing until we are ready for them. Until our greater force, our foot, come up. We know that the

English advance-guard has reached Stirling — and they can watch us from the castle. If we stand down now, they might conceivably start a crossing. And that could be fatal for us. They *must* believe that we are going to stand thus, all night. Tomorrow, also we must so stand, I say.'

There were snorts and mutterings from all around.

Wallace looked about him. 'Unless, my friends, you have a better strategy? Have you?'

Moray shrugged. 'We cannot meet them on a fair field, no. Therefore some device we must have. But this standing waiting . . . !'

'You will have more active work aplenty, tomorrow, my lord, I think! Or the day after,' Wallace assured him grimly. 'Myself, I am happy to do no more than stand, meantime.'

Graham, Ramsay and Campbell made loyal sounds — even though they also doubted.

It was a difficult situation for Wallace. Moray had brought six thousand men to Perth, one hundred and fifty of them well-mounted knights and lairds. So that in numbers of command, as well as of rank, he was superior. Moreover, he was an experienced commander of large forces, and of cavalry, which Wallace was not. In theory, he should have been in control, master of the Scots force — and certainly his officers so believed. Yet he had not assumed the leadership. Nor was Wallace disposed to yield it. Without vanity or conscious self-interest, he continued to make the decisions. He was careful to consult and in minor matters defer to his high-born colleagues — as to his good friends of whatever rank — but the final choices, he never doubted, lay with him. Now, he had to carry Moray with him, without seeming to dominate.

He had his way. They stood there until darkness, and the lights of the English watch-fires blazed all the way along the causeway and bridge below them. Then most of the horsed company moved back and down, into the valley behind Abbey Craig, to camp. Wallace and a group of his own, stayed there on the ridge.

The Scots foot were coming in all night, in troops and companies, forced-marching from Perth, done, all but exhausted. Campbell's and MacGregor's Argyll clansmen, used to swift, light-foot travel, were first.

In the morning, from the lofty stance, they could see the endless columns of the English main array coming down the

long slopes from St. Ninians, the Borestane Brae and Bannockburn, as far as eye could reach, under a forest of banners
and standards, a sight to make even Wallace's heart miss a beat.
The same ranks of Scots light horse stood on the same ridge of
Abbey Craig, all the new-come foot remaining hidden in the
valley behind. The foot were being brought in continually,
through the little Ochils pass from Sheriffmuir, by Hill of Logie
and Airthrey, hidden even from the topmost tower of Stirling
Castle by the mile-long ridge of Abbey Craig.

In mid-forenoon, with the oncoming enemy host still covering all the land to the skyline, southwards, Wallace declared
that he thought that they would not seek to cross that day. Their
destriers and heavy war-horses would be tired. Much of their
main host was still to arrive.

'Then we need no longer stand here,' Moray declared. 'This
standing in the sun, like wooden puppets, is no employment for
men of rank and spirit.'

'Stand down then, my lord — you and yours. If you must.
But leave your horses here, I pray you — so that *my* people, of
lesser rank perhaps but equal spirit, may sit them. They will
appear the same from Stirling Castle ramparts, I swear! Noble
blood will scarce be discernible at such range!'

The other looked at the big man narrow-eyed, opened his
mouth to speak, then thought better of it, and nodded briefly.
The exchange of saddle-sitters took place.

At near noon there was a diversion. A new force came
marching from the Perth direction, not secretly through the hills
but openly down the Allan Water, in full view of the enemy, to
skirt the English-held redoubt at Causewayhead and so to climb
the Abbey Craig. They came with banners flying and fifes playing, a brave show a score mounted at the front, the rest foot, the
great red-and-gold standard of the Earldom of Fife, so like
the royal Lion Rampant, at their head. It was the MacDuff,
at last.

Wallace was doubtful about this flamboyant reinforcement,
at this stage — despite the fact that it was perhaps one thousand
strong and every man counted. So much would depend on the
Lord Hugh's attitude. The MacDuff Earls of Fife could claim
to be the most senior nobles of Scotland, of the ancient Celtic
royal line. Theirs was the privilege of placing the crown on the
heads of the Kings of Scots at their coronation, as indication
that they could be the principal supporters of the throne. The

present Earl was only eleven years old, and held in King Edward's power. But his more warlike uncle could claim to represent him. As such he was, of course, much the highest ranking man present, and might well presume that he should have the over-all command, as of right — which Wallace was quite determined should not happen. MacDuff was evidently a showy and mercurial character, who might conceivably throw away all on a dramatic gesture or misplaced flourish.

However, although MacDuff turned out to be a large and rumbustious individual, all fiery reddish hair, bristling beard and hearty laughter, he seemed to assume from the first that Wallace was in sole command. He had come, indeed, to place himself and his contingent from Fife, under Wallace's banner. This, naturally, was of great advantage to the latter, especially vis-a-vis Moray. To that extent, a considerable weight was lifted from Wallace's mind — even though MacDuff's company was clearly going to have its trying moments, that braying laugh a particular trial.

This adherence had scarcely been assimilated when there was another and still more unexpected development. A small mounted party were seen to be advancing from the south side of Forth, over bridge and causeway, under a large white flag. It had never occurred to the Scots that the English, in their overwhelming might, would seek a parley.

But it was not quite that. When the newcomers were brought up to the ridge — where Moray, MacDuff and all the leaders of the Scots army were now drawn up under the Lion Rampant of Scotland to receive them — they turned out not to be Englishmen at all, but a little group of Scots nobles under James, the Lord High Steward and Malcolm, Earl of Lennox. Wallace was as surprised as the rest.

'My lords,' the Steward said thickly, gloomy and unsmiling as ever. 'Sirs, my friends — greeting. God be with you. Will — Will Wallace, I give you fair greeting. We are well met.'

Eyeing him askance, nobody answered at first, until Wallace spoke. 'Are we, my lord Steward?' he asked. 'I am ever happy to see friends. Especially my own lord. But . . . you keep strange company, I think!'

'Perhaps, Will — but *strong* company, I fear!'

'We come as friends, yes, Wallace,' Lennox asserted. 'For your best advantage. The advantage of all.'

'From . . . Surrey, my lords? We esteemed you prisoners?'

251

'Aye, prisoners,' the Steward agreed heavily. 'But still your friends. Hear us.'

'We will hear you, yes. But I, for one, will think twice before I *heed* you this day, my good lord. Since, if Surrey sent you — as he needs must have done — *he* plans nothing to our good advantage. That I swear!'

There was a muted growl of agreement from all on the Scots side.

'There you are wrong, Will,' the Steward said, with evident earnestness. 'You misjudge. Surrey is not your enemy, in this. Cressingham, yes. But it is Surrey sent us, not Cressingham.'

'To say what, my lords?'

'To say, Wallace, that you, and all here, should retire,' Lennox declared. 'That if you will retire from this position, disperse your men, and give assurances against further rising, Surrey will not proceed against you. Your actions will be forgiven, and you will be received back into the King's peace.'

'Whose peace, my lord? Which king?'

'King Edward's, man. There is none other, now.'

'Then I, for one, cannot be received back — since, God be praised, I was never in it! I have seen enough of Edward's peace!'

'You do not speak for all, in that,' the Steward pointed out.

Wallace looked around him.

'And if we do not accept these terms from my lord of Surrey?' Moray asked.

'Then he will crush you utterly, and without mercy.'

'If he can, sir — if he can!'

'Do not be a fool, Moray,' Lennox said roughly. 'You do not know what you say! Do you not perceive what you so witlessly challenge? Surrey has fifty thousand foot, four thousand Welsh archers, a thousand heavy chivalry. What have you to oppose to that? A handful!'

'More, perhaps, than you think, my lord of Lennox. This is not all . . .'

Hastily Wallace intervened. 'Did you think that we would accept these terms, my lord Steward?' he asked.

'I prayed that you would. For I do not wish to see good Scots blood staining the Forth. As it will, it must, if you oppose them. That is why we are come, why we agreed to this mission. To save our folk. Not for the English cause. We are prisoners, yes — but we have our pride.' There was a rather pathetic dignity in that.

'And you would trust the English? After all they have done? I would not!'

'Nor I! Nor I!' That was a chorus.

'We trust Surrey. Not Cressingham, no. That up-jumped clerk is evil. Surrey hates him. There is bad blood between them . . .'

'This also is why we are here, see you,' Lennox interposed. 'There is opportunity here for you, for us — the Scots. In their hatred of each other. Cressingham would not have had us come. Take Surrey at his word.'

'Tell me, my lords — is not Cressingham Edward's creature? Here to see that Edward's will is done? Edward does not trust Surrey — else he would not have dismissed him as Viceroy. What Surrey agrees today, Cressingham could disown tomorrow.'

'Nevertheless, most of the troops are Surrey's. They will do as *he* says, Wallace. Already Cressingham has sent messengers to turn back Percy, Surrey's nephew, and Clifford, with their ten thousand, coming from Carlisle — the Bruce carried with them. Saying that they are not required. That he will not pay for them. He is the Treasurer. Because he does not want more men who will do Surrey's bidding, as against his own.'

'That is good news, my lord. Dissension on the English side must help us, yes. But I do not see why we should therefore retire, give up?'

'It is because, if you do not, you will play into Cressingham's hands, man. And all Scotland will suffer. You cannot halt or beat this great host. They will trample you under, and afterwards Cressingham will wreak dire vengeance on the land. Retire now, as Surrey asks, and he will take his host back to Northumberland. He is a sick man, and weary of war. But once battle is joined, there will be no turning back.'

'As you say — once battle is joined there will be no turning back! *We* have not assembled here, my lords, to turn back. Nor to parley, as at Irvine! We fight. Under this Lion Rampant standard, the Scots stand. Fight and do not retire.'

Into the roar of applause, Lennox exclaimed. 'And who, Wallace, gave *you* authority to raise that royal standard? A simple knight's son. And to speak in the name of Scotland?'

It was Sir Andrew Moray who answered him. '*We* do,

Lennox — we all do. We lords, knights, lairds, chiefs — aye, and bishops, too — who have drawn the sword in the defence of our land, *we* give William Wallace his authority, this day!'

The cheers which rang out on Abbey Craig must have been heard in Stirling town two miles away, and set the English wondering.

Bishop Sinclair spoke up. 'In council, my lords, we have appointed William Wallace and Sir Andrew Moray, Lord of Pettie, joint generals of the Scottish host. They speak for all.'

'This host? Where is it?'

MacDuff could not restrain himself. ' 'Fore God, my lords, if you looked over this hill, you would not need to ask.'

Wallace bit his lip. He had taken great precautions to keep their great mass of foot hidden from the enemy. Now it was secret no longer.

'Ha — you have more, then? Many more?'

'Many, aye — many thousands. Let your English look to themselves!'

'My lords,' Wallace said urgently. 'Of a mercy, say naught of this to the English! You are Scots . . .'

'We are not spies or informers, Wallace! How many have you?'

'More than we seem. Let us leave it at that.'

'Never fear, we will say naught of this,' the Steward assured.

'You reject Surrey's offer, then? Think carefully, man.'

'Reject, yes. Here we stand — and Scotland's hopes with us!'

'Hopes . . .!'

The deputation took its reluctant leave, and most of the Scots leadership retired back into the valley behind the Craig. But not Wallace. He remained with the motionless horsed ranks, staring out, as though he would imprint every fold, wrinkle and feature of that waterlogged plain indelibly on his mind.

In the afternoon there was another deputation under white flag — this not unexpected, at least by Wallace. It consisted of but two friars — and that these were sent by Cressingham there could be little doubt. He would be anxious to find out what he could, on hearing of their defiance, as to their numbers and dispositions. The monks were given short shrift, and when they had delivered their purely formal demand for surrender, they were sent off with the request that their masters send no more such deputies, but come in person, when they would find the Scots ready to meet them, aye even to their beards!

At least there would be no assault that night. It was September 10th. Tomorrow, then.

*   *   *

When, at first light, and the morning mists lifting sufficiently to reveal the flood-plain of the Forth, it was also to reveal a massing of the English army to cross the river and causeway. So soon as he saw it, Wallace was a changed man, the irritation and reserve dropping from him, the long waiting all but over, at last. He gave orders for the first two moves to be made.

These were both to be invisible to the enemy. One was merely the sending of mounted messengers hotfoot, through the hills behind to west-about, to order the company of horse under Sir Richard de Lundin, from Dundee, stationed as precaution at the Fords of Frew, to take and hold the fords and then to move across and provide a presence on the enemy's left flank, a threat, however minor. The other order was for a tough task-force, some five hundred strong, under Kerlie, Boyd and Blair, to move east-about round the base of Abbey Craig, to opposite Cambuskenneth Abbey, and thereafter to work forward through the scrub woodland and bogland, as far as they could without being observed by the enemy, there to await Wallace's signal.

Trumpets neighing marked the commencement of the English advance. First came six companies of light horse, skirmishers not armoured chivalry, under knights' pennons. The bridge was narrow and would allow no more than two abreast, so that even six hundred trotting horsemen took a while to cross. The causeway was wider, slightly, and they could ride four abreast. All the causeway, like the bridge-head, was strongly held by permanent guards. This light horse was clearly to reinforce and expand the redoubt area at Causewayhead, to fan out therefrom and ensure that there was room for the thousands to follow.

Next came serried ranks of archers, in their green doublets, Welshmen in the main no doubt, amongst the most feared components of any English army, with their long bows and cloth-yard shafts. Then there were regiments of foot, their sloped spears like gleaming thickets, endless columns of these. Soon it was not only MacDuff who was urging action, before it was too late. Attack now, before too many had safely reached the head of the causeway.

255

Wallace advised patience — however little actual patience was in himself. Then came what he had been looking for, the enemy's pride, the massive might of fully armoured knights on heavy destriers, great horses themselves coated in steel-plating, slow-moving, ponderous, but colourful with blazoned shields, heraldic surcoats and mantling and banners. Here was the glory of the English power. No doubt the cream of her chivalry was with King Edward in Flanders; but there was sufficient more in the North country of Yorkshire, Lancashire, Durham, Cumberland and Northumberland, to provide this vast and frightening array of martial might. Of these were the thousand of heavy chivalry Surrey was reported to command, a strength of which the Scots had none. In fact, only some four hundred of these war-horsed paladins emerged at this stage; but over one group of them flew a larger flag than usual, the red St. George's Cross of England. Presumably Surrey or Cressingham, or both, rode beneath it. More foot followed.

At an hour before noon, after watching for three hours, and with most of the destriers well along the mile-long causeway, Wallace and Moray gave the long awaited signal.

Out from the valley behind the Abbey Craig the thousands of the Scots foot streamed, not to assail the enemy massed now at the head of the causeway, but to plunge straight down into the waterlogged salt-marsh on either side of it, and to struggle on, leaping, stumbling, wading, a ragged rabble in the mud, laughable compared with the disciplined English columns. On and on they struggled, parallel with the causeway, making as though for the river.

To keep the concentration of the enemy at Causewayhead occupied, especially the ranked archers, another horn-blast sent most of the Scots who had for so long occupied the ridge of the Craig, leaping down directly towards the redoubt area, westwards, MacDuff foremost. They went dismounted, however, for this was no terrain, or work, for horses; and they made maximum noise, shouting and distraction as they went. Their leaders were heedful, despite this, not to advance so far as to come within effective range of those dreaded bowmen.

All did not leave the ridge. Wallace, Moray and a group of the other leaders remained. This was Wallace's first taste of large-scale generalship — and he did not like it. To remain inactive, merely watching, while others fought and died, was galling. But this was how Moray conceived their part, meantime — and no doubt he was right. A general was other than a captain.

Nevertheless, it was not for long that Wallace stood there. Eagerly, anxiously, as he watched all the scene below, it was to one particular sector that his glance kept returning. At length he saw what he waited for — the task-force of his especial friends on the river-bank, hurrying from the east, from opposite Cambuskenneth. They had emerged now from the trees and scrub, and into view from the ridge directly above, many of them all but stripped naked to cope with the mud and mire, but burdened for all that, each with a shield of one sort or another. Straight for the bridge-end this five hundred raced, where it joined the causeway, already within arrow-shot from the southern bank — hence the shields. Some few fell. Their leaders reached the bank, and up on to the causeway they leapt, swords flashing, the marching infantry there, in the thinly-attenuated file necessary for crossing the bridge, cut and broken in moments by the concentrated attack on a short front. Slashed at its weakest point, the enemy column was severed, the bridgehead barred to further crossings, the permanent guard overwhelmed, and a redoubt formed, the shields used to make a barricade against the arrows. At a cost of some fifty fallen, mainly transfixed by arrows, the English host north of the Forth was separated from those to the south.

With a great shout, Wallace turned to Moray and thrust out his hand. 'God be priased — their line is cut!' he cried. 'We have an enemy we can match — and in a place where he can scarce match us! Now — you to your tasks my friend, I to mine. We shall meet, yonder in the midst, God willing!' And drawing his great sword, to use as staff meantime, he went bounding and slithering down the rocky and tree-clad hillside, towards his friends, followed by the Graham, Thomas Gray, Ed Little, Adam Wallace, Tom Halliday, MacGregor and MacFadzean, with a tight group of their veterans.

Suitable work for generals or not, Wallace was back to his old tactics — to seek out and destroy, if possible, the enemy commander.

The English chivalry was now strung out along the second half-mile of the causeway, the St. George's Cross flag towards the rear. The predicament of the war-horsed knights had to be seen to be fully comprehended. Cooped and cramped on the narrow causeway, they could scarcely move — even forward, now that

257

the front of the column was stationary and under heavy pressure at the Causewayhead. They dared not move aside, off the solid stone-and-timber base of the causeway itself; for the massive destriers, each carrying perhaps three hundredweights of steel as well as their riders, would have sunk to their bellies in the mire which made the causeway necessary. Backwards, they could not turn, for there the foot were packed tight. Immobilised they stood, the proudest arm of England's might, while the bare-shanked, mud-covered, yelling Scots canaille picked and poked and harried them from the marshland on either side.

Motionless and helpless, the knights and their colourful mounts might be, but they were also, of course, all but immune, behind their steel and chain-mail, from any hurt that swords or dirks could inflict upon them. Wallace had foreseen this — which was why he had allowed so many of the foot to cram the bridge and causeway behind the chivalry, before he gave the signal to attack. The English infantry were in the main, equipped with twelve-foot-long spears — and these were what were required against armoured knights.

The main attack, then, was against the foot, with their spears — difficult work for men hoisting themselves out of the marsh and on to the defended causeway. But there was difficulty also on the enemy side, for men tight-packed on a narrow base, twelve-foot shafts being exceedingly awkward to handle in a crush. The Scots were not long at gaining a foothold, although at a cost.

Wallace and his group made for the infantry immediately behind the last of the chivalry, pursuing the same tactics, grabbing at the spear-heads thrust at them, and seeking to pull the wielders bodily down into the bog. They suffered a few gashes in this process, but nothing vital, and managed to gain the causeway, there to battle to deepen their hold. Other Scots came to aid them, and presently Wallace was able to leave the general assault with sufficient spears collected, and to turn to his especial task.

Now their endeavour was to remove such foot as still separated them from the knights. This was not too difficult, for these unfortunates were not happily situated, only the front ranks being able to fight, all being pressed back upon the trampling warhorses, or else squeezed off the causeway altogether, into the marsh — from which they were being assailed all the time, anyway. Many died bravely; but most decided that their

258

position was untenable, and broke, throwing away their awkward spears, and turning to try to escape onward through the pack of the mounted knights, pushing, twisting, ducking under the trailing linen heraldic mantling which decked the horses' armour, beneath their bellies. The confusion became utter chaos. And so, at last, the proud leadership of the invading host was before them, the moment Wallace had envisaged and planned for. Now the tactics were sheerly mechanical, the negation of all knightly combat. The exercise was no more and no less than using the spears as long poles to push the great mass of horseflesh and riders, by main force, off the causeway and into the bog. This was to be achieved both by sustained pressure, and by jabbing and probing with the spear-tips at the joints and weak points of the armour, especially the eye-holes and mouth-pieces of the horses, also their lower legs. The knights, of course, chopped down at the spearshafts, and sheared many; but with a continuing supply to keep up the pressure, this could not be effective for long. Moreover, the major pressure on the great majority was, in fact, not the spears themselves but the weight of other horseflesh pushing back. And most riders had no opportunity to hit back.

It was by no means gallant warfare — but it was efficacious. As more and more Scots came to assist, and pressure commenced from the north side also, the knightly host quickly became a shambles, with screaming, rearing horses falling off into the mire — where dirks and daggers waited them and their riders. There was no escape and no surrender. It was total annihilation.

Wallace, after a period of spear-wielding, abandoned this, and following the example of many of the English foot, went ducking and scrambling beneath the horses' bellies, seeking to avoid the stamping of great hooves and entanglement in flapping caparisons, a breathless, double-bent and dangerous process, especially for a man of his dimensions. He was making, of course, for that large St. George's Cross standard. Buffeted, bruised, swiped at, he pushed on through the heaving press.

At length he could glimpse the man beneath the standard. Although it was difficult to distinguish features in fully armoured knights — hence the need for heraldic identification — with the bodies covered and the faces framed in chain-mail hoods and helmets, it was clear that this man, flanked by standard-bearer and esquire, was of heavy build, puffy-faced and early middle years. His coat-armour of yellow and black was unknown to Wallace — but it was certainly not the blue-and-gold checky of Warenne of Surrey; anyway, Surrey was an older man and fine-featured. Cressingham, then — it could be no other. Surrey was not here, had stayed to the south of Forth.

Stooping again, Wallace crawled on. Here in the centre of the press, the horses were jammed so close that there was little or no movement, and this crouching progress was actually less difficult and harzardous, however uncomfortable. Reaching his goal, the big man, his great sword left behind, as useless in this crush, used his dirk to rip upward at the unprotected belly of the esquire's destrier, dodging back under Cressingham's own mount to avoid the suddenly flailing hooves of the screaming creature. As the esquire and bodyguard fell from his collapsing mount, Wallace straightened up on the far side of the Treasurer's horse. Reaching up both arms, he dragged the unprepared and astonished Cressingham bodily from the saddle, crashing down amongst the stamping hooves. And there, on hands and knees, he drove his dirk into the open mouth of the yelling cleric, deeply, to sever the spinal column behind, as almost the only unguarded spot available. The most hated man in Scotland jerked to death within his armour.

Wallace, splashed with the man's spouting blood, found the esquire struggling to his feet nearby, dizzy from his fall, and dealt with him similarly. Then he wrenched the staff of the St. George's Cross from the standard-bearer's grasp, and thrust it away under the hooves, ducking away before the other could use sword against him. He kept on dodging and creeping now, removing himself from the panic and confusion, crabwise, side-ways to the edge of the causeway, to jump down into the marsh — and there found himself assailed by some of MacDuff's fifers, who did not at first recognise him. But, shout-ing his name, he won clear, and went plunging back to his own group.

It would be comforting to recount that, with the fall of both their leader and the English standard, the helpless chivalry col-lapsed entirely, and the battle with them. But this could not be, even though most of the knights had desired it. The circum-stances dictated only a slow, if steady, erosion of their numbers, mainly by the pushing-off-into-the-bog process, one by one, those in the centre merely having to wait their turn. It was weary, uninspiring work, after the first excitement and

elation — quite the most curious form of warfare Wallace and
his friends had ever engaged in.

In time, the big man wearied, and remembered his generalship, to withdraw himself from this seemingly endless slaughter.
He clambered up on to the back of a captured destrier, where
he could better survey the scene. Southwards he saw that
Kerlie's company still held the bridge-end, and had now advanced towards him along the causeway for a considerable distance. The enemy foot between were fighting bravely, but
hopelessly, cut off from escape, from their fellows, from all but
the marsh and the waiting dirks therein. Northwards, the situation was very different. Here, where Moray was in charge, the
redoubt area at Causewayhead was obviously much contracted;
but it was still a formidable position, strongly held — for here
was where the archers were massed. Moray had nothing to pit
against these. He was concentrating on the foot, and the now
dismounted light cavalry, and these were being more and more
pressed back upon the ranked bowmen, the object being to use
them to mask the archers' aim. This was only partially
achieved, and Moray was held up badly. Clearly the English
had a good commander here. The lack of archers was proving
more serious to the Scots than any lack of heavy chivalry.

Wallace perceived what he might attempt — even though it
was hardly general's work. Leaving Graham in command on
the causeway, dismounting, he called about a dozen of his veterans to him, and slipped down into the marshland once more,
on the west side, to go leaping and zig-zagging away across the
waterlogged levels, north-westwards.

They had about three-quarters of a mile to go, before the
land began to rise and dry out, to the vicinity of Cornton farm.
Behind this, well away from the fighting, they were some four
hundred yards west of the contained area at Causewayhead,
and on slightly rising outcropping ground, rough pasture.
Panting, Wallace drew flint and steel from his pocket, waving it
towards the others and pointing a jabbing finger at the whin-
bushes, bracken and long grasses of the long slope. His friends
understood. Spreading into an extended line, they knelt to apply
their own flints, steel and tinder, and to blow on the resultant
small flames with what breath remained to them.

It was mid-September, the bracken was beginning to turn, the
grass seed-heads were dry and yellow, and it had been a hot
summer. It all caught fire quickly, the whin-bushes going up

like torches, and in only a minute or two great yellow-brown clouds of smoke were billowing up. The wind was from the South-West, and down on the battle area, the choking opaque screen rolled. On and on the incendiaries went, using blazing whin-branches now, and ever the conflagration grew, and the smoke increased and thickened.

Scots and English alike soon were coughing, gasping, blundering, with eyes streaming. The archers could no longer see to aim. The great English advantage was neutralised.

Moray's trumpets shrilled.

After that, it was all chaos confounded — but the chaos worked for the Scots. Moray skilfully directed all from a high position on the flank of the Craig, above the smoke. The tight English control at Causewayhead could no longer hold the situation. Everywhere it became every man for himself. Arms, armour, banners were cast away, as impediments to flight.

The narrow causeway still being crowded and choked with men, horses and bodies, most of the fleeing English chose to take to the moss, making for the Forth, to try to get back across the river to their friends. Comparatively few succeeded, for Kerlie and his people now hurried to line the slippery mudbanks — and besides, the vast majority of the soldiery could not swim. The more intelligent and enterprising of the enemy raced off northwards into the Airthrey wooded hill-skirts, and most of these probably made good their escape. Some few groups sought to cut their way in tight disciplined fashion — but all were halted and confounded, sooner or later, by the extraordinary loops and convolutions of the Forth, which turned the plain into a vast series of traps.

In it all, only two men really achieved anything for their cause — Sir Marmaduke Tweng, the Yorkshireman who had commanded at Causewayhead, with his esquire. Tweng, seeing that all was hopeless at the front, turned his horse's head due southwards, and actually cut his way back along the packed causeway, closely followed by his esquire and armour-bearer, in an extraordinary display of horsemanship, initiative, courage and determination — for he had a whole mile to cover, scarcely a yard of it free from encumbrance, heaped slain and armed opposition. In the reaction from fierce battling, of course, he took most of the Scots by surprise — and there undoubtedly would be inevitable reluctance to venture within reach of his sweeping sword now that the day had been won and life preserved thus far. At any rate, Tweng managed to reach the causeway's end, and there was advantaged by the fact that, confident that no more English would attempt to cross the bridge from Stirling, in the circumstances, Kerlie and his people had left the bridge-end, to line the river-bank, east and west. Smashing through the barricade of shields there, Sir Marmaduke drove on across the bridge itself. And beyond, on safe and steady ground at last, he turned, and furiously drove the appalled watching English soldiery, who had never crossed, to break down the southern bridge-end, under cover of a company of bowmen. A brave, resolute and able man, his action not only saved himself but kept the Scots from following up their victory on the south side of the Forth.

Wallace meantime was at the wrong end of the smoke-shrouded battlefield, and knew nothing of all this. He and his group made their way through the mirk which they had contrived, to Causewayhead, and there learned that all was over save the pursuit; but also that Sir Andrew Moray was severely wounded. Apparently the only Scots leader to have fallen, he had been struck by an arrow at the very end of the fighting.

Hastening to Moray's side, Wallace found his fellow-general coughing blood and very pale, an arrow having pierced his right lung. But he retained all his wits, and urged Wallace strongly not to waste time with him, but to ensure that the enemy on the south side of Forth were not given time to rally — for they all knew that fully half the English army had never crossed the bridge. This was the big man's priority also. Leaving Moray in Thomas Gray's good hands, he hurried off down the shambles of the causeway.

Part way along this, he was vouchsafed a grim reminder as to the passions of men resulting from oppression, bloodshed and war. A group of Scots, who had had particular reason to hate Hugo de Cressingham, had searched for the Treasurer's body, stripped it of armour and clothing both, and were now in process of stripping it of skin likewise. This flaying was sufficiently well advanced, when Wallace came up, for the perpetrators to offer him a strip of the clerical hide, enough to make a swordbelt, when duly tanned. Shaking his head, the big man hurried on, wordless.

Before reaching the bridge-end, he was informed of Tweng's escape, and of the destruction of the farther side of the bridge — indeed that Tweng was now burning the timbers lest they be used again in repair. There was a gap of some thirty feet at the south end, and ranked English bowmen nearby to ensure that no close approach was possible.

Wallace expended no time on regrets. Blowing his horn, in a signal well known to all his veteran associates, he turned and went hurrying back long strided towards Causewayhead, his objective the horse-lines in the valley behind Abbey Craig. He yelled instructions to his lieutenants as he ran.

As a result, with a tough, mounted party some three hundred strong, he was presently riding hard, up Forth, the six miles to the Fords of Frew, leaving instructions for more to follow. Across the river, they met a messenger sent back by Sir Richard de Lundin, with the word that Surrey and the main mass of his force were in full retreat from Stirling, and that Lundin was following them, harrassing their rear and picking off stragglers. At Stirling itself, they learned still more surprising news. The Steward, Lennox and the Scots hostages, recognising that the English power in Scotland was at least temporarily in eclipse by this great victory, had rediscovered their courage and responsibilities to the nation, renounced their hostageship, and gone over to the attack, gathering their servants and such others as they could persuade, to assail the departing enemy rear, in company with Lundin — scarcely the noblest of gestures perhaps, but significant as to these supreme realists' assessment of the situation. Stirling town had been hastily vacated by all the English, save for deserters and some in hiding, leaving behind vast quantities of booty, gear and provision; but the castle was still held. Sir Richard de Waldegrave, its Constable, had apparently died on the causeway; and before he fled, Surrey had appointed his own bastard, young Sir Henry Fitz Warren, as Constable, with the redoubtable Sir Marmaduke Tweng as deputy and stiffener. Stirling Castle, then, was unlikely to yield quickly, and being more or less impregnable, might well become the only English toehold in Central Scotland, hereafter.

Listening to all this, Wallace perceived his opportunity. There was one other comparable Scottish fortress, almost as strong as Stirling, long in English hands — Edinburgh Castle, thirty-five miles to the South-East. If, in the panic of this surprising retreat, it could be taken, as it were in indecision, off-guard, the richest part of all Scotland, Lothian, which it dominated, might fall into their hands. Surrey must be dissuaded from stopping at Edinburgh.

So, leaving the prizes, riches and problems of Stirling to be coped with by others, Wallace drove on southwards. It was easy to follow the track of retreat, for any army of many thousands in flight does not fail to leave a vast trail of wreckage and ruin behind it — trampled fields, slain countryfolk, abandoned arms and equipment, their own wounded, foundered horses, especially slow and heavy destriers quite unsuitable for hasty flight. Pausing for none of it, Wallace and his people pressed on.

At Falkirk, with evening upon them, they came upon Lennox, the Steward and the other Scots nobles who had so clearly deciphered the writing on the Stirling wall, weary now of pursuit. They said that the English were still fleeing, with Lundin snapping at their heels. When they would stop, God knew — but Surrey would be well in front, intent only to be quit of an adventure which he had been against from the first. He might be making for Linlithgow that night — since he could scarcely get so far as Edinburgh.

Wallace did not remain long with the nobility. He had no wish to offend them, since inevitably he would have to work with them hereafter; but nor did he enthuse over their conversion. He had more vital work in hand. Hurrying on, he came to Linlithgow in another eight miles, in darkness now, to find Lundin and his company weary, glutted with slaughter, their horses foundered. The enemy was not far off, they said, moving only slowly now, and very scattered. It was still eighteen miles to Edinburgh. Even if they went on all night, they could not be there by morning.

His own beasts all but done. Wallace and his men flung themselves down to sleep, as they were, on the reedy banks of Linlithgow Loch.

He allowed them all only five hours. They were on the move again well before daybreak. As the light strengthened, they began to see groups and parties of the enemy lying exhausted where they had dropped, some in larger companies than their own — which had now reached some six hundred. For none of these did they halt. By Winchburgh and Kirkliston they rode, until at last, in mid-forenoon, the soaring towers of Edinburgh Castle came into view some miles ahead, on its rock so uncannily like that of Stirling; and all the land between strewn and dotted with the straggle of an army in disordered flight, a strange and indeed somehow terrible sight.

Wallace ceased to hurry, at last. His strategy now was to

harry and worry, not to overtake and bring to fight. He had no wish for the English to turn at bay, to his puny numbers; nor to arrive at Edinburgh before alarm and panic had had time to have its full effect. Their visible presence and threat was all that was required, meantime. Also, this gave time for reinforcements to catch up with them, from Stirling.

In the event, the Scots presence there, on the heels of the fleeing and demoralised host, was sufficient for their purposes. Whether Surrey was still with his people, or far ahead, the enemy commanders did not even pause at Edinburgh, but hurried on their ragged array. With the result that, when Wallace approached the western gates of the city, under the frowning ramparts of its great citadel, it was to be met, not by resistance but by a deputation of the citizens, led by the provost, magistrates, guild conveners and deacons of trades, assuring loyalty and obedience, offering every co-operation and praying that the town be spared the horrors of war.

The big man, still with less than one thousand behind him, decided to play for time, while he awaited support and news from his scouts. He turned a fairly hard face on the citizenry, and declared that he could by no means accept the surrender and fealty of the city, in the name of King John, unless the castle was yielded up likewise. Let the provost bring him the castle's governor, agreeing to surrender on honourable terms, and all would be well. Otherwise, city *and* castle would be proceeded against with every rigour of war.

It was, of course, a sort of blackmail — but it worked. In an hour or so, the agitated provost was back, with the deputy constable of the fortress, who announced that his superior was prepared to yield up the castle, on condition that he and the garrison were allowed to leave without molestation, with protection from the citizens, and with a safe conduct to the Border. Seeking to hide his surge of relief and satisfaction, Wallace acceded, in stern-faced fashion — but stipulated that the English should make no ceremony of their departure, fly no banners, and be off as quickly and inconspicuously as possible.

That night, William Wallace dined in the great hall of Edinburgh Castle, without a blow struck, his scouts assuring him that there was not a fortress or stronghold still held by the enemy between him and the Border, save only that of the English-biassed Earl of Dunbar and March, at Dunbar. And they would see about that, on the morrow.

But on the morrow, they had got so far as Haddington, in East Lothian, when Sir John Graham caught up with them. He brought word that Sir Andrew Moray's wound was not like to prove fatal, and that Moray urged Wallace's return, for there were many heavy decisions to be made. He revealed that the enemy dead at Stirling Bridge amounted to over five thousand, including over one hundred knights. That there were vast numbers of prisoners, many of them rich and powerful men, highly ransomable. The Scots casualties had been very small, with no men of note actually slain, though not a few were wounded. The spoil was enormous, and already there was much bickering over its division. Graham also had a message from no less than the Steward, Lennox and Bruce himself, who had apparently joined the others at Stirling, having escaped or decamped from Percy and Clifford — these last having turned back for Carlisle. The lords said that they had heard that Wallace was intending to pursue Surrey's host right into England, and to wreak vengeance there; and they besought him not to do so, as nothing would be more likely to drive the English into united and large-scale retaliatory action. They had suffered eclipse in Scotland, yes — but they were still ten times as many as the Scots, and, under better and united leadership, could quickly win back all they had lost. An invasion of England would be folly, at this stage. Moreover, Wallace's presence was greatly required back at Stirling, where much fell to be settled. They besought him to return thither, forthwith.

Wallace considered these messages and tidings thoughtfully. He had not, in fact, intended to invade England there and then, but only to try to take Dunbar Castle, and so ensure that the enemy had no foothold north of the Border strengths of Berwick and Roxburgh. However, Dunbar could be left until later, if need be. The important matter, he realised, was this communication sent him by the lords — no *order* to return, but a plea. They besought him, Graham assured — as did Moray. Wallace recognised the Bruce's politic line of thought in that message; recognised also that Bruce operated on a different level from the others. How far he could trust him, remained to be seen; but if Bruce was going to take a hand now, he, Wallace, ought to be there, on the spot, to look to his own, and the common people of Scotland's, interests.

He gave the order to turn around, from Haddington, to ride north again.

CHAPTER FIFTEEN

St. John's Toun of Perth seethed as never before. Even at coronations at Scone, when the town became almost a dormitory,
numbers were not on this scale. The quality, too, of the visitors
was more diversified, for here were not only the nobility, gentry
and high clergy thronging the streets, but representatives of the
burghs, trade guilds, parish priesthood, even the soldiery. On
invitations thereto, from all over Scotland, Wallace had insisted. Was it not these who had so largely made this council
and assembly possible? If large numbers of those present
tended to be hungry much of the time, that was unfortunate;
but Perth was little better than the rest of Scotland, that late
September of 1297, and notably short of food.

In the refectory of the Blackfriars Monastery, which was the
largest apartment in the town, Wallace himself stood amongst
the small men, in a lowly position far from the Prior's dais,
where the lords and bishops were seated — not out of any demonstrative modesty so much as because this was in fact his due
position. He was in a distinctly odd situation here in Perth, two
weeks after the Battle of Stirling Bridge. He was the hero of the
hour, hailed in the streets fêted, courted by deputations, lion-
ised; yet in this great council-of-the-realm, which had been
called very largely on his insistence, he had no official place or
standing. This could not be a parliament, since that required the
King's summons; nor yet a convention of the Estates, since that
demanded a statutory forty days notice. But call it what one
would, as an assembly and conference of the community of the
realm, it largely followed the normal official procedure, and
advisedly — since the last thing that anyone wanted was an un-
disciplined free-for-all. So the nobles sat in due order of precedence, earls, great officers of state, lords, with the bishops and
mitred abbots, known as the Lords Spiritual; then the sheriffs of
counties — such as had not fled with their English masters; the
knights and small barons; the priors and titled churchmen; the
few Highland chiefs who had deigned to appear; the governors

of fortresses and keepers of royal castles; the lairds and landed men; then the provosts and magistrates of the burghs, the deacons and conveners. In all this heirarchy there was no place for mere soldiers, fighters and non-representative citizenry, however worthy or even heroic. So these, such as could cram inside, stood in a pack at the bottom end of the refectory, Wallace towering amongst them; and no one knew whether they had a right to raise their voices or no — though few doubted that some at least would seek to do so.

William Sinclair, Coadjutor Bishop of Dunkeld, had been elected chairman or chancellor of the assembly, since this was a position which demanded an ability to write and read, something denied to many of the lords; also he was a lord's son himself, as well as one of the Lords Spiritual — these being in short supply, with Wishart still a prisoner in Roxburgh Castle, Fraser of St. Andrews not yet replaced, Crambeth in France, and Cheyne of Aberdeen a hunted fugitive. The Earl of Strathearn might have claimed the position of chancellor, as the highest-ranking man present, and of semi-royal blood — but he was also one of the most reluctant to be there, only attending because he had been forced to it, his lands nearby. There were others in that case amongst the nobility.

The proceedings had started with due thanks to Almighty God for their victory, and their preservation as an ancient and independent realm; also homage to those who had died in making this assembly possible, Sinclair by no means failing to remind the Deity of the part played by His servants William Wallace and Andrew Moray — whereat there had been a vigorous and prolonged cheering from the back of the refectory, highly unsuitable in an act of worship, and much frowning from the nobility. Thereafter the great debate had commenced.

There was much to discuss, military, civic and religious — and strangely enough, it was the civic authorities who, more used than were their aristocratic betters, to councilchambers and public discussion, at first made the running. The country was in chaos, near anarchy and incipient famine. The harvest had, in the main, not been ingathered, and in many areas not even sown — because of the harshness of the English occupation and the wholesale removal of grain, like beef and wool, to England. Granaries had been burned, mills destroyed, pastures flooded. The enemy administration had now broken down, and nothing raised up to replace it. Outlaws, broken men and deserters roamed at large, terrorising the people, and it seemed to be nobody's business to restrain and punish them. Courts of law had largely ceased to function. Piers, harbour-works, flood-banks, bridges and fords were everywhere neglected and damaged, often useless. Plague and pestilence were rife in certain areas, whole communities homeless, shel-terless. Half the parish churches in the land had no priests. And so on. The catalogue was endless. There had been no Scots parliament or convention for years — and now the flood-gates of oppression, woe and complaint were opened wide.

There was much stirring and muttering amongst the lords and knights; it was not for such as this that they had assembled. Bishop Sinclair was very patient. But at length, beating on his table, he had to refuse to hear more.

'My lords and friends,' he cried. 'Our land is in sorry state, yes. This we all acknowledge, and must weep over. But we must act, as well as weep. It is not for this assembly to set all to rights, to hear all the sorrows and shame. That must be done by coun-cils and officers, appointed by this assembly for these tasks. Today it is our duty to appoint to office, to discuss broad matters of policy and strategy, to look to the future rather than to mend the past. To such business I rule that we proceed.'

The cheers of most of the nobility were interrupted. John, Earl of Atholl rose. 'How can we appoint to office, my lord bishop?' he demanded. 'This gathering has no such authority. It is not a parliament, nor yet a council of the King.'

'We have no king. King John Baliol is abdicate, and left the realm,' the Lord of Crawford contended. 'Therefore we must do without. Or the business of the realm cannot be conducted.'

'No so,' John Comyn, Earl of Buchan, and Great Constable of Scotland, declared. As, with the Steward, one of the two remaining great officers of state, he spoke with authority, 'King John did not abdicate. He was deposed by Edward of England. Unlawfully and by force. Therefore he is still the King, even if furth of the realm.'

'Then he should have appointed a Guardian of the Realm, my lord Earl.'

'Not for John Baliol to appoint a Guardian!' Gartnait, Earl of Mar, brother-in-law of the Bruce, exclaimed. 'It is the Com-munity of the Realm of Scotland which elects and appoints a Guardian — not a craven fled to France!'

There was uproar.

Another Comyn, by banging a sword-hilt on the floor, made himself heard, John Comyn the Red, Lord of Badenoch and Locaber, and chief of the name. 'What is the Community of the Realm?' he snorted. 'This . . . this rabble!'

'My lord!' Bishop Sinclair protested, 'I ask you to mind your words. If this assembly does not represent the Community of Scotland, what does? Or could? No such representative company has gathered since King John's coronation. Or even then, I think!'

'It is a self-appointed rabble, Sir Bishop!' Comyn repeated. 'Lacking a head, or any authority. I came here to say so. You can appoint to no office. Only my uncle the King may so do. Or one appointed by him, as Viceroy . . .'

'Such as Red John Comyn of Badenoch!' Atholl jeered. In the absence of the Bruce, he and the Earl of Mar were the principal supports of the Bruce claim to the throne. Robert Bruce, Earl of Carrick, to Wallace's disappointment, had left Stirling for his own Ayrshire before Wallace had got back, with word of English attacks on Annandale from Carlisle.

'Why not, sirrah? Am I not nearer the throne than any . . .?'

There was further hubbub in that great chamber, with Sinclair banging on his table for order. 'My lords,' he shouted strongly. 'This must not, *shall* not, despoil into a dispute over who should wear the crown! Scotland has suffered enough on that score. I rule that since, meantime, there is no higher authority in this land than is assembled here, this gathering or council has, and must have, the right to appoint to office. That the realm's business may proceed. Such appointments to be confirmed later, by such due authority as may be established. My lord Steward, you are the highest officer of state in the land — do you agree to this?'

James Stewart licked wet lips, and nodded.

'I support that same,' Malcolm, Earl of Lennox declared.

'And I,' the Lord of Crawford added.

Clearly the great mass of the meeting agreed.

'Then, I make proposal that the first business of this assembly is the appointment of a Guardian of the Realm,' the Earl of Mar said. 'That there may be a spokesman and leader. And for that high position I propose the Lord Robert, Earl of Carrick.'

'I support that appointment,' Atholl seconded.

'My lords — I fear this is no place, no time . . .'

271

The Earl of Buchan shouted down the Bishop. 'And I nominate the Lord John, of Badenoch. He, at least, is not Edward Longshanks' favoured courtling!'

There was a storm of protest from the Bruce faction.

'My friends — this is folly!' Sinclair insisted. 'Such contest will gain us nothing. The realm is in no state to have another competition for the throne, under whatever guise.'

'Nevertheless, my lord Bishop, a Guardian is required.' That was a new voice, cool, precise, authoritiative, that of Sir John Stewart of Menteith. He had astonished the assembled company at Perth, the day before, by calmly arriving, as of right, in answer to the general summons to attend the council — and at the same time announcing the surrender of Dundee Castle, not to Wallace but to the lords assembled. Here he was assured, chilly, anything but apologetic. 'I support the Constable, my lord of Buchan's nomination of the Lord of Badenoch. I speak in the name of the Earl of Menteith, as Tutor thereof. And as Sheriff of the city and sheriffdom of Perth.' Stewart's mother had been a Comyn, Countess of Menteith in her own right.

There was an outcry of anger at this effrontery from one who had been so noted a persecutor of the patriots, especially here in Perth, as previously at Dumbarton. Sir William Ruthven was shaking his fist, and the Earl of Lennox was on his feet demanding action against such collaborators — despite his own recent associations. As for the burghers and commonality, they shouted and stamped and hooted.

Bishop Sinclair rose to the occasion. When he could gain quiet, he spoke firmly, reasonably. 'I cannot accept nominations for the high office of Guardian, my lords,' he announced. 'Such election would demand much longer notice and proposition. And we have no assurance that the Earl of Carrick, who has been named, would indeed accept office. I rule such discussion out-of-order. But none recognises better than do I the need for leadership in this pass, for spokesmen for the community. To that end, I myself make so bold as to suggest to you that the two notable captains who had so bravely led our forces to victory, and who before Stirling Bridge were appointed joint generals of our arms, be now appointed by this assembly commanders of the army of the Kingdom of Scotland and of the Community of the Realm. Until such time as a Guardian shall be duly elected. To prosecute our struggle against English domination. All leal men to aid them in that struggle. I name William Wallace, and Sir Andrew Moray, Lord of Petie and Bothwell.'

The entire chamber seemed to erupt as he enunciated those names. Everywhere, except on the lords' benches, men leapt and shouted and waved and cheered. Some even wept. 'The Wallace! The Wallace!' rang out on all hands — though some few remembered to add Moray's name. That young man sat, hunched, pale and frail, seeming, amongst his peers, clearly a very sick man. It was evident that his share of any joint leadership of the army and community would be very nominal for some considerable time to come.

'I support your proposal, my lord Bishop,' Sir John Graham cried, when he could be heard.

'And I! And I! And I!' Sir Neil Campbell, Sir John Ramsay and Sir Richard de Lundin competed in chorus.

'As representer of the Earldom of Fife, most ancient in this land, I support the same!' MacDuff roared, amidst further cheers.

Sincair turned, to look round at the glum ranks of the lords, eyebrows raised, and smiled thinly. None of them spoke.

'Passed with acclaim!' the Bishop announced, banging the table. 'Come forward, William Wallace.'

It took some time for the big man to fight his way through the tumult of that crowded chamber, with men clinging to his arms, slapping his back, struggling to touch him — till his own bodyguard of veterans pushed purposefully forward to gain him passage. At length, he climbed on to the dais platform, bowed gravely to the Bishop and then to the lords, and went to stand beside Sir Andrew Moray. Somebody found a seat for him, but he did not use it. He would not sit in the lords' seats, he who was no lord — but he would stand at Moray's shoulder.

When the shouting and applause died down, Sinclair declared that a first priority was the appointment of sheriffs for all counties where there was a vacancy — which included fully half of the total — that the rule of law and administration of justice might be re-established.

Atholl immediately rose to make the point that no sheriffs who had collaborated with the English should be reappointed, and all sheriffdoms where such obtained should be declared vacant. He looked hard at Sir John Stewart of Menteith.

The individual was not put out. He observed that the Earl of Atholl's stipulation was unreasonable and impracticable. For any sheriff who had *not* co-operated could not have held his position for a single month. The country had had to be managed; and it was better, surely, that it should be managed by native-born Scots sheriffs than by English nominees such as Heron, Hazelrigg, Arnuff and the like. Could any deny that?

Many could, and did, vociferously. Loud and long the argument raged, added to by the fact that many sheriffdoms had been hereditary privileges — such as Lennox's at Dumbarton — and the lords wished to make their own appointments. With much heat generated, much time spent and no single appointment actually made, and Sinclair hoarse and flagging visibly, William Wallace stepped forward, at length, to the Bishop's side, and held up his hand. He gained almost immediate quiet.

'My lords and fellow-citizens,' he said. 'This matter could occupy us all the day, and more. It is important, I agree. But there are more important issues before us — the defence of our realm against further invasion, which is bound to follow as night follows day. And the feeding of the people. Lacking defence and food, no sheriff can operate. I say, then, first things first. Let us leave such appointments to the morrow.'

It appeared that he now had the support of almost all, even the lords, in this postponement.

Since everyone clearly awaited his further suggestions, he went on. 'Defence first. Now that Dundee Castle has surrendered, and Stirling is suing for terms and should yield tomorrow, there are only three strengths still in English hands in all the land — or, more properly, two, Berwick and Roxburgh, since Dunbar is held by its lord, Cospatrick, Earl of Dunbar and March.' He paused at that name. 'I will refer to this great lord hereafter. I say, these castles must be safely in our Scots hands, before we can claim to be free of the invader ...'

He waited, while the cheers rolled on. This was what men had come to hear, rather than the election of sheriffs and the like.

'There may already be invasion of the South-West,' he went on. 'There is talk that Clifford has invaded Annandale, from Carlisle — and that is why my lord of Carrick is not here with us today. The English have been defeated only in one battle — not in the war, my friends. They will be back. I say, therefore, that if there is to be more fighting, it would be better on *English* ground than on ours! We have had sufficient of that. And nothing would be more like to turn Clifford around from his

274

assault on the South-West than a Scots sally into Northumberland and Cumberland, behind him. I propose, then, to assail Dunbar, Berwick and Roxburgh Castles, and then to invade the North of England, with such force as seems good.'

Again the deafening acclaim.

'Now as to food. We must divide up the land into food and forage districts. Officers to survey what each district has and what it needs, and then report. This must be done at once, swiftly. But, see you, more can be done than that. There is one area of this kingdom which has never been fought over, never suffered war or hardship — Lothian. The richest province of Scotland, the most fertile. Always it has been looked on by the English almost as their own. For two reasons — the strength of Edinburgh Castle, which they held; and the might of Cospatrick, Earl of Dunbar and March. He is of our old Scots Celtic blood, of the royal line indeed — but always he has chosen the English side. And he lords it over Lothian and the Merse. Of all the lords of Scotland invited to this assembly, not a few have not come — but only he has sent an insulting and challenging reply. He calls me a brigand and King of the Woods. But that matters nothing. What matters is that he defies the Community of the Realm of Scotland, and prefers English Edward's rule. I have just come from Lothian — and its fields are yellow stubble, its barns full, its mills busy, its pastures well stocked. I say, my friends, that Scotland needs what Lothian has, and must take it.'

It would have been a bold man indeed who disagreed publicly with that.

'Moreover, my friends,' Wallace continued, 'England has been robbing us of our treasure, our grain and our cattle, as well as of our blood, for years. Endless convoys of these have travelled south month by month — I know, for I have intercepted some! I say, it is time that such traffic was reversed. I have not heard that there is any want, or dearth, in the North of England. It is time their plenty fed empty Scots bellies! Convoys can travel north as well as south. I propose to go in for that trade — I who am brigand and outlaw!' He turned, to eye those behind him. 'So, my lords, while you appoint sheriffs and officers and the like, with your permission I will be off southwards.' He shrugged. 'Now — I have had my say, my lord Bishop. At too great length. I pray the forbearance of all.' And bowing, he returned to Moray's side

After that, there was little enthusiasm for more debate. The Earl of Buchan thought that it would be unwise to provoke the English into large-scale reprisals by an invasion — but he was howled down. Sensing the temper of the gathering, Sinclair wisely adjourned it until the morrow.

Wallace conveyed his fellow-Commander of the Forces of the Realm back to his lodging, for a more private conference.

* * *

A week later, the big man was back at Haddington, this time with a hard-riding, hard-hitting, multi-purpose force of about two thousand. He could have brought many more, but did not want any unwieldy army meantime. His requirements were speed, dash, and initiative. He had commandeered the horseflesh for these, mainly short-legged, broad-hooved hill ponies and Highland garrons, which could travel anywhere, leaving the captured English cavalry mounts for others who wanted them; and he had officered his corps with his own trusted lieutenants and friends. No single lord accompanied him.

From Haddington he sent a message to the Earl of Dunbar and March, at Dunbar Castle, eleven miles further east, demanding, in the name of King John and the Community of the Realm, the immediate allegiance of that stronghold — otherwise he would be attacked with all vigour, his lands wasted and his properties destroyed. Whilst he awaited a reply to this, he took into his charge the Earl's two other East Lothian castles of Preston and Dirleton, without opposition, and set his men to collecting grain from all the rich barns and granaries and mills of that fertile area, for despatch back to needy parts, well content that it was Cospatrick of Dunbar's grain, and therefore needed no paying for whilst he yet remained obdurate. He also wrote, at the instigation of certain Haddington merchants, to the mayors and councillors of Hamburg and Lubeck — with whom it seemed these merchants carried on a thriving trade, before current troubles — to inform them that the Kingdom of Scotland was again in good hands, and the harbours open to traders' shipping, with much of hides and wool ready for exchange for grain and foodstuffs. He was meticulous to sign this letter in the names of Sir Andrew Moray and himself as joint Commanders of the Army and Community.

He did not wait too long for the Earl Cospatrick. When no answer was forthcoming, he rode eastwards, his scouts informing him that the Earl had assembled a force in the Innerwick area some four miles east of Dunbar. But its size was estimated at only about four hundred — and for once Wallace was in the unusual position of much outnumbering his enemy. There was a brief sharp clash, in which Wallace's advance-guard only was involved — obviously only a token resistance — and after this gesture, the Earl with a small group, made off at speed, into the Lammermuir Hills, which here come down close to the sea. Leaving a sufficiency of men under Sir Christopher Seton, a Lothian laird who had joined them at Haddington, with instructions to avoid all unnecessary bloodshed of fellow-Scots, and to garrison the castle securely, Wallace set off in pursuit of the Earl.

The chase took them through the empty green hills, by Old-hamstocks and the Monynut and the Whitadder, and so down into the Berwickshire Merse, or March. Across that rich and undulating plain they pounded, marvelling at the wealth of cattle and corn, just managing to keep the Earl thereof's party in sight — for these were superbly horsed and knew the terrain — by Bonkyl, where the Steward's brother was master, and Edrom and Swinton, until at length they came to the wide and smooth-flowing Tweed, at Ladykirk, with daylight almost gone. There was a ferry here, a large flat-bottomed barge which, not unnaturally, the Earl had used, and left safely tethered at the far side, his party abandoning their weary horses in the process. Wallace cursed, but was checkmated. Strong swimmers, himself amongst them, might have swum the river and brought back the ferry-boat. But what use would that be in getting one thousand five hundred horsed men across? Norham Castle, a seat of Beck, Bishop of Durham, lay just over there — for that was England, across Tweed — and there almost certainly was where Earl Cospatrick was bound, a very strong place which it would be folly to approach in any small numbers. The nearest ford was at Coldstream, six miles south-west. Thither they rode and camped for the night. It had been a big day.

In the morning, Wallace sent scouts over the ford — which appeared to be unguarded — to discover the position, before he ventured his main force across. They came back with the information that Earl Cospatrick had indeed spent the night at Norham, but had moved on very early in the morning, whither was uncertain. The big man had to recognise that, meantime, the traitor Earl had escaped him.

Two challenges still faced him — the reduction of Berwick and Roxburgh Castles. At Coldstream they were roughly midway between the two. He selected Roxburgh for prior attention, since Bishop Wishart was still held prisoner there; but he sent Sir John Ramsay with four hundred men eastwards, to Berwick, to demand its castle's surrender. Berwick, although the chief seaport of Scotland, was said to be still very much a city of the dead, having little recovered from the terrible example Edward had made of it the year before, when he had left thousands of corpses in the burned streets, men, women and children, as a lesson to Scotland of what happened to those who opposed the King of England's peace. Its castle rose strongly above the shattered town, high above the stench and horror.

Wallace and the main body, riding up fair Tweedside, came at high noon to the little town of Roxburgh, on its spit of land where Teviot joined Tweed, near the larger town and great abbey of Kelso. With the Lion Rampant of Scotland unfurled above him, disdaining any white flag, Wallace personally rode forward to before the gatehouse of the castle, which stretched in strangely elongated fashion along the little escarpment which formed the spine of the peninsula, and presented only this one very narrow and moated front to any practical attack. Entirely courteously, he requested the presence of Sir Ralph Grey, the English governor, if it was convenient. Not unnaturally, Grey was there on the gatehouse parapet, waiting, presumably in some trepidation, however strong his fortress.

'Sir Ralph,' the big man called, 'I am Wallace. But I come in the name of King John, and of the Community of Scotland. You have, I understand, as guest, a friend of mine, the Lord Bishop of Glasgow. Of your kindness, I would speak with him.'

Grey, head just appearing above the crenellations, answered. 'Of the man Wallace I have heard — as outlaw and rogue. There is no King John, and no Kingdom of Scotland. King Edward rules a province called Scotland — perhaps you refer to that? As to the community thereof, I have no notion what that means — but I suspect it is a rabble of barbarians and savages. Master Wishart, of Glasgow, is here, yes — no guest but my prisoner. And he talks to none.'

'You are a brave man, Sir Ralph — though less than well-informed. Nevertheless, of your kindness, I would speak with the Bishop.'

'Very well — since you ask respectfully. I will give you the space of two paternosters, no more. Then, if you are not off, my bowmen will fill you with arrows, sirrah!'

'I thank you.'

Presently the small, stooping person of Robert Wishart appeared, between guards, on the gatehouse parapet-walk, even at that range to be seen as pale, shrunken, frail. But his voice was still crisp and clear.

'Will Wallace — I thank God for the sight of you!' he called. 'Bless you, for remembering an old coneman.'

'Who would forget my lord Bishop of Glasgow? All Scotland remembers you. I have *come* for your blessing, my lord.'

'That you already have, Will.'

'I thank you. But this is for an especial occasion. Something of a crusade. Worthy of a bishop's blessing. We invade England, you see.'

'Ha! Invade, you say? You do?'

'Not just this small company. A great army is on its way. It will be crossing Tweed here in a few days time.' He paused. 'Has Sir Ralph Grey treated you fairly?'

'Eh? Grey? Aye — fair enough, I judge. Scarce kindly, perhaps — but fair, yes.'

'Good. Then you must warn him, my lord — if you would not see him suffer grievous hurt. His position here is bad, bad. I do not wish to destroy him. My people are ill-disposed towards English governors. You may have heard how they flayed Cressingham, and sent his skin in pieces all over the land? Now Sir Ralph is the only English captain left in Scotland. I would spare him if I could.'

'Oh,' the Bishop said. 'Ah. I . . ah . . . yes.'

'Yes. And he cannot defend this castle, see you. It has strong walls — but it is very weak. In its water supply. We have a man here, from Kelso. One Haliburton, something of a mason. He helped build the present castle well-shaft. Good water — but the shaft leads down to no true spring, but to the pool of a small burn. We know where that burn goes underground. My men are already damming it. There will be no more water. I sorrow for you, my lord — and Sir Ralph.'

Wishart coughed, and glanced sidelong to see how Grey was taking all this.

'For the garrison I grieve also. I fear they will die sorely, to no purpose. Myself, I cannot wait here. We invade England, as I said, with your blessing. But I shall leave a sufficiency to keep this castle fast — but insufficient, I fear, to protect the garrison from the great army which comes. Seeking Englishmen to savage.'

'What ... what would you have me to do, Will?'

'Have Sir Ralph release you, and send you out to me. Then, perhaps, with the voice of Holy Church, you can persuade these angry men of mine, and those who follow, to deal more gently with him, and the garrison, when I have gone. Your great authority, in God, may save them.'

'To be sure. I will speak with Sir Ralph.'

The resultant conference was very brief, behind the fortifications.

'Will,' came the old prelate's voice, quite soon. 'Sir Ralph Grey seeks further enlightenment. If he was to consider leaving this castle, what terms would you offer him? And his garrison.'

'Since he has treated you fairly, my lord, I should be generous. He and his people may march out, unmolested, and cross into England — so be it that all is left in good order, all prisoners released in good state, and no spoil taken.'

'And if I do not accept such terms?' That was Grey's own voice.

'Then I must needs hang you, Sir Ralph, with much regret. From this same gatehouse. If I have time. But at least you should then be dead before any flaying!'

There was silence.

Presently the Bishop spoke again. 'Sir Ralph agrees, Will — if you will ensure safe-conduct over the Border.'

'Granted. But tell him that he must travel deep into England, if he does not wish for further encounters with me!'

Hoarse with all the shouting, but satisfied, Wallace dismounted and relaxed. It was the first time that he had *talked* a major fortress into submission.

That night, Sir John Ramsay himself arrived hot-foot from Berwick-on-Tweed, in the greatest elation. The castle there had scarcely waited for him to demand surrender, before yielding on terms. It seemed that its garrison had no ambition to be the last English toehold in Scotland — though there was some dubiety as to whether Roxburgh would yield first.

At any rate, the land was now cleared and cleansed of the

invader. The church bells rang all night in Roxburgh and Kelso, and beacons blazed on a score of Border hill-tops as the glad tidings spread.

Next day, with a considerable mixture of emotions, William Wallace led his force over into England.

CHAPTER SIXTEEN

The expedition into England was less haphazard than it might seem, Wallace's planning being careful, as ever. It took place in two stages, his light cavalry spearheading it and ranging far and wide, at speed, the main mass of the foot, from Perth, coming behind, slowly, consolidating, occupying. Not that there was any oral attempt to hold territory or to occupy towns and strongholds. The object of the incursion was threefold — to demonstrate that invasion could be a two-way process; to collect and send back food and treasure to Scotland; and to seek to draw back Clifford's assault on Annandale and the South-West, while inhibiting any other similar expedition. Unfortunately, not a few of the rank-and-file conceived of a fourth and very simple objective — vengeance. And from the first, Wallace was at pains to counter this. He ordered, explained, pleaded, punished, threatened even to hang — but detachments and minor commands still took their revenge, in no uncertain fashion, on the North of England, for the years of oppression and atrocity in Scotland. William Wallace was learning more of what it meant to be a general, as distinct from a captain.

He and his hard-riding company went through North Northumberland like a wind-fanned grass-fire, leaving a trail of burning villages, farmsteads, manors, peel-towers and lesser castles behind them. All churches and abbeys were to be spared — but it is to be feared that some of these went up in flames likewise, where Wallace was not personally present. They rode by Bowmont Water into the wide vale of the Till, and up it by Ford and Doddington and Wooler. Then seawards, by Belford and Wareford — Warenne, Earl of Surrey's own patrimony, which they destroyed — and on through Ellingham and Embleton to the

Aln, leaving the powerful castles of Bamburgh and Dun-stanburgh alone. Alnwick Castle, also, Percy's seat, they did not attempt — although they burned the town — for they had no means of dealing with such, without great delays. And all the time, the mounted force was growing smaller, as Wallace left behind parties to gather and convoy the great herds of cattle and the wagontrains of grain, back towards Scotland, until these should fall in with some of the main body of foot coming after, who would take over the duty. This was a foreseen prob-lem, but none the less hampering.

Wallace was surprised by the complete lack of any large-scale resistance or organised defence. Where was Surrey? Where was Percy? Where was Bishop Beck? Where was Sir Brian Fitz-Alan, the new Viceroy, another North of England man? King Edward's absence abroad, and the disaffection amongst the nobles, might account for disorganisation and lack of co-ordi-nation; but not, surely, such ordinary and spontaneous lack of defence of their homes.

Three days from the Borderline, Wallace halted, to make a base in the Forest of Rothbury, in Coquetdale, amongst the southern slopes of the Cheviots, to give time for his de-tachments to catch up again, and for the main force behind to draw nearer. From here his scouts probed deeply south and westwards. And not only scouts, but raiding parties, carrying the message of the Scots anger over a great arc of territory from the sea to the Pennines and the great valleys of North and South Tyne, through a golden October — a gold they turned to black and red. After the first elation and satisfaction of hitting back at the hated oppressors, Wallace quickly found the work to pall. This was not his kind of warfare, with no true challenge, no element and spice of danger, no pleasure in burning a fair land and terrorising an innocent population. But it was necessary, he was convinced — and if more authority and responsibility than he had ever conceived of, for the saving of his native land, had been thrust upon him, he must needs accept this along with the rest. At least he might, in the process, lessen the sheer savagery of it all just a little.

From Rothbury he led raids as far south as Morpeth and Newcastle — although the latter's fortress prevented him from making any large impact there. The mouth of the Tyne he laid waste, wrecking and sinking vessels to deny shipping passage.

On his return to Rothbury he found sufficient of his detachments rejoined, together with a reinforcement under Sir Richard Lundin. Leaving Ramsay in command in the Forest, with four hundred, he set off westwards with some one thousand five hundred. It was Cumberland's turn.

Carlisle, like Newcastle, a fortress-town and base for the North-West of England, was too much for them to tackle, so they headed well south of it into the rich area of the Cumbrian plain which lay between the high hills of Ullswater and Derwentwater and the Solway Firth. Throughout, Wallace was on the alert for attacking parties sent out from Carlisle; but they saw nothing of such, despite the fact that daily their progress was marked by high clouds of smoke to stain the autumn sky, which could not have been unseen from Carlisle. Whether because of Clifford's continued absence with a large force, or other limiting factor, Cumberland seemed to be as loth to try conclusions with Wallace as was Northumberland.

Then the weather changed abruptly, and the golden Indian Summer was succeeded by high winds and chill driving rain. Raiding and riding and ravaging became increasingly less attractive, even to those who had revelled in it previously. When the first snows began to whiten the heads of the high hills, clearly the time for this sort of campaigning was drawing to a close. From Cockermouth, near the rim of the Western Sea, they turned back for Rothbury Forest, in early November.

It was at Hexham-on-Tyne, halfway to Rothbury, that Wallace came to a decision on a fairly prompt return to Scotland. At the great Priory church of St. Andrew there, still semi-ruinous from Scots reprisals after the sack of Berwick, he was surprised to be approached urgently by three Augustinian friars to come protect their church property from thieving Scots. A company of Scots foot were indeed in control of the town. Fifers from MacDuff's command.

The clerics did not appeal in vain Wallace sent orders round Hexham that anything stolen from the Priory must be restored at once. If it was left in the oratory vestibule, no proceedings would be taken against the offenders; if not, a search would be conducted, and dire punishment meted out to the perpetrators.

Wallace indeed made much of these three friars, for they were in fact the first clergy he had set eyes on these last weeks. Like the nobility and gentry, all the churchmen had fled southwards into the Palatinate, and further, to Yorkshire, leaving their various establishments, locked and barred, but a major temptation to invading bands. He was pleased with this trio who had remained at their posts, and mindful also that their church was dedicated to St. Andrew, the patron saint of Scotland. Suffering from distinct conscience-prickings over the scale of devastation his eruption into England was inflicting, he requested that a Mass should be said, that evening, to be attended by as many of his people as could cram into the damaged nave of the church. The friars were happy to oblige — and happier still when, arriving later for the service, robed and ready, they found the vestibule filled to overflowing with piled up church valuables, chalices, pattens, candlesticks, crucifixes, censers and the like, in gold and silver, obviously culled from a vastly greater number of shrines than Hexham's. Wallace was highly embarrassd.

He was more than embarrassed presently, however, when, at the interval in the Mass consequent on the Elevation of the Host, he and his associates went outside for a brief spell, to remove their arms and armour, while the celebrants ritually washed their hands in the sacristy — and of a sudden the suitable holy hush was rudely shattered by a great outcry from within. Rushing back into the church, they discovered that, during this short interval, robbers had actually broken into the chancel and cleared the entire altar of its valuables — chalices, pattens, ornaments, the very missal from which the service was being read. In a great rage, Wallace stormed out, to discover that the vandals were a newly-arrived party of Highlanders, who knew nothing about Wallace's pronouncements or even of his presence there. Breathing executions and slaughters, he ordered a return of the loot for the second time — but in fact did not proceed too hastily to arrest the sinners, claiming difficulty in identifying them. Nevertheless, this incident taught him all too clearly how tenuous was his hold over his countrymen, how indisciplined were the forces he was letting loose on this land, how heavy was the responsibility of a supreme commander. A basically religious man, he conceived sacrilege to be the most deadly of all sins, a crime against the Holy Ghost. There and then he determined to reverse the tide of invasion he had loosed, and to begin the ordering of the main army back to Scotland forthwith. Only his own tightknit and mobile force of light cavalry would remain, for they had work to do yet.

Next day his messengers were spreading out from Hexham in all directions, with orders for retiral, taking all flocks, herds and grain with them — but leaving severely alone all ecclesiastical property, on pain of death. Rape and hurt to women and children also would be punished with death; he had been hearing reports of such happenings likewise. So he sought to salve his conscience. As solatium, and distinctly apologetic assurance to the three friars of Hexham, he gave a formal and comprehensively worded document, in the name of King John and the Joint Commanders of the Community of Scotland, declaring that all the property of the Priory of St. Andrew was sacrosanct, and that the bearers of this paper had the safe conduct and protection of William Wallace and Sir Andrew Moray for one year from that date. More he could not do.

He resumed his journey to Rothbury.

There he found that Ramsay had a prisoner, the knightly keeper of Morpeth Castle, who had revealed that King Edward had sent his son, the Prince of Wales, to summon a council-of-war at York, preparatory to large-scale re-invasion of Scotland. To this Surrey, FitzAlan, Percy, Beck and the other North Country lords had gone — which partly explained the lack of coherent defence against the Scots enterprise. It occurred to Wallace that a swift, hard-riding thrust at the city of York might be a worthwhile venture.

He was finding it more difficult than he had anticipated to get his wide-scattered units of foot turned back, with their convoys, to Scotland with most of them looking on the entire proceedings as one gigantic holiday — although the worsening weather conditions should help that. But the arrival of Earl Malcolm of Lennox on the scene enabled him to transfer responsibility for this turn-around operation to someone with the authority of one of the great earls of Scotland. Leaving Lennox in command, Wallace and his two thousand turned their horses' heads southwards.

It was not, of course, intended to be anything more than a demonstration — although a significant one. There was no thought of taking territory, sacking towns or collecting booty. So they avoided large centres of population and fortress-towns, such as Durham, Darlington, Northallerton and Thirsk, driving on at a pace seldom equalled by a force of such numbers. The river-crossings were their main problem, with bridges tending to be at towns, and fords not readily found in unknown country, with Tyne, Tees, Wear, and others to be negotiated. Nevertheless, their progress was such that they were across the

Yorkshire border the next day, and fifty miles into that great county the next.

There, in a secluded dale amongst low green hills, they rested their weary mounts only a dozen miles from York itself. And there heavy snow, highly unusual so early in the winter, caught them, and changed all. They were not equipped for hard weather, and the Yorkshire dales and moors no place for urgent travellers in snow conditions. They were nearly a hundred and fifty miles from the Border, and in bad country for drifting.

Reluctantly Wallace made his decision. They had to turn back.

One gesture they made, a swift sally to within a mile or two of York, where they burned a small village with its moated manorhouse, and left the flag of Scotland on its highest point. The smoke could not fail to be seen from the city, snow or none. So they turned their beasts' heads round — and hoped that the Prince of Wales' council got the message clearly.

It was a grim journey back, with the weather consistently atrocious, the country all but impassable. It took them eight dire days to win back to Rothbury — and by then all were in a state of exhaustion. There they found that Lennox had returned to Scotland, though some companies of Scots foot still were marauding in the area. In the comparative shelter of the forest, they rested, recuperating, whilst the last stragglers of invasion were rounded up and sent homewards.

At last, on Christmas Eve, Wallace was satisfied that all his errant and dispersed flock was safely out of England. Thankfully he moved north, to cross the Border himself. Whatever others might say of his first campaign as commander-in-chief, he did not assess it as greatly successful. He was beginning to doubt if he was a very good general.

CHAPTER SEVENTEEN

All Scotland appeared to be making its way, by various uncomfortable routes, into the Ettrick Forest. Which was a strange thing to see, especially in the early March of one of the hardest winters in living memory, with snow still lying in wreaths in the valleys, the tops consistently white, every stream in high spate, and the loftier passes still choked. William Wallace might well have been a proud man over this, since it was at his insistence that all came, that the great council-of-state was being held in so inconvenient and inhospitable a venue. The fact was that he resolutely refused to attend it anywhere else, on account of the security of the realm — now solely his responsibility, it seemed, since unhappily Sir Andrew Moray had died of his wounds. Although it was not Wallace's council, in that he had not sought it, the death of Moray and the threat of imminent English re-invasion was the ostensible reason for its calling. The move had come from certain of the lords, led by the Comyn Earl of Buchan — and since he was one of the remaining great officers of state, Lord High Constable, Wallace was in no position to object; especially as the call was supported by the only other extant great officer, the High Steward. Wallace had a strong suspicion that the real reason for the council was not the defence of the realm, at least not directly — and might even be concerned with undermining his own position, since he knew that there was plotting against him. But his army was assembled here in the Forest — and necessarily so, with Berwick and Roxburgh Castles already retaken, and a vast English army mustering at Newcastle, Holy Island turned into a sea-supply-base, since Wallace had blocked access to the ports. The council he had declared must come to him, and not he to the council. However unpopular that course was with most of the Scots nobility, the thing had been accepted.

He had decided on Selkirk as the meeting-place, since it was the most easy of access for the largest number — although it did mean that travellers from the South-West had a very difficult approach in these conditions. Also, Wallace had to be in a position from which he could move swiftly towards the East March of the Border, whence the enemy threat loomed, and Selkirk, opening on to the upper Tweed valley, was well-placed for that. His troops, of course, were scattered over innumerable valleys, with major problems of space and maintenance to be considered; but he had his own horsed brigade with him here, for immediate action.

Selkirk, although a small place, had two other advantages — a wide vale where many could camp, at a hub of drove-roads; and a semi-ruined abbey, to provide a meeting place.

King David, of all too pious memory, had established a Tyronensian monastery here in 1113, endowing it liberally and building great works. But it had been found to be too remote and inconvenient a spot for a successful abbey, and after about a dozen years the monks had removed some twenty miles down Tweed to Kelso, abandoning Selkirk. The remains were now in poor shape, used as a quarry for the town, but were still extensive and picturesque, providing a sufficiency of shelter, and some degree of dignity for an important gathering.

Wallace, without consciously intending it, found himself acting host to the many colourful parties and cavalcades, from all over the land. Not all of them appeared to appreciate his welcome, the various Comyn companies in especial; but when even some of their men-at-arms raised cheers at the sight of the national hero, the lords were at least discreet in their hostility.

It did not take long for problems to reveal themselves. One that grew in dimensions was the way that the nobility, in setting up their tented pavilions and horse-lines in the haughland of Selkirk Abbatis, appeared almost inevitably to divide themselves into two camps. It was soon clear that these were respectively the supporters of the Comyn and Bruce claims to the throne. No love was lost between them, with the Earls of Mar, Atholl and Lennox and the Lords Crawford, Maxwell and Sanquhar, having little to do with the Earls of Buchan and Strathearn and the Lords of Badenoch, Cumbernauld and Kilbride. It looked an ominous start for the council. Of the Earl of Carrick himself there was no sign. He was believed to be at his father's castle of Annan, repairing the havoc caused by Clifford's eruption and consequent retiral to Carlisle.

The actual conference was held in a sort of amphitheatre formed within the ruins of the abbey, its broken cloisters and the choir of the church together providing a central proscenium for the main actors in the drama, and ample raised if erratic accommodation for spectators. These latter were inevitably mainly the lords' men and other soldiery, but there were Selkirk townsfolk also, and herdsmen and foresters from a wide area. These were Wallace's people, almost to a man.

Bishop Sinclair opened the proceedings with prayer, thanksgiving for their recent deliverances and pleas for protection from further attack. This was heartily endorsed by all — but it was the last unanimity for a considerable time. On this occasion the Steward was appointed chairman — but only by a small majority vote against a Comyn nominee, Master William Comyn, Provost of the Chapel-Royal at St. Andrews, and a brother of Buchan, an able and ambitious cleric.

The Comyns were by no means set back by this initial defeat. Without any waiting for the sake of appearances, they plunged straight into action, the same Master William leading. He declared, without preamble, that in this crisis facing the nation, the people needed guidance above all else. Victories and campaigns were all very well, and of course necessary; and they thanked William Wallace and the late lamented Sir Andrew, Lord of Pettie and Bothwell, for their great contributions. But that was insufficient. The people must have guidance, leadership, direction. Holy Church could and did give much. But more was required, much more.

The man had a fine sonorous voice, a trained speaker, who knew just what he was at. Bishop Sinclair, who had come to stand alongside Wallace beside a broken pillar of the former transept, muttered that here was a man who would be more than Provost in St. Andrews, but Bishop thereof and Primate of Scotland, if they did not keep him under, a clever clerk — than which there was little worse!

'My lord Steward,' Provost Comyn went on, turning towards the chair. 'Who may speak with full authority, in the name of this kingdom of Scotland? Holy Church can only speak for its heavenly aspects. My lord — you occupy high office, and bear a proud name, of excellent repute. But you cannot speak in the name of the King's realm. My lord Constable — nor can you. You are one of the great earls of Scotland, and have authority to raise the realm in the King's cause. But you cannot speak in the realm's name, so that all men must obey. I say that it is entirely necessary for the governance and saving of this kingdom that one be appointed here and now, lacking the King's royal presence — appointed by the magnates of the realm here assembled — who may take fullest command in all matters, and speak for this ancient people. I do declare that this assembly is entitled to name itself a parliament of the Estates of Scotland, and that it should hereby appoint one to be Guardian of the Realm.'

There was considerable applause for this, especially amongst the Comyn faction, although some others looked at each other doubtfully. Wallace, who agreed that there should be a Guardian appointed, and the sooner the better, was glancing round to see who supported and who did not, when his eye was caught by a slight commotion, as a richly-dressed but mud-stained newcomer pushed his way forward through the tight-packed ranks of the spectators, to come to a halt beside a tall, black-robed Benedictine friar. Only when he turned his head from speaking to this friar, did Wallace recognise that the latecomer was indeed Robert Bruce, Earl of Carrick. He drew a deep breath. He had feared trouble this day; now he was certain of it.

Whether or no the speaker had noticed the new arrival, he went on confidently. 'The Guardian must be strong, else he is useless, my friends. He must dispose of large forces. He must be renowned as a warrior, yes, a man of repute, but also he must have powerful friends, allies, supporters. And be sure of the support of Holy Church. I say to you that such a man stands here amongst us. He is indeed the head of the family of which I am the humblest member. A family which, none will deny, is the strongest, the greatest, in the land. Which boasts three earls, three bishops and no less than thirty-three knights. I say to you that none is more fit to be Guardian of Scotland than Sir John Comyn, Lord of Badenoch.'

The reaction to this was predictable, loud, vociferous, from the Comyn faction as from many others, especially from the North and East of the country, for there was no question as to the power of that house, its influence, its widespread connections — and, of course, its link with the crown, through John Baliol. But the Comyns were not popular in the South, so that, as well as the Bruce faction, there was opposition from many, expressed in a ground-swell of mutterings and groans. The Comyns were indeed *too* closely identified with the despised Toom Tabard, King John, for the taste of many.

The Earl of Buchan, Constable, now seconded his brother's proposal. It may well have cost him some qualms to do so, for he was known not greatly to love his distant cousin. An older man and more experienced, as also outranking the Red Comyn, he could not deny that the other was head of their house. Their mutual Norman great-great-grandfather had married, a second wife, the heiress of the ancient Celtic mormaorship and earldom of Buchan. Red John of Badenoch was the heir of the first family, himself of the second. And in public, the Comyns always put up a united front. The Earl was no orator, as was his brother, a gruff, practical man. He limited his support to a brief few words.

The next speaker, with precedence important, was more subtle. A Comyn supporter also, the Earl of Strathearn proposed the name of the Steward, for Guardian. In all decency, someone had to. He made no encomium of it, just the bare nomination.

Men stirred uncomfortably everywhere. James Stewart was well enough respected, for his position, and as an honest if unexciting man. But he was certainly no warrior, and as a mouthpiece for the nation he could hardly have been less effective.

From his presiding seat in the choir he raised a thin, open hand, to wave it back and forth. 'I decline. I decline such nomination, he said thickly, sucking in his saliva. 'I am old. Of insufficient strength. A younger man is required. I decline.'

Strathearn exchanged a glance and nod with Master William. Clearly this had been anticipated.

Gartnait of Mar was clearing his throat to speak when he was forestalled by the mitred Abbot of Dunfermline, who suggested that a bishop of Holy Church might well prove the wise choice, uniting all classes and divisions of the people. He would have proposed their well-loved Robert Wishart, Bishop of Glasgow, who had acted Guardian once previously, before King John's coronation — but he was still a sick man from his privations as prisoner, and asked to be excused. The Primate, Bishop Fraser of St. Andrews, was dead, and no successor yet appointed. Bishop Crambeth of Dunkeld was next senior, but was still in France, acting as their ambassador to the French king, Bishop Sinclair, of good fame, was but Coadjutor. Therefore he proposed Thomas of Dundee, Bishop of Ross.

There was some applause amongst the commoner folk, for Bishop Thomas was one of Wallace's supporters. But there was no like enthusiasm amongst the ranks of the nobility; nor indeed amongst the higher clergy, where Ross was considered to be too junior a see to be thus exalted.

The Earl of Mar spoke up. 'My lords and friends,' he said, jerkily — for, though a good-looking youngish man and of proud Celtic lineage, he was basically diffident, and had to drive himself to public utterance. 'Hear me, Gartnait of Mar. I say that if there is one man who should be Guardian of Scotland, it is Robert Bruce, Lord of Annandale, who should rightfully be King. But since he is not, h'm, within the realm at this present ...' He coughed a little, at that. '... I say to you that his son

291

should be appointed. The Lord Robert, Earl of Carrick. He is not here, but is expected . . .'

Glancing over at Carrick, who still stood beside the black friar, in quite lowly position, Wallace noted the quick frown on that young but strangely rugged face.

'Bruce *is* here, my lords!' Mar's brother-in-law cried, coming forward in to the open flagstoned space which had once been the abbey's nave. 'I come late, by choked passes — but not too late.'

There was a great stir and exclamation on all sides now — by no means all of it enthusiastically welcoming. The Bruce was too lately Edward's darling, for most folk there. Yet there was no doubting his stature and authoritative presence.

'You give me leave to speak, my lord?' he asked the Steward.

At that man's nod, he turned. 'I have heard what is proposed, my friends,' he said. 'Not only as regards myself, but others. And I too say that a Guardian of the Realm should be appointed. Now. But not myself, who has fought no battles, earned no plaudits, am but untried amongst you. My father, were he here, would himself be no candidate for Guardian — that I swear! If he were to present himself to you, I say, it would be as your rightful King, not Guardian . . .!'

A wave of reaction, cheers and dissent, comment and question, greeted that, as a new vigour and excitement manifested itself throughout the great gathering.

The Earl held up his hand. 'But my father is *not* here. I have heard the names suggested as Guardian, and I say that, good and sound men as these are, they do not, cannot, meet the case. Only one man, at this juncture, can fill Scotland's need today. Only one man will the people follow. Only one man can speak with the voice that not only the folk, but England, Edward Plantagenet himself, will hear and heed. That man is William Wallace of Elderslie. I name you Wallace as Guardian!'

It was as though a dam had burst, and the emotion of men surged free in clamour. The shout that arose seemed to shake the very hills. Not all the vociferation was favourable, of course — but the broad mass of it was, wildly so. Almost to a man the common folk, the men-at-arms, the soldiery, the churchmen, the lesser lairds, roared their approval, hands high, or beating each other's shoulders, feet stamping. It was amongst the nobles, naturally, that the opposition was expressed. But compared with the mighty explosion of acclaim, this was a small thing, that faded where the other went on and on.

It was some time before Bruce could make himself heard again. 'I commend ... I say, I commend your judgement!' he shouted. 'This man has done what no other could do. He has rid us of the English ...'

Again the uproar.

'Hear me — hear me, my friends. He has rid us of the English, I say. Aye — once. But they will be back. And so he needs must do it again. Nothing on God's earth is so sure than that they will be back. I know Edward. Aye, some blame me that I know him over well! But this I do know, that when Edward himself comes chapping at our door again, then we shall need a united realm to withstand him And more than that — a leader whom all the people will obey and follow. Therefore, I say, William Wallace it must be. None other ...'

He was interrupted. 'And I say that this is folly!' It was Sir John Comyn the Red, himself a fiery, lean, hard-faced young man of bold good looks and a flashing eye. 'Here is confusion. It is a Guardian of the Realm we seek to appoint — not the commander of a host. Wallace has shown that he can do battle, yes. But he is no man for the council table, to meet representative ...'

His words were drowned in outcry and protest, angry this time, with an ominous underlying growl. Fists were shaken, even swords drawn and waved. Everywhere the nobles looked around them, apprehensively, at the gesticulating crowds.

Twice Wallace himself made as if to speak, and twice thought better of it. His mind, indeed, was in a complete confusion.

The Steward was also trying to speak, to restore order. But it was Bruce who prevailed. He had young and excellent lungs, and no impediments to speech.

'There are sufficient, and more, for the council-table!' he contended. 'Many to advise Wallace. All too many! But the Guardian must carry the people, not just the Council. If Scotland is to withstand Edward of England, in his might and wrath. Here is the heart of it. Only the nation in arms will save us, then. And only one man, I declare, can raise this nation in arms, lacking its King ...'

When the din was lessened, it was not the Lord of Badenoch but another Comyn, the eloquent Master William, who took up the issue.

'What my lord of Carrick says is not in dispute,' he claimed, with the careful moderation and reasoned appeal of the practised orator. 'None questions William Wallace's notable deeds, or his ability to arouse the people. That he must do. But he can do so in his present station. More than that is required of the Guardian. There are decisions of state and policy to be made. He must unite more than the common folk; he must unite the lords of this realm. Will Wallace do that? You say, my lord, that he must withstand King Edward. But he must speak with him also, in Scotland's name, treat, negotiate. Will the proud Plantagenet speak with such as William Wallace?'

'I say that he will. Edward is proud, yes. But he is a man of deeds, not of words. Because Wallace is of the same kidney, he will respect him, where he would not you, sir. Or myself, indeed. Think you he cares for any Scots lord? But the man who defeated Cressingham and Surrey, in open battle, is altogether different.'

The Comyns were not finished yet. 'I know Edward also, to my cost!' That was Buchan, the Constable. 'He does not eat his words. He has named Wallace outlaw, cut-throat, and promised to hang him. Think you he will swallow that, and deal with him? Never! Moreover, the Guardian speaks in the name of the absent King of Scots. How can this man do that? He is not even a knight. You, my lord, of all men, should know better. The kingdom cannot be represented by one who is not of the *noblesse*, the men of honour. How shall knights and lords follow and yield their voices to one who is not even of their order . . .?'

'By the Rude — is that what concerns you, my lord!' Bruce cried. 'Then we shall see to it.' He turned, and strode across the moss-grown flag-stones, spurs clanking, to where Wallace stood quietly amongst his own group, looking strangely out-of-place in all the finery, in his old chain-mail and leather arm-guards; all his friends now wore the best English armour, captured at Stirling Bridge or since, but he had found nothing of a size which would fit him. In front of the big man Bruce halted, and with a thin screak of steel, drew his sword, the short travelling sword which hung from a golden earl's belt.

'William Wallace,' he declared, voice vibrant, ringing, 'I, Robert Bruce, knight, earl of this realm, do hereby dub you knight. In the name of God and of St. Andrew.' He brought down the flat of his blade on one great shoulder, then on the

294

other. 'Earned on the field of battle, if ever knighthood was. Be you faithful, fortunate and bold. Stand, Sir William Wallace!'

There were moments of utter silence, surprise, elation, even consternation. Then, in that green, ruin-strewn vale of the hills, pandemonium broke out, to make feeble even the tumult which had followed Bruce's previous proposal of the Guardianship. In wild emotion men went all but crazy with jubilation, a sort of unholy glee. The thing was done, suddenly, dramatically, totally unexpectedly, there before them all — and nowise could be undone. Sir William Wallace!

While undoubtedly there were not a few present who questioned the wisdom, the propriety, even the taste of what Bruce had done, none could doubt his right to do it. In theory, any duly dubbed knight could himself dub another, provided that he had proved his prowess on the field of battle or in single combat, and was accepted as a man of renown; but in practice, only kings, princes, commanders of national armies and very great nobles ever did so, the last but seldom and in special circumstances. Nevertheless, as the holder of one of the ancient Celtic earldoms — and knighted most royally by no less than King Edward himself — none could contest the validity of Bruce's action, even without his claim to being second heir to the throne.

Wallace himself certainly had no doubts. He was dumbfounded, yes, his open features working, great hands gripped together in front of him, knuckles white. But he recognised what had happened to him, that he had, in those moments, become something other than he had been, a man on a different level, a knight, an undoubted member of the most basic of all orders of chivalry, a knight bachelor. Irrespective of whether he was worthy, or the bestower of it worthy, it was now a fact, and none could take it from him, even he who had conferred the accolade. Wallace was no respecter of persons, and the last to be impressed by empty titles and styles, mere forms and ceremonial; but he was very much of a man of his age, conceiving knighthood to be a proud and noble state, and was all too well aware of what this unlooked for metamorphosis could do for him. By one brief and simple rite, in that chivalric age, he had been made dignified, eminent, transferred to the ranks of the men of honour. Knighthood in 1298 was no empty honour. Much that had been inconceivable only a few moments before was now possible, William Wallace was no fool, and however reluctant to be beholden to young Bruce, or any other lord, he would not have rejected this accolade, even if he could.

The Comyns stood, at a loss, impotent, silenced by their own cherished code. Everywhere the nobility and chivalry of Scotland were in like case.

The Earl of Mar was the first to recover. As the din continued, he walked over to Wallace and clapped him on the shoulder, wordless. The Earl of Lennox came to do the same. These were the only other earls present, apart from Buchan and Strathearn. Bishop Sinclair wrung his hand again and again. Then, as though finally making up his mind the Steward stood, and came from his seat to congratulate his vassal. Crawford followed suit, and others, *some* others, likewise. Behind Wallace, his friends and companions were scarcely able to contain themselves.

Bruce, by that one act, had not only transformed the situation but had struck a notable blow for his own cause and claims. But he was not finished yet. Into the gradually ensuing quiet, he called, 'As Earl of Carrick, and therefore member of the high Council of this kingdom, I do now request of that Council to declare and appoint Sir William Wallace of Elderslie, Knight, to be Guardian of Scotland, as from this present.' He looked first at the Steward, and then nodded to his brother-in-law.

It was another shrewd thrust, addressing his nomination to the high or Privy Council. Such body undoubtedly existed, but it had not met formally for long. More important, for his present requirements, it had had no new members appointed to it for years. Therefore, save for one or two elderly men, only those who automatically belonged to it by virtue of their high office or position, could at the moment claim to be members. These were the great officers of state, the senior bishops and the earls. At one blow, Bruce had silenced much of the opposition. The Red Comyn, for instance, undoubtedly would have been a privy councillor if that body had been properly appointed; but lacking King or Guardian, no recent additions had been possible.

The Earl of Mar was about to speak, when Lennox forestalled him. As another of the old Celtic nobility, he had no love for the Normans in general and the Comyns in particular.

'I, Malcolm of Lennox, agree,' he said. 'I say Sir William Wallace for Guardian.'

'Aye, as do I,' Mar got in.

'No!' That was Buchan, gazing around him anxiously. As well he might. Apart from the Earl of Strathearn and the Steward himself, there was only one other certain privy councillor present, the Bishop of Galloway — Sinclair being only Co-adjutor — and coming from Galloway, almost bound to be a Bruce supporter. He was.

'I also say for Wallace,' the Bishop announced, briefly.

Malise of Strathearn was no hero or disinterested patriot. But he was a realist, and could see as well as the next when to jump from a sinking ship. 'As do I,' he declared, shrugging.

There was a pause, and the Steward, licking his lips, spoke. 'Does any other . . . of the Council . . . say otherwise, my lords?'

'I protest!' Sir John Comyn cried hotly. 'At this, of the Council. It is a trick, a ruse. Who knows who s of the Council? It has not met. These three years and more. Bruce would trick us all. I say all lords and knights may speak. And vote.'

There were cries of agreement from not a few, but Bruce shouted through them.

'I declare that the voices of individual knights and lords, however puissant, have no authority in this. Only a parliament, duly summoned, or else in its absence, the Council, can appoint a Guardian. This assembly cannot be a parliament — since who had authority to call one? Therefore the Council only may speak for the realm. And there are councillors enough here.'

'So . . . so I hold and sustain.' the Steward nodded, although obviously uncomfortable. 'Can you deny it, my Lord Constable?'

Unhappily Buchan eyed his cousin. 'In other circumstances . . .' he began and waved a helpless hand.

'I call the vote.' Lennox said.

'Aye,' James Stewart acceded. 'Does any other member of the Council speak?'

There was none other to speak.

'I see no need to vote, then. The issue is clear. Five had spoken for — no, six. One against. If I myself were to vote, nothing would be altered. My lord Constable — will you withdraw your opposition, that all may be more decently done?'

Buchan sighed, and nodded, in one.

'So be it. I declare Sir William Wallace, Knight, to be Guardian of this Scotland — in the name of the famous prince, the Lord John, by God's grace, King of Scots.'

Strangely, there was comparatively little acclaim and demonstration now. Men seemed to be sobered suddenly by what was done, what the implications were, what this dramatic action foreshadowed. It was as though an irrevocable step had been taken, an assured order all but overturned. All were for the moment abashed. Even Bruce, who should have protested about this being done in the name of John Baliol, did not do so.

All looked at Wallace.

That giant appeared to come out almost of a trance. Rather like a great dog shaking itself, he heaved his huge shoulders and raised his auburn head. He gazed round on them all, out of those vivid blue eyes, unspeaking still, a tremendous, vital figure, the very personification of innate strength, vigour and resolve. Then slowly, waving his supporters back, he began to pace forward from his transept.

Not a sound was heard as he stalked up the choir steps and came to stand before the Steward. That man, his own lord, rose, and after a moment, bowed deeply before his vassal. Then he moved slightly aside, and gestured to Wallace to take the seat he had vacated, the simplest of tokens, but fraught with significance.

Something like a corporate moan rose from the great company.

Wallace inclined his head, and moved into the Steward's place. But he did not sit, deliberately. He turned, to face them all, and raised a hand.

'My friends,' he said, and his deep voice shook with emotion — and made all other voices which had spoken there hitherto sound light, ordinary: 'I thank you. I thank you, with all my heart. For your trust. Your faith in me. I swear before Almighty God that it will not be betrayed. God and His saints aiding me, I shall not fail you. Much is needed. I shall demand much of you. But, for myself, I shall give all. This I vow — and you are my witnesses.'

The murmur which swept the crowd was like the distant surge and draw of the tide on a long strand.

For a long moment Wallace stood, staring straight ahead of him. Then, with a flick of his hand, he seemed to thrust all that had transpired behind him, behind them all. Emotion, by-play, ceremony, had had their moment. Typical of the man, all was now decision. 'And now, my friends, to work,' he said, still standing. 'There is much to do, I told you. Most can, and must, be done hereafter. But it is right that some shall be done here, before you all — and be seen to be done. The Council, for one. I know but little of these things — but it is clearly in need of renewing, of enlarging, as my lord of Badenoch says. My first duty, therefore, as Guardian, is to see to this. I now ask Sir John Comyn, Lord of Badenoch, to join it. Also Sir Alexander Lindsay, Lord of Crawford; Sir Alexander Comyn, Lord of Lumphannan; Sir Edmund Comyn, Lord of Kilbride; Sir Alexander de Baliol, Lord of Cavers; Sir William Murray, Lord of Tullibardine; Bishop Sinclair, Coadjutor of Dunkeld; and Master William Comyn, Provost of the Chapel-Royal.'

Even Bruce gasped at this swift recital, rapped out like the cracking of a whip. At first like the others, he might have thought it unsuitable, lacking in fitness, for Wallace to plunge so immediately into the exercise of his new authority. But now all men of any understanding could see how astute a move this was. Wallace had been appointed in the face of Comyn opposition; and since they were the most powerful family in the land, he would have them as a burden on his back. But, by this sudden move, he had changed the situation dramatically, and put the Comyns, especially Sir John the Red, into a position of acute difficulty. He had singled out four of them, five if Baliol of Cavers, a kinsman, was included, for advancement, in this his first official act. The Red Comyn had himself indicated that the Council was in need of new blood. Now, to refuse to sit on it, was almost unthinkable. Yet it meant that the mighty Comyns were thereby accepting favour at Wallace's hands, the very first to do so, demonstrating to all their acknowledgement of his authority. He had them in a cleft stick.

After an agonising moment or two, Sir John inclined his arrogant head, unspeaking. The other surprised nominees murmured varied acceptance.

Apparently satisfied, Wallace went on. 'Two other matters. This realm has an ancient alliance with France. The French are now attacked by the same foe as are we — Edward of England. We must see to it that both realms act in common against him. Make a treaty of aid, one with another. If Edward, as is said, does return from France to lead attack against us again, then the French should attack England in the south. It is our blows here in Scotland and into England, that will have brought him back. This must be our enduring policy. King John saw this three years ago, but was forced by Edward to denounce his treaty. We must renew it. I say that we should send envoys at once to King Philip, new envoys. Bishop Crambeth is there now, but new representatives are necessary. It is in my mind to send Master John Morel, Abbot of Jedburgh. And Sir John Wishart of the Carse, brother of our good Bishop Wishart.'

Men stared at each other — even Bruce looking wonderingly at Lennox. The proposal was obviously sound, and none could question the suitability of the envoys. But nor could any fail to be astonished at this naming of names, so soon. It must seem as though he had come prepared. Grimly, now, Wallace watched the effect of all this on his hearers.

Into the hubbub, he spoke further. 'It occurs to me, that it is always the practice, the sound practice, to send three envoys, never two — for sufficient good reasons! Therefore I would nominate the experienced Master William Comyn also, to proceed to France, as a member of our Privy Council, with such added authority.'

The Comyns looked at each other, questioningly; but Master William appeared to be pleased.

'We shall require a Chancellor, as senior officer of the government,' Wallace went on, almost inexorably. 'The realm has suffered from lack of such. I would suggest to you the Bishop of Galloway, Master Thomas Dalton, as first minister of state.'

None objected to that, for it was normal, almost essential, for the Chancellor to be a churchman, with so much of writing and Latinity involved; and Dalton was well-liked, and the most senior bishop present.

Then, although no hint of it was evident in Wallace's features or confident delivery, came his bombshell. 'Another important office, my friends, the lack of which has been a sore burden to the realm for long, is that of Primate of Scotland, to lead Holy Church in this land. It is normal for that office to be held by the Bishop of St. Andrews, the metropolitan see. Bishop Fraser of St. Andrews is dead. It is not for this Council or assembly to appoint a bishop or the Primate. But it can *recommend* one, for His Holiness the Pope to appoint. Having spoken with many churchmen on this subject, I have no doubt in suggesting to you the name of Master William Lamberton, Chancellor of Glasgow Cathedral, of the Order of St. Benedict. Bishop Wishart recommends him above all others — and who should know better? It will be necessary for the recommended nominee to

300

travel to Rome to be consecrated — and while there, Master
Lamberton should present to His Holiness the Pope the Scottish
realm's entire and leal duty and its request that the Holy See
declare its strong disapproval of Edward of England's invasions
and savageries in Scotland, France and Flanders, and threaten
him with outlawry from Christendom, anathema and excom-
munication, if he does persist in such wicked warfare.'

Quite overwhelmed, the company gaped. Never had anyone
present heard the like of this, such vehement forcing of the
pace, such high-sounding programme, such confidence of delivery — and all done by so young a man, before a great gathering of the people, not behind the closed doors of the council-
chamber.

The Comyns were largely silenced, with all those seats on the
Council, and Master William's prestigious appointment as
special envoy — Master William who undoubtedly had been
hoping for St. Andrews and the Primacy for himself, as senior
member of its chapter and brother of the Constable. Galloway,
who might have claimed the Primacy, as senior bishop, was
brought off with the Chancellorship. And Wishart's repute used
to recommend his own lieutenant, this Lamberton. Above all,
this skilful bringing in of the Pope as possible ally in the
struggle against England. Even the Bruce looked as though he
wondered what he had done in getting Wallace appointed
Guardian.

Amongst Wallace's group of immediate supporters, a tall,
strong-faced keen-eyed churchman stood beside the Benedictine
friar, John Blair. No large number knew him as William Lamberton, the power in Glasgow behind old Robert Wishart. A
long sword-hilt peeped from beneath this man's black robe.
Another Benedictine, and a fighting one, most evidently. None
could fail to recognise what the new Guardian was doing, if
they were knowledgeable at all. The Pope was a Benedictine
also.

There were murmurs, growls, alarmed looks amongst the
nobility and some of the churchmen, but no vocal or affirmed
opposition. That this was not the place, nor the time, any man
of discernment would appreciate — with the tide running too
strongly for William Wallace. This was his day. He had the
people entirely behind him, as well as most of the Church and
the entire Bruce faction. Any who openly opposed him would
go down.

Quietly the big man considered them all, waiting. Waiting for the outcry which did not materialise. At length he nodded, and turned.

'My lord Steward,' he said, in a different voice, 'it is enough, I think. I do thank you for your patience, your courtesy. I thank all. Let a feast, a great feeding, be prepared. For many are hungry. There is yet much food here in the Forest — the famine has not touched it. Many wild cattle, many deer. Sufficient beasts are already slain. All shall eat and drink tonight, at least. Tomorrow may be otherwise!' And, the King's representative and deputy, having given his orders to the King's Steward, bowed briefly, and waving to his own close group to follow, strode to the vestry door and out of the ruined chancel.

A new chapter in Scotland's story had commenced.

* * *

Wallace's friends carried him off to a celebratory feasting in their own corner of the great haugh of Ettrick, amidst scenes of wild rejoicing. If the big man himself entered hardly to the full into this jubilation, he might perhaps have been excused. It was not every day that a young man of twenty-eight, of comparatively humble birth, erupted into the position of supreme ruler of an ancient and proud nation, and a nation in crisis, attaining the status of knighthood in the process. If his colleagues and supporters believed it to be an occasion for unalloyed rejoicing, Wallace himself was not so sure. He was gratified, stirred, challenged, of course; but not for one moment did he fail to recognise the hazards, dangers, pitfalls, as well as the responsibilities. Therefore, throughout the subsequent junketings, he remained just a little preoccupied, his mind rather evidently elsewhere.

In this he was abetted by the cleric Lamberton, whom Wishart had sent to him soon after his return to Glasgow, and whom Wallace had quickly recognised as a man after his own heart, able, vigorous, practical, but also a thinker and planner — had indeed recognised him at once as one with whom he could work, and under whose direction the Church could play a positive and active, rather than a passive, role in the saving of Scotland. Wallace had decided to do all he could, through Wishart and Sinclair to advance Lamberton in power and influence — and when his own extraordinary and unexpected promotion to the Guardianship had been thrust upon him, he had seized the opportunity with both strong hands. Now, therefore, Lamberton was in a somewhat similar situation to his own, with suddenly the prospects of vastly increased responsibility, opportunities and dangers laid upon him. These two, of them all, were inevitably drawn closer.

Lamberton may have had his own preoccupations, but that did not prevent him from taking a share in Wallace's, there and then. Throughout the jollifications, he was never far away from the big man, and often they spoke seriously together. Some of Wallace's old and trusted lieutenants no doubt resented this immediate assumption of intimacy; but the more percipient amongst them recognised that here was a mind and character such as William Wallace was going to need urgently, in his new role of Guardian, offering something none of them had to give.

Later, then, in the March evening, with everywhere the campfires glowing and the rich smells of roasting beef and venison filling the night air, it was at Lamberton's suggestion that the pair of them went in search of the Earl of Carrick. They went wrapped closely in their cloaks, since it was none of their intention to be recognised and fêted, nor yet to have to encounter the hostility of a section of the nobility.

They eventually found Bruce, with his brother-in-law, pacing the shadowy, broken cloisters of the abbey, also in deep discussion. Indeed they rather startled the two earls with their quiet arrival.

'So, my lords,' Wallace said, 'You commune closely! As well you might. For in this Scotland, I think the very stones listen and whisper! And there will be much whispering tonight. How long, think you, before the word of this day's doings reaches Surrey? And Edward?'

The other two looked distinctly uncomfortable, and Wallace had a shrewd suspicion that they had, in fact, been discussing himself. 'What mean you by that, Sir William?' Bruce demanded, more tensely than was his usual.

'That wise men do well to look over their shoulders — that is all,' the big man assured, lightly. 'This is a notable realm for traitors, is it not?'

'Eh . . .? I do not take you, sir.'

'Then you are less shrewd than I had esteemed you, my lord! The House of Comyn may not love Edward Plantagenet. But they may prefer him to William Wallace. Or even to Robert Bruce!'

'So-o-o! You fear the Comyns will not accept what is done?'

'Only if they must, I think. And they are very strong. I ask you, my lords, as men of the same noble rank and station as they — should I feel secure, when Edward strikes, with the Comyns in arms at my back?'

Bruce glanced at Mar, and cleared his throat. 'I do not know.'

'Nor do I. Master Lamberton, here, believes that I should not.'

The tall priest spoke, in a crisp voice that smacked of the field rather than the chancel. 'I do not name them traitors,' he declared. 'But I hold that they believe themselves better suited to rule Scotland than is Sir William Wallace! And will not hesitate to stab him in the back, if by so doing they may take over the rule. And esteem themselves to have done Scotland service! To do so, they must be fully assembled in arms. As they can be, in answer to the Guardian's inevitable summons to the nation. The Comyns could raise ten thousand men. A sore host to have at your back, in battle!'

'True. But how may this be countered?' Mar asked. 'You cannot keep the Comyns from mustering their men. Nor deny them the right to fight for the realm.'

The cleric lowered his voice. 'My lord — you control the vast earldom of Mar, a mighty heritage in the North. My lord of Carrick, yours is the Lordship of Garioch, nearby to it, in Aberdeenshire — half a province! Moreover, Sir Andrew Moray — dead alas — has an uncle and brothers who are sound for Sir William here, and hold the great Moray lordships of Pettie, Innes, Duffus and the rest. All these abut on the Comyn lands. If you, my lords, were to go north, and with the Morays, muster the men of these lordships — as all will be called upon to do, the Guardian tells me — then you have a force assembled on the Comyns' doorstep, do you not? Men so mustered in arms are ever . . . restless. However firm you hold them in, there will be some small spulzie and pillage. Reiving, as we say in the East March of the Border, whence I come. On neighbours' lands. Comyn lands. I swear, so long as they are there, no Comyn host will come south!'

They could hear Bruce's faint whistle of surprise, as he looked from one to the other of them, assessingly. 'You would play the realm's nobles one against the other, Sir Priest?' he challenged.

'They need but little encouragement in that, my lord! I but

304

urge that, since all the land must be mustered in arms for defence, it is only wise that sound men muster alongside those who might be led otherwise. I, we, wish for no bloodshed, no fighting. But a due balancing of forces.'

'And *Bruce* is sound in our cause, to be sure!' Wallace put in, smiling into his curling auburn beard. 'Since he it was who made me Guardian. With my lord of Mar's aid.'

Bruce peered, clearly suspicious of derision in that, but only genial confidence was to be discerned. 'How do you know that I, that we, will not make common cause with the Comyns?' he demanded.

Wallace, who recognised that Bruce probably saw all this as a device to bring down two dangers with one arrow, to divorce him from his own great reservoirs of manpower in Carrick and Annandale, to cancel out Comyn in the North, actually laughed. 'Because John Comyn is Baliol's man,' he said simply. 'And you are . . . yourself!'

Mar spoke. 'If our hosts are up in Moray and Mar, facing Comyn, then we cannot be aiding you here against the English.'

'A nation's commander needs more hosts than one, my lord. It is wise not to put all at one throw. He requires a reserve. Your combined hosts in the North will serve well as that.'

'Beware, sir, that you do not estimate Edward Plantagenet too lightly!' Bruce said. 'If you think to fight him with your own common folk, without the lords' aid. That would be fatal, against his chivalry and archers. Have you any notion as to the numbers he will throw against you?'

'Some notion, yes. We know that three thousand heavy chivalry, four thousand light cavalry and eighty thousand foot, with very many archers, are assembled at Berwick and in Northumberland. It is a mighty host — but so also was that before Stirling Bridge. And the same commander. Meantime.'

'This time. Surrey will have learned his lesson.'

'Perhaps. But it is not Surrey that we have to fear, but Edward himself. Master Lamberton has kinsfolk at Berwick, and a priest there sends tidings that the word amongst the army's chaplains is that Edward is on his way back from Flanders already, and commands that no move into Scotland be made before he comes in person to lead it. That will take time. And then, it will be Edward we face, not Surrey.'

'And Edward is a puissant warrior, the greatest in Christendom.'

'No doubt. I do not under-estimate him — by God, I do not! But he is used to fighting great set battles, as I am not. Set battles are not for me, where all is won or lost in one throw. Perhaps we may teach even the First Knight in Christendom a thing or two!'

There was silence for a little, as the four men considered that prospect, and each other. Then Bruce shrugged.

'You are the Guardian of Scotland,' he said.

'Aye. Thanks to you, as I say.'

'I wonder.'

'You doubt my thanks, my lord? That is foolish. You did for me that which no other could, or would, have done. The knighting. I will not forget it. For that, at least, I do most surely thank you. Your reasons for doing it I do not know. But the deed was good. Of much value. I am in your debt.'

'It was merited,' the Earl said shortly. 'Never was knighthood more so.'

'Not all would agree with you. But ... that is no matter. What matters is the future. How long do you give Scotland? You who know Edward? Before he comes hammering on our gates.'

'If what you say is true — three months. A month to return to London. A month to set his own house in order — to bring the English nobles to heel. Another month to raise more men to march north with him, in strength. I give Scotland until June.'

'Aye. You have the rights of it, I think. Three months — and so much to be done. So much!'

'You can do it,' Lamberton said, in his crisp voice. 'You only. For the folk are with you.'

'We shall see, my friend. So you, my lords, go north — and be ready to hasten south again, at all speed, when I call. Much may depend on it ...'

Part Three

CHAPTER EIGHTEEN

Three months was just about right — three months for Wallace
to prepare, and to rule Scotland while he was doing it, the three
most testing months of that man's life. For it was not really a
matter of ruling, at all, but of struggling, battling, cir-
cumventing, not the enemy but his own people — or at least,
their natural leaders. There lay the trouble. Always the rule had
been in the hands of the *noblesse*, at every level, from the Privy
or Secret Council down to the sheriffdoms, the parishes, the
burghs. In these last the magistrates and deacons of trades were
of the common folk, certainly; but the provostships were nearly
all hereditary offices, and if the lairds did not fill them themselves, they appointed deputies. Likewise in the country districts, although the parish priests had their influence on the
people, the rule was almost entirely in the hands of the lairds,
who in turn were the vassals of great nobles, who gave them
their orders. And Wallace just did not have the co-operation of
the landed men, in much of the country. Even those who supported him in military matters were seldom prepared to yield an
inch of their privileges and authority in civil affairs.

And with a nation about to fight for its life, military and civil
could not be divorced. For instance, to gain maximum armed
manpower, over and above the levies of the lords, Wallace
sought to divide up the entire country into units of able-bodied
men between sixteen and sixty years. These were to be grouped
in fives, tens, twenties, fifties, and one hundreds, according to
population, with each appointing their own sergeants and
under-officers. And they were to adhere to specific regimental
cadres, under trained officers and veterans. The scheme was
excellent, and capable of rapid expansion — but it foundered on
the opposition of the lords and lairds, who saw it as an attack on
their own hegemony, their right to raise fighting tails of men-at-
arms — as to some extent it was. Also, since these local units
were to put down the prevalent brigandage in their areas, and
very often tribute from the brigands was accepted by the landed

gentry as price for turning a blind eye, this also was a cause of non-co-operation.

Then there was the matter of taxes and levies. The collection of these had always been in the hands of the sheriffs of counties, and these were not lightly going to give up so lucrative a right. The sheriffdoms were almost always a perquisite of the younger sons of nobles, and few indeed there were who considered the Guardian's great need for money as any concern of theirs. Even the cities and towns offered little co-operation, when it came to taxation, however much the citizenry cheered for Wallace. Only Dundee, in fact, came up to anything like its assessment — for which Alexander Scrymgeour was largely responsible, and whom, in a burst of gratitude, Wallace appointed Hereditary Constable and Standard-Bearer for Scotland. For years the country had not been self-governing, but controlled by a foreign power, and the resultant responsibility in such matters was not to be righted in a few months. Bruce himself demonstrated how little, really, the authority of the Guardian meant to him, for although he did go North, with Mar, to act as counterbalance to the Comyns, eventually, it was not until he had spent a month in Carrick dealing with his own affairs — and then, not long afterwards, sent a message to Wallace declaring that he had constituted himself governor of the South-West, appointing his brother, the Lord Edward, as deputy meantime. At least, as Wallace commented grimly, he had had the courtesy to inform him! Comyn was reported to have an army of six thousand assembled in the Laigh of Moray.

The fact was that, without the support of the Church, Wallace's Guardianship — as distinct from his commandership of the forces which meantime went unchallenged — would have been a mere ineffective travesty. The Bishop of Galloway, the Chancellor, Wishart at Glasgow, ailing but staunch, Sinclair of Dunkeld ever faithful, and Thomas of Ross, with a host of lesser clerics, the most able and educated section of the community, gave constant and consistent aid. Indeed, practically all the money and treasure which reached the Guardian's coffers came from the Church. Lamberton, after the first month's invaluable aid, was off to Rome for Papal consecration; and the Abbot of Jedburgh, with Provost William, to France; but Master Nicholas Balmyle, Official, and Archdeacon Fraser, a kinsman of the late Bishop, opened the hidden exchequer of the metropolitan see of St. Andrews to Wallace, to his great comfort. Making bricks without straw was no activity for any man, he had discovered.

Militarily, matters were in better shape. In theory, Wallace now commanded between fifty thousand and sixty thousand troops, with twice as many available to be called from their homes at short notice. As to arms, the situation was fairly good, for they had captured many English armouries in the fallen fortresses — although there was the chronic lack of bows, arrows and trained archers. Also, of course, no heavy chivalry to set against that of the enemy. But, though this was good as far as it went, these numbers were spread but thinly over the country. Wallace kept his main force in Ettrick Forest still, where it could be switched to South-East or South-West with fair speed, as need arose. But he had other forces sited at strategic points the breadth, if not the length, of the land. For he was very much aware of the English wealth in shipping, whereby they could land and supply armies by sea, at points of their own choosing — although this largely precluded cavalry. On this account he sent Sir Neil of Lochawe and his Campbells, with the MacGregors, back to Lorn, in case a landing should be attempted there, aided by Lame John MacDougall. For the same reason, MacDuff was back in Fife, Ramsay in Angus, Lundin in Aberdeen and Maxwell in Galloway, with a central host at Stirling, under Lennox, available to move where required. The Ayrshire and Clyde coast he entrusted to Bruce, while Sir Christopher Seton, at Dunbar, watched Lothian. With this dispersal, the numbers became all too small — especially with the Comyns' thousands in the North to be taken into account.

News came in fairly steadily, from reliable sources in Berwick and Northumberland; and also filtered up, less reliably, from England further south. King Edward was acting with his usual vigour and decision. With a judicious mixture of strength, realism and conciliation, he had put down the incipient revolt of his own nobles by first setting them at each other's throats, granting one offices previously held by another, lands likewise, imprisoning the least popular, conceding here, clamping down there — and then presenting the nobility with what amounted almost to another Magna Carta, enshrining their rights — or such of them as cost him little. All this in the space of some six weeks. Whereafter he began to turn his full attention to Scotland. Shipping was assembled in great numbers, provisioning collected, men mobilised and put in training, troops brought over from Ireland to Carlisle, and large contingents of Welsh archers mustered.

By mid-May it was evident that the Bruce's estimate was likely to be accurate. June 23rd was said to be the date chosen for invasion.

From Berwick came confirmatory news. The harbour there was now largely cleared of wreckage; but a large fleet of transports was already anchored in the sheltered bay at Holy Island, not far off, with cargoes of provisions and immense quantities of grain and baled forage for horses. Earl Cospatrick of Dunbar was appointed governor of Berwick and commander in the Merse, freeing Surrey and others for active invasion. There was constant coming and going between Berwick and Carlisle, across the hills, indicating a co-ordinated attack. All of which, although ominous, was of some comfort to Wallace in that it seemed to imply that the main invasion thrust would indeed come from the Borderline, and not from seaborne assaults elsewhere along the so-lengthy coastline.

Throughout all this period of waiting, Wallace's main force in the Forest did not stand by idly. They were set to implementing the grim and grievous policy of scorched earth, approved by the Council, so that food, shelter and forage should be denied to the vast numbers of the invaders. As well as cattle and sheep, all stocks of grain and hay and straw were to be sent northwards from the Border areas and Lothian, all growing hay trampled flat. What could not be transported was to be burned, barns, mills and grain-storehouses likewise. Armies the size of Edward's required enormous quantities of horse-feed in especial. The fleet at Holy Island might be laden with such — but it would all have to be sent after or with the army on more horses, an ever-increasing problem in logistics and a notable drag on progress. The invaders must find little or nothing to aid them in Scotland.

It was, of course, a difficult and heart-rending policy to enforce. No peasant, herdsman, farmer or laird will willingly see destroyed what he has laboured for or paid for. When men's livelihoods households and families are threatened, they will object, violently. Whole villages and communities fell to be cleared in the projected paths of invasion. Even the Church rebelled at the destruction of its glebes and the granges and fields of its monasteries and abbeys. Wallace's popularity suffered a drastic drop. The policy was not so difficult to enforce in the South-East, the Merse and Lothian, where most of the land was the traitorous Earl of Dunbar's; but in the South-West, where the lords were mainly loyal — to Bruce, if not to Wallace — the strategy was never really implemented, so violent the opposition. Fighting for one's home was one thing; burning it, before the attackers came, was altogether another. Moreover, the South-West was not yet recovered from Clifford's late incursion.

Thus the three months passed, with the Guardian a harassed man, and Scotland by no means prepared for King Edward's reception, until, on June 10th, Wallace received an urgent and alarming message, and from an unexpected quarter. It was from Alexander Scrymgeour, the new Standard Bearer, at Dundee. There had been an English landing on the north coast of Fife, across the Tay estuary from Dundee, from a dozen large ships and many smaller, said to be under the command of Sir Aymer de Valence, Earl of Pembroke. There was no cavalry, but heavily-armed and seemingly veteran foot, with many archers. The invaders were marching westwards along the south side of Tay, presumably heading for Perth or Stirling.

Much shaken, Wallace saw what he had dreaded materialising, after all — invasion at his back, north of Forth, to distract his attention from the main thrust. That he must not let happen. But, on the other hand, this eruption could be highly dangerous. It did not sound like a very large force; but Pembroke was a noted general, one of Edward's favourite commanders — and indeed last heard of leading a division in Flanders. A man of such rank and renown would never be sent on any mere token gesture. And if Pembroke got to Stirling and wrested that vital bridge and area from Lennox, he could cut Scotland in two. If Wallace dared not let this distract his main defence, neither could he afford to allow Stirling, or for that matter, Perth, to fall. He had little faith in Lennox's powers as soldier; and MacDuff, the commander in Fife, was not of the calibre to oppose a general such as Valence of Pembroke.

Wallace decided that he had to go himself. Edward was known to be at York. Therefore no main invasion thrust over the Border was likely for a few days at least. On the other hand, he dare not weaken his forces waiting poised in the Forest. He would take only a selection of his own old friends, as leaders, and a couple of hundred of his veteran light horse, and make with all speed for the Queen's Ferry over the Forth, to pick up

313

further men in Fife. Couriers he sent hot-foot to MacDuff, and Sir John Ramsay in Angus and Sir William Ruthven at Perth. These were scarcely gone when he was off at their heels.

In less than twenty-four hours, Wallace and his company were landing on the south shore of Fife, at Queen Margaret's Ferry, maintained by the monks of Dunfermline Abbey, having ridden almost non-stop through the June night, from Selkirk. There a messenger from Sir Duncan Balfour, Sheriff of Fife, awaited them. He said that MacDuff and his people were now in contact with the enemy, seeking to delay their progress westwards — but less than successfully. MacDuff had only about four hundred men available, and the English numbered fully three times that. Moreover a third of them were archers, of which MacDuff had none. The Fifers had captured one of the smaller English vessels, which had landed at the wrong place, in fog; and from the prisoners it was learned that this expedition had sailed direct from Flanders, on Edward's orders, all its soldiers being veterans of the Continental wars. The enemy were last reported in the Flisk area, west of Balmerino, halfway to Perth, with MacDuff falling back slowly before them.

It was grievous news that the English were all Flanders veterans, experienced in invasion warfare — and with so many archers. On the other hand, it was good to hear that they had not progressed further, only halfway to Perth. They were not fast-moving, therefore, or else markedly cautious.

Wallace did not know the North Fife coastline well. As ever, he recognised that if anything was to be achieved he must make the land itself fight for them. The enemy were slow-moving, heavily-armed infantry — for they could not have acquired many horses in Fife. Marshland would be little avail against such; nor would steep hillsides or ravines. But dense woodland would militate against archers — and if it was pine woodland, fire and smoke might confuse. He asked such Fifers as were present whether there was any large expanse of thick woodland along the terrain in front of the enemy line of advance. Earnside, he was answered in something of a chorus — Black Earnside Forest. At Lindores. Stretching for miles, seven or eight miles, between Abernethy and the hill of Norman's Law.

'And in that forest are there any of our good Scots pines, my friends? Pines will burn in June — broad-leafed trees will not.'

They asked what he thought it was called *Black* Earnside for? Because it was almost all dark pines and old oaks.

314

'How far from here?'

'Near thirty miles, east of the Lomond Hills, by Falkland and Auchtermuchty and over Lumbenny Hill, to Lindores,' the messenger said. 'And my master, Sir Duncan Balfour, is at Falkland.'

'Good. Then we have more hard riding to do, by the Powers! Whilst Pembroke walks!'

Horses all but exhausted, they reached the little grey town of Falkland, at the eastern end of the royal hunting-forest of that name, in the late evening. Here Sir Duncan Balfour, the Sheriff, had gathered a number of West Fife and Fothriff gentry and some two hundred men. Having been appointed by MacDuff, in the name of the young Earl of Fife, he was one of the few sheriffs favourable towards Wallace, a fortunate circumstance. He greeted them warmly, and gave them news of another sheriff, less loyal. Sir John Stewart of Menteith was said to have joined the Earl of Pembroke, and was now acting as guide-in-chief. If this was true that precise man had no doubts as to the outcome of the new campaign.

With the latest word, that Pembroke was now at Ballenbreich, only a couple of miles from the edge of the Forest of Black Earnside — indeed only some ten miles from this Falkland — Wallace allowed his weary company only some four hours sleep that night. Then they hastened on northwards through the half-light and the rolling North Fife hills, riding through thick mists over Lumbenny Hill, and so down to the Loch of Lindores, as the sun was rising. Before them stretched the vast dark blanket of Earnside Forest, covering all the hillfoots and the narrow coastal plain, right to the mile-wide Tay, streamers of mist still caught eerily amongst the tall trees. Within a wide enclave of this far-flung woodland, near the estuary shore, stood the Benedictine Abbey of Lindores.

Balfour said that the forest, about seven miles long by three wide, had quite large clearings and open cultivated patches throughout, mainly connected with the Abbey's activities in fruit-growing and wine-making. There were many tracks linking these; but the principal east–west road ran near the shoreline, passing close to the Abbey itself, naturally. The English advance would almost certainly follow that road, for the interior of the woodland was rough, hilly and cut up by small burns.

They entered the trees slightly nearer the west end of the

forest area than the east — and considering that this was a situation of active warfare, everything seemed notably peaceful in the early morning, with the woodpigeons croodling, the finches chirping, and squirrels and siskins darting amongst the dark pine boughs. Wallace was glad to note the large numbers of the pines; also that what wind there was came from the west.

He sent out messengers to try to contact MacDuff. Balfour said that the Earls of Fife had a small castle at Lindores, at the north shore of the Loch; the Lord Hugh might well be there. Wallace had his two hundred horsed men, and about fifty of his own lieutenants and the West Fife lairds, also mounted — the latter's non-horsed infantry coming on behind, from Falkland, more slowly. He explained what he was looking for — an area of particularly dense woodland which reached down to the roadside, where also the land was sufficiently broken to prevent co-ordinated infantry tactics, and where the enemy march would inevitably string out. They had not long to find this, for unless Pembroke was sluggard indeed, he would be on the move shortly now, and even slow-moving infantry, harassed by MacDuff's people, would not take more than a couple of hours to cover four or five miles. Balfour was uncertain as to a suitable location, so they sent Thomas Gray with a guide hastening to the Abbey, to enquire of the monks, who would be sure to know.

Reaching the road well east of the Abbey, they searched along it, ears alert for any sounds of battle, and scouts out well ahead. There were plenty of pine-trees for firing, but nowhere was the woodland sufficiently dense, nor the ground sufficiently broken, to please Wallace.

He was becoming distinctly anxious when the Abbot of Lindores himself arrived, with Gray and a score of armed servants, a stout, rubicund but breathless man, who was much relieved to see the Guardian come in time to save his Abbey, but concerned that they were much too far to the east for the sort of ground they wanted. Apparently there was such a place as Master Gray had described only half-a-mile from the Abbey itself, where the Red Burn came down to the shore, amongst wooded braes.

Back westwards they hastened, thankful to be going away from the enemy not towards him. When they reached the recommended spot, however, it was less good than Wallace had hoped — but would have to serve. The woodland was thick

enough, with much scrub birch, its young green vivid; but the
ground was so broken that any unified defence would be almost
as difficult as attack, with no levelish space to erect the redoubt
Wallace had planned. They would be unlikely to find a better,
now, nevertheless.

He dismounted his men, and sent all the horses back into the
deeper forest out of sight. Then he set all to gathering fallen
timber and cutting scrub and saplings with their dirks — they
had no time for felling larger trees. With this material they
made a very elementary redoubt on a minor ridge between two
ravines, overlooking the road, exceedingly uneven as to its sides
owing to the upheaved nature of the site, but with walls high
enough and thick enough to give a fair protection from arrows.
They made an elongated, narrow approach to this, with similar
walls — the only entry. In this enclosure would be forty of his
own men, whom he had instructed as archers during the
months of waiting, using captured English yew bows; also
another forty, with spears. Sir John Graham would command,
with Thomas Gray. The rest he would take into the dense thickets to the east, disposing them to best advantage along the line
of the road, about a hundred and ninety men all told.

The Lord Hugh arrived, during these preparations, arm in a
sling, having been wounded the day before by a spear-thrust.
He was thankful indeed to see Wallace, and to surrender his
responsibility. His people were all but exhausted, he declared,
and he had lost many. They could not have kept up this delaying action for much longer. Pembroke was able to treat
them as though they were flies, to be brushed out of his
way ...

Scouts returned to announce that the enemy were near, less
than half-a-mile off, with the scattering of Scots retiring before
them. About a dozen of the officers had acquired horses, but all
others were on foot, wearing steel breastplates, greaves and
helmets, with leather trappings, and armed with long spears or
pikes and short stabbing-swords — and of course, the bows and
arrows.

The subsequent ambush was much aided by MacDuff's
skirmishers. An experienced commander such as Pembroke, in
hostile country, would undoubtedly be on the look-out for just
such attack, but the constant harassing tactics of the Fifers,
always just in front of him, was almost bound to have the effect
of lessening alertness to ambush, in that the entire advance was

317

being made against opposition from ahead. In fact, most of the weary and jaded skirmishers themselves were not only unaware of Wallace's trap but went straggling along the road below at a tired trot, tending to glance behind them rather than to their left into the thickets, without ever perceiving the hidden ambushers. Some few, who threaded their way through the woodland above did stumble on the line of crouching, silent men — and were hushed to quiet, and promptly incorporated. Messengers were sent discreetly after the larger number on the road, to bring them back, inland. But not all of them, for in fact, a small demonstration of delaying tactics by these, say four hundred yards further along the road, would tend to help, to preoccupy the enemy's forward troops and distract attention.

Only a few minutes behind the last of the Fifers came the English advance-guard, two mounted officers, one of them with coat-armour, and about seventy men, mixed spearmen and archers, grim, professional-looking soldiers, alert and disciplined. But they were clearly concerned with what lay ahead rather than with the dense woodland on their flank. They certainly did not delay to probe the scrub. They were allowed to go past.

The main body appeared after a short interval, led by a colourful group of splendidly armoured knights, albeit on stolen horses, the banner of the Earldom of Pembroke, blue and red with three silver lions, at the front. These rode confidently, secure behind the advance-party, so that the watchers could even hear the loud-voiced, slightly arrogant chatter between these lordly ones. Behind, in orderly files, marched their troops, in platoons and companies, four abreast, stretching away out of sight round bends in the road.

It was rather like Shortwood Shaw again — though these would be tougher adversaries. Wallace had stationed himself at the hinge of his own line, where he could see the redoubt area and also some part of the roadway. Hidden behind the leafage, he watched the enemy leadership ride past, a bare hundred yards below. Some of the knights had their helmets hanging at their saddle-bows, others worn on their heads but their visors open. How would his new bowmen fare, with such small and moving targets?

Timing was again vital. Pembroke and his officers must be as far on as possible, without being out of range of the redoubt, before the signal was given. Wallace raised his hand.

Forty arrows sped from the leafage-camouflaged redoubt. A few, also, were fired from the hidden line in the thickets. A small number of men, mainly those with captured English mail, leapt out of their cover, to brandish swords, hurl spears and shout. Nine out of ten, however, remained in hiding.

It was a very elementary ruse, and might hardly have been expected to be successful with seasoned troops. But that would fail to take into account the effect of the attack on the leadership, the salvo of arrows from the redoubt. Aimed at perhaps a dozen knights, even with many misses and non-vital hits, the impact was great. Five men fell from their horses, and three others, though remaining in their saddles, were sorely wounded. Pembroke himself seemed to be unhurt; but he had lost most of his lieutenants at one stroke. The effect on the rank-and-file, in shock, anger and lack of direction, was dramatic and highly demoralising. Without any orders from in front, many turned automatically on the only enemy they could see. English archers, stringing their bows hurriedly, drew arrows and shot at men in view, or blindly into the foliage. Spearmen and sworders left the road to go bounding up to engage the demonstrating few — who promptly retired into the dense brushwood. In mere moments after that first signal of Wallace's, the disciplined enemy force was in complete disarray.

Disarray by no means meant defeat. But it did mean that much of the enemy's advantage in control, experience and concerted manoeuvre was dissipated.

Pembroke swiftly recovered from the initial shock. Soon he was shouting commands, and his trumpeter bugling to draw attention to them. But because of the strung-out formation imposed by the roadway through the woodland, only those comparatively nearby could hear the orders. Elsewhere, more and more of the soldiery were running up into the scrub and thickets after the deliberately shouting and jeering, if unseen, foe.

Pembroke lacked nothing in initiative or courage. Perceiving that he could not affect the rear of his column, he leapt down from his horse, and drawing his sword, led the forward portion uphill towards the redoubt, in gallant style. He lost many men, so doing, transfixed by arrows, but came on regardless, himself immune within full armour, visor now down. His own archers found very poor marks to aim at, although a few of Wallace's bowmen were hit, as they bobbed up, from behind the palisading, to shoot. Some English arrows, fired blind, did pierce the stockade, and found an occasional mark. But, naturally, it was the Englishmen, in the open, who suffered grievously.

By sheer determination and disregard for casualties, Pembroke's attack reached the redoubt. There, near the barricades, they were largely sheltered from the archery, and it was the spearmen's turn. But the spearmen outside were much more vulnerable than those within. They sought to pull down part of the walling, but lost so many men by spear-thrusts from inside that they gave up the attempt. Clambering over was equally unsuccessful, and although one or two got inside, they were quickly despatched. Eventually Pembroke, whose men still much outnumbered the defenders, recognized that only by assaulting the entry alley might they gain their objective. Behind an improvised barrier of knights' shields and the breastplates of the fallen, they turned to the grim task of battling their way in.

Meanwhile, the battle in the thickets proceeded very much as Wallace had anticipated. So dense was the scrub and so broken the ground, that no sort of line was possible on either side. The Scots tactics were to draw the enemy ever deeper into this woodland, away from the road. In this they were only partly successful, for some of the English under-officers kept their heads, and perceiving that their strength was being hopelessly dispersed, called back some proportion of their men, to reform as a fairly strong unit on the roadway where they took up a defensive stance. They would have no idea, of course, as to the numbers attacking them.

As for the rest, their advantages thrown away — for the thick scrub was no place for either archery or spearmanship — they were largely immobilised, made ineffective; and this accounted for more than half the invading force.

Well enough pleased, Wallace turned his attention back to the redoubt. When he came within sight of it again, it was to recognise that Graham and Gray were hard-pressed indeed. Pembroke and his people were now well up the entrance passage, solid behind their screen of shields. Moreover, the English advance-party had now returned, to add their strength. Some of these were seeking to pull down and demolish the walls of the enclosure, while the defenders were preoccupied with the frontal attack.

Hurriedly calling together a group of his men, from the dispersed fighting, the big man led then, shouting 'A Wallace! A Wallace!', to his friends' aid.

Thereafter followed the hardest fighting of the entire engagement. Sir Duncan Balfour fell at an early stage, with an
arrow in the back of his neck, above his harness. Wallace,
wielding his great brand, sought as usual to reach the enemy
commander, but could not get at Pembroke on account of the
press in the alley. He did seek out and slay the knight who had
commanded the advance-guard. More and more men joined
this battle, on both sides, from the woodlands and from the
roadway — which was not what Wallace had planned, for the
English still outclassed them both in numbers and in exper-
tise.

He began to reckon that it was time to fire the forest.

It was at this stage that he became aware that the knight
fighting at his left hand, replacing his cousin Adam who he had
seen wounded, was Sir John Ramsay. As the significance of this
dawned on him, he disengaged for the moment, and fell back,
signing to the other. Gasping, Ramsay explained that the messengers had found him at Arbroath, on the Angus coast, and he
had gathered a horsed company and ridden almost non-stop.
The ferry across Tay at Cairnie could take no more than six
horses at a time, so, first over, he had raced on ahead, to Lindores Abbey, with his half-dozen, to seek news. The monks had
told him of this fight. He had sent back two of his men to bring
on the rest . . .

'How many have you?' Wallace demanded.

'Near two hundred.'

'Then back. Now. Bring them. Along the road. All speed.
And much noise. Remain on the road. Drawn up. I will fire the
woods. Off with you . . .'

Wallace detached a small party to go and set alight the pines
and fallen brushwood to the west, and then, shouting his slogan
hoarse-voiced, rejoined the fight.

The dense smoke-clouds which soon came drifting down
quite quickly had their effect on the struggle, slowing it up,
causing men to look around, eyes to stream and throats to
choke. The tempo flagged, and as the smoke grew worse, men
on the fringes started to break away. It all took some time, but
when the crackling roar of the flames, and the lurid light tinging
the smoke, added to the ominous threat, Pembroke recognised
that this section of Earnside Forest was no place for fighting in.
His trumpeter sounded the Recall.

This was where training, discipline, experience, proved their worth. Everywhere the English sought to break off the engagement, from redoubt and forest, and to move back down to the road. By no means all were able to do this. With less well-trained and veteran troops it would almost certainly have degenerated into a rout, a shambles. But these, some of England's best, supporting each other, retiring in leap-frogging groups, using the very ground which Wallace had used against them to protect them now, made their retiral to the road, through the billowing smoke, to Pembroke's repeated Recall.

At a rift in the dense blue-and-brown clouds, Wallace was dismayed to see how many of them there still remained.

It was at this juncture that Ramsay's Angusmen put in an appearance, coming jingling through the smoke at a trot, along the road from the Abbey. Their arrival was the last straw for Pembroke. He could not, of course, tell how many there were; but they clearly were a large party and made a lot of noise, as instructed. They were cavalry — Pembroke had no cavalry to face them. Moreover, they were fresh to the fight, and his men were weary, with many wounded. The trumpeter sounded again — this time not Recall but Retiral.

It was a fighting retiral, and no panic-stricken flight; indeed as a retreat, it was masterly — and William Wallace saluted Aymer de Valence of Pembroke as a commander after his own heart. But it *was* a retreat, nothing could alter that — and inevitably it would deteriorate the longer it went on.

Wallace handed over to Ramsay, MacDuff and Sir William Ruthven, who had just arrived from Perth, with instructions to keep up the pressure on the retiring English until Pembroke was either overwhelmed, or, more likely, reached his ships and departed. For himself, weary as he was, it was an immediate right-about-face and back to Ettrick Forest without delay. All the time he had been dreading what Edward Plantagenet might be doing, whilst he was far from the Border.

Before he and the small tight group of his faithful veterans rode off southwards, he took a few minutes to pay his respects to the dead and commiserate with the wounded. Sir John Graham was amongst these — fortunately not seriously — as was Adam Wallace and Thomas Gray. Both Kerlie and MacGregor also were hurt, but not sufficiently to keep them from riding with their leader. There were not a few dead on the Scots side, other than Balfour the Sheriff, including a promising young knight of Moray's ranks, Sir William Bisset. Wallace

grieved to have lost so many good men, proportionately more
than in any of his former battles — an ominous indication of
what happened when confronted with first-rate English troops.
Amongst the English dead, the knight whom he had slain personally, commander of the advance-guard, proved to be Sir
John Siward, a noted captain of King Edward's. No doubt it
was his name, which had been mistakenly reported as that of Sir
John Stewart of Menteith.

It was a tired and concerned victor who rode southwards.

CHAPTER NINETEEN

At Selkirk, Wallace found all in a stir. King Edward had arrived on the Border, and was now at Beck's castle of Norham,
after having made pilgrimage to the shrine of St. John at Bev-
erley, in East Yorkshire, to make his devotions and pray for the
speedy success of this campaign in Scotland. News of the actual
invasion was expected hourly. It was emphasised that Edward
had declared repeatedly that the Scots were to be treated as
traitorous rebels, and proceeded against with maximum
severity — which, from Edward Plantagenet was grim warning
indeed.

At least the King would not be long in learning that his first
move, to assail the Scots rear, had been a failure.

There was also news that Edward had written severally, and
at great labour, to all the major Scots nobles, the lords temporal
and spiritual, informing them that they had failed him grievously, and commanding their immediate return to their due
allegiance — since all had sworn fealty to him, as required. He
was coming in person to put to rights his province of Scotland,
and commanded all to submit themselves to him at the earliest
moment. Those who failed to do so would be adjudged forsworn traitors, and treated accordingly, irrespective of name,
status and position.

Wallace, for one, did not underestimate the effect of this
pronouncement.

Two days later, couriers brought the expected tidings.

Edward had crossed Tweed at Coldstream in strength and was proceeding westwards, by Kelso and Roxburgh. Seemingly he was going to take the inland route northwards, by upper Tweed and Lauderdale rather than the normal coast road — no doubt because he anticipated that the scorched earth policy would be less effective a handicap in the hilly regions on the edge of Ettrick Forest than on the fertile levels of the Merse.

Waiting only long enough to confirm that this was indeed the main English invasion route, Wallace gave the orders for retiral. He might have held out almost indefinitely, embattled in the inner fastness of the Forest; but he was no longer Will Wallace, guerilla captain, but Guardian of Scotland, supreme commander and representative of the King of Scots, however unworthy. He had a whole realm to guard and sustain, not just a handful of youthful irregulars.

So he moved his army of some ten thousand down Ettrick and Tweed to the entry of the Gala Water. He dared not go further down the main river, to Melrose and Leaderfoot, for fear of entanglement with Edward's advance units, no part of his tactics meantime. He marched up Gala Water northwards for a few miles, to Buckholm, where he cut eastwards across the hills, by Colmslie and Langshaw, to Ercildoune in mid-Lauderdale, where was the main castle of Cospatrick's Earldom of March. If this was going to be Edward's path, then the burning and trampling could start here, again, with a will.

With word of the English burning the abbeys of Kelso, Dryburgh and Melrose, to say nothing of these and other townships, and the wholesale slaying and hanging of the citizenry, Wallace's force retired slowly northwards up Lauderdale, themselves leaving a wide and blackened trail of destruction behind them, seeking to lure the English on as well as to starve them. Not that Edward Longshanks required much luring; but the knowledge that Wallace was just in front of him might hasten him, cause him to extend his huge, slow-moving and cumbrous host to its own disadvantage, and possibly to lessen its impact on the unfortunate towns and villages around. If Edward's four thousand light cavalry could be tempted into a premature encounter, on ground of Wallace's choosing, amongst the hills, a serious blow might be struck which could much unbalance the rest of the force.

But the First Knight of Christendom was an old and wily campaigner, and not to be provoked into indiscretion. Sternly

324

he kept his people in hand, and his mighty array in careful and implacable order of march — however much they might be tempted to hasten, on account of increasing hunger and lack of forage for the thousands of horses. They had to move at the pace of the infantry and of the heavy war-horses and destriers under their weight of steel armouring. Twelve miles a day was the maximum. Edward used his light horse, not for catching up with Wallace but for ranging far and wide in search of food and unburned and untrampled hay. And for condign punishment of the rebellious Scots lieges.

So both armies slowly climbed out of stricken Lauderdale and over the high moors of Soutra, at the western end of the Lammermuir Hills, down into Lothian's wide, rich and lovely plain. Wallace could not burn all of Lothian, of course — although much had already been scorched — and Edward could now choose his own path across it, no longer confined by hills and river-valleys.

Wallace's first tactical venture had scarcely succeeded.

In fact, Edward surprised the Scots by not making for Edinburgh but striking well to the west of the fortress-city, skirting the base of the Pentland Hills. Wallace had assumed that he would make for Leith, Edinburgh's port, in order to try to reach his supply-ships; therefore the harbour of Leith had been blocked by wrecks. Perhaps Edward knew of this, and had other plans.

Wallace's own long-term strategy, of course, was to retire before the enemy until they both reached that great and unavoidable hazard of any northwards invasion, the Forth at Stirling. He did not for a moment imagine that he could thus repeat his success over Cressingham and Surrey; but if he could reach the vital crossing, and contest it, serious disadvantage must accrue to the English. Edward would know it well; but that was not to say that he could avoid the consequences. Wallace had sent out messengers all over the land, ordering all commanders of troops and districts, and all lords with their levies, to converge on Stirling with all speed. How many of the latter would in fact answer his call, remained to be seen; but he could rely on his appointed commanders, such as Ramsay in Angus, MacDuff in Fife, Ruthven in Perth and Gowrie, Seton in East Lothian, Campbell in Lorn and Maxwell in Galloway. And if Sir John the Graham was not sufficiently recovered to lead the Stirlingshire men, he would send his uncle. It would be interesting to see if Bruce came, from the Garioch, or wherever he was.

In time it became apparent that Edward was in fact heading for Queen Margaret's Ferry — a shrewd move, for although he could by no means ferry any large proportion of his host across Forth, he might send over a cavalry flanking-party, to try to reach Stirling from the north, and capture the bridge. Moreover, the harbour of Queensferry, if it was to remain clear for the great ferry-scows of the monks, would also be clear, as a port of entry, for the English supply-ships.

Wallace therefore hastened to South Queensferry, and sank the ferryboats, and any other shipping he could lay hands on, in the mouth of the harbour.

Foiled in this, Edward halted his hungry host at Kirkliston, three miles to the south, to await his very slow moving, ox-drawn baggage-trains.

They both waited, now, Wallace for his forces to gather from the far corners of the land. Edward did not entirely waste his time — although he was reported to be ill of a fever. He sent a force under one of his favourite captains, Sir John Fitz-Marmaduke, to aid Bishop Beck in reducing the East Lothian castles of Dunbar, Dirleton and Preston, all belonging to the Earl of Dunbar and March but held for Wallace by Sir Christopher Seton. He also made continual demonstration of his well-known severity, on the Lothian countryside, as warning and example.

In the end it was Wallace who required the longer waiting, for the great numbers of his scattered forces just failed to appear. Some did, to be sure. Graham, looking much the worse for his wound, came, with almost a thousand, MacDuff had managed to raise only five hundred, after his Fife losses. Ramsay arrived with two thousand Angus infantry plus his two hundred horse. Scrymgeour brought over a thousand of the Dundee train-bands. Ruthven had halted at the far side of Stirling Bridge, with another two thousand of his own and Bishop Sinclair's men. Campbell sent messengers to say that he was on his way, from far-away Argyll, hastening across the mountains; Maxwell likewise from the South-West. But from the lords, in the main — silence.

As for King Edward, his oxen-trains arrived — and the oxen themselves were slaughtered for their beef. One or two of his ships managed to put in at small fishing havens along the Forth coast, and unloaded; but he was still desperately short of food

326

and forage for an army of a hundred thousand and more. There was a near mutiny amongst the hungry troops, and a serious fight developed between Welsh archers and English spearmen over who was getting the most food, in which not only were eighty Welshmen slain but no fewer than eighteen priests died — peacemakers sent in by Edward from the large contingent of churchmen without which he never campaigned. The Plantagenet decided against further waiting, for ships or forage-parties. Hungry or not, they would advance.

Wallace recommenced his retiral.

But now Edward changed his tactics. He moved fast, recognising the dangers and problems ahead at Stirling, now only twenty-five miles on. His aim clearly was to bring Wallace to bay before that. No doubt he was well informed as to the Scots numbers, or lack of them. And Wallace, now burdened with thousands of slow-moving infantry, perceived that the four thousand English light cavalry could reach Stirling before him. He had waited just too long for his reinforcements.

He would have to make a stand somewhere before Stirling Bridge, or else disperse into the great Tor Wood Forest and leave Edward master of all Lowland Scotland, failing the realm which had made him Guardian, without a blow struck. Then a messenger arrived from Sir William Ruthven bringing word that a Comyn host of six thousand foot and three hundred horse had arrived at Stirling, from the North. Bruce was also said to be making his way south. That decided it. Wallace certainly did not trust the Red Comyn. Better to fight before the Comyns could join him — or join Edward!

So the die was cast, for better or for worse.

*   *   *

Even though they were prepared for it and were well aware of the dimensions and scale of the confrontation, the Scots were appalled. Wallace himself grew very tense, silent, as he watched. His immediate companions on the braeside, nobles and knights as well as lesser men, stared, almost awestruck, as the might of England deployed itself before them in seemingly endless array. An army of a hundred thousand and more may be a sufficiently impressive mental concept; but when actually seen spread out, and formed up in its serried ranks, to cover an entire plain, is something to daunt and bludgeon the imagination.

327

The setting was a vast declivity at the very South-Eastern end of Stirlingshire, not far from the Lothian border, west of Linlithgow but east of Falkirk. Wallace had done the best that he could by choosing the battleground. The great Tor Wood which clothed most of the high ground south of Stirling, sent out a spur just below the town of Falkirk, eastwards, called Callendar Hill, a long, low wooded ridge only some three miles inland from the flat Forth shore. Wallace had selected the southern re-entrant of this to make his stand, guided by the Graham, who knew every yard of this country. He had his back to the main Tor Wood heights, and his left protected by the Callendar ridge. Across his front, at the foot of the whin-dotted braes, ran the Westquarter Burn, to round the east end of Callendar Hill and so reach the flats of Forth. This quite sizeable stream itself would not form any very effective barrier; but in the centre of this declivity it had become dammed up, to form a reedy loch, surrounded by an area of marshland. On the western slopes above this, the Scots were drawn up. Wallace's preoccupation had been Edward's three thousand heavy armoured chivalry. Here he was protected from them on his east-facing front, and on the north; only by a southerly circuit might they approach him *en masse*, and even then only over fairly soft ground — although the Westquarter Burn itself they could splash through.

At the last moment Wallace had had two accretions of strength — although strength might not be the most apt word. The first had been the arrival of the Earl of Lennox and the High Steward, with sundry knights and about a hundred and fifty horsed retainers — late, but welcome, as providing an aspect of noble support for the Guardian. The second should have been still more so, for this was the appearance on the scene of another of the great officers of state, with four hundred horse. But it was the Constable, the Earl of Buchan, and his men were Comyns. They had left the main Comyn host at Stirling, on hearing that Wallace was making his stand at Falkirk, and had ridden hard to be here in time. The Guardian, making a show of welcoming these also, would have been happier without them.

He had, of course, never fought a set battle such as this, and was well aware of his inadequacy and lack of training for the mighty task. He was offered no lack of advice, needless to say — but he recollected that the last such great fight on Scottish soil had been the Battle of Dunbar, three years before, when many of the men now authoritatively giving him guidance had been spectacularly routed by the same opponent, Edward. Buchan, Lennox, the Steward, his brother Sir John of Bonkyl, and others of the lordly band had all been there, to suffer one of the most shameful defeats in Scotland's story. Perhaps he was to be excused for scarcely slavishly following their far from united but vigorously expressed advice.

He had formed up his main force in four great schiltroms in a row, literally shield-rings, tight, oval formations like human redoubts, each of a couple of thousand men, kneeling, crouching, standing, shoulder to shoulder with their long spears out thrust in every direction like vast hedgehogs. Around these a sea of long wooden stakes were driven into the ground, linked with roughly twisted grass ropes, to entangle cavalry hooves. Between the schiltroms, both protected and protecting, he had placed his precious bowmen, mainly Border foresters from Ettrick, whom he had been training for months, though direly lacking suitable yew bows. Immediately behind, he ranked his own veteran horse, as a mobile force to go wherever most required. These were not cavalry in the true sense, in that they were not trained for fighting on horseback. Their mounts were for getting them swiftly to their targets; in nine cases out of ten they fought on foot. His only true light cavalry were the lords' men-at-arms, some seven hundred of them all told, including the Comyns. These he placed well to the right, on the higher ground, where their evident presence might tend to inhibit the southern flank attack by chivalry which he feared; and where, whatever they did, they would be in little position to endanger his schiltroms. As added security, Wallace placed Ramsay and his two hundred horsed Angusmen between them and his main array.

He had plenty of time for this proceeding, for the tremendous English host took infinitely longer to marshal — and Edward appeared to be in no hurry; indeed, the Steward said that he had had word from the enemy camp to the intent that, during the night, owing to a page's carelessness, a war-horse had trampled on the sleeping King, damaging his knee. The big man was interested — but more interested still that his own lord should be in a position to know what went on in the English camp. Personally, he was eager for a start to the engagement, not so much out of natural impatience as out of fear that the Red

Comyn himself, and his six thousand foot, might have time to arrive, from Stirling, and possibly change the entire situation. He recognised that his suspicions of the Comyn chief might be unworthy; but he also knew that, while he was fighting for a people and nation, the Red Comyn, if he fought at all, would be fighting for a crown — which could well mean a notable difference in alignments.

For two weary hours, on either side of noon that Day of St. Mary Magdalene, 22nd of July, the Scots waited and watched, with misgivings. Bishops Dalton and Sinclair had led prayers to God for divine aid — they did not stipulate victory — and all possible dispositions were made. The prevailing tension was marked by irritations and petty disputes, symbolic of the realisation of what was at stake that day. Buchan claimed that, as Constable, he should have had the marshalling of the Scots array. The Steward, no warrior himself, nevertheless contended that he, being the senior officer of state, should have command of the right wing — which, since he was not one to fight amongst the sweaty foot of the schiltroms, meant the horsed levies on the right, in which the Comyns predominated. In an effort to restore harmony, Wallace appointed Buchan commander of the horse — which command he would have assumed anyway; and Stewart in command of the centre — which, since each schiltrom had to be an independent command, under his own tried lieutenants, and the veteran horse was under Wallace's own personal control, really meant only the bowmen grouped between the schiltroms. The Steward, mollified, accepted this as suitable, but preferred to appoint his brother, the more truculent and warlike Sir John of Bonkyl, as deputy. Sundry other similar adjustments had to be made, with such patience as might be mustered.

'I vow Edward Longshanks does not have to suffer such follies, over yonder!' Sir John Graham asserted, low-voiced. 'He would have a short way with the like!'

'There is a difference, my friend,' Wallace answered. 'Edward is born master, where I am appointed servant.'

As though to emphasise his unassailable superiority and security, King Edward had had tents and pavilions erected over there, and from these now, across the half-mile gap came the tuneful sounds of chanting. Evidently some religious observance was going on. The Scots listened with a certain apprehension. Mary Magdalene was a somewhat doubtful saint, as far as they were concerned — a reformed whore, some said. She had a shrine at Linlithgow, where the English leadership has passed the night. Could this be an ill omen?

At last the sounds of sweet singing changed to a more martial trumpeting. This was presently drowned by prolonged cheering, as out from the mass of the enemy array rode a mighty phalanx of armoured chivalry, all colour and gleaming steel, under — Wallace's heraldic experts assured him — the standard of Bigod, Earl of Norfolk, Earl Marshal of England, and those of the Earls of Hereford and Lincoln. The first two had been the leaders of the recent nobles' revolt, but here they were leading the English van. Their solid ranks of knights and barded horse, the most dreaded corps in Christendom, moved slowly, deliberately forward, as though nothing on God's earth could stop them. The very ground beneath the Scots feet began to tremble under that terrible advance and the massive hairy hooves of the destriers and war-horses.

'Two thousand of them, for a wager!' MacDuff cried. 'The main assault, already!'

'God save us!' Kerlie breathed. 'Oh, for the likes of Stirling Bridge!'

'Wait you,' Wallace advised, quietly, from under the Lion Rampant of Scotland, held aloft by Alexander Scrymgeour, Standard Bearer. 'My lord Hugh — get you to your schiltrom. You also, Sir Richard, Sir William and Sir John — and may God strengthen your arms this day!' He lowered his voice to Ramsay. 'And to your place, my friend. And watch you the Comyns like any hawk!'

The implacable pacing advance of the war-horses reached the edge of the slight dip to the dark green hollow, and the tempo increased to a lumbering trot. Only when halfway down would the gleam of water amongst the rushes reveal that there was a loch of sorts in the centre of the great reed-bed. Abruptly trumpets sounded, and with much waving of arms from the leaders, the heavy host ground to a gradual halt. After a pause, a single reconnoitring troop moved cautiously down to investigate.

The Scots waited, silent, almost breathless.

In only a few moments the troop of destriers was in serious trouble. Not quarter-of-a-mile from their foe, and long before they could reach the water, they began to stumble and flounder and rear. With those furthest advanced sinking almost up to their bellies in the soft slime of the reed-bed, the situation was established sufficiently clearly for all. With much further trumpet-blowing and shouting of orders, the huge knightly array went through the cumbersome manoeuvre of turning left-handedly at right-angles, in column, to go pacing away southwards.

From the watching Scots ranks arose a vast yell of relief, jeering, and cheering.

Wallace did not join in. Eyes narrowed, he traced the route the enemy must now take, calculating, timing. They had only to go far enough, to get round.

More bugling from the main English host heralded the second line of battle. This also mounted, but differently composed and much larger, if less fearsome of aspect. Under the great two-staffed banner of the Prince-Bishop of Durham, a gold cross on blue between four silver lions, supported by no fewer than thirty-six knightly flags of lesser commanders, the four thousand light cavalry, reinforced by another five hundred heavy chivalry, moved out.

These advanced on a more northerly bearing, making as though for the wooded flanks of Callendar Hill.

Wallace looked in that direction. There lay infantry, with trenches and pits dug, amongst the Callendar trees, and roped stakes all along the burn-sides; but these would not delay such a force for long. He sent Robert Boyd and his own cousin Adam, with four hundred of his veteran horse, to seek to increase that delay.

Whilst keeping these two cavalry advances very much under his regard, the big man had also to consider the English centre. Edward still had perhaps one thousand light cavalry and half that of heavy; and of course the ninety thousand and more of foot were still drawn up in their endless companies, unmoving. The King himself, presumably, was commanding these — and fever, injured knee or none, Edward Plantagenet remained the greatest menace William Wallace had to fear. If Edward was prepared to wait, Wallace must wait likewise. His role, on this occasion, unfortunately had to be defensive only.

Edward waited until his right, under Bishop Beck, was fighting in the Callendar trees, and his left, under the Earl Marshal, was on firm enough ground, to the south, to cross the burn and turn back northwards. Then he sent forward his Welsh archers, twelve thousand of them the Scots counted, in endless green columns.

Wallace groaned — but inwardly only.

The archers marched down steadily, and were by no means confounded by the reed-beds as the heavy chivalry had been. They could not wade the loch; but although this was over half-a-mile long it was only about a hundred yards wide. Down into the reeds their ranks plunged, and although they sank up to their knees, they did not halt until they could advance no further. And there they were within fifty yards of the water, one hundred and fifty yards of the far side, two hundred and fifty yards of the western edge of the reeds, three hundred yards from the Scots line. The effective range of the yew long-bow was three hundred and fifty to four hundred yards.

This was what Wallace had dreaded. He had sited his schiltroms as far back from the soft ground as he could, and yet give them levelish land — for without that the formation lost most of its effectiveness.

The deadly archery began. At first it was all concentrated on the Scots bowmen, grouped between the schiltroms. These shot back; but their shorter bows had a range of only two hundred and twenty yards or so, and their arrows almost all fell hopelessly short. The men went down in their scores under a vicious hail of shafts that was like driving rain. Sir John Stewart, who had insisted on commanding them from horseback, quickly had his mount shot under him. Thereafter he stalked to and fro, encouraging the men, on foot, the arrows striking but failing to penetrate his armour — until one shaft found a crevice at his visor, and transfixed eye and brain.

By that time Wallace had been forced to order the bowmen to withdraw to higher ground, from this useless dying. The schiltroms were left the more vulnerable.

Now the massed Welshmen turned their bows on the vast targets of the schiltroms themselves. The arrows were somewhat less effective here, for Wallace had put all the men with steel breastplates and helmets in the outer ranks, and these, close-packed as they were, presented something of a wall of steel. But even so, the deadly cataract did great havoc — and was, moreover, grievously bad for the morale of men who could only stand and take it, with nothing to hit back at.

As much on this last account, as any, Wallace mounted some seventy of the surviving bowmen behind his chain-mailed or semi-armoured veterans, and sent them dashing down to the edge of the reeds, where they were within range with their shorter bows, the horses there wheeling and coming back, to repeat the process. This did some considerable damage amongst the equally tight-packed, immobile and unarmoured Welsh — but at great cost to archers, riders and horses. And with all the ranked thousands of the enemy, the impact was pitifully small, for the lives lost — although it did cheer the schiltrom spearmen somewhat.

Wallace was forced to recognise that this would not do. He was throwing away his best and most effective, to aid the less effective. He just had no answer to the English and Welsh long-bow. His beloved fellow countrymen were dying all around him, without being able to strike back — and he was their ap-pointed Guardian. He began to consider ordering a general re-tiral to the Tor Wood. It would be admission of defeat, yes, and might have incalculable effects on the nation's spirit, especially on the nobility's will to resist. But at least he could thus save large numbers of his men — and thereafter return to the guerilla tactics of which all men said he was the master. The fighting of this set battle had been forced upon him; would he not be wise, then, despite morale, to withdraw from it before further disaster overtook them?

It was at this juncture that all eyes were turned towards the left, the north. There, streaming out from the Callendar wood-land came Bishop Beck's light cavalry, yelling. They had broken through the defences there more quickly than anticipated, and there was now no barrier between them and the Scots array. At the sight and sound of them, a great cheer arose from the ranks of the Earl Marshal's chivalry, on the other side, now advancing again, although slowly. The cry was taken up by the Welshmen in the marsh, and further back, by the great mass of the still uncommitted infantry under the King.

Behind the schiltroms and Wallace's remaining veterans, the High Constable of Scotland saw the writing on the wall, and was not surprised. He raised his hand high. And at the signal, led by the Comyns, nine out of ten of the cavalry, and the lords' men-at-arms, wheeled their horses' heads around, and spurred from the field.

The English shout of triumph seemed to shake the very heaven.

Wallace himself had no time for recriminations and heart-burning — whatever the reaction of most of his men. He was facing the other way altogether, and deciding on priorities. He

334

had still some hundreds of his veteran horsemen; but to throw them directly against the oncoming host of Bishop Beck would be folly. They were not fighting cavalry, and would simply be overwhelmed, and swiftly, to little purpose, without breaking the charge of the thousands. That was what the schiltroms were designed for, breaking charges. The schiltroms had lost their supporting bowmen. His horsemen, too few now for independent action, would be best taking the bowmen's place, between the formations. Once the English cavalry came up, the Welsh archers would have to stay their hands, or else risk killing their own people — there was that small advantage in the situation.

He shouted to his immediate lieutenants to divide his veterans into three groups, and place them between the schiltroms. There was just time. He himself remained with the central group.

There, awaiting the impact, with arrows still hissing around him, Wallace was surprised and heartened again to find not a few of the Scots nobles and knights rallying to his side, after all, having either refused to ride off with Buchan, or else turned back ashamed from that retiral. He rejoiced to see the unmartial Steward, still here despite his brother's death, Lennox, Crawford and others. Their adherence, in this desperate pass, lifted his spirit, which direly required some lifting. He raised his great voice in a sudden accession of emotion, to bellow, above the thunder of those oncoming hooves.

'Friends all! I have brought you to the ring, God forgive me! Dance, now, I say — dance the best you may!'

There was no time for more. With a crash of steel, a roaring and yelling of men and a screaming of horses, the Bishop's onslaught was upon them. The flood of arrows dropped away.

*   *   *

As when a great river in mighty spate thunders down on an immovable midstream rock, was the impact of that assault. The northernmost schiltrom took the brunt of it, naturally, but stood firm, even though it seemed to wilt somewhat at the first shock — although this was caused mainly by the sheer weight of hurtling horseflesh crashing on mere men, as the animals fell in sprawling ruin, hooves entangled in the outlying network of stakes and ropes, or else skewered themselves on the bristling spearpoints. Pressed on by those charging behind, there was no

335

escape for the front ranks, as men and beasts went down in bloody chaos. Quickly, moreover, the barrier of dead and wounded piled up in such lashing, screaming havoc that it was into this heaving wall that the oncoming riders crashed, rather than on the spearmen behind.

Inevitably the torrent of cavalry divided, to stream down the front and rear of the schiltrom line, still largely held at a distance by the network. Inwards on the defenders the horsemen sought to turn, but to little effect. And as they swept past the gaps in the formations, they were assailed by the veterans, and such of the Border bowmen as survived. Their leading ranks met each other at the far, southern, end; and thereafter the impetus died away, and the attack was forced to change character to individual assault — vast and crowded numbers of individuals, but each man basically for himself. The horses proved to be of little aid in this, meantime, for though they gave the attackers height and reach, they got hopelessly entangled in the ropework, and moreover presented large targets which could not dodge the spears. More and more of the English jumped down, to use their lances afoot.

The first change of the Bishop's array, then, was a failure. The schiltroms remained unbroken, and the enemy lost large numbers of men and horses. But, of course, their casualties represented only a small proportion of the whole, and the majority kept circling round the Scots formations like wolves frustrated of their kill. They still prevented the Welsh archers from continuing with their deadly hail.

But Wallace postponed elation. He kept glancing left and right. When the heavy chivalry came up, there would be a different story to tell.

The five hundred or so which had started out with Bishop Beck arrived on the scene first, at a ponderous, hulking trot. These did not charge. Instead, they drew up at a little distance from the northern schiltrom, formed up in closest order and, many files deep, began to advance, on a single trumpet blast, at a steady, slow walk, a solid mass of sheer weight, steel-clad, impregnable, in pacing majesty. Nothing, it seemed, could withstand this deliberate tide. The stakes and ropes were stamped flat, the bristling spears were knocked aside and snapped like sticks, and human flesh and blood gave way — but could not give way for any distance, hemmed in as men were. The defenders went down under the great trampling hooves, and the first schiltrom collapsed in shattered wreck. MacDuff himself fell, shouting defiance.

Watching, helpless, Wallace was forced to dire decision. He had to take a tremendous risk — or else accept certain annihilation. He ordered the three remaining schiltroms to move, in formation so far as they might, down into the soft ground flanking the loch, down towards the waiting archers.

It was, of course, only a desperate throw. There was only some fifty to seventy yards to go, but for thousands of men to do so, in their tight formations, and under attack, was asking much. Had the Earl Marshal's larger force of chivalry been on the scene, and interposed itself, it would not have been possible, at all. But the Bishop's heavy force was still entangled in the ruin of the first schiltrom, and by its very nature was a difficult and slow body to reform, turn around, and set on a new course. The English light cavalry, of course, plunged into attack to disrupt the movement; but to some extent these were still held off by the long spears and the rope network. The same ropes and stakes were now a grievous impediment in the way of the men who had erected them — though less grim for men on foot than for horses. The flanking veterans strove heroically to protect them in their move — and died in their scores.

It would be inaccurate to say that the schiltroms achieved their transference in formation. In fact they became all but a stumbling, streaming rabble in the process. But two did manage to form up again, in something like order, although with sad losses, on the lower ground; the third, Lundin's command, next to the broken MacDuff's and assailed by some part of the heavy chivalry, disintegrated wholly under the pressure and never reformed — although many of its men attached themselves to the other formations.

Two schiltroms only now, and within close range of those archers. The latter did not neglect their opportunity.

The light cavalry would have been wiser to leave it to the Welshmen. But there was great animosity between them, the enemy horse despising all infantry, especially Welsh-speaking barbarians. They bored in, soft ground or none, again tending to mask the bowmen, so that only individual targets could be selected.

But now King Edward had moved forward the great mass of his foot; and while the major numbers of these were marching left and right, as the cavalry had had to come, some bolder companies were hurrying down straight for the marshland and loch, clearly intending to wade or swim their way across. The loch, in fact, had been discovered by Wallace to be no more than three or four feet deep, although muddy-bottomed.

Wallace's own veteran and knightly force was now so sadly decimated, from its protective efforts, that it was no longer an effective fighting unit. Recognising realities, the big man ordered its remaining numbers to dismount, and to join one or other of the schiltroms. He himself went to the south, Sir John Graham's, with most of his close friends.

Even that was not easy, under the cavalry attack, for the tight-packed ranks of spearmen were not in a position or inclination to open up at various points to let newcomers inside. Indeed not a few of the knights and nobility who sought entry into Ruthven's formation were unsuccessful, being cut down before any opening could be formed for them. So died some of the most renowned in Scotland.

Kerlie, Gray, Boyd, Little, Adam, Blair and MacGregor, some wounded but all still on their feet, managed to get Wallace inside the right-hand schiltrom, where, in trampled slime almost up to his knees, he gazed round upon the ruin of the Scots army. Broken men were streaming off in all directions, climbing over the heaps of dead — and often adding to them, as Welsh arrows found them — the most successful ploughing through the marsh itself, southwards. Less than three thousand, he calculated, remained of some twelve thousand. He, the Guardian, had thrown away Scotland's shield, that day.

The Earl Marshal's mighty chivalry array had now come up, but found itself unable to do very much. Some few rash knights did drive their destriers down towards the schiltrom, but were quickly bogged down and had to retire, some minus their mounts. Fortunately for the Scots, the light cavalry kept up their harassing tactics, or archery would have finished the Battle of Falkirk at long range but in shorter time.

But once the English foot arrived . . .

Just what caused the collapse of Ruthven's northern schiltrom was hard to say. It may have been under somewhat heavier attack, being on rather firmer ground. Possibly it had not reformed so adequately. More probably it was more a collapse of morale, the hopelessness of the situation becoming ever more evident, until something snapped. At any rate, one minute it was still some sort of fighting formation, the next it was only a horde of unhappy men, fleeing down into the marsh, archers or none, throwing away weapons, armour and anything which could hamper them. The Welshmen gave them their entire attention.

There was now no disguising the fact that the battle was lost, and it was only a question of the remaining schiltrom standing and dying where it stood, or of following the disintegration of the other. The uncountable hosts of the English infantry were now near; some had already negotiated the loch and bog — although these were mainly chasing stragglers.

Wallace had lost his helmet, and was bleeding from an arrow-graze on his brow, his head dizzy from the blow which had knocked off his helmet. Sore at heart, he leaned, panting, on his long sword, just behind the kneeling rank of spearmen, still under the Lion Rampant Scrymgeour held high above him. Despite all, he every now and again shouted a sort of general encouragement. This schiltrom would not break and run, yet awhile.

Alexander Scrymgeour grabbed his arm, and pointed. Up on the high ground westwards a force of light cavalry was emerging from the Tor Wood, some hundreds strong apparently. It drew up there, at gaze.

'Not, not Buchan ... returned?' the Standard Bearer gasped. 'Never that!'

'That banner,' Kerlie cried. 'Not the Comyn sheaves on blue. It is a red saltire and chief on gold. That — save us, that is the Bruce device!'

'Come late!' Wallace muttered. His temple wound made him distinctly light-headed. 'Bruce come late. Too late, to save us now — even if he would!'

'He will not try,' Thomas Gray said. 'How many? Five hundred? Six hundred? Against thousands down here. Even if they loved you well enough — think you they would dare, Will?'

Another surge of the enemy attack put a stop to such discussion. Thereafter they were much too preoccupied for talk or observation.

Presently, through the clash of steel, the shouts of men and the whinnying of horses, some part of Wallace's reeling mind registered another sound, a cry from many throats, oft-repeated. It was some time before he recognised it for what it was — the slogan 'A Bruce! A Bruce!' Despite what his head told him, his heart lifted to the sound, a little.

When he could pause in his furious slashing swordery, to look up, it was to see that the company under the red-and-gold banner was indeed driving down into the battle. In a tight arrow-head formation, and clearly under superb discipline, they came at a full gallop, heading apparently straight for the schiltrom, lances lowered, swords flashing. They were taking a line to avoid the two great masses of the English chivalry — and all else scattered before their narrow-fronted headlong charge — as well they might, for only two or three men would in fact have to take the brunt of the impact, and few would be eager for the honour. Moreover, there was no evident united control of the English forces, as yet, lacking the King's personal presence.

Wallace could spare only moments for his glance; then he was involved again. He heard Kerlie yelling that Bruce might have changed sides again, and be riding to redeem himself in Edward's eyes.

When next the staggering Guardian could look about him, it was to discover Bruce himself savagely drawing up his pawing horse only a few yards away, beyond the fringe of spears, and seeking to halt the hard-riding band behind him in some sort of order, though with only partial success, some of his men already cannoned into the waiting, and thrusting, spearmen. The chaos was indescribable.

'Wallace!' the Earl was shouting, beckoning from his saddle. 'Quickly! Come! A chance. To win free. To me, man!'

Blinking, staring, the big man sought for words. None came. He shook his head.

'Hurry, I say!' Bruce cried. 'Do not stand there. We cannot wait. I say, we cannot wait, or all is lost. They will rally. Come!'

Wallace gave a single dismissive wave of a large bloodstained hand.

'Fool!' The other, striving to control his horse, while his brother the Lord Nigel, controlled those behind, was leaning forward as close as he might. 'Do you not see? You must break out. While you may. Or you are a dead man . . .'

Wallace dredged words out of his reeling consciousness. 'You . . . you would have me leave these? Abandon my folk? Away with you, Bruce!' That was thickly, unevenly, but not uncertainly said.

'You can do no good here, now. Come away. And fight again.'

340

'No. Run from my friends? Never!'

Others were pleading with him now — Scrymgeour, Gray, Kerlie. Even the Steward and Lennox, from deeper within the schiltrom, with Wallace scarcely aware that they were there.

Hotly, desperately, Bruce remonstrated, his voice breaking as he heard the battle joined behind him, the English recovering from their surprise and beginning to hurl themselves against the Scots horse.

'Wallace!' he yelled. 'You are the Guardian. Of Scotland. All Scotland. Not just these. If you fall now, Scotland falls. Mind who you are — the Guardian!'

The Lord Nigel Bruce added his voice. 'For God's sake, hurry, man! These others can break Into the marsh and away. Where horse cannot follow. Many will escape. They will not, while you stay. All will die.'

'Aye. Aye.' All around men saw the sense of that, and cried it. Hands were pushing and pulling Wallace forward, towards the Bruces.

The brothers' cavalry now formed something of a barrier between the schiltrom and the enemy, on the west side, those towards the rear turned to face outwards, and taking the brunt of the so far disorganised English assault. Others were mounting fellow-Scots behind them.

It was this last fact which seemed to sap Wallace's resolution.

'Get the Steward.' Bruce ordered his brother. He waved to others. 'Crawford. Lennox. Scrymgeour. Graham. The rest of you. Up behind, I take Wallace . . .'

One of his men pushed forward with a riderless horse, in the desperate jostle.

Eager hands were propelling the big man onwards, all but lifting him on to the head-tossing wild-eyed garron. He was not really resisting now, when he saw his lieutenants mounting behind the riders. It required no lengthy survey to realise that the only possible route of escape now was along the edge of the soft ground, south-westwards, where the Earl Marshal's host did not block the way. Then behind this, uphill, before the oncoming English foot closed the gap. There were enemy in the way, yes — but not in the numbers behind them, no massing everywhere, trumpets blowing urgently. 'Come!' Bruce commanded. 'After me. A wedge again — keep close.' He was shouting to his men.

A cheer, an actual cheer, arose from the men. Wallace was

deserting. Perhaps they saw that, individually, they might have a chance of life yet. It was a ragged wedge which began to pound away south-westwards, most of the horses now double-laden. Not all who had set out on that rescue attempt however, were alive to ride off.

They went at a very different pace, too, the beasts burdened, the ground underfoot soft and slippery. Nevertheless, they kept up a determined canter, and though the enemy closed in at sides and rear, none actually sought to bar their menacing way. They were riding northern hill ponies from the Garioch, not lowland charges; and these were a deal more nimble on the soft ground.

Behind them, the last schiltrom began to break up at once, as men took their chances in the marshland.

Wallace, swaying alarmingly in the saddle, his long legs practically trailing the ground, was pounding along behind the Bruce brothers. The Lord Nigel now had the Steward clinging behind him, heavily armoured and a great added weight.

Then came the inevitable development. Once it was clear what was happening, the Welsh arrows began to fly. They were at long range, and a moving target; but the archers needed only to loose off into the brown, the mass.

Havoc followed fast. The Lord Nigel's horse was the first to fall, pierced through the neck, throwing both riders — to be all but ridden down by those following. Bruce himself reined round violently to the right, uphill, in front of the massed heavy chivalry, risking their slow reaction and movement, in the interests of increasing range and the change of direction of flight, yelling for his brother and the Steward to be picked up; but he did not himself slacken pace or leave grip of Wallace's reins. A young man of decision and determination, obviously. Somehow the pack behind swung after him, formation much broken, and not a few fallen. And still the arrows hissed down on them, amidst the screams of men and horses.

Wallace was still dazed. He clung on, clutching at his great sword — and found that as much as he was fit for.

The hail of arrows at least had the advantage of effectively inhibiting over-eagerness on the part of their English pursuers.

Bruce was now heading up for the line of the Tor Wood, although a quarter-mile southwards of where he had come down. The rear files of his wedge were having to take the major punishment from the archers, with only the odd spent shaft now falling amongst the leaders.

At last they were out of bow-shot, and strangely, with no major pursuit.

In the blessed shelter of the trees presently, Bruce pulled up. All around him thankful men did likewise, on trembling, spume-lathered, near-foundered horses. Wallace gripped his saddle bow, and stared blindly ahead, wordless. Scrymgeour, Blair and Kerlie jumped down from behind rescuers, and came running to him. Scrymgeour still had the Lion Rampant standard, torn from its shaft, wrapped round his arm.

'You are well?' they panted. 'Not sore hurt, Will? Thank God you came away! Your head — it is not a grievous wound?'

He shook the blood-smeared head. 'Where ... where is Sir John? The Graham?' he got out, as though from a great distance, at great effort.

'He fell, Will. An arrow. In the throat.

'Dead?'

'Dead, aye. At once God rest his soul.' That was Thomas Gray, himself wounded.

Wallace did not speak further, although they questioned him about his own hurt.

Bruce took an authoritative hand. 'You are wounded, Sir William? Can you go on? Sit that beast? Or ... shall we make you a litter?'

The big man stared down at him distantly. 'I am very well,' he said.

'That you are not! But can you ride further?'

'I am very well,' he repeated heavily. 'But others ... are not. Those who looked to me ...'

'Here is folly, man! A battle lost, aye — but others to be fought. And won. What good repining?'

'I left my brave spearmen ...'

'And thereby did them kindness! They could not flee with William Wallace there. Now, they are fleeing every one, to every airt. Three out of four will escape. Which they would not have done had you bided. Nor would you. Now, you, and they, will fight again.'

Most there acclaimed the Earl of Carrick's assertion, though men repeated the names of those they had seen to fall, friends, kinsmen, companions-in-arms.

'Quiet!' the Bruce burst out, cutting the air with his hand. 'Here is no time for such talk. Men have fallen, yes. Fighting. They came to fight, did they not? And fall, if need be. Time

343

enough for talk, after. But what now? What to do? *Edward* will not wait and talk!'

'Aye.' With a great effort, Wallace pulled himself together, drawing a quivering hand over his bloody brow. 'You are right, my lord. And I thank you. I fail in my duty. We fight on. But not here. We cannot stand, south of the Forth. Even at Stirling. Not now. We must rally again, in the hills to the north. And burn the land behind us. Burn Stirling. And its bridge. Burn Dunblane. Burn Perth, if need be. Starve them. Starve England's war host. That is Edward's weakness now. No more battles, backed by nobles that I cannot trust! I was a fool to think that I might out-fight Edward Plantagenet, his way. No more. I fight on, my own way again. Wallace the outlaw! The brigand . . .!'

'You are Guardian of this land,' Bruce reminded, tightly.

'Aye — and I shall fight Edward with the land. What he can ride over but never defeat! Would God I had used my own wits, instead of listening to others! But it is not too late, God willing. While Scotland lives, it is never too late. And Scotland will not, cannot die.' The man's great voice shook with a mighty emotion.

Bruce scarcely shared it. 'So it is Stirling, now? Stirling and beyond?'

'Yes. Take me to Stirling, my lord. But watch you for my lords the Comyns! But not for *you*, beyond. The North. The lurking in the hills. The raids by night. The ambuscades. The knife in the back. This is no work for great lords! Go back to your West, my lord of Carrick — back to your own country. And mine. You claimed to be the Governor of the South-West, did you not? Go there, then. Hold the South-West. Harry the English West March, if you can. While we starve Edward. Raid into England. Nothing will harass hungry men more than the word that their homes are threatened, endangered. Go west from Stirling, my lord — and such other lords as are not fled! I shall require the West at your hands.'

Bruce eyed the man he had saved, levelly, for long moments, and then nodded. 'Very well, Sir Guardian. Now — Stirling!'

CHAPTER TWENTY

If Scotland had a capital in these evil days of autumn, 1298, it could be said to be the Ettrick Forest, in the Borderland. Here great armies could not penetrate, and there was little or nothing to burn, save trees and whins and turning bracken. Here were almost a thousand square miles of uplands, alive with game and wild cattle, conveniently set between the East and West Marches, but secure from both, a sanctuary for broken men and outlaws — and that well described Scotland's Guardian and legitimate government in those months. Wallace made it his headquarters, after a brief scorched-earth campaign north of Forth — and indeed had little choice in the matter. Methven Wood, the Tor Wood and suchlike, were all too small to hide and shelter for any period even his sort of guerilla force. Most of the rest of Lowland Scotland was a blackened, smoking desert, with the strong castles reoccupied by Edward's garrisons. Behind the Highland Line, the Red Comyn reigned — if anyone did — and Lame John MacDougall of Lorn again controlled the Hebridean Sea. If resistance to Edward of England, and the small flame of freedom, burned anywhere in Scotland that autumn, it burned brightest in the Forest of Ettrick. Edward himself, with his starving if victorious thousands, had been forced back over the Border on September 6th — by sheer hunger, not by force of arms. Wallace's grim policy had had that success, at least. He had indeed made the land, rather than the people, fight for him.

And now, strangely, the Forest was for the moment transformed. At least, certain roads and droving-tracks into it were, hotching with people, travellers — not the Forest folk but nobles, lordly ones, knights, clerics, lairds, all making for the Forest's one little township of Selkirk, on Ettrick. Despite all the dangers and inconveniences, they came in answer to a summons, an official summons, from the Guardian and Council of the Realm. How many would have answered that summons had it not been for the business stated, who could tell? Not one in five, probably. But the agenda was stated clearly and succinctly — to appoint a new Guardian of Scotland. So even the Comyns came, from their northern fastnesses.

The old castle of Selkirk, on higher ground across the Ettrick from the ruined abbey, was a ramshackle, sprawling place, built as a hunting-lodge for David the First, draughty and bare. But at least it had a roof on it, and covered accommodation of a sort for gentlefolk not used to the rough living of the Forest; and who, owing to lack of forage for horses, had had to cut down drastically on their transport animals for carrying tents, pavilions and the like.

Wallace might not have considered this as sufficiently important; but William Lamberton did. And Lamberton, returned from Rome, duly consecrated Bishop of St. Andrews and Primate of Scotland, was a thoughtful man, and had all in hand. Indeed, this assembly was largely of his urging. Once he had realised that he could not change Wallace's decision to resign the guardianship, a quietly able and determined individual, he had made it his business to organise and arrange it all — at least so far as was possible. Personalities might well change what he planned and hoped for. Lamberton was undoubtedly something of a showman, despite his apparent gravity of manner — where Wallace was not.

He had set the scene in the castle's great hall, and had convinced Wallace that, for Scotland's sake, he must continue to play the role of principal actor, meantime, however uncomfortable he might feel, and even look. And the timing was important — as important as in one of the big man's own more energetic productions. Keen-eyed watchmen on the castle's topmost towers kept Lamberton informed.

Certain of the lofty arrivals were admitted to the Guardian's presence without delay, others were not, known allegiances being the Primate's criterion; the Steward, Lennox and Crawford, for instance, with Bishops Wishart, Sinclair and Dalton, and the Abbots of Scone, Jedburgh, Lindores and Melrose. Lamberton had ensured a major attendance of churchmen.

It was important for their plan that the heads of the two factions which sought to claim the throne, Bruce and Comyn, should not meet, and possibly clash, before the situation was prepared for them. Fortunately, as anticipated, the Bruce entourage arrived first, having come from Annandale. The Earl brought his brothers Nigel and Edward with him, on this occasion, as well as a train of knights and lairds.

346

Wallace had not seen this young man, to whom he probably owed his life as well as his accolade, since the grim aftermath of Falkirk. When Lamberton ushered him into the hall, the big man strode forward to greet him, warmly.

'My lord, my lord — you have come! I thank God for it!'

The other looked surprised at the fervour of this welcome. He had never gained the impression that the Guardian thought so very highly of him.

'I could scarce do otherwise — when the Guardian called,' he said.

'No? I wonder! But — I have not had opportunity to thank you for what you did that day, at Falkirk, my friend. If I may so call you? I was less than grateful then, perhaps — having much on my mind. But it was nobly done — and boldly. I was in your debt before — now, the more so. I am grateful.'

'I did what needed doing — for the realm's good, Sir Guardian. Then, as previously. That was all.'

'The realm's good. Aye, that is the touchstone, for us all. I rejoice that you name it, my lord. Today. Not all will do so.'

'Meaning . . . what?'

'Meaning that some may see a throne as a greater prize than the realm's good.'

The Earl eyed him levelly, at that, unspeaking.

Wallace reached out to grip the younger man's shoulder. 'But not the Bruce! It is good to see you here — for much depends on you hereafter.'

The other looked doubtful. He turned to survey the identities of the others in that great chamber.

'The Lord of Badenoch is not yet come.' Wallace said, reading his mind. 'But he comes, he comes. He has agreed to come.'

'The Comyn's coming here, like mine, is the least of it, Sir Guardian!' Bruce commented shortly. 'We shall never agree on aught else — that I vow!'

'Do not say so. If sufficient depends on it, any two men can seem to agree, however ill-matched. Even I have learned that lesson! Think you that I have loved all that I have had to deal with, work with, this past year and more? And enough depends, here, on my soul! The future of Scotland, no less.'

'Scarce so much as that, I think . . .!'

'Yes. So much as that.' Wallace spoke urgently. He had

changed much since Falkirk, aged somehow. He was thinner, more gaunt, but none the less authoritative as to presence — even though the finery in which he was dressed for this occasion seemed to sit but uncomfortably on his huge frame. 'See you, my lord — the magnates of this Scotland are divided. By many things, many feuds, much jealousy, warring interests. But in the end, all depend on the Crown for their lands and titles. You know that. And the Crown is vacant — or nearly so. I act in the name of King John Baliol, since the Crown must be vested in some name. *De jure*, he is still king. *De facto* he is not, and the throne empty. One day, if Scotland survives, she will have a king again. That king will be either a Baliol, a Comyn or a Bruce. This all know. John Baliol has a son, Edward — a child. Held, like his father, hostage by the King of England. King John has renounced the throne, for himself and his son, at the demand of King Edward. Renounced and abandoned. Therefore, it is scarce likely that John or his son shall ever reign. So the king shall be your father, the Bruce. Or John Comyn, Baliol's nephew.'

The Earl made a half-impatient gesture at this rehearsal of facts only too well known to him.

'Aye — you know it. All men know it, my lord. Therefore, since the nobles hold all they have of the Crown, they must take sides. For Comyn or for Bruce. In order that they may retain their lands from the winner of this contest. Divided, as I say. And Scotland cannot afford a divided nobility today, see you, when she fights for her very life. So, your father being none knows where, only you, and Comyn, can heal that division. By acting together. Joint Guardians. Nothing else, and no other, will serve.'

That was a long speech for William Wallace, who was not notably a man of words. All others in that apartment watched them, fallen silent.

Bruce could not refute the validity of any of it. But it was personality not validity, that was his trouble.

'John Comyn will not work with me,' he said flatly. 'We have never agreed on any matter. Nor are like to.'

'But when the matter is the saving of the realm? For whoever may eventually sit on its throne? Can you not, at least, *seem* to agree, my lord? Since neither of you, I swear, would wish the other to be Guardian alone!'

'*You* are Guardian, sir. The best we shall have.'

348

'After this day I shall no longer be Guardian. Whoever else is. On that I am decided.'

'Why, in God's name?'

'As Guardian, I failed the realm. As Guardian, I did not guard. At Falkirk, I knew myself for what I was — a captain of bands, no more. No commander of great armies, no Guardian of a nation. In part, *you* taught me that, my lord, that day! But it was not only Falkirk. Before, and since, I did not measure to the task. I was not bred for it, as are you. Or trained. I have lost the trust, if not the love, of the people. I have burned their fields, trampled their corn, made them homeless, hungry, led them to defeat. I lay down the Guardianship this day.'

Bruce inclined his head, recognising that he would not alter nor shake that resolution.

'A Guardian there must be,' the other went on. 'And Comyn comes to claim it. Nothing surer. Will Bruce have it so?'

The younger man was silent looking away, his strangely expressive features working.

Lamberton, choosing his moment, joined them. 'The Comyns have been sighted, my friends,' he told them. 'They are riding down from Tweed. A great company of them. The Constable's banner alongside that of Badenoch, the watchmen say. They have come far. From Spey. I do not think they have come for nothing! John Comyn intends to be Guardian, I swear — whoever else may be!' And he looked at Bruce.

That man bit his lip.

*   *   *

The Comyn arrived with splendid circumstance, in magnificent clothing and array, confident, assured, and with an unmistakable appearance of prosperity and lack of tension which contrasted notably with the demeanour of most of those assembled — for, of course, they came from the North, untouched by famine and war. The drawn, guarded, battered look which had become so much part of the others showed in them not at all. They brought a train of over a score of knights, their own clerics, standard-bearers, pursuivants, trumpeters, entertainers, even a group of Erse-speaking, colourfully clad West Highland chieftains — though not Lame John MacDougall. There was no doubting that they had come prepared to take over the rule in Scotland.

Although they resented and deplored the arrogance of it all,

Wallace and Lamberton were not dissatisfied. If anything would force Bruce into line with their own wishes, this display should.

The new arrivals did not trouble to make any formal approach to pay respects to the Guardian and Primate. They pitched their own tented camp nearby — seemingly having no lack of provision for man and beast — and set up their court there. There was no lack, either, of visitors to it, from the rest of the assembled company. The Bruce entourage and supporters kept their distance, each eyeing the other warily, like stiff-legged dogs considering the same bone.

All watched — but none so keenly as the Guardian and Primate. These did more than watch. They manoeuvred, they guided, they tempered skilfully, unobtrusively, their policy to channel support towards Bruce rather than Comyn, amongst the uncommitted, and to ensure that the principals of the factions, at least, did not come into any sort of clash before the thing could be brought to a conclusion. Wallace was less adept at this than was the Bishop, perhaps.

So soon as might be, the Seneschal and King of Arms summoned all to sit down to a repast in the great hall, the victuals procured with much difficulty from the ravaged land. All the fussing over precedence and the like was now to be seen in a new light. Everything had been thought out, so far as the great ones were concerned. Normally, in any castle-hall, the dais-table stretched sideways across the head, while the main table ran lengthwise down one side of the apartment, leaving the rest free for the servitors, entertainers and the like. Now, since practically everyone present in Selkirk's castle would have felt entitled to sit at the dais-table, this had been brought down to add to the length of the other. Moreover, at its head, where the Guardian's great chair, with the tattered Lion Rampant standard from Falkirk spread on the wall above, was flanked by two others, two further small tables had been placed at right angles, each with only a couple of seats. At that to the right was set Buchan the Constable, with Lamberton at his side; on the left was seated James the Steward, with the King of Arms. There was some doubt as to which great office of state was actually senior; but Buchan was an earl, and the Steward was not. In the same way, at the main table-head, Bruce was placed on Wallace's immediate right, and the Red Comyn on his left; again there could be no quarrel, for Carrick was an earldom

and Badenoch but a lordship. Other nobles found themselves
equally heedfully disposed. There were no solid groups of pro-
Comyn and pro-Bruce supporters. And everywhere Lamberton's clerics were set between, to act as both catalysts and
buffers. The Scots lords, used to jockeying for the best places,
by initiative or sheer weight, were taken by surprise, and strategically seated where they could cause least trouble.

Bruce and Comyn thus were sitting in isolated
prominence — but the mighty figure of Wallace was between
them. Moreover, Bruce had Buchan sitting at the little table,
next on his right, while Comyn had the Steward to contend with
on his left. Seldom can there have been less general converse at
so illustriously attended a meal.

Wallace spoke to each of his immediate companions, and
sometimes to them both, seeking to involve them in mutual talk
which he might control. But they were a mettlesome pair to
drive tandem, and it was a somewhat abortive exercise. The
Guardianship issued was not mentioned.

'How long have we, think you, before Edward attacks once
more?' Wallace asked, presently — a safe subject, surely? 'How
serious are his troubles with his lords?'

'Do not ask me, Sir Guardian,' Comyn returned quickly. 'I
have no dealings with the English. Ask Bruce. He knows
Edward passing well. Or his friend Percy may have told
him!'

Bruce drew a swift breath. Then he let it out again slowly, and
raised his wine goblet to his lips.

'My Lord of Carrick has put himself more in Edward's dis-
favour than any other in Scotland,' Wallace said heavily. 'He
burned the South-West in Edward's face, forcing him to call off
his campaign. Much of the land burned is Bruce's own. As for
the Lord Percy, I think he is scarce like to call my lord his
friend, now!'

'Yet the woman Bruce is like to marry is Percy's kinswoman.
And bides with him at Alnwick, does she not? While her father
fights for Edward in France. Against our French allies.' All
knew of Bruce's relationship with the Lady Elizabeth de Burgh,
daughter of Edward's old comrade-in-arms, the Earl of Ulster,
and indeed Edward's god-child.

'Curse you, Comyn! I am not like to marry Elizabeth de
Burgh. Edward would have had it once — but now would not,
you may be sure.'

'Yet she is a comely. And well dowered, I swear! Edward's god-child — a useful go-between . . .'

'I'll thank you to spare the Lady Elizabeth the soiling of your tongue!' Bruce exclaimed, leaning forward to glare round Wallace.

'My lords! My lords — of a mercy!' the big man cried. 'Moderate your words, I beg you. Here is no way to speak to each other.'

'Have I said aught against the lady? Save that she is Edward's god-daughter. Bruce has a guilty conscience, I think, to be so thin of skin!'

'What knows a Comyn of conscience!'

'My lords — at *my* table no guest of mine will be insulted. By whomsoever. I ask you to remember it.' Wallace brought down his great fist on the board with a crash, to make the platters, flagons and goblets jump — and not a few of the company also. Pushing back his chair, he rose abruptly to his full commanding height. All eyes upon him, he raised his vibrant voice.

'My lords and friends, fellow subjects of this realm. I, William Wallace, Guardian of Scotland, crave your close heed. I took up that duty and style seven sore months ago. Now the time has come to lay it on other shoulders than mine. No — hear me. They have been ill months for our land. We have survived them only at great cost. But there are as bad, and worse to come. Let none doubt it. The man Edward Plantagenet is set on this. He will make Scotland but part of his crown. A lowly, servile part. If he can. Whilst breath remains in him. That is sure. And he has ten men for every one of us.

He paused, and though all present were aware of it all, men hung on his careful words.

'I say to you that I know now what I should have known before — that *I* cannot fight Edward the King. I can fight his underlings and minions. I can, and have done, and I will. But not Edward himself. Only Edward's own kind can fight Edward — I see that now. And I am . . . otherwise. Scotland's own king it should be who fights him. But since that is not possible now, it falls to the Guardian. Therefore, I cannot remain Guardian, Falkirk proved that.' Deliberately he looked round on them all. 'In this realm today there are two men who could, and should, be Guardian. Two men whom all must heed, respect and obey. For what they are and who they are. They are here at my side. Sir Robert Bruce, Earl of Carrick, grandson of

Bruce the Competitor; and Sir John Comyn, Lord of Badenoch, nephew of the King, King John. On these two, who are both of Edward's kind, I lay my burden. Jointly and together. These two can, and must, unite this realm against the English usurper. These two I charge, in the name of God and of Scotland — fight Edward! Save our land,' He pointed. 'My lord Bishop of Galloway — the seals.'

As men exclaimed, from further down the table the Chancellor rose, to bring up the two silver caskets which were his charge, and set them before Wallace, opening them to display the Great Seal of Scotland and the Privy Seal.

The first, the big man took out and raised up — and it required both hands to do it. Not because it was so heavy, but because its bronze was in two parts, two exact halves. He held them high.

'My friends,' he cried, 'here is the Great Seal of this realm and nation. I broke it. This day I broke it. For the good of all. Now, before anything may be established and made law, bearing the Seal of Scotland, these two parts must be brought together and set side by side. One, in the name of the Crown, the magnates and the community of this ancient realm, I give to Sir Robert the Bruce, Earl of Carrick. The other to Sir John the Comyn, of Badenoch. I do now declare them both and together to be Joint Guardians of Scotland. To them I hereby pass the rule and governance. Declaring that I, William Wallace, will from now onwards be their leal and assured servant. God save them both, I say!'

As all men stared, Wallace thrust his chair far back, and bowing to Bruce first, then Comyn, turned and strode down the length of that great table, right to its foot, where he gently pushed aside his own Standard Bearer, Scrymgeour, modestly seated there, and sat himself down in his place.

Something like uproar filled the hall.

Each holding his half of the Great Seal, Bruce and Comyn gazed at one another, before all, wordless.

Gradually the noise abated, and men fell silent, all eyes upon the pair at the head of the table, clutching their half-moons of bronze. All knew that these two hated each other. All knew that they represented mutually antagonistic claims to the throne. Moreover there could be few indeed who could have accepted Wallace's dramatic gesture in itself as any kind of valid appointment. It was not for the outgoing Guardian to appoint a successor; that was for the council of the Realm to choose, its choice to be confirmed by a parliament. What Wallace had done in itself carried no real authority. Yet, if these two indeed elected to accept it as such, none there were in a position to contravene it, even if they so desired.

The hush was broken by the scrape of Bruce's chair on the rush-strewn flagstones, as he rose. 'My lords,' he said, thickly, 'here is a great matter. Here is the need for decision. I, for myself, do not want this duty, this burden, that Sir William Wallace has laid upon me. I am young, with no experience of the rule of a realm. I have much to see to, without that. My lands are devastated, great numbers of my people homeless. Winter is coming upon us — and in the spring, Edward will return. But ... all this, if it is true for Carrick and Annandale and Galloway, is true also for much of Scotland. Save, perhaps, the North.' He glanced down at Comyn. 'The land faces trial. Destiny. All the land. The people. The need is great. And in this need, unity is all-important. Only unity can save us from Edward of England. None shall say that Bruce withstood that unity. If you, my lords will have it so, I accept the office of Guardian. With ... whomsoever.' He sat down abruptly.

There was acclaim. But it was tense, almost breathless, and brief. Every glance was on John Comyn.

That man sat still, toying with the segment of bronze. He seemed to be under no strain, no sense of embarrassment that all waited for him. His sardonically handsome features even bore a twisted smile, as he examined the broken seal. The seconds passed.

When a voice was raised, it was Bruce's. 'Well, man?' he demanded.

'This of the seal was cunning,' the other said, almost admiringly amused.

He looked up, but not at the Bruce. 'How think you, my lord Constable?' he asked his fellow-Comyn conversationally.

Buchan huffed and puffed, looking towards his brother, Master William the cleric, some way down the table. Almost imperceptibly that smooth-faced man nodded.

'Aye. So be it,' the Earl grunted. 'In a storm a man may not always choose the haven he would!'

'Ha — neatly put kinsman!' John Comyn acceded. 'No doubt you are right. So there we have it. Joint Guardian — heh! With Bruce! God save us all!'

It was moments before it sank in. That this was acceptance. That Comyn was, in fact, going to say no more. That, smiling and still lounging in his chair, he was reaching for his goblet, to drink. And that he had pocketed his half of the seal. The thing was done.

As the recognition of this dawned, the company broke forth in excited chatter, comment, speculation. Order and precedence were forgotten. Men rose from their places and went to their friends and fellow-clansmen. Chiefs and lords beckoned their knightly supporters, prelates put their heads together and rubbed their hands. Down at the foot of the table, Wallace sat expressionless.

But, after a while, as the noise maintained, the big man signed to the Bishop of Galloway. That cleric raised his hand, called out, and when he could make no impression, banged a flagon on the table for silence.

'My lords — this matter is well resolved,' he declared. 'But it falls to be confirmed. To be accepted and duly made lawful. By a parliament. I, therefore, as Chancellor of this realm, for and on behalf of the Guardianship, do call such meeting of parliament for tomorrow's noon, in the former abbey here. To be attended by all and sundry of the three estates of this kingdom who can so attend. So be it. God give you a good night.'

Bruce rose, and looked again at Comyn. 'This means ... no little ... accommodation, my lord,' he said slowly. 'It will tax our patience, I think, ere we are done.'

'You think so? Patience is for clerks, and such folk. It is not a quality I aspire to, Bruce.'

'Nevertheless, you will require it, if I am not mistaken. As shall I!'

'If you esteem it so high, then I shall leave it to you Myself, I see the case calling for quite different virtues. Valour, daring, resolution, spirit. These, and the like.'

'Such as the Comyns showed at Falkirk field?' That erupted out of Robert Bruce.

The other was on his feet in an instant, fists clenched. 'By the Rude — you dare speak so! To me! You — Edward's lackey!'

'For that, Comyn ... you shall ... suffer! As God is my witness!'

For moments they stared eye to eye. Then John Comyn

swung about, and stormed from the hall. Few there failed to note it.

There was a deep sigh at Bruce's back, from William Lamberton. Wallace still sat silent, watchful, eyes narrowed.

* * *

Next day, in the abbey, a tense and anxious company assembled, anticipating trouble naked and undisguised. And they were surprised, relieved, or disappointed, according to their various dispositions. A night's sleeping on it, second and third thoughts, and the earnest representations of sundry busy mediators — mainly churchmen, and Master William Comyn in particular — had produced a change of atmosphere. Nothing would make Bruce and Comyn love or trust each other; but it was just conceivable that they might sufficiently tolerate each other to work, if not together, at least not openly in opposition.

At any rate, John Comyn arrived at the abbey, with his supporters, apparently in a different frame of mind. He favoured Bruce, even, with a distant inclination of the head, did not address him directly, but seemed to be prepared to co-operate in some measure with Wallace, Lamberton and the Chancellor. He allowed himself to be escorted to the Guardians' seats, by the Steward, while Buchan stiffly, did the same for Bruce. They sat down, a foot or two apart, not looking at each other but not quarrelling either. The Primate said a brief prayer over their deliberations, and Bishop Dalton, as Chancellor, opened the proceedings by asking if it was the former and proposed Guardians' will and pleasure to declare this parliament in sitting — even though lacking the normally-required forty days' notice? Two nods from the chairs, and a deep 'I do,' from Wallace, established the matter. Whereupon the latter retired to a lowly position in the nave — where, however, he still somehow continued to make a dominant impression. There was considerable routine business to get through, administrative detail which had piled up during Wallace's regime, and which required ratification by parliament, much of which the big man had to speak to, and much of it uncontentious. There was, in especial, the new French treaty and its ramifications to discuss. Master William Comyn, of the Chapel-Royal, naturally, had much to say on this, having been on the embassage to France — and spoke well and soundly, for he was an able man, however smooth. Lamberton also, newly returned from Rome,

356

via France, had items to add. The King of France's promises regarding armed help and intervention were noted and approved, and rounded off by Lamberton, who declared that King Philip had asked him specifically what was needed in matters military, and was apparently willing to do all that he might — if not for love of Scotland, at least to embarrass Edward. Not being a military man himself Lamberton could not inform the King in any detail, and had suggested sending a soldier-envoy from Scotland to make all plain. King Philip had thereupon asked particularly that Sir William Wallace himself should be sent, of whom he had heard so much. He, Lamberton, had doubted whether this was possible, with the Guardian; but in the changed situation, he believed that it was not only advisable but greatly in the realm's interest. No one knew better Scotland's military needs than the former Guardian: and because of his fame and renown, no one would be more likely to gain the very maximum for his country's benefit. He therefore proposed that Sir William Wallace be sent forthwith as special envoy to the King of France.

This was accepted by all, even the two new Guardians — who no doubt each would feel more comfortable without Wallace looking over their shoulders, in the early stages of their reign.

The big man, features schooled to expressionlessness, bowed briefly in acknowledgement. A period of exile was probably best. He saw no place for himself, meantime, in the Scotland led by Comyn and Bruce, when he might serve the realm in France.

Lamberton went on to give some account of his negotiations with the Pope, at Rome, on Scotland's behalf, with assurances of Papal sanctions against Edward. He had to announce, indeed, that these, plus France's representations, had already resulted in Edward releasing King John Baliol and his son from strict ward; they were now more or less free, in the custody of the Vatican, at Malmaison in Cambrai.

No cheers greeted this announcement. Indeed, a pregnant silence fell, as men looked at Bruce to see how he would take it. He sat motionless, stiff. In a parliament it was normal for the King to preside, but not to intervene in the actual discussions unless to make some vital and authoritative pronouncement. The Guardians were there as representing the King. Bruce could scarcely express forebodings about John Baliol's limited release, however much he deplored the deposed monarch.

Lamberton, to fill the silence, proposed that Sir William

357

Wallace should also go on to visit the Pope after seeing the King of France. His Holiness could, no doubt, be persuaded to greater aid to Scotland — for which, in his own position as new bishop seeking consecration, he himself had been unable to press. None objected to this — although John Comyn yawned cavernously.

There were a number of appointments made by Wallace which fell to be confirmed, few of any prominence. But one raised noble eyebrows. Alexander Scrymgeour, of Dundee, had been appointed Hereditary Standard Bearer of the Realm and Constable of Dundee — the former a new office of state.

Buchan got to his feet. 'My lord Chancellor,' he said, 'Here is a strange matter. A new office. Is this the time to create new offices of state? Such should be by the King's own appointing. And ... if Standard Bearer there must be, it should be one of the King's nobility. I move against.'

There were a number of ayes from the assembly, but some growls also; the first sign of a clash.

'Do you contest the right of the Guardian to create such office, my lord?' the Chancellor asked mildly.

The Constable hesitated. 'No,' he admitted, after a moment. 'But it requires confirmation by this parliament. And by the new Guardians. I move that confirmation be withheld.'

'Noted.' The Bishop of Galloway looked round. 'Does any other wish to speak on this matter?'

'Aye, my lord Chancellor — I do,' Wallace spoke up. 'With great respect to my lord Earl, I would say that the creation of this office was no whim or caprice. Nor the filling of it by Alexander Scrymgeour. In this our realm's warfare, none I swear, will question who suffers most. The common people. Few will deny who has achieved most in it, as yet. The common people. Even you, my lord Constable, will not gainsay that if the people of Scotland lose heart, or fail in their full support, then the realm is lost. The common folk, then, must see that they are considered, represented, given their due place. I say, who is more fitted to bear the Royal Standard of Scotland than one of themselves? And of them, who more fitted than Alexander Scrymgeour, descended from the ancient bannermen of our Celtic realm, under the MacDuff Earls of Fife? Who has fought in every conflict with the English, fought with valour — and stood his ground, unlike some! I crave, my lords temporal and spiritual, barons of Scotland and gentles all — confirm the office and appointment both.'

There was a curious sucking noise as the Steward, rising, sought to control his copious saliva. 'I so move,' he got out. And sat down.

That was it, then. So soon. The moment of decision. All eyes were fixed on the new Guardians who sat side by side, looking straight ahead of them rather than on the Chancellor, Wallace or Buchan.

Galloway, fingers tapping on the recumbent stone effigy of a former abbot, which had to serve him as desk, looked in the same direction as all others. 'Before putting this to the vote, I think, the minds of the two Lords Guardian should be known,' he said, and for once his confident and sonorous voice was uneven.

Promptly Bruce spoke. 'I accept the office, and agree to confirm Alexander Scrymgeour as Royal Standard Bearer of Scotland.'

Seconds passed as all waited. Then John Comyn smiled suddenly, that brilliant flashing smile of his which not everyone, always found an occasion for joy. 'Why, then, we are in happy accord, my friends,' he declared easily. 'For I too accept and accede. Let the excellent Scrymgeour bear his standard ... so long as he can!'

The sigh of relief that arose was like a wind sweeping over the Forest outside. Men scarcely noticed the Chancellor's declaration that he thought that there was no need for a vote; or Buchan's snorting offence, and the angry look he cast at his kinsman. Everywhere the thing was seen as much more than just the Scrymgeour appointment; it was the sought-for sign that these high-born rivals might yet sink their personal preferences for the common good.

But as even the Chancellor, like the others, relaxed a little, he was abruptly alert once more. John Comyn was speaking again.

'Since appointments are before us,' he said crisply, sitting a little forward in his chair. 'Here are some that I require. For the better governance of this kingdom. My lord of Buchan to be Justiciar of the North. Sir Alexander Comyn, his brother, to be Sheriff of Aberdeen and keeper of its castle. Sir Walter Comyn to be Sheriff of Banff, and keeper. Sir William Mowat to be Sheriff of Cromarty, and keeper thereof. Sir Robert Comyn to be Sheriff of Inverness. Sir William Baliol to be Sheriff of

Forfar. And Master William Comyn, of the Chapel-Royal, to be Lord Privy Seal, and elect to the next bishopric to become vacant. All that due rule and governance may be established in the land.'

Bruce could be seen to all but choke, as all around men gasped and exclaimed. Never before, it was safe to say, had a parliament been presented with such demands from the throne, such an ultimatum. For clearly that is what it was. This, then, was Comyn's price for superficial co-operation with Bruce. He had come prepared. Already the Comyns possessed enormous power in the North; with these key positions additionally in their hands, they would become complete control of all the upper half of the kingdom, not only theoretical but actual control.

Keenly Wallace, like all others, considered the Bruce. He had been prepared for trouble — but scarcely so blatant, brazen, as this. Had he made a great mistake? Again. Like Falkirk. He had thought to gain Scotland a second chance, to rally the nobility with the rest, against English domination, by using these two to give a surface impression of unity, a unity which might strengthen under the hammer-blows of actual attack. He had well known the risks and the difficulties. As had Lamberton. But what choice had they? What other combinations and alliances were possible? For any that excluded Comyn, or Bruce, or both, was doomed to failure, and the opposition of the other. But was Bruce going to prove strong enough? To cope with this arrogant opportunist. Bruce was his one slender hope, for Scotland. But could he survive against John Comyn? Was the Joint Guardianship finished before it ever began?

Wallace found Bishop Lamberton at his side. 'Think you we have calculated amiss?' he murmured. 'This man Comyn is a devil. Is all to be wrecked on account of his self-seeking folly?'

'One gleam of hope,' the big man answered, after a moment. 'It is all the North. Apart from the Privy Seal, all he demands is in the North. Thus far. It may be that he intends to divide the kingdom — divide, rather than rule it jointly. Comyn, King of the North! If he but leaves the South to Bruce . . .?'

'Ha! It might be so. Always the land has been so divided, in some fashion. The Highlands and the Lowlands. It might serve our turn. It might just serve . . .'

'So long as the North does not attack the South, while the South fights Edward for both!'

'No. That is the danger.'

'It is that, or nothing, I fear.'

The Chancellor had been speaking, suggesting that this was scarcely the time or place for appointments to sheriffdoms and administrations. That could best be done by the Privy Council, surely? As was usual. The Lord Privy Seal, yes — that was fair. Relevant. Was there other nomination for that office . . .?

Lamberton went forward again, to speak. 'My lord Chancellor,' he said, 'You are right in declaring that such administrative appointments as sheriffs and keepers of castles are scarce apt for this parliament. Or for piecemeal filling. But, in this special case, and since such appointments as have been named undoubtedly would strengthen the rule of the Joint Guardians in the North, to the internal peace and security of the realm, I would concede them. And suggest that a similar list of nominations, made by the Earl of Carrick, for the South, and presented to the Council, would be to the advantage of all. A . . . a balanced responsibility. Of the Joint Guardians. For North and South. On such joint security the kingdom might rest firm. In this pass.' He was looking hard at Bruce, as he spoke.

That young man saw the look, and heard the unspoken as well as the spoken message. He took a deep breath. 'Very well,' he said shortly. 'I accept these appointments. And shall produce my own, in due course. Proceed.'

In the buzz of talk that followed, John Comyn turned in his seat, to stare at his companion long and levelly. But it was at Lamberton and William Wallace that his kinsman, Master William, looked.

After that there was little more than formalities. The main confrontation and decisions had been made, and all knew it. In effect, Scotland would be partitioned into two mighty provinces, North and South, as there had once been the Northern and Southern Picts. It was the natural, age-old division, and in line with the two great houses' spheres of influence. And there was the unspoken corollary, which few failed to perceive. When Edward of England over-ran the South, and might be held again at Stirling, as once before, then the North would become all there was of Scotland. In which case there might well be a new king in the land. When Edward struck, the South would have to face him first. And it would be wise, then for Bruce to look back over his shoulder — as Wallace had had to do.

The parliament in the Forest broke up. It was arranged that the Guardians should meet again at Stirling, where North and South joined, in a month's time, to confer, and sign and seal edicts, charters and the like, with the two halves of the Great Seal.

Robert Bruce sought out William Wallace before he departed again for Annandale. 'So you leave us? For France?' he said. 'I am sorry.'

Wallace was surprised. 'Are you, my lord?'

'Yes. I think Scotland needs you here, more than in France.'

'I think not. Meantime. Your lot, my lord, will not be an easy one. My presence, I fear, would but make it more difficult.'

'Why, man?'

'Because of the people. The common folk I spoke of. Do you not see? Although I failed them, they still look to me. See me as one of themselves. All who should know tell me so. Think you they will love the men who displace me? Especially in the South. *You*, my lord.'

'I care not whether they love me, or no!'

'Then you should. You *need* their trust, at least. You must have it if, you would fight Edward. You will gain it sooner lacking Will Wallace's presence, for a while. Believe me, I have no wish to go, God knows! But . . . it is meet.'

The other sighed. 'I hope that you, and Lamberton, know what you have done, these last two days!'

'We know what we have *tried* to do, yes. And believe it for the best. Believe also that yours are the hands best fitted, now, to guide this unhappy realm. I commend your patience and wisdom this day, my lord — in sore circumstances. And will pray God, daily, that your hand be strengthened.' He held out his own hand. 'Be you a better Guardian than Wallace was, Robert Bruce! For Scotland's sake.'

CHAPTER TWENTY-ONE

They sailed from the harbour of Dundee after considerable, inevitable, delays — Dundee, because that city and fortress remained firmly in Scrymgeour's hands, where Edinburgh, Glasgow, Ayr, Lanark, Stirling, Dumbarton even Perth, were back under English control. Scrymgeour saw them on their way, bewailing the fact that he must not accompany his master and friends — although Wallace declared that surely it was evident to all that his place was there at Dundee. Most of Wallace's surviving companions had elected to accompany him to France, partly for love of him, partly in that they recognised that there was little place for them in Scotland now, lacking their leader. Since the parliament, in a typically swift campaign of movement and guerilla tactics, they had cleared Angus and Fife of the English precariously re-established there; but the Red Comyn clearly considered that this was encroaching upon his territories, and was disowning Wallace. Further activity could only exacerbate the precarious balance of power, and superficial co-operation, between the two Guardians. So the embassage was now being made, on Lamberton's advice, with Bruce's agreement — although Comyn was said now to be against it, presumably merely because his rival was for it. Such was the state of Scotland as the party took passage in a vessel of some Montrose merchants, found for them by Sir John Ramsay, trading to the Low Countries' port of Sluys, hides, tallow and salt-herring, to bring back grain.

It was with mixed feelings indeed. then, that William Wallace watched the shores of his native land dwindle and sink away, as they ploughed in spirited style before a fresh westerly breeze. He was going because he honestly believed it best, not for himself but for his country and people; and because William Lamberton, with the keenest wits he had discovered in Scotland, clearly thought that he could usefully serve the nation. But he did not want to go. Indeed, his heart was sore, for he felt that he was leaving behind the task he had set himself, unfinished, the invader still desecrating the land, and Edward Plantagenet's grim shadow diminished no whit, leaving behind a divided country, with jealousy and self-seeking rampant. And moreover, leaving behind all that was sacred to himself, the soil for which he had adventured all, times without number, the very soil which held the earthly remains of so many he had loved and who had died because of him — of Mirren herself, of Andrew Moray, of John the Graham, of Hugh MacDuff, of Bryce Blair, of Meg Drummond even, as of so many another. And what was he going to do? No less than to pit his poor wits against those of the highest in Christendom, the Most Christian King of France, and the Holy Father himself — he, Will Wallace, younger son of a small Renfrewshire knight (he seldom thought of himself as Sir William Wallace. Knight) who had failed his people, and had to give up his Guardianship after only eight months.

His friends, by mutual consent, left him fairly consistently alone in the stern of the vessel, as he watched the blue hills of Scotland recede.

They sailed well out into the North Sea, past the menacing rock of Inchcape with its constantly tolling bell, and far beyond, before turning South-Eastwards; for the threat of English pirates and privateers was ever present, the principal hazard for Scots merchants trading with the Continent, much more potent than mere storms and fogs. They made excellent time, before the stiff breeze, and the traders were happy — however uncomfortable some of the passengers. The pirates tended to operate fairly close to the English coastline, so that the further out they were into the open sea, the better. Ten hours after leaving the mouth of Tay, on a night of a myriad stars, the shipmaster, a Fifer from Dysart, named Duncan, felt it safe to turn southwards.

But in the early hours of the morning, the wind changed drastically, right round to the South-East — which was not only awkward for a vessel sailing in that selfsame direction, but was apt to bring bad weather with it, cold rain, sleet and bad visibility.

Sure enough, conditions worsened steadily, and the master was hard put to it to maintain even an approximate course. For three days and nights they were battered and blown and tossed, seasick and unhappy, with little headway, or notion of where they were — save that the shipmen feared an inevitable westwards drift. Then on the fourth night the weather cleared and the wind sank, and by morning there was crisp air and strengthening sunlight, with scudding white clouds giving a wide view — and a long coastline on the starboard bow.

Concerned, the master turned his prow into the east again, but not before he had recognised the landfall as the mouth of the Humber, no more and no less. He had hoped to be over one hundred miles further to the South-East.

If the passengers were grateful for the calmer seas and more clement weather, after being boxed-in below in misery for so long, Skipper Duncan saw it otherwise. It was no time to run into clear weather off that coast, in the morning, with all day before they could be hidden by darkness. He watched every sail that he glimpsed, like a hawk — but a fearful hawk — seeking always to keep his distance, and gave ill-tempered answers, or none at all, to any questions and comments.

Then, in the afternoon, with land almost out of sight, he came to the merchants with Wallace, saying that there was no point in hiding the matter any longer. They were being pursued by a bark faster-sailing than themselves, had been for the last hour and more. He had changed course three times, and each time the other had done likewise. There could be no doubt about it. And it would not be dark for almost three hours yet. Wallace bid him be of better cheer. They were not going to let some wretched English pirate upset them. With the odds one to one. Why not turn about, and send these busybodies back to the Humber or wherever they came from?

The master, while endeavouring to display a veneer of respect for the former Guardian of Scotland, indicated that land-lubbers with no experience of seafaring would be well advised to keep their own counsel — as would *he*, when matters of state were being debated.

An hour later, the Fifer was more agitated still, and the Montrose merchants with him, as the strange ship bore down upon them hand over fist. Calling on all saints, he declared the pursuer to be none other than the dreaded privateer John Bishop, of Lynn, a scourge of the seas, enjoying the protection of King Edward, who was said not to be above sharing spoil with him. He had made an end of many a fine Scots ship and its crew — although he normally harassed the French and Low Country shipping, all conveniently the King's enemies. Wallace once more pointed out that, since they obviously could not outsail this ruffian, they might as well turn and face him, putting themselves into a better position to defend themselves.

Personally he much preferred attack to defence, in any confrontation, as a matter of military principle.

They continued to flee, however, with the shipmaster pointing out that there would be at least a hundred and fifty armed scoundrels aboard the pirate, practised at boarding tactics. He scoffed at Wallace's assurance that he had eighteen heroes on this craft which he would wager gladly against any hundred and fifty Englishmen soever, afloat or ashore. The big man suggested that his friends go below and don such armour as they had brought with them — and which they had scarcely thought to use so soon, if at all, on this embassage.

When they regained the deck, it was to see that the pursuer had run up the three leopards of Plantagenet England, a sure sign that she was a privateer and of hostile intent. The ship was a two-masted carrack, with particularly high fore and stern castles, for fighting from, actually no larger than their own bark but more slender, and built for war. Soon the other was close enough to hail to them to strike their colours and heave-to, in the name of the King of England.

The man Duncan wrung his hands, helplessly — and already many of his crew had discreetly disappeared below. When it seemed that he was, in fact going to obey the order, Wallace stepped in, announced that he hereby took command of the vessel in the name of the King of Scots, and ordered the shipman to follow his men below decks — which the other seemed ready enough to do. Then he raised his voice, to shout across the water, to the carrack, that he was getting uncomfortably close for good navigation, that there was plenty of room in the sea for both of them, and that he had better be off about his legitimate business.

The answer to that was a shower of arrows, as warning, and loud yelling of threats.

Wallace had not come prepared for warfare; but there were two or three bows on board — and now an increased number of arrows. Master John Blair had made himself something of a master with the weapon. At a sign from Wallace therefore, part-hidden behind the main mast, he loosed off a shaft, with sufficiently expert aim to drop the English helmsman beside his wheel. In the confusion that followed, with Wallace turning their own craft's bows eastwards, the Benedictine shot two more arrows, each of which brought down a man on the enemy aftercastle.

The two vessels veered apart, to a mixed exchange of shouts and jeers.

Soon the arrows were coming thick and fast from the Englishman, his high fighting-castles giving him an advantageous field of fire, so that Wallace's companions had to crouch behind the bulwarks for cover. He had some of them fetch bales of wool and sheepskins from the cargo, using these as shields as they ran, to build a protective barrier round his own position at the wheel, into which the arrows plunged but did not penetrate. As he twisted the vessel this way and that his friends hurried to bring out more bales, hides as well as wool, to line the bulwarks also.

During Wallace's years at college in Dundee he had done much sea-fishing, and was accustomed to boats and steering — although he had never handled so large a craft as this. But he quickly got the feel of it, and kept zig-zagging their ship sufficiently to prevent the other from lying alongside for long enough successfully to cast his boarding-nets, the very unpredictability of his helmsmanship something of an asset. Once the wool and hide bales were positioned fairly consistently, the defenders were able to shoot back with good effect.

When this running fight had continued for some time, Skipper Duncan and his mate reappeared on deck, somewhat shamefacedly, presumably perceiving a gleam of hope in the situation — and Wallace gladly surrendered the wheel to experts. Bent double, he ran to Blair's side, two arrows striking his chainmail in the process, but doing no hurt.

'John,' he panted, 'Fire-arrows! Could you contrive them? Lamp-oil and rags. Shot at their sails. If we could set the sail ablaze . . .?'

The monk was scuttling below before ever that was finished.

It was not long before Blair was back with oil and cloth, flint and steel. Wallace tied the soaked rags to arrow-shafts and lit them. Blair shot these at the foot of the great main-sail of the carrack. The first was extinguished in passage, the second struck the canvas but fell to the deck, the third penetrated and burned away harmlessly. But the fourth, the burning rag close against the canvas, did set it alight. As quickly as they might, they put in more, and soon the huge sail was blazing at three points, fanned by the breeze.

While this had been proceeding, the carrack had managed, for the third time, to draw close enough to cast the heavy boarding-nets. One of these had caught, towards the stern, making a precarious gangway. This had happened before, and the defenders had managed to toss the ropework overboard. But this time Wallace shouted to desist — but to prevent any more nets getting a hold. Then drew his sword.

The Englishmen were no cravens, nor backward in their desperate trade, actually fighting with each other to be the first across that swaying, awkward catwalk, on all fours, clutching swords, hatchets, spikes and daggers. Wallace and his people could not stand openly to receive them, because of arrows; they had to hide behind the wool-bales until the boarders were masking their own archers, then rising up and smiting. Even so they had the advantage, and few Englishmen got more than a yard or two inboard.

The blazing main-sail was having its effect, preoccupying the enemy leadership, making steerage difficult and cutting down speed — indeed, the Scots vessel would soon be towing the carrack by its boarding-net. Wallace was content to deal with the boarders in small numbers, and only so could they swarm over the narrow access; but when presently the huge sail came crashing down on the English deck in flaming ruin, spreading devastation and chaos, and he heard the English skipper shouting for his people to cut the net free with their hatchets, he decided that it was time for a change in tactics. Shouting his slogan of 'A Wallace! A Wallace!' he leapt up, and went staggering across the network himself, reeling but just managing to keep his feet, using his sword as balancing-rod. Behind him his friends were not slow in following.

So unexpected was this turning of the tables, plus the fire and consequent confusion aboard the enemy, that there was little coherent opposition at first. Wallace was able to cut down two men, chopping with axes at the net-cables, before they could sever them. He then held a bridge-head with his furiously-sweeping sword, until sufficient of his people were across to present a menacing phalanx of steel-clad veterans. In tight formation they moved forward, smiting.

The English captain, John Bishop of Lynn, or other, clearly was not used to repelling boarders himself, especially when at the same time fire-fighting and seeking to manage a vessel with most of its motive-power gone. Individuals fought bravely, but to no unified plan — and chain-mailed knights were rather beyond their experience. It became almost child's-play for the Scots.

Wallace had no difficulty in distinguishing the captain, up on his forward-castle, and fought his way directly for him, up the steps. It was quite a difficult ascent — but once up, the Englishman died shouting defiance.

It was all over in little more than an hour from the first shower of arrows, with the Scots in undisputed control of the carrack. The captain did prove to be the notorious John Bishop. They proceeded to throw the English dead overboard, batten down the prisoners below, and extinguish the fire. Some of his people actually urged aiding the fire and abandoning the vessel; but Wallace declared that it might be of service to keep it. Duncan, elated now, put aboard a small prize crew, and rigged up a jury-sail to make the carrack manageable. They found that she had a considerable cargo of valuables, no doubt stolen from less prickly victims.

Although they had one or two slightly wounded, the Scots had not lost a single man.

They resumed course South-Eastwards, the carrack trailing astern, with a rampant Lion fluttering above the three leopards.

Three days later they reached the port of Sluys, without incident, down its six mile estuary. There was a large Scots merchant colony here, and great was the excitement when these discovered that they had no less than Sir William Wallace in their midst, and that he had brought John of Lynn's blood-soaked vessel as prize. The Flemish authorities were almost equally happy, for John Bishop had long been a menace to the port's trade. They feasted and made much of their Scots visitors, to the extent even of suggesting that they spent the winter with them — since they would find winter travelling across Northern Europe scarcely to their taste, and there was no lack of suitable targets for Meinherr William's energies close at hand. But Wallace explained that he was on a mission to the King of France and must not delay. Moreover, as was right and suitable, he must first make a call and pay his respects to his own monarch-in-exile, King John, whom he understood was presently domiciled at Cambrai in Hainault. He presented the Lynn carrack to the burgomeister and council, and shared out all its cargo, save the gold, amongst the Scots merchants. After a week's stay, he and his set off southwards to cross the Flanders plain on big-boned Flemish horses.

* * *

Their journey was a strange one, of mixed pleasure and pain, ease and hardship, satisfaction and disgust, part triumphal progress, part nightmare. Where the harsh hands of Edward of England and Philip of France had not fallen, they were welcomed as heroes, feted, feasted, honoured, in the great trading cities of Bruges, Courtrai, Lille and Douai. But much of the intervening and vast fertile plain had been the scene of fierce and prolonged warfare, and was now an extensive and evil desert, worse than the deserts these travellers had deliberately made in their own Scotland, for there the land was ravaged but the dead were few; here the dead were legions, everywhere, unburied, mutilated, hanged, crucified in whole manors, villages, small towns even, woods in which every tree bore swinging corpses of skeletons, ponds overflowing, canals choked. On these stretches of their route not only were there no lords, burgomeisters, mayors, trade guilds and the like, to provide hospitality, there were not even inns surviving to give them food and shelter. They understood now what the Sluys folk had meant about finding winter travel scarcely to their taste. Moreover, great bands of broken men, robbers, cut-throats, ghouls, roamed the once fair and fruitful wastes, and terrible hands were these for travellers to fall into. Wallace's party was large enough and sufficiently stalwart to look after itself; but they saw no lack of examples of what could happen to less wellendowed companies. They hastened over these great areas, and lingered over others where they were treated with deference and honour — to their surprise, for Wallace certainly had never realised how far his fame had spread.

In this way they crossed the Belgic plain, and into the low green hills of Artois, out of Flanders and into Hainault, southwards one hundred or so miles, more or less following the line of the ever-winding Scheldt. Hainault was much less devastated than had been Flanders since, though in theory within the Empire, its Count adhered to France in the wars. The walled bishop's city of Cambrai lay in the wide valley of the Scheldt, perhaps halfway between Sluys and Paris; and at the request of the Pope, under whose protection and keeping he now was, the Bishop had made available the old, crumbling palace of Malmaison, as refuge for John Baliol, former King of Scots.

Wallace had no doubts about the duty that lay upon him to call upon King John before he sought audience with King

Philip. There were many who contended that he was no longer King of Scots, but Wallace maintained that, since the abdication papers which he had signed had been imposed upon him, a prisoner, by Edward Plantagenet, they were not valid, any more than was the deposition order from the same source. There must always be a King of Scots, while Scotland remained a kingdom; and until another was forthcoming and crowned, John Baliol was all they had. He himself had accepted the Guardianship only in King John's name. He would not refuse the man his due homage, even if only a formality, now that he was in his country of exile.

It is safe to say that no one could have been more surprised to see William Wallace, or any company from Scotland, than was John Baliol. They found him, in company with the Bishop of Cambrai, studying books and parchments concerned with religion, which appeared to be his stay and consolation; a tall, stooping, slender man, of middle years and great dignity, richly but soberly dressed. When Wallace was announced, in the library of the episcopal palace, and came to drop on one knee before him and take his hand between both of his own, in the gesture of fealty, Baliol was quite overwhelmed, and could find no words. Clearly no one had done this for years.

Wallace had to speak first, therefore. 'Your Grace's humble and devoted servant, William Wallace,' he said. 'I greet you, Sire, with my leal duty. And that of these my friends.'

The other was so overcome with emotion that he could only stammer and shake his head. But when Wallace remained kneeling, he glanced almost furtively at the Bishop and servants, and found his tongue.

'Get up, man — do not so. It is not meet. I am King no longer. Stand, Sir William. I . . . I rejoice to see you. But call me not Grace, or Sire. That is past and done with.' Again he looked at the Bishop, clearly alarmed. He had noble features, a lofty brow, deep dark eyes, but all above a slack mouth and a delicate chin — no face to confront that of Edward Plantagenet, undoubtedly.

'You are crowned and anointed King of Scots, Sire. Initiated on the Stone of Destiny,' Wallace said, deep-voiced. 'As such, you remain my liege-lord, lacking any other.'

'Edward . . . Edward is king in Scotland now, man. All must acknowledge it. Folly to do otherwise. I am abdicate. That is all done with. An old story. Is it not so, Monseigneur?'

371

The elderly Bishop, Baliol's keeper under the Pope, nodded. 'That is so, my son,' he said, gravely.

'Edward is King of England — no less, but no more,' Wallace insisted. 'I shall not speak you as King, if that is your royal will. But . . . if *you* are not King of Scots, who is, my lord?'

'None. None, now. The style and title is abolished. There is no longer a King of Scots.'

'How can that be? Since there is still the ages-old *Kingdom* of the Scots. Of which, until lately, I had the great honour to be, all unworthily, the Guardian. Can the King of England, a foreign monarch, abolish the Kingdom of Scots, by a stroke of his pen?'

'Not the kingdom, perhaps, but the king. *Edward* is King of Scotland now.'

'*You* say so, my lord? You, of the blood of a hundred ancient Celtic kings? Who ruled when Plantagenet, Angevin, Capet, or even Charlemagne's line, walked behind the plough!' Baliol, although to all intents an Anglo-Norman, was the son of the Lady Devorgilla, heiress of the ancient Celtic Lords of Galloway, who had married the Lord John de Baliol of Barnard's Castle, in Durham.

The other sighed. 'My friend — the sword and the strong right arm speak louder than many dead generations of ancestors! *You*, who use a sword passing well, should know that! But . . . enough of this, meantime. Such debate is discourteous to our host, the Bishop here. Present your friends to me. And then we shall repair to my own house — or the house His Holiness is kind enough to lend me — and I shall endeavour to welcome you more fittingly. My quarters are modest, but at your service . . .'

And so they settled at the Malmaison of Cambrai for a time — and found John Baliol an excellent and attentive host, a good talker and a better listener. Even Kerlie and Ed Little, who had been much against coming here, and frequently referred mockingly to the former monarch as 'Toom Tabard', 'Empty Coat' and the like, were converted to a sneaking affection for the kindly, courteous man who had had the misfortune to come between the First Knight of Christendom and one of his ambitions, and was not equipped to deal with the results. Only a very strong man could have dealt adequately with Edward — and Baliol was clearly not that. But he was intelligent, friendly, with a certain nobility of character, even

courage of a sort — although he was a frightened man. Pope
Boniface had gained his release, meantime, from Edward's
close imprisonment and continuing insults; but let the Plantagenet get the least notion that Baliol was still thinking of
himself as a King, or providing any sort of possible rallying-
point for Scots dissidents, and he would be under lock-and-key
again, if not worse. He had given his word to Boniface that he
would indulge in no intrigues or political moves whatsoever.
His episcopal keeper here was helpful and understanding — but
wanted no trouble. This visit of Wallace would undoubtedly be
communicated to the Vatican by swift messenger, at once.

Wallace swallowed as best he could his bitter disappointment
over Baliol's defeated attitude, of which admittedly he had been
warned, but which he had not really accepted as possible. He
was duly concerned, however, that his well-meant gesture might
have the possible effect of adding to his former monarch's
troubles, and offered to leave Cambrai right away. But Baliol
showed his own kind of courage, refusing to hear of it, and
declaring that if any ill was to follow, the damage had been
done already. They must stay, and regale his ears with word of
Scotland, a land which he still could love however much he had
failed it. If they could but find opportunity to assure the good
Bishop that they had no schemes for restoring him to his throne,
nor indeed any desire to see him back thereon — that was all he
asked.

Wallace readily agreed to this — recognising indeed that this
was no king for Scotland in her present situation, that certainly
Bruce, and possibly even the Red Comyn, would serve better,
where a fighter was needed above all else. He agreed, also to
Baliol's quite pressing invitation to stay at Cambrai over Yule,
when he heard that King Philip was at present at Guienne, in
the South-West, where there was an English thrust, and was not
expected to be back in Paris until February, at the earliest.
Wallace had not come to the Continent lavishly endowed with
money. John Bishop's pirate gold was a great help; but maintaining a score of hungry Scots in Paris, awaiting the King's
arrival, would be bound to be expensive. Better to wait at Cambrai.

It had never occurred to him that King John Baliol would be
lonely. He had two young sons; but on the principle of not
keeping all eggs in one basket, these were maintained by French
kinsfolk at Bailleul-en-Vimeu, in Picardy.

373

It was not long before the exiles were longing for news of Scotland; but it seemed that Cambrai in Hainault was not the best place to gain it.

It seemed strange to pass Yuletide at peace and leisure, strange and somehow wrong, shameful.

CHAPTER TWENTY-TWO

They parted from John Baliol with real regret and in mutual esteem — although certainly not esteem as a monarch for Scotland. It was hard to know what future to wish for him, save perhaps peace to live a quiet and inoffensive life in freedom — and that was hardly a wish they might express to him, in the circumstances. But wish him well they did. And he, on his part, was almost pathetically grateful for their company, their goodwill, and for all they had been able to tell him of Scotland. He gave them a letter for Philip le Bel Capet, King of France.

That quicksilver, ebullient and unpredictable monarch had returned to Paris by the time they reached the city. But gaining his royal presence proved to be a different matter. His Most Christian Majesty seemed to keep himself surrounded by layer upon layer of the most ignorant, arrogant and unhelpful officials and functionaries, each of whom had to be negotiated — and negotiated was the due word, since each palm had to be greased, on an ascending scale — before the next could be approached. Wallace quickly grew tired of this expensive and time-consuming procedure. All citizens could inform him that the King, watched trials of strength, man against man, beast against beast, or man against beast, over which he could wager with his princes and courtiers. The big man perceived a possible approach to the unapproachable.

He presented himself, therefore, to the royal Master of Entertainments, at the Louvre Palace, describing himself as a wrestler, and when asked for an identity, gravely declared that he was William Wallace, the Scots Champion. This drew laughter; but his great size gained him a ready acceptance. He had, in fact, been something of a wrestler since boyhood, and although he had had little practice of recent years, he occasionally engaged in a bout with any of his friends sanguine enough to take him on. He believed that he could acquit himself reasonably enough to pass muster — and it seemed to be a sure way of gaining the royal presence. He was told to report at the palace stables the very next morning.

The great fortress-palace of the Louvre stood in many-towered splendour on the north bank of Seine, with a broad moat from the river led around its extensive perimeter. Wallace's previous attempts to gain entry, at its imposing front, had never got him past the gatehouse range — where the King's bureaucracy seemed to sit enshrined. But he had no difficulty now in entering the domestic wing behind, almost a separate establishment, with its own bridge over the moat, its spreading kitchens, bakehouses, brewery, storerooms, laundry, even slaughter-house and blacksmith's forge. Here were the stables and kennels, the former, it was said, with accommodation for five hundred horses. Here the Master of the Entertainments had his premises. The contests themselves were held in one of the many courtyards of the palace, overlooked by windows and galleries where the King and his guests could watch at ease. Wallace found that he was to be pitted against an enormous young mulatto, part Moor apparently, and presumably the largest they could find to match him. He seemed to be an amiable youth of limited intelligence, with a wide, white-toothed grin, not quite so tall as Wallace but much heavier, being somewhat gone to fat. He declared cheerfully that he had broke a dozen men's backs, but doubted whether he could break this Scots one; but so long as he was well paid, he cared not.

They had to wait for long hours for, though the King liked almost daily contests when in Paris, it was never known just when he would call for them; but all had to be in readiness, in case. Moreover, there were always a number of bouts, and the monarch himself would choose the order of appearance.

It was early afternoon before the summons came for the wrestlers, and, wearing only short trews, and greased copiously with hog's fat, Wallace found himself on the sanded flagstones of a central courtyard, already stained with clotted blood from previous contests of unspecified sort, facing the mulatto. He looked up at the overlooking windows and balconies, and although most were crowded with spectators, he had no difficulty

375

in placing the King's window, less packed than the others, indeed with only three seated figures thereat, one a woman.

Then the bell rang for the bout to commence, and he devoted all his attention to the task in hand — for it would serve him nothing to lose this contest. But hardly had he got to grips with his dark and high-smelling opponent, than he realised that he had little to fear. For all his size and weight, the fellow was flabby and in poor shape for his years. No doubt for too long he had relied on sheer bulk to win his battles, few contestants being able to compete. When he had noted his large belly, Wallace had guessed something of the sort; too much ale there. The muscles would be strong enough, but the bellows would be faulty and the reactions slow.

In fact, the Scot found himself quite quickly presented with a very unexpected problem — how to prolong the fight sufficiently to make it seem a worth-while victory; for his object, after all, was to come face to face with Philip, and it seemed quite probable that the King would not trouble to congratulate too easy a winner. Twice in the first few minutes he could have put the mulatto on his back, and once have broken the said back. He would have to be wary.

So he heaved and twisted and huffed and puffed and seemed to strain, groaning loudly on occasion — but all the time equally wary not to become careless, to throw away his superiority by being too confident. And all the time he wondered whether his efforts might not appear noticeably false to the knowledgeable spectators above.

At length, he decided that it might be non-productive to continue this, as there was a distinct lack of cheers, indeed the occasional jeer. He exerted himself, then, in a spectacular gesture, lifting the other right off the ground, and staggering a number of paces with him so, before dropping to his knees before the King's window, and there forcing the other's shoulders to the sand. It seemed to him that the mulatto was quite content to let him do this, without too much struggle, no doubt having long recognised who was the master, and being glad to finish with the business, unhurt.

Wallace rose, to only very moderate acclaim, and bowed to the royal window. He stooped to raise his fallen opponent. And then the deputy Master of Entertainments, with a bull-necked attendant, came out, waving them both back to the door from which they had emerged.

Wallace was much put out. He had not done all this for nothing! Retreating before the pair of them, he looked up, raising a hand towards the King.

'Sire!' he called, in excellent Norman-French, 'Hear me. I humbly seek your royal face. I am William Wallace, from Scotland. Audience, I pray you.'

There was laughter at that, from all around the courtyard — but not from the pair trying to corner him, who cursed him roundly. The mulatto had already made off.

The Deputy Master managed to get his hands on Wallace — but greased as he was, they slipped off. The big man dodged away — but the attendant flung himself low to grab around the knees. Keeping his feet with difficulty, Wallace picked the fellow up and threw him far from him, to crash all his length on the sanded flags.

More men came running out now, in answer to cries for help. Wallace dealt with these easily enough, knocking a pair of heads together. The Master of Entertainments himself then appeared, holding out imploring hands alternately towards Wallace and the King. He got no comfort from Philip, who was now laughing heartily; nor from his errant wrestler, who breathlessly demanded that he be taken into the royal presence. Instead of that, however, the Master beckoned out four more men, bearing between them one of the heavy nets used for entangling the wild beasts when they had to be withdrawn from the arena at baitings and displays. Seeing this, the big man's heart sank. He could not hope to beat a net.

Nevertheless he tried, gallantly. But after four or five attempts, the throwers managed to get the net over him, and that was the end of the interlude. But now, strangely enough, there were loud and enthusiastic cheers from all sides; and the King, standing up in his first-floor window, beckoned imperiously, obviously for Wallace to be brought before him. Cursing, the Master had to cease his fist-hammering of the bound wrestler, and obey; but he took the precaution of keeping the net wrapped securely round Wallace's upper parts.

Thus, all but naked, glistening with sweat and hog-grease, and entangled in netting, Scotland's special envoy to the Court of France was led upstairs, pushed and kicked in the process, and at last came into the august presence of His Most Christian Majesty.

Philip the Fair was a man of Wallace's own age, handsome as

his name implied, with a long nose, out-thrust chin and glittering restless eyes, stockily-built and wide-shouldered, though beginning to incline to fleshiness. He was magnificently but most carelessly dressed — he might indeed have slept in these begemmed and gold-encrusted velvets and satins. And the lady at his side, rather evidently not his Queen Joanna, looked as though she also might have just risen from a bed, not so much on account of untidiness but that above the waist her clothing was almost non-existent, her large, well-formed white breasts scarcely veiled anywhere. She had bold eyes to match, that appraised Wallace's stalwart figure expertly. The third person in that royal ante-chamber was oddly neat and sober for the company, a greying, spare, shrewd-looking man of middle years, dressed in modest greys.

'What is the meaning of this unseemly display, in our royal presence, rascal?' Philip demanded, with seeming severity — although the woman smiled reassuringly. 'Mishandling my servants and creating an uproar. I could have you hanged for this.'

'No doubt, my lord King. I regret the necessity. But necessity there was — since it was the only way I might attain to Your Majesty's presence.'

At the other's manner, and the way that was said, the King looked at him more keenly. He glanced also at the older man at his side. 'You speak boldly, fellow. Watch your words.'

'He speaks as he fights, I think — well,' the woman murmured.

'What is so important that you say to His Majesty?' the grey-haired man asked, in a thin, crisp voice.

'Only that I must believe that His Majesty wishes speech with me — since I came at his royal invitation, sir.'

'Eh . . .?' Philip frowned. 'Is the fellow mad?'

'Your name, sirrah?' the other man demanded.

'As I said earlier, sir. William Wallace, from Scotland. *Sir* William, if it pleases you.'

'What . . . what folly is this?' Philip cried. 'Dare you cozen *me*, fool?'

'I dare not that, Sire. Nor would I. As to folly, Your Majesty must be the judge. I came from Scotland, at your royal behest. And on the orders of its parliament. To speak with you, on Scotland's needs in this war. That I could not reach your royal

378

presence past your, your guardians, was my misfortune. Not possessing a bottomless purse! Though I tried.'

The older man drew a quick breath; and the woman laughed softly.

'Precious Saints of God!' the King exclaimed. 'Do you say ... do you tell me ... can it be true? That you are truly Wallace? The, the *Protecteur*? The Scottish hero. The general . . .?'

'As to hero, Sire, I fear not. Nor true general. But I am William Wallace, who was Guardian of the Realm of Scotland, in the name of John, King of Scots, until some months ago. From whom I bear a letter. Sent now as envoy of Scotland to your royal Court.'

'Mary Mother have mercy!' Philip swallowed — and in his need transferred his attentions elsewhere. 'Fool! Imbecile! Dolt! Get that net off him!' he commanded the unfortunate Master of Entertainments. 'God in Heaven — are you deaf, man? Palsied?' He turned. 'Marigny — do not stand there. Fetch a robe. My own cloak, there. Get it. This, this is beyond all!'

'Do not distress yourself, Sire,' Wallace urged, as they divested him, with some little difficulty, of his coils of rope. 'No harm is done. I am pleasantly exercised, have provided some small entertainment — and have reached your royal side, to my joy. All is well — if you will forgive my appearance . . .'

'Heads shall fall, for this!' the King snorted. But he came forward, and actually helped in the last freeing of the ropes. The lady came too, and though she did not do much disentangling, she stroked Wallace's gleaming skin assessingly.

The man Marigny came with a handsome cloak, which he placed around Wallace's broad shoulders, while the Master of Entertainments and his servants went scuttling off. 'Do we understand, Sir William,' he said, carefully, 'that you have been denied audience of His Majesty, by his servants and chamberlains? Having made yourself and your mission known to them?'

'I have, sir. My slender means did not reach their charges!'

'H'rr'mm. They knew who you were?'

'They were told. Moreover, I handed in letters addressed to His Grace.'

'Damnation, Marigny — here is a fine state of affairs!' Philip spluttered. 'Your precious arrangements! This is *your* responsibility. You are my Intendant. This of payment — it is an outrage! You will see to it, and swiftly. I will have all put to rights, and the guilty punished. You hear me? I hold you answerable. You will report to me fully. My honoured guest has been insulted. So notable a man! By *your* venial and insolent servants — yours, not mine!'

'I take full responsibility, Majesty. And make profound apology to Sir William,' Marigny said, bowing stiffly — but not looking noticeably apologetic. 'All shall be dealt with, suitably.'

'Sire — do not allow such slight misunderstanding to affect you, I pray you. Nor to embroil Monsieur, here, and myself further. No doubt I am much to blame, being unfamiliar with your arrangements and proceedings.' Wallace cleared his throat. 'With your royal permission, I will retire. And seek Your Majesty's presence on a later occasion, more suitably garbed . . .'

'I approve of the Sieur de Wallace as he is!' the young woman declared, moistening her red lips.

Philip chuckled. 'I'd swear you would, Hélène! Madame Lanfranc is a notable judge of men, Sir William!' He paused. 'But, tell me — is it not, h'm, unusual that you should fight so? Wrestle so excellently. A man of your standing. To have thought on this? Such device . . .?'

'My standing, Sire, is only what I make of it. I do what is called for. I am but a small knight's son — which has many advantages. I have no dignities, to bind me!'

'Ha! Hear you that, Marigny?'

'A philosopher, Sire! We are to be edified!' There was no doubting the coolness there. 'Shall I conduct Sir William to his quarters?'

'Do. He will dine with me this night. We have much to discuss. See that he has all that he requires. France must make amends. You have a company with you, Sir William?'

'Yes, Majesty. Near a score. Of my friends, companions-in-arms. Warriors all.'

'Ha — the heroes! The Scots paladins I have heard much of. You shall present them to me. To my . . . what was the word, Marigny? Edification, yes? To my edification. Meantime, my Intendant will install you all. In the Chambrier Tower, I think — that would be apt. Eh, Enguerrand? The Chambrier — with all comforts and servants. A captain of my Guard, to attend on Sir William at all times. See to it. Until this evening then, my friend. . .'

As Wallace rose from his bow, he caught the lady's eye — although, to be sure, she it was who did the catching.

'His Majesty says France must make amends, Monsieur,' she observed. 'Even I might be permitted to ... assist! Who knows?'

'Sir William is warned!' the King commented, grimacing. 'As am I!'

Later that afternoon, when, in company of an exquisite captain of the Royal Guard, Wallace brought back his companions through the main gatehouse portals of the Louvre, with deep bowing servitors on every hand, on the way to the Chambrier Tower of the fortress, it was to discover two bodies dangling on either side of the doorway thereto, still twitching. These had not been there when Wallace had left to fetch the said friends. They were floridly dressed gentry, chamberlains at a guess — although their features, being contorted and swollen, were not recognisable by the Scots.

King Philip's amends, it seemed, were comprehensive.

* * *

The dining with the King, that evening, proved to be a large-scale and magnificent banquet, greatly more ambitious than anything the Scots had ever experienced, held in one of the many halls of the palace, and attended by hundreds. Presumably this was a quite normal proceeding, since there had been no time to arrange any special feast or guest-list.

Philip made good his declaration regarding Wallace's companions and friends, by having them all presented to him, in an ante-room, before the banquet began — with his Queen Joanna at his side, this time, Queen of Navarre in her own right — and no sign of Madame Lanfranc. The King was most amiable towards them all, and on more than one occasion indicated that he could use the services of such renowned champions here in his own realm. Then they all went in procession into the hall, Wallace walking between the King and Queen, his veterans immediately behind in a solid phalanx, notably plainly clad for that scintillating company, while all around men bowed deeply and women curtsied low. Wallace found himself seated still between Philip and Joanna; while his companions were allotted a table to themselves, set at right angles, but close, to the royal dais table — or not entirely to themselves, for beside every vacant chair already was seated a young woman, making up an attractive and saucy company. This dispensation, needless to say, was appreciated by the visitors.

Wallace himself would have preferred a similar provision, Madame Lanfranc perhaps — who no doubt was not on view when the Queen was present — for he found Joanna of Navarre heavy going, a large, slightly masculine woman, with few graces and little to say. Not that her husband left him much opportunity for converse with the Queen. He seemed to be a man with a questing mind, his enquiries flitting hither and thither, as dartingly restless as his glance. Wallace quickly realised, however, that the King had a central theme to all — and that he was not particularly interested in Scotland. It was theory in the main that concerned him — although with many side-issues — military theory in particular, demanding details and tactics of battles, campaigns, ambuscades, marches, feints, burnings, sieges. No aspect or manoeuvre was too small for him, or too large — but it became evident that the Scottish application thereof was of little concern; it was theory in general he was interested in, and the relevance to the French military needs in particular. The Guienne situation preoccupied him clearly, and much of what he was gleaning from Wallace he immediately applied to that province's problems. It was, of course, an extremely galling position for any monarch to have to suffer. Edward of England, an Angevin, was also Lord of Aquitaine, or Guienne, a province of South-West France, which Henry the Second of England had gained by marriage to Eleanor of Aquitaine. It was a hereditary fief, held of the French crown, a difficult situation. What made it worse was that the nobles and landowners of Guienne actually owed, and paid, a double fealty, to Edward as lord and to Philip as king. With a man of the Plantagenet's aggressive and forceful character, it was an insupportable state of affairs. Philip had, on the whole, managed to keep the Norman-English territorial claims in the North of France under control, using Flanders as a battle-ground; but in the South-West Edward could sail in, with an aspect of legality, and find much of the population prepared to accept him. So a state of chronic if undeclared war prevailed. Edward did not deploy large forces in Guienne, with the long sea journey an inhibiting factor, relying on local support stiffened by English bands and captains. Great battles were seldom fought, but a war of attrition went on, with constant small engagements, harassments, encroachments, a running sore on the body of France, which Philip found intolerable.

As the banquet wore on, with the King's ever increasing emphasis on the parallels between Scotland and Guienne, it began to dawn on Wallace that Philip saw his arrival in France in rather a different light from his own; that while Scotland had sent him here to negotiate French aid, France was probably considerably more interested in *his* aid, in Guienne. Admittedly, a dinner table was no place to list and amplify Scotland's military needs; but the big man saw himself being manoeuvred into a situation where anything he gained for Scotland might have to be earned in France. He began to recognise a form of indirect pressure.

The actual meal over, and he gained some relief. There followed entertainments, and although Philip was no doubt quite capable of talking all through such, he was himself partly involved; for, amidst the turns of jugglers, acrobats, dancing-bears, dwarfs and the like, were interspersed troubadour items, something new to the Scots, although they had of course heard of them. These consisted of songs and ballads rendered to the accompaniment of lute, viol, zither or harp, not by professional singers or minstrels but by knights, nobles, even the King himself. This was part of the knightly tradition in France — where clearly knighthood meant something other than in Scotland, or England either. The songs and verses were not concerned with war and battle, except incidently, but with love, fair ladies, broken hearts and romantic dreams, all strangely stylised and far removed from reality, but tuneful, attractive and often hauntingly lovely. Each troubadour had his own jongleur, or instrumentalist, very often his squire or page, and usually rather beautiful young men who were apt to gaze soulfully at the singers and often be caressed by their principals as the song or recitation went on — which seemed to the Scots sometimes at variance with the devotion to the ladies being sung about. They found much of it odd, indeed; but Wallace at least thought it some improvement on the aftermath of banquets at home, whereat hard drinking was apt to be the order of the night, and gross drunkenness the result. There might be drunkenness here also, later, for there was no lack of wine; but perhaps most present were reserving their capabilities for appreciating other delights, for there was a great deal of pairing off observable, male and female and otherwise, although all within the confines of the great hall itself meantime. Presently Philip and Joanna rose — as, of course, must all others — and made a ceremonial departure, with no special gesture towards Wallace or the Scots; which likewise seemed odd. However, everyone sat down again, relaxing, and the entertainment resumed. But now people began to drift away, in their pairs. And presently Philip came back again, having discarded certain of his splendid robing, this time with a different lady on his arm, a tall and statuesque beauty — and nobody stood up. It was apparent that this was a device to get over the strict convention that none might leave any gathering before the King did so. Philip was back incognito, as his change of partners demonstrated. They arranged some matters in civilised fashion, in France. The new lady proved to be the Countess D'Eastramont, and she absorbed the King's attention fairly comprehensively. After a little of it, Wallace decided that his attendance was no longer vital. He excused himself, to Philip's wide wave. He noted that most of his colleagues at the Scots' table had already disappeared, and their female table-mates with them.

Outside the hall, lovemaking was going on in uninhibited fashion in every corner, niche and ante-room of the palace, it seemed, all rather unsettling. When the big man got back to the Chambrier Tower, past the hanging chamberlains, he found a guard in the royal livery outside his bedchamber door — who certainly had not been there when he left. This individual bowed.

'That Monsieur is not disturbed,' he said.

'Am I like to be, my friend?'

The other shrugged, with Gallic non-committment. 'Orders, Monsieur.'

Within the apartment, the big man found Madame Hélène Lanfranc sitting before a well-doing fire of scented logs, wine at her elbow. She was wearing a voluminous robe of sorts, distinctly better clad than when last he had seen her. She did not rise as he came in.

'Here is . . . an unexpected pleasure,' he said, carefully.

'We were concerned that you should be comfortable, Sieur William,' she answered.

He noted that "we", and wondered whether it might be royal, or otherwise. 'Kind,' he said. 'All seems to be in order, Madame.'

'Hélène, I am called. Wine, Sieur William?'

'A little, if you please. And my friends call me Will.'

'Ah. Will is good.' She pronounced it Vill. She rose, with his wine — and her robe, falling open, revealed her to be wholly naked beneath. 'I am glad that we are friends, Will. I like strong men — and you are very strong, are you not?'

'There are more strengths than one,' he declared. 'I would scarce think that you are weak, yourself! Or lacking in any ... advantage!'

'Perhaps, then, we make a pair?' she said. And she moved a little to the side, so that the robe swung wider, without actually holding it open demonstrating more of the splendid body within. Her breasts had already been made fairly explicit; now the remainder of her shapely, graceful amplitude, gleaming white with strong black triangle, made its emphatic statement.

Wallace cleared his throat. 'And ... His Grace? The King?'

'Philip is otherwise occupied tonight. And would have his guest well cherished, I am assured. You perceived the guard at the door?'

'I see.' He nodded. Uncertain still whether this was French royal hospitality, or private initiative. he was not the man to adopt any unseemly caution before a spirited and willing woman, any more than a spirited enemy. 'Very well, we shall put it to the test, Hélène,' he said. 'With joy.' And drank down his wine.

Her chuckle was deep, promising. She threw off her robe with frankest satisfaction, and came to him, arms out. 'Allow that I help you with your clothes, Champion of Scotland. Come wrestle a bout with me. Or two. Or three!'

CHAPTER TWENTY-THREE

So commenced a period at the French court which Wallace came to look upon almost as one more of his campaigns, rather than any social or diplomatic interlude, a prolonged campaign wherein were both successes and failures, but which, like most warfare, consisted mainly of frustrating inactivity and waiting. The objective was never in doubt — to get King Philip firmly committed to substantial armed aid for Scotland, both in men and arms; the hazards and difficulties, in convincing that mercurial monarch that this was to his own advantage, as well as being his kingly and knightly duty — and at the same time, to avoid entanglement in the Guienne situation, for which Philip was clearly working, assisted by his closest adviser, Enguerrand de Marigny, entitled his Intendant of Finance, an able but, Wallace judged, totally unscrupulous man. Another aspect of this campaigning was a sort of continuous sexual tournament with Hélène Lanfranc, who seemed to be concerned, in the most pleasant way possible, with proving that, in one form of warfare at least, Wallace had nothing to teach the French, either in tactics or in staying-power. Although Philip never actually alluded specifically to this, it was certain that he could not have remained in ignorance of it; and the big man sometimes wondered whether, in fact, it all might not be another of his favoured wagering contests, this time performed in private, but presumably reported upon.

Complicating this Franco-Scottish duelling was the intermittent arrival of news from Scotland, the effects of which were seldom advantageous to Wallace; and unfortunately it was to the King that the messages and tidings came, rather than to the Scots. These told of constant bickering between the two Guardians, almost to the extent of armed clashes; the Comyns were attacking their old rival of the Highland West, the Lord of the Isles and his Clan Donald federation, with the aid of Lame John MacDougall, and laying waste their lands; widespread famine in the country, and no revenues being collected — indeed only the Church supplying sufficient treasure to keep any sort of administration going; monthly meetings of the Guardians, held at either the Tor Wood or Inchaffray Abbey in Strathearn, just south and north of the Forth alternately, which were more confrontations than conferences — and these only held, apparently, on the persistent urgings of Bishop Lamberton and Provost Comyn. Militarily, Bruce had instigated a siege of Stirling Castle, with sundry raidings, some deep into Lothian; but these were clearly small-scale efforts. Edward had shown no sign of major re-invading meantime, although he kept large forces at Carlisle and in North Yorkshire, tidings from England indicating that he was having renewed trouble with his nobles over political and constitutional disputes, especially with the powerful Earls of Norfolk, Northumberland and Surrey, whose influence in matters military was paramount. He was seeking to

offset this by judicious forfeiting of the lands of Scots nobles
whom he could identify as having opposed him at Falkirk, and
conveying these estates to his own English nominees, to make
them more enthusiastic for a return to Scotland.

In these circumstances, Philip the Fair declared that he saw
no urgency for French military aid. Whereas there was much
need for his arms in Guienne, here and now. If Wallace would
aid him against Edward in Guienne, then when that province
was cleared of the English, he could afford to send more
significant help to Scotland.

It was evident that this was the only way Wallace was going
to gain the required assistance. Reluctantly, he agreed —
especially as many of his friends were finding the idle life at the
French court beginning to pall.

One thing he did achieve, before he set off southwards; he
saw gathered and on its way to Scotland, a consignment of three
ship-loads of grain for his hungry countrymen. Contemplation
of the continuing famine at home tended to come between him
and appreciation of the sumptuous meals which were their daily
lot at the Louvre.

So commenced one of those unsatisfactory interludes in
Wallace's life, unproductive for himself as it was protracted.
Despite his flair for the war of movement and guerilla tactics,
he was in fact far from a born soldier, in that he had no love for
fighting and bloodshed, as such; quite the reverse. He had to be
stirred deeply by a cause before he was inclined to draw his
sword for it; he required to have his heart in any warfare he
undertook. He certainly did not feel that way in the case of
Guienne, either in theory or in practice; and throughout the
long months of campaigning which followed, he grew ever less
enthusiastic over the part he was forced to play. Moreover,
someone else's civil war is seldom other than a distressing experience, save for the hard-hearted; and this one was particularly unappetising. Both sides behaved with a degree of
callousness and savagery that was quite shocking — and it
seemed clear where Edward the Angevin had heired his ruthless
cruelty. But as time went on, Wallace found himself, if anything, more sympathetic towards the local Guiennese than
towards Philip's forces, since these at least were defending their
own territories and homes, and held to a loyalty to their hereditary lords which they clearly did not feel towards the crown of
France, of which the ancient dukedom of Aquitaine had

387

formerly been independent. Moreover, Philip's methods and reprisals were so harsh that Wallace became increasingly loth to be in any way connected with them.

Not that the King was present in person; he had his own kind of campaigning to conduct, it seemed, when winter was well over, consisting of a marshalling of forces of one sort or another against his three other prime enemies, the Pope, the Knights Templar and the Jews. These causes he pursued, if in fits and starts, by every means in his power, fair or foul, largely for financial reasons, advised by the grave-faced Marigny. So he sent with Wallace his sixteen-year-old eldest son, Louis, a weak, petulant and obnoxious youth whom the older man quickly came to loathe. Unfortunately, the Prince looked upon himself as commander-in-chief in the Guienne campaign; and needless to say, most of the French captains and knights elected to take the lead from the King's heir rather than from the foreign hireling, however renowned.

Very early in the business Wallace contracted severe disillusionment when, less than two hundred miles South-West of Paris, and still over a hundred and fifty miles from Bordeaux, capital of Guienne, they were held up at Chinon, where town, castle and road were held against them. This was only at the south of Touraine, so that the entire province of Poitou, between them and Guienne proper, was evidently in English or Aquitainian hands — something not previously hinted at. Chinon, where had died Henry the Second, who had gained Aquitaine by marriage, was an ancient walled town with a castle on a high rock. It was being besieged in a half-hearted fashion, and had been for months.

Disturbed, not only by the vastly increased task this opened before him, but by the lack of frankness and trust implied, Wallace set about invigorating and reorganising the siege arrangements forthwith — although siegery was no speciality of his — and so successfully that the town and castle fell after only five days. This initial triumph, naturally, produced notable reactions, and a fairly general acceptance of Wallace's leadership and authority — which authority was in fact exceedingly vague, Philip having appointed him, apparently, more as adviser to young Louis than anything else, an intolerable situation for a man of his temperament.

They settled in at Chinon, as possibly the best base for the conquest of Poitou, and from here Wallace commenced the lengthy process of bringing that province under the royal control, by a series of raids in depth. He fought no pitched battles and avoided sieges wherever possible, preferring to outflank, isolate and negative fortresses. Prince Louis, an indolent youth, seldom accompanied him on these forays — although he frequently criticised them as insufficiently large-scale and effective. In fact Wallace seldom had more than a thousand men at his command, spear-headed by his own veteran Scots, finding this a manageable, fast-moving and logistically self-supporting force, and quite large enough for most tasks required of it. Gradually Poitou was won over. Like Guienne itself, it had once been part of Aquitaine.

Ralph de Monthermer, Earl of Gloucester, was the English commander, with his headquarters at the port of Bordeaux, some fifty miles up the Gironde estuary, where he could be supplied readily by sea. But it was on the far western edge of Guienne, and a poor base for controlling a province a hundred and fifty miles long by a hundred wide. Nor was Gloucester by any stretch of the imagination a military genius. He did not make any very effective defence against Wallace's swift and unpredictable inroads.

Thus spring passed into summer, and the French royal forces drew ever nearer Bordeaux, with most of the country behind in their hands, although some pockets of resistance remained. Louis was now eager to press on to Bordeaux, drive out Gloucester and proclaim France free of the invader. But Wallace pointed out, not once but many times, that this was no such simple matter, that it was a heavily-defended and well-sited seaport, which could not be surrounded because of the estuary, but could remain supplied and reinforced, by water. They had no fleet to blockade it, and no heavy siege machinery to reduce it. Bordeaux would be a hard nut to crack. Moreover, there were rumours of Edward sending reinforcements from England.

The Prince, however, would listen to none of this, and they moved in to invest the city.

Of all this unsatisfactory campaign, successful as it might seem superficially, the following two months were the most burdensome. There was little or nothing to do but sit around the beleaguered town, hoping to wear out the patience of the defenders and citizens. They managed to requisition and sink a number of coastal craft in the harbour entrance, as Wallace had done at Berwick; but though this prevented large ships from entering, it could not prevent them from unloading cargo or men into small boats and coming ashore. Wallace sent messages to King Philip for battering-rams, sows, ballista and the like; but none materialised. He sought to build engines out of local materials, but these were inadequate. Gloucester sat tight, secure in the knowledge that he could sail away at will, if the city eventually had to capitulate.

By late October young Louis's scant patience was exhausted. Deteriorating weather conditions made camping-out around Bordeaux, with its chill wet winds off the Bay of Biscay, little to his taste. Winter was no time for campaigning, he declared, and Paris the only place to spend it. Wallace could have argued otherwise, and dug in his heels; but he was insufficiently enamoured of the entire business so to assert himself. He bowed to the youthful commander-in-chief's orders.

Back in Paris, it suited King Philip's purposes and policies to treat them both as conquering heroes, it being declared that the English were now driven out of France and the nation cleansed. Honours were conferred, speeches made, and festivities the order of the day: even a special tournament, at which Wallace did manage to distinguish himself — though for the rest he felt a fraud, whatever were young Louis's reactions.

But Philip, despite all the acclaim, seemed as reluctant as ever to commit himself to a Scottish expedition, or even any substantial shipment of arms. Discussions took place with Marigny and other ministers, as to what was required, Wallace stressing the great need for archers in especial, and destriers and heavy cavalry likewise. He had found the Poitou men notable bowmen, and proposed to enrol an entire regiment of them. But discussion was as far as it got. No firm decisions were made — save in that Philip decided that no French ships should be hazarded in winter seas; besides, he seemed to agree with his son about the unsuitability of winter campaigns of any sort, especially in a land of snow and ice such as he deemed Scotland to be. Nothing could, or should, be done until the spring.

Wallace had been away from Scotland for a full year, and appeared to be little or no further forward in his mission.

Admittedly that winter passed pleasantly enough, with a continual round of junketings, hunting, play-actings, contests, bear-baitings, horse-racing and the like, Wallace and his friends contributing, in jousting, wrestling, feats of strength and Scots dancing and songs. They were popular, especially with the ladies — and Hélène Lanfranc was assiduous in her private contest with Wallace himself. They retained the Chambrier Tower of the Louvre, and could scarcely have been more comfortable. But they had not come to France for comfort.

So the century turned.

Wallace, out of his depth in this world of courts and intrigue, wrote to William Lamberton for advice.

CHAPTER TWENTY-FOUR

The Scots were back at Sluys. It would be safe to say that they almost all wished that they were waiting for a ship to take them back to Scotland. Wallace most certainly did. But that was not their objective here. They were waiting for a ship indeed, and had been for a full week; but it was Bishop Lamberton's ship they were awaiting, much delayed by contrary winds. Lamberton had answered Wallace's letter, pleading with him not to return to Scotland meantime, not to be discouraged and lose patience with King Philip, not to be distressed that he had apparently achieved so little in the year. Diplomacy was a slow and devious business, he insisted; but nothing stood still, nevertheless, and there were constantly changing situations and aspects of events which required assimilation and adjustment — as at present, when much that was important was going on out of sight. Little might seem to be gained, on the surface; but the results of patient pressure and influence could be great, for good or ill. Wallace could achieve more for Scotland by staying in France, close to Philip, than he could by returning home, in present circumstances. Of this he was assured. So delicate was the situation, and so vital for Scotland's future, that he, Lamberton, was himself going to see the Pope again, and would hope to confer with Wallace *en route*. He intended to sail from Dysart towards the end of that month, March, and should be at Sluys, the first fairly safe port east of the English-dominated narrow seas, the first week in April.

Not only Wallace awaited the Bishop's arrival, but so did

Enguerrand de Marigny. For Philip was concerned at any Scots exchanges with his enemy Boniface, and wanted to know what was involved and intended. Since Lamberton had had to apply for the required safe-conduct through the King's territories, on his way to the Vatican, the King had only granted this on condition that he should be kept informed.

When the Bishop's ship at last made its landfall, it was therefore to a mixed Flemish, French, Scots welcome. And it was a considerable time before Wallace could see Lamberton alone. In a room of the Sluys Guildhall they eventually relaxed over a jug of Rhenish wine.

'So much talk, my friend — and most of it saying nothing. Or worse, saying less, or more, than the truth! Hiding the truth, indeed. One wearies of it.'

'Churchmen are good at that, are they not; my lord Bishop?'

'Is that the reputation we have? God forgive us, then! But . . . someone has to talk diplomatically. Or the business of nations could not be transacted.'

'No doubt. I fear that I scarce have the art. Or the taste for it. You should have sent a churchman here, to deal with the French. Not William Wallace.'

'Not so. You were the right man. Still are. We did not mistake.'

'I have achieved nothing . . .'

'You have achieved more than you know, my friend. More than any other could. More than I could, certainly. All is not on the surface, visible.'

'What have I achieved, my lord?'

'You have won Philip's confidence — a great matter. You have kept him from doing much that would have been to Scotland's hurt. Not for love of Scotland, but for fear of offending *you*, and bringing you back from Guienne.'

'Ha! Guienne – that unhappy province. Where I wasted six months!'

'Not wasted, Sir William. You were fighting for *Scotland* in Guienne. And to good effect. Not only against Edward Plantagenet and his English, but keeping Philip from succumbing to other pressures, which would have been to our injury. He has been under great stresses, His Most Christian Majesty. While you were winning Guienne for him, he could hold his head higher. He lacks successful generals. That is why it was necessary for *you* to come to France.'

'You mean ... that you knew? That this is why I was sent? That you knew that I would be forced to fight. In Guienne?'

The other inclined his head a little. 'I knew that it was likely, my friend. That Philip greatly needed one such as yourself — and such are scarce, are they not? That he must be sustained and strengthened, if he was to continue to stand out against Edward.'

'I came here, then, to fight Philip's wars — not to gain troops and arms for Scotland?'

'Both. But the one was necessary before the other was possible. I perceived. And in the first, you were serving Scotland as well as in the second. For if Edward could ensure that his rear was safe, that France was no danger to him, then he could turn his full might and attention on Scotland. And nothing would save us then.'

Wallace was silent for a little.

'Guienne is important, therefore,' Lamberton went on, earnestly. 'It is not just a French province which Edward has invaded — it is his own property. He will never give up Guienne. And you are making him fight for it. Philip would have given up, by this, without you. For sheer lack of military skills and commanders. That is why you must go back there, Sir William. Continue the fight. We know Gloucester is being reinforced . . .'

'No! Not that. I fight, my lord bishop, for what I believe in — not other folk's squabbles. I am no paid mercenary . . .!'

'Have I not told you? It is Scotland you fight for, in Guienne. To keep Edward preoccupied, and to keep Philip on Scotland's side.'

'He is in treaty with Scotland . . .'

'Ink on paper — nothing more! See you, apart from Guienne, Philip is more interested in fighting the Pope than Edward! That is why I am here. I must try to turn the Pope's wrath away from Philip and on to Edward. And turn Philip's away from the Pope and back to Edward. No easy matter, my friend — but why I am come to this land. That, and to see you, persuade you to stay on, and go back to Guienne. For it is most needful, believe me.'

Seeing all too clearly the doubt, disbelief and objection in the younger man's strong features, the Bishop leaned forward, to clasp his forearm urgently. 'Hear this, man — and judge if I speak true or false. Edward has remained at York, all these months, and his great armies with him. Why? Facing Scotland — but looking back over his shoulder. Just as Bruce faces southwards — but also looks back over his shoulder, towards the Comyn. Edward does not like to lose a battle — and this is what he has been doing, in Guienne. Thanks to William Wallace! No great battle, no — but his own birthright being filched from him! Think you Edward Longshanks the man to stand for that? It is given out that he holds back because of his earls — Norfolk, Northumberland, Surrey and the others; but that is but excuse. He has not moved against these — as, with a snap of his fingers he could have done. No — it is France that concerned him. Not only Guienne, but the North — Normandy, Picardy, Flanders also. If Philip, encouraged by success in Guienne, were to turn his eyes thither, and *you* with them, Edward could be in serious trouble.'

'Is Philip so thinking? He has said naught of it to me.'

'I do not know his true mind. That is why I spent so much time with Marigny — although I got little out of that close man. But so it is rumoured. Even these Flemish burghers of Sluys believe it. As a move against the Pope and the Empire, as much as against Edward. More, probably. But Edward would require to marshal all his forces at the Channel if full scale war erupts in Picardy, Artois and the Low Countries.'

'Dear God — this is all too great a coil for me!' Wallace said. 'This folly of war and threats of war. For what?'

'It is how kings reign in this Christendom of Our Lord's new 14th century! For power. Playing one kingdom against another. An evil game. But, if that is how kingdoms are won and lost, it behoves Scotland to take a hand — for her own freedom's sake.'

'You say this is but rumour . . .?'

'Aye. But informed rumour. From sources I trust. And substantiated in highly significant fashion, my friend. Few know of this yet, but I have it for fact. Edward, to halt Philip's ambitions, and to safeguard his rear, has proposed matrimony. A widower of sixty-two years. And to whom? To Philip's fifteen-year-old step-sister Margaret!'

'Saints save us! Not that! Edward? Not to that pale slip of a lassie! Still in the school-room. Edward of England?'

'It is true, my spies assure me. Nor does Marigny deny it.'

'And Philip? What of him? He would not throw his daughter to that . . . that ogre?'

'Philip considers the matter. Weighs and balances. He cannot hope to fight both Edward and the Pope, and win. That is also why I am here. I go to seek Boniface make concessions. Soften his hostility to France, so that Philip may feel free to turn wholly against England, And if you went back to re-open the campaign in Guienne — that would much help sway Philip.'

Wallace stared at the older man, and all but groaned. 'You would have me but a pawn in this game you play!'

'Scarce that, my friend. A knight indeed! Your part is strong, positive, honest — much more so than my own bishop's moves! To seek to drive the English out of France, as you sought to drive them out of Scotland. And by so doing keep Philip Scotland's ally. No light task, but a worthy one. While there is naught for you to do in Scotland.'

'And there is not? I have had enough of exile and foreign ways. I would return to my own place. Fight the English there, as I have done before.

'I understand very well your wishes, friend. But what could you do there, meantime? Bruce and Comyn are all but at each others' throats. It would not take much to provoke civil war. I spend my time mediating. The English hold the great fortresses of the South — Berwick, Roxburgh, Lochmaben, Ayr, Lanark, Bothwell, Stirling, Edinburgh, Dunbar. But they do little else, waiting for Edward — as he has commanded. No campaigning until he comes to lead it in person. He will have no more mistakes made in Scotland. You could not win these great fortresses, any more than can Bruce. You might harry a few convoys, slay a few English officers, play the bandit again. But what is that, for Scotland's greatest soldier, compared with what you may do here? It will not keep Edward away.'

The other was silent.

'You do not find France to your taste, Sir William?'

'Not altogether. Oh, we are comfortable enough, well treated, even honoured above our deserts. But French ways are not our ways. I weary for my own folk.' He shrugged. 'But — tell me of the Bruce? I hoped for better things from that Earl of Carrick.'

'Do not blame Bruce, friend. He is hamstrung, whichever way he turns. By the Red Comyn. It has never worked. The country is not being governed. Cannot be, while one Guardian counters the other's every move. And that, in some measure, is your doing, Sir William. Since you it was who broke the Great Seal in two. Nothing the Bruce can do has the force of law — without Comyn's half of the seal. And Comyn withholds, on principle.'

395

'I did it for the best. That they must co-operate . . .'

'It requires two to co-operate! And Comyn will not. It matters not so much for him — for he controls the North and the Highlands, where the sword has always ruled, rather than the crown and the law. But in Bruce's South, it is different. He is a man near driven to distraction. It had been better, I think, had you never resigned the Guardianship.'

'That was necessary. But what does Comyn hope to gain?'

'Supreme power. And then, possibly, the throne itself. If he can so harass and confound Bruce that he gives up as Guardian — as has been near enough these many times — then he will have taken a great step towards his end. You must see it.'

'Leaving Comyn sole Guardian? Would a parliament, or the Council, agree to that?'

'They might. To see a unified rule, an end to this chaos, a firm hand at the helm — even Comyn's. For he is an able man enough, and a fighter.'

'*You* say that? It would be disaster for Scotland.'

'I say that others might so think — not I. For myself, I would do almost anything to stop it. I would not trust Comyn, ever.'

'Nor I. But . . . you say, my lord Bishop, that you would do almost anything to stop him ruling Scotland alone? Would that include turning Guardian your own self?'

'Eh . . .?' Lamberton blinked.

'Might that not much help? Get Scotland out of this impasse? And be none so strange. You are the Primate. Head of Holy Church, in Scotland. Already you say, you constantly mediate between these two — and, I suspect, largely rule. Bishops have been Guardians before. Wishart was one. If we can have two Guardians, we can have three. A triple rule — one earl, one lord temporal, one lord spiritual. And, see you, two Guardians together could always out-vote the third!'

Lamberton moistened his lips, staring hard at the younger man.

'I say that this would resolve much,' Wallace insisted. 'And, I swear, you would be elected, if so be you allowed your name to be put forward. Bruce, your friend, would agree, and all his faction. The Comyns would vote against — but you would have the Church vote. And all would hear that Wallace favoured it, if that means aught.'

'This . . . that would be a large step. It would require much thinking on. Me, Guardian! I have sufficient to do, as Primate . . .'

'Think on it then, my lord — while I think on Guienne! Perhaps we may have to strike a bargain . . .?'

*　　*　　*

So Wallace went back to Guienne, while Lamberton journeyed on to Rome. In a way it was good to be moving again, in action, away from the inactivity, fleshpots and smelly confines of Paris, in the breezy May weather. And, blessedly, the Prince Louis was not present on this occasion, and Wallace in effect commander-in-chief. But nothing could make that man joyful or enthusiastic over this warfare, and he had no sense of duty fulfilled.

As might have been expected, they found the situation in Guienne much deteriorated since autumn, Philip having obviously done nothing to consolidate the gains of the previous campaign. For so ambitious and aggressive a monarch, he was singularly lacking in military sense. Gloucester had indeed been reinforced — and presumably warned by Edward to be a deal more active — and his forward units had repossessed much of the territory taken from them the year before. They had also made examples of many of the seigneurs, landowners, mayors and townsfolk who had co-operated, or insufficiently resisted Wallace and the French, in gruesome fashion. All had to be done again, and under more difficult conditions. Whoever won Guienne eventually, it was going to be for sorry reward, a devastated, blood-soaked ruin of a once-fine and populous province.

As spring passed into summer, Wallace once again, if more slowly, pressed the enemy forces back towards Bordeaux. This time he had a promise of siege machinery, from Philip; but despite urgent messages to Paris for its delivery, it failed to materialise. The King was not at Paris, it seemed, but pursuing an active campaign of his own, of intrigue, manifesto and threat, against the Pope and the Knights Templar — who seemed to be in alliance — in the Dauphiné and Provence, and was presumably otherwise preoccupied. Also his brother, the Duke Charles de Valois, had started a new, if so far very tentative attack, in Flanders, against the Empire forces allied to the Vatican. It all looked ominous for Lamberton's mission.

Wallace reached the outskirts of Bordeaux in early August,

still without the means to reduce that fortified city. This time, he was determined that he was not going to spend a frustrated summer and autumn sitting ineffectually around the walls and estuary-shores. Leaving his cousin Adam in control — who, since he bore the Wallace name, might have the more authority, under the nominal command of sundry French grandees — he set off eastwards by south, with most of his tight group of friends, plus the troop of the royal guard allotted for his personal protection, in search of the monarch.

Once they were out of Guienne, and riding pleasantly through an undevastated and variedly fair countryside, Rouergue, Gevaudan, the Languedoc and Venaissan, they began to hear everywhere of the great struggle going on between His Most Christian Majesty and His Holiness of Rome. Clearly this was filling the minds of men to the exclusion of almost all else; certainly the campaign in Guienne was seldom mentioned, or even that in Flanders; and Edward of England might not have existed, so far as the folk of these southern parts were concerned. It all sounded highly dispiriting.

It seemed that, after a sort of truce for a couple of years, the struggle between these two had flared up again in no small way. Boniface had apparently fired the first shots, as it were, by threatening to excommunicate Philip for taxing Holy Church in France — allegedly to pay for his war against England. Philip had retaliated by prohibiting the export of all precious metals from France — evidently Rome's main source of supply, and a serious blow. Whereupon the Pope proclaimed that year, 1300, a special jubilee year, if belatedly, and decreed that all who could physically travel to Rome must do so, and there receive plenary absolution, after due expression of contrition, from all their sins — offerings to be brought, in gold, where convenient. He sent the Bishop of Pamiers, as legate, specifically to convey this Papal summons to the King of France. Philip clapped the Bishop in prison. Boniface hastily called a Vatican council, and had all taxation of Church property wheresoever declared a mortal sin, and had a bull to that effect issued, and a copy sent direct to Philip. This was duly burned in court, and an epistle in reply headed 'To Your Illustrious Stupidity ...' pointing out that even His ignorant Holiness should know that in matters secular, such as taxation, the King of France was subject to no one on earth. This produced two more bulls, *Salvator Mundi* and *Ausculta Fili*, one declaring all King Philip's privileges null and void, and the other declaring the Holy See's supremacy over all states and princes, even in secular affairs. Philip's jurists cleverly made a translation of this into French, but altering it in the process, so that it acquired a totally different meaning. All this, and more, appeared to have been going on that warm summer — and Wallace and his friends had to admit that they could produce nothing equally dramatic or competitive from Guienne. Small wonder that they could not get their rams and sows and ballista.

King Philip was variously reported to be at Lyons, Valence and Arles, on the Rhône. But the travellers having changed course southwards for the last-named, obtained news, seemingly factual, at Castres Abbey, on the Agout. The King, apparently, had gone to take order with the Knights Templar, who dominated the area of Bigorre in Gascony from their fortress-church of Luz-St. Sauveur, a good hundred miles to the southwestwards. And there was a Scottish bishop travelling the land looking for Walois le Maréchal, heard of only a couple of days previously at Carcassonne, thirty miles to the south.

They turned southwards, for Carcassonne, and met Lamberton half-way thereto.

The Bishop was in no happy state, his mission a complete failure. He had been able to achieve little with Pope Boniface — whom he described, with little clerical respect, as an unscrupulous and unreliable man, but whom Philip's war-of-nerves was pushing ever more in Edward's direction. There was no point in him remaining longer at Rome. All he had gained was that the Vatican would continue to recognise John Baliol as King of Scots — this in order that Boniface might have some bargaining-card with Edward, rather than out of sympathy or principle; but at least it enabled Holy Church to support the Guardians of Scotland as legitimate, representing King John. For the rest, it had been a wasted journey and interlude.

Now he, Lamberton, was hastening back to Scotland — but had had to see Wallace first. Edward had at last made his invasion, in July. But not in his full strength. He had left his major force at York, and taken only that assembled at Carlisle. He was at present campaigning in Galloway. This was an unexpected move and a very secondary objective. And starting thus late in the campaigning season, it must mean more of a gesture than preliminary to a full-scale invasion. Presumably, even with Philip embroiled with the Pope, and making placatory moves towards himself, he was still uneasy about the Continental situation. Charles of Valois' moves in Flanders might be concerning him a little — but certainly the Guienne situation much more so. He was giving the Scots warning, therefore, that their time was coming; but still keeping his main strength uncommitted, in case of need to send it to Europe. Galloway had been chosen, probably, not so much in that it was convenient to Carlisle, but that, while it was in the main Bruce territory, the Comyn Earl of Buchan also owned lands there, and so Edward's invasion might further help to estrange the two factions — indeed, Lamberton had already had an unconfirmed report that the Comyns were approaching Edward privately to spare these lands. Bruce was to be taught a lesson on the inadvisability of tangling with Edward Plantagenet.

Wallace saw all this as good reason for his own return to Scotland, forthwith. But Lamberton was of the contrary opinion, and vehemently. It was more vital than ever, he insisted, that Wallace should continue with the Guienne campaign — the only advantage for Scotland on the entire complicated scene. Wallace and Guienne were the only hold Scotland now had on King Philip. So long as he had hopes of the English being driven out of Guienne, Edward could not be sure of him. Otherwise, the Plantagenet could let the Pope fight his battles for him, and devote his whole attention to Scotland.

When the big man protested that this was surely too sweeping, that Philip, and France, were still forces to be reckoned with, and Scotland's nominal allies, the Bishop paused, looking searchingly.

'My friend,' he said carefully, 'I think, in your remote Guienne, that you cannot have heard all that has transpired in this murky business of kings and statecraft? King Philip, to free his hands for the Papal struggle, has agreed that his sister *shall* marry Edward. And has signed a secret two-year truce with England, to remain in force until November 1302.'

'Dear God! The serpent! The deceiving, lying hypocrite! To use me thus — and to do this behind my back! You are sure . . . ?'

'Oh, it is true enough. Though true is perhaps scarce the word! Lies, deceit, hypocrisy — all these are true, too. But that is statecraft, see you, as practised by the Most Christian King! But take comfort, my friend, in that it is not all practised against Scotland, and you. For he equally deceives Edward himself. Not in the matter of his sister, no — poor child! But in his intentions. He will keep this truce not a day longer than suits him. Just so long as you remain useful to its king!'

'What do you mean?'

'I mean that one of the clauses of the truce agreement, signed and sealed, was that you, William Wallace, were to be apprehended and held in custody, my friend. Edward, if he believes such documents, thinks you to be safe under lock-and-key — at Amiens, to be sure!'

Wallace stared, speechless.

'Such are princes and diplomacies! But here you are, roaming France free, with a royal guard — Monsieur le Maréchal! And will almost certainly remain so so long as you appear to be winning Guienne for Philip. But . . . seek to leave this country, my friend, for Scotland or otherwhere, and it will be a different tale to tell, I vow! Overnight, your guard will become your gaolers!'

'You mean . . . that I am little more than a prisoner, here? Sweet Mary — we will see about that!'

'Say a hostage at large, rather. Who will remain at large, so long as he fights Philip's battles for him.'

'And you think that I will do that? Fight the battles of a man who betrays and deceives me?'

'I do, friend. For not only do you thereby preserve your freedom and comfort — and that of your friends, I'd remind you — but you serve Scotland well, as nobody else can. It is as important as ever that the English be harassed or expelled from Guienne. You only can do this. I believe only this had kept Edward from full invasion. He must continue to be kept looking southwards, from Galloway To his threatened birthright. If you would continue to serve your country, Sir William, to best effect, you will return to Guienne. And stay there.'

'Saints of God — for how long?'

'That I do not know. The situation may alter, and in many ways. But meantime, if you value my counsel — back to Bordeaux. No ill place to seek to leave France from, see you — should the situation require it! For, believe me; you will not be allowed to leave, from elsewhere.'

'I see.' Wallace took a turn about the inn courtyard where they talked. 'And you?'

'I will seek to return to Scotland forthwith. By way of the Low Countries. Philip has no cause to halt *me*. I have his safe-conduct still. And in Scotland I will see Bruce. At once. And offer myself as third Guardian of the Realm.'

'A-a-ah! That, at least, is good. Bruce will rejoice, I swear. And others likewise. I salute you, my lord Bishop — although I scarce felicitate! The Guardianship is no bed of roses!'

'Of that I am well aware. I do not know but that *you* may have the happier lot! Exile as you may be.'

They eyed each other soberly.

*   *   *

Wallace took the Primate's advice, went back to Bordeaux, and remained there. The city and port did not fall, for the necessary engines were still not forthcoming; but that was the King's responsibility. As autumn progressed, the Scots moved into a nearby manor-house; and the French senior officers likewise found themselves comfortable quarters. For Wallace was not going back to winter in Paris, this time. They would do exactly as Lamberton had said, and sit tight. But they had a small vessel, ostensibly for supervision of estuary landings, kept provisioned and ready to sail at short notice. It would not serve to take them to Scotland, but at least it would get them out of the King of France's territories, if need be. They were not willingly going to suffer further restrictions on their freedom in the cause of devious French diplomacy.

Not that any overt moves were made which might seem to endanger their liberty and privileges. Occasional visitors arrived from the King and his ministers; but whatever these may have said privately to senior French officers, they were nothing less than friendly and respectful towards Wallace and his Scots, with nothing which could be construed as a hint of double-dealing. None of them had any information regarding siege machinery; but likewise none made any suggestion of a retiral to Paris.

It was an unsatisfactory situation, to be sure. But once accepted as inevitable, it was not insupportable. The Scots lacked for nothing. They were comfortably housed, had ample leisure, their duties nominal; they could hunt boar and deer and hares, or hawk wildfowl in the estuarine marshes; there were women in plenty, and wine — for this was, of course, one of the principal wine-producing areas of France. They certainly would have been a deal less comfortable in Scotland; and they could console themselves with the thought that Gloucester's English, cooped up in the beleaguered city — with the unfortunate citizens — would be much less happily placed. All of Guienne, save only this Bordeaux, was now firmly in French hands.

So autumn turned to winter, and it was 1302.

Word reached them intermittently of what was happening in the wider world; but this was primarily about Philip's struggle with the Papacy, with little relevant to Scotland. Boniface, it seemed, had dismissed from office the entire clergy of France, at least in theory, thus more or less excommunicating and damning the entire nation. Philip had called on the College of Cardinals, and also the princes of Christendom generally, to unseat the Pope and appoint another. It was difficult to see what either protagonist could do further, short of outright war.

In February a letter came, by devious channels, from Scotland. Lamberton wrote that he was now the third Guardian — but that he did not think that he could much longer hold Bruce in that thankless position. Edward had left his army in control of Galloway and Annandale, and returned to the South to wed his new young bride. So there was a sort of uneasy interval. The Comyns had indeed sought an agreement with Edward, in Galloway, advocating the restoration of John Baliol as a sub-monarch; so that now there was still greater suspicion and tension between them and the Bruce faction. Indeed Bruce was now more concerned with fighting John Comyn than Edward Plantagenet. In this unhappy situation, he would be glad to hear that Alexander Scrymgeour, with other of Wallace's old colleagues, was playing a noble part, having gathered together an army of no fewer than fifteen thousand irregulars, mainly from Dundee, Angus and Fife, and was keeping it mobilised as a buffer between North and South, protecting Bruce's rear. On the diplomatic side Lamberton was sending a new Scottish deputation to the Pope, under Master Baldred Bisset, Official of Lothian, to counter the efforts of two special English envoys to the Papal court, the Earl of Lincoln and Sir Hugh Despenser, who were seeking to overturn Boniface's support for King John Baliol, and to reverse the Pope's generally favourable attitude towards Scotland. Master Bisset, a sound man and a church lawyer — as indeed was Boniface himself — had been instructed to try to see Wallace, if at all possible.

Wallace was not particularly interested in conferring with lawyers, clerical or otherwise. But Master Bisset's legalities were to make a greater impact on the situation than anticipated by the men of action. For, at Rome, he managed to persuade the Pontiff to make a declaration that the Kingdom of Scotland was in fact a Papal fief, directly under the authority and superiority of the Pope himself, and as such must be inviolate from the invasions and attacks of Christian rulers. Consequently, Edward of England's warlike acts against a Papal fief must cease forthwith, or the full wrath of Holy Church would be turned upon the aggressor. And this, of course, included the wrath of Holy Church in England — and the withholding from Edward of all dues, taxes and payments soever by the said Church, and all co-operation by bishops and clergy.

What Edward Plantagenet, Bishop Beck and other English clerics thought of this, did not penetrate to Guienne — although Archbishop Winchelsey of Canterbury, who had supported the dissident earls, might well be none so displeased. Obviously serious disturbance of Edward's revenues must follow. The Plantagenet could not ignore this. But, strangely enough, the promptest reaction came from King Philip. He was very angry. For this of Papal fiefs, if insisted upon, involved superiority in law in all the courts of Christendom. The holder of a feudal fief was superior of the territory concerned, which superiority was recognised, in law, both by fee and military service, a basic principle of the feudal society. If Scotland officially accepted that the Pope was its feudal superior — worse, if Edward accepted it — then France's position was undermined in law. For the Papacy also claimed fiefs in France — notably the small province of Gevaudan, the county of Melgueil and the viscounty of Narbonne, with its important port. Philip might not care what Boniface *said*, in his bulls and pronuciamenta; but feudal law was a different matter, with involved international ramifications. Scotland must be persuaded to drop this ridiculous and highly dangerous course, and at once. King John Baliol must immediately deny that he was in any way tributory to the Vatican — which meant, of course, that Baliol must continue to be recognised as lawful King of Scots. And, Wallace, the most distinguished Scot available, and former Guardian, must go at once to Rome, confront this wretched Bisset, and emphasise Scotland's complete independence of the Pontiff.

A command to this effect duly arrived at Bordeaux, from Pierrefonds in the Forest of Compiègne, where Philip was hunting enclosing a safe-conduct for his beloved Sir William le

Walois of Scotland, Knight, to pass through and travel out of the French dominions, to Rome

The busy lawyer from Meigle, by chance, had gained for him what he so sorely needed, a passport to leave France. Nothing new was happening at the siege of Bordeaux, and Wallace felt no least twinge of conscience in leaving all there in the hands of his senior French officers. He and his friends rode away from Guienne with carefully concealed elation, South-Eastwards. Unfortunately they still had their royal guards.

They journeyed to the afore-mentioned port of Narbonne, near Carcassonne the nearest point to take ship to Rome, a haven constantly in touch with the Italian states. Here they learned that Bisset and his deputation had in fact already left the Holy See, returning urgently to Scotland, no doubt for further consultation on this momentous development. Wallace was well content with the news, and not in the least offended that Bisset had not found it necessary to seek him out at Bordeaux.

Because of their guard escort, they had to make at least a gesture of heading for Rome; anyway, there was no direct traffic between Narbonne and far-away Scotland. They embarked, therefore, on a vessel bound for Rome via Genoa — from which great port, they gathered, it would not be difficult to find a ship for the Low Counties or Norway. And the Genoese Republic was in trade relations with England, a source of wine, silks, paper and marble — important, in that any ship therefrom was unlikely to be attacked in the narrow seas by English privateers and pirates.

They said goodbye to their royal guard, with relief. It might take the travellers a long time to get to Scotland — but they were on their way.

Part Four

CHAPTER TWENTY-FIVE

If Wallace's last sight of Scotland had been with very mixed feelings, his glimpses of his homeland once more, eventually, were little less so. For when at long last he and his companions reached these northern latitudes, after most round-about and wearying journeyings, it was to see, intermittently through the driving rain squalls, the cliff-girt coast of Caithness slipping by, to port, harsh and forbidding after the suns of Southern Europe, but, however unwelcoming this seemed, it was galling indeed to behold it thus slipping by, and not to be drawing into land. For nothing would make the Norwegian skipper alter his allotted course for Orkney. Scotland it seemed, was now in the hands of Edward of England, and no Scottish port was safe for foreign shipping. Too many good vessels had already been seized and their cargoes confiscated. They would sail on to the Isles of Orkney, as stipulated, and his passengers must find their own way back to Scotland from there, as best they could.

This last frustration was typical of the entire journey. Throughout, it had been characterised by delays, detours, distractions and discomforts seemingly endless. It was now March of 1303. After waiting for months at Hamburg, with no shipmaster prepared to sail direct to Scotland they had finally taken passage with this Norseman, of Orkney, in desperation. Orkney was part of the domains of the King of Norway, and considered safe from the English pirates who, now that the Scots seaboard was under Edward's control, operated at will over the entire length of the British Isles. Their skipper, congratulating himself on having managed to avoid attack so far, was not going to risk any dangerous diversions at this stage.

They put into Kirkwall two days later. They had no difficulty in obtaining safe-conducts from the Earl Magnus, representative of the King of Norway. But obtaining suitable passage to Scotland was another matter, for the same restraints lay on shipmen here as had prevailed in the Continental ports. Eventually they were forced to make use of another halfway-house, the Hebrides. The Western Isles were still under considerable Norse influence, ruled by the practically independent Lord of the Isles. In time, they managed to find a skipper who would take them to Angus of the Isles' port of Tobermory, on Mull. From there, surely, they could reach the Highland mainland without difficulty.

And so, it was early summer before they finally set foot on Scottish soil, on the peninsula of Ardnamurchan, in Argyll, with heartfelt thankfulness. But even here they had to walk warily indeed, for the Lord of Argyll was, of course, Lame John MacDougall's old father, and Lame John was now very much in the ascendant in these dangerous if beautiful territories. Very discreetly, Wallace's party made its way by as unfrequented ways as possible, through the clan lands, heading for Sir Neil Campbell's stronghold on Loch Aweside. It was strange to journey through the dark Pass of Brander, from the west, to be challenged by the Campbell's permanent guards, at its mouth.

Sir Neil was at home, in a state of armed readiness for attack by Lame John, and welcomed them warmly. But he was sorely depressed about the state of Scotland — as, indeed, well he might be. The newcomers had heard nothing factual and detailed for a long time, only rumours and suppositions, much of which they had discounted as over-dramatic and gloomy. Now they learned that the worst of these had by no means been exaggerated. Bruce had resigned as Guardian more than a year before, frustrated at every turn. He had been succeeded by Sir Ingram de Umfraville, a cousin of the Earl of Angus and kin to Baliol, more or less a puppet of the Comyns. This triumvirate had not lasted long either, even Umfraville being unable to stand the Red Comyn's behaviour, while Lamberton had all but lost his wits. After less than a year, with a two-to-one vote, they had dissolved the triple Guardianship, and a desperate parliament had appointed Sir John De Soulis of Liddesdale as sole Guardian. De Soulis was a moderate and inoffensive man, allied to no faction. He had done his best — but by then, unhappy Scotland was overtaken by events. Edward had invaded again in full force, content that the French situation was secured at his rear, and risking the Papal fulminations. He had swept through the land in fury. This was after his new Governor of Scotland, Sir John de Segrave, had sustained an early and totally unexpected defeat at Roslin in Lothian, when moving north to take up his office. The Red Comyn, and Sir Simon Fraser, with eight thousand men, managed to surprise the English array of twenty thousand, when it was split into three sections, over forage difficulties. It was Scotland's only major victory since Black Earnside, and Edward's rage had been terrible. Scotland had had to pay, thereafter, the entire country to be occupied and savaged, including Comyn's northern area. And pay not only in invasion. For the Roslin victory had the immediate effect of making something of a popular hero out of Comyn — something he had never been before — and this put him, for the time being, in a strong personal position. He was not the man to neglect such opportunity, and used this to introduce a new policy — namely that John Baliol should somehow be got back to Scotland, and reinstalled on the throne. But only for a brief period. He would then formally abdicate, after naming his successor — who naturally would be his nephew John Comyn . . .

'Save us! It would be the end of Scotland, with the Red Comyn on the throne!' Wallace declared. 'Bruce would have something to say to that!'

'He did,' the Campbell nodded. 'He made submission to Edward again!'

'Dear God — no! Not that?'

'He did, yes. They say on Bishop Lamberton's advising.'

'But why? Why?'

'It is said that they are seeking to use Edward to put down Comyn's threat. Then, when Comyn is down — as he will be — Bruce will throw off Edward's yoke again, and claim the throne for himself. His father, the old lord died in March, in England. So Bruce himself could now be king. And he has married his Elizabeth de Burgh, Edward's god-child — with Edward himself at the wedding.'

Wallace groaned. 'I like nothing of it,' he said 'Whom can we trust?'

'Myself, I trust only you, I'm thinking,' the Highlander said simply. 'I thank God Wallace is back in Scotland. Perhaps Lamberton is an honest man, enough. For a cleric! If too clever!'

'Yes. I believe Lamberton to be a true man. If something devious. If indeed he advised Bruce so, then there may be some good in it. Where is he now? The Bishop? I must see him.'

'That you will not do. For he is fled to France. With the

Guardian, de Soulis. And the Steward, Umfraville, Crawford, Buchan and others. To escape Edward's wrath.'

'God's eyes! All these? Gone? Left the country . . .?'

'Aye. That, or be hanged! Edward has all under his hand, now — save only close Highlanders. And even here his lackey, Lame John, rides high! I am telling you, my friend, all that you have done is undone, whatever! This land was never in so ill a case. Edward drove his way north from Berwick — but he also was after sending a great fleet, with soldiers, to land in Fife, and so get behind the Forth crossing at Stirling. All the south fell and Bruce made his submission. Edward accepted him like the Prodigal, they do say — for his own ends. Then the English marched on, taking Perth, Brechin, Aberdeen, even Elgin and Inverness, right to the Black Isle of Ross, before Edward was after turning. Now he is back, settled at Dunfermline, and ruling the land from there with an iron hand. Bruce with him, with his new wife — but sorely unhappy they do say . . .'

'And Comyn himself?'

'Yielded on terms, at Strathord, north of Perth, in February. Terms . . . if you can be calling them that!'

'Terms? What terms would Edward grant to Comyn?'

'These. That he, and all others, must accept Edward only. As liege lord. And Scotland as no longer a realm, but part of his English dominions. That all who had led in opposition to him be exiled from the King's dominions for up to three years — Lamberton, Soulis, the Steward, Buchan and the rest. But not Comyn — like Bruce. These were to remain, and to find and deliver to the King the man William Wallace, on pain of death! Not were any of those exiled to be permitted to return to their lands until you, Wallace, are taken and punished. These are the terms, friend.'

Wallace drew a deep breath. 'I see. Aye — I have been over-long away, to be sure!'

'That — or insufficiently long!'

'Yet you said that you were glad to see me back, Sir Neil?'

'Aye. But for Scotland's sake, perhaps, not your own. Never yours.'

*   *   *

In no very hopeful frame of mind, therefore, Wallace's party headed South-Eastwards from Loch Awe. Campbell provided them with an escort, to see them through the turbulent clan lands — indeed, he would have given them two hundred Campbells to form a nucleus of the fighting force Wallace was going to have to raise again, and MacGregor of Glenstrae another hundred of his own men — generous, in view of the ever-present threat from Lame John; but the big man, thanking the chiefs, said that he would wait, and send for them later. He would prefer to slip into Lowland Scotland quietly, with no large following, to spy out the land and decide on his course of action.

Through Mamlorn, Strathfillan, Glen Dochart and upper Strathearn, they came down to the edge of the Highland Line and the settled lands, in high summer, a country lovelier than any they had seen for years — and no signs of Edward's hated hand as yet. Wallace headed for his old haunts in Methven Wood, so near to Perth, as good a sounding-board for Central Scotland as any they would find. But they found it not what it had been, like all else. Still some broken men haunted its glades, but they were vastly reduced in numbers and low in spirits. English patrols frequently combed the Wood, it seemed, as they did all other sanctuaries and refuges. It seemed that Edward Plantagenet was an infinitely more effective usurper than any of his underlings, and markedly hard on what he termed outlaws and brigands. His anti-brigand patrols were everywhere — it was said, largely in the hope of catching none other than William Wallace. The newcomers took due note. Presumably Edward's spies had reported their departure from Guienne, and assumed a secret return to Scotland.

They did not stay long at Methven, therefore — but long enough to learn that only the one major fortress or castle held out against the invader — Stirling, under the gallant young Sir William Oliphant, straitly besieged. In the Lowlands, only one other man of note appeared to be in open resistance — Sir Simon Fraser of Oliver, joint-victor, with Comyn, of the Roslin fight. Oliver, of course, was on the skirts of Ettrick Forest, near Peebles, and Sir Simon had the resources of that great wilderness to hide in. For the rest, they learned that almost all Bruce's faction had submitted when their leader did, including the Earls of Lennox and Mar. The Earl Patrick of Dunbar and March was now Governor of all South-East of the Forth; Sir John Stewart of Menteith, Sheriff of Dumbarton, was Governor of the West; and all the South-West, Bruce's territory, was under the direct English rule of Sir John Segrave.

All offered rewards for the capture of William Wallace, dead or alive.

Two choices, or three perhaps, appeared to be open to the returned exiles. They could return whence they had come — although, in fact, this was never considered. They could go to ground here in Central Scotland, with an escape-route to the Highlands, either in the vast Flanders Moss or the almost as large Tor Wood. Or they could head south for the Ettrick Forest to join forces with Sir Simon Fraser. It did not take Wallace long to decide on the latter course.

Secret ways and river-crossings well known to the travellers brought them unchallenged to the northern outskirts of Ettrick, in a few days. Here they found that the Selkirk area was no longer available to them, the English having destroyed what was left of the abbey and used its stones to rebuild and strengthen the old castle, which was now garrisoned. But further down Tweed, in one of the remote side-valleys of the Stobo area, deep amongst the green rounded hills, they ran to earth Sir Simon Fraser, with a company of about four hundred, tough foresters and Border mosstroopers — the only force in arms, apparently, against the invader, in all Scotland.

It was a strange meeting, for these two did not know each other, and were inevitably a little wary, in the circumstances. Wallace was unsure of Fraser's devotion to the cause of Scottish independence. He was an associate of Comyn's, and had taken little part in the struggle, before Roslin — indeed he had been a friend of Edward's, fought for him with distinction in his foreign wars and been knighted by him. On the other hand, Wallace with all his fame and seniority, as former Guardian, might have sought to assume command; and undoubtedly his adherence, with a price on his head and all Edward's forces searching for him, could not but tend to draw unwelcome attention to any company he kept.

Fortunately the two men quickly took to each other, and decided that there was no clash of interests. Fraser had sickened of Edward's ever-increasing cruelties and savageries — he said that he was now a great man gone sick in his mind — and he, Fraser, was now committed against him, for better or for worse. Wallace did not seek to challenge the other's leadership, but set about recruiting a force of his own. He sent messengers back to Loch Awe for the promised Campbells and Mac-Gregors.

414

It was both gratifying and disturbing how quickly the word spread over Southern Scotland that Wallace was back. If men did not actually come flocking to join his standard, that would be because to have done so would have been all but suicidal, for most. But everywhere he went, around the wide rim of the Forest area and throughout the Borderland, he was welcomed by the ordinary folk almost as a saviour — and all seemed to know of his return. When he left any village or hamlet, however small, a proportion of its young men left with him. Especially after, as demonstration, he took and destroyed the newly-rebuilt peel of Selkirk, putting the garrison to the sword. Having lived in that castle, he knew its weaknesses and exploited them.

Sundry other exploits they achieved, in a comparatively small way, both jointly with Fraser and separately, as it were flexing their muscles and showing the flag, partly as training for their new levies under the veteran officers — all the attacks discreetly spread over a wide territory, so that attention should not be drawn to their base area. Nevertheless, in the half-light of one still night, their camp at Happrew was surprised by a large force, on three sides, approaching in stealth, the sentries being able to give only the briefest warning. They had no time to establish any sort of battle or formation before the enemy was upon them, with overwhelming superiority, clearly a carefully planned operation.

It was hopeless from the start, however furiously Wallace and his veterans, with Fraser, fought, however gallantly they sought to rally their surprised, scattered and sleep-bemused ranks. The lofty hollow in the hillside of Harrow Hope was surrounded by an outer ring of steel, which closed in and in. Of those who bolted, few won clear; most others died where they stood. In the end, Wallace gathered such as he could into one of his wedge formations, and with himself and Fraser at its head, flanked by his stalwart friends, cut their way out by sheer concentrated sword-slashing force, against a chosen and limited section of the perimeter. They got through, with most of the wedge, and managed to lose themselves in the shadowy hills to the north. But they had lost two-thirds of their total strength.

The repercussions of that night's betrayal — for betrayal it clearly was, some of the survivors having recognised one John of Musselburgh, who had been with them two weeks before, now fighting beside the English leaders — was serious indeed for

Scotland, comparatively minor defeat as it was. For Sir Simon Fraser began to lose heart, and was in fact never the same again. In the council held later in the safety of the Broughton Heights, he did not fail to make it clear that he held Wallace's presence at Happrew to be responsible. This John of Musselburgh was one of the men whom Wallace had recruited. Anyway, with all Southern Scotland talking about Wallace's return, it had only been a question of time before attempts were made to win the rewards offered for his capture. If he had not come, Fraser's force could have remained unassailed and ever growing in strength in these Ettrick fastnesses. Now, all the Forest area would be combed for them — or, at least, for Wallace. There was no safe refuge for the rest of them here, any longer.

The big man had not the heart to counter the other's reasoning, however angry were his friends denials. Clearly it was all true. Segrave the Governor himself, and Sir Robert Clifford, recently promoted Lord, had been identified as leading the fighting. These great ones would never have been sent out against a comparatively small band, in the wilderness had Edward's prime and hated foe not been the prize. And it was true, too, that there was likely to be little security in Ettrick hereafter; for these important lords, having failed to capture their quarry, would not dare return to their master without having made the most stringent search. And they would have ample men to do it, nothing surer; nor would their methods be gentle.

What to do then? There was no other place of sanctuary large enough to hide, shelter and feed a substantial body of men for any time, save the Tor Wood, behind Falkirk, and the Flanders Moss in the upper Carse of Forth, both in the Stirling area — that was admitted by all. There were plenty of empty hills, but such lofty barren heights would not support men in any numbers, especially with winter coming upon them; there must be farmlands to supply the basic essentials of life, quite apart from shelter from rough weather. It was agreed, although reluctantly by Fraser and his Borderers, that they should move north to the Tor Wood meantime. There they might seek to aid and encourage Sir William Oliphant, besieged in Stirling Castle. And perhaps return to Ettrick when the present hue and cry had died down.

Wallace remained cheerful, outwardly assured, determined,

however grave his inward doubts. But there was an atmosphere of gloom and foreboding as, travelling only by night, they made their secret way northwards again.

CHAPTER TWENTY-SIX

The months that followed were scarcely conducive to hope and cheer; faith alone had to sustain them — and it was insufficient for some. They were unable to help the beleagured Stirling Castle, for that fortress was forced to yield, partly by the most tremendous concentration of siege-machinery, partly through starvation, and Sir William Oliphant sent in chains to the Tower of London. It was a hard winter, and conditions in the Tor Wood were less than pleasant. Fairly soon, Simon Fraser had had enough of it, and announced that he was going back to his own Ettrick, with his Borderers. Wallace did not seek to detain him, for the other's presence, in these circumstances, was little asset. He was sorry, for he liked the man: and given any other conditions of warfare, he would have made a fine commander and good colleague. But hard living and guerilla tactics and crudities were not for him. A few weeks after his departure from the Tor Wood, they heard that he had made his submission to Edward, and was sentenced to exile — although if he aided Bruce and Comyn to capture Wallace within twenty days of Christmas, his exile would be reconsidered.

Now there appeared to be only William Wallace and his group assembled in arms against Edward Plantagenet, in all Scotland. There was no longer even a Guardian, Soulis having demitted office when he fled abroad. They were back where they started eight years before.

There were certain gleams of light in the darkness, however. Alexander Scrymgeour managed to join them, with over one hundred of his faithful Dundonians — a mere token percentage of the fifteen thousand he had marshalled to protect Bruce's rear; but it was hard indeed now to convince even the most sanguine that there was any point in actively continuing the struggle. Others of Wallace's former comrades-in-arms found their way to the Tor Wood or the Flanders Moss — both of which were used as bases — but none of the nobility or knightly class, who of course were all carefully watched by the English. Bishop Sinclair sent secret messages of support, however, as well as moneys, with promises of men for the next campaigning season. And all the time, small-scale but effective forays, raids and ambushes were kept up, effective enough for their purpose of keeping the flickering flame of hope alight in the hearts of the Scottish people.

That seemed to be as much as was possible, that winter of 1304–5.

King Edward went south, at last, with his Court, breathing threatenings and slaughters against Bruce, Comyn and all others who had failed to deliver up to him the traitor and outlaw Wallace. But he would be back.

A letter reached Wallace, in March, from France. It had taken months to come, from William Lamberton, written in November. He declared that he, and all other Scots exiles, sent their warm greetings, esteem and admiration. That they had heard of the setback in Ettrick, but not to be downcast. All might seem to be going Edward's way, but all was by no means lost, for Scotland. King Philip was already regretting his truce with Edward — if not his sister's marriage — and there could be hostilities again. Gloucester was recalled from Bordeaux and a new commander being appointed, identity as yet unknown — but it looked as though there would be a renewed campaign there, which could mean general war. This must distract Edward's attention from Scotland. Also, there was rumour that Edward was not well, that he had had some slight seizure — God's hand on him, it might be, with too much blood and a young wife. It was believed that he had appointed his nephew, the Lord John of Brittany, Earl of Richmond, to be Lieutenant and Viceroy in Scotland — and all France knew this John to be a weak, pompous man, and no soldier, markedly different from his uncle. It could well be that, in the spring, Wallace would find conditions in Scotland easier — for as they all knew, it was Edward himself who was the dire menace, rather than the generality of the English. Meantime he, Lamberton, had sent orders that all moneys required by Wallace for his continued resistance to the English should be met from the funds of the bishopric of St. Andrews, whose officers would issue it as required. And it might well be that they would meet, before over-long, since it was his intention to return secretly to Scotland when opportunity offered. God's blessing on William Wallace and the land he so nobly fought for! As postscript, William Lamberton added — trust Bruce!

Considerably comforted by this delayed communication, and by the thought that he was less alone than he sometimes felt, and that the Primate even now might be back in Scotland, Wallace put new heart into his endeavours.

It seemed as though much of what Lamberton prophesied and adduced was accurate. The new Viceroy, John of Brittany, Earl of Richmond, turned out to be a stiff, sour man, but not really harsh, nor indeed very effective. His main preoccupation appeared to be with imposing English-style laws and collecting taxation; matters military suffered a declension. Much of the vehemence went out of the punitive patrolling in general, and the anti-Wallace campaign in particular. As a consequence, the Scots began to stir again, men plucked up courage for small resistances. More came to join Wallace in the wilderness, even some of the aristocracy. Sir John Ramsay, who had been hiding in the Angus glens, arrived with four-score men; the Bishop's contingent duly appeared from Dunkeld; and Sir Henry de Haliburton, one of Fraser's Border lieutenants from the Kelso area, came back to continue the struggle. By early summer, Wallace had a thousand men under arms. He kept half of them in the Tor Wood and half in the Flanders Moss, these two great empty areas all but communicating. They raided from each, sometimes jointly, and between them made the vital fords of Frew and Drip unusable by the English, and this enabled their own strike-forces to operate north or south of the great dividing line of Forth, at will.

That entire summer Wallace spent in consolidation. He was not yet strong enough for large or ambitious thrusts; and none of the great lords, on whose shoulders Edward's hand rested most heavily, had moved to join him. But he pushed westwards into the Lennox lands, and indeed made all the central area of Scotland, west of Stirling Castle, something of a redoubt, where the English dared not penetrate save with a large armed force. Glasgow he came very largely to control, his patrols coming and going almost as they would, the English garrison seemingly content meantime to keep strict guard over Bishop Wishart, and to hold certain key-points and Clyde crossings.

All this large and important area came within the vital

sheriffdom of Dumbarton, of which Sir John Stewart of Menteith still was sheriff. He made no very evident moves against Wallace however. It was said that the new Viceroy had rebuffed and offended him; indeed John of Brittany did not like the Scots, whatever their policies and allegiances, and made it evident. He did not like the situation his uncle had pushed him into, either, and made constant requests to be relieved of his position. But Edward, whose health was giving cause for anxiety — although not to the Scots — was adamant. One member of his family must represent him in Scotland — and he made no secret of the fact that he could not trust his son, Edward Prince of Wales.

So the summer progressed, with no spectacular developments, but Wallace steadily gaining strength, with many more men of rank finding their way to his side. Sir Neil Campbell came, with another contingent of his clan; and though he dared not remain too long away from Loch Awe and Lame John MacDougall, he left his men with Wallace. When the Lord Maxwell of Caerlaverock turned up, one of Bruce's most senior vassals, Wallace felt that perhaps, at last, the tide might be beginning to turn. He brought a message of support and admiration from Bruce — of little material benefit, but of real moral encouragement and comfort to the man whom he had knighted.

Amongst those who joined him that summer was one man with a reputation — Ralph de Haliburton, brother to the aforementioned Sir Henry. He had been one of the heroic garrison of Stirling Castle, with Oliphant, which had for so long defied Edward's might, and on the fortress's surrender had been sent to prison in England. He explained that he had escaped from durance, and found his way northwards, with many adventures. Wallace made much of him, out of policy. An adherent such as this could be a valuable magnet for drawing in others. Moreover, he had with him a squire, whom he declared might be useful, a slight and slender young man of diminutive stature, one John Stewart, rejoicing in the nickname of Jack Short — who was indeed nephew to Sir John Stewart of Menteith, a brother's bastard son. This youth, personable and talented, was a fine fiddler and singer, an asset at a camp-fire of an evening; moreover, having been brought up in the foothill country of the Campsie Fells and Kilpatrick Hills, north of Glasgow, he knew every yard of that rather difficult terrain, which in present circumstances was of strategic importance. Wallace found these two useful recruits.

In July there was a council meeting held in Perth, under the chairmanship of Master William de Bevercotes, Edward's Chancellor for Scotland, Earl John of Brittany being absent in England — a frequent occurrence. It was attended by most of those who now ruled in Scotland, as nominees of the English; and Wallace judged it a suitable opportunity to make one of his demonstrations — not a serious attack but a gesture, to alarm and upset the councillors, sheriffs and the like, to remind them that all was by no means secure in the realm of Scotland, and that they might yet have to pay for their co-operation with the invaders.

So, for two nights, Wallace's people created uproar around and even within St. John's town of Perth, firing haystacks, thatched roofs and buildings with fire-arrows, riding round the walls blowing horns and trumpets, terrorising the townfolk, lighting Sir John Stewart's beacons on the surrounding hilltops, burning the whins and brushwood on the rising moorland to the South-West so that the smoke billowed down all day to envelop the city, on the westerly breeze — and disappearing, themselves, by day, into the depths of Methven Wood. The assembled magnates and collaborators had plenty of men-at-arms with them for protection, but these were nevertheless insufficient for any large-scale penetration and combing of the extensive woodland; and any lesser attempt would have been suicidal.

After the second night, Wallace believed that his conflagration was going sufficiently well for him to leave all in the care of his cousin Adam, Ed Little, Sir John Ramsay and others, so that he might make a swift excursion into the South-West, with a small party, to do something he had been intending for some time. He believed that he could rouse much of his own calf-country of Renfrewshire, to take an active part in the struggle for freedom, if he could convince and enroll certain key figures there. The Steward, overlord of all this area, was still an exile in France, his brother slain at Falkirk, his sons Andrew and Walter only children. So there was a hiatus in the power structure in this important area, and Wallace had plans to fill it, by mobilising a group of the Steward's senior vassals, including his own brother, Sir Malcolm Wallace of Elderslie, his cousin Ronald Crawford the Younger, of Crosbie, Sir Thomas Randolph, kin to Bruce, and others. This seemed a good opportunity to make the attempt, with so many of his enemies isolated at Perth. Accordingly, he set out, with a mere fifty or so men, taking Thomas Gray and Kerlie with him, and also Ralph de Haliburton, whose Stirling celebrity might be of value. The squire Jack Short accompanied his master. They went by their accustomed secret routes by the fords of Earn and Allan and the Braes of Doune, to the Flanders Moss, and then southwards across the Campsie Fells to the Kelvin valley and the wide plain of Lower Clyde. Here it occurred to Wallace that it would be much to his advantage to have the support and co-operation of the Bishop of Glasgow in this enterprise, for as well as his spiritual authority, the Bishop owned large lands and baronies in the area. But Wishart's palace was kept under close guard by the English. Some stratagem was required.

Leaving his party at the Clachan of Campsie, in the mouth of the Campsie Glen, under Thomas Gray, Wallace took only Kerlie and the squire, John Stewart, the ten miles on to Glasgow, on foot now and dressed in the nondescript clothing of packmen. They would all meet up again at Bishop's Riggs in Cadder parish, three miles north of Glasgow, at first light the next day, whereafter they would continue on their journey, skirting well to the east of Glasgow, so as not to draw any attention to themselves, to cross Clyde at a quiet ford they knew of between Rutherglen and Carmyle. There were a number of small lochs in the Bishop's Riggs area, amidst rough swampy moorland, ideal for a quiet rendezvous. They would meet at the west end of the Robberstone Loch, at dawn.

The trio entered Glasgow by the Drygait Port, in the Townhead vicinity, without difficulty, young Stewart now wearing the ragged dark habit of a wandering friar over his other clothing. They made their way to the Cathedral graveyard, haunt of packmen, wanderers and idlers generally. The Bishop's Palace was nearby, somewhat dwarfed by the vast mass of St. Mungo's Cathedral. Wallace dared not approach nearer, for fear of being recognised; and even Kerlie was now a fairly well-known figure. But Jack Short would not be known, and ought to be able to gain access to the Palace, as a monk, with his message.

They had a long wait, and were beginning to become anxious for the youth's safety, as well as uncomfortable — for the weather had turned to rain — when at length, in the late evening, Stewart returned. He had had great difficulty, he said, in gaining the Bishop's presence, for the old man was ill and confined to his chamber. At length he had been forced to disclose that he was from Wallace, and had then been admitted to Wishart's side and had deliverd his message. The Bishop himself had been kind, eager to hear all that he could tell him of Wallace, and had had a clerk write a paper, which he had signed and sealed. This was an open episcopal letter, commending to all who read it his good friend and son-in-God Sir William Wallace, and urging all to assist him in his present endeavours by every means in their power, especialy those who bore any duty or responsibility towards Holy Church.

Well satisfied, the trio left the city as they had come.

Darkness overtook them in the Garngad area, but they reached the Robberstone Loch quite soon afterwards, in driving rain. They had over seven hours to wait before the rendezvous time, and it was going to be a chilly and unpleasant interlude. Young Stewart announced that he knew of an alehouse not far beyond the other end of the loch, a poor place enough but where at least they might find shelter and refreshment. Nothing loth, Wallace told him to lead the way. The squire had been reared, apparently, not five miles away.

Unfortunately, they found the low-browed, thatch-roofed cottage shut up and barred, with its little farmery deserted, presumably a casualty of war. But the byre-cum-stable attached stood open, and there was some boghay therein, old but dry. They would do well enough there. They could sleep in fair comfort — although one would remain on watch. Wallace took the first two-hour watch. Kerlie would take the last.

The squire did not sleep. Wallace heard him tossing and turning and sighing, on the hay. At length, well before his time was up, he rose, saying that, since he could not sleep he might as well start his watch and allow one who could to rest. The big man did not deny the sense of that, and went to lie down.

When Wallace, by his regular breathing, had been asleep for some time, Jack Short quietly slipped out of the byre, and made off into the wet, dark night.

It was some ninety minutes before he came back — and not alone. Silently a quite large group of men approached the house. Detaching himself, young Stewart came forward on tiptoe, to peer in at the doorway. All seemed to be as he had left it. He made a sign to the others.

The squire now moved inside. The sleepers had laid their dirks a little to the side, for comfort, but close enough to grasp

423

in an emergency; being dressed as packmen they carried no swords or other obvious weapons. Infinitely carefully the young man gathered these up, and took them outside.

Handing the dirks over to one of the men, there was a slight clink of steel. Kerlie, prepared to awake early for his watch, sat up, peering around him. Perceiving no sign of Stewart, in the gloom, he presumed that he had gone outside probably for natural causes. He was turning over, to sleep again, when he heard the faintest murmur of a voice. He reached for his dirk, and found it gone. In a single movement he was on his feet, and in three strides was at the doorway, peering out. The squire was there in front of him, two men at his back.

'Ha, Kerlie,' Jack Short said, quietly. 'Our friends are come, early. No need to wake Sir William.'

Kerlie moved out further — and an arm crooked round his throat from behind, choking off his cry of surprise. And a dagger drove between his shoulder-blades, deep to reach the heart. He sank down on the wet grass, with only a faint bubbling groan.

Perhaps it was that groan which wakened Wallace; or it might have been some sixth sense belatedly warning of dire danger. He started up, also automatically reaching for his dirk. But men were now streaming into the byre, silence no longer necessary, to hurl themselves upon him, before he could rise. Two fell upon him bodily, grappling. He tore free of their grasp, and flung each aside in an explosion of fierce strength. As another gripped him, he managed to get to his feet, wrenching himself free. Stumbling on the uneven floor of hay, he kicked over the little milking-stool which was all that survived of the byre's furnishings. Grabbing it up, as weapon, he smashed it down on one man, felling him to the floor; and then on another. But there were half-a-dozen more in the byre now, and they had ropes to entangle him. Thrash and struggle as he would, it was not long before they had him encoiled and bound, after a fashion, helpless. They dragged him outside.

There were fully fifty more men there, waiting in the rain. The August night was not so dark that he could not perceive that they wore a lord's colours, the wavy barred blue-and-white of the earldom of Menteith. Three men stood a little apart, and to them Wallace was brought. One was the young Stewart, the squire; another was his master, Ralph de Haliburton; the third was a stranger.

Panting, straining, Wallace stared at these. 'You!' he gasped. 'Haliburton! The hero . . . of Stirling.'

That man turned away, shrugging. 'Bring him.' he said, briefly, and led the way to the horses, hidden some way off.

As they went, Wallace, searching faces, perceived Kerlie's body lying sprawled on the grass, disregarded. He wept for his friend as he stumbled on, pushed and prodded.

*   =   *

They rode westwards through the rain-shrouded low hills, fording the Kelvin near where the old Roman Wall crossed it, and on by Boclair and Duntocher to the Clyde estuary shore. It did not require any major exercise in deduction to perceive that they were making for Dumbarton Castle. Tied securely on a horse's back, and surrounded by men-at-arms, Wallace rode sunk in grief — not so much for his own plight but for Kerlie's slaying, and for the fact of treachery.

It was some seventeen miles from Robberstone to Dumbarton, and it was daylight of a thin watery sunshine at their backs before they reached the towering fortress-rock guarding the widening estuary, to clatter up the winding causeway and wait while the great gates were opened to receive them. Wallace was thereafter flung into a vaulted basement cell, and left to his own thoughts.

It was not until the late afternoon that he was taken, wrists bound, and led up the winding turnpike stairway to a room of the castle where two men awaited him — that calmly precise individual, Sir John Stewart, Tutor of Menteith, Sheriff of Dumbarton, and the officer who had assisted at Wallace's capture, evidently one of his minions. There was no sign of Haliburton or the squire. For long moments these three considered each other, unspeaking.

'Sir William Wallace,' Stewart said, at length. 'I am but new come, from Perth. A surprise, to find you here.'

'Scarce a surprise, surely, Sir John — since you contrived my capture. By treachery.'

'Not I, sir — not I. That was Haliburton's doing.'

'With some assistance from a young kinsman of yours, I understand? And from this man at your side.'

'This is one of my sheriff-officers. And if my brother's bastard son is squire to Haliburton, and serves his master, that is no concern of mine. Haliburton sought the aid of my officers, as was right and proper, within my sheriffdom. I am concerned in this solely as Sheriff of Dumbarton, in which jurisdiction you have been apprehended. As former Guardian, Sir William, you must be fully cognisant of the due procedures.'

'I am fully cognisant of traitors when I see them — however judicial their speech!'

'Silence, sirrah! I will have no such talk. I but do my plain duty, here. As Sheriff, and a loyal subject of King Edward.'

'Loyal to King Edward, aye — in King John's realm!'

'There is no King John, as well you know. Nor has been these years. I represent the only lawful authority there is in Scotland . . .'

'And Haliburton also? Another loyal subject of King Edward? Although he defied him at Stirling siege. And later joined my company. You will scarce deny *him* the title of traitor, sir?'

'I do, indeed. Traitors and treachery are concerned with the betrayal of loyalties. Where no loyalty is held, there can be no treachery. Haliburton saw the error of his ways. He was released from his English prison on the express orders of the King, took oath of allegiance to His Grace, and was brought back to Scotland with the sole duty of apprehending yourself, sir — his brother being known to be of your outlaw band. This he has done, and delivered you to me, the Sheriff, as was his plain duty. Without injury to yourself. Now I must do my duty, likewise. I have to send you, under secure guard, to England, to London, again by express orders of the King's grace, there to stand trial for your many offences and slaughters.'

'So! You do not try me yourself, Sir John — as could also be your duty, as Sheriff?'

'Not so. Your offences, sir, have been committed not only in Scotland, but in England and in France and on the high seas. You are to be tried in London, by the King's command.'

'I see. King Edward is . . . prudent!'

'King Edward is just. And merciful. You could have been slain out-of-hand last night, man, in yon tulzie — as was your henchman. An outlaw — many would have so done. But the King's commands were stringent — you were not to be harmed. You will go to a fair trial — that I am assured. The verdict will be just — and any sentence tempered with mercy, I have no doubt. I am satisfied that all will be well done.'

'So speaks the son of a Scots earl, of ancient lineage! How

much, Sir John, will you receive for this day's work? In lands and moneys? I heard that even the man John of Musselburgh was given ten shillings by Edward for his betrayal at Happrew in the Forest!'

'Be silent, sir! How dare you speak me so! Away with him, Sandy. I do only my duty . . .'

'A basin of water, for you to wash your hands, Sir John, would be apt! Would it not? Forby, I think that you will need more than water to wash your name clean, hereafter!'

'Take him away, man!' Stewart shouted at his officer, strangely agitated for so exact and calm a man. 'And have all ready to ride, at dusk. Begone!'

'So you eschew the daylight for our journey!' Wallace called back, as he was hustled out. 'I think perhaps that you are well advised . . .!'

That night, as the last of the sunset faded seawards, a small group of men and horses were ferried across the darkling estuary to Langbank, on the Renfrew shore, Stewart himself amongst them — but keeping well away from the bound Wallace. At Langbank two troops of cavalry were drawn up, awaiting them, bristling with arms. They set off southwards without pause, climbing the low green hills by unfrequented ways, Sir John still with them. Wallace smiled to himself wryly; this progress was as determinedly inconspicuous as were apt to be his own night marches.

Dawn saw them in the Ayrshire hills east of Kilmarnock — not so very far from Loudoun Hill, where this long struggle had commenced. They crossed the River Irvine near Galston, before halting for a few hours; then on by more lonely moorland drove-roads by Cessnock and Sorn and Cumnock, empty country, much of it belonging to Bruce, ironically. Wallace did not seek to buoy himself up by any hope of rescue. His friends would undoubtedly try to deliver him; but it would take time to arrange. Thomas Gray would move heaven and earth, once he discovered what had happened; but by bringing him away from Dumbarton so quickly, and with his force still at Perth, the thing was next to impossible. And Stewart was wasting no time on the journey, either, to be sure.

They were another twenty miles southwards, by Sanquhar and Thornhill — Douglas country now — before the next rest, into Dumfries-shire. Thereafter they went more slowly, the pace telling on horses and men. But nightfall found them halfway down Nithsdale, fairly safe from even the most swift and furious pursuit. The following day, Sir John Stewart, white-faced with fatigue and tension, handed over his charge to Sir Aymer de Valence, Earl of Pembroke, and Robert Lord Clifford, at Carlisle, across the Border, without ceremony or even farewell, duty done.

He was a stickler for duty, was the Tutor of Menteith.

CHAPTER TWENTY-SEVEN

The English Lords were a deal more respectful towards Wallace than had been Sir John Stewart. Of course, they were soldiers, and he had defeated them both in the field, on occasion. Not that they were any less careful to keep him secure. But they were civil, and did not seek to humiliate him. Unfortunately, their charge of him lasted for only three days, as they escorted him speedily South-Eastwards across the Pennines, to York. For they were, as it were, on active service, their place with the army facing into Scotland — and not in Scotland itself only because of food and forage shortages there. At York, they handed him over to Sir John de Segrave, who had been withdrawn from his post as commander-in-chief in Scotland and created Grand Marshal of England. He was to conduct the prisoner to London.

Segrave was a hard, tough man, as befitted an old fellow-campaigner and crony of Edward's own, and Wallace received no kindnesses from him. But there was no deliberate mal-treatment either — and the big man had journeyed in less comfort many a time when his own master. His only cause for complaint was that, when they passed through large towns, he was forced to dismount and a rope was tied round his neck, the ends held by mounted men-at-arms, as a sight for the populace to stare at. Clearly all were warned in advance of his coming, and this was an exercise in boosting public morale — which made the captive thoughtful. That such was considered necessary was surprising; and presumably it would build up still further, in that case.

It took a week to reach London, in this fashion. In the capital the crowds were enormous. It was Sunday, August 22nd, and every citizen seemed to be in the streets for the occasion. Here attitudes and atmosphere were different, the folk not content merely to stare and point. They jeered and hooted and shook fists, even threw stones and dirt and offal. Segrave and his men had to force a way through the press — but they did not seek to check the demonstrations. Wallace survived, with some filth on face and clothing, and a woman's nail-scratches on his cheek. He had not realised that he could be so hated by ordinary London citizens, so remote from all the strife and warfare. Most of the Englishmen he had slain, he imagined, were North Countrymen.

He had expected to be put into the Tower, where so many Scots had been, and were, immured. But to his surprise he was taken through the city, somewhat northwards, to a large house at the end of Fenchurch Street, beside the church of All Hallows, Staining, apparently belonging to an Alderman of the city, one William de Leyre. Here he was installed in the wine-cellar, under lock-and-key, guards at the door, but in fair comfort. He had often done a deal worse than this, on campaign.

But nothing in his years of campaigning had prepared him for what developed the next morning. He was awakened by church-bells ringing all around — and London seemed to be notably full of churches — in a jangling cacophony which went on and on. He was brought food, but told to hasten with it, as all was almost in readiness. What all represented, he was not informed. But presently his guards took him upstairs to street-level, and outside. Here he was astonished to find the entire street packed with people — not just gaping townsfolk, these, but official-looking personages, dignitaries and soldiers. Sir John Segrave was there again, and appeared to be acting master-of-ceremonies. He ordered Wallace's wrists to be unbound, and then had him mounted on a splendid white destrier, richly caparisoned. Then he demonstrated towards a large group of waiting personages, as splendidly garbed, in full rig of office. He did not exactly introduce them to the prisoner, but intoned their names and styles impressively. Sir John le Blount, Mayor of the City of London; Master Geoffrey de Hartlepool, Recorder of the City; then the Sheriffs of London, one by one, followed by the Aldermen, including his hitherto unseen host.

Then there was the Common Sergeant, the Master of the City Guilds, the Captain of the City Guard, and others. Wallace missed many of the names, owing to the jangling of the bells. Bewildered over what all these could have to do with himself, he sat his mount and occasionally inclined his head towards some particularly impressive figure. He was the last to have recognised that he himself was far and away the most impressive figure present.

It appeared that they were all going to ride in procession, westwards, flanked by marching soldiery, a major cavalcade. They had to make a very lengthy and attenuated procession, for the streets were narrow, and crowded with waiting citizenry. It seemed to be some sort of public holiday, for everybody was in the streets, including the apprentices — who made their presence felt in much shouting and capering. Again there was the vehement hostility as on the previous day — but at least the press of accompanying dignitaries prevented any major casting of rubbish and missiles.

They rode by the Poultry and Cheapside, past St. Paul's Church and down Fleet Street to the Strand, and thence by the Tilt-Yard to Westminister Hall, the church-bells ringing all the way, as though for some triumph. Whatever the reason for the holiday, their procession appeared to be the main attraction. There was a ceremonial dismounting outside the great hall, built by Canute and William Rufus, much bowing amongst official personages, and Wallace was led within, heavily guarded, now, by men-at-arms wearing the royal livery of Plantagenet. The hall was part of the King's palace. The prisoner was conducted to a sort of bar and bench at the south end of the huge and handsome chamber, to wait there.

He had quite a long wait. The hall was crowded already, so that there was scarcely room for the newcomers who had accompanied him, important folk as they were. Some of the sheriffs and aldermen had almost to share Wallace's stance with him and his guards. At length a flourish of trumpets introduced some even loftier people to the dais, or platform, at the opposite end of the hall. Each had his style and title shouted out by a colourfully tabarded herald. The first was Sir Peter Mallory, Lord Chief Justice of England. Then Sir Ralph de Sandwich, Constable of the Tower of London, Sir John de Backwell, a Judge of the High Court, and again Sir John Segrave, Grand Marshal of England and Sir John le Blount, Mayor of London.

These five took their seats on the dais, behind a table, the Lord Chief Justice in the centre.

Wallace, perceiving the composition of this party, began to wonder if it could possibly be his trial, already, the very day after his arrival — although that seemed highly unlikely, with no time or opportunity having been allowed for a defence or even a spokesman to be instructed by the accused. His wonderings on this were rudely interrupted by a guard coming with a laurel wreath, to clap it on the prisoner's head — a proceeding which convulsed the huge company with mirth. Wallace took the thing off, and handed it back to the guard with a slight bow; but the man slapped it on again, somewhat askew — to the added delight of the assembly. The big man removed the garland, put it on the floor, and stood on it, amidst howls and shouts of anger.

Lord Chief Justice Mallory raised a hand to still the tumult. 'The accused will wear the chaplet,' he intoned. 'Or else his hands will be bound fast, so that he may not remove it.'

The laurel was once more thrust on to his brow, where perforce Wallace had to let it remain.

When the maximum of elation had been extracted from this humorous gesture, Mallory signed to the herald, who thereupon read out a commission from His Grace the most excellent, high and mighty Prince Edward, King of England, appointing the aforementioned five judges, under the Lord Chief Justice, to try for his many vile, shameless and insensate crimes, the notorious murderer, brigand and outlaw William Wallace. And having tried him, to pronounce due verdict and to execute justice upon him, as was right and proper. Given by the King's hand the 18th day of August, the year of our Lord 1305. God save the King!

Wallace took a long breath, noting that not only was he apparently to be tried and allowed no defence arrangements, but that the verdict was assumed to be guilty before they started, and that sentence would follow automatically. And the commission had been signed four days before ever he reached London. Edward, although not present apparently, was in a hurry, it seemed.

The Chief Justice, perhaps to emphasise that this was no ordinary trial, chose to read out the indictment himself, a lengthy process. In impressive tones he declared that the charge was of a composite character, including sedition, homicide, spoliation,

431

sacrilege, robbery, arson and other damnable felonies, all undoubtedly committed by the accused. But worse than these, the
prisoner was charged with the horrible crime of high treason.
This offence was above all others damnable ...

A great shout of indignation arose from the company; and
Mallory paused, nodding, to dab his lips. But as the noise died
away, it was Wallace who spoke first, and strongly.

'My Lord Justice,' he said, 'Before we proceed further, I
declare that I cannot be tried on a charge of treason. Not here,
in England. I could not be a traitor to the King of England, for I
was never his subject, and never swore fealty to him. It is true
that I have slain many Englishmen; but it was in defence of the
rights and liberties of my native country of Scotland ...'

'Silence, sirrah!' Mallory exclaimed, banging his table. 'How
dare you raise your insolent voice! You will not speak unless I
give you leave ...'

'Is this a *trial*, my lord? *My* trial?' Wallace had a more
powerful voice than the Justice, than probably anyone in that
hall, and used it. 'I am not conversant with the law of England.
But in every other nation of Christendom, a man standing trial
may speak in his defence, or be spoken for. Is it otherwise
here?'

'Be quiet, man! This is outrage!' the other cried. 'If you inter-
rupt again, I shall have you silenced by force, fellow! You may
not speak, for good and just reason. You have already been
outlawed and placed beyond the King's peace, in His Grace's
Scottish realm as well as in this. Therefore you have no rights
soever to plead or to defend. Do you understand? You are
beyond the law, and may not invoke it. Remember it.'

'What is this array of the law then, my lord?' Wallace gestured with a hand at the bench of judges. 'Why are you here?
This is not a trial — it is a play-acting, a mummery. But, if so be
it amuses you, and these — and the King of England — then
proceed, sir.'

Swallowing, and clearly having difficulty in enunciating his
words, Mallory pointed a trembling finger. 'More ... more
from you, and you will be removed. Do you hear? You can be
dealt with, in your absence, very well. Another word from you,
and you will be removed, I promise you.'

Wallace bowed slightly, half-smiling, and waved permission
to continue.

'Very well.' Carefully the Lord Chief Justice addressed the

company, his fellow-judges, the back of the hall, anybody but the accused. He pointed out that their liege lord Edward, on the forfeiture of the subordinate King John Baliol, whom he himself had set up and appointed, and therefore could reduce, had also reduced all Scots to his own royal power, in place of the man John's, since royal authority there must be. He had publicly received the homage and fealty of all prelates, earls, barons, sheriffs and a multitude of others, had proclaimed his peace throughout Scotland, that rebellious land, and seen justice done. Yet this Wallace, forgetful of his fealty and allegiance, had risen against his lord, had banded together a great number of felons and attacked the King's wardens and men; had in particular attacked, wounded and slain Sir William de Hazelrigg, sheriff of Lanark, and in contempt of the King's Grace cut up the said Sheriff's body in pieces . . .

Groans of horror filled the hall. at this enormity, fists were shaken at the prisoner, and Almighty God called upon for judgement. Mallory waited, more patiently now.

When he could, he went on. The felon Wallace had then assailed towns, cities and castles in Scotland. He had made his writs to run through the land as if he were Lord Superior of that realm, instead of the mighty Prince Edward. And having driven out of Scotland all the warders and servants of the Lord King, had set up and held parliaments of his own. More than that, he had wickedly and presumptuously counselled the prelates, earls and barons, his adherents, to submit themselves to the fealty and lordship of the King of *France*, to aid that sovereign to seek destroy the sacred realm of England . . .

Shouts of 'Shame!' and 'Traitor!' and 'Dastard!' prevailed.

Furthermore, the Lord Chief Justice went on inexorably, he had actually invaded the realm of England, entering the counties of Northumberland. Cumberland and Westmorland, and committing horrible enormities. He had feloniously slain all that he could find in these places, liegemen of the King. He had not spared any person that spoke the English tongue, but put to death with all the severities he could devise, all — old men and young, wives and widows, children and sucklings. He had slain the priests and nuns of Holy Church and burned down their churches, together with the bodies of the saints and other relics of them therein placed in honour.

The outrage of piety was well demonstrated.

Mallory suddenly seemed to grow weary of reciting this

catalogue. Holding up his hand, and speeding up his delivery, he fairly rattled through the last bit. In such ways the man Wallace had seditiously and feloniously persevered, to the danger alike of the life and crown of their Lord King. For all that, when the Lord Edward invaded Scotland with his great army, and defeated this William, who opposed him in a pitched battle, and thereafter granted his firm peace to all that land, he had mercifully had the said William Wallace recalled to his peace. Yet William, persevering in his wickedness, had rejected his royal overtures with scorn, and refused to submit himself. Therefore, in the court of the Lord King, he had been publicly outlawed, according to the laws and customs of England and Scotland both, as a misleader of the lieges, a robber and a felon. Thus it was impossible that he could be allowed the normal defences of the law. None could say otherwise.

The Justice sat back, pushing the indictment paper from him. He seemed to recollect that he had four fellow judges, and made a pretence of consulting them. Then he drew forward another paper, and resumed.

'This commission appointed by the King's Grace, declaring the said William undeniably guilty of all the aforementioned wicked crimes, hereby announces the sentence of the King's judges upon him. To wit. That the said William, for the manifest sedition that he practised against the Lord King be drawn from this Palace of Westminster to the Tower of London, and from the Tower to Aldgate, and so through the midst of the city to the Elms. And that for the robberies, homicides and felonies he committed in the realm of England and in the land of Scotland, he be there hanged; and afterwards taken down from the gallows.'

A long sigh, as of relief, rose from the assembly. Wallace stared straight ahead of him.

Forming his words slowly and carefully, the Lord Chief Justice went on. 'And that, inasmuch as he was an outlaw, and was not afterwards restored to the peace of the Lord King, he be decollated while he yet lives. Before ... before being decapitated.'

There was silence now, breaths seeming to be held, every eye fixed on the tall, massive and upright figure wearing the laurel wreath, to see how he took that atrocious sentence. He granted them not so much as a flicker of an eyelid.

Mallory frowned, and cleared his throat. 'And that, thereafter, for the measureless turpitude of his deeds towards God and Holy Church, in burning down churches, with the vessels and litters wherein and whereon the body of Christ, and the bodies of saints and relics of these were placed, the heart, the liver, the lungs, and all the internal organs of William's body, whence such perverted thoughts proceeded be removed out of his person, and cast into fire and burnt.'

This time a prolonged moaning sound came from the company, a strange noise which seemed to hold a kind of pain and ecstasy combined, but with neither sympathy nor protest. Everywhere men leaned forward, eager, avid, intensely aware, alive indeed as seldom they were.

'Furthermore and finally, that inasmuch as it was not only against the Lord King himself, but against the whole Community of England, and of Scotland, that he committed the aforesaid acts, the body of the said William be cut up and divided into four parts; and that the head, so cut off, be set up on London Bridge, in the sight of such as pass by, whether by land or by water; and that one quarter be hung on a gibbet at Newcastle-upon-Tyne, another quarter at Berwick, a third quarter at Stirling, and the fourth at St. Johnston, as a warning and a deterrent to all that pass by and behold them. This for doom, by order of the High Court of England. God save the King.'

In the stir and buzz of talk, Mallory stood up, and the other four with him. The trumpeter sounded a flourish, and as the entire company rose to its feet, the King's commissioners of judiciary filed out.

William Wallace stood motionless, head high, the very picture and epitome of a strong man, calm, and armoured in his strength. But he was praying to God for fortitude, as he had never prayed before.

*   *   *

Wrists bound again, he was the last to be allowed to leave Westminster Hall. Outside, all had gathered once more, to watch, even Mallory and the other judges. Now all was entirely different from heretofore. Gone the formality, the dignity, the official attitudes. The time for that was past. Now was the time for sport, diversion, the reason for the public holiday. Yells and catcalls and hooting greeted Wallace's appearance, and continued. He was barely brought through the doorway when men, some of them dignitaries, surged forward to slap and punch and spit, others to start to tear his clothing off him. Fighting each other to get at him, men — and women too, now — grabbed and wrenched and ripped. Soon he was completely naked, save for his laurel crown, to the high delight of all, new opportunities for sport and pleasantry now presented. A due interval for this was allowed, and then Wallace was dragged and driven further out. With difficulty a couple of horses were brought forward through the press, not handsome destriers these but rough and shaggy work animals. At the tails of these was attached a sort of narrow hurdle of wood, with a single central spindle, no wider than a man's back; and to this the prisoner's naked body was bound, head downwards. Then a team of kitchen-boys and scullions was marshalled, given sticks and ropes-ends, and amidst jeers and cheers set to their task.

With yells and slogans and much enthusiasm, the lads laid about them, at horses and man indiscriminately, and away the brutes ran, the hurdle bouncing and bumping and twirling behind, over the cobblestones. The youths raced after, with a hasty mounting of better steeds on the part of all who could, that none of the fun be missed. Those on foot could scarcely keep up, of course.

So back the way the very different procession had come, they went, through the shouting, screaming crowds, jolting, spinning, the hurdle dragged this way and that — for no one was leading the horses and these, terrified by the noise, the crowd's thrown missiles and the beatings, bolted anyhow, anywhere they saw an opening, often pulling against each other, to the excited huzzahs of the youthful drovers.

Wallace, after the first terrible few minutes, was less than wholly aware of what went on. Because of the narrowness of the hurdle and its single central spine, it tended to rotate as well as to bounce and slither. He was therefore frequently face-down to the causeway, and his head bumping on the stones; indeed he suffered more and harder knocks from this than from the sticks and hurled stones and filth of the crowd, which missed more times than they scored hits. With the continual spinning round and the jarring and shaking, as well as the knocks and buffets, he was soon only semiconscious — a mercy indeed, since he became little sensible of what he found almost worse than the mere physical pain and indignity, the disgust and nausea produced by the dung, ordure and foulness of the causeways themselves, with which his face and body quickly became plastered.

So he was dragged back along King Street, the Strand, Fleet Street, and by Ludgate Hill and St. Paul's to the Tower. What he was taken there for he neither knew nor cared. Such part of his mind as was still aware of anything, was concerned only that an end should be made, and quickly. The sooner he reached Smithfield Elms, the sooner he might reach a much better place than that.

In fact, there was little delay at the Tower, where an additional contingent of grandees was waiting, to join the procession. They turned up the Minories to Aldgate, then westwards by Leadenhall Street, Cornhill and Cheapside to Newgate, where they passed outside the city wall to the great open space of the cattle market at Smithfield Elms. All the way, the crowds were as dense and vociferous as ever. They went more slowly, now, not so much because the horses were tiring but in that the youths and apprentices were, and so did not race and beat so eagerly — after all, they had come over three miles. Which allowed the bystanders better scope for striking and throwing, of course. But long before Smithfield was reached, Wallace was quite unconscious, and such attentions immaterial.

He came to again, after a fashion, with cold water being thrown over him — not to rid him of the filth but to revive him, for there would be no sport in hanging an unconscious man. Unbound from the hurdle, he was raised upright — but had to be held up, dizziness overwhelming him. Hating this weakness, this so evident inability to control his splendid body, almost more than anything else, he strove desperately to keep his feet, to maintain some sort of stance. All his effort went into this, so that he scarcely saw the gallows rearing above him, nor the fire blazing at its foot.

He told himself that he must make a really mighty effort to stand straight, upright, be his own man. It would be only for a little while, after all and then he need no longer strive and fight with himself. God would surely give him the strength, that these guards need not hold him up . . .

The thought of God's so necessary aid reminded him. With a great exertion, sweat bursting from his brow, as much mental as physical, he looked around him, seeking to control and concentrate his gaze. In the reeling, red-hazed fog before his eyes,

437

he thought that he could recognise one face. Segrave, who had brought him to this London. He tried to speak — and did not know whether words came or not. Moistening blood-encrusted, filth-encrusted lips, he tried again and again.

Frowning, Segrave deigned to notice. 'What ails you, man?' he demanded, shortly.

'A priest,' the other got out, thickly. 'A priest. To shrive me.'

'No,' Segrave snapped. 'Forbidden. For an outlaw.'

'Edward's outlaw. Not . . . God's! A priest . . . of a mercy.'

'No, I say. You have desecrated Holy Church. Such as you can have no priest, no shriving.'

'Who says so, Sir John?' a quiet voice asked, from the side. 'Since when have *you* spoken in the name of Holy Church?'

The Grand Marshal turned. 'My lord Archbishop — I did not perceive you there. I crave pardon. I but told this outlaw that he cannot both despoil Holy Church and expect Holy Church's blessing.'

'*Expect*, no, Sir John. But even he might be granted it, at the last.'

'It is expressly forbidden, my lord. I have my orders.'

'Orders you may have, sir — but not from Holy Church. Where *I* am present, I give such orders.' Robert Winchelsey, Archbishop of Canterbury said firmly. 'This sinner seeks the Church's last comfort. *You* shall not deny it.'

'Not I, my lord — but the King.'

'In matters of state, I am the King's humblest servant. But in matters of Holy Church, only God's! I myself shall shrive this sinner.'

Wallace had swooned away again during this exchange, sagging limply on the arms of his guards. Now when the Archbishop spoke to him, he was only vaguely aware of it, and could by no means answer the formal questions as to belief and repentance. But Winchelsey chose to interpret the head jerkings for due acceptance, made the sign of the Cross, and pronounced a brief benediction — to the growls of not a few of those present.

As the Primate stepped back, Segrave signed angrily to the guards.

Four of them dragged and pushed Wallace's all but inert person up the earthen mound to the actual gallows-platform. The hangman had his rope ready, and slipped the noose over his victim's lolling head, being careful to ensure that the knot was well to the side, not at the back, lest the neck should be prematurely broken. Then he made the rope taut — to much advice from the large company. All was ready.

Or not quite. The sentence of the High Court had to be read out again, in full, at this stage. Wallace, having made the supreme effort to remain master of his senses to the end, was cruelly disappointed. As the words droned on and on, he could by no means retain full consciousness. His mind slid away into another kind of consciousness. He was back on the north shore of Forth, opposite Cambuskenneth Abbey, not at his triumph at the Battle of Stirling Bridge but earlier, in dire trouble, seeking desperately for means to cross that broad river, to safety and better things. He was longing for that other side, for he was sore and weary, and he had betrayed his friends, caused the deaths of many who had trusted in him, and slain a companion-in-arms, the man Fawdon. If only he could get to that other shore, he might know peace. The water was dark and swift-running and fearsome, and looked cold . . .

He knew abrupt choking, terrible constriction at his throat, no breath, a roaring in his ears, red seething clouds before his eyes — that water, he realised, was red, not black, not cold. He was in. He must swim now, swim with all his might, swim to the good, far shore where the Abbey rose serene, strong, beckoning. He must swim, not drown in this red flood, swim, fight struggle, as always, as always.

The goodly shore was nearing. He was winning, winning. He would not go down yet awhile. The Abbey bells were ringing him in, welcoming, drowning the river's roaring. But a few more strokes. At last. How good, how good and fair . . .

William Wallace was joyfully on his way to a wider, kinder realm than Scotland.

* * *

Man can command, plan, ordain, decide, and with the utmost authority. But he cannot always ensure. William Wallace was indeed alive when his twitching, jerking, naked body was run down from the Smithfield gallows, and dragged to the fire below. He was still alive, ever his eyes wide, when the hangman drew his great knife and slashed open the belly with one fierce cut, and then, turning the blade, ripped upwards to open the rib-cage — although the fellow had more difficulty there — to extract the still strongly-pumping heart. But he might as well have

439

been dead, since God can have greater mercy than man created in His image, and the human body, too gravely maltreated, can be shocked into insensibility. Numbers of the onlookers undoubtedly felt the knife's slashes, experienced the griping at their own stomachs as the hangman plunged gory hands in and drew out the steaming, pulsing entrails, to cast on the fire, and later shrank and winced as the axe hacked off the head and dismembered the limbs. Not a few indeed heaved and vomited, women laughing hysterically — though none protested and not many looked away. But William Wallace was no longer concerned, with more important matters to attend to, a suddenly and wonderfully wider scope for his decisions, and friends awaiting him.

He left these others to it.

Historical Note

Some confusion surrounds the actual destination of the parts of
Wallace's body, chroniclers variously giving Dumfries and Aberdeen as alternatives to Stirling and Perth as sites for their
exposure. The head certainly remained on a pole at London
Bridge for a considerable time. The Sheriffs of the City presented an account for fifteen shillings, for the disposal and car-
riage of the body, to Sir John Segrave, for onward transmission
to the King; but Edward considered this exorbitant, and gave
them only ten shillings.

Sir John Stewart of Menteith did better over his share in the
earlier proceedings, being granted lands to the value of one
hundred pounds, and the temporalities, that is the secular revenues, of the bishopric of Glasgow, for his services in de-
livering up Wallace. The 'valet' or squire, Jack Short got forty
merks, and other helpers sixty merks between them — which
presumably included Ralph de Haliburton. He, of course, had
obtained his reward in advance, on being released from his
English prison.

King Edward, however, made but a poor bargain. Within six
months, no more, Robert Bruce, sickened by what was done to
Wallace, and recognising that there could be no living with such
a Lord Paramount, donned not so much Wallace's patriot's
mantle but one of his own as rightful king, and rose in arms
once more, and to good effect. Slaying the Red Comyn, whom
he found to be in treacherous negotiation with Edward, he was
crowned at Scone Abbey, in March, 1306. Edward was forced
to go north once again to deal with the Scots, fell ill in Cumberland, and was taken to the Solway shore where he could see
the Scotland he hated so fiercely, and so might die cursing it.
Which he did, with his last breath directing his son Edward,
Prince of Wales, the moment he was dead, to boil his body in
water in order to separate the flesh from the bones, the latter to
be carried at his son's side into Scotland and never to rest until
that unruly country had been totally and finally subdued to

441

England's might. Edward the Second, lacking his sire's venom, broke his vow and did nothing of the sort, taking the body back to Westminster for burial, unboiled. But he continued the war against Scotland, and it was not until 1314, nine years after Wallace's death, that the great defeat of the English by Bruce, at Bannockburn, marked, not the end of the war but the final turn of the tide for Scotland's independence.

William Wallace's dream came true seventeen years after he set himself to make it a reality. Who shall say that he lost his final battle?

NIGEL TRANTER

DRUID SACRIFICE

King Arthur's niece, sister to Gawain and daughter of King Loth: Thanea was high-born and privileged.

But when, as a devout Christian, she objected first to the druidical practice of human sacrifice and then refused to marry the man her pagan father had picked out for her, her execution was ordered.

Then, after a miraculous survival, she was cast adrift in an oarless coracle as a sacrifice to the sea-god.

Yet, again, she was saved, cast up on the Fife coast and rescued by the monks of St Serf . . .

The life of Thanea, and of her son, St Mungo, the founder and patron saint of Glasgow, is a dramatic, action-packed story from the early centuries of Scotland's history.

HODDER AND STOUGHTON PAPERBACKS

NIGEL TRANTER

CHILDREN OF THE MIST

'Our race is royal,' was the proud claim of the MacGregors. Yet for all their history and fighting qualities, they were a small clan and their lands too close for comfort to the great Clan Campbell.

So by the end of the sixteenth century, the heritage of their new young chieftain, Alastair MacGregor, was a poor thing indeed. Not only was much of the land lost, but their principal threat, Black Duncan of Cowl, Campbell of Glenorchy — as clever as he was unscrupulous — had the ear of the king . . .

HODDER AND STOUGHTON PAPERBACKS

NIGEL TRANTER

MACBETH THE KING

Across a huge and colourful canvas, ranging from the wilds of Scotland to Norway, Denmark and Rome, here is the story of the real MacBeth.

Set aside Shakespeare's portrait of a savage, murderous, ambitious King. Read instead of his struggle to make and save a united Scotland. Of his devotion to his great love, the young Queen Gruoch. Of the humane laws they fought for, the great battle they were forced to fight. And the price they paid.

HODDER AND STOUGHTON PAPERBACKS

NIGEL TRANTER

CRUSADER

Alexander the Third of Scotland was just seven when he inherited the throne. South of the border, England's King Henry the Third saw this as his chance to assert his paramountcy over the kingdom. At the age of ten, the boy was married to Henry's daughter.

But when, as a devout Christian, she objected first to the druidical practice of human sacrifice and then refused to marry the man her pagan father had picked out for her, her execution was ordered.

Whether it was shooting the wild geese, helping him escape from the prisonlike confines of Edinburgh Castle or teaching him to stand up both to his ever-threatening English father-in-law and the unending feuds of his own countrymen, David de Lindsay, of Luffness in East Lothian, was his one true and constant friend.

The rolling Lothian and Border country and its compelling history are both brought marvellously to life in Nigel Tranter's magnificent account of a young boy and his destiny.

HODDER AND STOUGHTON PAPERBACKS

NIGEL TRANTER

FLOWERS OF CHIVALRY

Once again Scotland was fighting for her survival as a free and independent nation.

Robert the Bruce's legacy, three years after his death in 1329, was in danger. With a five-year-old heir guarded by an ageing and diminishing band of lieutenants, the English king, Edward III, had seen his opportunity. War was renewed, a puppet king set up.

In the years of struggle that followed, two men stood out as leaders of their people: Sir William Douglas, the Knight of Liddesdale, known as the Flower of Chivalry, and Sir Alexander Ramsay of Dalwolsey.

Friends and comrades-in-arms, by their gallantry and daring, they did more than any others to save their country. Yet something was to happen between them that would cause one of the most cire and desperate happenings in Scotland's violent and dramatic history . . .

HODDER AND STOUGHTON PAPERBACKS

NIGEL TRANTER

UNICORN RAMPANT

The year 1617 was a fateful one for Scotland – and especially for young John Stewart of Methven, bastard son of the Duke of Lennox.

King James VI of Scotland and I of England made a rare and disastrous visit to the homeland of which he had been an absentee monarch for fourteen years. Knighted in a rash moment by the eccentric King Jamie, John became the reluctant servant of the Court. Much against his will he was commanded to return with the King to London, and was soon caught up in a net of murky political intrigue.

'I recommend it strongly'

Books in Scotland

HODDER AND STOUGHTON PAPERBACKS